First published in 2023 by Kimori Books

This edition published in 2023 by Kimori Books

Copyright © 2023 by Louise Holland. All rights reserved.

No part of this publication may be reproduced, distributed, or transmitted in any form or by any means, including photocopying, recording, or other electronic or mechanical methods, without the prior written permission of the author. For permission requests, contact lahollandauthor@gmail.com or visit kimoribooks.com.au

The moral right of the author has been asserted.

An electronic copy of this book is available from the Australian National Library catalogue.

No AI was used in the production of this publication, including any interior or exterior artwork. No part of this publication may be used to further any algorithm or learning techniques of any AI-based programs.

The story, all names, characters, and incidents portrayed in this production are fictitious. No identification with actual persons (living or deceased), places, buildings, and products is intended or should be inferred. This includes the original characters as imagined by their players at the personal home TTRPG game, the actions carried out by said characters, and any divergence from in-game canon.

Cover illustrations by Mike Knot https://mike.tattoo | @mikeknot on Instagram

Interior design & maps by Louise Holland

ISBN 978-0-6458896-1-1 (paperback)

ISBN 978-0-6458896-2-8 (hardcover)

ISBN 978-0-6458896-0-4 (electronic)

SPARK OF THE DIVINE

THE KALARAAK CHRONICLES
BOOK ONE

LOUISE HOLLAND

KIMORI BOOKS

PRAISE FOR

SPARK OF THE DIVINE

"I genuinely got this magical and almost nostalgic feeling that I can only describe as 'coming home'... Holland gently eases you into this world, entrancing you with her magical prose and expertly trickling in just the right bits of organic world building at exactly the right times to continuously spark wonder."
ESMAY ROSALYNE, *BeforeWeGo blog*

"Subverting typical high fantasy, where nothing much happens beyond worldbuilding and plot, the themes within Spark of the Divine intertwine together and pay off beautifully. It had something to *say*, and meant it."
LUCAS LEX DEJONG, AUTHOR OF *DELUGE*

"...[an] unapologetic love letter to a personal DND campaign, exploring friendship, love, loss while still managing to incorporate some of the humorous insanity that the game can bring."
KRIS, *TheFictionalEscapist*

"I was absolutely absorbed in Holland's worldbuilding... Fondly influenced by Holland's adventures at the DnD table she assembles a cast of characters that exhibit delightful and at times volatile chemistry that feels incredibly natural and satisfying... Louise's prose is lyrical magic."
BOB, *BlueSmokeFire reviews*

"Wow, your book has LOTS of words."
KIRA HOLLAND, AGED 3

For the Weaver, without whom this world would never have existed; and for the original members of the Sunday Kalaraak D&D crew, who first brought their characters to life within it.

This isn't quite that story, but I hope you like it anyway.

"Our belief is often strongest when it should be weakest. That is the nature of hope."

Brandon Sanderson

THE SEVEN REALMS

KALARAAK
CAL-ah-rack
THE REALM OF EARTH

IGNATIA
ig-NAY-she-uh
THE REALM OF FIRE

ADRAI'ICA
ad-RAY-eek-uh
THE REALM OF CURSED FAE

KEANOS
kay-AHH-noss
THE REALM OF WATER

ANTITHIIA
ann-TITH-ee-uh
THE REALM OF THE DAMNED

TAE'VALIK
tay-VAHL-eek
THE REALM OF FORGOTTEN GODS

REQUIEM
REH-kwee-em
THE REALM OF THE DEAD

AELMORE

ISLANDS

CAPE KIRAA

INNIT

HEARTGATE

THE
RUBY
ISLES

MOITERVAL

PORT SALTE

SOLACE

JARAHEIM

BOLDEN

SAL

CROSSROAD

The West Keep

Falcon's Wat

ALSURAN OCEAN

ROOST KEEP

KINGDOM OF
ALTAEA

GREENVA

MIDHOLD

BATEFORD

JEN

TALON

VERES

MOENGRAAN

SHIBA'S REST

GRENGLADE

MOENGRAAN

OLGSTAAD

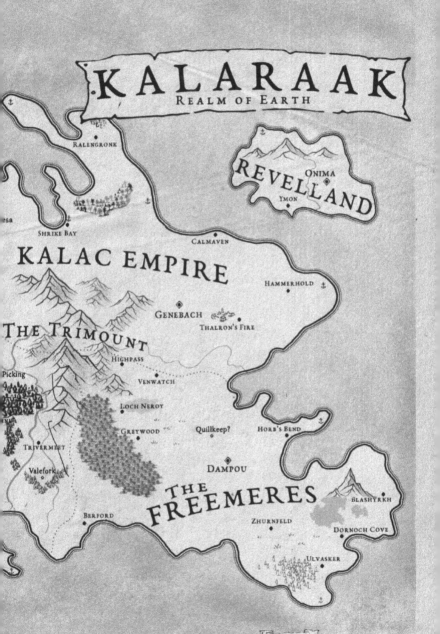

KALARAAK
REALM OF EARTH

RALENGRONK

REVELLAND
ONIMA
YMON

SHRIKE BAY
CALMAVEN

KALAC EMPIRE
HAMMERHOLD

GENEBACH
THALRON'S FIRE

THE TRIMOUNT
HIGHPASS

Picking
VENWATCH

LOCH NEROY

GREYWOOD
QUILLKEEP?
HORB'S BEND

TRIVERMEET

DAMPOU

VALEFORK

THE
FREEMERES
BLASHYRKH

BERFORD
ZHURNFELD
DORNOCH COVE

ULVASKER

PROPERTY OF

PROLOGUE

THE KIVERI CZAI

The man was dying, but he had to be sure.

He shifted, concealed in a dark corner of the study. Most of the candles had already burned down to stubs, and the oil lamps had not been lit that night. The fireplace was barren and dark. The only light came from the barest hint of the moon peeking through the heavy curtains, leaving patterns on the carpet from the iron intersecting over the windows.

The dying man sat behind his desk, an impressive hulking slab of wood much too grand for the chaos that it held. Ledgers, maps, reports covered in rushed, cramped handwriting all vied for room amongst stacks of thicker books and precariously balanced ink pots. A half-full glass of mulled wine lay on its side, the remnants of the warm liquid seeping carelessly onto papers that had been strewn across the desk, as if the owner had been searching through them earlier. Perhaps the papers contained valuable information that warranted being destroyed, the dying man using precious last moments to conceal their contents. Or perhaps the man had simply already lost the use of his arms. Poisons could be unpredictable.

The hooded figure lingered, spectral, in the shadows of the room. He watched with an intensity many had witnessed, but none had lived long enough to describe. The dying man knew he was there because he allowed it. He always stayed to watch the light leave their eyes. Killer though he may be, he firmly believed that nobody should depart this world alone.

Among the mess of the desk, a single stubborn candle clung to life, sputtering in the draught an ajar window pane had invited in. The warm light flickered across what little could be seen of his face. A pointed finger raised towards him. The skin was scarred and mottled from the strange transition from middle into old age; a process it would now no longer be troubled with.

"I know who you are."

The voice was weak, as if the man's soul was already preparing a graceful exit to make its way to the Silver Stream. It had two minutes, at the most.

He sneered at the man's comment, what insufficient light the room offered glinting on his white teeth. He said nothing. Not a single soul knew who he really was. To think otherwise was laughable.

"They call you the Kiveri Czai," the dying man continued. "The deadliest of Kalac's assassins. I suppose I should be honoured."

He blinked, impressed. The man knew his moniker, at least, and had done a decent job of pronouncing it despite the foreign tongue it hailed from. Still, he said nothing. Death didn't comment. He simply collected what was due.

"At least this confirms it," the man murmured to himself, eyes beginning to glaze over. "So questioning the Arcane one's motives poked the hornet's nest, after all. I knew there was a connection between them. Now Braak sends you to clean up the mess."

That got an eyebrow raise. The dying man knew who had orchestrated his demise, and who had commanded the Kiveri Czai to carry it out. This was possibly why he had been instructed to use poisons, to make the death as slow and painful as possible. His master did not like being interfered with. As for the 'Arcane one', he did not know them at all. His master did not discuss plans with him.

"I wonder if the Arcane one will share what he has stolen, or if he has other intentions. I should have known they would—"

The dying man's words cut off as his body heaved with a violent, hacking cough. Blood joined the wine, splattering onto the pages in a blend of mahogany. It was quite impressive, really, that his body had not yet succumbed to the various poisons currently travelling through him. Playful killers, racing to see who could reach the vital organs first. Too many antidotes had been made in recent times. It was better to be sure.

"I'll be replaced. High Marshal is but a title," the dying man gasped, spitting blood onto the parchment before him. He seemed to realise each word could be his last, and he wanted to make them count. Most did. And most wasted their final words on pointless declarations.

"Above all, I was a good man."

Another sneer. These people were all the same, illusions of grandeur and power. How he despised them—powerful men who controlled the lives of those beneath, in the name of society and order. All to lord it over one another how polite and demure, how productive and obedient their subjects were.

They were all slaves. Some were just more aware of it.

The High Marshal was breathing hard, still determined to give his own eulogy. From experience, most of those cursed with slower assassinations acted similarly. Men longed to be profound in the moments before death, like they could override a lifetime of meaninglessness.

"I lived as honestly as I could. I took no bribes, I—tried to keep the soldiers with the most to lose from the grittiest battles. I fought with honour." The dying man's tongue must have begun to succumb to paralysis, for his words began to falter. "I h-have served my realm, the kings and the gods, and... ensured the safety of th-those within this city's walls. I protected them. I did more good than bad. I... I go to Requiem knowing that."

The High Marshal's words gave him pause. This man really thought himself a grand protector of the mewling crowds and tittering nobility? That he had been more than a puppet for whatever king lined his coffers? That he had spent his life keeping them safe? How honourable, indeed. He attempted another sneer, but it felt hollow. He had no true quarrel with this man. He was only the messenger.

The High Marshal had lost the use of his limbs now, and was struggling to keep his head up. His neck muscles ceased to function and collapsed, and his eyes squeezed shut as he braced for impact. Instead, the dying man found his head being gently lowered onto the desk. It was an apt ultimate resting place for a man married to his position. No partner, no children, no family to speak of had been discovered. Either the High Marshal had not cared enough to forge those connections, or cared enough to make them untraceable.

The Kiveri Czai found these unattached kills less soul-scarring, somehow. Usually.

The light began to leave the High Marshal's face, and he found himself staring into it, determined to bear witness. The harsh wrinkles around the man's eyes had softened, but the lines remained—a permanent homage to years spent squinting towards the horizon. Though his last decades had been spent behind a desk, at heart, the man was still a fighter, and had deserved a more glorious death.

As he removed his gloved hands from the dying man's neck, the hood of his robe fell back. It revealed little of a face that could have been handsome, if not for the utter void of emotion. It wasn't human.

"I made Altaea safe," said the High Marshal with his final breath.

The single remaining candle snuffed out, and as the room plunged into darkness, the dying man's ears caught the last sound they would ever hear. The faintest chuckle, humourless and bleak. The laugh of one who must do what he has been ordered, or face worse.

And for the first time, the Kiveri Czai spoke to his victim.

"My good man, of this I can assure you. From death, no place is safe. Death comes for us all."

PART ONE
THE GOD OF LIFE

1

LESSIE

We're going to get ourselves killed.

Lessie Shilling pushed the morbid thought to the back of her mind with a sigh and attempted to focus on the task at hand. She had been observing the occupants of a run-down fort from the forest for the greater part of the past three days, and the monotony was wearing on her. The rest of her crew were expecting her to catalogue everything; not only to find the best way in, but also to know where to hit should things go south. One wrong move could see all of them fighting for their lives. A miscount of the guard detail could result in failure. An overlooked escape route could spell death.

So she watched, and she assessed, and she memorised. The crew had built their plans from the information she gathered, and they were more likely to succeed because of it. It was gruelling, thankless work, but it was vital.

It was also, for the most part, extremely boring.

The rest of the crew didn't know Lessie well enough yet to know that if it were her alone, she'd probably have given up and stormed in by now. Every so often, her fingers twitched towards the shiny revolver strapped to her hip, though it was currently unloaded. Only the promise of vindication kept her from leaping from the large branch she perched upon. She had managed to convince them this kind of preparation was necessary. Now she had to prove it.

They need to see how much smoother things run with my plan.

Lessie had only just started working with a crew, and at first it had been frustrating, since nobody had been willing to change the way they operated. But after completing a couple of low-stakes jobs and proving her worth, the others seemed to trust her enough to let her put in the preparation. Since joining them, it was the second time she had insisted on full reconnaissance—and the first time they had listened. The catastrophic failure of their last job had helped to convince the others. They couldn't afford to mess this one up.

Even if her last couple of meals had been interrupted with pointed questions of when she would be finished.

I don't know what they're complaining about, anyway. They get to relax, while I get to be stuck up a godsforsaken tree for half the week.

Lessie suppressed a groan, readjusted her footing, and forced herself to survey the situation once again. She listed the human elements aloud under her breath. It was easier to relay information if she remembered saying it. Her father had taught her that.

Her father had taught her a lot of things, while he could.

"Single guard on the larger roof of the tower. Three on the parapets; two patrolling, one stationary, focusing east. Two at the door to the east entrance, stationary. Four at the main entrance, to the west, stationary. Another four on the outer edges, moving laterally, never lingering together long at any crossover. Shift change every eight hours, rotation every four."

Lessie dug around in her pack for a minute before producing a small notebook. Balancing it precariously on her lap and squinting at her own messy handwriting, she compared today's figures with those from the ones before. They matched. It was a pattern.

"Twenty-eight total, minimum," Lessie whispered to nobody, "though by how rested the soldiers look, more likely closer to forty."

Gods help us.

Practically a legion of guards, for a broken-down piece of rubble in the middle of nowhere. It had to be the right place. The fort itself was not worth guarding. The derelict building gave the impression it had been uninhabited for at least a full cycle of the Kingswitch. Dark, abandoned, falling apart. Nothing fancy to look at.

The fort's newest occupants, in contrast, wore bright, unfamiliar colours, denouncing them as outsiders. The tension was palpable, a living thing roiling over the fort. Those inside knew what they guarded would not remain unchallenged for long. They weren't bothering to hide their numbers. They were anticipating an attack—maybe even welcoming one. Why not take their prize and disappear?

Lessie's thoughts wandered again as she glanced at the twin suns, already beginning their lazy afternoon descent towards the horizon.

Mae should have checked in by now. She's not usually late.

Stiff and uncomfortable from the tense hours of inactivity, Lessie shifted her weight, the bark of the ancient oak scraping against her boots and snagging on the thick material of her trousers. Tendrils of chestnut hair caught the breeze and swayed into her vision, having escaped from the long braid down her back. The gentle wind brought with it the heavy, woody scent of the forest, along with something familiar she couldn't quite place.

Sick of looking at the fort, Lessie let her eyes wander. She had chosen her vantage point for its high ground, the forest flowing over the hills like a great green river before bursting its banks into the fields. The fort itself stood around a mile away, but the enemy's bright tunics made it easy to follow their movements, even from a distance.

Gods, it's like they want *me to track them.*

Away from the building, trees and patches of colourful wildflowers dotted the landscape before being swallowed by the massive forest she lurked in. Something about the fields reminded her of home, although she still missed the lighter hues of the plains behind her house; the way the browns and yellows blended together in summer. It was too green here. A quiet, picturesque countryside, where nothing much happened.

Until now, she supposed.

Lessie shook herself. She had been watching a small bird as it flitted from branch to branch and had not focused on her task for a good few minutes. Forest this thick was a liability. There were too many distractions. She closed her eyes and allowed her breathing to slow, bringing her back to the present moment.

In for six, hold for three, out for six.

Another old trick of her father's. He may have never left their tiny hometown, but that hadn't stopped him from being full of useful information on all walks of life. She missed him so much it felt like a physical pain in her chest.

If only he could see this. He'd never question my patience again.

A single twig snapped and Lessie's eyes flew open.

A shifting of movement in the trees below. Her adrenaline spiked as she caught the barest hint of movement from the corner of her eye. She strained through the thick undergrowth of the forest floor, scanning and disregarding information until she found the source of her sudden discomfort. There.

Two amber eyes, faintly glowing in the dappled light. They belonged to something large. Feline. Carnivorous. And stalking straight towards her. The beast stopped under the tree, sniffing the wind, and Lessie subconsciously held her breath. It sat back on its haunches, pausing momentarily before powerful hind legs launched it halfway up the oak in one leap. The animal—a mountain lion—reached the branch she occupied within seconds. Lessie shuddered at the sound of sharp claws embedding into the tree's trunk, scraping the bark loose like skin. It growled softly as it placed one monstrously oversized paw onto the bough.

But as Lessie locked eyes with the creature, she offered it a rare smile.

"You're late."

The mountain lion huffed as if offended. It padded elegantly towards her, then paused, hearing the creak of the branch as it protested their combined weight. Lessie was treated to the odd sight of chagrin on the predator's face, before there was a flash of greenish light and the creature disappeared. In its place, a human woman crinkled her nose and adjusted her skirts to prevent her skin from making contact with the branches.

"This forest all looks the same," Mae said, stretching as she adjusted back into her human body. "I had to rely on scent alone. Of course, that was relatively easy, since I just had to follow the reek of gunpowder and resentment." She cocked her head at Lessie, the movement still oddly feline. Gentle amusement glimmered on her face.

Lessie rolled her eyes, but the corners of her mouth tugged upwards at the comment. Mae made fun of her the way she imagined an older sister might, or maybe a mother who was less highly strung than her own had been. It was an odd dynamic, but Lessie welcomed it.

As with her real sister, however, it was impossible not to draw uninvited comparisons. Mae's face was kind and soft, whereas her own was angular, all cheekbones and frowns. Mae's hair shone, brilliant fiery waves that tumbled past her collarbones, and her amber eyes were deep-set and framed by long, dark lashes. Even the way Mae held herself, perched on a smaller branch with inhuman grace, suggested a quiet calm Lessie couldn't even comprehend after a week of hiding out in the woods. Mae might as well have been elven. There was probably Fae in her bloodline, somewhere, but that would be rude to insinuate.

It didn't matter. As a Divine of the goddess of life and nature—whom she referred to only as the 'Mother'—Mae preferred four-legged forms more often than not. Lessie envied the ability to escape.

People are too predictable. They only look out for themselves.

"I've been sent to get you. Grundle wants to go in," Mae said, gesturing towards the large fort as if Lessie hadn't spent the past few hours staring directly at it. "They're done waiting."

Lessie only raised an eyebrow in reply. Since when did Grundle call the shots?

Mae gave her an imploring look. "I know, I know, but he made a good point. There's only so much planning we can do before we must take action and adapt to the circumstances as they arise."

Lessie snorted. "Grundle said that?"

The idea of the sullen, unrefined rogue spouting words so poetic was laughable. He'd sooner spit on the floor than recite words with more than three syllables.

Mae laughed with her, an airy sound that conjured summer breezes.

"Well, I cleaned it up a bit," she said. "I believe his exact words were 'Grundle thinks this will all go to shit anyway, so we might as well get on with it.'"

The sound of Grundle's jarring words floating out of Mae's mouth elicited a true bark of laughter from Lessie, one that could have easily given away their location had she not been so meticulous about scouting. That was the point of reconnaissance. To keep them all safe. Lessie knew they were all itching to act, just as she was, but a bounty like this—with a payment this high—couldn't be run blind.

"This is the biggest legitimate job I've had," said Lessie. "By myself or with a crew. I don't appreciate Grundle trying to rush the most important part of the assignment. He's just bored since I've forced y'all to not jump straight in and actually plan it right for once."

Mae gave her a gentle smile. "And that's exactly why we needed someone like you to join us."

Us. Right. Lessie was still getting used to that.

When she'd become desperate enough to join a crew, she'd had trouble finding one that would accept her. Meeting Mae and the others had been pure luck, and Mae had been warm and welcoming, enveloping Lessie into the ranks as quickly as possible. Naturally, this had made Lessie immediately suspicious. Her first theory was that Mae had latched onto her because they were vaguely similar in age, with the Divine appearing only a handful of years older than Lessie's twenty-five seasons. But a few innocent campfire conversations had Lessie thinking Mae was a lot older than she had first guessed.

Divines are rumoured to be ageless, after all.

Mae was the first Divine Lessie had ever met; with strange abilities gifted to her by the goddess she followed. Divines were uncommon, especially in Altaea. Mae's gifts were coveted, sought after by the powerful and godless, and most chose to work for the nobility. Mae could, theoretically, live a life of luxury serving the highest of Altaean society. So why was she in a common mercenary crew, earning a pittance and sleeping on the ground more often than not? Lessie wondered, but she didn't have to know the exact answer to know.

The same reason any of us do this. Because in this line of work, nobody asks too many questions. Plus, the gold is easy enough to earn, if you're not a complete moron. It's the best option we have out here.

Even if some crewmates were easier to stand than others. Lessie swallowed, the bitter edge to her thoughts leaving a bad taste in her mouth.

"Look, I know it's taking longer than I said it would, but I don't think we're ready," she said. "I want at least one more night to establish the pattern. Grundle can moan all he wants. He'll thank me later when we're all alive and actually paid this time."

"That may be true, but it's not just Grundle who thinks we've got enough information to move on," Mae said carefully. "Valandaras wants to move by sunset. I must say, I think he's right. You've done really well, Lessie, but there's only so much we can plan. Besides, Val has always made the right calls before. I trust him."

Lessie glanced at the sky. The twin suns still shone, albeit lower than when she had last made note of it. The light had taken on a soft, diffused quality, bathing everything it touched in an ethereal glow. Sunset couldn't be more than half an hour away.

"Well, if he means tonight's sunset, he's cutting it godsdamned close," Lessie muttered.

For the first time in the conversation, Mae bristled. "He's waiting for me to come back with you. Val wouldn't leave without either of us."

Lessie willed her eyes to stay looking straight ahead, resisting the urge to roll them. He absolutely would, if he thought it was the right move.

Lessie's overall opinion of Valandaras was still undecided, but if she voiced any of her concerns, she was sure to hurt Mae's feelings—not that Valandaras needed any help in that department. The experienced fighter and de facto leader of their little crew was talented in many areas, but noticing Mae's affections for him apparently wasn't his speciality. It was the first thing Lessie had picked up. Sometimes, watching them interact made her want to scream in frustration. It was just so... obvious.

Other people's relationships made her uncomfortable.

You don't have to do this mercenary work for long. Just until you have enough gold to keep searching. Then you can set off on your own again, and nobody can tell you how long to take.

"Sunset it is, then, since apparently Valandaras knows everything," Lessie muttered, irritated, already reaching for her pack to take stock of her belongings.

Her revolver, by far the most valuable item she owned, was first to the touch, hands dropping to her side to check automatically before she had even opened her pack. The vast farmlands of a sleepy border town like Picking had been a strangely ideal setting to hone such a skill, and Lessie had been using more primitive versions of a firearm since she could walk. The shooting had come naturally. The killing was another thing, but she couldn't afford to think about that anymore. Lessie traced her fingers over the cool metal, letting it ground her and bring her tasks into focus. Her expression softened as she felt the slight indentation etched into the smooth wooden handle. Two letters, in an impossibly elegant hand.

'T.S.'—her sister's initials.

Her hunting bow and quiver were next to be checked. Lessie ran her fingers over an arrow's fletching, feeling the feathers resist the touch. Most people still used weapons such as these, and she'd favoured a bow for years. It was good to have a backup. Firearms were rare, and ammunition was hard to procure. Lessie was lucky to own one, although her sister still insisted it was 'on loan', since she had been the one to make the weapon.

Lessie's journal lay tucked at the bottom of her pack, wrapped within her sleeping roll. She felt for it blindly, and the knot in her chest relaxed slightly as her fingers brushed the outline within the fabric. In a way, the simple leather book was worth even more than her gun.

Trixie would kill me if anything happened to either.

In some ways, it was even harder to think of her sister than it was of her parents. The happy memories were now stained with a coating of fear, an uneasy uncertainty. They'd shared a room for most of their lives, spent every day together, and now Lessie hadn't set eyes on her sister in over a year. It felt wrong.

Trixie was safe, most likely. Halfway across the world, but happy and completely safe. But what if she wasn't?

What if she's lying to me?

Lessie heard her father's words more often than ever since she and her sister had parted ways. His very last words to them had been largely inconsequential, but his repeated phrases over the years had been branded into her brain, her soul, and became her creeds to live by. The ones about Trixie had been said the most.

Take care of her. Family is irreplaceable. Trust each other. You're sisters. It's your job to keep her safe.

Lessie made a mental note to write to Trixie later that evening, to make sure she was as safe as she claimed to be. If the crew didn't all die horrible deaths when the job inevitably went sideways, that is. Satisfied that her belongings were all where they were meant to be, Lessie swung her pack over her shoulder and started climbing down from the tree. It felt good to have her feet touch solid ground again.

"Let's go," she said.

Mae hadn't moved. She had been picking absently at her fingernails, judging by the tiny flakes of turquoise paint that now drifted from them, disappearing into the folds of her skirts. She seemed hesitant to voice what thoughts troubled her. As if saying them aloud would cause them to become reality.

Of course, when you were Divine, that might be exactly what happened. Lessie had no idea how that sort of thing worked.

"What is it?" Lessie asked.

"I just have the oddest feeling that it's all going to go wrong," Mae replied, a slight quiver in her faraway voice. "Like this is a path that leads to the Silver Stream. To death."

Lessie felt a cold sense of dread wash over her. Since joining the crew, she had worked a handful of jobs with them before the current one. She may not know them as well as they did each other, but she had picked up enough to know when something was off. Mae was usually optimistic about a job's outcome, to the point of irrationality. This seemed different, and it was unsettling.

"I'm sure it's all in my head," Mae said doubtfully. "We've taken the time to plan it all out. We all know what we're supposed to do. Nobody's going to get hurt."

Lessie nodded in agreement, but Mae kept staring off into the distance, her strange amber eyes full of apprehension. Like she could see a hundred possible outcomes and was worried about all of them. It reminded Lessie of her mother, despite the two being nothing alike. The comparison was like a punch to the gut, knocking the breath from her momentarily.

It was too easy to find them in everything, now.

Mae shook herself. "I'm just nervous because of what happened in Holdfast. Right?"

Lessie flinched at the reminder. Their last contract had left quite a few new scars on them all. It had been an utter failure—there had been some metaphorical wounds to lick, as well as a few actual broken bones to mend. It had taken them weeks before they'd felt ready to take on a new bounty. The delay in work had cost them, and Lessie's personal gold was running dangerously low.

I joined a crew to make money, not lose it.

"Right?" Mae repeated. They both needed to believe it.

"Right," Lessie replied. She tried to make her voice strong and reassuring, and it came naturally. Mae may be quite a few years her senior, but for the moment Lessie pictured her little sister, eyes wide, convinced a demon was lurking under their bed. How many times had she whispered in the dark, chasing fears of a nightmare out into the sunlight?

"Of course we'll be all right," Lessie added. "We've done the work. In and out. Nobody will even know we were there."

She finished her thoughts unspoken.

As long as the others don't do anything too godsdamned stupid.

At that moment, as if planned by some escaped god to mock her, the serene silence of their surroundings was shattered. A muffled explosion thundered towards them from a mile away. The ground shook. The forest came alive, with small creatures scurrying away and birds taking flight, eager to escape the unfamiliar noise that carried the promise of a distant threat. Mae gasped, her hands flying to her face.

"Oh, Mother," she exclaimed, pointing towards the horizon.

Lessie launched herself back up the trunk of the tree. Not bothering to go as high as before, she could still spot the cloud of billowing smoke already rising from the fort, partially obscuring the tower. She couldn't be certain, but it appeared to be coming from the east entrance's stone wall. Close to the thick, impenetrable wooden gates reinforced with steel.

The very point Lessie had spent days assessing, and the crew had agreed when she said it would be the absolute worst place to position their attack.

"Looks like they decided to start without us, after all," said Mae, a burst of anger clouding her features. Her skin had already started to glow with a faint emerald hue.

Lessie swore as she jumped back down from the low branch. Her boots hit the forest floor with a soft thud.

You've got to be godsdamned kidding me.

They were miles away. It would take her forever to get there. She wondered, selfishly, if perhaps this way they could avoid the majority of the bloodshed. Of course, if they couldn't get there fast enough, the blood being shed would be theirs.

Lessie blinked and Mae was gone, and the mountain lion in her place gave a gruff nod before leaping from the branch and tearing into the fields. She would be there in half the time it would take on human legs.

Lessie forced herself to unclench her jaw, swallowed her scream of sheer frustration, and loaded her revolver. The bullets slid in with a satisfying click as she rotated the chambers.

She could yell at the rest of the crew later. Right now, there was only the job.

Get in, get out. Nobody sees us. That was the plan.

As she steeled herself to run, the distant sounds of panicked shouting coming from the fort told her the last part of the plan would already be impossible.

Amidst the stream of muttered curses that fell from her mouth, her father's favourite popped into her mind. The only time he swore around his girls. He would always apologise profusely afterwards, all the while knowing they were using words much worse, but never around him.

Words Lessie would give anything to hear one more time.

Well, hell.

2

REEVAN

Reevan observed the chaos with unblinking calm.

He lingered outside the entrance of the western gate—an ambitious name for it, since it was more of an oversized archway in the stone wall. Pulling his dark robes closer around him, concealing his sandy fur, Reevan kept one clawed hand on the hilt of his dagger beneath his cloak. He stayed still and silent, poised to strike at the first enemy unfortunate enough to exit the keep from this direction. None came.

Reevan cleared his throat, a sound that no ordinary man would pick up—but the small, dark-skinned goblin standing on the other side of the archway noticed it immediately. Grundle made no noise at all as he met Reevan's eyes, his only reply a sharp nod confirming they were soon to be alone.

It had worked. Guards were shouting, all moving towards the east entrance of the fort. Towards the explosion. Away from the western gate. Away from them. Just as Valandaras had said they would.

Reevan sniffed. The plan-within-a-plan had been risky, since Lessie had not finished her reconnaissance, and Reevan had been averse to rob the women of their chance to weigh in on the move. All were involved, so all should get a say. But Valandaras's reasoning had been sound, what little of it he had shared with them, and it appeared to have paid off. Still, it was a little irritating. Although not the type to gloat, success would reinforce Valandaras's belief that he knew best, which would of course make him insufferable the next time someone disagreed with the way he planned a job.

Grundle would be even worse to deal with, as it had been his idea to utilise the small amount of explosives he had managed to procure. He would relish in the fact that some may have already lost their lives to his carefully constructed booby trap. Most people mistook Grundle's lack of eloquence for a lack of intelligence, and the quiet goblin was happy to let them. Grundle was small and easy to dismiss—which made him the deadliest of them all.

Smoke rose from the eastern wall in thick clouds, floating up and over them and marring what had been quite a beautiful sunset. It flooded Reevan's kitskan senses with the reek of destruction. Harrowed screams, audible even from this distance, suggested multiple injuries. Grundle gave him a smug smile.

Reevan let his focus pull away from the last disappearing group of guards who had vacated their post outside the western gate. His eyes trailed upwards to assess the fort from the inside now, vertical pupils dilating in the fading orange light. It was impressive how much of Lessie's information matched up with what he could now see. A single cylindrical tower in the east gave the only proper height to the architecture, patches of ivy trailing hopefully up the sides of the uneven stonework. Otherwise, it was as standard as forts of its time could be, rectangular and utterly commonplace. Small windows interrupted the cold greys of the masonry only occasionally, dotting the three storeys. What remained of a partially crumbling wall had hidden most of the lower levels, and a makeshift palisade had been constructed in places around the fort, albeit sloppily. Large gaps had betrayed where the enemy felt most comfortable, where they thought they could defend without effort.

So Valandaras and Grundle had hit the most fortified part of the keep. The unfamiliar men who squatted in this keep had panicked from the explosion and taken to the parapets to cross the large compound faster.

Leaving the rest of its entrances clear.

And in the pandemonium, not a single guard noticed the two hooded figures move inside behind them. One tall, one diminutive, neither strictly human—in a regular setting, they would make quite the odd couple. It was a pity nobody was around to see it.

Reevan now stood by the rickety door of what they had marked as the servant's quarters, the half-crumbling building as disused and forgotten as the rest. He remained impossibly still, the only movement his tail twitching, peeking out underneath his robes. A reflex he had unfortunately failed to train out of. He readjusted his long robes around his lithe body, repressing a shiver. The cooler season had already begun descending upon the majority of the land, though this close to the border resisted it longer. Some leaves on the trees were already turning various shades of red and gold, though most stubbornly clung to green. Reevan was used to intense summers and mild winters, and had not expected to spend his twenty-first season in Altaea. At least it didn't get too cold in this part of the country. He had experienced much worse.

Reevan glanced down at Grundle, who had taken out a small leather-wrapped parcel full of gleaming silver tools and was picking the ancient lock on the door to the side of the building. The lock was older than them both combined, and flakes of rust drifted down onto the weathered stones that surrounded the building. Reevan, for his part, flipped his dagger into the air, catching it in a pawlike hand, before using it to scrape non-existent dirt from the razor-sharp claws at the end of his fingers.

"Could you quite possibly accomplish your task any faster?" Reevan asked, the delivery polite and melodic as if he were commenting on the weather. "We're a bit exposed out here."

The only response his question elicited from Grundle was the sound of sharp teeth grinding together. Perhaps his small colleague had not heard him correctly.

"This sort of thing usually takes you much less time," Reevan added. "Are you having extra difficulties with this simple mechanism? I can attempt to help if you like."

Reevan was rewarded this time with an irritated grunt from the goblin.

"Grundle thinks the cat should be quiet," Grundle muttered around the small tool wedged between his teeth. His gravelly voice matched the glower on his pointed face. "Grundle is nearly in."

Reevan snorted. Ah, of course Grundle would refer to a kitskan as a cat. How delightfully pedestrian. Reevan was a cat in the same way a human was an elf, the way an orc was a goblin. Distantly related? Most likely, but it was deeply offensive to suggest they were one and the same. Granted, his entire body was covered in fur, he did have claws, and he was quite adept at seeing in dim light. However, he'd never met a house cat over six feet tall who could speak three languages.

No matter. If calling Reevan a cat was the worst taunt Grundle could come up with, Reevan would allow it. An insult only carried weight if it were true. Besides, he was only trying to help. An emotional outburst was quite uncalled for, really. They had known each other for years, been working together all their lives. Grundle was the closest thing Reevan had to a friend.

A slight click and the lock finally acquiesced, granting them access to the room within. Reevan's casual stance shifted into a deadly calm, revealing what he truly was.

A predator.

Grundle rolled up his tools back into their pouch, stowed them safely in his belt, and edged the door open. Reevan slipped inside and quickly scanned the room, the green of his eyes disappearing into pools of black as they adjusted to the lack of light. This fort had been long abandoned, but there was no true way to know which areas inside were currently being occupied. The sight of his sandy furred face caused no angry shouts or screams, which was a good sign. Having deemed the room devoid of life, he signalled that it was safe to enter.

Grundle shuffled into the keep, causing tiny flurries of dust to swirl around his feet. A thick layer of it coated the bare room; items of value or sentiment would have been removed whenever the staff had left. Little remained beside a few cots, resting in the corners like skeletons in their tomb. An empty vase sat next to one, the flowers it might once have held long crumbled into dust. Whoever owned this keep was either long dead or long past caring about it.

Reevan had been in enough castles to know that these quarters would be directly connected to the kitchens—but more importantly, there would be passageways that would take them anywhere inside the keep without being seen. After all, nobility didn't want to see their slaves scurrying around, attending to their every whim. That would be improper.

Stepping out into the kitchens, Reevan observed the silent tells. This room, unlike the one they had just vacated, had been used recently. A large, rusting pot sat near the hearth, which contained embers from a dying fire. The scent of rudimentary spices in the air rushed Reevan with an unexpected pang of homesickness, which he quickly dismissed. Crude metal bowls and cups lay haphazardly on the large benches, suggesting some guards had taken their afternoon here to replenish. Someone had attempted to make a stew. Reevan crinkled his nose as the smell of something burnt beyond recognition assaulted his nostrils, the long white whiskers brushing against the side of his hood. The cooking of the stew had gone quite poorly indeed.

Among it all, the information he had counted on. A set of rusted brass chimes, their holders embedded in the stones, delicate chains disappearing into the walls. Tarnished plates attached below each one, denoting in the common tongue which room they hailed from. The names were simple, intended for even the uneducated to recognise.

Hall.

North Bed.

Bath.

Tower.

Courtyard.

Dungeon.

He took a moment to collect himself, digging through his mind for information that had been gathered over the past few days, mainly by the new girl. Lessie was young to call herself a ranger, but had so far been quite a useful addition to their little crew. Valandaras had been right to offer her a place with them, though she had claimed it was to be a temporary arrangement.

Reevan hoped she would reconsider, for her style of reconnaissance had been quite useful. Their earlier attempts to assess the fort had been rudimentary at best. Mae had taken the form of a sparrow and attempted to map the keep from the air, but she had confessed the tiny wings fatigued faster than was optimal. Reevan had been perplexed at that and had asked why then did she not simply become a larger bird?

Mae had reddened and fallen silent at his question, and Valandaras had spoken sharply to him for the rest of the afternoon. Reevan still hadn't gotten an answer. Perhaps this was why Mae did not serve in any of the houses of the high nobility, as most Altaean Divines did. Perhaps the king's courts demanded larger birds.

Despite lacking in aerial surveillance skills, Lessie's intel had been most beneficial to this operation, tracking movements of all guard personnel and where they congregated. The trick, she said, was to look for the human elements in the mechanical decisions. Reevan, being a kitskan, had felt the vague impression he should be insulted, but had listened anyway.

Lessie had pointed out that most of the guards crossed over the eastern entrance more often than the others, suggesting that the reason they were there dwelled in that quadrant. The need for presence both on the roof of the tower and below it showed they feared the tower being breached. Hastily constructed palisades had all been positioned around the south and west, implying the enemy felt they could better defend themselves to the north and east, where they wanted the majority of their forces to be.

Fascinating, really. How anything could become a pattern.

It was clear. All signs pointed to getting inside that tower, and that it would be extremely difficult. Getting back out again would be a nightmare. Reevan felt his skin prickle with excitement. It had been a while since he'd been presented with a challenge. He turned to Grundle and gave the goblin his best approximation of a smile. It looked painful, as if he was unused to it.

"Try to keep up, my short friend," Reevan stated plainly, as if it weren't obvious that the goblin would fail spectacularly at doing so. "We've got a tower to climb."

Valandaras had given them seven minutes to find what they came for.

Reevan would do it in five.

3

REEVAN

Reevan knew he had found the right room when he discovered two guards outside it.

They were currently doing a spectacularly poor job of guarding the door, instead gaping out of the nearby window at the commotion below. One guard looked as if he would gladly jump from the top of the tower itself if it would bring him closer to the fight, itching to join the fray. The other seemed like he was close to vomiting, pale and clammy beneath his ill-fitting armour.

Reevan assessed the area. The stairwell was circular, winding around the rooms within. He had opened the servant's passageway directly onto the bottom level, but the open stairs gave no shadows to slink unseen. The top floor had presented him with a quaint hallway leading to a singular door, to what had most likely been the master room of the keep.

With the majority of the guard occupied outside, Reevan had only dispatched two others unlucky enough to cross him in the secluded halls. If any had fallen to Grundle, he hadn't heard it, since Grundle was no longer behind him. He wouldn't be surprised if the goblin had given up and gone back to wait for him in the servant's quarters. Grundle was quiet and ruthless, but keeping up with Reevan was not his strong suit. Nobody could move quite like a kitskan with somewhere to be.

Two clean strikes and both guards would fall. Reevan tensed, readying his dagger. The eager guard jostled his companion for a better view of the ground below. Reevan caught a clearer glimpse of their faces.

They were young. Much too young. Still in the twilight of their teenaged years. The elder of the two looked as if he was attempting to grow a moustache, if the ten or so hairs on his upper lip were any indication. Eager volunteers, perhaps, or forced to leave the family nest to support a struggling household.

Reevan was young, too, but he had known no other life. This was no place for children. He sighed aloud, cursing his own bleeding heart, before drawing in a deep breath. Out of sight in the stairwell below, he bellowed in an authoritarian voice unlike his own usual drawl.

"All guards to the east entrance, now!"

His declaration announced, Reevan immediately tensed his powerful back legs and shot straight up into the air. Pinning himself to the ceiling with his clawed hands and feet was quite uncomfortable, but murdering children was a line he had never crossed.

He wished he had his staff, his usual weapon of choice, but it had been too conspicuous to bring along. His tail helped with little more than holding his robes from falling, but hopefully the guards would be too enthusiastic to leave their tedious post to notice. He held his breath and focused on the feeling of his paw pads gripping the ancient stone.

Reevan's ploy was successful. Both young guards practically tripped over each other to race down the stairwell, the eager one dragging the other by a fistful of his tunic. Reevan kept still, listening to their retreating steps until the sounds were swallowed by the commotion outside.

He was alone. Perfect.

Reevan retracted his claws and dropped silently to the floor. He didn't like to use them often, preferring less unique and traceable methods, but it was very unlikely anybody would think to check the ceiling.

Now his only adversary was the door.

He should have attempted to locate and swipe a key from his junior companions, but there was a high chance they wouldn't have had access to the room itself. He certainly wouldn't have entrusted them to. Cursing Grundle, who was much better at opening locked doors and who clearly had declined to scale three flights of stairs, Reevan stared at this last obstruction and cracked his knuckles.

First, he tried the obvious. He gripped the door handle. It was locked. Well, at least somebody in this establishment took their security seriously. Reevan poked a sharp claw into the keyhole, more out of curiosity than anything. It was an old mechanism, designed to be operated from the inside, only requiring a key when the occupant wished their belongings to remain untouched within. He tested the top and bottom of the door, letting his claws scrape along the stone of the framework.

"Is someone out there?"

A male voice, muffled, came from within the room.

Reevan stayed silent, continuing to poke around the door. There had to be another way in. He inspected the hinges.

"If you're here to rescue me quietly, you've done a rather awful job of it," said the voice, speaking louder this time. The accent was Altaean and lilting, the tone a mixture of bored and amused. "They'll have heard that blast halfway to Roost Keep."

Reevan, who had one claw embedded in the top of the rusty hinge pin and was attempting to coax it out from the bottom with the tip of his dagger, let out a snort. He had been to Roost Keep, and it was much too far away for the noise to travel. Whoever this was, perhaps they should leave him in there.

When the pin had emerged enough to get a grip on it, Reevan used his dagger to slide it free. He turned his attention to the other hinge, which came loose much faster now he had figured out the angle and force needed. He clawed his way between the wood of the door and the stone of the castle's wall, bent the door in the opposite direction it was meant for, and finally accessed the room.

It had been four and a half minutes. A new personal best. Reevan was quite pleased with himself.

This room had indeed been intended for the master of the keep, with large windows providing what was left of the fading sunset's light. They had been left open, panes of glass dulled with years of dirt. A worn tapestry depicting a bird of some kind adorned the north wall. A shabby desk and wardrobe were the only furniture besides the bed, a giant four poster that would have once been grand. It had threadbare blankets and a moth-eaten mattress, as well as a solitary figure who lay upon it. Reevan evaluated him, tail twitching.

The man was human, twenty-five seasons or so, lying on his back with an air of regality only those born into coin could manage. Dark brown hair brushed the collar of his nightshirt which, although stained, was finely made and embroidered along the edges. He seemed to be in reasonably good health, despite his current living arrangement, as well as reasonably good spirits—in fact, he looked as if Reevan had merely awoken him from a pleasant nap. Only the bound hands and the gag around his mouth marked him as a prisoner. The material had pooled around his chin, like he had been fighting it for hours and only recently won.

Reevan greeted him with a deep bow.

"My lord, your cavalry has arrived."

The man snorted in amusement. "Forgive me, my good man, but you resemble a cat, not a horse."

Reevan blinked. "Is it always your first inclination to insult your rescuer's race? That seems like a poor choice. If you do not want to be rescued by a kitskan, I can leave you here if you so wish."

The man's face remained jovial, but Reevan caught the flash of panic easily. Although his posture suggested ease, his eyes darted warily from Reevan to the door. Humans wore all their emotions on their faces.

"No, no, not my intention at all," the man said hastily. "My apologies. I would be delighted to be rescued by a kitskan. Shall we go, then? I have missed my own bed. And wine. And decent conversation. Nobody here can cook worth a damn, either."

A hint of a smile playing under the half-fallen material that had been secured around his mouth, the man swung his legs towards the edge of the bed and attempted to stand before falling awkwardly back. He gestured to where he had also been bound at both ankle and thigh.

"I'm afraid you'll have to carry me, my good kitskan. I hope that isn't too much of an inconvenience for you."

Reevan moved towards the man, his dagger still out from the improvised lock picking. He spun the blade between his claws with a flourish.

"I suggest you hold very still, my lord," Reevan said, "or you shall find yourself wishing I had not been the one to liberate you."

All joking aside, the man went still as death. Reevan chuckled. He certainly seemed to value some parts of his body more than others. Reevan made quick work of the bindings on the man's legs and was moving to his wrists when a clattering sounded from the hall.

Reevan spun to find the youngest guard—the queasy one—returned to his former post. He had stopped in the hallway, momentarily distracted by the simple wonder of seeing a door off its hinges.

Time to improvise.

"It appears you were right," Reevan whispered to the man on the bed, "I will have to carry you. I hope you're not afraid of heights."

Reevan allowed his newest friend a moment of confusion before lunging towards him and hoisting him up in a lightning-fast movement. The young guard faltered as Reevan turned towards him, drawing up to his full height with his human cargo in his arms. Luckily, the captured man did not struggle, which gave Reevan the chance to adjust to carrying his weight.

The guard drew a shining sword, but it was plain that he had barely been trained to hold it, let alone use it. Reevan locked his emerald gaze on the guard, who seemed to be fighting the urge to run.

He should have listened. When confronting a predator like Reevan, it was best to follow instincts.

"Let this be a lesson to you, child, before we go," Reevan said politely to the guard, back-stepping across the room. He used the movement to shift the man around onto his back, and the bound wrists of his passenger to keep his arms looped around Reevan's neck. The guard's confusion only increased. Where would they go? He was blocking the tower's only exit.

Or so he thought.

"Don't blindly follow orders," Reevan continued, "or you'll find all of your free will goes out the window."

With that, so did they.

The guard's aghast face vanished as Reevan launched himself backwards out of the window's open frame and plummeted down alongside the tower. His human companion let out a terrified shout before his own self-preservation kicked in, locking his legs around Reevan's middle and mumbling a string of barely coherent curses into the kitskan's back. Reevan concentrated on scraping his claws along the stone, sparks flying as he attempted to slow their descent. His dagger wrenched from his grip and clattered to the ground below. The keening of nails against the stone made Reevan's ears ring, and the friction of his hind claws dragging along the tower gave him the strange sensation of wanting to vomit, but thankfully his limbs remained attached to his body and they made it to the bottom of the tower relatively unscathed.

Leaping the last few feet off and rolling forward to soften the landing, Reevan landed lightly on his feet. He supposed he and cats had that in common, too.

His unwilling passenger was not so lucky. The man came over Reevan's head and sprawled into the dirt, the bindings on his hands preventing him from catching his fall. He narrowly missed a patch of thorny bushes growing at the tower's base.

"Perhaps it is best to lie low for a while, my lord," Reevan remarked, patting his new friend on the shoulder. "You've got cover here."

The man gave him a withering look as he shuffled further behind the bushes. He looked like he regretted being rescued.

A fallen guard lay motionless to Reevan's right, and the smoking remains of a large hole in the eastern wall showed where Grundle had decided to announce their entrance into the keep. Bits of wood from the palisades and other debris from the blast littered the courtyard between the keep's heavy main doors and the wall that surrounded it. Ash floated through the air, guards shouted frantic orders, metal clanged as weapons clashed, and all around was chaos.

And in the centre of it all stood Valandaras.

Wielding a curved sword; the deadly falchion already dripping with red, and a heavy silver shield, Valandaras moved with the grace of a seasoned fighter decades older than he appeared. The piece of off-white cloth covering his eyes from view did nothing to impede his vision or technique. His steps were deliberate and unhurried, parrying over and over as men tried to cut him down from all angles.

Reevan paused as he took in the scene, mentally calculating how likely they were to emerge victorious. At least ten guards lay slain. Valandaras showed signs of fatigue and minor injuries, but he held strong, and that in itself was enough to intimidate those he faced. His opponents seemed to be steeling themselves to fight him a few at a time, after rushing him at once had proven unsuccessful. A sharp clang sounded as one guard's sword smashed down upon Valandaras's shield, and the smell of blood and sweat mingled in the air. Valandaras was severely outnumbered, and his silver armour was already coated in ash, dirt and blood, but he was well-trained and formidable. His very skin emitted a faint light as he spun between his opponents. Flashes of brighter light came from beneath the cloth on his face. It was mesmerising.

Reevan was so distracted watching the deadly dance unfold that he almost missed the crossbow bolt flying towards his left ear.

His reflexes caught up before his brain did, snatching the projectile from the air as if it were no more than an errant moth daring to flutter past his vision. Reevan followed the arrow's trajectory and locked eyes with the guard who had fired it, perched upon the damaged outer wall and looking rather shocked.

Reevan grinned.

He had crossed the courtyard and was halfway up into the parapet before the guard had realised what had happened. He sauntered up to the man, a picture of nonchalance.

"It is quite rude to attack when your opponent is distracted," said Reevan conversationally.

The guard, at least, had the common decency to look vaguely ashamed. He could see the man's pulse beating wildly in his neck. All men died the same. Terrified. The guard was backing up along the wall, but the blown-out portion had made the structure unstable. There was nowhere to go.

"Of course," Reevan continued, strolling closer, "it's also quite effective."

The guard had dropped his crossbow and was trying to unsheathe his sword. Reevan jammed the crossbow bolt into the man's neck.

Crouching and keeping steady as the guard collapsed, Reevan stayed to watch the man's soul depart for the Silver Stream. It was quick, as he had intended it to be. Then he turned his attention back to the dance.

Valandaras was not looking so well. He had been fighting since the initial explosion had drawn all the attention, and he was wearing down. Lessie's intel had confirmed at least thirty guards. It was a miracle a marksman hadn't already taken him out.

Looking around, Reevan noticed a suspicious lack of archers. He wondered if they had all decided to take the day off, or if they felt it would be dishonourable to defeat a foe like Valandaras with a coward's shot to the back. Neither option was likely. He didn't have to wonder long, as his vision caught the flash of colour from a guard's uniform as they plunged over the side of the far wall to the ground below. They didn't rise. Reevan caught a glimpse of a tiny black head moving in between the parapets.

Not a miracle, then. A goblin.

Reevan, still perched next to the body of his would-be assailant, was about to make the leap back to ground level when a number of things happened at once.

A particularly strong fighter smashed into Valandaras' shield so hard he finally lost his grip, dropping it into the dirt.

Sensing an opening, the guard made to deliver a blow, raising his heavy warhammer high.

And lost the arm that held it as an enormous mountain lion closed its jaws around it.

The guard's blood-curdling scream as the massive animal landed on top of him was enough to make everyone on the field pause. The sound of tearing flesh pierced the air.

When it was satisfied the man had been thoroughly disarmed, the lion stood and paced in front of Valandaras, snarling, as if daring the remaining guards to make the first move.

Mae was a different kind of formidable.

She and Valandaras worked in tandem, covering each other, exploiting weaknesses in their enemies. Valandaras seemed to get a second wind from having a companion to fight with, and the remaining guards fell quickly.

Reevan didn't even feel the need to step in. They looked like they had it handled. In a manner of minutes, the courtyard was near silent; the only sound being faint groans from the wounded. Reevan sniffed. They'd been quite successful, really.

"STOP," came a voice from the edge of the courtyard, "or I'll kill him!"

Reevan's head whipped around, and his eyes came to rest on a most unpleasant sight. His newest friend had evidently decided against Reevan's advice to lay low, and the other young guard from the tower had found him. The captured man struggled against the sword at his throat, but his hands were still bound.

The eager guard seemed disoriented, as if he had never seen true combat before, but he had tasted bloodshed and liked it. There was a fervour in his eyes that had been only embers in the corridor, now fanned into a flame.

This was a dangerous new step to the dance.

"I mean it," he called to Valandaras, eyes bulging. "I'll slit his throat right here. We all know he's what you came for."

Valandaras made a show of wiping the blood from his blade before putting it back into its scabbard. The seasoned fighter took a step towards the guard, who yanked his captive back. The captured man whimpered as his bare feet scraped on the ground.

Valandaras spoke in a clear, calm voice. "You don't want to do that, boy," he said, his mouth a hard line. "Killing changes a person. Murder most of all."

Reevan rolled his eyes.

The guard seemed to be psyching himself up to commit the atrocity he threatened. Reevan noticed the signs. His grip on his sword had adjusted, he had planted his feet and lowered his centre of gravity. He truly believed he was doing the right thing by denying them their bounty.

Valandaras had stopped moving closer to the guard. Mae had stilled. No sign of Grundle. They all knew this was dire. They needed to do something, or this would have all been for nothing. Also, they wouldn't get paid.

The guard laughed, a harsh sound for one so young. His eyes darted wildly between the two foes in front of him. Reevan saw a glint of fanaticism spark within them as the guard took in Valandaras's armour, the golden glow emanating from him, the coverings over his eyes. All markers for who and what he was.

"Realmshifter," the guard sneered at Valandaras, spitting onto the ground before him. Mae growled, hackles rising.

Reevan sniffed. At least the child was educated on obscure holy factions.

"The Master spoke of ones like you. I'll be commended when he learned I spilled this noble's blood right in front of you. He'll be so pl—"

The sentence hung unfinished in the air. For a second, Reevan wondered why he had stopped. Then his brain caught up to his eyes, and he realised the guard was missing one. The sound thundered through a moment later.

Where the guard's left eye had been moments before, now only a crater of splintered bone remained. Reevan could see through it to the castle wall behind. It was an off-putting sight.

The guard seemed to crumple in slow motion, his brain not having time to register half of itself was now missing before he hit the ground.

Ninety feet away, breathing hard, revolver still smoking, stood Lessie.

Reevan sniffed in approval. Not bad. Yes, the new girl had made an excellent addition indeed.

4

MAE

The smell of death was overwhelming in this form.

Mae's tail swished around her, trying to clear the air, and she fought to keep her focus. Breathing didn't help, as every inhale flooded her senses. Blood and sweat stained the ground, dark patches forming under fallen enemies. She could taste the emotions that still lingered. They were simplified, in their rawest form—rage, terror, guilt. She couldn't voice the feeling while in her human body, but life and death seemed more real when experienced in another form. Animals had a way of understanding what it meant to die that people couldn't truly grasp.

Most people, anyway. She wouldn't shift back until she had to.

Mae forced herself away from the courtyard to prowl around the grounds, checking for signs of other guards. They had neutralised the threat for now, but the Mother only knew what reinforcements could arrive at any moment. When she was satisfied that there would be no immediate second wave, she allowed her attention to rest where it belonged.

Valandaras.

He kneeled in the dirt of their makeshift battlefield and was leaning heavily on his shield. The fighter looked exhausted, drenched in sweat and blood. Most of it wasn't his, but Mae could smell that he'd been wounded, and the thread of worry tugged at her. Covered in scaled armour, what little of his skin was visible held a luminous golden glow. It was usually faint and imperceptible, but the fading light of dusk made it stand out. He looked otherworldly.

Reevan and Lessie had approached the former captive and were assessing his injuries. There was no sign of Grundle anywhere. For the moment, they were alone.

Mae padded towards Valandaras, who always took this time to be silent after a fight. He was still breathing heavily. She watched through slitted pupils of amber as a bead of sweat glistened upon his forehead before rolling into the stained cloth covering his eyes. He never removed it. Mae had asked once, long ago, and he had not given her an explanation for why he wore it, only that he had to. Over the years, it had become normal, and she barely even noticed it anymore. The cloth itself was a thin fabric, not truly opaque, merely muting the light that poured from his eyes—so his face was still somewhat readable, if one knew how to look for the expressions beneath the cloth.

Mae had a lot of practice reading Valandaras's obscured expressions.

A very dim light came from beneath the cloth, which Mae understood meant his eyes were closed. Valandaras shifted towards her as she came closer. A casual movement to most, but to Mae it was acknowledging and welcoming her presence.

"You fought well, lioness," he said. His low voice was strained, and he winced on every inhale. "This form suits you."

She chuckled, but what came out was an odd growl. The main frustration of wearing another form was that communication was difficult at best and impossible at worst. It was time to return. Mae sighed. She didn't like this part. It felt wrong, somehow.

In her mind, a silent prayer formed. *Thank you once again for your Gift, Mother. I release it.*

She contorted in pain as the transformation took place, tearing her bones and muscles apart before weaving them together again. Her body glowed with a blinding emerald hue, forcing her eyes shut. The strange sensations of claws turning to fingernails, of fur becoming hair, of a tail disappearing, were all minor notes in the symphony of Changes. Her Gift was no illusion, she truly became what she wished to, if the Mother willed it so.

More than once, she had wondered why it only hurt coming back.

Mae blinked as her human eyes struggled to adjust in the failing light. She had been sitting on powerful feline haunches when she released her Gift, and now found herself kneeling on the sodden dirt with Valandaras, her yellow dress already dirtied. She barely noticed, already reaching towards him. He needed her.

Valandaras leaned away from her touch, and Mae shoved down the stab of rejection that flared in her gut. *It's not you. He's not ready to let go of the pain yet.*

"Val, don't be ridiculous," she chided. "Let me help."

Her eyes roamed his body with the precision of a healer, someone who had seen countless wounds and tended to all she could. Judging by how many injuries she found, he should have been in agony despite his stillness.

Valandaras's eyes remained closed. "Pain is a necessary part of battle," he said. "It is penance for the life that was taken today."

Mae huffed. "And healing is a necessary part of my job," she replied, rolling her eyes in an exaggeration of annoyance. "Show me the worst of it."

Valandaras didn't respond, but she caught his mouth twitching as he smiled at her retort. Releasing his grip from his shield, which was planted firmly on the ground, he gestured to his side. Mae gingerly unbuckled the side of the breastplate, lifted the dark red undershirt, and pressed one delicate hand to the flesh underneath. Valandaras' sharp intake of breath told her all she needed to know.

"Broken ribs," she murmured, more to herself than to him. "Internal bleeding. And a lot of cuts and bruises."

Her hands hovered above his luminescent skin; the glow even more noticeable in the dark. She waited for his permission. He gave her a curt nod, eyes still closed.

Mae prayed. *Mother, please help me to help him.*

For a moment, nothing happened, and Mae felt a jolt of panic that she had overused her Gift and would be unworthy of any more for today. Being a Divine was not without its limits, and she had been leaning on it heavily the last few weeks. Then she sighed in relief as she felt the faint, familiar warmth of the Mother slowly spreading down to envelop her hands. She pressed them to Valandaras' side and concentrated.

The emerald gleam from her fingertips pulsed against his skin and appeared to merge with his own glow, as if playfully greeting each other. She'd healed him enough times that their sparks were old friends by now. It wasn't much, but she gave all that she could. She knew it had mended the cracks in his ribs, and the worst of the internal damage had been reversed. With rest and time, Valandaras would be all right. Mae exhaled heavily.

It was never enough.

No matter what some in the Altaean nobility believed, Mae wasn't a miracle worker, and could not undo injuries truly fatal. If one of them lost a limb, she could not bring it back. She could mend bones and stop bleeding, but she was no master of death. There was no stopping a soul who had already crossed into the Silver Stream. She knew that for certain.

Energy spent and Gift running dry, a sudden wave of exhaustion crashed over her. She always felt a bit faint after using her Gift to heal, as if it took from her to give to others. Her vision blurred, and she swayed forwards, grateful she was still kneeling.

Two strong hands shot out and grabbed her by the shoulders, steadying her. Mae opened her eyes and immediately blinked, squinting.

Valandaras had moved to mirror her position, his arms on hers to prevent her from falling, his eyes fixed on her. His cloth dimmed the light that poured from his open eyes, but to face him this close still stung her own. Valandaras seemed to sense her discomfort from his gaze and turned his face away.

The strangest sense of sorrow always flooded her when he couldn't look at her. Like he thought she was afraid of his light.

He thinks I should be afraid of it. Of him. Can he not see the true monster?

"Thank you," Valandaras murmured, and Mae detected a note of bitterness in his voice. Did he resent her for having to heal him? She took a steadying breath and willed her voice to be light.

"It was nothing. I've seen worse," she replied. It was tough to keep her thoughts straight with him this close, and she attempted to laugh off her nerves. She was too old to be reacting in this manner. "In fact, I've seen worse just on you. Somehow this is less damage than last time. You did an incredible job handling this many guards."

"He had help from Grundle," came a low, gravelly voice from directly next to them. Mae's heart jolted in her chest before she recognised it.

The goblin, dark-skinned and dressed in black leathers, blended in so well with the evening that now blanketed them that he was almost invisible. Few could hold a candle to Grundle's level of stealth—he was completely silent when he wanted to be. His small stature put him at eye level with them kneeling, and Mae felt oddly exposed as the goblin's overlarge yellow eyes bored into her. Valandaras dropped his hands from her shoulders and she felt a sudden rush of cold.

"Grundle took care of all the archers," said Grundle, while checking his assortment of knives and poisonous powders in various pouches strapped all over his leathers. "Grundle thinks it would be not right for Valandaras to die from an arrow. Too sneaky."

"My dear friend, it appears you had missed one," said Reevan, sidling up to the three of them as if they were having a picnic he was fashionably late to. "I had to reacquaint him with the crossbow bolt he aimed so rudely at my head."

Grundle glowered, offended that his work had been declared less than perfect. Reevan seemed not to notice.

Mae glanced between them, smiling. She had met Reevan and Grundle almost a year ago, now, when they had crossed paths for a job. The unconventional pair were both from Kalac, across the border, and were so different from anyone she'd met before. She found them fascinating, and often amused herself by comparing the two.

Grundle was calculating and meticulous, preferring to silently increase their odds in any fights by sneaking around the shadows. The tiny goblin would never survive open combat, so he made it that he didn't have to. Clever as a fox and twice as stealthy.

Reevan was oblivious to social cues and often seemed rather bored in most polite conversation, but he was just as deadly when needed, and approached every task he was given with an air of detached confidence Mae desperately wished she could have. His kitskan heritage made it impossible not to compare him to a cat, but she had come to think of him as more of a mountain lion. Quiet, striking quickly, but also prone to moments of silliness. Mae had been using his colouring for her last few Changes, she liked how the sandy fur blended into different surroundings.

At first, they had been wary of one another, and she had been just as likely to not see the two for weeks between jobs. Reevan in particular had a tendency to disappear. The last few months, however, they had all come to know each other's strengths and weaknesses and taken jobs accordingly. They had carved out a decent living working together.

Survivors, all of them.

Mae scanned the goblin and the kitskan for injuries, but detected none. The front of Reevan's robes were very dusty and torn, but otherwise, they both appeared unharmed. They were only hurt if they were caught. She found herself smiling, proud of them, and also relieved that her Gift would not be required. She was empty.

"That was so exciting. I almost forgive you for cutting Lessie and me out of it," said Mae, glaring at Valandaras with no true malice behind her eyes. "I wasn't sure how fast mountain lions could run. It was kind of... fun."

There was no use holding onto a grudge for a decision like this. Valandaras had done what he thought would give them the best chance at success, and he had been right.

"If y'all are done chatting, we need to move. Now."

Lessie's sharp voice echoed across the courtyard, cutting through the light-hearted moment like a dagger. She moved towards them with the grace of a hunter and the temper of a wild boar, half-dragging their rescued captive with her. Mae noted that she had not removed the bindings on his hands. Lessie didn't trust anyone.

The young man seemed to have recovered from his attempted assassination and was grinning at all of them. It appeared as though he had been trying to engage Lessie in conversation. Knowing her, it hadn't gone well.

"My gallant rescuers," he declared, with a sweeping gesture tempered by his bound wrists. "Wonderful work on my liberation. Except perhaps for the part where the cyclops over there attempted to sever my head from my shoulders."

He jerked his head backwards at the one-eyed corpse behind him, flashing them a mischievous grin. He had very straight teeth, and reddish-brown stubble grazed his sharp jaw. Underneath the layer of grime from his imprisonment, the young man was quite handsome, but it was clear he knew it.

"I'm going to go ahead and assume we now have a long, perilous journey ahead of us," he continued. "Fantastic. I'm sure you've a carriage stashed somewhere nearby, since walking the whole way will be... refreshing."

There was a hint of sarcasm beneath his words. Cynicism wrapped in grandiose. A dangerous combination if he knew how to use it. He was also obviously used to those around him falling over themselves to grant his every whim.

Mae hid an amused smile. Whoever this boy was, he was not going to like how their crew reacted to him. She'd never met a group less inclined to respect authority born of privilege, be it of noble birth or fair face.

"Forgive me, my ordeal seems to have robbed me of my manners," the young man said, clearing his throat dramatically and addressing them as though they were adoring fans who had gathered to hear him speak. "I haven't even introduced myself properly. I am the Lord Camden DeFalcone of—"

"We don't care," Lessie interrupted, snapping at him.

Camden blinked. A lock of dark hair fell into his eyes, and he frowned as he swatted at it with bound hands. Mae stifled a giggle. Yes, this was a man who was accustomed to people treating him like royalty. He had to be from a high noble house, most likely one of the Seven. They were easy to spot. The fine clothes and the accent weren't the giveaways; anyone who could muster enough coin and instruction could play the part. It was the sense of entitlement—the attitude of one who thought he was always the most important person in the room. Irritation flickered on Camden's face, like a house cat denied the hospitality of a warm lap it had every right to.

Sometimes, for Mae, it was easier to read people if she searched for the animal in them.

Camden recovered quickly. "Well, I do hope you're not all this awful," he said, shooting a look of distaste at Lessie. "Or it's going to be a terrible journey."

Lessie ignored him completely. She was staring back towards the fallen body of the guard she had sent to the Silver Stream. The pool of blood grew steadily as it soaked the ground, travelling further away from underneath the remains of the mangled head. Her face paled beneath her freckles.

She is still uncomfortable with taking life, Mae thought. *Good. It means she still has a soul.*

Placing a hand back onto his shield, Valandaras rose from his position on the ground, towering over the others. He didn't say anything to Mae, or even look at her, but he extended one faintly glowing hand towards her and she took it. Rising from the ash and mud of the battlefield, Mae dusted herself off.

For a moment, the six of them stood together silently.

For once, Grundle spoke first. He always referred to himself in the third person, which Mae had thought strange at first but come to find oddly charming.

"Grundle thinks we should retreat to the camp, rest, then move quickly at first light," said Grundle, his low voice harder to catch with human hearing. Mae chastised herself for wishing she could shift only her ears into a design better equipped to deal with low tones.

Valandaras fixed his obscured eyes on each of them in turn, reading the agreement on their faces, before stepping towards Camden. To his credit, the young man made a show of not being intimidated by the glowing, bloodied warrior in front of him, and only flinched lightly when Valandaras drew his falchion from the sheathe. The blade itself was ordinary and most likely owned by many before, but in the hands of a Realmshifter, it may as well have been crafted by the gods themselves.

Valandaras motioned for Camden to hold out his arms, and severed the bonds around his wrists. Lessie narrowed her eyes, like she expected the man to pull a hidden weapon from his stained clothing and attack.

"Let us go, then," Valandaras said quietly, picking up his shield from where he'd wedged it into the ground and hoisting it onto his back. The movement highlighted the simple design that had been etched into it, barely visible through the blood and grime that had coated it. A lion's head, mouth open in a ferocious roar, eyes glowing faintly with an everlasting pulse of light. It was duller than Valandaras's own eyes, which he kept covered at all times. Another mark of who he was and where he belonged to. Just one of a dozen clues when all taken into account became obvious what he was.

A Realmshifter.

Realmshifters were few and far between in their realm, but most people had still heard of them. Legends whispered about in taverns had a way of twisting—what the holy warriors could do, where they came from, who they served; there were more myths than solid facts. Valandaras himself rarely referred to anything before the years in which they had worked together. He had told Mae some of his tale, the bones of what it meant for him, but he seemed reluctant to share more than he deemed absolutely necessary. Mae wondered what it would take to earn his trust for that particular story, for him to open up to her.

Of course, they all had secrets. She had first met him many years ago now, and he had never once asked her anything about her former life, only that she wished it to remain so. Mae didn't know if he had questioned the others more thoroughly—if it were only her whom he had accepted with no explanation. A lone Divine in the middle of nowhere, unsupervised, with nothing but a flimsy excuse and the clothes on her back. Unimaginable in Altaea.

Mae had heard that in other parts of Kalaraak, Divines came and went as they pleased. Controlled by nobody but their own whims. It was a myth, a frivolous daydream whispered between Divines of neighbouring noble houses. Divines were fairly uncommon, with only dozens chosen in the century since the Godprison had splintered, so any who showed signs of being Gifted were carted off to the capital before long.

Mae also knew that there were other lands that considered anyone Divine to be a perversion of humanity, and they were hunted. There was always something to be afraid of.

"Lioness, are you planning on taking point?" said Valandaras without turning back.

Only Mae would take that for what it was—a gentle push out of her own mental loop.

They can't take anything else from me. I will not be afraid.

Mae shook herself out of her thoughts, gave the others the most reassuring smile she could muster, and followed the Realmshifter into the darkness.

5

MAE

It was easier to forget the day's horrors when staring into flame.

The night was unseasonably cold, and so was the food, but the small fire Lessie had built kept the worst of the shivers at bay. Mae cupped her hands around her tea, letting the warmth from the steaming liquid seep into her bones and the sweet scent of peppermint fill her head. It was worth not drinking it. Her fingers no longer felt like ice.

The six of them had made it to the secluded clearing a few miles from the fort; travelling straight through the forest itself to avoid any of the small homes around the fort. They had not dared to get close to any of the homesteads, or what remained of a tiny village nearby that had probably sprung up around the fort when it had been new and impressive. The homes could have offered shelter, but they also could harbour more enemies. It was not worth the risk of discovery.

Lessie had done her job well, scouting ahead and declaring their previous campsite safe, before doubling back and making sure they were not followed. Mae had been secretly relieved. The task of rearguard usually fell to her in another form, but her energy had been too depleted to Change. Valandaras had her lead the expedition instead, and the girl had taken over both jobs without complaint.

Mae suspected Lessie had done it not only to help her, but to get away from their newest companion, the Lord Camden DeFalcone. The handsome young nobleman had complained gloriously the entire way to their camp, about anything and everything. His blood-soaked tunic. How the nights should not have turned so cold this early into the autumn. The lack of light causing him to walk into low-hanging tree branches. Mae had tried hard not to giggle when she'd noticed Lessie's fingers twitching towards her weapon every time he opened his mouth.

Camden had finally fallen silent about his poor bare feet bleeding on the forest floor when Valandaras had turned around and picked him up, hoisting him over a shoulder and carrying him a good thirty feet before the younger man's pride had insisted he was returned to walking.

Mae had openly laughed at this, and Valandaras had turned his golden glare in her direction. She'd clapped a hand over her mouth, sheepish at unintentionally mocking their important bounty. However, Valandaras's face had softened, and he had given her a small smirk in return. She knew he'd done it partly for her reaction—to make her laugh.

She couldn't explain how she could read the expressions of a man who covered half his face with cloth. She just could.

There were a few attempts at conversation, mainly from Camden, who seemed accustomed to being entertained and had not enjoyed his weeks of solitude. Mae indulged him in niceties while the rest of the crew remained quiet. Now they sat in silence, the only sound the crackling of wood, the flickering of the flames their only light. It was the most peaceful night they'd had in weeks.

Grundle and Reevan stepped away from the group to set up their bedrolls for the night. Lessie rummaged through their haphazard collection of supplies and managed to find a pair of old boots that looked as though they may fit Camden. Mae suppressed another giggle when the ranger dumped the dirty shoes into the lord's lap, ignoring his blustery protests as she stalked away to ready her own bedroll.

Mae felt the weariness pulling on her bones. It joined the familiar ache in her soul that always felt stronger when her Gift ran dry. It was enough to make her feel alone, adrift—disconnected from who she truly was.

Mother, please let tonight's rest be enough.

She didn't know how she would get through the following day's journey without her Gift. It was the only thing that made her useful to the other crew members.

There had been a time in her life when she had felt isolated from her Gift for months. It had been like living in a fever dream bathed in eternal night. It had taken everything she had to pull herself out of it. Now the tiredness from a regular job came with the haunting of that time, and Mae's exhaustion threatened to pull her under right at the fire's edge.

A strong hand rested gently on her shoulder.

"Go to sleep," said Valandaras quietly, standing behind her. He had leaned down so that he could address her alone, his warm breath tickling the skin of her neck.

"Val, I'm all right," Mae protested, but her wobbly voice betrayed her.

"You're not. I'm taking the first watch," he said, straightening up. He seemed to have recovered from the worst of his wounds. Sometimes Mae thought he had healing powers of his own. She hadn't been able to give that much; he would have to have still been hurting.

She opened her mouth to argue, but a yawn escaped instead. Valandaras's mouth twitched in amusement.

"Sleep. Now," he said quietly.

"All right, all right, General," Mae replied, raising her hand to her brow in a salute and attempting to sound teasing, but her thoughts had already begun to drift away towards the bedroll she'd laid out. "Promise me you'll wake me for the next shift, though. You can't do the whole night alone."

A tiny sliver of light shone more brightly through his cloth as he fixed her with a pointed stare, before he softened and gave her a small smile. It was a beautiful sight.

"Go to sleep, lioness," he repeated. He avoided her statement completely.

Mae chuckled. She was no more a mountain lion than a sparrow, or a deer, or a house cat. She was all of them and none. But she liked the way it sounded coming from him.

She got up from her position, her muscles protesting as she stretched. Her body screamed for sleep. She glanced over her shoulder as she began the short walk to her bedroll.

"Promise me, Val," she said.

He simply replied, "Goodnight."

She didn't wake until sunrise.

The path to their destination—a town that connected paths to many of the major cities, aptly named Crossroad—was uneventful, taking five days on foot. If they'd had a cart or horses, the travel time would have been slashed, but it had been both too conspicuous and too expensive.

Valandaras kept them all to a strict schedule and a marching order that saw Camden protected on all sides, wanting to make up for the time they lost each night. Mae knew Valandaras would have preferred to travel through the nights, but the crew were more drained from the rescue than any of them would admit.

Her Gift was always slow to replenish, especially after a big job, and she was using what little she had left to ease the other's aches from the extended travel. Camden's feet were bloodied from his barefoot travel, though the boots Lessie found for him helped. Valandaras' injuries from the fight lingered in his slowed pace and stiffness. Mae gave everything she could, which fortunately felt like more than she had managed before. The fourth night, she had been so tired she had fallen asleep before returning to her human body.

Mae spent most of her time on the edge of the roads, ahead of the rest, having Changed into a hunting dog used for tracking. The heightened sense of smell and hearing made her able to pick out other travellers well before they were spotted, which enabled the crew to avoid curious eyes or prying conversation. Whether innocent merchants or something more sinister, they were better off melting into the trees unseen than risk being remembered. It was second nature to her.

The Mother has blessed us with this weather, at least, she thought, letting the cool breezes and scents of autumn wildflowers wash over her canine senses. *We've been lucky to avoid the rain.*

It was equally peaceful and lonely, to stay in a Changed form for so long. As the fifth day passed, Mae found herself running closer to the rest of the crew, keeping one ear on the road and the other on the conversation. One-sided as it was.

Valandaras didn't speak as he walked. He kept his eyes on the road ahead, constantly watching for 'complications', as he called them. Ever the soldier. Grundle, too, was mainly silent. Reevan and Lessie chatted somewhat, but mainly exchanged looks, the former quizzical and the latter annoyance.

The Lord DeFalcone, however, had taken it upon himself to regale them all with grand tales of himself, the surrounding land, and his family's wealth and influence. He peppered in a few stories of debauchery and wine-sodden bad decisions, for flavour. For a man Mae judged to be in his mid-twenties, he had quite a collection of them. She had listened to most of it.

To pass the time, she told herself. Not to check for anything amiss in the nobility's circles.

Camden mainly spoke of his own house, of which Mae was the least familiar. Therefore, some of the information was new and interesting. She still surprised herself with how much she remembered, how many words sparked a glimmer of recognition inside of her.

Recognition—and dread.

Mae had been correct in her initial assessment of Camden; the DeFalcone family were part of the Seven—the common term for the high-born families that made up the majority of Altaea's nobility. Most of where they had travelled through were Camden's ancestral family lands, he told them. That was interesting, at least. The fort they had rescued Camden from belonged to the DeFalcones, but it had been in disuse for decades. His father preferred to live in the sprawling city of Verestead, though he split his time around a few other keeps. It was proper for one in line for the next Kingswitch to reside in the capital for more than a year before the handover occurred. Camden had expressed shock that his father had come to rescue him, since Verestead was so far to the south of Altaea.

Mae tuned out the history lesson. She was well-versed in the intricacies of the Kingswitch and the nobility it revolved around. Most Altaean Divines were sworn to the noble houses, and their services were guarded fiercely. A single Divine could mean the difference between a house's rise or fall. Depending on which god they served, some were granted Gifts of creation, others of terrible destruction. Some, like Mae, were healers, keeping the young strong and the old in good health. The Seven high noble houses relied on their Divines and kept them safe, but it came at the cost of their freedom.

Mae had spent many years of her life in Verestead. She hoped to never see it again. Even hearing it mentioned sent a shiver through her, her hackles rising.

"And of course, I am grateful for your gallant rescue, but I must admit I thought it would be quicker," Camden said, in the middle of an impromptu speech on the importance of his father's time. "Two weeks is a long time to be away from home, and with the reascension less than a year away–"

"I don't understand," said Lessie, interrupting. "If you're so important, why did your rescue have the misfortune of falling to a mercenary crew hired off the street?" She narrowed her eyes as if trying to detect a lie.

"Couldn't your daddy have sent half the Kingsguard marching down to save your pretty face?"

For a moment, silence hung in the air. Mae's wolfhound ears pricked up. Lessie had obviously had enough of Camden's rambling and decided to engage him.

This should be interesting. The girl has no more love for nobility than I do.

Camden's jaw set momentarily, as if he were clenching it, before arranging his face into a pleasant smile.

"It is simple," he replied, a hint of a smirk crossing his features. "If my father was currently our king, perhaps he would have done so. As an Archduke, he does not have the power to command the Kingsguard, as they are busy guarding the king."

Lessie's eyes narrowed, and Camden only smiled wider. Mae got the impression that both of them knew what she had originally meant, but he had taken the literal meaning of her sentence and ran with it purely to annoy her.

"I suppose Father could have sent the house guard down," Camden continued, "but it appears as though he elected to go the quiet route of rescue. Why he chose such an interesting group remains to be seen. Perhaps there were no others available on such short notice. I know better than to question his motives."

Camden looked down pointedly at the tunic he wore, still stained with the blood of the guard who had almost killed him. "Perhaps if the Kingsguard had orchestrated my retrieval, it would have been a little... cleaner."

Lessie paused briefly as she looked over at Camden, as if deciding which of the words inside her mind would sting the most. Or perhaps she was regretting her impressive aim.

"I get it," she said as they continued walking, shoulder to shoulder. "Your father doesn't actually like you. Maybe he took so long to have you rescued because he forgot that you existed. Are you the fourth son? Fifth?"

Camden blinked. "Second."

"Ouch."

"My father is a very important man."

"Gods, maybe he left you there so he didn't have to hear you talk."

"This might be hard for you to understand, but Father knew whoever took me wanted a fuss made, so he refused to give it to them."

"Doesn't that usually piss off spoiled brats like you?"

Both had stopped walking and turned to face the other. Camden was glaring at Lessie with a look of incredulous venom in his eyes, like he was shocked somebody would dare speak to him that way. A wolf distracted from a kill, puzzled that its prey would confront it rather than run.

Lessie held the gaze, challenging it. The expression on her own face had grown dangerous. She had been insulted, and Mae had seen before what happened when the girl felt threatened or looked down upon—it usually ended in a fistfight. She was territorial, quick to anger, and never hesitated to strike back. A rattlesnake.

Mae smelled no fear from either of them. She growled. A warning for them to play nice.

The rest of the crew were doing their best to pretend the conversation wasn't happening, except for Reevan, who was observing the barbed exchange with mild interest. Mae moved her wiry wolfhound's body closer to Lessie, feeling protective as she noted the height difference between the two. The younger woman was practically covered in weapons, but Camden was a head taller, broad-shouldered, and unpredictable, not to mention an important lord from an extremely powerful family. He could very well order Lessie executed the moment they set foot in town.

Mae still wasn't sure who she was more worried about.

"Why would it enrage a man," Camden asked, avoiding the original phrasing of Lessie's last comment, "to have a fuss made of them?"

She scoffed. "Not that. I'm talking about not getting exactly what you want all the godsdamned time."

At this, Camden's face unexpectedly brightened, and he threw his head back laughing. Lessie cocked her head, brow furrowing at his odd reaction. He only smiled at her, teeth flashing. She raised an eyebrow.

Mae held her breath.

"Honey, I've never had a single problem getting what I want," said Camden, brushing dust from the shoulder of his jacket dismissively. "Perhaps you've had more experience with that. It would explain your charming demeanour, my *lady*."

There was an unmistakable patronising tone to his voice as he gave her a title she did not hold. Mae felt the hair on her hackles rise despite the barb not being directed at her. She would not have been surprised if the younger girl pulled her weapon at this point.

The rage in Lessie flared behind her eyes, and her fingers balled into fists, but to her credit, she simply threw Camden a disgusted look and stalked ahead to catch up with Valandaras.

Mae huffed a sigh of relief and whined at Camden, who was staring after the girl with an expression like he'd smelled rotten meat. He flinched, startled, as if only just remembering he was not alone. It looked as if he were coming back to himself after getting caught up in the moment, not entirely sure why he'd been so offended.

Reevan chose this moment to sidle up to Camden.

"I'm afraid Lessandra doesn't like you, my lord," he said pleasantly. "I suggest you refrain from speaking to her from now on if you wish to remain whole and unshot."

Mae discovered dogs could laugh.

Camden opened his mouth to reply, but Valandaras's clear voice cut him off as they rounded a corner in the path.

"Enough. We'll reach Crossroad before sunset."

Mae sighed, a strangely similar feeling in a canine body. Finally, they would return to Crossroad, deliver their bounty, and move on. She could stop worrying about lords and nobility and their petty quarrels. They would get a new job, travel to a new city, and she would remain invisible. She could keep avoiding anything to do with the Seven, like she'd done so for a decade now.

A single thought froze her. *What if Camden's father recognises me?*

6

VALANDARAS

The cloth itched, but Valandaras ignored it. He had a job to do.

They had reached the outer rims of Crossroad before sunset, as he had predicted. The town was a hub of activity, even as the last rays of the twin suns glowed faintly on the horizon. A collective sigh came from the surrounding crew, and pride glimmered underneath his exhaustion. They had done well to make it this far with no complications.

The sound of his boots on the neatly packed gravel of the main thoroughfare was a welcome change. Valandaras had walked the surrounding roads for many, many years, and knew the favoured ambush points of the various banditry and racketeering that happened outside of city walls. Through his careful plotting of the route, they had avoided it all. A well-thought plan was a well-executed one.

Valandaras's decision to leave some crew members out of the initial attack was a perfect example. It was simple. He had needed the guards to believe he was alone and that they could defeat him, or they would have simply removed Camden, or killed him. Valandaras had considered that Mae and Lessie would be hurt by the decision to sideline them until the last moment, and that they would not have agreed to it. But the success of the move had relied on their ability to shake off that hurt and play their parts.

Which they did, he thought. *Even if that last guard's actions almost undid us. Mae was brilliant as always, and the girl arrived precisely when she was meant to.*

Valandaras also knew part of him was trying to keep the rest of his crew from direct bloodshed. Sometimes, though, it was inevitable.

No matter. He had been given a task, and the final step to accomplish it would be to deliver their human bounty to the client. Then the crew could rest—stay a few nights in Crossroad before seeking another bounty or job, likely a more lucrative one due to the gossip that would spread of their success. Two, perhaps three nights could result in a higher interest in their services.

Always calculating. Even a rest was part of the plan.

He took in the sight of the glowing windows, inns and homes lighting lamps as the last light faded. The smell of stews being brewed and ale being poured filled the air. Snippets of conversation drifted from windows left open to let in the crisp evening breeze; children's laughter rang like bells as they chased each other towards their homes. Crossroad was a quaint town, despite its size, with no true walls and a sense of homeliness that kept the residents content and the travellers frequent.

Surrounded by the sounds of camaraderie, Valandaras allowed himself a moment to wonder how the rest of his Pod were faring without him. He imagined their reactions to the recent events. Elastrad, their leader, would have disapproved of his needing Mae to help him finish off the final guards at the crumbling keep. Xiclaar would have been jealous that he missed out on the battle. Saelin would have laughed and congratulated him with a bone-breaking clap on the shoulder. Valandaras could practically hear it, the voice booming too loud as always. *That last one nearly got you there, brother!*

He missed them all. His family, in oath rather than blood. But his Path—the mission for which he walked in this realm—was unfinished, and he could not return to them until he completed it. He would catch up to whichever realm they had found themselves in eventually.

I need to find a Sliver that even Saelin will covet, Valandaras mused. A small smile formed at the memory, and his eyes crinkled under his cloth. *He's been waving Aasimon's Fang in my face for far too many years.*

A small, deliberate cough caught his attention, and Valandaras looked down to see Grundle. The goblin had been at his side since they had reached the outer limits of the city.

"Grundle thinks the dog needs something," said Grundle.

Valandaras looked back. The rest of his crew were close, Reevan having decided to walk in between Lessie and Camden since their earlier exchange. Judging by the huffs and venomous looks shooting between the two, it had been a wise decision. Reevan, however, seemed to have done it purely for amusement, attempting to engage both in conversation and not having much luck with either. The three had followed along behind Valandaras into the town and now lingered in the street; just a group of weary travellers deciding on which inn to bed down in for the night.

Grundle, who missed nothing, was right. They were one short. Mae had stopped a few paces into the town, still in her Changed form. Her hackles were raised and her ears flattened. She was clearly in distress.

"I'll handle it," Valandaras said, voice low.

Grundle shrugged, turning his attention back to the other members of the crew. Nothing really phased the goblin.

Valandaras approached the wolfhound in the street. He kept his voice low and calm, the way one might address an animal. Did people address animals at all?

"Do you not wish to enter, wolfhound?"

Mae whined. Her tail had tucked between her legs. The signs were not difficult to decipher. Valandaras had known many hunting dogs in his years, and Mae for over half a decade now—she was afraid. Of what, he couldn't be sure, but a leader didn't need a reason to hearten a soldier.

Valandaras crouched down, so that he was at eye level with Mae. The massive dog sat on her haunches, before laying down on the gravel with her head on her front paws, huffing, eyes pools of liquid sadness. It was unnerving how perfectly she could become an animal—their mannerisms couldn't simply be built into their being, there had to be study and practice to it. An art.

He had noticed, however, that the amber of her eyes was always the same. Like it was the one part of herself she could never truly change. It was fortunate, then, that they were such an extraordinary colour. Like melted gold.

Valandaras tried not to look too long at Mae's too-human eyes.

"You will be safe here, wolfhound," he said. He kept his voice in a whisper, trusting her canine ears to be enhanced enough to hear him. "No man will question a warrior wishing his prized hunter to be near him."

There was a thump on the ground as Mae gave a small wag of her tail, showing she understood. He did not need her to be herself. She could remain as she was. Changed. Invisible. Safe.

Valandaras stood and beckoned with an obvious command signal.

"Come, hound," he said, louder than necessary, feeling foolish at the wooden words. He tried not to laugh as the wolfhound shot up from her position, legs flailing and tail wagging wildly as she bounded ahead to catch up with the others. She played her part too well sometimes; now the people of this town would think him the owner of a boisterous puppy. But it was a small price to pay for her easement.

Valandaras watched her run towards Grundle, her giant dog's body almost as tall as the goblin. She was indistinguishable from a regular beast. He wondered how many Divines were out there, quietly serving their gods in altered forms to avoid the hysterical questioning of the masses or the servitude the Altaean nobility asked of them. He would not be surprised if there were dozens, depending on which gods granted a Change. Too many of them had suffered, even after the Godprison was breached. A memory surfaced of the insurmountable pain he had seen when he had first seen Mae's face. It was years ago, and it still stood out to him. Hollow eyes, so different to the sparkle he now knew. Haunted eyes.

Any chance she gets to be happy is a moment well spent.

Valandaras re-joined the rest of the crew, Mae now prancing between them all and sniffing the air excitedly. He gestured to a tavern at the other end of the street. Large, faded letters had been painted onto the tavern's many windows, proclaiming it to be Blue Bernie's Bed & Bread. A wooden sign hung above the door depicted a sapphire woman merrily pouring an ale. It was like the rest of Crossroad—a little shabby and unrefined, but functional and well-loved.

"That is our rendezvous point," he said to the group. "Same place we secured the contract. The agreed meeting was this evening."

Reevan sniffed. "Ah, a fine establishment," he said, looking at Camden expectantly. His eyes were pools of black in the fading light. "Do your family own this too?"

Lessie snorted.

Camden searched the kitskan's face for ridicule, but found only polite interest.

"No," he replied, somewhat bemusedly. "My family does not own Crossroad, despite it being well within our rights to do so, since most of it is on our lands. The entire point of Crossroad is that it falls within multiple territories, therefore belonging to no singular lord. My father has partial ownership of the stables and a few of the more refined taverns, though." He looked around, as if trying to find his bearings. "Our main estate is to the west," he said, pointing grandly in a direction more to the south.

Mae disguised her wolfhound's huffing chuckle with an odd choking noise.

Lessie gave an exaggerated sigh as she placed her fingers on the outside of Camden's elbow, pushing it until his still outstretched hand pointed due west.

"There you go, my lord," she said, patting his arm with a practised grimace. She gave him a mocking curtsey before stalking off towards the tavern. Camden sputtered as he hurriedly put down his hand, attempting to hide the embarrassment of his mistake.

Grundle trailed after Lessie, choosing not to comment, proving again to Valandaras that the goblin was smarter than most men he had ever known. Mae, remembering to commit to the part of warrior hound, stood silently at Valandaras's side, but even in the dog's body he could sense her shaking from holding in laughter.

The woman is always giggling about one thing or another, even when her form proves difficult to, he thought. *It's impressive that she finds so many reasons to laugh. Especially in our line of work.*

Reevan's own chuckle died as his eyes narrowed at Camden. "It must be exhausting to have so much land you forget which direction your home is," he said. The beginnings of a storm swirled in the kitskan's eyes, but it was gone as quickly as it appeared. "I cannot imagine the responsibility you must bear for it."

Valandaras cleared his throat, cutting off Camden's reply. "Let us go. You are all in need of warm food and drink after our journey," he said, already striding towards the tavern, trusting the rest to follow. He pushed open the heavy wooden door and let the warmth from within wash over him. The smell of ale and roasting meat hit immediately.

The tavern was modest, with worn wooden tables and mismatched chairs taking up the majority of the floor space, as if the owner wanted the opportunity to cram as many patrons in as possible. There were a decent number of people already claiming tables, dining or clinking glasses together after a long day. Uneven candles shone brightly from repurposed wine bottle holders, and the oil lamps hanging from the exposed beams of the ceiling had not been cleaned in a long time, giving the establishment a warm, muted glow. Semi-circular booths took up the far corners of the small inn, offering more privacy to those who occupied them. It was early in the evening, and most were empty.

Valandaras strode directly for one that was not.

Moving between the cramped tables was difficult, but he managed. He ignored the few furtive glances he received from the patrons he passed. His appearance was a novelty on Kalaraak, the realm of earth, and he was used to people staring at him out of fear or curiosity. The stares were usually at his dimly glowing skin, which he kept mostly concealed, or his cloth, which he found frustrating since he wore it out of respect for others. His inner realmlight could be deadly when exposed, and was never to be revealed to anyone but a Realmshifter. Valandaras had gone decades without a single soul seeing his uncovered face.

Valandaras reached the furthest booth and slid into it, joining the lone patron already inside it. Lessie followed a moment later. She gave the stranger a wide berth and a tight-lipped smile of social obligation, but her dark eyes were full of mistrust.

The man in the booth was trying very hard to be nondescript, with his hood up and most of his attention on the dark liquid he was nursing. He barely looked up when Valandaras joined him, although his eyebrows raised at the large wolfhound who was now sternly guarding the entrance into the booth.

"Did you succeed?" the man asked quietly. He addressed his glass as he spoke, like he was afraid to hear the answer.

"The keep suffered extensive damage, but we got him out," Valandaras confirmed. "He is safe with us."

The man visibly relaxed. "Oh, thank the gods," he said, throwing back the hood of his cloak and running a scarred hand through his hair. Streaks of grey peppered the brown at his temples. "I've been sitting here for twenty minutes imagining how to tell my father that my little brother is dead. That would not have gone well. Where is the idiot, then?"

Reevan joined them at the booth, and having caught the last of the conversation, answered the question before Valandaras could.

"I believe our newest travelling companion made a brief stop at the bar before joining us," he said, sliding in next to Valandaras. "He remarked that his throat hadn't gone so long without whiskey since he was a child. That seemed odd. Do children in your family often drink whiskey?"

Valandaras heard a bark of laughter from Mae, who quickly stifled it when she drew some worried looks from other patrons. He wasn't entirely sure if animals were allowed to be inside the inn, and the less attention she got, the better. He gave her a stern look. She lay down, her canine grumbling causing him to suppress a smile.

Camden sauntered up to the table last, his hands full with five perfectly balanced glasses of the same golden liquid. He crouched to offload them onto the table, sliding the fifth onto the wood before untangling the others from his splayed fingers. He didn't spill a single drop, revealing a surprisingly deft hand.

Camden shoved into the booth next to Lessie, who looked impressed despite herself as she reached for one of the drinks. Her expression turned to outrage when Camden placed his hand over hers and slid the glass back in front of him.

"No, honey, these are all for me," he said, downing one in a single swallow. "Apparently you can't just pour five whiskeys into an ale mug, that would be uncouth, but you can put them into five glasses and serve them all the same. I'd offer you one, Druitt, but you seem to be taking a while with yours." He grinned at the stranger and raised his glass in a mock toast. "Captain."

The older man—Druitt—sighed again and pinched the bridge of his nose like he was warding off a headache.

"Nice to see captivity hasn't destroyed your spirit," he said.

"Just my sleeping patterns," Camden replied, rubbing at an eye. "As well as a frightfully long stint of sobriety and silence I will be doing my best to end tonight. I've never been alone without at least some form of entertainment since we were children. It's been mind-numbingly dull."

Druitt scoffed at Camden's complaints, and as the two brothers argued, Valandaras noted the resemblance between them. It was subtle, but they had similar features—in the sharpness of the jaw, the shape of the nose, the eyes of the same cloudy grey. Druitt looked to be at least ten years Camden's senior, though Valandaras knew more than most how looks could be deceiving of age. Valandaras himself was approaching ninety years old. Time worked differently in some of the other realms, as well as his bond to the Pod gifting him with strange abilities he didn't truly understand. He knew Mae was also decades older than she looked. It was a bittersweet side effect of housing a god's favour. He had once heard a rumour that some Divines were older than the Breach itself.

Apparently satisfied that his brother had been returned in one piece, the elder DeFalcone pulled a large pouch from his belt and slid it across the table towards Valandaras.

"Your payment for rescuing my dear brother," said Druitt.

"I hope it's decent," Camden quipped. "What am I worth to Father, anyway?"

"This isn't Father's money," Druitt snapped. "It's mine. He was content to let you rot, and perhaps he was right to, since you appeared to have such a boring time of it."

Valandaras glanced inside and shook the bag. It was more out of habit than any true mistrust, to make sure it was not padded with copper or silver. Some crooks tried to mess around and conceal smaller coins or rocks by putting all the gold at the top. Druitt did not seem the type, but Valandaras always checked regardless of the client.

The gold seemed above board, but the amount was concerning. At least three times what had originally been agreed upon.

Valandaras frowned. *Either Druitt is being extremely generous,* he thought, *or we're not finished.*

7

VALANDARAS

Valandaras did not need to say anything about the extra gold. Druitt noticed his assessment of it immediately.

"I have another matter that would require your services," Druitt said, shifting uncomfortably in his seat, "if you are all able and willing. I have taken the liberty of including it in your payment tonight."

"Grundle is listening," said Grundle. His small, dark face peered over Valandaras's arms into the pouch.

Camden jumped at the sound of the goblin's voice, spilling whiskey onto the table, the silver signet ring on his finger cracking against the glass. Lessie snickered despite her own flinch. Druitt maintained his composure more carefully than his brother, the only sign of alarm in his widening eyes.

Even Valandaras hadn't noticed the goblin join the rest of the crew. He tried to ignore the huffing chuckles from the wolfhound at his feet, who had been privy to Grundle's methods, and gave Druitt DeFalcone his full attention.

"There are many theories as to why my brother was taken," said Druitt. "My father's steward is convinced it was to weaken or threaten my father before the Kingswitch; our head of house is telling anyone who will listen that it was to extort gold from the family." He pinched the bridge of his nose again, as if his headache were worsening. "I keep telling Royce that would require a ransom demand to be made. The correspondence we intercepted showed only that they were instructed to move him from Falcon's Watch into Kalac, not to demand payment. Whether their eventual plan was to kill him across the border, or to ransom him once they were home, we don't know."

Reevan sniffed. "Would you like us to find out exactly why Lord Camden was taken?" he asked, peering at Druitt from around his mug full of milk. "We are a mercenary crew, not a band of investigators, although I'm sure we will try our best. We can be quite resourceful. I could ask around."

Camden scoffed. "Maybe they just liked my company."

Druitt shook his head, ignoring his brother. "The mystery is of no concern to me, so I'm not asking you to solve it. What I need is for you to accompany my brother on his journey home to our estate, and to stay with him while I complete my obligations between here and Roost Keep. The death of the High Marshal has put all of us in the legions working overtime."

Valandaras gave the captain a small nod of respect. "I heard about that. The assassin from Kalac?"

"It is an open secret," Druitt said darkly. "Never officially confirmed, of course, but the Kiveri Czai has distinctive methods."

A hush descended upon the table. They had all heard of the famous killer, who had been unofficially terrorising Kalaraak for over a decade. Rumours circulated constantly, blaming the demise of practically any high member of Altaean society on the Kiveri Czai and those who employed his services. There was once even talk of him assassinating a king who had died while ascended. Most of the rumours were terrible and cruel, bordering on fantastical, but there was sure to be truth in them.

"It's been a tough year," said Druitt, "and without divulging too much sensitive information, Altaea's conflict with Kalac appears to be reaching a boiling point." He placed his elbows on the table and massaged a temple.

Valandaras looked closer at the elder DeFalcone. There were dark circles under his eyes, and the growth on his cheeks and jaw suggested he hadn't shaved in weeks. The man took his job seriously. Valandaras had heard of Druitt refusing to serve his mandatory time in the Altaean military behind a desk—the easy route most heirs of noble houses took—choosing instead to join as an infantry guard. When his service had finished, Druitt had stayed, and had worked his way up to the rank of Captain within the Roost Keep guard on his own merit.

This man, noble birth aside, is the kind of man soldiers follow out of respect, not because they have to.

Druitt drained the last of his glass. "I want to see my brother safely home," he said, staring into the empty glass as if contemplating whether to have it refilled. "But I cannot abandon my duties. The men who took Camden were from Kalac, and that alone tells me the borders aren't secure."

At that, Reevan and Grundle exchanged an uneasy glance. Valandaras didn't blame them for keeping their origins quiet; relations between Altaea and Kalac were strained at the best of times. Most people came from one to the other to leave their former lives behind altogether.

"So you're paying these thugs to babysit me?" Camden exclaimed; words still mostly clear despite the amount of alcohol he'd rapidly ingested. "What am I, seven?"

He threw back the last mouthful of his fifth drink and slammed the empty glass down on the table too loudly, like he had misjudged the distance. Mae let out a startled yelp, limbs flailing on the wooden floorboards.

"You think you don't need it?" Druitt snapped, turning an ice grey stare on his brother. "They stole you from your bed, in our family home, while surrounded by our guards. Then you were taken to another estate, also owned by us, but neglected so long it's practically crumbling to dust, and held without ransom demands. What does that tell you?"

This is not the captain talking, but the brother.

Camden fell silent, so Valandaras answered for him.

"It means your family's estate is compromised," he said. "Somebody within it has either been actively working against your family, or is too loose with their lips and has spoken to someone who is. Either way, people who mean you harm knew exactly how to get to you and where to take you."

Druitt nodded. "I don't have time to weed out the traitor—or idiot—from our staff, because I'm busy trying to prevent a war. So I'm sending you home with outside protection I can trust had no part in it."

Camden glowered into his empty whiskey glass and did not respond.

With that, Druitt made to rise, and Valandaras and Reevan both moved out of the booth to make way. The elder DeFalcone put out his hand and Valandaras shook it.

"We will guard your brother with our lives," Valandaras said quietly.

"Speak for yourself," Lessie muttered under her breath.

"I am in your debt, all of you," said Druitt, raising a rough hand in farewell. "Thank you for this. I have already paid for a few rooms here tonight, so you can rest before leaving tomorrow. There are clothes for you—" he pointed at Camden, "in one of them. Try not to die before you get home."

Camden gave his brother a hazy smile and a merry salute, bumping Lessie with his elbow as he did so. The alcohol he had consumed appeared to be catching up to him. The look on Lessie's face suggested the lord may not make it home in one piece.

I hope she learns to control her fire, Valandaras thought, *or it could consume her.*

Valandaras walked Druitt to the entrance of the tavern, as was polite. The wearied man turned to him and spoke in a voice so low he could barely hear it.

"War is coming," Druitt said hurriedly. "We have reports of border skirmishes, spies, and numerous attacks in the planning stages. The fact that my family's estate was so easily infiltrated bothers me, as well as that they used Falcon's Watch to harbour him. It feels personal. Crossroad is the closest town—Kalac forces could attack it at any time, and I fear that time is soon."

Druitt fastened a thick travelling cloak around his shoulders and put one heavily scarred hand on the door. A silver ring, identical to Camden's if not for the dark stone embedded in it, glinted in the firelight.

"He's a pain in the ass, but he is my brother," said Druitt. "Keep him alive, Realmshifter. I chose you not because of what you are, but because you have a reputation for staying alive when you shouldn't. I expect you to live up to it."

Valandaras simply inclined his head with respect. Druitt took this as assent and exited the tavern into the cold evening.

Valandaras turned back towards the booth, viewing them as an outsider for a moment. Camden was loudly complaining about the lack of music in the inn. Lessie was scowling and absent-mindedly petting Mae, who had edged under the booth and placed her giant wolfhound's head into the girl's lap. Reevan was lapping at his milk, and Grundle was barely visible over the head of the table.

A far cry from a trained battalion of guards, but they're what Druitt needs to keep his brother safe. We should rest immediately so we can leave at first light.

Valandaras headed to the bar to confirm they had rooms, and the barkeep rummaged around under the bar for a while before she handed him three keys. At one point he turned back to the booth and thought he caught a glimpse of a wolfhound's tail disappearing into the lavatories.

Mae must feel more comfortable now we know the meeting went well, he thought fondly. *It was a good plan to keep her disguised in case things didn't go as we intended. She could have been the edge we needed in a fight.*

The 'real' Mae emerged a few minutes later, bright blue dress swinging around her legs as she bounded back to the booth. Something of the wolfhound remained—the playfulness, the somewhat uncoordinated movements as she adjusted back to her human body.

Valandaras found himself turning back to the barkeep and ordering two ales. Perhaps one more drink couldn't hurt. It would be good for morale.

They ended up postponing their travel for an entire day.

Sharing a room with Camden—who had proceeded to become inebriated beyond what Valandaras thought possible for a human man—was not a relaxing experience, and he needed his wits about him if they were to make their journey safely. He was also still hurting from remnants of the fight, though a combination of Mae's Gift and his own odd ways of healing had seen to the majority of it. None of the crew had complained. They were grateful for the rest.

Travelling west towards the DeFalcone's estate would take much less time, with the substantial payment Druitt had left them able to procure horses. Grundle had refused to spend his portion on a horse, instead opting to share Reevan's, but the goblin weighed so little that it was not an issue. Camden had suggested sharing as well, but the contemptuous hiss Lessie had given him had left the lord stone-faced and Mae collapsing into a fit of giggles.

Valandaras did not understand exactly what was so funny about Lessie's dislike of the DeFalcone boy, but what mattered was that Mae was happy.

I suppose I should thank the young lord for being her new source of entertainment, Valandaras thought as they mounted their horses for the journey. *Her laughter is as refreshing for the crew as clear stream water. Even the girl has stopped frowning so much.*

As they came upon the close of their second day of hard riding, they crested a particularly large hill and were rewarded with the sight of the DeFalcone's West Keep looming on the horizon.

Unlike the one they had liberated Camden from, this keep was well maintained, surrounded by high stone walls and teeming with men patrolling diligently, wearing the grey-and-blue tabards that announced them as members of the household guard. A similar coloured flag waved proudly from the roof of the highest tower. The keep itself was twice the size of the abandoned one, but much wider, giving the feel of a sprawling stone manor. The grounds themselves were well-manicured, sterile in their uniformity, and the surrounding orchards had been planted in perfect rows. What looked to be a mine stood much further in the distance, with a structured, mechanical line of workers with carts moving slowly between it and the outer gates of the estate.

Valandaras halted their progression for a moment, letting the horses rest after scaling the hill. Camden had stopped at the edge, and now stared down at the keep with a hardness in his eyes, as if the sight of it chased away all merriment. He looked much more his age as he exhaled dramatically, before gesturing grandly at the buildings below.

"Ah, no place like home, right, my friends?" said Camden, a false grin not reaching his eyes. "Welcome to the West Keep. My favourite prison. I'm sure you'll find the amenities to your liking, but the guards don't take kindly to anything out of place, so you'll probably find they'll question every little thing you do to make sure it's in accordance with my father's wishes."

The young lord sighed again before turning back towards the others. Eyes darting between their faces, he smirked at Lessie.

"My lady, it's not polite to gawk so openly at another's fortune, no matter how fortunate it may be," he commented drily.

Valandaras expected the girl to explode, but she did not respond. She did not even appear to have realised Camden had spoken to her at all. Camden noticed too, puzzled, and whatever other jabs he had prepared for her died on his tongue as he took in her expression—which was not on the estate, but on the coast beyond it.

Lessie was staring at the open ocean with a look of incredulous wonder.

The far west of the DeFalcone estate was unwalled, with the pebbled beach forming the fourth boundary. Light from the twin suns glistened off the water as they set, half-submerged, staining the sky pink, and the air that rushed towards them smelled of salt. Far beyond the walls of the estate, to the very edge of their vision, at the end of the land that jutted out into the ocean itself, an immense lighthouse tower stood proudly. It was a beautiful sight, but Valandaras didn't quite understand the need for revere until the girl spoke.

"I... I've never seen the sea before," she said quietly.

Camden scoffed. "Surely you're joking. Never?" he asked, more in disbelief than true cruelty.

Lessie shot him a look of pure venom, even as her freckled cheeks reddened with embarrassment.

"Not all of us have giant castles in cities all across the realm, you puffed-up pompous prick," she snapped. "And I wasn't gawking at your stupid fortune, which is what, to be born? To have an impressive view? Well done. Someone, hundreds of years ago, decided to build here. Congratulations. You did it."

"It's not a castle," Camden sputtered in indignation. "It's not about an impressive view. It's just a keep. It's a godsdamned summer home. Am I not allowed to have a home?"

Anything else he planned to say was drowned out by Mae's laughter. She had been trying to keep it from interrupting them, but the shaking of her sides became more obvious as eyes turned to her. The fact that everyone now knew only set her off more, and she dissolved into another fit of giggles.

"I'm so sorry, I don't mean to. You both just... remind me of someone," Mae said, shaking her head, and taking big breaths to calm herself. She even wiped a tear from her eye. Her amusement was infectious; before long Reevan and Grundle were smiling, and even Lessie had lost some of the hardness to her face, though the girl was clinging to it stubbornly.

Mae moved her horse up so that she was alongside Lessie. She gave the girl a motherly pat on the back.

"I didn't see the ocean until I was around your age," Mae said kindly. "It is normal to not have, especially coming from where you do. But you never forget your first time. I'm glad it was here with someone special, so you didn't waste it." Through her kind words, Mae's eyes glittered with amusement at the double meaning, as if she couldn't help herself. Lessie rolled her eyes, but the corners of her mouth tugged upwards.

Mae turned her attention towards Camden. "And it's easy to forget what you've seen from your own window your whole life might be a novelty for somebody else. That doesn't make you pompous, only a little... inexperienced with other's perspectives."

Lessie snorted. Camden looked mollified, though he still shot the girl a dark look, which she ignored. Mae nudged her horse closer to Camden's.

"But I have to say, my lord," she whispered loudly, intending for everyone to hear, "if this is not an impressive view, then you simply must show us the others. They would be to die for."

At that, Camden smiled, running a hand through his hair sheepishly.

"It is a bit ridiculous," he said quietly. His eyes were still hard when he looked down at the keep, but the creases around them had relaxed.

Valandaras shook his head in amazement. Trust Mae to break the tension, to make everyone feel heard. He found himself smiling. This was not a Divine skill, but a human one. For all she brought to the crew in the manner of her Gift, it was this that was priceless. This ability to care for people who do not care for each other. To make them feel like their feelings matter.

Besides, her smile is blinding, he thought. *It is impossible not to feel important when she smiles at you.*

Catching his small smile, Mae looked towards him and beamed. The emerald glow of her Gift glimmered behind her eyes, and Valandaras was wrenched by a sudden pang of hurt. Like a knife twisted into his side that he had forgotten about.

Her eyes glow without the threat of danger behind them. With a Gift that only helps, only heals. I doubt I can even feel such levels of joy at the risk of hurting someone.

Mae's own smile faltered for a heartbeat. Valandaras pushed away the ugly thoughts and, for once, let himself return it. She lit up even more.

Mae was still grinning at him when the arrow took her in the chest.

8

LESSIE

Shit.

Lessie heard the projectile land with a sickening thud before she saw it. Mae had been knocked backwards off her horse, and there was a godsdamned crossbow bolt sticking out of her shoulder.

Valandaras whirled around and charged his horse in the direction the arrow had come from. Reevan followed; Grundle jumping from their horse's back as it whinnied in alarm. The other horses nickered frightfully, ears back, tasting the fear that had surged through their riders.

Lessie moved without thinking. She dismounted, boots slamming into the packed earth of the path.

Time slowed. This was what she was good at.

Camden had frozen in panic, staring at Mae and trying to rein in his horse, which was tossing its head about and blowing in fear. Lessie yanked her pack from her saddlebag and clicked her fingers to get his attention, but he didn't seem to hear her.

"Hey," Lessie said sharply, and his focus snapped to her. "Ride to your front gate, now. Tell them what happened." When he didn't move, she raised her voice. "Get help, you idiot!"

Camden swore and took off, his horse galloping downhill towards the keep, kicking up dust.

Grundle had moved behind Mae and taken a defensive stance, anticipating further attacks, and Lessie threw her pack at him.

"Get out the small brown stoppered bottle and some cloth," she barked. Her father's voice—*hope for the best, prepare for the worst*—pulsed in her ears like a heartbeat. "Put the liquid onto the cloth. Soak it."

Grundle did as she asked, long fingers making quick work of the task.

Lessie kneeled next to Mae, who hadn't moved from her back since she hit the ground. She was awake and breathing; winded by the double impact. The bolt had taken her in the right shoulder, just below her collarbone. It looked clean, but it was hard to tell. Blood blossomed onto her yellow dress and stained the ground below. Her eyes were wide and full of shock.

Lessie spoke as calmly as she could. "I'm going to sit you up, and it's going to hurt like hell, you hear me?"

Mae, breathless, nodded. Lessie eased her up, one hand on her back, trying to brace her, and Mae let out a small hiss of pain. Lessie assessed the wound as clinically as she could. The glint of metal shining showed the arrowhead of the bolt had gone through to the other side of Mae's body, piercing clean through the muscle of her shoulder.

At least it missed her heart.

Lessie steeled herself for what she knew came next. She had little experience with Divines, but what little she'd observed over the past few months spoke volumes. Her brain emptied of everything but the bones of the truth.

Mae could heal herself, but not with the bolt still in her body. The wound was leaking blood at a concerning rate. They could all soon be facing similar injuries. She had to get Mae back up.

Because if Mae went down, they all did.

"I'm going to have to break it to get it out," Lessie muttered, low and calm, more to herself. They were godsdamned lucky the bolt's shaft was wooden.

"Do what you need to," Mae whispered. She seemed surprisingly composed given the current circumstances.

Lessie inspected the bolt, trying to find the best purchase point. Mae winced when any contact was made, but voiced no complaints. Only her sharp intake of breath betrayed how bad it was. Lessie found her gloves and yanked them on. They wouldn't do much, but they were leather, so at least she wouldn't end up with splinters. She tried to judge where she could get a decent hold on the arrowhead. It was wicked looking, long and serrated.

Grundle braced himself against Mae's back. It was all he could do to help. Mae's breathing was even, but shallow. Her face had gone pale. Too pale.

Lessie was out of time. She gave herself fifteen seconds. In for six, hold for three, out for six.

"On three," she said. "Keep her still."

Grundle nodded.

Mae squeezed her eyes shut.

Lessie gritted her teeth.

"One—"

Lessie threw all of her weight into her arms and snapped the tip from the spine of the bolt. Mae gasped from the pain of the jostling and the shock, but Lessie had already reached around and yanked the rest of the arrow out from the original impact point.

"Two—"

She tossed the arrow to the side and ripped the soaked cloth from Grundle's hands. She placed it on either side of the wound, pressing the material into the puncture to staunch the bleeding that had surged from the arrow's removal.

Lessie exhaled. "Three."

Emerald shimmered over Mae's body as she called upon her gift from the Mother. It was like the light came from within, rushing over her skin and becoming brighter when it reached the injury. Mae sighed in relief.

Lessie pulled the cloth away and watched, fascinated, as the glittering light sunk into the wound, filling it until there was nowhere left for it to go. A faded pink scar and a hole in the dress were all that remained. It was like it had never happened.

Lessie peered at the puncture, the puckered mark now only faintly visible beneath Mae's collarbone. She still held the blood-covered cloth, so heavily soaked it had begun to stain her gloves an odd shade of maroon. Her mind flashed with an old memory; an image of red wine splashing onto their table at the bar, soaking into the wood, forever altering its colour. There would be more evidence of that spill than this injury.

I could have sworn she takes so much longer to heal a wound like this. After Holdfast, she had to rest for days.

Mae sat up straighter, exhaling loudly. "On three, huh?" she questioned, eyebrow raised, eyes still dancing with faint emerald sparks.

Tossing the bloodied rag aside, Lessie shrugged. It was how she'd been taught. People tended to tense on three. Luckily, Mae seemed to accept the shrug as an apology.

"Well, that wasn't exactly the warm welcome I was expecting," she said, reaching a hand to her hair and brushing the dust from it. She looked down at the non-existent wound and frowned at the damaged fabric. "Oh, Mother. This is my favourite dress."

A bubble of hysterical laughter rose in Lessie's throat. She had rebuffed Mae's offers to borrow one of the dresses for a meal in some dingy backwater inn, but if damage to one could provoke a reaction like that, then maybe they were worth it. Perhaps she would finally indulge Mae and try it out.

I can't shift into an animal when I get sick of wearing the dress, though.

Adrenaline wearing off, Lessie clamped down on the laughter, offering Mae a small, close-lipped smile instead. She balled her shaking hands into fists and looked over Mae for any other signs of injury, relaxing only when she found none. If there had been, the Divine's Gift had already taken care of them.

But the relief was tinged with the quiet suspicion of someone trained to notice small differences. Mae was not only healed, she seemed completely fine. If anything, she looked healthier than she did when they had started the journey from Crossroad.

Hell, maybe I should start praying.

Lessie shook her head, trying to ease the slight ringing in her ears and take herself out of survival mode.

"I wouldn't worry about your dress," she said. "I'm sure someone in the giant castle we're about to stay at can lend you a needle and thread."

Mae laughed. "Thread spun from gold, perhaps? I should be so lucky. Perhaps the needle will be made of diamonds."

Grundle shifted behind them. "Valandaras and Reevan return."

Lessie and Mae both twisted their heads at the sound of thundering hooves, all merriment forgotten. *Have they brought the fight back to us?*

Lessie stood quickly, fingers floating over her revolver, but their crewmates were not fighting or fleeing. There was no edge of panic in their riding; they spared no glance over their shoulders to see if they were followed. Their horses were sweating and blowing hard, and the riders weren't much better, but there was no imminent combat.

Reevan arrived first, panting, tail twitching under his cloak. He looked uncomfortable in the saddle. He didn't like riding, preferring his own two legs, and had yet to admit that the horses were slightly faster.

"I'm afraid our assailants did not feel the need to stick around," Reevan drawled, as if delivering a report on the weather. "They opted to simply vanish instead. It was rather disappointing. I had hoped we would find them hiding in a bush and could trample them to death with our mighty steeds." He gave the horse beneath him a look that questioned its capabilities to do so.

Mae snorted, but Lessie's eyes moved to Valandaras, who looked like he wanted to storm back into the forest and tear apart every tree just to make sure. The Realmshifter stared down at Mae, searching for her injuries, forehead creased with worry.

Mae caught her breath and brushed dirt from her dress where she'd fallen as she got to her feet.

"I'm fine, Val, thank the Mother," she said brightly. "Wish I could say the same for my dress, though." She pinched the torn fabric together, as if expecting the material to knit back into a single piece the way her skin had.

Lessie had never seen Valandaras look so angry. A muscle in his jaw twitched as he clenched it. The storm on his face could level a city.

And that's with half of it covered. People are easier to read than they think.

"Whoever it was, they have completely disappeared. Left no trace at all," Reevan continued, oblivious to the tension rolling off of his nearest companion. "I must say, if this was another attempt on Lord Camden's life, they were a terrible shot. I suppose if I missed that badly, I'd disappear too. I wouldn't want anybody to know how awful I was at aiming."

Mae laughed, and Valandaras's shoulders loosened a bit. Lessie allowed herself to relax, but kept her guard up. There could still be danger.

More pounding of hooves sounded as Camden made his way back to the group. Lessie fought the urge to roll her eyes, irritation prickling as she saw the panic on his face despite their own calm demeanours.

He might as well be the Lord of Molasses for how long he took. We could have all been dead already.

Camden brought his horse to a screeching halt, looking around at them wildly. Another man had joined him on his horse, sitting uncomfortably on the back of the saddle.

"I... I brought help," Camden blurted, clearly perplexed to find Mae in perfect health. He had seen her heal them all, been healed by her, but maybe he wasn't familiar with how powerful some Divines could be. On this, at least, Lessie could understand the confusion.

Hell, I've seen it a hundred times by now, and it's still hard to believe.

The man behind Camden dismounted awkwardly and brushed the horsehair from his trousers. He was short and middle-aged with thinning hair, and wore an expression like he was facing down a pack of rabid sewer rats and trying to conceal his unease about it.

Camden, still atop his horse, swept out a hand dramatically for an introduction. "My father's Head of House for the western estate, Royce Ackermane."

Lessie narrowed her eyes. "And what was he going to do to help, exactly?" she asked, glaring at Camden. "Offer Mae a cup of tea? Ask the bandits to pay their tithe before committing any more murders?"

Gods, it's like he hasn't got a single drop of common sense in his body.

She wasn't sure what role the Head of House played in the running of an estate, but she knew they were unlikely to be out on border patrol or well-versed in healing. Royce Ackermane looked as if he'd never seen a fight in his life.

Royce removed a pair of small round spectacles from his pocket and perched them on his nose before giving her an up-and-down look of distaste.

"My lady, I have merely come to assess the threat Lord Camden has informed me of," he said. His voice was nasal, but it was the tone that made her immediately dislike him. "I have already dispatched some of the West Keep's guard to sweep the surrounding grounds for any assailants. I have also ordered the staff to prepare a room to treat the wounded in—though that seems to no longer be necessary. I delegated."

So that was what a Head of House did.

Determined to keep the redness out of her cheeks, Lessie looked once again to Valandaras, ignoring Royce's words and Camden entirely.

"So whoever attacked us disappeared?" she asked, a bit louder than necessary.

"Into thin air," Valandaras replied darkly. The adrenaline still pumping through his body made the glow of his skin brighter, and his knuckles were white as his hand gripped the hilt of his falchion. He was furious that he had been unable to confront the attacker. Valandaras's horse mirrored his unease, blowing hot air from its nose and throwing its head as it stamped at the ground.

Royce Ackermane looked up at the angry Realmshifter, shuddered, and took a few steps back. A few of the keep's guards arrived to report on their surroundings. There seemed to be no sign of the attackers—if Lessie didn't have the broken crossbow bolt in her hands, they would have struggled to prove it had happened at all.

Royce scowled at the guard's words. "Since the... threat has passed, my lord," he said, addressing Camden, "then I shall accompany you all back to the grounds and instruct the guards to return to their posts."

He gave Camden an exasperated look, as if he didn't quite believe anything dire had happened and the lord had been playing a trick on him. Camden was oblivious to the tone of the statement, nodding dismissively as he stared down at the keep. Lessie watched a muscle in the Head of House's jaw twitch as he accepted a mount from a guard and trotted back to the keep.

At least I'm not alone in thinking the lord is a pompous twit.

Mae had been standing with her horse, stroking the animal's side and murmuring to it, ignoring everyone around them. Once it had calmed, she swung into the saddle with the grace of an experienced rider.

"Let's finish our journey, then," Mae said lightly, declaring the matter closed. "I want to see Lord Camden's lovely castle."

Camden sputtered. "Like I said, Miss Mae, it's not a castle. It's a summer home. It's a pity we've just missed the perfect season, actually, as it's most beautiful in the warmest months."

However polite Mae was, she had not listened to Camden's response, as she was busy staring intently at Valandaras.

"It wouldn't be a proper journey for us if we didn't get attacked at least once, right?" she said, smile too wide, determined to convince him that she was perfectly fine. Lessie shifted her eyes from Mae to Valandaras, interested to see if he saw through Mae as easily as she did.

Valandaras merely glowered, his attention fixed on the distant treeline, even as he directed his mount down towards the keep. The others followed. Lessie waited until the rest of them had made it halfway down the hill before she could breathe normally again.

Tearing her eyes away from her companions as she remounted her own horse, she let herself take in her surroundings properly. The serene copse of trees looked completely ordinary. The leaves were green, and the trunks were solid, with not a single hint of malice lurking within. She squinted, hoping to glimpse something, anything, but the woods offered no answers. Her father's voice echoed in her mind, as usual. *Never miss the forest for the trees.* She still had trouble understanding that one.

Lessie returned to looking upon the water, watching how the dappled light of the twin sunsets glistened off the waves, trying to commit it to memory. It didn't matter what Camden said; it was nothing to be ashamed of. There were thousands of people who had not seen the ocean before. Millions, probably. She would have never seen it if she hadn't left home. Would have preferred not to, if it meant she could have her old life back. But she was closer to that than ever, now.

It had been a rough year. Of the few solo jobs she had managed to pick up, none had offered even a quarter of what she would earn for this one. For this, she could afford to move on. To get back to what she was meant to be doing—tracking down the monster responsible for turning her life upside down. It had to be worth it.

Even if it meant keeping an insolent lord alive far longer than he probably deserved to be.

Lessie sighed and urged her horse forward, catching up with the others, and found herself staring at the back of Camden's head. His dark hair was curlier near the nape of his neck, where the sweat from hard riding had dampened it. Maybe they could ask for even more gold since he had nearly died twice already.

I have a feeling this job is going to be harder than we thought.

9

LESSIE

The West Keep definitely looked like a castle to Lessie.

They dismounted at the stables within the first wall, and as they entered the second, the uncomfortable feeling of confinement settled into Lessie's gut. The entrance was heavily fortified with iron portcullis barricades, and to the east, she saw one other, which was fitted with large oil pots at the top of the wooden doors reinforced with iron.

The main building was immense, dominating the space inside the double walls of stone. Large watchtowers were built into both the walls and the keep itself. The whole place reeked of steel and discipline. Camden had referred to it as a 'summer home', whatever that meant, but she couldn't help but count the guards patrolling the walls. Before long, she was in double digits.

This is too much fortification for a simple summer home.

Reevan noticed too, whistling in appreciation, which was difficult for a kitskan. Tiny droplets of spittle flung from his lips onto the ground before him. Lessie pretended not to notice. *Never mock someone for something beyond their control,* her father had said.

Every time another piece of his sage advice popped into her mind, she drifted back to thoughts of home. Time and time again she and Trixie had gotten into mischief, sometimes on the receiving end of cruel words and other times dishing them out. Her father believed all beings deserved respect and had expected them to behave as such. Her mother had more unconventional advice. Lessie had done her best to combine the two, but she'd privately agreed with her mother more often than not.

Her mother's favourite weapon was words, and she had wielded them well. The truth could cut sharper than any blade.

Reevan was oblivious to the glazed expression on Lessie's face.

"I'm beginning to think you kidnapped yourself, my lord," said Reevan, obviously impressed with the keep's defences. "I don't believe even I could get you out of here. I suppose we could test it, though, if you get bored later."

Camden chuckled. "Only if you promise not to throw me out another window. I'm really not much for heights." He glanced around at the towering walls, and Lessie thought she saw a flicker of resentment cross his annoyingly symmetrical face. "My father had this keep built after he descended from the throne when he was my age. He's just begun living in Verestead again for the next few seasons, though. It's easier when you're about to take over again."

Lessie searched her mind for her mother's history lessons. She remembered struggling with the concept as a child; a temporary king. A shared throne.

Altaea had once been split into territories—seven tiny kingdoms independently governed, seven high noble houses who all fancied themselves royalty. Somewhere along the line, their neighbours had become too powerful to ignore, and after years of war and invasion, the seven small rulers joined their forces and united to become a single, sprawling kingdom. But all seven were unwilling to give up their crowns.

Now, the heads of the houses each spent seven years ruling as king, before passing the duty to the next family in line—a practice commonly referred to as the Kingswitch.

In Altaea's history, there had been a handful of kings who had ruled twice, once in their youth and again as they entered their twilight years. Camden's father was one such ruler—becoming head of his house and first serving as king at a very young age. He was due to take the throne again at the next Kingswitch, and this time would do so as a powerful and experienced man having ruled over his territory for the past fifty years.

"My mother always said this was her favourite of the estates," Camden remarked quietly. "Commissioned countless Divines to decorate it. I suppose she had become used to living in gated luxury, or perhaps Father expected vengeance for whatever decisions he made or laws he passed as king. It wouldn't be the first time an Archduke's family got caught in the crossfire."

Lessie looked up at the heavy doors before her, painstakingly whittled with filigree, no doubt toiled over for months to be barely glanced at. The fortifications began to make more sense.

The reason she remembered so much about the history of the Kingswitch wasn't because it was interesting, but because of the endless tirades her mother had gone on in criticism of it. The idea behind the Kingswitch was to keep one noble family from having total control over the entire country, but there were endless loopholes. Advantageous marriages, squabbles over land, assassinations and vendettas and alliances between the Archdukes and their families. Each one pretended they were smarter and richer than all the rest.

They're all as bad as each other. None of them care to look past their own noses, let alone outside the walls of Verestead. It's the same no matter where you go. Mama said all those in power care about is protecting it and getting more, while the regular people suffer.

Camden cleared his throat and Lessie pulled herself back into the present, trying to ignore the sting imagining her mother's voice had brought to her eyes. He had also been lost in his thoughts, pausing on the threshold of the beautiful main doors, but he seemed to shake it off as Mae looped her arm through his.

"Well, I think it's lovely," Mae exclaimed merrily. "You must give us the grand tour, my lord."

Camden latched onto the role of a guide like he had been born to it. He pointed out useful rooms and favourite paintings as they traipsed along behind him, tracking mud and dirt from their journey through the halls of the first floor. Lessie made a point to keep a watchful eye on Grundle, who was prone to slipping off when something interesting caught his eye, but even the goblin stayed close in the maze of hallways.

Lessie tried not to gape as they wound their way up a staircase and down yet another hall. Everything—from the candlesticks to the painting's frames, from the lantern brackets to the long rugs that ran along the corridors and deadened their footsteps—was of fine make and in impeccable condition. It was opulent, but not gaudy. Rich, and yet tasteful. She had expected Camden's home to be more like him. Loud. Obnoxious. Not to her taste.

The crew were shown into a room that was dominated by an immense cherrywood dining table. It was gleaming like a mirror, as if someone had polished it moments before they entered, and it could easily seat thirty. Matching chairs rose up around it like spires. Lessie's face burned with a rush of unexpected heat as she took in the sheer quiet extravagance of it.

This godsdamned table is probably worth more than my entire home was.

The western wall of the room was made entirely of glass doors that opened out onto a balcony, the sky inky blue and dotted with the first evening stars. A fire had already been lit in the hearth, chasing away the beginnings of the late summer chill, and well-dressed servants were in the process of setting out a large plate of biscuits and pouring tea from a steaming pot.

Camden fell into his chair at the head of the table, groaning aloud. Royce had remained silent throughout their passage, but now instructed them all to sit as he lowered himself into the chair at Camden's right. Lessie frowned as Camden pulled out the seat to his left, gesturing towards her with a mocking smile—then bit her lip to keep from laughing as Reevan slid into the open chair instead.

"Thank you, my lord. It is a relief to finally rest my paws after such a long trip," Reevan purred, raising his teacup and delicately sniffing it.

The others chose seats at random—Lessie noticing with amusement that Mae had bounded into the seat next to Valandaras—and the crew sat in silence for a few minutes. The only noise came from the clinking of teacups and the crunching of biscuits. Lessie preoccupied herself by staring at the table. The intricate carvings along the edges had been made to resemble hunting birds in flight. It was the most beautiful woodwork she had ever seen up close.

This could only have been crafted by a Divine, she mused. *One of... the Maker? He makes things, right?*

Lessie's religious education had been far more rudimentary. With no Divines in their small town, her mother had thought them as useless to the common people as the nobility, and hadn't deemed it important to teach her daughters about them. Their father had tried to answer their curious pestering with the basics, but he knew little himself. Lessie could hear his frustrated tone, repeating the same sentiment.

"They were in the Godprison for thousands of years, girls. How am I supposed to know who has returned? All I know is the one we had first lied about the rest of 'em."

Trixie had found it interesting, but Lessie had tuned out everything to do with gods. There were so many, it was hard to keep track. Thinking about gods made her head hurt. Blasphemous as it now was, it had probably been easier back when everyone believed there was just one.

Lessie closed her eyes and let the fragrance of the tea she held distract her from how overwhelmed she felt. There was lavender and something vaguely citrusy in it. Coupled with a faint scent of cinnamon and the wood-smoke of the fireplace, she felt herself relaxing for the first time in weeks.

Royce cleared his throat, and Lessie stopped letting her spoon clink against her teacup. Her tea swirled like a tiny tornado.

"My lord," Royce said, speaking to Camden as if he were the only one present in the room. "I do have some things to discuss with you once your... guests are settled. I have organised rooms for them to sleep." He sent an uneasy glance around the table, clearly wishing for the rest of them to leave so that they wouldn't hear privileged DeFalcone information.

Lessie narrowed her eyes. Did Royce know why they were here? What did he not want them to hear? Was he the one who had sold Camden out? She knew it was logical for him to not trust them—she didn't trust him, either—but the dismissal was pointed.

Camden had been stirring his own tea without drinking it, staring blankly into the whirlpool he had made, but now his eyes crinkled as he gave his Head of House an easy smile.

"Royce, my good man, my guests are here on Druitt's payroll, so I wouldn't worry about keeping anything from them," Camden said. He leaned back in his chair and stretched his arms above his head, a loud crack resounding from one of his shoulder blades. "I'm sure they'll probably find anything you have to say about this place infinitely more interesting than I do."

Royce bristled. "Very well, sir. There have been reports of strange happenings near the mines. Some of the workers reported seeing lights and movement in the trees they couldn't track. We suspect spies from rival mining houses."

That piqued the interest of most.

"Couldn't track, how?" Valandaras interjected.

Royce seemed irritated by the questioning, but answered as if the query had come from the lord to his left rather than the dirtied, faintly glowing warrior to his right.

"Our miners are not trained fighters. They know the ore is most vulnerable moving between the mines and the outer walls, so they continued their route without investigating further."

They knew they'd be punished for stopping their work, you mean.

Lessie kept her face impassive, though her eyes begged to roll.

Valandaras addressed Camden directly, ignoring Royce. "Lord Camden, we should look into this. It could be connected to the earlier attack."

Camden looked like that was the last thing in the world he wanted to do, but he nodded his agreement.

"We shall investigate in the morning, then," Camden declared. "For now, let us take wine out on the terrace and then head to bed. I've missed having more than one blanket. Royce, you can retire."

Barely masking his annoyance, Royce Ackermane excused himself from the room. Lessie made a mental note to ask some of the other staff about Royce's temperament, his movements, his loyalty. Perhaps there was more to Camden's kidnapping being an inside job than they first thought.

Camden swept from his chair and threw open the doors of paned glass, stepping out into the open air. The crew followed him out onto the balcony, where goblets of dark red wine appeared, presented to them on a large silver serving platter. The servants had heard Camden's offhand request and fulfilled it immediately. They were good.

Lessie sniffed her glass and wrinkled her nose.

"Is there a problem?" Camden asked and she jumped. She hadn't realised anyone was watching her. "It's not poisoned, you know."

Lessie shook her head hurriedly. "It's fine," she mumbled, holding the wineglass awkwardly by the stem. "I'm just more of a whiskey person."

He raised an eyebrow, and she could feel his eyes stay on her even as she raised the glass to her lips. She refused to make a big deal out of it. Camden might be used to getting exactly what he wanted all the time, but she could drink one glass of red. It wouldn't kill her. She sipped from it stubbornly until his attention finally slid from her.

Camden brandished his glass in a belated toast. "Well, my esteemed rescue crew, you've seen me safely home," he said. "Well done. Now I suppose we'll try not to die horrible deaths to assassins before my brother comes to relieve you of your babysitting duties." He inhaled deeply from his glass and sighed, the night sky at his back.

Grundle snorted.

"To death," Mae said, voice light, as if she hadn't faced a sliver of it that very day. She raised her glass to Camden, but her eyes found Valandaras. "May it claim us when our time is truly up, and not a moment before."

They all drank. Some sipped, others gulped.

Lessie watched the sky.

And was momentarily blinded as a ball of emerald light streaked across it.

Lessie squinted against the brilliant brightness. One sideways glance into Mae's delighted face confirmed it wasn't a hallucination. The others had fallen silent, mesmerised, and Camden regarded them all quizzically before he turned to follow their gaze. Together they watched the pulsing light as it arced across the night, in stark contrast to the surrounding black. The ball of emerald shimmered as it descended, and they lost sight of it among the treetops. Lessie cocked her head. Judging by the trajectory, it would have landed a few miles outside of the estate, near the shoreline of the sea.

"Whatever that was, I do hope that it didn't damage the mines," said Camden drily. "Father will be livid."

Lessie looked to Valandaras, who was the only member of the group not reacting in awe. Instead, a calm sort of weariness blanketed his features, like he had seen it all before.

Of course, he's a Realmshifter. He probably has.

Mae noticed it, too.

"Val, what was it? What do you know? What does it mean?" She shot the questions at him in rapid succession, not waiting for an answer before the next escaped her. Her face was alive with joy at seeing something new and unexpected. Lessie's stomach flipped as she was shunted into a memory of her sister on the morning of a birthday, tearing into wrappings as her parents laughed, her mother squeezing her shoulder, feeling warm and alive, not cold and glassy-eyed and—*no. Stay in the now.*

Valandaras remained quiet, but the lack of light beneath his cloth told them his eyes had closed. He shook his head, pinching the bridge of his nose, leaving yet another new mark on the heavily stained cloth.

"It means another god has returned to this realm. From the prison."

Camden blanched, choking on his wine. "I beg your pardon?"

Reevan patted him on the back. "My lord, surely you know about the Godprison? It's all anyone's been able to discuss over the past century or so. Would you like a refresher?" He sighed dramatically and cleared his throat as if preparing to lead a sermon.

"Once upon a time, most of us believed there was only one God. He protected us all, gave us life, love, and laughter, and then disappeared for millions of years and so on. So of course everyone was very surprised when the Godprison broke open and the others began to return. Everyone got very mad at the first god and those who followed him, especially the Elven people, who had spent the last eon singing his praises. They were wiped off the map by the angry gods and their even angrier followers, and the False God never returned to defend them or his title."

Lessie suppressed a shudder. She had never even met someone who openly claimed to have Elven heritage. Overnight, they had disappeared from Kalaraak, and only wisps of their bloodlines had survived. She had a vague memory of her sister being questioned once—due to Trixie's Arcane ability or her beauty, Lessie wasn't sure. Either way, it hadn't been a compliment, and their mother had stopped speaking to the friend who'd made the comment.

To be Elven was to be untrustworthy, like the False God. Even Lessie knew that.

"Of course, I've always found it to be nonsense," Reevan continued. "They say the Betrayer locked all the gods up for millennia, but they've been leaking out for the past century like tree sap. If the gods were really betrayed by one of their own, how on earth was he powerful enough to imprison all of them at once?"

Reevan sniffed disdainfully, shrugging like he found it hard to believe his own words. "I think they were just tired of being asked to do things all the time. Perhaps they needed a break. Tens of thousands of years does seem rather excessive, though."

Impromptu speech completed, Reevan gave a slight bow. Mae giggled. Reevan's brow furrowed at Camden, trying to read the lord's exasperated expression.

"Or was it the concept of the realms you needed explaining, my lord? There are seven—"

This time, Camden held up his hands. "My education included both history and geography, thank you," he said firmly, cutting Reevan off.

Lessie snorted. *Apparently not cardinal directions, though, or you'd be able to point to the West Keep from Crossroad.*

Mae was bouncing on the balls of her feet, her whole body quivering like she was restraining herself from leaping from the balcony.

"Can we go and see the god?" she exclaimed, grasping Valandaras by the arms and smiling with unbridled enthusiasm. "Imagine it, returned to Kalaraak, and we're the first to welcome them home. It would be so special! Val, please?"

By the time Valandaras nodded wearily, Grundle was already at the door.

"We should go," the goblin said, one hand on his belt, long fingers searching for the comfort of his daggers. Of course, Grundle would never miss a chance to see something new. Or stab someone new.

Despite her fatigue, Lessie was equally interested in a chance to see exactly what had fallen from the skies. *A year ago I'd never left home, and now I'm out chasing fallen gods. Mama would be shocked.*

Camden looked to be the only member against the idea of an impromptu excursion. "I do believe I'd like to sit this one out, thanks," he said, running a hand through his hair and stifling a poorly staged yawn that fooled nobody.

"If we go, we all go," Valandaras said firmly. "You're safer with us."

Camden sighed. "Fine. But if we meet a god, then can we go to bed?"

Lessie almost laughed aloud. Men like Camden were always complaining of boredom, but then shied away from any experience. Maybe he was the Lord of Hypocrisy, instead. She met his eyes and found herself smirking.

Camden frowned at her, reading the mockery of her mouth as she extended a hand and offered him the doorway. When he didn't react, she shrugged and breezed through it, following Grundle back into the dining room.

Candles flickered within elaborate sconces, sending shadows dancing along the walls. A portrait Lessie hadn't noticed before caught her eye. Both DeFalcone brothers, a few years younger, dressed in their finest regalia. Even the oil-painted version of Camden seemed to sneer down at her; the artist had done an excellent job of capturing the arrogant glint in the grey of his eyes.

Lessie upended her travelling pack onto the priceless cherrywood table and began to take stock of her weapons.

Maybe meeting a god will finally humble him.

They made their way down the coast, following the path Camden explained was used for transporting ore from the mines into the castle. It had been easy enough to leave the estate, with Camden cheerily waving away any guards who questioned them. Maybe Royce Ackermane had not informed them of the true nature of Camden's recent journey, but Lessie couldn't help but notice that not a single one seemed concerned for their lord, only that he had a reason for leaving.

He probably irritates them all as much as he does us. Still, aren't they supposed to be loyal to him? Or is it just his father?

As they moved, Lessie kept her senses focused on the road ahead. She thought of the strange lights the workers had reported. Was it a precursor to this? Did gods show signs before they returned?

After walking for a while in silence, Mae veered sharply off the trail into the woods and disappeared into the forest. Lessie quickly realised that the faint glow of the fallen god had centralised on a point in the direction Mae was heading and crashed after her. The rest of the crew followed, pushing through bramble and low-hanging tree branches as they left the man made path behind in favour of the Divine's. Lessie caught up to Mae, panting, intending to chide the older woman for leaving them behind.

The words died on her tongue when she saw Mae's eyes.

They were glowing.

The emerald luminescence of Mae's eyes was so bright it lit up the surrounding woods. Green sparks shimmered over Mae's body, skittering over her like flames, and beneath her skin the essence pulsed like a heartbeat. The woods were thick and the path treacherous, but Mae had moved through the difficult terrain with a graceful purpose bordering on inhuman. The wind blew playfully around her skirts and ruffled her hair. It was like she was a part of the forest around them, the leaves of the trees swaying gently towards her, calling to her.

Mae turned to Lessie and Valandaras, beaming with joy.

"It's her," she whispered. "It's the Mother. I can feel it."

Mae looked as if she wanted to break into a full sprint and was only holding herself back because of her companions. Her body trembled with anticipation. Her illuminated eyes were otherworldly, alien, but it suited her.

Mae turned back towards the glow, hair rippling like embers of a fire with the reflections of emerald light.

Valandaras smiled. Not the tight-lipped ghost of a smile he usually offered. An open, broad, genuine smile.

Lessie allowed herself a moment to marvel at the sight of it, before the tiny voice of the goblin at her side spooked her so badly she nearly elbowed him in the face.

"Grundle found a problem," said Grundle, pointing the way they were heading. He put the spindly finger to his lips, and they all froze.

Following the goblin through the silent path he had created, they found themselves overlooking a cove. Lessie tried to suspend her wonder at the sight of the beach, illuminated by the full moon slowly making its way across the sky. Light danced on the rippling tide, washing onto the shore gently. White sand mixed with shells and pebbles, pushed gently back and forth by a low tide. What was left of an ancient ship had washed up onto the shore, barnacles still clinging hopefully to the side of the hull.

Most trees from the forest had not bothered to venture far onto the sand, save for one—a behemoth of an oak that shouldn't have been able to survive on such soil. It had to be centuries old; its branches outstretched majestically, like it was praying to the sky. Some leaves had already turned golden, but most were stubbornly clinging to their greenery. They glittered in the darkness with the same emerald that coated Mae's skin. A glow was pulsing deep within the massive trunk, bright enough to illuminate the entire cove.

The sight of the tree was so overwhelmingly magnificent that Lessie almost missed the figures that had gathered around it. She couldn't make out much, but some of them were in the process of driving heavy metal objects into the ground around the tree. The simple act triggered a memory she'd been trying to forget.

Her mouth went dry.

Mae growled. Even in her human body, the sound was primal, animalistic in its rage.

Lessie gritted her teeth. The scene was eerily familiar, only this time she knew what it meant. The sudden pang of wishing her sister were there threatened to knock the wind from her lungs. She tried to breathe, feeling the panic and grief rising, willing it to subside for the moment. She could deal with it later. Her crew needed her now.

We came to meet a god. These people came to destroy one.

10

REEVAN

The strangers were from Kalac.

That much was obvious to Reevan, though he supposed one who had never set foot in Altaea's closest neighbour could miss the signs. They all wore clothing best suited to the harsh, unforgiving heat of the deserts, and they had no trouble moving on the sand. He eyed their robes, noting colours and patterns and storing the information away. He didn't recognise them, but whoever these men were, they were working for somebody important.

The crew had a decent vantage point to assess from, at least. With the forest growing right to the edge of the small cliff they huddled upon, they were concealed, around fifty feet above the cove. The cove itself was rather spacious, the only interruption to the curve of the shoreline being the broken hull of the ship that had washed up there. Embedded in the sand, the rotting wood marred the landscape somewhat, but it was still beautiful. The majesty of the giant oak tree dominated the space, as if commanding all attention, the emerald pulsing in the trunk clear even from a distance.

Reevan took all of it in without really thinking about it, focusing on the human element. He crouched next to Grundle, who had also marked the strangers as fellow homelanders and was no doubt plotting how to murder them all to prevent a single one from recognising him.

A wise decision, if he was being honest with himself. Reevan sighed and sized up his newest adversaries.

There were around ten of them, all heavily hooded and masked, with some busying themselves hammering in large metal spikes deep into the sand around the tree. If he had to guess, Reevan would bet there would be a full circle created before long. The glow from the immense oak reflected off the silver, casting odd lights around the cove. A couple of the figures stood away from the rest, speaking in hushed tones. One appeared to be giving orders, others relaying them.

Reevan cocked his head. Something about the stature of the one in charge... It was wrong.

"Y'all, this is bad," Lessie whispered to the group, the tone of her voice pulling Reevan's attention. The girl was frowning, which was quite regular. What was highly irregular, however, was how distressed she appeared. A light sheen of sweat had broken out over Lessie's brow, her jaw was clenched, and Reevan watched as she seemed to be fighting her own breathing, like she was forcing the air out of her lungs against their will. It was altogether a bit worrying.

Valandaras kept his eyes on the beach. "Tell us what you know," he said, gently, but still a command.

Lessie fixed her gaze on a faraway point as she let an incoherent explanation fall from her mouth, like the words would hurt less if they escaped quickly enough.

"I've seen this before. It's why I left home." Her voice broke on the last word, and Reevan's tail twitched. "The men down there, the leader—I've seen them. In the Maw. I've seen him attack a—a god? The tree? Whatever that is."

Mae had not torn her eyes away from the pulsing oak from the moment they came upon it, but Lessie's words finally broke the Divine's gaze. She whirled on the younger girl, emerald skin flaring, blurring her outline. Reevan squinted against the odd light. Was it the reflection pulsing from the tree, or was she turning green? He had not noticed her Gift having that effect before.

"What do you mean, attacked?" Mae hissed, grasping Lessie's wrists and causing the younger girl to flinch. Mae's eyes were backlit by the glow, and fear and fury raged inside them.

Lessie glared back at Mae, yanking her hands away like they were burned.

"I mean attacked," she shot back in a heated whisper. "We came across a giant tree growing in the middle of a cave. I saw the men, the spikes—some kind of weird ritual. It seemed like he was killing the tree, and my sister and I tried to shut it down." She balled her hands at her sides before the rest of them could see how badly they were shaking and refused to meet their eyes. "He didn't like having his work interrupted."

Reevan sniffed. It was clear that the girl had experienced something traumatic, although he didn't understand why she wouldn't relish a chance to shoot at the people who had traumatised her. The retribution for the interruption must have been brutal to spook the girl so badly.

What was also becoming quite clear was that they needed to interrupt this one, too.

Valandaras had turned back to watching the strangers, whilst Grundle had never stopped. Lessie ran a shaking hand through her hair, shoving stray pieces behind her ears violently.

Reevan glanced over at Camden. The young lord looked ill, and seemed to be weighing up whether it was worth walking back to his estate alone to not have to participate in the confrontation.

"Should we return to the keep and alert the guards?" Camden suggested, eyes darting between Lessie and the glowing tree nervously.

Grundle snorted. "Grundle thinks these ones will be long finished by then."

Mae continued to stare at Lessie. The prolonged eye contact made Reevan uncomfortable, despite not being involved in it.

"What are they going to do to her?" Mae whispered, eyes pleading.

Lessie only shook her head. "I don't know. It had already started when I saw it. Trixie—my sister, she's Arcane. She tried to counteract it. I don't know what she did. It worked, though. I don't even know what the tree is."

Valandaras put up a hand, and they all fell silent. He spoke calmly, not to anyone in particular, but Reevan noted the way he moved closer to Mae.

"It is a vessel," he said, "a cocoon for the god's power, before they can manifest their physical form within this realm. Some are drawn to ancient trees like this one." The words hung heavily, for once the exhaustion of his true age showing through. "Nature has a magic all of its own. But it is one of the only times gods are vulnerable."

Lessie's face was grey. Behind the raging power brimming, Mae's eyes were full of terror.

"So they are planning to kill this god tree, then?" asked Reevan. "In that case, we should probably stop them."

The men below had finished their work—the gleaming spikes now spread equally around the base of the glowing giant. The tallest, who had been conversing with the one Lessie had marked as the leader, had stepped towards the base of the god tree and turned to face the others. He seemed to be addressing them. Reevan itched to get closer, to hear what was being said below.

"Get the spikes out," Valandaras muttered. An order. Reevan nodded.

Mae bristled. Her whole body seemed wound too tight, like a tripwire begging to be sprung.

The hooded stranger turned to face the oak, raising his arms above his head as purple lightning crackled within his fingertips. An Arcane, then.

Reevan had met a few in his time, individuals who relied not on gods for their power but manipulating the Weave itself, where the very essence of magic was believed to come from. They were just as uncommon as Divines, and even more persecuted unless they showed true mastery of their abilities. Some provinces in Altaea had gone as far as outlawing the practice altogether.

Most Arcanes were self-taught, if they survived long enough to teach themselves. Magic had a way of bursting out, of being almost impossible to control. There were a few dedicated schools of the Arcane arts across the realm, but they were heavily guarded and shrouded in secrecy to protect those who attended them.

Reevan had never understood it, despite being curious. It was beyond his knowledge.

A deep voice boomed across the clearing, originating from the one giving orders. Reevan's ears twitched, but even he was too far away to make out the words. Two of the figures stood before the Arcane, presenting him with something, and as the Arcane took it and lifted it high, dark steel glinted in the light. The wicked looking blade looked to be half the man's height, and he sent a wave of energy through it as he plunged it into the ground at his feet, completing a perfect circle around the tree.

The lightning began to build, and sparks shot out, creating glass divots of violet in the sand. One hit the spike closest to the figure, and the metal clanged as the energy coursed through it. The amethyst glow grew brighter as the lightning streaked through the surrounding spikes, searching, like fingers grasping for an anchor.

When it had spread through all the spikes, creating a perfect ring around the god tree, the light within the blade surged—and Mae screamed in pain. Her body twisted unnaturally, like her spine was trying to escape her skin.

Valandaras moved.

The warrior hurled himself off the cliff, rolling onto the sand on impact before barrelling towards the men. Some of them looked alarmed, drawing weapons and shouting.

Reevan sighed. So much for the element of surprise.

He sprung, not waiting for the others, clearing the fifty-foot drop with little thought. Taking a second to welcome the familiarity of sand beneath his paws, Reevan adjusted his gait and sprinted in an arc towards the god tree, hugging the line of the forest. The men had closed ranks around the Arcane with the blade, looking to their leader, crying out.

Valandaras had drawn his falchion as he charged towards the one giving orders, the blade glinting as it reflected off the glow of his skin. Reevan watched out of the corner of his eye as Valandaras swung a deadly strike straight for the man, who did not attempt to block the blow, or even react in any way. At least this would be a short fight.

Valandaras's blade passed through harmlessly.

The Realmshifter stumbled, carried forward from the force of his powerful attack.

The figure did not move.

Reevan skidded to a stop. His left ear twitched as he picked up the sound of laughter, low and humourless. A voice came from the figure—male, low, but it was hollow and muffled.

It still made every hair on his back stand on edge.

"Once again, I am so carelessly interrupted. Once again, I shall be forced to teach the interrupters a lesson," the figure murmured, thoughtfully, as if musing to himself. His voice was low, void of any true emotion, sounding mildly inconvenienced.

He raised an arm—slightly transparent, Reevan could see now—and waved a hand dismissively towards the beach behind him.

There was an unmistakable creak of groaning wood. Reevan turned back towards the shoreline and watched in disbelief as the sunken shipwreck *moved*.

The water rippled, disturbed, as the remains of the once proud ship that had washed up there shifted. It rose from the waves, forming rudimentary limbs from the splintered pieces of its hull, until it resembled something of a human shape, albeit mutated and eerie in its haphazardness. It was taller than the cliff they had been on. Reevan craned his neck upward as the gargantuan construct tested a leg and took a heavy step onto the beach. A pair of rusted cannons perched upon the shoulders. Barnacles and multicoloured coral clinging to the hull gave it an odd sheen in the fractals of light bouncing around the cove. Reevan even spotted a terrified octopus clinging for dear life around its neck. It was altogether quite disturbing.

The cloaked, transparent figure smiled beneath his hood. The smile of a shark who had scented blood in the water.

"Go," he said, and the shipwreck lurched towards Valandaras.

Valandaras, to his credit, simply raised his weapon higher towards the monstrosity.

Reevan stood frozen in the sand, momentarily torn between carrying out his original task of interrupting the ritual and not leaving his crewleader to face down this sailor's nightmare alone. Then a feral snarling cracked across the cove, louder than he'd ever heard before. Perhaps he would not have to. Of course, Mae would go straight for Valandaras. Reevan glanced over his shoulder and his heart skipped a beat.

The creature stalking over the sand towards them was nothing short of terrifying. The feline form was familiar enough that he recognised Mae—yet the massive, hulking stature of the beast she had become still made the survival instincts embedded deep within Reevan's psyche scream at him to run. She was at least three times the size of a regular mountain lion, reminiscent of ancient dire beasts long extinct.

Mae's amber eyes glowed green, brimming with raw energy, like she could barely contain it within her even in such a monstrous form. She reached Valandaras in a few bounds, muscles rippling under the fur, and as she stood beside the Realmshifter—dwarfing him—the sheer power radiating from her...

Reevan gave himself a moment to wonder.

Was it the strength of the god that mattered, or the strength of the Divine's belief in them?

The other strangers had frozen, waiting for direction from their leader. Even the colossal shipwreck had paused. The hollow figure of their leader looked rattled for the first time, taken aback by the sudden appearance of Mae's form. His cold eyes glittered with malice under the hood as he assessed her. Whatever he saw in Mae, he must have decided that his unholy shipwreck was a match for her, since he turned back to his followers and resumed his place as overseer.

But Reevan noticed a tension in the figure that had not been there before.

"Get it done," the leader said, voice taut, waving a dismissive hand. His disciples all scattered, returning to their places around the god tree, the Arcane one gripping the black sword's hilt so hard his knuckles turned white. The shipwreck resumed its awkward shambling towards the shore, planks of rotten wood breaking off and plummeting into the shallow waves below.

Mae sized up the living shipwreck before her, growling, teeth bared, saliva pooling around the wickedly sharp canines. Valandaras twisted in the sand beside her, finding his footing, grounding himself. The Divine and the Realmshifter, side by side, were ready to take on an abomination of an enemy.

Reevan made his choice. They could handle it.

He bolted for the god tree.

11

REEVAN

Reevan refused to look backwards as he ran.

The possessed shipwreck's eerie creaking was jarring, especially coupled with the sounds of waterlogged wood meeting claws and steel, but Reevan kept his focus towards his goal.

Take the spikes out.

He rounded the edge of the forest and attempted to attack from the side. Two of the strangers rushed forward to meet him, both carrying wicked-looking shortswords.

Reevan drew his own dagger, a simple blade, but before any of them could make a move, a sharp crack pierced the air. One man dropped, swearing and gripping his thigh, which had begun leaking blood. Reevan spied the bullet wound and grinned.

At least the girl had pulled herself together.

Lessie's next shot went wide, missing them all, but they flinched at the sound and Reevan pounced.

The hooded man tried to keep both threats in his sight, his attention divided, and Reevan quickly dispatched him. Pulling his blade from the man's chest, Reevan whirled to miss a second sword coming down on him by inches. He threw himself to the right, rolling in the sand, spitting it from his mouth.

Reevan dug his paws into the sand and let the momentum take him back to standing before he launched himself at the man, tackling him. They grappled on the ground before a sudden sharp intake of breath told Reevan his favourite blade had found its mark.

Watching the light leave their eyes was always the hardest part of killing, but he could never look away.

Staying low, Reevan glanced around. The living shipwreck was thrashing in the shallows, creaking and groaning, sending sprays of seawater high. Mae had climbed it, trying to find purchase in the rotten wood with razor-sharp claws and teeth, pieces of the ship breaking apart under her. Valandaras stood beneath it, narrowly avoiding being crushed as he swung his falchion into the construct's lower limbs over and over.

Some of the robed strangers had attempted to face him, and Valandaras fought them, too, but the shipwreck was unpredictable and just as likely to hurt them. One hooded figure already lay face down in the water, unmoving, an unlucky victim of the giant's flailing.

The sound of bullets racing past stopped and started again as Lessie reloaded her revolver, still high on the cliff, giving them cover. If Camden knew what was good for him, he would stay up there with her. Reevan hoped the lord would have better self-preservation than he had shown at Falcon's Watch.

The remaining hooded figures had closed ranks around the Arcane, trying to shield him from the projectiles. No sign of Grundle, but that was always a good sign.

For the moment, Reevan had been forgotten.

Reevan turned to face the nearest silver spike. The energy from the god tree seemed to be fading, as if it were feeding into the spikes, the emerald bleeding into the amethyst. The light intensified, crackling around him, making his fur stand up. He grimaced as he reached towards it.

Take the spikes out. That is what Valandaras had said.

Reevan closed one paw around the base of the metal, and for a moment, the world was calm. Then he was blasted off his feet.

Reevan hit the ground, thirty feet away, his skidding backwards halted by a thankfully young and pliant tree, which had bent to his body rather than broken it. His vision swam.

"Grundle thinks you shouldn't touch the spikes," a low voice murmured. Reevan sniffed.

The goblin was rummaging through his pockets, searching. Reevan shook his head and tried to stop the ringing in his ears. He tasted metal. Or perhaps it was blood.

"What do you suggest, then, my sneaky friend?" Reevan replied, blinking rapidly to clear the spots, trying to restore his senses to normal. "I don't particularly wish to fry, but we're running out of time."

It would be seconds before they were spotted. They were lucky the lion and the shipwreck were putting on such a show, holding the attention of the remaining acolytes. Mae's furious roaring was deafening.

Grundle pulled a blackened dagger from its sheathe and ran his hands along it. Discarding the blade, he shoved the leather scabbard towards the spike and grunted when it made contact. He was not launched backwards, which was an improvement.

Reevan watched, curious, as the goblin returned the dagger inside, and made to reach for it again. Reevan threw out an arm to stop him.

"It's the metal," he said, realising at the same moment Grundle did. The goblin swore. Reevan cursed himself for leaving his staff at the keep and turned for the forest. He snapped a large branch from the nearest tree, hoping it would be thick enough, gesturing to Grundle to move as he angled it downwards. The goblin stepped aside, and Reevan slammed the end of the branch into the spike. It shifted slightly. And he didn't die.

Reevan aimed again, panting, throwing all of his weight into the branch. The spike jolted again, now sticking at an angle. The lightning flickered, as if angry its path had been altered. He was sweating as he brought the branch down a third time. If he left it too long, the energy surged up the branch towards him and he felt his paws start to sizzle. The spike did not come out.

Reevan glanced over towards the remaining Arcane, still standing before the blade he had driven into the sand. His companions had fled, whether to join against Valandaras and Mae or simply to preserve their own lives, Reevan did not know.

At first Reevan had thought the Arcane was simply keeping the sword steady, but now he wondered if the black blade had frozen the unfortunate soul's hands around it. The dark steel seemed to be filling with energy, syphoning it from the crackling ring it had created. The Arcane's hands shook as they, too, glowed brighter.

Reevan's eyes met the Arcane's as a booming voice cut across the night. They were frightened.

"I hope you have learned that you should not meddle in what you cannot understand," the hollow figure intoned, thunderous voice rolling over the cove as if amplified. "This world has no place for gods who were too weak to return when they needed to."

Grundle cringed away from the voice, and even Reevan grimaced. He had heard enough leaders speak to sense the rage that simmered beneath the suspicious calm. Whoever this was, they were angry. Even the tone held an ominous promise of violence. The purple light, as if hearing the words, crackled between the spikes, converged on the sword, and glowed so bright

Reevan had to force his eyes shut. The last thing he saw was overwhelming fear fill the Arcane's face.

"Power belongs to those worthy to wield it," the hollow voice declared. "And I intend to."

The Arcane holding the sword exploded.

Reevan threw an arm over his face as flesh and ichor splattered towards him. The light surged, filling the sword, glowing so hot it could have burned. Reevan skittered backwards as the sudden heat singed his whiskers. Feeling Grundle at his side, Reevan grasped his arm and yanked them back. The entire cove lit up, and the force that radiated from the god tree knocked them from their feet. He heard wood crack, the great oak groaning as if in pain as the power within was wrenched from it.

Trying desperately to get his bearings, Reevan felt at his side for a weapon—a sword, a dagger, anything—and instead felt his claws close around the tree branch.

He moved before he could second guess his decision.

Reevan smashed the tree branch into the silver spike one more time, wincing as the heat from the lightning coursed through his fingers, and felt the spike finally come free. The light around it wobbled, as if no longer certain where to go, and streaks of the energy flailed out wildly, hitting the surrounding trees.

Reevan had no time to admire his handiwork as he felt a tug on his robes.

"Move, now," Grundle all but shouted, the loudest Reevan had ever heard him.

They ran blindly, unsure of the direction, unaware of the others, fuelled purely by survival. Streaks of energy soared over their heads. Smoke filled the air. The scent of burning filled his nostrils. Reevan glanced behind him once as he thought he heard a high-pitched screaming. But neither of them stopped running until they were at the base of the cliff.

When they both noticed how it had become eerily quiet.

Reevan rolled, panting. All of his senses engaged as he searched for his crew. Boots crunched in the sand next to him and his nostrils were assaulted with gunpowder.

"You all right?" Lessie asked, voice thick, in the middle of reloading her handgun. She barely glanced up to see him nod. "Were they with you? Where's Mae?"

Reevan frowned. Could she not see—

Reevan looked back and was met with a most disturbing sight. The cove was covered in smoke, roiling over the sand, obscuring everything from view. There was no sign of the remaining robed figures, the shipwreck, or of Valandaras and Mae. Only overlapping, indistinct sounds of fighting. Flickers of orange glinted within the smoke.

Reevan took a single step towards it when a roar shook the earth and the scent of burning wood overwhelmed him.

The god tree was on fire.

Reevan sprinted back towards the oak, Lessie and Grundle falling behind as he threw everything he had into his gait, becoming little more than a blur. The kitskan's prowess for speed was well deserved.

Reevan flew over the sand until he had reached the base of the god tree, as close as he dared get. The flames engulfed the mighty oak, branches once raised in prayer now a silent plea for help as they blackened and turned to ash. He felt his breath catch in his throat. The fire must have been magical in nature, for it did not spread to the neighbouring forest despite the wind that whipped around them. But there was no way to slow it. He could do nothing but watch, helpless, as the god tree burned before him.

"A minor setback."

Reevan snapped his head towards the voice. Somewhere in the haze of smoke, he had not realised how much further out to sea he had arced as he ran. He now found himself directly in the path of the attack's orchestrator.

Close up, the figure was clearly not physically present, with some sort of Arcane projection magic allowing him to be there. He was hooded, keeping the stature and features concealed, and what little of his face not covered by the hood was wearing a ceremonial mask that resembled some sort of sea creature. His eyes reflected the burning of the god tree as he regarded it with mild disappointment.

"You would do well to remember this moment, kitskan," the hollow voice mused.

The apparition glowed more brightly now, sparks of amethyst skittering around him. He lifted a transparent hand. Grasped between his fingers was the sword that had been part of the ritual. The blade was wide and jagged, steel so dark it appeared black. It glowed, too, with a faint greenish hue that was achingly familiar.

Reevan resisted the urge to look back, to confirm the blade was no longer on the beach. Every instinct in him roared that this was a dangerous adversary, one to never take eyes off.

There seemed to be something in the sand at the figure's feet. Reevan sidled closer to it, feigning mild interest in the stranger's words.

"Such a strange thing, Divinity," the figure said, twisting the sword as if checking the balance of the blade. "How it can manifest from the smallest belief, how it can be begged and borrowed. Taken from those gods who took too long to reclaim it. How with enough Divinity, a mortal could surpass a god themselves." He pointed the sword at Reevan.

Reevan barely ducked in time as the blast of Arcane energy soared over his head into the forest beyond. How had the figure cast it through the sword, or through the illusion? Neither seemed possible. It went against what little Reevan knew of Arcane skills.

"Remember who holds the power, and who serves, kitskan," he droned, turning the sword over in his hand, inspecting it. "And remember what happens to those who interfere."

Reevan spat damp sand out of his mouth as he stayed in a crouch. This was a person who relished being in control, and who believed above all that they were right. Which made them incredibly dangerous.

He needed to get off this beach.

The figure regarded him, eyes glittering cruelly under the mask.

"Tell the Divine that her fallen god's power will be paramount to a new age upon this realm," he said. "She was unusually strong. Perhaps she will survive its loss." His voice sounded, of all things, oddly impressed.

Reevan let out a snarl, but the figure had already dismissed him, instead looking over his shoulder. A flicker of surprise crossed over the hooded man's face.

"You," he spat angrily.

"Me," replied Lessie, aiming her revolver at the small object at the figure's feet. She fired and the apparition sputtered. Reevan felt a rush of smug satisfaction as the hooded man's face contorted into true rage just before it vanished.

The atmosphere around them immediately felt lighter. Lessie holstered her weapon, balled her fists at her sides, and strode to the object. She kicked it over to inspect it, frowning.

"Arcane bullshit," she muttered. "I thought the others were with you. Did you find them?"

Reevan shook his head. He looked up at the charred remains of the tree. It was no longer on fire, but there was no saving it.

A a shout pierced the air. Lessie spun and ran towards it, and Reevan followed, quickly outpacing her. Seawater splattered onto his robes as they reached the edge of the waves, the feel of the salt water on his skin momentarily paralysing him as he felt a very old, fractured memory attempt to resurface. He pushed it aside as the smoke finally cleared enough to see.

The remains of the transformed shipwreck lay stationary once more, returned to its grave now whatever magic that had animated it had been revoked. Pieces of it littered the shoreline, as if it had been torn apart during the fighting. In the shadows of the hull, Reevan spotted two human figures amidst the wreckage. A pale golden light glowed softly from one of them.

From the other, nothing.

Reevan approached cautiously, but there were no other threats lying in wait. The bodies of fallen strangers bobbed in the shallow waters, drifting lazily in the flow of the tide. It had receded somewhat from when they had first beheld the cove. Patches of darkened scarlet stained the surrounding banks, marking the places where their life's blood had spilt into the ocean, souls already departed for the Silver Stream. Reevan's tail twitched as he moved closer, and for once felt no words come to him.

Valandaras, bloody and drenched, knelt in the retreating waters, cradling a lifeless Mae in his arms. What Reevan had initially thought was blood was thankfully only her auburn hair, unbound and half-submerged in the water, floating gently in the movement of the tide.

The Realmshifter was shouting, not for them, but to the woman he held, only the glow from his eyes illuminating her limp form. She must have returned to her human body when the Arcane's siphon had completed, or perhaps when the god tree caught alight. Reevan watched, frozen, feeling helpless for the second time that night, as Valandaras screamed at her to open her eyes, to breathe, to come back—

Reevan's ears twitched backwards at the sound of Lessie catching up to him, footsteps faltering.

"Mae? Mae!" Lessie's voice, frantic, carried out over the sea. She barrelled past him and skidded to a stop in front of Valandaras, water spraying over them both, neither of them caring.

Reevan watched closely as the younger girl placed her hand on the woman's neck and gasp, though with relief or grief he could not tell. He felt like a stranger, intrusive as he inched closer; his ears twitching as he struggled to pick up the younger girl's words.

"Her heart is beating," Lessie said, looking around as if for her pack and finding nothing. "And she's still breathing." She levelled Valandaras with a glare that would make most men cower. "Whatever you can do, you better do it now."

Valandaras stared at Lessie for a moment before giving her a small nod. He rose to his feet, carrying Mae out of the water and onto the damp sand of the cove. Placing her gently down, Valandaras removed the gauntlets from his arms and untwisted the cloth wrappings underneath them. Reevan's curiosity peaked, and he wondered if Valandaras had every inch of his skin covered in one way or another.

Valandaras took Mae's face into his bare hands and closed his eyes, the light beneath the cloth growing dim. For a moment, all of them collectively held their breath. Reevan had only seen the Realmshifter attempt this once before, after their disastrous bounty in Holdfast.

Golden light seeped from Valandaras's hands into Mae's body, glittering within her, and Reevan could have sworn he saw a faint flicker of emerald respond.

12

MAE

Mother?

Strong hands, holding her, carrying her like a child. A soft golden light. The gentle sway of footsteps.
Fear. *Mother?*

A cool breeze upon her skin. The sounds of the forest.
Despair. *Mother, you can't leave.*

Worried voices, speaking in hushed tones. The crunching of gravel.
Utter desolation. *Mother, please, I'd rather die than lose you.*

A soft bed. Warmth settling over her. The scent of chamomile.
Mother, come back. I can't feel you here anymore.

A whisper in the abyss.
I am always here, even when I am not. That is a Mother's love.

Mae awoke.
The first thing she felt was the aching emptiness inside of her.
She cracked an eye, a ceiling of stone greeting her, and felt the softness of wool covering her. She flexed her fingers, gathering the material between them. The movement felt foreign. Her muscles felt wearied, atrophied, like she'd spent years asleep in this unfamiliar bed.

Every bone in her body felt like it had broken. Her muscles were sore and strained, her lungs felt crushed—every single part of her hurt. But none more than her heart as she reached for the well of power within her and found nothing but a trickle of her Gift.

Empty.

Mae watched specks of dust float across a sunbeam as her eyes adjusted to the daylight streaming into the room from the open window. Time drifted with the warm, enveloping light of early autumn. An afternoon breeze sent the dust motes scattering as it drifted lazily through the window. Birds sang merrily outside of it, twittering as they foraged. A sparrow alighted momentarily on the windowsill before gliding away again.

How strange, that the suns should still shine. That the moon would rise when they set. That the world should still burst with life, when the reason for its existence had been stolen from her again.

Someone shifted, the scraping of armour on wood echoing off the high ceiling. Mae propped herself up on her elbows, gritting her teeth at the pain, and found Valandaras.

He was sitting in the corner of the room, leaning against the wall, a spindly stool creaking under his weight as he shifted in his uncomfortable sleep. The glow from his eyes under the cloth was dimmed, and his chest rose and fell steadily. His arms were crossed; his falchion and shield, priceless to him, lay carelessly at his feet, as if he had thrown them to the ground without a second thought. He was bloodied and bruised, coated in sand and seawater, his clothing dried in places and still damp in others, the coverings on his face filthy and blackened with ash and sweat. He looked terrible.

Mae felt her brow soften, the corners of her lips tug upwards. She didn't remember smiling requiring this much effort.

I should help him heal, she thought, seeing him wince as he breathed. She tried to sit up, but her limbs were heavy. She reached again for her Gift, subconsciously, but felt nothing more than a whisper where there should have been a symphony.

Empty.

The grief that swelled inside of her was overwhelming. She only vaguely registered her head hitting the soft pillow again before the darkness claimed her once more.

"I brought you soup."

The low voice roused her, but it was the heavenly scent that made her open her eyes. Lessie perched beside her on the bed, a steaming bowl in her hands.

"Mae, come on. You need to eat," she said, holding up a spoon. Her tone was casual, but Mae registered the worry in the younger girl's eyes.

A spike of grief shot through her. It was her job to worry about them.

Mae sighed. If she searched herself, she was starving, but the sadness that blanketed her made her numb to such needs. She couldn't move. Her body felt like lead. It took all of her energy to keep breathing. She ran a hand through her hair, fingers snagging in the tangles. Even her scalp felt sore.

Lessie helped her into a sitting position, rearranging the pillows on her bed. Mae took the bowl but did not eat. The sides of the bowl were much too hot, but she barely felt the burning. Her eyes darted towards the empty corner. She tried to speak, but her throat swallowed the words. Why did it feel like she hadn't spoken for a century? She cleared it and tried again.

"Where's Val?"

Lessie spoke softly, like she were afraid of spooking an animal. "I dragged him out of here about an hour ago. Said that you would never wake up if your nose was under constant assault. He's down in one of the bathing rooms." She shook her head, rolling her eyes as if quietly outraged by the opulence. "Of course the West Keep has multiple bathing rooms. One might as well be a lake. I think I've got the hang of it now, but I nearly drowned the first time I went in."

Mae tried to smile, but the effort of it nearly wiped her.

"How long have I been out?"

Lessie's brow furrowed. "A week. We thought we lost you," she replied, her own half-smile sliding from her face. "When I saw you on that beach..."

Empty. Aching. *Mother...*

Shutting down the hurt was almost as painful as the hurt itself, but Mae managed. She focused on the bowl in her lap, on raising the spoon to her mouth, letting the smell of the hearty broth flood her senses and keep her from breaking. She ignored the part of her that wanted to hurl the bowl across the room and watch it shatter on the stone floor.

Lessie watched her, eagle eyed, as she ate half of the stew before setting it aside, her stomach queasy. Breathing slowly, Mae fought the nausea, saliva pooling in her mouth as the stew threatened to make a reappearance.

Lessie reached down beside her chair and handed Mae a glass of water. Mae gripped it harder than she needed to and counted the lines on her knuckles.

"Druitt DeFalcone is arriving tomorrow," Lessie said, trying to take her attention off her sickness, an attempt at a normal conversation. "I sent word to Roost Keep that he was needed here. That stuffy Head of House seemed angry that I handled it, but he was dallying and Camden was... occupied. He can take it up with Druitt. I'm sick of him looking down his nose at me." She wrinkled her own nose, the freckles upon it dancing. "We've got more pressing matters now than babysitting the Lord of Whining."

Mae felt another tug at her lips. It was safe to assume Lessie and Camden had not become fast friends in the week since she had been asleep. The young lord had survived, then, but the others... Mae felt a stab of guilt as she realised she had not given them a single thought.

"Is... is everyone all right?" she asked, choking on the words.

Lessie nodded. "Reevan's been running laps of the keep, trying to figure out how Camden managed to get himself kidnapped, and Grundle's attempted to break into every single locked room just to prove he can, spooking the snot out of the servants. Safe to say they are perfectly fine," she sighed, but there was a flicker of affection behind the exasperation.

Mae sighed in relief. *Thank the Mother they're all safe.*

The tiny prayer escaped her mind without thinking, and a wave of anguish crashed into her. She closed her eyes, but the scene still played as if pasted over her eyelids—the pulsing of the god tree as it bled out, feeling the pain of the Mother's essence as it was absorbed by the Arcane's lightning, feeling her own Changed form shatter as her Gift was ripped from her—

The room swayed. Her cheeks felt too hot. Her skin felt clammy. She wanted to curl into a ball and die.

Oh, Mother, I can't do this again.

The door opened, creaking, and Mae willed herself not to crumble.

Valandaras stood in the doorway, wearing a clearly borrowed tunic. His skin glistened with the dampness of someone who had recently bathed, and he looked the cleanest she had ever seen him, although the same dirty cloth covered his eyes. He had belted his falchion at his side, but was otherwise unarmed and unarmoured.

He hesitated, having not expected to find Mae awake and sitting up.

"I'll take this to the kitchens," said Lessie, picking up the bowl and the untouched mug of tea Mae only just noticed had been sitting on the small table beside her bed. The younger girl gave her a look of apprehension, like she had half a mind to stay, but after levelling Valandaras with a hard stare, she exited the room.

Valandaras remained motionless in the doorway. Mae looked up at him, afraid of what she would find on his face. Was he disappointed? Did he think her now useless to the crew?

What good is a Divine with no Divinity?

"Val, I—" her voice wobbled and she cut herself off, tears pricking at her eyes. Her careful reconstruction of her psyche was already splintering.

Valandaras crossed the room in a heartbeat, sitting beside her, searching her face, and the full force of his gaze bored into her despite the cloth. Her vision swam, eyes so filled with tears that the light didn't hurt. Her voice was hoarse, barely more than a whisper.

"I can't feel her anymore."

Valandaras did not speak. He simply pulled her towards him, enveloping her completely. The pressure of his arms around her felt like the only thing keeping her from shattering. He stroked her hair softly and murmured words she couldn't properly hear.

She could not remember ever being held like this.

Mae buried her face into his chest and sobbed.

It took Mae another three days to leave the room.

Lessie led her straight down to the grandest bathing room, promising she would feel better after finally scrubbing the grime of the fight from her skin. Mae had been given cloth and water to wash with, but it was a poor substitution, and she had not found the energy to do so.

The girl had exaggerated on the size of the room, but not by much. Mae was unsurprised. Many of the noble houses, especially the Seven, liked to flaunt their wealth in odd ways, and unnecessary luxuries like these baths were a popular way to do so. It must have taken the servants hours to carry in enough buckets to fill it.

Mae felt a vague sense of irony—the idea of being waited on in a noble's house should have been amusing to her, but she had forgotten what amusement was supposed to feel like.

All she felt was cold.

The bath itself had been built from the same stone as the rest of the castle. A ring of stone created raised edges before sinking into the floor, and it took three steps down before she fully entered the water. It was deep enough that Mae had to stand if she wanted her head to remain above the surface.

Lessie had lingered, uncertain, and only left once she seemed satisfied that Mae was not going to drown herself. Mae felt affection for the girl glimmer under the crushing sadness.

She did not look at her body as she peeled away her clothing. The ache that coated her bones, coupled with the sharp spikes of pain that lanced through her with every mild movement, was enough to know she would be covered in bruises, or possibly worse. New scars.

The invisible ones hurt most.

The first step into the water stung, and she yelped as she reflexively yanked her foot back out, which sent another wave of pain crashing over her. She tried again, wincing, the warm water feeling scalding against her icy skin. She had to sit for a while with just her feet dipped in, watching the skin turn bright red as blood rushed back to where it was meant to.

Her hands were next, fingers protesting, knuckles aching. The sight of her horribly chipped polish sent a weak pulse of disgust through her, but it felt far away. How had she ever cared about something so frivolous as the colour of her nails?

Mae took her time, and eventually managed to enter the pool through a combination of deep breathing and moving very, very slowly.

Submerging herself in the fragrant waters, Mae closed her eyes and concentrated on the feeling of her hair swaying around her.

Of her body's temperature, at first so cold the bath had threatened to boil her, now beginning to adjust, to feel her fingers and toes again. Of the weightlessness her bones felt, suspended in the warmth. Of how all sound had become muted, muffled, far away.

She floated, letting her face disappear beneath the surface. Pure silence.

She was completely, utterly alone.

The Mother can't be truly gone. Even when she was imprisoned, she came to me. The Hollow God himself could not keep her away.

Mae had felt this disconnect once before in her life, but that was when she had been so lost and desolate the Mother had struggled to reach her. When grief had broken over her like a tidal wave, washing away any trace of herself. When the connection had severed on her end.

When I couldn't find myself, she found me. Now, I have to find her.

Mae reached inside herself.

She searched through every inch of her soul. She silently called, seeking the spark that had flowed with such abundance for as long as she could remember. She stayed under the water longer than she should, and delayed coming up for air until her lungs were burning. She floated, searching, praying, calling, until the water went cold.

Somewhere in the abyss, a small flicker of the Mother's power responded.

It was damaged, muted, a tiny fraction of what had once been available to her.

But it was still there.

The tiniest of emerald sparks, glowing deep within.

13

MAE

Mae spent the next few days in the bathing room.

While she was floating, the ache in her muscles didn't feel so pronounced. When she submerged herself underneath the surface, it was harder to see the discolouration that peppered over her skin. Even the screams that echoed in her skull felt slightly muted with her head under the water, drowned out by her own heartbeat.

And if she strained her ears—or her soul—hard enough, once or twice she thought she might have heard the Mother's whispers.

As the twin suns descended past the horizon on the fourth day, Mae broke the surface of the water and accepted that it was too cold to continue. She could call for more hot water, but the guilt at the amount she had used already had been weighing on her.

She dressed slowly, having found her favourite yellow dress neatly folded at the foot of the bath when she finally exited. The tear in the fabric from her earlier attack had been mended—a near-invisible line of perfectly blended cotton pulling the hole closed, similar to how her Gift had knitted her own wounds together. There was barely any trace of it happening.

I suppose I healed so quickly because the Mother was closer than before.

Mae traced her fingers over the raised stitches in the fabric that laid over her collarbone, brushing against the marred skin underneath that matched. She didn't want to think about how long it might take her to heal from an injury like that now.

It was a strange feeling, to be vulnerable.

Mae ventured down the stairs, struck by the sudden need to be around people, and followed the sound of familiar voices to the room with the grand cherrywood table. She knocked, feeling suddenly timid as the voices ceased, before the door swung open violently. Lessie sighed in relief and beckoned Mae into the room impatiently, while a lone servant melted back into the shadows, their task having been usurped.

"Mae, thank the gods," Lessie said as she circled the table back to her own seat, ripping an empty chair out on the way. "I need somebody level-headed in this room. Druitt's the only one here with any sense. Nobody else seems to listen to a godsdamned word I say."

The other occupants of the room expressed varying levels of disagreement at her words. Reevan and Grundle both looked like they were supremely bored and were attending the meeting against their will. Reevan nodded along with Lessie, as if agreeing to his own lack of caring.

Valandaras was staring intently at the parchment before him, not looking up at her or anyone else. Mae recognised his handwriting all over the pages around him. Straight, uniform letters; even pressure. Careful. Deliberate.

Camden lounged in the chair next to his brother, a picture of nonchalance. He feigned outrage at Lessie's comment, but Mae noted the way his fingers gripped tightly to the glass of whiskey he held, despite the time being not long into the afternoon.

Druitt DeFalcone had indeed joined them, having managed to find time away from his duties at Roost Keep. Or perhaps he had brought them with him, judging by the maps and papers strewn across the table. He looked just as tired as he had in Crossroad, if not more so.

Mae felt the edges of panic try to rise within her, knowing the reaction she should be having, but the aching emptiness had dulled even the fear of him recognising her. Still, more out of habit than true worry, she gave the unfamiliar Druitt a wide berth as she took the empty place next to Valandaras.

"What were you trying to make sense of?" she asked, her voice feeling hoarse and unfamiliar after not speaking for days. Had she always sounded so small?

Druitt gave her a courteous smile, clearly meant to put her at ease, but a tug of warning came low in her belly as she met his eyes. She managed to push the numbness of her soul to the side and contemplated the likelihood that he could connect her to the person she had once been—and the repercussions if he did so.

Druitt was the heir to a house of the Seven; he would have spent time in Verestead, even briefly. Some members of the Seven kept a semi-permanent residence in the capital, while others preferred to return to their own territories when their reign completed. Occasionally, an Archduke would fall ill or otherwise be unable to attend various matters, so the heir would represent them.

There were too many variables. Verestead was an immense city, home to hundreds of thousands of people, and most of the Seven were discreet about their Divines. It was unlikely Druitt and Mae had crossed paths. But a single remembered whisper could be her undoing.

A wave of fear tried to wash over her, but the sadness, tired of being ignored, murmured in her ear.

It doesn't matter. I have no power. I have nothing left to be afraid of.

Mae took an odd comfort in the bleak realisation.

If the handsome captain recognised her, he gave nothing away as he inclined his head politely.

"My lady, I do not believe we have met," he said, eyes warm above his strained smile. "You were not present at the inn for the delivery of my brother."

Camden snorted into his whiskey. "Yes, she was."

Lessie shot him a withering look, and Camden raised his glass to her with an exaggerated wink.

Druitt looked puzzled, but decided that his brother's odd comment was not worth an explanation.

"Among many things, we are currently discussing the connection between what happened to my brother and what happened to you," he said. "I now believe Camden's abduction may have been an attempt to draw the house guard away from the West Keep, so that the... harvesting of the returning god would not be interrupted."

Mae flinched at the choice of words, but Druitt appeared not to notice, pinching the bridge of his nose. He looked weary.

"The attack as you arrived was probably them, too. Camden told me of how you took a crossbow bolt meant for him," Druitt glanced sideways at his brother before meeting her eyes once more. "You kept my brother safe. I cannot thank you enough."

Mae inclined her head gently, not trusting herself to speak.

"Of course, it could have been a coincidence or unlucky timing," Druitt continued. "Forces from Kalac are known to be planning attacks on our borders. There is one heading for Crossroad within the fortnight. Perhaps god-harvesting is their newest plan to get power. This man on the beach you described certainly sounded like he intended to continue his work."

Lessie looked up sharply—not at Druitt, but at Mae. She saw her own panic reflected in the younger girl's face.

Mae's heartbeat thundered in her ears. Her breath caught in her throat. She heard the voice, hollow and cold, like she was still on the sand, feeling the Mother rip away from her.

Power belongs to those worthy to wield it.

Valandaras had been silent while Druitt spoke, but he shifted now.

"Long have there been mortal men who sought the Mantle of a god, even before the Betrayer," he said quietly. All eyes turned to him. "It could be that this person has taken it upon himself to try to steal enough power to claim one for himself. I do not know if it would be successful, as he would be combining the powers of different gods, but it is still extremely dangerous. It is pure luck he has been thwarted in both of his recent attempts."

Mae blinked. Thwarted? The Mother was gone. They had utterly failed.

"What do you mean?" Lessie asked, also confused. "This time, at least, he seemed pretty successful from where I was standing."

Valandaras nodded towards Reevan. "Reevan knocking out that spike was enough that the ritual did not fully siphon the power. It was only a minuscule interruption, but it stopped the god from being completely absorbed."

Mae felt tears prick her eyes. The tiny speck of power in the depths of her soul flickered in response.

Reevan looked around, uncomfortable that they were all staring at him.

"You're welcome, I suppose. My blackened paws are at your service," the kitskan drawled, raising his goblet in a toast to himself. "Grundle was the one to figure it out, though," he added, shifting the attention onto the goblin, who glowered.

"Grundle also did not fight a shipwreck," the goblin muttered, gesturing to Valandaras.

Lessie looked mildly annoyed that none of them had mentioned her part in the fight, but Mae did not mind being left out. She supposed the sidelines would be a more common place for her, now. The thought hurt more than she expected it to.

Druitt held up his hands.

"Very well, then," he said, sounding mildly exasperated. "We've established that you are all capable under pressure—a crew with, shall we say, interesting talents? You've discovered some sort of plot to harvest the powers of returning gods. I don't know what this stranger's end game is, but this coupled with the news of planned attacks in Altaea... whatever the Emperor of Kalac is planning, it can't be good."

Reevan and Grundle exchanged an uncomfortable glance.

"I have confirmed that the group were dressed in traditional Kalac attire, but nothing more," said Reevan, sitting up straighter than before. "It would certainly be unwise to assume they are working for the Emperor. Their robes leaned towards the styles the southern cities favour, like Saluo and Heartgate. I highly doubt the Emperor would have sent them for this."

"Grundle thinks parts of Kalac outside of the control of the Emperor, anyway," the goblin added.

Reevan's tail twitched uncontrollably under the table. "My tiny friend is right. Kalac is vast, with hundreds of miles of desert separating the Emperor from the majority of his subjects. Many of the southern cities answer only to their Perqeit, and even then, it's more about who has the most coin. As I've noticed is true of most places."

Druitt levelled both of them with a hard stare. "You are both from Kalac, I take it?"

"Oh, no, actually, I was born on one of the Ruby Isles," Reevan responded politely. "But I was taken to Kalac at a young age, and did most of my growing up there, and have only spent the past year or so in Altaea, so I suppose you could say I am familiar."

Camden snickered into his whiskey. Mae shook her head, but she felt amusement brush against the numbness. *I wonder if it is all kitskans who are so literal, or if Reevan is a special case.*

Druitt frowned. "You say these people could have been from Saluo? How well do you know the city? Could you navigate it?"

Reevan contemplated this for a moment before nodding. "I have been there many times."

Mae glanced down at the largest map on the table, depicting the entire realm of Kalaraak on which they lived. Altaea was meticulously filled in, with rivers and forests marked as well as the major cities and some smaller towns. Kalac and the Freemeres were more of an outline, with only a few points marked on each of the countries, and further countries like the Ruby Isles had barely been mapped at all. Tracing her finger inwards from the coastline she knew they currently resided, she found the city Druitt had mentioned, Saluo, just over the Altaean border.

All these years, and I've never been to Kalac.

Druitt appeared deep in thought, leaning back into his chair and staring at the map.

"This could be useful," he muttered, pulling a hastily scribbled list towards him and reading the words upon it. Mae watched with vague curiosity as he dipped an elegant quill into an inkpot and marked a few places on a smaller map, mumbling under his breath. A few minutes passed in silence before Druitt spoke again.

"I have a proposition for you all," he said, standing and leaning over the map. "I have information that soldiers already march from Kalac towards the border, with the intent to take Crossroad. The town is poorly defended, and the acting High Marshal cannot spare more soldiers. I am underhanded, and quite frankly, desperate for anyone who could give us an edge. You've proven you're all more than capable. Help me defend it."

"You want us to fight in an army?" asked Lessie. Her voice squeaked a little, betraying her nervousness at the prospect. "That's not really the kind of mercenary work I signed up for."

"How does this help with... our problem?" said Valandaras. Mae kept her eyes on the map, but she still felt his flicker to her.

He can't even say it. I'm the problem.

"I have a connection in Saluo," said Druitt. "The man knows everything—costs me a fortune to stay on his good side, but he's never been wrong. It borders on supernatural."

Druitt circled the tiny town on the map before them with his finger, then dragged it across the border. "Help me defend Crossroad, and I will place you in contact with him. Vouch for you. You could go to Saluo, speak with him and find out what he knows about this group and why they are gathering god's power. He might even be able to find out if you could reverse it."

Reverse it? Free the Mother?

Mae gasped, the colour draining from her face. She hadn't thought that was a possibility. Valandaras and Lessie both snapped their attention to her, Valandaras's sword arm lurching as if to draw against an invisible enemy.

Druitt regarded her with eyes full of pity. "My lady, I am not saying it is possible. I have no knowledge of gods. But there are many out there who know things I cannot begin to imagine. Those who spend their lives studying the ways of gods and the Divines who serve them. Perhaps one of them will be able to help you restore your Divinity."

Mae smiled weakly, trying to calm the roaring in her ears, the panic filling her mind, the urge to bolt from the room. Even the numbness could not contain it.

He knows what I am. What else does he know? Does he know who I am?

A hand closed over her own, cutting through the storm of fear that swirled inside her. A gentle golden light glowed from underneath the wrappings. Mae exhaled shakily.

Druitt gave her a kind smile. "The Divine who serves in my father's household was always warm to me. He mended my elbow when I shattered it in my first week of training, even after Father had told him to let me suffer my stupidity," he chuckled.

Camden gave a snort of laughter, mimicking his brother's sentiment. "That man had his work cut out for him, having to tend to the two of us. He threatened to leave for another house at least once a month." For a moment, the two shared a fond look of nostalgia.

Mae relaxed.

Then Druitt's brow creased as he turned to her with a quizzical look. "Did you ever serve in a House of the Seven?" he asked her. "I haven't heard of a lot of Divines outside of the courts these days."

Mae's heart skipped. Her throat turned to lead, and fear churned in her belly. Adrenaline flooded through her veins as her instincts screamed at her to run. The burning eyes of her companions slowly slid towards her.

Valandaras squeezed her hand.

"I did, once," she managed to reply, struggling to keep her voice steady. "But no longer."

Even to her own ears, it sounded weak. A flimsy answer, worthy of further scrutiny. Druitt was an Altaean general, trained to interrogate and uncover falsehoods. He would be sure to—

Druitt nodded absently, accepting her non-answer, his attention already back to the map before him. Mae's mind was overwhelmed by the flood of relief, and she blinked away the first prickling of tears that formed. The sadness whispered to her once more, casually cruel in its honesty.

It doesn't matter now. They would not want a Divine with no Gifts.

Valandaras stood from the table, the sword at his side clinking in its scabbard. He did not look at her, but placed a gentle hand on her shoulder as he addressed Druitt.

"We will aid you at Crossroad," he said quietly.

Lessie nodded her assent, though her face was pale. Reevan and Grundle looked at one another before Reevan shrugged, sniffing.

"It appears I do not have much of a choice in this matter," said Reevan, before inclining his head towards her. "But if it will help Miss Mae, then I am glad to offer my service. In the short time I have known her, she has patched me up more times than I can count. Who am I to not attempt to do the same?"

The swell of emotion was too much for even the numbness to hold back. Mae looked around at her companions, willing to place themselves in danger, to fight in part of a war. For *her*. Her vision blurred as her eyes filled with tears. She fought the urge to bury her face in her hands.

"Thank you," she murmured, trying to keep her voice from shaking. She didn't know what else she could say, how to convey to them just how much it meant to her.

The tension in the room broke when Camden slammed his glass down on the beautiful table and clapped his hands together like a child about to plan a dessert heist.

"Right. Excellent. Where do we start?"

Valandaras settled back into his seat, and the discussion turned to battle tactics and information on possible movements.

Mae focused instead on that tiny spark of her Gift, dwelling deep inside her, blanketed by numbness. She felt a scrape on her arm begin to heal, but it took everything, the power running dry in seconds.

A colder sense of dread washed over her, settling in the cracks of her soul. Her deepest nightmare was now a very real possibility.

What if I can't keep them safe anymore?

14

VALANDARAS

Another petty war between nations. They will never learn until they've obliterated one another.

Pacing the stairs of the West Keep, Valandaras thought of the battles he'd seen, the land barren and destroyed, the carnage and lives lost. It didn't matter what realm; it was always over the same thing—power, and the belief most held that they deserved more of it than those around them.

The gods were no different, though their wars usually went unnoticed by the common folk. Realmshifters had been created purely because of one god's thirst for revenge. Valandaras had been born into it, chosen as an infant, his quest predetermined. Every move he made had to propel him towards accomplishing his task. His Path to walk.

He told himself that helping Mae recover the Mother's power would do just that.

The journey to Crossroad would happen in a week, giving Mae time to restore her strength. Valandaras kept an eye on her as she regained some semblance of her regular self, but she seemed muted, like she was in shades of grey compared to her usual burst of colour. She picked at her food, she rarely spoke unless spoken to, and she no longer sang or danced or laughed.

It was clear she was struggling, and he had little idea of how to help her. He did not know what to say, what to do that would see her blinding smile break across her face once more.

Perhaps she simply needs to feel the grief.

Over the next few days, Valandaras found himself in the West Keep's dining room more often than not. Druitt was experienced in warfare, but he also knew of Valandaras's reputation and had requested his presence in order to pick his brain. An outsider's perspective.

Valandaras was glad for the distraction. When he closed his eyes at night, he had to fight the image of Mae's lifeless body in his arms. It became necessary to fill his days with planning, with complications and hard questions, to exhaust his mind and keep the nightmares from haunting his waking hours. The threat of a looming battle was strangely welcome; it gave him something to focus on.

Sleep still found him less often.

Occasionally, the others joined him in the temporary war room. Reevan and Grundle offered up bits of knowledge of their homeland here and there, but neither of them had volunteered anything about Kalac's motive for the attack. Reevan had been quick to explain how hailing from the southern cities made their knowledge of Kalac's Emperor almost as rudimentary as any Altaean.

Druitt had seemed vaguely suspicious, but Valandaras doubted they knew much. Besides, he had travelled with them for over a year. Any information they had would be woefully out of date.

Surprisingly, Lessie had been the most helpful. The girl had no experience with open warfare, but her years of tracking and hunting gave her insight into enemy movements and placements of protective measures even Valandaras himself had not thought of. Druitt had seemed impressed with her contribution.

She often left the room early, however, if Camden was also present; her patience with him was limited and quick to drain. It was always the same before long—Lessie's expression would sour as Camden twisted another of her serious phrases into a loaded double entendre, and her chair would scrape as she shoved it backwards to stalk from the room.

Camden, for his part, seemed to delight in antagonising her. He would grin up at her like a devil, having received the reaction he'd looked for. She bit back every time, never learning, never holding her tongue. Valandaras had not missed the way Lessie's fists would ball up after twitching towards her revolver. Privately, he wondered if the lord had a death wish.

Camden DeFalcone has much to learn about playing with fire.

The day before departure, they all gathered around the cherrywood table and spoke of whatever came to mind. The planning had been completed. They would leave in the morning. Nobody said it, but they were stalling for Mae.

Valandaras said little. He felt disconnected from discussions like these, of mundane life and politics. Realmshifters were considered a separate entity—respected enough that they had not been forced into any kind of servitude with the nobility, and rare enough to not be prohibited from using their power.

Based on what he knew of the lives of the Divine and the Arcane, Valandaras supposed he should count himself lucky, as the ones he served were benevolent at worst and absent at best. He enacted Haropheth's will in his own way, on his own time. There was only the Path.

"Wait, who is Claudette again?" asked Camden, picking up a discarded map and squinting at it. "I'm guessing it's not the same Claudette from that charming little tavern in the third circle." He sighed wistfully. "She really knew how to overpour a whiskey. Dreadfully clingy, though."

Druitt paused, frowning at his brother. Valandaras glanced at Mae, who had let out a small sound of amusement, her eyes on Lessie's face. The girl was glowering with disgust. Hopefully, it would take more than a few crass comments to get her to leave the room today. Mae stayed longer when Lessie was present, out of a somewhat motherly sense of duty.

"Claudette *DuBois* has been acting High Marshal since Terrill's assassination," Druitt answered, the exasperated expression showing he had already explained this at some point. "She's been working overtime, investigating his death as well as handling all the work he was doing—and he was doing less of it than anybody realised. Apparently, he was putting all of his time into researching some odd conspiracy in Kalac and neglecting the work he was actually responsible for."

Druitt shook his head in pity. "So Claudette's taken over and discovered a backlog of issues, one of which being that our recruitment of soldiers into the garrison has been declining hard over the last decade. We barely have enough to guard the major cities. And if that wasn't enough, she has to deal with some of the Seven not recognising her authority. She hasn't been officially sworn in as High Marshal, which won't happen until next year. Until the Kingswitch."

Camden and Druitt shared a brief, dark look at the mention of the Kingswitch, before Druitt ripped the map out of his brother's hands, smoothing it over as he placed it back onto the table.

"Of course," Druitt snapped, "you would know all of this already, if you ever paid attention to Father's advisors."

Camden rolled his eyes. "Why bother to listen to political prattle when there are so many more interesting stories out there?" The younger DeFalcone rounded on Lessie, eyes glittering. "For example, how the lovely

Miss Shilling here is in possession of a firearm, when the Altaean military is still trudging around with longbows? Care to explain that, my *lady*?"

Camden fixed the girl with a pointed look, as if expecting her to confess to a crime. Lessie only glared at him.

"Because my little sister is smarter than everyone in this room put together," she retorted. "Not that it's hard, since you're in here dragging down the average."

Mae snickered, and Valandaras felt the corners of his mouth twitch upwards. Reevan looked deeply offended.

"Your sister?" Druitt asked.

Lessie looked as if she regretted her outburst. "Trixie," she said carefully. "She's been taking things apart and putting them back together since we were kids. A traveller came to our town once who specialised in firearms. Trixie wanted one, so she made one. Then she made me a better one." Lessie's hand fidgeted as if she wanted to check the gun was still beside her.

"Where is she now?" Druitt asked.

"The Freemeres," said Lessie, reluctantly. "Studying. Trixie's brilliant, but she's Arcane, so she's always been at risk."

"An Arcane?" Druitt questioned, voice frank. "And you thought a single firearm was adequate to control an Arcane's dangerous nature? She could have exploded out at any moment, injuring herself and innocents around her. Why wasn't she sent to training?"

"I never said I needed it to control her," Lessie snapped. "Trixie has never been dangerous to anyone who didn't deserve it. We kept her magic secret; she always practised where she wouldn't hurt anyone. We couldn't afford to leave, anyway. The big cities have training, but small towns like Picking..."

Lessie jabbed a finger down onto the map, onto a tiny dot that marked her home town. Valandaras peered at it. The ink had smudged, like she had recently added the marker herself—the town would have been too small to have been included by the original cartographer. It was closer to the Trimount than he had expected. He had not realised how far she had travelled from her home in such a short time; she had only been working with them for a couple of months.

"People talk," Lessie said. "The townsfolk already considered us outsiders. They avoided us. They would be godsdamned shocked if they knew how many threats we took care of within a mile of their doorsteps. That's what I needed the gun for. Not Trixie. Never her. Trixie used her magic to keep them safe. And she didn't need *training* to do it."

Valandaras had heard of Altaea's way of handling Arcane users—or at least, the methods their nobility preferred. It usually involved suppressing their magic, sometimes so much so that the Arcane would implode and lose access to it permanently. Some outstanding students were heralded, but it was an open secret that only high-born Arcanes were given leniency to hone their skills. No wonder Lessie's sister had been sheltered.

Mae stiffened beside him. He knew she felt the same.

Druitt sat back in his chair, folding his arms. "If the townsfolk treated you all so poorly, why bother to protect them?"

A flicker of confusion crossed Lessie's features. "Because we could," she answered, frowning. Druitt looked unconvinced. "We lived on the outskirts, near the Maw, which has all manner of danger spewing out of it. My father taught us how to keep ourselves safe. We had the means to protect the town. Why wouldn't we?"

"Lessandra, what exactly is the Maw?" asked Reevan. "You've mentioned it a few times now. It sounds delightful."

Lessie snorted. "It's a giant hole in the ground. Caves that were there long before the first houses went up in Picking," she explained. "It's a maze. People like to say it's the gateway to the realm of the damned."

A prickle of curiosity Valandaras had not felt in a long time shivered over him. He had not heard of this place, and he had never heard Lessie speak so much.

"It's forbidden to enter the Maw without permission," Lessie continued. "But people go down there anyway, seeking glory or riches or whatever they think they'll find. The town even holds a festival for it once a year, challenging visitors to brave it. Sometimes, they return with trophies, but most of the time they don't come back up."

Lessie's eyes met Mae's and then quickly darted away again.

"When I met him—the first time, I mean," said Lessie, flustered, "that man on the beach. He visited Picking during the Opening Festival. He knew straight away, what Trixie was. He tried to recruit her into some Arcane school in Kalac, but my father refused him. After that, he entered the Maw. Trixie had a bad feeling about it, so we followed him in. He knew there was a... god down there. A returning one."

Lessie's hands balled into fists, and she crossed her arms over her chest, slumping back in her chair with haunted eyes. "I didn't think I'd see him again so soon," she muttered. "He has a lot to answer for."

Camden was staring at Lessie, his head tilting. Even the young lord must have read the pain in the girl's expression, for he kept whatever flippant remark he had no doubt thought of to himself for once.

Valandaras was hyper aware of Mae's breathing next to him, how it had hitched in her throat at the mention of the god tree. She did a decent job of holding it together, but she still folded into herself, like she wanted to disappear.

"What do we know of him?" Mae asked, voice barely more than a whisper.

"Not much, I'm afraid," drawled Reevan. "I did not recognise him, but his choice of attire would have made that difficult, anyway. Hooded robes and masks are so dramatic." The kitskan sniffed in disapproval, before rising from his chair to pour another cup of tea. The irony of his own hooded robes billowing around him was lost on him.

Reevan raised the fine ceramic cup to his lips and inhaled deeply before sipping. He seemed to be debating whether to speak his thoughts.

"Saluo was not my home, but it is one of Kalac's more important cities," he said. "It is known for its temple dedicated to Arcane studies and Divine worship—the Arcane school Lessie spoke of. Given his interest in god power and Divinity, it is very likely we will find him there. Perhaps Druitt's friend will be able to shed some light on his plans."

Mae nodded absent-mindedly, eyes on the table, tracing the carved birds with her fingertip. "Perhaps," she replied.

"I did not recognise the sword, either," Reevan continued, missing the cue that Mae no longer wished to speak of the stranger. "It was extremely ornate, made of obsidian steel, and seemed to be the main conduit for the god's power. A blade like that is not mass produced by the military. Perhaps we can find the man through the weapon."

Reevan had mentioned the sword before, after they had returned to the West Keep from the beach—how it had disappeared from there to wherever this stranger had been. There was something about the way it had been described that tugged at Valandaras, like trying to remember a phrase in a long-forgotten conversation. He could practically hear Saelin's voice, mocking in jest, waving Aasimon's Fang just a bit too close to his ear. *Brother, you only wish you could wield a Sliver as beautiful as mine!*

He had a theory, but it would have to remain untested, for now. If it was meant to be his Path, if a thread of the invisible string that governed his life was truly tugging him down this road, then he could always come back to it, once he had time.

If he didn't die defending Crossroad.

Their travel back to Crossroad was smooth, with their horses well-rested and their provisions well-stocked. Druitt had selected six members of the West Keep's guard to accompany them, and even the boldest of bandits had not dared to approach. The only hint of trouble was the shouting match between the brothers before they left, with Camden wishing to remain in the West Keep and Druitt insisting his brother was safer with them. Druitt had won, and the younger lord had sulked for the majority of the travel.

Walking through the main thoroughfare for the second time in a fortnight, Valandaras took in the telltale signs of a town preparing for an attack. The atmosphere of Crossroad had changed. It was most noticeable in the behaviour of the inhabitants. Laughter and an easy slowness had been replaced by fearful faces and quickened steps. Nobody lingered in the streets to chat. These were simple people accustomed to being left alone, who had now found themselves in a warpath.

A woefully small army of soldiers from Roost Keep had arrived the day before. Druitt effortlessly issued commands in between welcomes, assigning duties and roles as per their careful plans in the West Keep. Valandaras admired how easily Druitt slipped into the role, and how thoroughly the men followed his orders.

The man may have been born into nobility, but this was where he belongs.

Valandaras toiled with the men for most of the day, helping to erect palisade walls around the northern and eastern outskirts of the town, along with a few raised platforms for the archers. The soldiers themselves should be able to keep approaching invaders from entering the town proper, but it was prudent to add a physical barrier. The overlapping wooden fences would not withstand much force, but they were better than nothing. The enemy would have to weave through them, slowing them greatly, and preventing a rush into the town.

It was tough, gruelling work, but it gave the soldiers something to do, rather than sit and contemplate their own mortality. The force totalled less than a thousand men, so there was plenty of work to be done, but it was easier to face an opponent in battle if one felt it had been prepared for. It was long after sundown when they completed their work.

Returning to the quaint tavern they had previously stayed in, Valandaras felt a weariness to his bones that told him he should retire early. Most of the soldiers would sleep in tents for the night, but for now they had crowded around inside the inn, filling their bellies and drinking as much as they dared.

Word of who Valandaras was—what he was—must have circulated the camp, for most of the soldiers gave him a respectful but wide berth as he crossed the floor of the inn. He noted their overfilled tankards with quiet disapproval, but would not comment.

Many of these men will die tomorrow, he thought. *Might as well spend their final night with a belly full of ale.*

Valandaras found some of his crew at the same quiet booth already—Lessie and Grundle deep in a card game, Reevan watching as if he could deduce the rules without asking. Empty whiskey glasses left rings of condensation upon the tabletop, and someone's meal lay abandoned in the corner, the plate shoved aside to make room for the cards.

Valandaras saw no sign of Mae or either DeFalcone brother. He slumped into the booth next to Lessie, who did not look up from the cards in her hand, her brow knit in concentration.

"She went to bed already," Lessie muttered out of the side of her mouth, as if pre-empting his question, before shoving a handful of copper coins towards the goblin. "Raise."

Grundle stared Lessie down with an intensity mostly reserved for the victims of his daggers. His yellow eyes darted between the cards in her hand and her face, which was currently an impassive mask.

They stared each other down, neither speaking. Seconds ticked by.

Reevan peered over Grundle's shoulder. "If your cards match, that is fortunate even if they are a low number, correct?" he asked politely.

Grundle threw his cards onto the table in frustration, one of them spinning and landing in the forgotten food. Reevan, oblivious to the goblin's snarl of betrayal, sat patiently waiting for an answer to his question. Lessie smirked and dragged the pile of coins towards her, scooping them into a small leather pouch.

"We can double or nothing the next round if you want," she said to Grundle. He scowled, but wordlessly began retrieving the scattered cards.

Valandaras watched them play for a while, not participating in any conversation, before he bid the rest of the crew goodnight and traipsed up the narrow staircase to the inn's bedrooms. His footsteps felt heavy as he let himself into the tiny room, the floorboards creaking under his step.

Sitting at the foot of his bed, Valandaras thought of his brethren. Wished they were here with him to face yet another unknown enemy. He thought only of them as he went through his pre-battle preparations. Those he loved most.

He inspected every piece of his armour for damage and oiled the blade of his falchion. He polished his shield until it shone, the simple design etched into its surface more visible with the layers of dust and grime removed. Valandaras stared into the face of the lion upon it, the mouth open in an eternal roar. It helped to ground him, to remember his duty. The other Realmshifters were far from here—they could be on any of the seven realms—but knowing they all carried an identical shield brought him immeasurable comfort.

Valandaras meditated, eyes closed beneath the cloth, thinking of those he had fought beside and those he had lost, willing for their strength to guide him. He stayed motionless for a while, on the floor of his room, the only sound his steady breathing and the distant hum of drunken revelry. But even in his relaxed state, he couldn't shake the feeling that something was missing. This fight had to be part of his Path, or he would not feel compelled to be there. But it felt like he had forgotten something important. It tugged on his mind like a loose thread, threatening to unravel all the work he had done to settle it.

Finally, he rose and decided it was time to sleep. He crossed to the open window, intending to close it before he put out the lantern at his bedside, but stopped when a flash of colour caught his eye.

Below in the garden behind the inn, a fire-haired woman in a bright blue dress knelt beneath the night sky.

Valandaras knew Mae was praying, and part of him felt as if he should look away, that even witnessing it was to intrude. But he could not.

The night breeze picked up, ruffling Mae's clothing and blowing her hair about, though she did not move. Fireflies danced around her head, wreathing her in a crown of gently glowing stars. The surrounding greenery seemed to sway towards her, like it was beckoning, welcoming her presence. The sounds of the leaves rustling mixed with crickets merrily singing gave the scene a peaceful quality, in stark contrast to the chaos within the inn itself.

Valandaras was so accustomed to seeing Mae's emerald light that the lack of it was jarring, and he felt a stab of anger hot in his chest.

She should not have to bear this pain. Not after all she has suffered.

Mae finished her prayer, rising and brushing away the dirt from the garden that clung to her dress. He couldn't quite tell from this distance, but she seemed happier, more grounded. She stood a little taller, her shoulders a little less slumped.

Valandaras was about to blow out his lantern when Mae looked up towards his window and their eyes met. He inclined his head, a silent acknowledgement. She returned the gesture, giving him a small wave, and he glimpsed the beginnings of a smile. It was not the beam of light he was longing to see return to her face.

But she smiled.

And all at once, it was enough.

15

VALANDARAS

Valandaras awoke before the dawn and was on the edges of their chosen battlefield before the first rays of sunlight had melted the morning dew.

He gazed over the plains that rolled out before him, tall grass and wildflowers that would soon become trampled and bloody. The voices of awakening soldiers filled the air, the scent of oiled leather and hastily cooked breakfasts drifting over the campground before the sky had fully lightened.

Those who have never seen combat are quick to imagine chaotic glory. An enemy appears out of nowhere, weapons are brandished menacingly, and a violent dance ensues until the victor emerges, all foes slain. The truth was that most battles were about calculated positioning. Lines were drawn days ahead of time. Whoever has the upper hand, the better ground, or the superior numbers instigates the fighting. Armies would fall back long before half of their troops fell.

Valandaras stood with Druitt, listening to the reports of the dawn scouts, who had returned with news of a Kalac force camped around five miles from the edge of Crossroad. The scouts had seen long lines of infantry, along with a small unit of cavalry and a few archers, all readying themselves to march forward.

They had not noticed any magic users, no robes like those that had been present for the god tree attack, but that was of little comfort. Arcanes did not walk around with sparks flying from their hands. It was unlikely, but for all they knew, every member of that force could be wielding the power of the Weave. Kalac did not frown upon the use of the Arcane arts the way that Altaea did.

The good news was that the Kalac army, although well-rested and formidable, did not appear to outnumber them by many. It sounded like they had not expected much resistance from the tiny town, and had only brought along enough soldiers to drive out the common folk.

It would have disappointed them to hear from their own scouts this morning.

Valandaras shifted, testing the pliancy of his armour, listening to the captain as he threw out orders to his gathered leaders. Druitt had assigned Valandaras a group of men to direct, but had not given them a position in the front, instead trusting him to see where the lines needed support and use his team accordingly.

As a Realmshifter, Valandaras was used to working either alone or as one part of a highly attuned group, and he relished the chance to be back within a trained unit. People who would obey his instructions without question were less likely to die on his account.

The crew had discussed their separate roles in the skirmish only briefly. While Valandaras had been busy building palisades, the rest of them had worked together over the course of the previous day. They had organised what little evacuation they could, bundling the most vulnerable of Crossroad into wagons and sending them towards the West Keep.

Lessie had been assigned to a group of archers. Druitt, having heard of her impressive aim, did not refuse her request to fight, although he had already considered her contributions to the defence strategy as fulfilling her promise of helping. Valandaras had been concerned, but Druitt had assured him that the girl's group were far from where the actual fighting would occur. Lessie would be as safe as someone participating in open warfare could be.

Tough as she is, she should not have to see the gore of a battle like this up close.

Reevan and Grundle, both better suited to the shadows, were to linger behind the palisades, tasked with stopping any foe from entering the town proper. A last line of defence for the townsfolk who remained. They accepted their roles gladly.

Mae had not been assigned a task. Valandaras had made sure of it. There were no Divines in Crossroad, but they would make do with mundane healers, as well as what little restorative draughts had been hurriedly brewed and donated by the local alchemist. She would not need to set foot on that battlefield. She would be furious when she found out, but he would rather have her angry than dead.

It was for the best.

She has barely begun to heal from what she went through, Valandaras thought. *She would destroy herself trying to save others.*

The men who had been assigned to him were of varying height, build, and age, but they all shared the same look most soldiers wore before facing possible death or glory. Their eyes shone with fear, but their bodies thrummed with adrenaline; they had a hard time keeping still. Some of them paced around their tents, others fidgeted with armour or weapons, checking them over and over again.

When the call came through to mobilise, Valandaras signalled the men to wait for the front lines to move out before they were to follow. He was staring hard into the horizon when he felt a soft hand upon his arm.

"Val," Mae said softly, his name a plea too quiet for those around to hear, like she were embarrassed. "Why haven't I been asked to heal? I can still help."

Valandaras kept his obscured eyes towards where the cresting suns met the distant plains. He couldn't look at her. If he strained, he could make out small figures moving on the horizon, a blur of dark against the pale pink of the morning sky. He tried to ignore the way his stomach swooped at the sound of his name in her mouth.

Nobody had ever shortened it before. Nobody had bothered to learn it well enough to.

"Lioness, it is too dangerous," he replied, voice low.

Mae huffed. A rush of joy flooded him in that simple expression, because he had not heard it in too long. But the dismissiveness beneath it worried him. She was not trained in combat. Mae did not know how to use a bow or sword, she had never had any reason to. She had no business being out on the front lines, but he wouldn't put it past her to attempt to join him there regardless. To try to take on an enemy when she could not Change, could not heal. To throw herself in the path of an enemy that threatened the girl, or the kitskan, or any of these people.

Valandaras finally turned to her, and he saw it written all over her face. Mae would do exactly that. Would martyr herself, if she deemed it necessary.

Mae squeezed a delicate hand in the crook of his elbow and lifted her chin proudly. She flashed him a false smile that didn't reach her eyes.

"Even in my current condition, I'm perfectly capable of fixing some scrapes and applying a few bandages," she said. Her expression was soft, like she expected him to agree and send her off into the midst of the carnage. Unprotected. To die.

No.

He needed to keep her safe. Even if it would hurt her.

Valandaras kept his voice neutral and quiet, so those around them would not overhear. It still felt like shouting.

"Right now, you are a civilian and a liability," he said sternly. "You should have gone with the evacuated children. It would be a distraction for you to be too close to the fighting. You can only help us by staying out of the way."

Mae cringed at his words. The betrayal in her eyes stung him so badly he wanted to flinch away from it, but outwardly he stood strong, unyielding. He said nothing as she took a step backward, her mouth open as if to begin arguing, before spinning on her heel and stalking away.

Valandaras turned back to the squad of soldiers awaiting his command, eyes forward, but ears still focused on the retreating sound of her footsteps on the gravel.

It had to be done. She will forgive my words when this is all over.

But he couldn't shake the sickening feeling in the pit of his stomach as he marched towards the oncoming enemy. There was always a chance he would not walk away from a battlefield. He didn't like the idea of crossing the Silver Stream with his last words to Mae being ones of cruelty. He closed his eyes, the glow under the cloth growing dimmer. He took a deep breath and centred himself, before bidding the soldiers he commanded to follow him towards the wildflower plains that would soon become a killing field.

Valandaras unsheathed his falchion, adjusted the grip on his shield and drove all thoughts not of survival from his mind.

The Kalac force had gathered where Druitt's scouts had said they would, and the soldiers mirrored their own; mainly infantry, with a smattering of mounted archers towards the back. He felt a rush of relief as he saw no catapults or siege weapons. This was not a fight to destroy—this was a trial run of a conquest. Invasions like this from Kalac were designed to gauge their reactions, to see how quickly they could defend the land around them, or how easily it might fall or be abandoned.

Valandaras squared his shoulders. They would not concede an inch. The innocent people of Crossroad deserved that much for their home.

The first part of a fight was always tedious. Orders were shouted from both sides as each group advanced slowly, testing the waters. A few arrows were loosed.

Waiting. Waiting.

Who would crack first? Who thought they had the upper hand?

The fighting began in earnest after one particular Kalac general—a massive, hulking behemoth of a man—gave the order to charge, and the majority of the Kalac forces rushed towards them at once. Most of the foreign soldiers seemed to take their orders from him.

Valandaras fell into the rhythm of warfare. Directing his team of men, ordering them to join other groups, filling gaps in the lines where others fell, dispatching enemy soldiers all the while. He swung his blade sparingly, using his shield to deflect blows, conserving his strength. He attracted many desperate attacks, probably due to his size and the gleam of his armour. The lucky Kalac soldier who presented his head back to that general would be heralded. He only engaged them if he needed. Most of the time, a block was enough. He only killed when necessary.

Valandaras pushed his shield into an eager kitskan soldier, who had come flying towards him. The fighter went sprawling into the dirt and snarled viciously as he jumped back to his feet, the poleaxe in his hands dripping with blood. He tried twice more before changing tactics, circling Valandaras and trying to goad him into swinging blindly. Valandaras parried his next attack and shoved with the shield once more, knocking the soldier to the ground again. Valandaras dropped his falchion momentarily, snatching up his opponent's poleaxe and driving it into the kitskan's chest. Blood spurted from the impact. The kitskan's body jerked twice before stilling.

The enemy soldiers seemed to give him a wider berth after that.

At one point Valandaras saw Lessie, longbow fully drawn, loosing arrows into the Kalac army with a precision he had not expected for a fight this chaotic. Her aim was true even with a lesser favoured weapon in her hands, and soldiers fell just as hard to her arrows as they would have to her bullets. As much as he had wanted to keep her out of the fight completely, he had to admit she was making a difference. Druitt had been right to put her on the back line, but she had left that line with good reason—most of Druitt's own archers had fallen, and now Lessie patched the hole in their defences. Their side seemed to be driving back the Kalac forces with the least amount of trouble, the tide of the battle beginning to turn in their favour.

Some of the fighters turned and tried to retreat, and those who were left fought with less fervour; the scent of fear rising with the sweat and blood from their bodies. More than one Kalac soldier gave Valandaras an uneasy look before fleeing, not engaging him at all.

It will be over soon. Their panic is starting to override their sense of duty.

Valandaras had made it towards the other end of the fields when a smaller group of Kalac soldiers caught his eye. They were moving quietly, much too slow, and they were too clean to have been part of the initial wave of fighters. This group had not fought their way through to where they now were, about to enter the first of the palisade maze the Altaean soldiers had constructed. They must have sneaked around the edges of the battlefield, trusting the chaos to hide them.

Valandaras almost pitied them. Reevan and Grundle were both lurking in those palisades. The goblin and the kitskan would dispatch them all before they saw it coming. They would never set foot in Crossroad.

He was about to turn back to oversee the rest of his soldiers, but one final glance towards the group had him stop dead. Fear coursed through his body for the first time since the battle had begun.

An obsidian sword flashed in the morning light, clutched in the hands of the largest of the Kalac mercenaries. It had a faintly glowing, serrated blade.

A familiar blade.

Before he could think, Valandaras was running.

16

LESSIE

"God*damn* it!"

Lessie swore aloud as she released her grip on an arrow, knowing even before it had left her bow that the shot would not hit the mark she'd aimed for. As predicted, it went wide, disappearing into a group of Kalac soldiers advancing on some of the Roost Keep guard, but hitting none of them. She resisted the urge to scream in frustration.

I should've brushed up on my longbow last night instead of losing all my copper to Grundle.

Lessie hadn't used a bow for some time, and her aim was rusty. To make matters worse, the simple iron breastplate she had been given to wear wasn't made for her size; it was bulky and restricted her arms. She gritted her teeth violently as yet another arrow fell short of her target. A bullet would have hit. She understood the request for her not to use her revolver—it would have deafened the surrounding soldiers, as well as painted a much larger target onto her own back. It made sense. Just how she understood that her own bow, compact and made for hunting, was not big enough to handle the thick, heavy arrows designed to pierce metal armour. She had to use the weapons given to her.

But they weren't *hers*. The longbow was awkward and heavy, and her lower accuracy made her look incompetent. She cursed her complacency, her failure to keep up with her training in the longbow. She'd been using her revolver for so long that it felt like an extension of her own arm; now the bow felt alien and clunky in her fingers.

It would have been embarrassing if anyone was paying any mind to her, which they weren't. The other members of the group she had been assigned to were too busy shaking in their too-new boots. Lessie tried not to judge the rest of her little squad too harshly, but it was hard not to. A couple of them looked like they had barely handled a weapon at all.

They had been stationed in a spot so far back from the battlefield that it might as well have been inside Crossroad itself. She would've had a better vantage point from a rooftop than where she was—covering the last of the entrance into the town proper; the hastily constructed palisades looming in the peripherals of her vision. Where new recruits were sent to be kept out of the way of the real fighters. Most of the Kalac army had no idea they were even there. The few that strayed too close were already dying, staggering away from an earlier opponent. The archer next to her blanched at the blood spreading from the fallen bodies, his face turning a peculiar shade of grey she hadn't known was possible on a human.

Lessie sighed heavily before reaching for another arrow.

I know I got put back here because Druitt and Valandaras think I can't handle a battle. Maybe I should have gone into more detail about what comes out of the Maw. At least this army is human-shaped.

But Lessie knew if she were honest with herself, she hadn't seen anything quite like this. For a battle of this scale, it was a scrappy fight. The neat rows of soldiers quickly devolved into chaos, with squad leaders on both sides bellowing orders she was too far away to hear. The low grass and patches of wildflowers churned beneath their feet, dirt turning to mud as the sweat and blood mingled.

In between picking targets, she found herself focusing in on tiny, seemingly mundane details. Her brain had already started compartmentalising the horror of watching so much death, but noting the human elements of the battle kept her strangely calm. She saw an Altaean soldier slip on the uneven ground, lurching forward before another grasped the neck of his armour and hoisted him back to his feet, patting him on the back in encouragement.

Thankfully, there was little cavalry on either side, and most of the fighting was happening in the middle of the plains. To her untrained eye the two armies seemed evenly matched, with the invading force pushing their strongest fighters immediately to the forefront, hoping to rush the Altaeans and overwhelm them.

The roar of swords meeting shields, of soldiers screaming as they fell, of warhorses neighing as they came down upon their riders—the noise was intense. Lessie felt a rush of gratitude towards her father, who had taught her to pack her ears with cotton. The habit formed from years of shooting a firearm at close range, which she ignored more often than not, had come in handy on the battlefield. Even muted, the wails of the wounded were haunting.

Most of the Kalac forces seemed to be using the same weapons as the Altaeans, with some bearing wicked looking warhammers and one with a particularly deadly poleaxe. It was odd—she had always been taught that the citizens of Kalac were barbarians, a bloodthirsty lot who fought with primitive weapons and no regard or respect for human life. The enemy in front of her seemed just as disciplined as their own force. Most of them wore the same crest, the same colours, many of them with cords of dark leather wrapped around their throats. Some Kalac fashion, she supposed, or a way to appear more cohesive.

She kept track of Valandaras easily. Even from a distance, his faint glow was like a beacon of death, leaving fallen enemies in his wake. The soldiers in his unit fought with a tenacity only a Realmshifter could muster from them. They weaved through the battle, patching holes in the weaker soldiers' defences. The Kalac soldiers around them seemed to shy away.

Valandaras, at least, was making a difference in this fight.

Lessie found herself inching forward, frustrated. Before long, she had left the rest of the novice archers behind. She'd always preferred to be a little closer to the action, anyway. She squared her shoulders, nocked an arrow, and plunged into the fray.

Lessie had a vague thought of joining another group of fighters and blending into their archers, but she quickly found a gap in the Altaean defences. From within the pockets of breakaway fighting, it was easy to miss, but approaching from the side, it became obvious that the experienced archers this side of the field had been focused down. Lessie's boot caught on a discarded bow, half-buried in the mud, and she cursed as she shook it free. Where were they all?

Without the threat of arrow fire, more of the Kalac soldiers were drawing closer to the edges of Crossroad as they slipped past the Altaean infantry. Lessie swore under her breath. This was a problem. She had to find Druitt or Valandaras; they would know what to do about the missing archers. The other problem was that she was now the only one left.

Which made her a target.

A flash of wood and metal to her left and Lessie ducked. A Kalac soldier swung at her, wind whistling as his heavy polearm sailed past her head and slammed into the earth beside her. She hastily brought her bow up as a makeshift shield to block his second strike. The impact jolted down her forearms as the weapons clashed. Luckily, the soldier was lithe, and Lessie managed to hold her ground, but it took everything she had.

The arrow she had nocked stayed trapped between the weapons, useless. She couldn't reach for her gun.

Bile rose in her throat.

The Kalac soldier wore no helmet, and she took in his gaunt face, his eyes glinting with desperation, the black cord around his throat like a noose. He pushed down on her bow with all his strength, grunting with effort, trying to disarm her.

Reacting on instinct, Lessie let her own pressure on the weapons go, sidestepping as the soldier stumbled forwards past her. Thrown off-balance by his own momentum, he flailed, gripping his polearm tightly for support as the weapon sunk into the ground. The Kalac soldier turned back towards her, panting, wild eyes betraying a hint of surprise, like he had expected an arrow in the back. He ripped the polearm free to swing at her again.

Lessie dropped her bow altogether and punched him square in the face.

She felt the satisfying crunch against her knuckles and knew his nose had broken. Blood streamed from both nostrils, and the man howled in pain as he collapsed. Shaking her hand to get some of the stinging to stop, she hissed at the pain and kicked away the enemy soldier's polearm before picking up her bow.

She could kill him. Probably *should* kill him. But something about the look on his face made her think that at least some of the Kalac forces were not volunteers. Lessie left her enemy lying in the dirt, clutching at his nose, one eye already beginning to swell shut.

A flash of blue and grey caught her eye. Druitt DeFalcone fought nearby with his group, by far the most graceful and effective on the field, but the archers assigned to cover him were nowhere to be seen. Lessie drew another arrow, wincing as her smallest knuckle protested, and squared her shoulders.

I guess that's my job now.

Lessie didn't know where the archers who were part of Druitt's own squad had disappeared to, but it didn't matter. She focused on her technique. There was no enemy. Only another target. Only drawing another arrow, testing the pull of the bow before exhaling and letting it fly.

She quickly found a rhythm. Her shots landed more without the other novice archers to impede her positioning, and she focused on slowing down the biggest threats to the captain and his team, who were carving their way through some of the most intimidating Kalac fighters.

Lessie made sure to never lose sight of Druitt as he ducked and spun around enemy soldiers, a beautiful silver longsword glinting in his hand, the pommel's cross guard designed to mimic a falcon's wings. After a few arrows sailed over his head, Druitt looked towards her, concern creasing his brow beneath his helmet at her proximity. He disapproved of her being there. She didn't let it break her concentration, and followed through with her next shot before he could order her otherwise.

He can disapprove all he wants. I'm keeping him alive to do it.

Lessie couldn't hear the impact over the clash of steel, but she knew she'd found her mark as a Kalac soldier dropped in front of one of Druitt's men, sword clattering to the ground where it had faltered in mid-swing.

Druitt paused long enough to allow a glance of acknowledgment in her direction. She couldn't hear him, but she read his lips.

"Good shot," he yelled over the din, in between parrying strikes and repositioning soldiers.

Lessie threw the captain a rare smile of pure triumph before pulling her attention back to the fighting. She couldn't afford to take her eyes off the enemies for too long, lest they find their mark before she found hers. She drew another arrow from her quiver and nocked it, but did not loose it. In the brief glimpse around the battle, she had noticed something else, and registering what it was had the grin sliding from her face as quickly as it came.

A flash of golden light. Running at full speed.

Moving *away* from the battlefield.

Valandaras was heading back into Crossroad, leaving the group of soldiers he had commanded to blend into other lines. Lessie frowned as he vanished behind the first of the palisade walls. There was only one reason Valandaras would leave in the middle of a fight.

Lessie sent her last arrow flying into a charging Kalac soldier and was moving before she saw it land. Hastily throwing her longbow onto her back, she brought her fingers to her lips and let out a piercing whistle that got Druitt's attention. The captain was successfully driving back the enemy, some of the Kalac men breaking and outright retreating. Lessie gestured wildly towards the town, hoping he could read her intention.

Understanding bloomed on the older man's face as he gave her a curt nod before turning back towards his soldiers. He didn't need her anymore.

The tide was turning, and this battle was practically over. Lessie heard him shout to rally the men to him, to push harder, to press the advantage of the upper hand they had managed to take.

A wave of fear rolled off the Kalac force as the Altaeans surged.

Lessie tore off, leaving the main fight behind to follow Valandaras. Her lungs burned as she sprinted, her worn leather boots crunching as they hit the gravel of the outskirts of the town. The wooden walls stood unchallenged, the placement staggered, designed to slow and confuse an invading army rather than keep one out indefinitely. She ducked behind a palisade, panting, willing herself to catch her breath, and unbuckled her iron breastplate. It hit the ground with a dull thud. It was a risk, but she needed the full range of motion of her body more than the rudimentary protection the armour offered. Where did Valandaras go?

Lessie knew the answer, of course. He went to Mae.

She's not even supposed to be out here. Something bad has to have happened.

Lessie drew her revolver.

The feel of the weapon in her palm helped to ground her, to steady her—and the groove of her sister's initials on the handle calmed her more than she'd ever admit, especially to Trixie, unless she wanted to be teased for the next decade. She checked she'd loaded the chambers and deactivated the safety mechanism built into the trigger. There was an angry bruise already forming on her swollen knuckles, and she winced as her fingers closed around the grip of the gun.

She had to be smart about this.

Edging around to the front of the palisade, she tried to listen for any trace of where Valandaras had gone. She pulled the cotton from her ears, ignoring the imagined tut of her father's disapproval, and shut out the sounds of the dying battle raging behind her. She ducked behind one wall after the other, trying to remain unseen. Was the sound of clashing weapons getting quieter or louder?

Lessie reached the final palisade closest to Crossroad when an unmistakable shriek pierced the air.

That was Mae.

Lessie bolted from her position, following the sound, throwing herself behind the wall of the first building on the outskirts of town. The blacksmith's forge, currently unoccupied, its owner having joined in Crossroad's defence. The smell of steel and fire lingered around the place, even with the embers of the forge dulled.

Lessie peered around the building's edge. A small group of Kalac fighters had peeled off from the army, and now only the rest of the crew stood between them and Crossroad. Valandaras duelled with two of them, moving with deadly intent as he slashed his falchion into one foe, their shield only just making it up in time. Mae was wide-eyed with terror, dress stained with dirt and something darker as she crouched over an unconscious Grundle. A cloaked figure in Kalac colours lay on the ground beside them. Reevan fought nearby, robes billowing as he danced around the enemy's attacks, his staff whistling as it cut through the air.

One of the Kalac fighters was laughing—*laughing*—as he swung an obsidian sword at Reevan. Lessie's throat went dry at the sight of it.

It's that godsdamned blade from the beach. His blade.

Lessie watched in horror as Reevan barely corrected himself and ducked, narrowly avoiding being beheaded. The sword glistened in the sunlight as it passed over Reevan's head, and the wielder of the black blade feinted to the right before slashing at him again. This time, the steel found its mark. Reevan doubled over, holding his side, his blood spattering from the arc of the sword onto the packed earth. His staff clattered to the ground, rolling out of his reach.

The fighter shoved Reevan aside, sparing the kitskan no glance as he went sprawling into the dirt, and stalked towards Mae and Grundle.

Valandaras let out an enraged shout as he threw himself in between them, attempting to engage the wielder of the black blade while still covering his back as he twisted away from the two men he already faced.

The sound of the ever-calm Realmshifter's visceral roar shook Lessie out of her stupor. She could even the odds, but she had to do it now. She gave herself three seconds to aim—she needed to be careful, lest she hit Valandaras or one of the others. Then she could swing back behind the wall and reload.

Breathe.

The thundering of her revolver rang in her ears as she fired in rapid succession. Crouched at the building's edge, she saw with grim satisfaction that her first shot had taken one of the Kalac fighters out with a clean round through the head.

Papa would have been proud of that one.

She hadn't hit the wielder of the black blade, her shots at him going wide, and he still advanced on Valandaras with a feral grin etched across his face.

The third man had dropped his heavy crossbow to hold his thigh, groaning, a trickle of deep scarlet soaking through his fighting leathers. He turned, seeking the reason for his new injury, and his eyes met hers.

Lessie froze. There was no going back behind the wall now. He knew exactly where she was. The stranger's face was human, completely ordinary and unfamiliar, but the eyes were hollow. He spoke, and she felt a prickle of dread down her spine. She had never seen this man before in her life, but his voice still sent alarm bells pealing through her.

Like it didn't belong to him.

"The Mournblade's drain is incomplete," he said quietly, and yet she heard it perfectly, like it had been amplified, as if he had spoken directly into her mind. "The Divine still holds the last of it."

Still smiling, the black blade's wielder swung again, and the sword sang as it crashed into Valandaras's falchion. The Realmshifter buckled onto one knee from the parry. Lessie knew that something was terribly wrong—she had seen Valandaras fight, many times, and although he was exhausted and distracted by the injured crew around him, there was more to it. The glow within him seemed muted in places where the black blade had pierced his armour, like it had absorbed the light itself.

Reevan had not moved from where he had fallen, his blood staining the packed earth and gravel; only the exaggerated rise and fall of his chest showed he was still breathing. Mae sobbed as she grabbed at the front of Grundle's body, clutching handfuls of fabric in her fists, faint sparks of emerald sputtering over her fingertips.

The injured Kalac fighter lurched toward Lessie, slowed by the bullet wound in his leg, dragging a sword from its sheath at his side. A predatory smirk appeared on his face as he assessed her.

Lessie struggled to keep her hands from shaking as she levelled her revolver at the man's chest, willing herself to remain calm. There was exactly one bullet left in her revolver. She didn't have time to reload again before he would reach her, so she needed to make the shot count.

"You need not all die," he said. "Only the Divine has what we seek."

Lessie's eyes flicked between the man advancing on her and the scene behind him. She raised her gun until it pointed directly at his head. He didn't flinch.

All sound had emptied from the street except for Mae's sobs and Reevan's laboured panting. Valandaras still stood between them and the enemy, but he had been driven almost to the ground. His fighting stance was purely defensive; his shield battered and dented before the obsidian sword.

Lessie's finger curled tighter around the trigger.

The tip of the black blade pointed skyward as the wielder held it aloft, intending to bring it down upon Valandaras. The Realmshifter could barely raise his shield in response.

He needed help. They all did.

Lessie exhaled shakily.

I can't lose them, too.

Lessie shifted her aim to the left and fired at the wielder of the black blade.

The bullet struck exactly where she intended—into the back of his left hand. The man's hiss of pain was drowned out by the clattering of the sword as it fell to the ground.

The other fighter swung for her. Lessie threw herself backwards, swearing under her breath at the sting of gravel cutting into her palms. She hoped Valandaras had enough strength left to take advantage of his opponent being disarmed. He could get the rest of them out.

The hollow-eyed stranger smiled mirthlessly as he advanced on her. Sounds of a scuffle came from behind him, but she couldn't see anything beyond the longsword now pointed towards her throat. She had half a thought to try to reload, but the sharp blade moved with her as she attempted to reach for her ammunition, so she stilled.

"Noble," he said, smirking again, playing with her like a cat who had trapped a mouse. "To sacrifice yourself for another. Pity it will be just as pointless as the last time you dared to cross me, girl."

Lessie frowned. The last time?

Something about the stranger's voice was familiar.

He drew his sword back to plunge it into her heart. The man's face contorted, smiling cruelly, before a flash of movement behind him distracted them both. His eyes lost their hollowness and widened in fear just as Valandaras's falchion severed the fighter's head from his shoulders.

Lessie skittered away in horror as blood spattered and the decapitated figure collapsed towards her. The body thumped onto the ground, weapon falling harmlessly at his side, a pool of blood soaking into the ground. A flurry of dust whirled into the air.

Lessie tried very, very hard not to look for where the head had gone.

As the dust cloud settled, she could see past the hollow-eyed fighter now to the wielder of the black blade—or what Valandaras had left of him. He looked as if he had been carved into pieces. Mae had crawled to Reevan, her sputtering healing sparks coursing over his body.

Valandaras was breathing hard, like the fight had drained him beyond what should have been possible. He was still holding his falchion in the move that had ended the fighter's life and saved her own.

Lessie looked up at Valandaras, blinking hot blood out of her eyes and trying not to be sick.

"Good shot," Valandaras murmured, before he fell to his knees.

17

LESSIE

The blood had dried on her skin before she had a chance to remove it, so she left it.

Lessie picked her way through the now quiet battlefield, searching for signs of survival from the fallen. Occasionally she came across an Altaean fighter, wounded but still breathing, and helped to move them into the town for treatment. Not a single Kalac soldier had been left alive on the field. Those who had retreated had either carried their injured with them or finished them off to prevent prisoners of war. Crossroad's mundane healers were doing their best to keep up with the string of injuries they were seeing to, but it was slow work, bloody and thankless. The alchemist quickly exhausted their meagre stock of healing draughts.

A month ago, Mae could have healed them all without breaking a sweat.

Mae had been given her own tent to treat the others in, and Valandaras had ignored his own injuries to help take Reevan and Grundle into it. Lessie left them only after Mae had assured her that they were all going to be fine. Mae's Gift was weak but steady, and she had managed to bring Grundle back to consciousness after a short while.

The wounds inflicted by the obsidian sword—the Mournblade, the Kalac fighter had called it—seemed to temper any healing, even when Divine in nature. Valandaras had not let the sword out of arm's reach since the fight, having wrapped the obsidian blade in a discarded cloak before strapping it to his side. Lessie hated it. A dark hum of power seemed to emanate from it, and it made her want to be sick if she focused on it for too long.

The argument between Mae and Valandaras within the tent as they worked together to heal his injuries had been legendary, if only because neither of them raised their voice above a whisper. He was furious at how Mae had not listened to him and been anywhere near the battleground at all. She was adamant that if she hadn't been, Grundle and Reevan would have both died. They both had points.

As the only crewmember who had not been hit by the Mournblade, Lessie soon left the tent to help the soldiers with more menial tasks. She felt restless after the fight, like the adrenaline still coursing through her would have her jump out of her own skin if she didn't move. She needed to do more than sit around and watch her friends bicker as they were slowly pieced back together.

My friends. Is that what they are?

Lessie focused on her search, but there were no more survivors to rescue. Only a sea of bodies, who would hopefully see a proper funeral rather than be left for the crows. Kneeling over the crumpled form of an infantry soldier, a memory of her mother citing an old superstition floated into her mind. Most of the common folk believed that without a proper send off, souls of the recently passed would have trouble finding their way to the Silver Stream to pass into Requiem, the realm of the dead. Whether they were buried or burned, someone had to speak the prayers to guide them on their journey. She wished she could for the fallen soldiers, but she had never learned the words.

Lessie couldn't remember the name of the god of death, but she hoped they had left the Godprison and reclaimed their mantle. They would be busy today.

At least she had enough gold to break away now. The payment for the Lord of Complaining's rescue and guard duty had been beyond what she could have hoped for. There was no more need for gruelling mercenary work. She'd stick around for a short while, maybe travel with the others to Saluo for safety, then break off and pursue her quarry. It was as good a place as any to start.

Footsteps to her left. Lessie looked up to find Druitt DeFalcone approaching her. There was a large gash above the captain's left eye that would probably require healing, but he had not sought treatment for it yet. He came to stand beside her, looking out onto the plains, following her gaze into the horizon where the last of the Kalac soldiers had vanished back across the border, abandoning their tents and fallen brethren.

"Well, as far as skirmishes go, we couldn't have hoped for much better," he said by way of greeting. "We successfully pushed back the Kalac invaders. Crossroad is safe."

Lessie nodded her agreement. "Except for the part where we all almost died, I think it went pretty well," she replied, trying not to keep the wave of guilt from washing over her. "Sorry I left my post."

"You made a call, and it was the right one," Druitt said. He seemed a little on edge. "We had already won. They might have all fallen. It was the same decision I would have made." He looked her over, taking in the blood spatter that still stained her clothing and dried on her face. "As for leaving your post, I apologise for underestimating you. Sticking you in the novice group might have killed me, but you trusted your own abilities. It was a brave choice."

Druitt reached into the satchel he carried, shuffling belongings around before drawing out a yellowed piece of parchment. His face was unreadable as he offered it to her, and she frowned as she took it.

"What is this?" she asked.

"A reward, and a favour. For all of you, really."

Lessie's eyes narrowed as she skimmed over the document. Parts of it were new, the letters still glistening like they hadn't fully dried, while others looked like they had been written and rewritten for years. She could read, but most of it was written in the old language, stuffy and mind-numbing to interpret. Her full name was written in fresh ink near the top.

"I don't understand."

Druitt looked uncomfortable, like he was fighting within himself. His fingers curled around the hilt of his longsword in its scabbard, toying with the filigree embedded in the handle. Birds in flight.

"This is the title to Falcon's Watch, and the surrounding lands," he said, motioning to the parchment. "It's DeFalcone land, but it's been neglected and ignored by my family for decades. I was tasked by my father to make sure the next lord who occupied it was someone honourable, logical, protective. A lord who knew how to make the right calls."

Lessie searched his face, her concern only deepening. Druitt gave her a mischievous smile that took years off his face and forcefully reminded her of Camden.

"Or lady, as it turns out."

Oh, gods.

Lessie stared at him in shock, fingers trembling as she clutched the ageing paper.

"This is a joke, right?" she said, eyes darting between Druitt's face and her name on the page, skimming over the other lines without really reading them.

Druitt shook his head. "I've been toying with the idea for years, but I've never had a good enough reason to put it into place. I recently found one."

"But I'm not highborn," Lessie protested. "I don't know the first thing about running a—a keep? A village? How many people live there? What am I supposed to do? You can't be serious. Aren't nobles supposed to handle this kind of thing?"

She resisted the urge to fling the parchment into the mud. The gore of the battle had not phased her for the most part, but now she felt sick.

Is he insane? Are all DeFalcones complete idiots?

Druitt sighed and rubbed at his eyes, wincing as his fingers brushed against the cut above his eyebrow.

"I assure you, I am serious. As of right now, I have the authority to name whomever I see fit to hold those lands. I could pick any highborn member of my father's court and be done with it, true, but they just squabble over power. They don't care about the common folk. I want that keep, and those people, to be looked after. You've proven you can do that."

Lessie snorted. "Why not sign it over to Valandaras, then? Surely he can take care of it better than I would. Why me?" *What are you not telling me?*

Druitt looked back towards Crossroad, to the tents set up on the outskirts. "Old prejudices are hard to shake in Altaea," he said. "The Realmshifter and the Divine cannot hold titles of their own, being that they wield power; the others are not Altaean born. It had to be you. But we both know that they will take as much responsibility for the lands as you will. All of you together will make Falcon's Watch a place of safety for its people."

It made sense, but Lessie still frowned.

"Do I even get a say in this?" she snapped, the words sounding harsher than she intended.

Druitt fixed her with a hard stare. "You can refuse, of course," he said. "But please consider it."

He began the walk back in the direction of the town. The battlefield was silent except for the sound of his careful footsteps. Lessie stared after him, fingers still clutching the old parchment. They were shaking slightly.

"It would be good for your sister to have a home to come back to, after all," Druitt added over his shoulder. "Especially if her training doesn't go as well as you hope."

Lessie's heart lurched. *I should never have told him about Trixie. People use who you love against you.*

She cursed internally, wishing she could return to the minutes before he had found her. Where she was alone, with minimal responsibility and nothing but her desire for revenge to guide her choices. *Godsdamn it.*

"Fine, I'll do it," Lessie shouted after Druitt. He turned back to her and gave her a solemn nod of approval as he waited for her to join him, extending a hand. She ignored it completely as she stalked past him.

"But I want help cleaning it up."

It was past sundown when Lessie finally made her way back to the crew.

After begrudgingly accepting his proposal and signing the cursed parchment, she'd followed Druitt into the ranks of resting soldiers. He had introduced her to a few in his company who were on the edges of retirement, and Lessie had taken a liking to one soldier in particular—a rough man with kind eyes who had shaken her hand and introduced himself only as Cutty before Druitt had intervened and given her his full name, to the man's dismay. Cuthburt Remmingford Brix was in his mid fifties, with close-cropped greying hair and skin that had seen more than its fair share of sunlight, and he spoke in a thick lowborn accent. He seemed interested in the chance to settle down in one place, although he had been quite taken aback at Lessie's immediate offer to be captain of her guard.

She had her reasons.

I remember him on the field. He stopped fighting to help another man up.

With the new captain of the guard secured, Druitt had spent the afternoon discussing the main elements of Falcon's Watch—the tiny village surrounding it, how they survived and what they produced, what they lacked by not having had a lord to watch over them for the past century. Druitt had also promised to make arrangements for the fort to be restored. He would not fund all of it, but he would make it inhabitable. It was more than she had expected from him, especially since Druitt had made it very clear that by her accepting the title of this land, it had ceased to be part of the main DeFalcone family's holdings. Her title fell under the DeFalcone house, but once the keep was functional, she would be on her own. Druitt had also mused about what plans she could make of the fort, how she could utilise it as an extra port of protection for Altaea, as it was so close to the Kalac border. He offered her advice, speaking of improvements to the town that she agreed to but had no idea how to pay for, and assured her over and over that none of the Seven would challenge her claim to it. It was too small, too remote—dead weight, he said, that no noble would have wished to reside over it.

Lessie tried to pay attention, but she caught herself glazing over. Regret washed over her like a waterfall. It was too much, all at once.

He seems too glad to be rid of it. This feels like a trap, but I'm already in it.

Having finally escaped Druitt to see to his men, a red tinge of exhaustion clouded Lessie's vision as she made her way to the tavern and pushed through the heavy wooden door. Spotting the rest of the crew, muscle memory had her heading towards the booth they occupied every night now, and she groaned as she collapsed into it. Mae scooted inwards to make room for her, and Valandaras shifted uncomfortably as they brushed up against each other. Lessie felt too tired to even roll her eyes.

Reevan was there, which surprised her. She hadn't known the extent of his injuries, but she'd also never seen him be taken down quite so easily before. It was a good sign that he was up and about from the healer's tents. Grundle's absence from the table hung in the air, an uncomfortable silence as they glanced towards where he had sat the night before.

"Ah, Lessandra, there you are. We were about to send out a search party," said Reevan, looking supremely unconcerned as he curled his large clawed hands around his mug of milk. He held himself at a particular angle, so as not to aggravate the wound he nursed. His persistent use of her full given name irritated her to no end.

"Yeah, yeah, you look distraught," replied Lessie, resting her head on her arms at the table. She had been seated mere moments before an angel in the form of a pretty barmaid placed a glass of whiskey in front of her, smiling and leaving without asking for payment.

Lessie glanced around, attempting to see where the drink had come from, and sniffed it suspiciously. A single sip chased away any lingering paranoia. It was the kind she could never afford paying extra for, rich and spicy, and she drank deeply, savouring the feeling of the liquor flooding through her and momentarily turning her limbs to lead. Draining the glass, she placed it back on the table and cleared her throat. The alcohol rapidly coursing through her veins gave her just enough liquid courage to share her news.

"Druitt gave me a title today," she mumbled. "I own Falcon's Watch."
And I'm already scheming of ways to be rid of it.

All eyes were on her instantly. Lessie resisted the urge to shrink away from the undivided attention. She wished her sister were here. Trixie would have bathed in it.

Maybe I should ask her to come and run this godsdamned keep instead. She'd have the townsfolk eating out of the palm of her hand in no time.

Lessie sighed inwardly. She'd already thought of that. Altaean law wouldn't let a common-born Arcane like Trixie hold a noble title. There would be too much talk of if she'd manipulated the Weave to get it. Besides, her sister was finally safe and accepted, was getting to experience her Arcane nature without threat. Lessie couldn't take that away.

But I will write to Trixie tonight. She needs to know. Maybe she can help me get out of this.

"Congratulations," Reevan drawled. "I suppose this means you will be leaving our little crew to live a life of luxury as a noblewoman?"

Lessie snorted. "Absolutely not."

Mae and Valandaras shared a glance she recognised from her own parents, like they weren't sure who should first broach the subject. Mae put her arm around Lessie, a trace of her usual beaming smile playing around her lips.

"That's wonderful," she said, squeezing Lessie's shoulder affectionately. "It will be a lot of work, but I'm sure we can all help you. Does this make you a lady now?"

Lessie rolled her eyes. "A Viscountess, apparently, based on the amount of land. It's ridiculous and completely unnecessary. The first one of you to refer to me as Lady Shilling is getting a bullet in their ass."

Mae giggled at her crass words. Valandaras shifted, like he was monitoring her every move, keeping track of her bursts of joy, once so abundant but now rare. Lessie knew because she looked for it, too.

I never realised how much Mae's happiness affected us all until it wasn't there.

"Did Druitt say anything about his contact in Saluo?" Valandaras asked. They both pretended not to notice that Mae had gone still, the laughter sliding from her face.

Lessie shook her head. "He did say that he would stay in Crossroad a few more days before returning to Roost Keep, though. So he'll probably tell us tomorrow, and then we can plan our journey."

They fell silent for a while. Mae had wilted, eyes fixed on the untouched mug of ale in front of her. Lessie searched for something to distract her with.

"How is Grundle?" Lessie asked.

Mae's demeanour improved somewhat. "He is resting. He was struck by that horrible sword straight away, and it crumpled him immediately. I heard Reevan's shouting, and I managed to get to them when Valandaras showed up. I got there just in time to heal him." She shivered, as if picturing the scene again. "I only have a fraction of what I'm used to, but it was enough to stabilise him. That sword is nasty."

Reevan sniffed. "I'd say I'd be happy to never see that blade again, but I'm assuming Valandaras will be dragging it around with us for the foreseeable future."

Lessie glanced to where the Mournblade, still wrapped in the discarded fabric, had been placed next to Valandaras's falchion, both weapons stored neatly beside him. She thought she was imagining it, but even concealed within the cloth, it was like there was a coldness emanating from the blade. She opened her mouth to speak of what the Kalac fighter had said to her, to muse on what it meant, but stopped short as a small pointed face appeared in the booth beside her and spoke.

"Grundle found a problem."

Lessie tried to disguise her jump of surprise by redirecting her hand, which had flown to her revolver, to adjust her stained clothing instead. Mae shrieked before clapping a hand over her mouth and throwing an apologetic look at the surrounding patrons who had jumped at the high-pitched noise. Reevan and Valandaras had not reacted, but Lessie could tell that the goblin had surprised them, too.

"Grundle! You are supposed to be resting!" Mae chided him, looking him over, assessing his injuries like a mother would a child. Whatever they were, they had not impacted his stealth, though he was breathing hard and wincing at every inhale.

"Grundle was. Grundle felt better," he said, pulling himself up to his full height, which still barely reached over the top of the table. "So Grundle went for a walk to see what Kalac left."

He reached into his leathers and pulled out the remnants of a few pieces of parchment. They had been burned, as if someone had tried to destroy them, and what little remained was indecipherable. They were nothing more than scraps.

Valandaras reached for one. "There is nothing on here I recognise," he said, turning the burned piece over in his wrapped fingers.

Grundle silently placed the largest parchment in front of Reevan. Lessie peered at it. There were a number of symbols scrawled onto the page, hasty and violent in the splatters around them. It was not in a language she recognised, unless it was a code. There was a crest inked on it at the top. The pattern on it reminded her of iron chains.

Reevan went deathly still.

Lessie waited impatiently, eyes flickering between Reevan and the parchment, before she glanced at Mae. The Divine's curiosity shined through the numbness that blanketed her features more often than not. They all waited anxiously for an explanation.

"What does it mean, Reevan?" Lessie asked, breaking the silence.

Reevan gingerly picked up the parchment, turning it over in one clawed hand. His expression was unreadable. He shifted uncomfortably. Grundle seemed to have been waiting for his confirmation, and now shrank down into the shadows, as if he wanted to disappear entirely.

"Of course he would be involved. It's been one of his plans for years," murmured Reevan.

"Who?" asked Mae and Lessie together. Valandaras remained silent.

Reevan's tail twitched as he placed the parchment back down upon the table. "This is the crest of the house of Braak. They are one of Kalac's largest and wealthiest families. They are cunning, ruthless, and feared among the majority of the Kalac Empire." All emotion had drained from his face, like he was a living statue. "Grundle and I are familiar with them."

"How familiar?" asked Valandaras.

Lessie flinched as Reevan's claws scraped into the wood he sat upon. The kitskan's emerald eyes glittered with a quiet violence she had never seen before.

"Ashendi Braak owned us. We were his slaves."

18

REEVAN

When compared to the weeks Reevan had recently experienced, the next few were uneventful.

He spent most of his time exploring their new home, the fort of Falcon's Watch. It was the most domesticated he had ever been, and he found it oddly comforting. He had never had a room to himself before. It was strange, to know that only he would sleep in the bed, only he would touch the furniture, that only his belongings would be stored in the drawers of the tiny side table in the corner.

Once Grundle had recovered well enough to travel, they had left Crossroad. On the journey back to Falcon's Watch, Reevan managed to successfully avoid most questions about his life as a slave. It was a touchy subject, and both Mae and Valandaras had been quick to drop it. Lessie had pressed for more information, but given up when the details of her new home threatened to overwhelm her. She had made it clear that although the title was hers, Falcon's Watch belonged to all of them—like the idea of sharing made her less weighed down by her newfound nobility.

Valandaras had mused that being closer to the border would give them a few days' head start when they decided to make the trek to Saluo, and that they owed it to both Druitt and Lessie to restore the keep before they left. Reevan knew that Valandaras was simply stalling to allow Mae to store up the power she had drained from the battle of Crossroad. But with his own wound from the Mournblade taking a stubbornly long time to heal, he was inclined to agree. Mae was a ghost of her former self, but she could still be the difference between life and death. It was prudent to wait.

The keep of Falcon's Watch was as they had left it, with the only difference being the small group of workers toiling with mops and brooms. They had slowly scrubbed a century's worth of grime from the stone, piecing the fort back together room by room. Reevan and the rest of the crew had joined the workers, happy for the mundane tasks to take their minds from the horrors of the past few weeks.

Reevan wondered what they had done with the bodies of the enemy soldiers that had been killed here. If they had been buried, or burned, or dragged away to rot.

The crew had then ventured into the small village—Lessie to reluctantly introduce herself as their new noble caretaker; Valandaras to gather the supplies they would need for extended travel. The townsfolk, by all accounts, took a strange liking to Lessie, perhaps because they had been ignored for so long. She was soon inundated with requests and suggestions to improve the town's standing.

Reevan had felt mild curiosity for the village, and had accompanied the two on one trip, but it lacked most of the necessities required for an interesting outing. There was no tavern, no blacksmith, no alchemist—the people had made do with living off the surrounding land, supplemented by the one general shop in the vicinity. Reevan supposed they travelled to Crossroad when they required more than the village could provide, but he made a mental note to suggest to Lessie to commission a tavern as soon as they could afford to. He rarely partook in alcohol himself, but it seemed to be the quickest way to get people to like one another.

Grundle had commandeered the dungeon, transforming it into his own personal workshop. The goblin spoke little and explained nothing, but the others accepted his tinkering and were happy to leave him be. Reevan visited him a few times, head tilting as he skimmed over designs for prototypes, rolled papers collected over years and now left under heavy stones to smooth. Rough drafts of weapons and ingredient lists for potions and poisons, annotations and variations crossed out or written over the top. Grundle had been infamous back home for his unique take on blending mundane weapons with elixirs.

The third time Reevan ventured down to visit, Grundle showed him a secret door concealed in a wall at the very back of the dungeon. Reevan, delighted, immediately inspected it, prying the door open to reveal a narrow passageway. He followed it for a while, Grundle trailing behind him, and when they finally came to the end of the passage, a trapdoor above had them scrambling out of a disused well, of all things. It was delightfully cliché. Sensing a pattern, Reevan poked around inside the keep, too, and found several hidden passages and false doors over the three storeys. Falcon's Watch held many secrets, and it would be years before they discovered them all.

In the evenings, he rested his injuries and prepared for their long journey. In the mornings, Reevan would rise with the dawn, and often wandered the outside of the keep on his morning walk. Most days it was peaceful.

On one, it was not.

Distant shouting drifted towards him, coming from the main gate—or rather, what was left of it after Grundle's explosion. He was too far away to make out the words, but the tone suggested trouble.

Reevan sighed and meandered towards the sound, picking his way around the side of the keep, careful not to move too quickly lest he attract attention. There had been no raise of alarms and he heard no clashing of weapons, so he wasn't too concerned. He located the source of the commotion as he neared the front of the keep; two men were scuffling in the dirt just inside the entrance like children squabbling over possession of a toy.

Reevan rounded the corner at the same time Lessie barged out of the heavy wooden doors.

"What is going *on* out here?" she barked, wearing an oversized plaid shirt and brandishing a spoon, clearly in the middle of breaking her fast. Valandaras and Mae both stood on the steps to the keep; the Divine's hand lingered on the Realmshifter's arm, like parents unsure when to intervene in a child's quarrel. Reevan sidled up to them, smirking sideways as Lessie stalked towards the men arguing in their courtyard.

One was their newly appointed captain of the guard. Cutty had subdued his quarry, pinning the other man's arms behind him, and had been marching him back toward the gate. The newcomer's protests became louder the further he was dragged.

At the sound of Lessie's voice, Cutty swung his captive around to face them. "Apologies, milady, but this young man tried to enter the fort without me, kept brushin' me off, talkin' about how he was a personal friend to you all, but he wasn't on the list of names you gave me."

Reevan suppressed a chuckle as he recognised their first official visitor. Red in the face from the exertion of trying to break Cutty's hold on him, dusty from travel, wearing expensive clothing and an expression of complete incredulity.

"And I keep telling *you*, I don't need to be on a list," Camden DeFalcone exclaimed loudly, "I'm the godsdamned reason they even have this fort."

Lessie sighed. "It's all right, Cutty," she said. "I do know him. Unfortunately."

Her new captain released his hold on Camden immediately. The lord made a big show of dusting off and straightening his clothing.

"Seven realms, if this is how you treat guests, don't expect to have many," he said, shooting a look of distaste at Lessie.

She glared back. "Guests are invited."

Cutty looked mortified at his mistake. "Apologies, milady," he said again, his low-born accent thick and tone regretful. His ruddy skin managed to turn even more red. "I didn't mean to hurt your friend. I only wanted to protect this keep, and I figured if you knew he was comin', you would've told me."

Lessie pinched the bridge of her nose before she gave him one of her half-smiles, like she wanted to put him at ease.

"Don't worry about it," she said, ignoring Camden's exaggerated look of outrage. "You were just doing your job. We'll handle him from here."

Relief bloomed over the older man's face. Cutty nodded and offered Lessie a small, stiff incline of his upper body, like he was unsure how low he was supposed to go for someone with her title. He excused himself back to his duties, boots crunching under the earth as he walked away.

Camden watched warily as Cutty passed, before turning back to Lessie and sinking into a formal bow that would have been respectful if not for the mocking gleam dancing in his eyes.

"My... lady," he said, letting the tone of surprise linger within the title, "it seems congratulations are in order. It's not every day a commoner rises to the ranks of nobility."

Lessie frowned. "You came all this way to congratulate me? That was unnecessary. You could have written a letter," she replied, ire dripping from every word. "And then thrown it in the fire, because I wouldn't have opened it, because I don't care."

Mae giggled from the doorstep.

Camden gave Lessie a dry look as he brushed the hair out of his eyes. It was shorter than when they had first met him, though it still reached past his jaw, and he was clean-shaven. He brushed past Lessie to address the rest of the crew lingering on the keep's doorstep.

"As much as I do love these conversations with the delightful Lady Shilling, I actually came to speak to you, Miss Mae," said Camden, ignoring Lessie's huff at the use of her title. "I bring with me the gift of information.

Not all of it is good, but knowledge is power, I suppose. Druitt found some rather interesting crossbow bolts from your little stand-off in Crossroad that matched the one she—" Camden gestured behind him to Lessie, "wrenched out of your shoulder. Those men at the West Keep were never after my head. They came for you."

Mae put a hand to her collarbone reflexively, no doubt feeling for the scar that now dwelled there from the attack. Valandaras took a step forward, angling himself in front of Mae like he could shield her from the invisible threat he had already taken care of. Reevan glanced between the two. Interesting that the wielders of the god-syphoning blade would seek to kill the Divine before they had even begun their attack on her god. It suggested prior knowledge. Very interesting.

Camden cleared his throat and continued.

"So, the good news is, you successfully kept me safe, and I am no longer threatened. Well done. Oh, and also, my brother's contact has finally responded to his letter. He's agreed to meet with you. We can leave for Saluo at any time, so you can get some answers."

Mae tensed beside Reevan, processing the news that had been dropped upon them so suddenly. They could leave for Saluo. Reevan thought perhaps Camden should have led with that information first.

Lessie's eyes were like ice. "I'm sorry, *we?*"

Camden glanced back over his shoulder at her and gave her a beaming smile, teeth flashing.

"Of course, we. You all need someone who can vouch for you with Druitt's man, and gods know *you're* going to need help to not offend the wrong person and be thrown in jail for it. It'd be a terrible blow for your shiny new noblewoman's reputation."

It was Lessie's turn to sputter, and Camden smirked at her confused expression. He wore leather riding boots and carried a well-made travelling pack. It looked brand new; it had probably never been used.

"So I volunteered," Camden said. "I've always wanted to see Kalac, and I hear it's beautiful this time of year. I've been meaning to broaden my horizons, as they say."

Lessie seemed momentarily unable to speak. Reevan chuckled again. It was interesting to watch her sort out what she was going to say before she said it, since she had been making an effort to curb her impulsive outbursts around so many new people.

"You're coming along with us because you wanted... to travel?" Lessie finally asked, voice incredulous, like she couldn't quite believe what she was hearing. "Can't you go visit one of the other castles you own? Are they all too boring?"

"Something like that. It was time for a new adventure," the lord replied pleasantly, looking to Valandaras. "So when do we depart, Realmshifter?"

Valandaras seemed torn between delaying the trip as long as possible to spare Mae's health, and the allure of fixing the problem that plagued her altogether.

"This will not be a simple journey, Lord Camden," Valandaras said. "There may be danger, and we may not be able to protect you. You will need to defend yourself."

To Reevan's surprise, Camden did not argue, but nodded solemnly. He patted the sword at his side, the leather of the scabbard well crafted with a familiar design of birds in flight.

"I have been trained in the longsword since I was a boy," Camden replied, ignoring the snort of disbelief from Lessie behind him. "Mostly in the art of duelling, and for ceremonial purposes, but I can handle a blade." He looked back at Lessie, who now stood with her arms crossed and eyebrow arched. "And I've been involved in enough tavern brawls to know how to throw a punch if needed," he added, smirking.

Reevan's tail twitched. It was risky to take Camden at his word. True, he was tall, broad-shouldered, and seemed relatively fit and healthy underneath his fancy clothing and bravado. But they had never actually seen him fight. If they brought him along and he were killed, it could bring the wrath of the DeFalcone house down upon them, not to mention the might of the entire kingdom once his father reascended the throne.

There could be no doubt. What they needed was proof that the lord could take care of himself.

"All right, my lord," Reevan said, stepping forward. "I have a proposal. Hold your own, and we will no longer question your ability to survive."

"Hold my own?" Camden asked, face puzzled. "Against what?"

Reevan grinned. It was purely predatory. "Me."

He pounced.

Robes billowing as he launched himself forwards, Reevan was pleasantly surprised to see Camden react quickly enough to twist away from his first attack, boots shuffling in the dirt and stirring up dust. He struck again and Camden ducked, avoiding his punch by mere inches. Lessie stepped aside as Camden backed up, throwing his pack to the ground and drawing his blade hesitantly from the throat of its scabbard.

Reevan flashed a dagger and grinned, letting Camden find his footing.

"Very good, my lord," he said. "Now let's see how much of your training you remember."

He struck high, slower than usual, not intending to end the man's life but to test his instincts in blocking. Camden brought his sword up and across his body in a fairly decent parry before shoving against the dagger. The heavier weapon pushed the lighter one away, and Reevan raised his eyebrows in approval. He cut low, faster, and Camden panted as he barely swung his sword in time to block the blow.

Reevan wielded the dagger like it was an extension of his paw. He would have preferred to use his staff for this demonstration, as there was less chance of stabbing his opponent with it, but his favourite weapon remained leaning against the wall in his new room.

At one point, Mae made a small noise of concern, and Reevan noted that Camden did not let his focus be pulled by it, which was a good sign. Reevan drove him back, testing his footwork. It was a little clumsy, but the instinct to mirror an opponent kicked in and Camden copied Reevan's movements, holding him out of reach with a few more parries. Satisfied, Reevan ceased his attack.

"Well done, my lord," he said, stepping away, the dagger glinting in the morning sunlight. "Now try to take me down."

Camden blanched. "I'm sorry, what?"

He continued to hold his sword defensively, switching between guards like he had no doubt been shown by his brother or some grizzled instructor. They seemed stiff and clinical, like he had been forced to cycle through them for long enough that it had become mostly muscle memory.

Reevan flicked the dagger from one paw to the other.

"Try to hit me," he repeated.

Camden hesitated, but raised his blade high as he went on the offensive. He swung it at Reevan weakly, like he was terrified that it would connect and he would hurt Reevan, but it was not for nothing that kitskans were known for their blinding speed. Reevan did not even need to parry the attack, as he had already stepped out of reach, shaking his head.

"You will not hit me, my lord, but please at least try," he said, a faint hint of amusement in his words.

"This is insanity," Camden muttered, before swinging a series of more powerful blows towards Reevan. The cuts were well made, and although it was clear it had been a while since he had wielded a blade, his aim was adequate. A less skilled opponent would have struggled to parry them.

Of course, Reevan was not a less skilled opponent. He dodged them all, but brought his dagger up to meet the last one, feeling that the lord's pride would be damaged should he fail to land a single blow onto the kitskan's blade. They met with a resounding clash of metal. Reevan calmly held up a clawed hand, signalling that they had finished.

"Well done, my lord," Reevan said, his demonstration complete. Camden had proven himself quite nicely. He would not immediately die if they were attacked on the road, at least.

Wiping a light sheen of sweat from his brow, breathing hard, Camden looked to Valandaras for approval. The Realmshifter stood unmoving for a moment, his face unreadable. Reevan supposed it was always unreadable, anyway, since it was always covered, so there was no difference.

After a tense silence, Valandaras gave Camden a small nod of commendation.

"We will leave in three days," Valandaras said, voice calm and low. He turned and strode into the keep. Mae gave them all a small smile before following Valandaras inside. It was nowhere near as blinding as her usual smile, but a smile nonetheless.

Reevan turned to Camden and offered a paw in respect.

"You fought honourably, my lord," he said. Camden eyed his clawed fingers, but shook his outstretched hand firmly.

"Thank you," Camden replied, eyes twinkling with pride as he slid his blade back into the scabbard at his belt and wiped the sweat from his brow. "It's nice to know I haven't forgotten it all. I was top of my class when it came to longsword, but I suppose my only issue is I am a little out of practice. Duelling with honour is—"

Reevan caught the blur of movement at the last second.

A small silver projectile collided with the side of Camden's head. Camden's voice cut off in a small yelp of pain. The young lord flinched, ducking too late. He brought his hand up to cradle his ear, searching around wildly for his attacker.

"What in the seven realms..."

Lessie strode towards the keep, not looking at Camden, but as she passed him, her eyes rolled so far back it looked painful.

"Your *issue* is that you expect not to be hit because you're you," she hissed. "You were top of your class because your opponents were too scared to piss off your father. Real enemies won't give a shit that you're the Lord of Honourable Duelling, they'll just stab you."

The spoon from Lessie's interrupted breakfast lay in the dirt from where she had thrown it. Reevan's whiskers twitched with amusement. She had a point. Somewhere, an invisible tally between the two had recorded another mark in Lessie's column.

Camden prodded his temple and winced. He pulled his hand from his head and inspected it, as if expecting to see blood. Lessie yanked open the heavy doors and glanced back over her shoulder.

"You want to stay alive? Get your head out of your ass," she said, dark eyes flashing. "Pay less attention to yourself and more to what's going on around you."

She disappeared into the hall, letting the heavy wooden door swing shut with a loud thump. Another tally mark.

Camden stared after Lessie, rubbing his temple and frowning.

"Gods, what is her problem?" he exclaimed loudly, throwing his hands into the air. The interaction had unravelled some of his carefully charming demeanour.

Reevan tilted his head, contemplating. It seemed like Lessie had quite a few problems. To Reevan, they were obvious, but perhaps Camden was not aware of them.

"Lessandra has lost most of her family, my lord, and worries constantly for the sister she has left, who resides on the other side of the continent. She took a title and charge of this keep at your brother's behest without knowing how to properly run it, which she regrets, but she fears failing the people around her. I believe she is under a great deal of stress. Furthermore, I have my suspicions that the being who took the Mother's essence also took something Lessie cherished, so although she craves revenge, she is terrified of facing him, as we saw on the beach."

Camden stopped walking. His brows knitted together.

"I meant with me, kitskan," he mumbled, his face pensive. "Her problem with me."

Reevan sniffed. He should have been more specific, then.

"My lord, it appears that Lessandra thinks you do not take anything seriously, and therefore that you will end up getting yourself or others hurt on this journey. Furthermore, she finds you to be spoiled, selfish, and irritating, as well as undeserving of your high standing, since you do not seem to want or appreciate it."

Camden's eyed widened slightly.

"Seven realms, Reevan," he said with an incredulous laugh. "Tell me what you really think. Don't pull your punches."

"I was not, my lord," Reevan replied, confused. "I merely thought you would appreciate the truth."

Camden sighed, reaching to pick up his travelling pack from the ground where he had thrown it. He attempted to brush some of the dust off. A futile effort considering where they would soon be travelling.

"I do, Reevan. I appreciate the candour more than you know," Camden said, sighing again as he stared up at the closed doors of the keep. "But it's going to be a long adventure if I have to dodge cutlery the whole time."

Reevan gave his best approximation of an easy-going smile. It felt uncomfortable.

"Not to worry, my lord," he said, patting Camden on the back. "Lessandra will come around. She may even possibly grow to be fond of you."

Camden looked unconvinced, but Reevan simply pulled the door to the keep and held it open for him. He gestured grandly, bidding the younger DeFalcone welcome inside the place that had so recently been his prison.

"After all," Reevan added, "her telling you your faults is her way of making sure you are aware to correct them."

"What does that prove, exactly?" Camden asked.

"If Lessandra truly wished you harm, she would have kept her observations to herself and allowed your weakness to become your cause of death."

19

REEVAN

On the last night in their new home before travelling to Saluo, Reevan found himself climbing the spiral stairs of the keep's tower.

He headed for the chamber which had once held Camden DeFalcone captive. The stairs were mildly more welcoming now, with the alcoves lit by lanterns in the evening. Reevan smirked as he crossed under a ceiling that bore the faint marks of his claws, and let out a low chuckle as he surveyed the door to the room, which had been placed back onto its hinges slightly crooked. He knocked politely; the sound muffled by the fur on his clawed hand.

"What?" the voice from within snapped, annoyed by the interruption.

Reevan took this to mean he had permission to enter and swept into the room. It had changed little from the last time he had been here, with the only difference now being a small fire burning merrily in the hearth and no bound, smirking nobleman sprawled upon the bed.

Instead, a young woman sat at the desk, hunched over a book and scribbling furiously onto the parchment. A low burning candle perched on a nearby stack of dusty books, wax spilling onto them without her noticing.

"Good evening, Lessandra," Reevan said politely.

"Sorry. I thought you were—never mind."

Lessie did not look up as he entered and continued to write. She was once again wearing the soft plaid shirt, several sizes too big; it appeared to be her sleeping clothes. It looked older than she was. Her eyes had dark circles under them, and her chestnut hair was pulled back into a haphazard ponytail, strands of it falling loose and brushing against the pages. She pushed them behind her ear, irritated, and finally looked up at him.

"What do you want, Reevan?" she asked, voice weary.

Reevan's curiosity had momentarily distracted him from what he had come to ask her.

"Are you writing a novel? Or is this your diary?" he asked, crossing the room and peering over her shoulder. "I'd love to read your take on recent events. Although judging by your handwriting, it would be quite a challenge."

Lessie sighed and slammed the book shut with a thump. The front was made of soft leather, the kind that folded over itself to close completely with cords meant to tie it on either side.

"Do you really want to know?" she asked, forehead creasing as she frowned up at him.

"Why would I ask a question if I did not wish to know the answer?"

Lessie regarded him warily, but she opened the book once more.

"It's a journal. My sister has one the same. I guess you could say it's ours," she said, turning the pages. Reevan peered at it, noting that some entries were in Lessie's careless scrawl, but others in a clear, unfamiliar handwriting. On some pages, the writing changed multiple times, flowing back and forth. Lessie flicked through too fast for him to read more than a few words before closing it again.

"One of Trixie's more brilliant inventions," she explained. "When one is written in, both journals bear the words. It's how we stay in contact even when she's on the other side of the godsdamned continent. She studies at the Quillkeep now. Probably taking apart some magical contraption and putting it back together as we speak."

Reevan was impressed. He had limited knowledge of how the Arcane functioned, but most who had wielded it in his presence could do little more than concentrate it in short bursts of destructive energy. To craft with it, to create a lasting enchantment that existed without the Arcane there to control it—it was exceptional. Especially for one who had not attended an Arcane school before creating it.

"Your sister is very talented," he commented.

Lessie gave the book a rare smile. "It's the result of a hundred failed attempts, and she's never been able to replicate it. It drives her mad. The first time she got it working, I wrote three sentences before the entire book burst into flames." Her face softened, and her eyes had a faraway look, like she could still see the paper burning before her. "Mama was pretty upset about the scorch marks on the kitchen table."

Reevan snorted in amusement. "And what does your mother think of your sister's Arcane skills now?"

Lessie's eyes shuttered. "Nothing. She's dead."

"My apologies." Reevan inclined his head in respect, tail twitching. He had suspected, of course, since any brief mention of either parent by Lessie had been in past tense. But she had never elaborated, so there had been a small chance of distance or estrangement being the reason her mother and father were no longer around.

Lessie sighed again, rolling up the sleeves of her shirt to her elbows before stretching her arms, her fingers lacing together behind her head.

"I haven't exactly made it common knowledge." She kept her eyes on the ceiling. "My father is gone, too. Last year."

Reevan's instinct was to stay silent. But this was the most Lessie had ever spoken about her past, at least in his presence. If she trusted him enough to tell her story, perhaps then, one day, he could trust her with his. He should relate to her, then ask her more questions.

"I do not know if my parents are still alive, but I cannot imagine the pain of knowing for sure that they are not," he mused. "Was it peaceful?"

Lessie's face darkened. She shook her head.

"The day we found the stupid god tree in the Maw, Trixie and I returned home to nothing but ash. Our homestead had burned to the ground. Mama and Papa were barricaded inside." A muscle in Lessie's jaw twitched. "Everything was just... gone. We didn't grow up with much, but... that farm was passed down for generations. Now our family's legacy is destroyed. All because we tried to stop that godsdamned ritual."

Pain and anger glittered in her eyes as she stared past Reevan into the flames of the fireplace. Reevan knew that look; she had not let herself feel the pain of the loss yet.

"It was him," Lessie spat. "That... person from the beach. I can't prove it, but I know it was. He wanted to punish us for interrupting his god harvesting." Her voice was rough, like she was trying to keep it from shaking. "He's a monster."

Reevan looked over Lessie's face, at the freckles spattered over her cheeks and across her nose that would have made her look much younger if not contrasted by the haunted look in her eyes. Her youth overshadowed by her ghosts. He supposed he looked much the same—they had both seen too much in their short lives.

In an odd way, Lessie reminded him of his own sister, albeit with much less fur. He knew he was taking many creative liberties with the comparison, considering he had not seen his sister since he was a child, and the memories were clouded. But he allowed the feeling of companionship, of familiarity, to take root. He had been alone too long. Maybe it was time to try to care about someone else. To make a friend.

Reevan did not know what to say about her loss, so he elected not to say anything, instead focusing on the facts of the conversation.

"Monster he is, but a man just the same," he said. "Perhaps it will be easier to stop him now that we have that cursed sword of his."

Lessie shivered. "I hate that thing. I wish Valandaras had left it at Crossroad, or given it to Druitt, or thrown it off a cliff. I swear, if I focus on it too long, I can hear it whispering to me."

Lessie's expression suggested she expected him to mock her, but Reevan merely looked thoughtful. The Mournblade had been used as a conduit to funnel the power of at least one god. It was not entirely far-fetched that it could hold some sinister power of its own.

"I never thanked you for coming to my aid on the beach," said Reevan. "I was dangerously close to becoming much more acquainted with the sword than I'd like."

Lessie waved away his thanks. "I can't stop thinking that he'll come for it," she muttered. "It's obviously important, and now we have it. He won't like that. And he has a way of knowing how to make you suffer. I don't have much else to lose, but he could go after Trixie, and who knows what he'll try to take from you all." She pulled her legs into the chair and hugged them, as if she wanted to curl into a ball and sob, but was stopping herself either because of his company or out of sheer spite.

"I keep dreaming about it," she whispered.

Reevan stood awkwardly next to her for a moment before reaching out and placing his hand on her shoulder. He was not sure if it was the right thing to do, but she did not shrug it off, so he supposed it offered her some small comfort.

"We will stop him, Lessandra," he said, tone matter of fact. "Because we should, and because we can, and because I, for one, do not want to take this long to heal from a wound again." He gestured to his stomach, knowing his robes concealed a jagged scar held together with the combined effort of Divine magic and mundane medicine. "Having Miss Mae at full power again has become my top priority. However, a side of revenge is always a good motivator."

Lessie did not seem comforted. Reevan looked her over, noting the exhaustion on her face, the defeat in her posture. His tail twitched. There had to be something he could say to cheer her up. That was what friends did. He glanced around, as if the walls could give him a hint on what to say, and his eyes fell on Lessie's gun, inside the holster, placed carefully around one of the bed's posts. He gestured to it and her eyes followed.

"The last thing that man will see will be your revolver pointed at his head," said Reevan.

Lessie did not reply, but the look in her eyes turned from worry to pure fire as she nodded. Even the flame of the candle flickered. Reevan decided that his work here was complete.

"It is late, you should retire," he said. "We will soon be back sleeping under the stars. It would be prudent to take advantage of a bed while you can."

He made to leave the room, but Lessie called out to him before he could.

"Hey, Reevan," she said. "Thanks for coming to talk to me. I needed it." She looked embarrassed at the admission.

"Lessandra, I am always 'here for you', as they say," Reevan replied, already halfway out the door, glancing back to see her face a bit more at peace than it was when he had entered. Her lips upturned in a half-smile of dismissal, she let out a long exhale before rubbing at her eyes and opening the journal once more.

Reevan smiled back, the gesture unfamiliar to him, before disappearing behind the heavy wooden door into the dim corridor. The latch clicked gently as he closed it. It caught slightly, since the frame did not line up anymore, and he thought about offering to fix it.

It was hours later when Reevan realised he had not brought up the one thing he had gone to Lessie to discuss. It did not matter.

They were friends now. They had time.

PART TWO
THE GOD OF WAR

20

MAE

How strange, that I should already miss Falcon's Watch.

Mae stared into the horizon, thoughts wandering as they crossed into unfamiliar territory. The journey to Saluo would take twelve or thirteen days on horseback. She had been itching to go, of course, to finally *do* something to help the Mother, but part of her had just began to feel a semblance of usefulness back at the keep. It had almost begun to feel... homely.

It was strange to think of anywhere else as home, but the thought of their plans for it gave Mae comfort. She saw the empty plains around the keep and pictured lush gardens, herbs and vegetables growing underneath wise old oaks, wildflowers exploding with colour. Some of her plans had already been set in motion. Before they had left, Lessie instructed Cutty to gather information on what the townspeople wished to improve in the area. She had encouraged Mae's vision, asking her to pick areas where they could plant certain crops, foster gardens, breathe life back into the place.

All in all, there was great potential at Falcon's Watch. Mae had felt a tendril of hope blossoming underneath the incessant numbness.

One day, I will see the entire estate in bloom as if the Mother's hand itself has touched it.

Their days were long, with little conversation between them. Mae had expected Camden to do the bulk of the talking, but to her surprise the young lord was as subdued as the rest of them. He occasionally shot furtive glances at Lessie, avoiding her, but also keeping his horse alongside hers most of the time. His behaviour reminded Mae of a wolf she had once encountered and offered to share her rations with—wary, skittish, but also inquisitive, like he was trying to gauge if she were friend or foe without getting too close. A pinch of curiosity prodded at her through the numbness at the way he watched the ranger. Lessie, for her part, did her best to completely ignore him, though her silence seemed pointed. Something had changed.

If the tension between Lessie and Camden wasn't enough to make the travel uncomfortable, both Reevan and Grundle became noticeably tenser with every step they took. It was a stark contrast to how they had been at Falcon's Watch—Mae had never seen either so relaxed. Now the dread coated them like sweat, and worsened once they crossed the border into Kalac. There were no fences, no markers; only slight changes in the climate and terrain indicated they were leaving Altaea behind.

It had been heading towards the colder season back home, mild as their winters were near the border, but the further north they travelled the more the twin suns shined brightly upon their backs. The air became drier and warmer, and the winds whipped around them, sending flurries of dust around in tiny whirlwinds.

For the most part, they were forced to keep to the roads, especially as the sparse plains of Northern Altaea gave way to the shifting sands of Southern Kalac. Their horses were hardy, but balked at the uneven footing the sand gave. Other travellers were few and far between, and seemed just as eager to avoid contact as they did. They broke for camp in the evenings, after the dusk had blanketed the land in a soft navy glow. The temperature plummeted at night, so they still lit small fires, warming themselves around them and heating their food. Lessie searched the surrounding land whenever they camped, sometimes getting lucky and returning with a rabbit she had brought down with an arrow. Sometimes Reevan or Valandaras joined her. The nights nothing was caught, they made do with hard cheeses and increasingly stale bread, but their moods suffered.

It was a surprisingly simple, peaceful journey, but it was the incessant silence that Mae had not expected. Even Lessie had resigned herself to gloomy monosyllabic conversation, when the girl usually became so uncomfortable within silences that she broke them with the first thing she could think of. Despite Mae's own thoughts being focused inward, stoking the tiny ember of the Mother's spark to make sure it stayed alight, the lack of talking began to bother her.

Mae did what she could to ease the aches of travel with elixirs she had purchased from the meagre stock of the general store down in the village. She knew better than to deplete her woefully small store of her Gift on trivial pains. Not when they had no idea what could be greeting them in

Saluo—one wrong move and they could be facing their deaths. Mother knew what they might find at their destination.

Reaching into a place within her that had once felt limitless and now felt strangely hollow was terrifying. Mae had not attempted to Change, and did not dare risk it.

I cannot even remember the last time I stayed in this fragile human body for so long. It feels wrong.

The days dragged on.

On one of the better nights, their bellies full of rabbit stew and a relatively calm day of riding behind them, Camden reached into his fine leather travelling pack and pulled out a dusty bottle of whiskey. He presented it to Lessie with a flourish, like a medal of honour after a battle. Mae hid a smile as the younger woman's eyebrows raised, tentatively accepting the bottle like it might have contained poison.

Lessie squinted at the label, eyes narrowing in the firelight.

"This is nearly a hundred years old," she said, fingers brushing over the markings. "And you're passing it around like it's nothing?"

Camden shrugged. "Only the best for us, my *lady*," he replied, unable to keep the hint of mockery from his tone as he addressed her by her now legitimate title. Lessie scowled and rolled her eyes, but uncorked the stopper and inhaled deeply before taking a mouthful.

"Godsdamn it, that's good," she said, an edge of disappointment to her voice like she was loath to admit it.

"It had better be. It's practically pre-Breach," Camden remarked, taking the bottle from her and throwing his head back as he drank. He offered the bottle to Valandaras, who shook his head.

Camden shrugged and took another swig. "I may have visited the cellars of the West Keep after deciding to join you on this adventure. The Dwarven distillery where this was made predates the gods' return, but I find it hard to believe they could make something this good without Divine intervention. Either way, my father won't notice the disappearance, so we might as well enjoy it."

Camden turned to Mae and wiggled the bottle back and forth in silent invitation. She hesitated, before reaching delicate fingers out to grasp the neck. She took a small sip and sputtered at the burning sensation. The whiskey tasted faintly of honey and wood-smoke, and something about the smell reminded her of a forge.

Mae looked at the Dwarven runes on the bottle, the golden lettering on the label faded with age, and a giggle of delight passed her lips before she knew what was happening. Valandaras's attention snapped to her, and her cheeks heated as she felt a blush rise.

"What is it?" asked Lessie, perplexed by her reaction. "Can you read Dwarvish? I could only make out the numbers."

Mae nodded. "Only a little, but enough to get the joke."

A range of curiosity and confusion bloomed on her companion's faces. Mae smiled, a warmth spreading that had little to do with the alcohol now coursing through her veins. It was the most they had interacted in days.

"It's nothing," Mae said. "They called it Kharodrum's Revenge."

She got mostly blank stares from her translation, but it was Valandaras who chuckled. Mae met his obscured eyes across the firelight and grinned, letting the amusement wash over her, coating the pain, rounding the corners of the sharp edges of her misery.

Reevan, next to her, sniffed loudly. "If you would be so kind as to explain the joke," the kitskan said politely, shifting his body to face Valandaras. "We could all use a laugh."

Valandaras shook his head, muttering something about the nuances of Dwarven humour, so Mae handed the whiskey back to Camden and approached Valandaras. She avoided the Mournblade, still wrapped in cloth and strapped to Valandaras's belt.

"Oh, go on," Mae said brightly, smoothing the skirts of her dress as she sat. "I would tell it, of course, but I think I would butcher the meaning of the story. Please, Val?"

She tried to tell him with her eyes what she could not say aloud. *We've spoken so little on this journey. It will be good for us.*

Valandaras sighed deeply. "I only know what I have been taught. To understand this, you must first know the history of the Godprison, and of the Betrayer. Do you?"

Reevan's nod was confident, while Lessie's and Camden's were much more hesitant. Grundle did neither, focused on finishing off the last of his stew, indifferent.

"I only know the basics, the same story everybody knows, and I don't remember much of it," Lessie admitted quietly, eyes on the ground. "It wasn't my father's forte."

Camden scoffed, but in agreement for once rather than ridicule.

"Count yourself lucky. It's frightfully boring, and impossible to memorise. I barely stayed awake throughout my lessons." He took another heavy swig of the bottle.

Valandaras sighed again, rubbing at his eyes over the cloth. A new mark appeared where his knuckle had brushed against the already stained fabric. Reluctantly, he began the story.

"Millennia ago—tens of thousands of years—the seven realms were much more interconnected than they are today. Gods from each realm interacted freely with each other and with those who followed them. Gifts were bestowed freely. Many gods crafted weapons of great power, sometimes even bestowing them upon their most loyal as ceremonial gifts. Every god had a domain and a purpose, whether large or small—all the Mantles were filled. The realms and gods existed harmoniously. Until one of their own sought to destroy them all.

"Vry'iin—the False God. The Betrayer."

Valandaras spoke the name like a curse. A ripple of tension flowed from him, like even mentioning the god had repercussions. The rest of the crew stilled, sensing it.

"He had many followers—hundreds of Divines, and millions of regular folk, which amplified his power. The Elven people in particular. Worship of him has now, of course, been outlawed, to the point that the true gravitas of what he accomplished is lost on those who did not witness it. This is a mistake. We can never forget what he did, for Vry'iin was the god of lies and deceit. He tricked the others into containing their power, into leaving their mantles empty. He trapped them within the great Godprison, and took all of their power into himself."

A wrath radiated from Valandaras underneath his calm demeanour, almost separate from him entirely. Mae watched him closely.

Mother, it's like it's personal for him.

"Vry'iin splintered the realms, severing the connections between them, and left them cut off from any Divinity. I do not know what happened in the others, but in Kalaraak, people believed their gods had abandoned them. They stopped their worship before forgetting them entirely. Without the power of the Divines, people died from ailments once healed without a second thought. Crops withered. The Weave itself became weak, those previously able to wield its power finding it unstable and uncontrollable. Even now, Arcanes struggle."

Which is why the Altaean nobility fears it so, Mae thought. *They cling so desperately to the advantages a Divine brings them, and persecute the Arcane they can't control.*

"In the millennia that followed, most of the gods were forgotten, as were the powers wielded by the Arcane and Divine among regular folk. Vry'iin set himself up to be the only being worthy of worship, but in doing so, he cut off the very essence of magic. He is the reason there were barely any Divines of other gods until a century ago, when the Godprison was breached and those inside managed to start reclaiming their Mantles, to regain their influence on this realm."

Mae shivered. It had been a long time, but that was one of the first shared facets of Divinity she had learned from other Divines. They all held fear that Vry'iin would return again to take their gods—and their Divinity—for himself.

"Most people are terrified to even invoke him. There are some who still refuse to speak his name to this day, calling him only the Betrayer or the False God. But he was Vry'iin, and he does not deserve the reverence these names place upon him. He imprisoned all the gods, split the realms, caused great suffering for countless lives, and then vanished. He has never been held accountable for these despicable acts."

Valandaras paused, as if steeling himself. Mae lay a hand on his forearm, feeling the soft wrappings, seeing the faint glow underneath. He did not look at her, but he breathed deeply. Although uncomfortable with his role as storyteller, he had a captive audience.

Camden sat cross-legged next to Lessie and offered her another swig of the whiskey bottle. She took it absent-mindedly, forgetting to scowl at him, eyes locked on Valandaras. Both absorbed in the story.

Reevan snorted. "I had thought this was all common knowledge. What does it have to do with the whiskey?"

"There were some gods who tried to defy Vry'iin," replied Valandaras, "once his plans became clear. Some gave up their Mantles, released their power and confined themselves to a physical body, immortal or otherwise. Others fled this realm, favoured though it was, attempting to hide from the Betrayer's curse. But there was one god who simply did nothing, and it saved him. Saved us all."

Mae smiled at the look of wonder on her companion's faces.

"The Maker?" she asked, though she knew the answer.

Valandaras nodded.

"The Maker had always been known for his... inability to connect with his brethren. Or his followers, for that matter," Valandaras said, his tone of amusement lifting the atmosphere. "Those who worship the Maker do so quietly, by creating—by forging things of great beauty and utility. His power comes from the accomplishment of a job well done. He was not one to come down to talk. The Dwarven people are especially fond of him, and did not forget his teachings. His rituals and worship are some of the most well-preserved, as they were not lost to time like most of the other gods' were."

Camden nodded gravely. "That's why the Dwarven make the best liquor," he said. "I would know. I've tried them all."

Lessie flailed her arm and smacked him in the chest, quietening him without taking her eyes off Valandaras. Mae felt her eyes crinkle as she watched them, as captivated as children being told a fairytale.

"Part of Vry'iin's plan involved claiming the realm of the damned for himself," said Valandaras. "He built a castle there, a great fortress, and in the thousands of years since his disappearance, it has never been breached. Vry'iin has his second-in-command still guarding the Vault of Whispers at this very moment. Many believe he is holed up inside, hiding from the gods he imprisoned. The realm's previous occupants were... unwelcoming. The battle for Antithiia rages on, even today. Hordes of demons and immortal beings, locked in eternal combat."

"Most people won't even call it by name," Lessie interjected. "It's bad luck, even to curse with it. Papa always said 'hell' instead."

Camden smacked her on the shoulder in an imitation of her earlier objection to his own talking, and she glared at him in outrage. Mae hid a smile behind her hands.

"I have seen Antithiia," Valandaras said. "Many Realmshifters have died there. It is a desolate wasteland, littered with the bodies of the fallen. Requiem may be the realm of the dead, but Antithiia is truly a hellscape unlike any other."

For the first time, he looked troubled. Mae shivered. Grundle had paused from eating, his bowl balanced in his lap, food forgotten. Reevan's tail twitched.

Valandaras cleared his throat. "The Maker was not happy about the realms being disconnected. He had long used the forges of Ignatia, the realm of fire, as well as the blackened demon-fires of Antithiia, to craft weapons of great power. Legend tells that it was in the realm of the damned where Vry'iin approached the Maker, spinning his web of trickery, attempting to bind him to the prison so many others had fallen for—and that the Maker did not speak a single word. He simply walked away. And when the Betrayer tried to follow him, the Maker lifted his great warhammer and cleaved the ground so completely that it tore a piece of Antithiia apart."

The only noise came from the crackling of the fire. Not a single sound came from any of them.

"The Maker claimed this piece of Antithiia for himself, renaming it Kharodrum, and has existed on it ever since. Vry'iin never challenged it. Even when the Betrayer held the power of all other gods in his hands, he could not touch the Maker, and some believe that it is because of this that the Godprison was eventually breached."

Camden whistled, leaning back on his hands in the dirt, all decorum forgotten. "The Maker sounds like my kind of god," he said. "He just wanted to be left alone."

Mae grinned, reaching for the bottle, which Lessie passed to her. It was considerably lighter than when she had last held it. She took another drink, deeper this time, and then pointed at the faded Dwarven runes on the label.

"That's exactly what he wanted," Mae said. "'Kharodrum' is Dwarvish for 'solitude'."

Valandaras gave her a tight-lipped, amused smile. "And many believe it was the creation of Kharodrum that eventually led to Vry'inn's plan falling apart, to the prison failing to hold the gods, and the reveal the False God's trickery. A piece of the Godprison cracked, splintered, just as Antithiia had. It took millennia, but the spark was there from the beginning. Vry'iin sought to be the only god, but that kind of solitude can only bring misfortune. The Maker was the immortal proof of Vry'iin's lie, and the Dwarven people never forgot him."

A smirk spread across Lessie's face as she understood the double meaning of the alcohol's name. Camden groaned.

Reevan tilted his head. "But what does Kharodrum's Revenge have to do with whiskey?" the kitskan repeated, obviously perplexed.

Mae laughed, holding the bottle high in an impromptu toast to her companions. She understood Dwarven humour, strange though it was. As the warmth of the whiskey flowed through her, she welcomed the fuzziness around her edges. The numbness receded, just enough for her to feel the glow of the eyes that now fell upon her.

"Because if you drink enough of it, all your plans will fall apart and you'll end up alone in your own personal realm of the damned," Mae proclaimed, a little louder than she had been in weeks.

The tiny spark inside her sang as the expressions around her turned from puzzlement to amusement. Eyes rolled and heads shook. Mae giggled, draining the last of the bottle.

To her delight, the one who laughed loudest was Grundle.

21

MAE

By the time the first glimpse of their destination appeared on the horizon, the crew were tired, hungry, dirty, and thoroughly sick of each other.

Even Mae's usually endless patience had worn thin, mainly due to the incessant sniping from Lessie and Camden. The perpetual silence had been broken and replaced with heated debates. Surprisingly, they had similar views on larger issues—women's place within the ranks of the Altaean military, the circumstances of the Seven's rule, Arcane rights—but more than once, a seemingly innocuous topic had devolved into an argument, which then deteriorated further into an insult-slinging match. It got so bad that Mae moved her horse up to ride beside Valandaras in silence, but she could still hear their low voices muttering behind her.

Mother, why do they disagree on the most inconsequential of things? Their arguments are pointless. If I could Change right now, it would be to something with smaller ears.

Perhaps she imagined it, but she felt a glimmer of amusement from the trickle of her Gift inside her. Like the Mother herself agreed.

As they traipsed towards Saluo, their view of the city itself was obstructed by the high sandstone walls that surrounded it, with twin guard towers framing the main gates into the city. Only the pointed spire of a single pyramid-shaped building could be seen beyond the wall, towering above, the sheer size of it dominating the skyline.

Outside of the walls, the land was dotted with dwellings—what Mae understood to be the slums of the city existing outside of Saluo itself. It was consistent with most great cities she had seen, where the less fortunate were not granted the protection of the walls the nobility had commissioned them to build.

The slums of Saluo consisted of few meagrely constructed permanent buildings interspersed with a sea of travelling tents, which spread out along the main road into the city. It looked as though there were a great many people visiting the town. The contrast of the colourful fabrics of the tents against the sands was oddly beautiful.

Valandaras halted his horse, the others quickly falling in beside him.

"Where does your brother's contact call home?" he asked Camden.

Camden put a hand to his brow, trying to block the harsh sunlight of the twins from his face. The travel had already stained the young man's skin a more golden brown than it had been before, but it suited him—like his regular pallor suggested he had spent too much of his life cooped up indoors.

"Druitt said he runs a tavern in the slums," he replied, gesturing to the buildings outside the city gates. "I figured it wouldn't be too hard to locate. Guess I was wrong."

Mae glanced back at Reevan and Grundle, both perched on the same horse. The kitskan's face was hard to read, but part of her recognised the fear that he worked hard to conceal.

The group wound their way down the hill towards the outskirts of the slums, dismounting from their horses and leading them towards the assorted tents. Valandaras located some sort of makeshift stables at the very edge, and a tawny-coloured kitskan attending them happily led their horses away once a few gold coins had made their way into her pocket. Mae lingered to watch her horse as it drank deeply from a trough, satisfied that they would receive the proper care. She adjusted the travelling pack on her back and followed the others into the labyrinth of tents.

It was delightful chaos.

People from all walks of life chatted with each other. Young children shrieked with laughter as they chased each other through the tent poles and the legs of the adults around them. Most tents appeared to be for sleeping, but some had been set up as market stalls and shops, the vendors proudly displaying their wares at the open fronts. Makeshift paths had been made between them, but they were all over the place. Various smells of food being cooked made Mae's stomach growl, and one in particular had her mouth watering as the scent of garlic and onions filled the air.

"Grundle thinks it is the wrong time of year to come," the goblin remarked from behind Reevan, shadowing the kitskan as if trying to make himself even less noticeable than usual.

Reevan sniffed. "On the contrary, my small friend. The Festival of the Falling Star is exactly the kind of cover we need."

"The what?" asked Mae, feeling a flutter of excitement. She looked again at the colourful tents. Many of them had constellations woven or painted onto the fabrics.

Reevan approached one of the nearby vendors, conversing in low tones before the kitskan offered a few gold coins in exchange for a long, lightweight robe. Reevan threw the colourful fabric around his shoulders casually. The constellation pattern woven into it glittered in the sunlight as he pulled the hood low over his head, concealing most of his face. Although now more vibrant, he immediately blended in better with those around him.

"I had forgotten this would be happening," said Reevan. "Every year, the city holds a week-long festival in celebration of the first returned god."

Valandaras stopped dead in the street.

"Haropheth?" he asked, voice a dangerous whisper.

Reevan's brow knitted in confusion, both at Valandaras's demeanour and his question.

"Lai'ireal," he replied, with an air of correcting a mistake in a small child's arithmetic. "She was the first to return to Kalac. The scholars speak of her falling from the Godprison in the middle of the night, lighting up the sky like a great burning star. I suppose we can attest to the accuracy of that depiction, now having seen one for ourselves."

He gestured to another tent, which was selling carved figurines and painted pieces of parchment that all depicted the same figure, a humanoid female wearing elaborate armour and wielding a spear.

"She is the god of war and battle," said Reevan. "It is fitting, I suppose, given that she fought her way out."

Mae knew there were many gods, of course, but none other than the Mother had ever spoken to her, and she had not deigned to learn much of their individual histories. There were so many details lost to time—after thousands of years, it was impossible to know what was real and what was embellished. The Betrayer had also stolen many stories and warped them to fit his own purpose.

Intrigued, Mae moved closer to the tent and picked up a small wooden statue. It was unpainted, beautiful in its simplicity, and she felt a glimmer of her Gift smile as she marvelled at it. There was a great level of detail that had been carved into the statue, but the woman's face had been left blank, with no features beyond her flowing hair and delicately pointed ears that suggested Elven heritage.

"Lai'ireal," Mae murmured, letting the unfamiliar name roll off her tongue. "Why does she not have a face?"

Reevan shrugged. "The Battle Maiden has many faces as well as names, whichever she chooses to wear. Personally, I think it is so more can claim to have met and been blessed by her. But it is offensive to attempt to depict her true face. Something about daring to capture her godly beauty."

"I thought you weren't a believer in gods, Reevan," Lessie commented wryly. She browsed nearby stalls casually, her fingers lingering on a lightweight robe similar to his.

He scoffed. "I am not. I have little love for the gods themselves. But it became a special interest of mine to find the discrepancies in the stories. I do not believe they have done most of what they profess to. It all seems quite... well, unbelievable."

Reevan looked around, oblivious to the scowl he now received from the carver of the statues. Mae gave the vendor a weak smile and replaced the small carving, falling into step beside the kitskan as he kept talking.

"I do not claim to be knowledgeable of the majority of the gods' hubris, but is difficult to escape here. Lai'ireal is worshipped so fervently because she appears to the city at this festival every year. It is hard to deny the existence of a god who makes herself known."

Camden, who had been transfixed by a tent selling tiny crystals strung from wire, casting brilliant rainbow reflections of light as the twin suns' rays shined through them, snapped back to their conversation.

"The god shows up to her own festival?" he asked, an edge of curiosity in his voice. "I've never heard of such a thing."

Reevan sniffed, but it was Grundle who replied.

"Grundle thinks it is not really her," he said curtly.

Mae looked down at the goblin, who was doing well at hiding the terror he must have felt at being back in his former homeland. But one hand had disappeared beneath his robe, no doubt permanently curled around the hilt of his favourite dagger. "Every person wears a mask, including the god herself. Could be anyone behind it."

Many of the makeshift stalls had indeed been offering masks of all kinds—some to cover the entire face, others just the eyes, ranging from plain and featureless to bejewelled and shimmering.

Valandaras suddenly straightened and strode forward, clearly having noticed something the rest of them had not. A flicker of irritation coursed through Mae. He could say something before barrelling off and leaving them, at least.

The crowd parted for the intimidating warrior as he walked directly towards one of the few permanent buildings that stood between the tents. It was shabby, with parts of the sandstone crumbling at the edges of its two storeys, and it had no front door, only a wide archway that was guarded by a large man who had to be of orcish blood. The massive man dwarfed even Valandaras, who stood well over six feet, and had to stoop to hear the Realmshifter as they spoke.

Mae watched as the guard nodded gruffly before gesturing inside. Her eyes drifted, noticing a few figures gathered around the side of the building, raising large mugs of ale and singing as they sat with their backs resting on the wall. A great deal of noise could be heard coming from inside.

A tavern in the slums.

Valandaras looked back at them, raising a hand to beckon them closer. Mae could feel the apprehension roll off her two companions like waves, like cornered beasts ready to lash out. She turned to Reevan.

"That robe covers you so completely, I can barely recognise you," Mae said brightly, trying to put him at ease. "Perhaps you should get one, too, Grundle."

"Way ahead of you," said Lessie, coming up behind them and tossing a bundle of fabric at the goblin. It was a brilliant purple with silver stars painted onto the hood. It looked much less elaborate than Reevan's, and the proportions were a little odd; the arms short and square. Mae stifled a smile as a couple of young children ran past wearing similar designs.

Oh, Mother, I hope he doesn't realise.

The goblin scowled but donned the robe, pulling it so low over his head that he would have been partially blind. Together, they walked towards the tavern, the giant orcish guard eyeing them warily as he let them pass inside. Valandaras lingered in the doorway, continuing to speak with the guard. Mae hesitated, then followed the rest of the crew into the tavern.

An explosion of sound met her ears, like the walls of the tavern had been treated to absorb the noise before it polluted the surrounding streets. What they had heard from outside was nothing in comparison. Sweat and alcohol assaulted her nostrils, mixed with a strange, sweet scent that might have been from the haze of smoke coming from one of the corners. It was dimly lit, with the only windows high and narrow. There were spindly chairs surrounding wooden barrels, as well as cushions strategically placed around the edges of the room, with overturned wooden crates serving as tables.

The tavern was filled with people—chatting, yelling, smoking, singing, playing cards. A group of bards in the corner played an upbeat tune made for dancing at an ear-splitting volume, and a few drunken souls were attempting to remember the steps, jostling each other and anyone who dared get too close. The bar at the far end of the room was packed, with three servers behind it, frantically making drinks for the patrons. The afternoon was young, but it seemed like time had no business here. It might as well have been the middle of the night.

Camden grinned, reminding her again of the wolf.

"Now this is a tavern," he remarked, grabbing Lessie's wrist and dragging the younger woman towards the bar. Mae smiled as she watched Lessie rip her arm out of his grasp and hiss at him, before they were swallowed up by the crowd and Mae could no longer see them. Reevan and Grundle shifted towards the edges of the room, whether to hide or simply observe, and for a second, Mae stood alone.

She realised her mistake too late and panic gripped her. She hated crowds. There were too many people. Too much sound overlapping, too many voices. She closed her eyes and tried to breathe, but her stomach lurched like she was going to be sick. Desperately, she reached inside for her Gift, to soothe herself. Warmth skittered across her palms, the emerald glow too dulled for anyone to notice, but it was enough to bring her some small comfort. She breathed in deeply before a jolt of unexpected physical contact had her eyes flying open.

A sweaty patron had broken away from the impromptu dance floor and bumped into her, reaching his hands to her shoulders to steady himself. The half-empty ale he had been drinking clattered to the floor, splashing both of their legs.

"Ah, sorry, love," he slurred, eyes unfocused as he gripped her, hands sticky and hair plastered to his face.

Mae froze.

"Lemme buy you a drink," the drunk said. He gave her an exaggerated look up and down, and he was much too close, and Mae felt her pulse thunder in her neck. He ignored her protests and swung an arm around her. "Whatever you like. 'S an apology."

It was all right; he was just intoxicated and unbalanced, and once he got another drink, he would wander off—

"Yer too pretty to be alone in here, Red," he leered, showing yellowed teeth. "What's a lovely thing like you doin' here? You lost?"

He reeked of ale, and Mae tried to suppress the revulsion she felt, the rage of knowing if she could Change, she would grow fangs and claws and scare him sober. In all her years, she hated how these situations still made her freeze—the urge to scream stifled by the subconscious need to be polite. She could feel her pulse beating wildly, instinctual warnings flooding through her.

She tried to duck out from underneath his arm, but the drunk's fingers dug into the exposed skin of her shoulder.

"You look like you've got Fae in you, Red," he slurred, frowning. A jolt of adrenaline surged through Mae as a new level of panic hit her.

Mother, help me.

The drunk let out a sudden howl of pain.

Mae felt a tug backwards as his hand disappeared from around her, fingers catching in strands of her hair. Somehow, even in the pandemonium of the tavern, she heard the sickening crunch of bones as the drunk's fingers were crushed inside the iron grip of Valandaras. He stood behind them, fury radiating from him like his very glow was laced with it.

"She is not alone," he said, voice quiet as death. "And she is not lost."

The drunk had fallen to his knees, sobbing as he cradled his broken fingers. Valandaras leaned down, towering over him.

"Put a hand upon her again, and you will mourn the loss of both," he murmured into the man's ear. The drunk seemed too far gone to respond, tears streaming down his ruddy face, holding his now useless hand in his lap. A number of people nearby gave him disgusted looks. Mae could not meet their eyes. A flush stained her cheeks and burned her eyes, the panic still coursing through her veins, screaming at her to run while rooting her to the spot.

Valandaras straightened, dismissing the man, and silently offered Mae his arm without looking at her. Breathing deeply, she took it, latching her fingers onto him and trying to calm her racing heart.

"Thank you," she whispered, barely audible in the din.

Valandaras merely nodded. A few nearby patrons who had noticed the altercation gave them a wide berth, and they carved a path towards the bar, which was little more than an oversized wooden plank resting upon a series of barrels.

There were three bartenders working behind it, two humans and a kitskan. The kitskan was tall and dark-furred, with brilliant violet eyes that sparkled with quiet intelligence. She moved around the other two with ease, preparing drinks at twice the speed they did, and most of the tavern's patrons seemed to gravitate towards her end of the bar.

They melted away for Valandaras, however, so Mae soon found herself staring into the face of the kitskan girl, who smiled warmly.

"Welcome to Bueno's, best tavern this side of the Trimount," she said, half shouting above the noise. "What can I get for you?"

Valandaras did not return her smile. "Bueno."

22

VALANDARAS

Rage.

All Valandaras could hear was the thundering of his own heartbeat pounding in his ears. All he could feel was vehement fury rushing through his bloodstream. Adrenaline surged through him, warring with the logical knowledge that Mae was safe, that he had protected her, that she was usually perfectly capable of protecting herself. What had gone wrong? What if he had taken too long speaking with the guard? What if he hadn't found her in time? A dozen scenarios swirled in his mind, each ending with him committing acts of outrageous violence he would normally advise against.

He waited at the end of the bar in silence, trying to still his mind. Trying to keep his feet planted, instead of striding back into the crowd to finish what he had started. Mae shifted uncomfortably next to him, smoothing at her skirts, her golden eyes darting around the packed room. He knew she was looking for the one who had accosted her. The interaction had rattled her, though she pretended to be unaffected.

The black-furred kitskan had disappeared at his request, to find Druitt's contact and inform him of their arrival. Whether this Bueno would have anything useful for them was yet to be seen, but for the moment, all he could do was wait while his instincts screamed to tear the place apart.

Valandaras had to fight to keep a snarl from escaping his lips, clenching his hands into fists as the image replayed in his mind of the man's grubby fingers gripping Mae's shoulder, the fear that had coated her as they pulled at the fabric of her dress.

Those fingers will not grip anything again without difficulty and pain, he thought, willing the wrath in his chest to settle to a simmer. *I should have broken the other hand for good measure.*

Being a Realmshifter had a cost. His anger was often not his own, and when it was, it was enhanced beyond normal reasoning. He had reacted without thinking. He knew his Pod leader would be disgusted with him for such an overt display of violence, for dealing such harsh justice in full view of the public. He could practically hear Elastrad berating him, insisting in an icy voice that interfering in the lives of others is forbidden, that it would only bring pointless anger to distract him. There was only the Path to walk.

Her objections would have fallen on deaf ears. Valandaras had never faltered from his Path. Despite walking it alone for the past few years, he was as focused on it as the day he had stepped into the realm of Kalaraak and left his Pod behind for the first time. He had been raised to be separate from regular society, but that did not mean he could wilfully ignore wrongdoing. Being a Realmshifter did not exempt him from a moral conscience.

He had also never vocalised what he had come to suspect—that Mae was put in his Path because she was part of it. Protecting her *was* protecting his Path.

Mae relaxed visibly as the rest of their crew converged on the spot where they stood. Camden held his arms high above the people around him, a glass in each hand, and Lessie's scowl alone parted the crowd of revellers before her. Reevan approached from the side of the room, having slunk around the edges, Grundle concealed behind him like a deadly shadow.

"If this is how they celebrate during the day, remind me never to come here at night," Reevan remarked, holding his new robe aloft to prevent it from dragging along the floor. "I cannot imagine—"

The black-furred kitskan reappeared behind the bar.

"Thank you all so much for waiting," she half-shouted above the roar of the crowd. "If you go through that door over there, next to Orembar," she pointed to the very back of the tavern at an unassuming door with a grumpy-looking kitskan standing beside it, "and head up the stairs, then he will see you. He's in a pretty good mood today, so you should be fine, but don't touch anything on his shelves, he doesn't like that. Good luck!"

Her eyes glanced over all of them and lingered curiously on Reevan, who stood with his mouth still open, staring at her. She smiled at him, giggling awkwardly before returning to her duties. Reevan continued to watch her, transfixed, and did not move when the rest of them made to walk away from the bar.

"I have decided I am extremely parched and in desperate need of a drink," Reevan said quickly, but Lessie had already grabbed his forearm.

"Come on," she muttered, pulling him towards the door.

Reevan fought it, letting his feet drag as he was ushered away, eyes locked on the kitskan behind the bar like he did not want to look at anything else now that he had seen her.

Mae's eyes sparkled with amusement as she watched Reevan struggle in Lessie's grip. It chased away the lingering stress from her earlier encounter.

"Do you believe in love at first sight, Val?" she asked, with a playful grin so reminiscent of before her Gift had left her that he felt a hitch in his chest.

There she is, he thought.

"I am not sure I believe in love at all, lioness," Valandaras replied honestly. Too much of what people called 'love' seemed to bring only pain. It was more akin to an addiction or dependence than any true connection.

The smile on Mae's face faltered, and he silently cursed himself.

"But if I did," he added hastily, "I would agree that Reevan has just found it."

Why can I never hold my tongue around this woman?

The grumpy-looking kitskan guarding the door gave them all a glare before opening it, and they filed through one by one. They made their way up a small flight of stairs to the tavern's upper floor, which consisted of a number of doors that led to rooms that would be rented out to travellers. The kitskan did not speak to any of them, eyeing them suspiciously, but he marched towards a door at the far end of the hall and knocked curtly before opening it to allow them to pass.

Valandaras stepped through last. The kitskan pulled the door shut behind him, and all the noise from the bar was silenced so completely it was unsettling. The door—or perhaps the room itself—had to be enchanted by Arcane means for it to be that soundproof.

The small room seemed to be an ostentatiously decorated study, dominated by bookshelves and a large desk. A thick rug woven with rich purples and greens blanketed the floor, as well as a number of cushions large enough for sitting. Shelves lined both the walls, with shiny knick-knacks and potions full of glittering mystery liquids interspersed between the thousands of books. Colourful weaves of fabric draped over the ceiling, creating a canopied effect. In one corner was a tiny, curved bar, made of rich wood and surrounded by cushion-topped stools.

Behind the large desk hung a tapestry of a map. It commanded the focus of the room, drawing the eye. It was meticulously plotted, depicting the various lands of Kalaraak in stunning detail. Kalac, Altaea, and the Freemeres were all covered in markers and landmarks. Even the lesser-known regions and remote islands were filled in.

I have never seen such a rendering of the entire realm before, Valandaras thought. *Most of these countries care little for their neighbours.*

There were two people already in the room when they entered. An impeccably dressed human man sat at the desk, his slippered feet balanced on a stack of books as he perused one. The other, a young woman with shaggy dark hair, looked them over and gave them all a sly smile as she lounged on a stool at the bar. A toothpick danced between her lips as she chewed on it casually.

"I guess that's my cue to leave," she said, hopping down from her seat and giving the man behind the desk an elaborate bow. The amusement in her eyes gave the impression it was not entirely respectful. "We can talk about it later, boss."

She breezed past them quickly, but not before Valandaras caught sight of the deep scar running vertically over her right eye. She yanked open the door, the commotion of the tavern spilling into the room once more as she lingered in the doorway, seemingly waiting for approval.

The man at the desk waved a hand in a dismissive shooing motion, light glinting off the rings he wore.

"Yes, yes. Time is money, Greyholme, so go make some more," he said, not looking up from the book he currently held open on his lap. "You may not keep track of what you owe me anymore, but I do." His voice was pleasant, with no underlying malice, but the message was clear.

The woman merely smirked over her shoulder as she left the room. Total silence fell upon them all once more as soon as the door clicked closed.

The man made no movement to acknowledge their presence, flicking through the pages of his book, until Mae cleared her throat nervously and his eyes snapped up to them.

"Ah, yes, of course," he said, his face breaking into a wide smile, and he closed the book and rose from his seat. "Welcome, friends. Welcome to Bueno's. I am the one and only Bueno himself. Eyes and Ears of Saluo, and indeed perhaps all of Kalac, as well as the owner of the finest tavern this side of the border."

Bueno was of average height, with coppery-brown skin and dark hair that curled past the collar of his tunic. His sparkling eyes were such a deep brown they were almost black, framed with dark lashes and rimmed with kohl. The clothes he wore were clearly of fine make, his robes embroidered with glimmering thread, the fabric a stark white—which in itself was a statement. It meant he could afford to keep the fabric clean. A powerful message to send in the slums.

Bueno's dark eyes roamed over them all, sizing them up, and he gestured to the cushions on the floor as if they were thrones.

"Please, sit," he said, leaning on the front of the desk. "Tell me of your travels. Was it a long and perilous journey? Did you encounter any strange beasts? I hear the roads between our two great lands can be most dangerous. Sit, sit, make yourselves at home."

Valandaras elected to stay standing, leaning against the far wall, and Grundle shadowed him, the goblin's glower marred by his colourful children's robe. Mae and Reevan made themselves comfortable on the floor, though the kitskan kept his hood up, casting shadows upon his face, and his tail twitched repeatedly. Lessie's eyes had narrowed, like she was trying to decide if Bueno's tone was mocking them or if that was simply how he spoke. She sat next to Mae and fidgeted with her clothing, uncomfortable with the positioning.

Camden's eyes darted between the cushions and the stools at the bar. He was still holding the glass from the tavern, and he finished the drink inside before he approached Bueno the way one might approach a strange dog. Cautiously.

"My brother Druitt sends his regards," he said, offering his free hand in greeting. "He is most grateful you agreed to host us."

Bueno shook Camden's hand firmly and gave him an exaggerated look over.

"Ah, yes, I see it. You DeFalcone men do have such sharp jawlines," he commented, winking at the young lord before returning to his seat behind the desk. "Druitt spent some time in Saluo a few years back, dealing with all that unpleasantness with the border skirmishes." He waved a hand at the elaborate tapestry behind him. "I had to update the map three times. Most annoying."

Bueno steepled his fingers and glanced at each of them in turn, as if expecting them all to introduce themselves. Names were exchanged—some given freely, others muttered reluctantly—as well as a few pleasantries. Valandaras could tell that Bueno enjoyed the dance, but that he also valued his time. He did not allow the conversation to drift before getting to the heart of it.

"Now, let us discuss what has brought you to me," Bueno said. "Druitt asked for a favour, but he would not speak of what it was. I must say, it piqued my interest. It must have been big for you all to travel so far. I hope it's not about that strange rock formation out in the desert? My scouts never come back from that one, I'm afraid. Most disappointing."

Mae had wrapped her hands around her knees, curling into herself. She seemed overwhelmed. Her glow was dimmed.

"We seek a way to return the stolen power of a god," Valandaras said quickly, cutting off Bueno's tirade about the loss of good adventuring scouts. Bueno blinked at him before smiling again—the grin of a man who knew too much.

"Ah, a Realmshifter," he remarked, reaching for a half-empty glass on his desk. He drained it, smacking his lips together loudly, before placing the glass carelessly onto a stack of papers. "I'd have thought Haropheth would be running out of realms to put you all on by now. Has he finally given up on his vengeance? Or has he simply branched out into helping lesser gods?"

The tension in the room shifted.

"This does not concern Haropheth," Valandaras said firmly, tone suggesting the subject was not open to discussion. Mae twisted to face him, her eyes brimming with questions, but he did not dare to look at her. He worked hard to keep his face neutral as the mention of Haropheth, thrown out so casually, thundered through him. Druitt had said that Bueno could be trusted, and that his knowledge of Kalac's secrets was unmatched. It stood to reason that he would know many things others would not.

But it concerns me that this man speaks of the purpose of the Path without a second thought.

Bueno waved a hand dismissively. "Yes, yes, you're all very mysterious. I suppose I can put a pin in that. Which god do you seek? And how was the power 'stolen', exactly?"

Together, Mae and Lessie described the events of the Mother's essence returning, of the rituals they had tried to prevent. They were occasionally interrupted by Reevan, who added details neither had been close enough to see. Valandaras remained silent, watching the strange man, gauging his reactions.

Bueno listened for the most part, chiming in to clarify a point or two, but was mainly content to let them speak. When they had finished, he said nothing as he crossed the room to the bar. He disappeared behind it, and the crew shared glances between them as they heard rummaging and the clinking of glass. Bueno straightened, holding two bottles of dark wine, a single bottle of light wine and one of a dark golden liquid, and placed them onto the bar with a clunk.

"This calls for a stronger drink or two, my friends," he said, opening one of the wines, flinching dramatically as the cork rocketed out of the stem and struck the far wall. He took a swig from the bottle before pouring them all a glass. "What a delightful mess you all have stumbled into."

Camden, who had seated himself at one of the bar stools, took one of the wines and drank deeply.

"It's been an interesting few weeks," he commented drily.

Bueno laughed. "That, my boy, is an understatement. I cannot say for sure, but it appears as though you have all become entangled in a plot to disrupt the hierarchy of the gods themselves. Yes, yes. How exciting." He opened the bottle of golden liquid and began pouring it into smaller, square glasses. "Some of the Mahejerai have always been ambitious, but I did not think they would go quite this far. Their new leader has certainly been making waves."

Valandaras frowned at the title, the term unfamiliar.

"Who are the Mahejerai?" he asked, fixing Bueno with a hard stare, the cloth over his eyes doing little to disguise his intensity.

Lessie twisted back at him, eyes widening. "Is that who we saw on the beach? The *Majaheri*?" she asked, struggling to pronounce the foreign word. "Do they work for the Emperor?"

Bueno delicately sniffed at one glass filled with honey-coloured liquid before taking a small sip.

"Mahejerai, love. Say it with me. Ma-heh-ZHER-eye," he said, deliberately over-enunciating each syllable. Nobody spoke with him, but Bueno seemed not to notice. "Wonderful. The Mahejerai are the order who study the powers of the Arcane and Divine, have been doing so for millennia. They have factions and temples all over Kalac. I'm sure you've spotted the one in Saluo. Even without entering the city, it's impossible to miss. Dreadful, pointy eyesore."

Bueno grimaced toward the window, where the spire of a pyramid could be seen even from a distance, looming over the city wall. The building had to be thirty stories high.

"I have my theories about them, of course," said Bueno, "but they tend to be quite secretive about their research. Most frustrating. They are not governed by the Perqeit—the lord of our city, as you would call them—or the Emperor, really, though he would not wish you to know it."

"They don't answer to your Emperor?" Lessie asked, tone incredulous. "How is that possible?"

Bueno shrugged. "Arcane power is sacred in Kalac. Anyone who shows a disposition to it is recruited into the ranks of the Mahejerai before long, where they learn to wield it to further Kalac's success. Divinity is even more revered. They are closest to the gods, and therefore worthy of worship. A powerful Divine in Kalac could do practically anything they wished to; they answer to no-one but their gods."

Valandaras felt the attention in the room shift towards Mae, who looked uncomfortable with so many sets of eyes on her. What a life she could have led, had she simply been born north of the border. In Altaea, Divines were little more than indentured servants.

"As it is, there are plenty of Mahejerai across Kalac who lead perfectly normal Arcane lives," Bueno continued. "But as for Saluo, let us just say that their faction has always been... fanatical, both in their recruitment and their practices. It does not surprise me that they would make a power grab for Divinity."

"Can you help us?" asked Mae, voice cracking. She rose gracefully from her cushion and crossed the room, standing in front of the bar. She looked at Bueno with pleading eyes. "Can you help me?"

Bueno gave her a kind smile and pressed a wine glass into her hands.

"I will do what I do best, my Divine dear," he replied. "I will help you acquire the knowledge you seek."

Valandaras glanced between them. Was Bueno offering them knowledge to put back together a god, or how to stop a madman from becoming one?

"Of course, you will be doing me a service, in return for my generosity," said Bueno, smiling merrily. "Call it a verbal contract, or a favour if you must, but this is my price. I wish to know as much as possible about what goes on inside that pointy little palace the Mahejerai call home. It has long irritated me to have such an unforgivable gap in my knowledge."

Lessie frowned. "How are we supposed to get inside there if you can't?" she asked, voice barely concealing her frustration. She stomped over to stand beside Mae, the luxurious rug muffling the thud of her boots. "Do you even know how to help us stop them, then? I thought you were supposed to already have the answer to everything."

A weaker man may have crumbled under Lessie's glare, but Bueno's smile only widened. He began to slide her a glass of the dark wine, but Camden put out a hand and blocked it, shaking his head casually and gesturing to the honey-coloured liquid. Bueno shrugged before offering the whiskey to Lessie instead.

"I deal in favours and secrets, girl. What kind of businessman would I be if I gave them all away at our very first meeting? Tell me one of yours, and perhaps I'll give you one of mine."

Lessie took the glass but did not drink, staring him down.

Bueno seemed unperturbed. "Part of having the answer to everything is knowing where to ask questions." He raised his own glass to his lips and drank delicately. "And I know where you should ask them."

Mae glanced back at Valandaras, the hope blossoming on her face so beautiful it nearly brought him to his knees. *I cannot let her down.*

"Where?" she asked excitedly. "Where should we go?"

Bueno gave her a knowing grin. "In this case, it is not where, but who. Who better to ask of restoring a god's power than one of their own?"

Mae's face was blank. Lessie crinkled her nose in confusion. It was Reevan who first understood the meaning of Bueno's words.

"You are suggesting we speak with Lai'ireal?"

Bueno gave them all an amused smile. "My furry friend, that is exactly what I am suggesting. How fortunate that you should find yourselves in Saluo during the festival, on the eve of the Night of Many Faces. I will ensure your attendance."

The Battle Maiden. The god of war herself. Of course, where else in Kalaraak could they speak with a god directly? Lai'ireal was one of the very few gods who appeared in their realm. Valandaras knew little of her, but had heard stories. She was ruthless, intelligent, and would not take kindly to a plot to steal her power.

And Bueno was promising them an audience with her.

This is certainly an interesting twist in the Path.

Bueno's face held the smugness of a man who held an unbeatable hand, and his eyes twinkled as he raised his empty glass in a toast to the room.

"To the success of my newest employees," he declared. "Tomorrow's festivities could prove illuminating in more ways than one."

23

VALANDARAS

Valandaras sat at the end of the modest bed, staring at the far wall without seeing. Truly alone, for the first time in what felt like weeks. The lack of privacy had been exhausting.

Bueno had given them all rooms, insisting that they rest after their long journey. He had waved away their objections, but had also made a point to mention that they would enjoy a discounted rate, so they would not mistake his generosity for free lodging. They were not in a position to argue, since their other option was to make the long trek back to the outskirts to set up their sleeping rolls. The self-proclaimed Eyes and Ears of Saluo had also presented them all with a small token before retiring once more to his study.

Valandaras turned the small silver coin over in his hands, not looking at it, but feeling the raised edges as his fingertips brushed the engravings. One side depicted the pyramid of the Mahejerai, the other a series of falling stars over a palace of some kind. Bueno had said the coin held no monetary value—it could not be spent or traded—but it would grant them access into the city of Saluo itself.

How we gain an audience with Lai'ireal is still yet to be determined, however, Valandaras thought. *I doubt it will be as easy as flashing a coin.*

His attention drifted to the Mournblade. He had placed it next to his shield and falchion, still wrapped in cloth. A dark power seemed to hum from the blade. Usually it was barely noticeable, but the silence of the room seemed to amplify it. Valandaras had his theories about what it could mean. He closed his eyes, letting thoughts of the Mournblade drift across his mind untethered. He needed to relax to sort through them.

The Mournblade allowed the Mother's essence to be syphoned through it, so it is a conduit for the power of the gods. The damage it inflicted seemed worse than regular wounds, and the recovery from them took much longer, even with Divine healing. It thrums as though it is alive, it whispers.

It could very well be a Sliver.

Slivers were ancient artefacts forged by the gods themselves, and they contained an infinitesimally small mote of the Divinity of the god they had been created by. The few Valandaras had seen had been blades, but there were records of some gods fashioning shields, warhammers, or other types of weapon. Most had passed into myth, lost relics of the millennia before the Godprison.

Slivers were sought by the Realmshifters—and others—for many reasons; the main one being they were the weapons of the gods. Immensely powerful, but dangerous to wield, and they could easily kill a mortal being if mishandled. The notion that one could currently be sitting in the room with him was alarming, and a tinge of guilt washed over him as he contemplated it.

If the Mournblade were indeed a Sliver, then his mission on this realm was complete. He would be expected to return to his Pod as soon as possible, now that he had procured a weapon capable of aiding him in his Path. Capable of hunting the Betrayer.

If it is what I think, then I must—

A gentle knock on the door startled Valandaras out of his thoughts, the silver coin slipping from his fingers and clattering to the floor. He cleared his throat before answering.

"Enter."

The small wooden door creaked inward, and a sheet of auburn hair poked around it.

"Hey, Val. I thought I'd find you in here," Mae said, lingering in the doorway. "I'm in the one across the hall. Can I come in?"

Valandaras nodded his assent and she swept into the room, skirts swishing as she leaned down to pick up the coin, which had stopped short on its roll for the exit. She flicked it towards him, her eyes crinkling in delight as he caught it reflexively. She looked physically refreshed, clean, like she'd managed to shed the stress of the travel.

"Bueno's bathing rooms aren't quite the luxury of the West Keep, but any water is welcome after that journey," Mae said, running a hand through her hair. The waves were still damp, the colour muted.

Valandaras nodded again, turning the coin over absently. He hadn't thought about bathing yet. It hadn't seemed important.

Mae paused before perching lightly on the side of the bed. She did not face him, but he noticed her slight hesitation, like she was toying with saying things she was unsure of. He kept his eyes on the Mournblade.

Finally, Mae spoke. "Thank you for earlier, in the bar. I... I just froze." She shook her head, like she were annoyed with herself. "I can take on a possessed shipwreck without breaking a sweat, but one drunk in a bar and I completely lose my head."

Valandaras gave her a small smile. "We all have our weaknesses, lioness. It does not make you weak."

Mae sighed. "It took me to a different time. Where I could not speak up, for fear of being seen as impolite." Her voice wobbled.

At this, Valandaras turned to face her. He did not let the light from his eyes fall directly on her, but he shifted so that she knew she had his full attention.

"People like that do not deserve courtesy," he said. "You owe them nothing. Never be so polite that you forget your power."

She smiled, but her face was forlorn. "What's left of it."

"You grow stronger again every day," he said, slightly louder than necessary. "I can feel it. The Mother grows stronger as you do."

Mae smiled again, a sad smile that did not reach her eyes. One he saw too often now, that he could tell she was faking.

"We can only hope."

They sat in silence. It was an easy, comfortable thing, borne of many nights with only the other for company, when neither wished to speak. Most people found silence jarring, the need to fill it with idle conversation winning out before long. He knew she loved to talk, but to sit with him like this was her gift to him, in a way. The silence that only comes when two people understand each other.

They said nothing for a few minutes, but one glance told him Mae was looking at him sideways from underneath her lashes. Valandaras held in a laugh. She was not subtle in the slightest.

"Whatever you came here to ask of me, ask it, lioness," he said quietly, and her cheeks flushed. A crooked smile blossomed on his face before he could stop it. Perhaps she would—

"Who is Haropheth?"

Valandaras blinked. *That is... not the question I expected.*

Mae looked embarrassed, like she felt she had infringed on his privacy to ask. In a way, she had. But to see her curious again, to see her eyes light up...

Valandaras cleared his throat. He could tell her. The stories were sacred, but not explicitly forbidden. It was merely frowned upon to speak of them to outsiders.

"The simple answer is that he is my god," he said. "But the reality is much more complicated. Haropheth is the father of all Realmshifters."

Mae's eyes widened. He suddenly found it much harder to look at her.

"According to our teachings, he was the first of the gods to Breach—though I suppose that is now of some dispute," Valandaras said. "He was once the god of wisdom and judgement. But he was close with Vry'iin, like brothers, and the betrayal hurt him beyond most gods. He struck a deal with another while in the Godprison, allowed them to bind their power to his, to unravel his carefully constructed system of core beliefs. Some believe he went mad inside the Prison, or he would have never agreed to it.

"Haropheth gave up everything he was, even his former Mantle, and became a being of pure vengeance."

Valandaras felt a simmering rage that did not belong to him shiver underneath his skin, glowing brightly.

"But once he made the Breach and cracked the Godprison, Haropheth could not find Vry'iin, and it drove him even more mad. He interrogated the Divines of the False God. He cursed the Elven people, banishing them to Adrai'ica when they refused to answer his questions. He searched for the Betrayer for a decade, roaming between the realms, struggling with the failing sanity of his conjoined form—before conceding he would need others to help fulfil his vow."

Valandaras looked down at his arms, uncovered and unarmoured, the gentle golden glow humming underneath the skin. The disconnected anger simmered beneath the surface.

"That is why the Realmshifters exist. We are chosen as infants and raised as his warriors, as Haropheth himself is too unstable to hold a mortal form for long in any one realm. He will never rest until he finds Vry'iin and the Betrayer is made to answer for his crimes. Haropheth blesses us with some of his own Gifts to aid our search, and we burn with the light of his holy vengeance."

Valandaras tried not to focus on how Mae's eyes were alight with interest, how her full lips had parted in awe, how her whole body had turned to give him her undivided attention.

Mae had been silent the entire time he spoke, but she now tilted her head curiously.

"So you do not choose to serve him?" she asked.

Valandaras considered her question carefully. Strangely, it sounded like more than one.

"No. I was born to it; I cannot walk away. It is my Path."

"I see." Her tone was unreadable.

His brow furrowed beneath the cloth. "Could you choose to stop serving the Mother?'

A touch of grief blanketed her features and he regretted the question.

"I have done so before," Mae said, smiling wistfully. "She did not mind. She welcomed me back when I was ready."

They fell into another peaceful silence. Valandaras had long noticed how Mae did not take away his feeling of being alone, in a way he could not quite explain. But he welcomed it. His primal need for solitude, his simple relief at not having to hold himself a certain way, was not interrupted by her presence. Like she simply passed through the shield he held around himself from the rest of the world. As if it did not exist.

After a time, Mae pulled a folded bundle of material from her pocket. She fiddled with it nervously before shoving it into his hands.

"I found these in the bathing rooms. I thought you could use them for your eyes—your coverings."

Valandaras took her offering, turning them over. The long strips of white cloth were soft, like they had been washed a hundred times, but still sturdy, with no fraying or weakening of the fabric.

"I already have coverings," he said.

She gave him an exasperated look he didn't quite understand. "Yes, and they're filthy. They must have at least a decade's worth of grime coated on them. I thought it might be time for a new set."

Mae reached out a delicate finger, as if to run it along the cloth covering his eyes, and he tried to contain his instinct to jerk away. She hesitated, then placed a fingertip onto his cheek, where patches of skin were sore and angry underneath his glow. The slightest pulse of emerald settled into the raised edges of the largest scratches and smoothed them away. The effect was soothing, like she had spread ice-cold water over his face.

"They seem to irritate you. I thought it might help."

Valandaras reached a hand to his cheekbone, feeling the rough fabric scrape against his newly healed skin. The cloth he wore had not been removed since he set foot on Kalaraak. It was a Realmshifter's duty to protect those around them from their raw power, to keep it contained. They were given their cloth to wear before they even truly understood what it meant, and it was his Pod leader's responsibility to supply them. He had never thought to change them himself.

But Mae had seen this pile of fabric, and thought of him. A strange feeling bloomed in his chest.

"You are right," he murmured. "I shall change them after I bathe."

Mae beamed. "You might want to do so soon," she laughed, rising from the bed. "From the way Camden was talking, I think he intends to spend the rest of the afternoon in there. He asked Bueno if drinks could be brought in to him."

Valandaras watched her as she crossed the room to the door, at how her long, delicate fingers grasped the handle but lingered.

"Thank you, lioness."

She looked back at him over her shoulder. "I can look out for you, too, Val. Don't forget that."

She gave him a final wisp of a smile before disappearing, the latch of the door clicking gently behind her. The silence in the room became strangely lonely.

Valandaras sat in solitude, staring at the Mournblade once again, feeling the soft cloth in his hands and the ghost of her fingertips on his skin. The obsidian steel offered no answers. He closed his eyes.

Yes, the Mournblade could possibly be a Sliver, but even if it was—it could be unstable after having been used as a syphon, and they did not know which god it claimed allegiance to. It would be unwise to attempt to wield it, to bring it to his Pod, without first learning more about where it came from. If he were wrong about it being a Sliver, he would simply be sent back to Kalaraak to continue his search, having wasted valuable time. Elastrad would chew his ear off, and Haropheth himself would be furious at the delay in his search.

I cannot stray from this Path, he thought. *Not just yet. I need to ground myself, to think about what this could mean. I cannot risk being incorrect about where following this particular Path might take me.*

Valandaras knew his reasoning was logical. That if he were to explain it to his Pod leader, she would accept it.

But as he settled himself onto the floor and began to meditate in earnest, his thoughts continued to drift towards the door across the hall.

24

LESSIE

Lessie awoke to the first rays of sunlight streaming across an unfamiliar ceiling, and it took a few moments before she remembered where she was. She fought the urge to pull the blanket over her head and pretend she hadn't.

She vaguely remembered coming back to the room she was to share with Mae after bathing, intending on a short rest before going to find something to eat. Instead, she had passed out before the Divine had even returned. She rubbed the sleep from her eyes and her stomach growled.

Lessie dressed quietly, trying to not disturb Mae, who was fast asleep curled up on the other cot. She padded across the wooden floor in her socks, holding her boots as she eased the door closed. The familiar process reminded her painfully of home, where her sister had not appreciated her early risings from their shared room.

I don't think Mae would have thrown anything at me if I woke her up, though.

Lessie descended the narrow stairs, the sounds of the tavern becoming louder with each step. It was a different kind of din in the early hours. There were groups of patrons enjoying breakfast; gathered around the low tables piled high with an assortment of food. In an amusing contrast, a number of ale-soaked revellers remained on what was left of the dance floor, some still nursing the last of their drinks, others sleeping on what had been the stage where the band played.

Lessie spotted a familiar face and headed to the bar, where Reevan sat perched upon a spindly stool, eating what appeared to be porridge. One of the kitskan's ears twitched in her direction, but he gave no other indication that she had approached. His attention was fixed solely on the black-furred bartender from the night before, who now poured milk into a dusty ale glass and set it in front of him. She smiled warmly as Lessie took the stool next to Reevan.

"This is one of your friends, isn't it, Reevan?" the bartender said, giving him an expectant look as if he would formally introduce them. Reevan missed the cue entirely. Lessie frowned, her eyebrows creasing together before she caught herself.

Friends? I didn't think Reevan considered us that close.

She didn't know if the customs in Kalac were different, so she did what felt natural. She extended a hand to the woman and gave her a polite nod.

"Lessie."

"I'm Callira," the bartender replied, taking Lessie's hand in her own, careful to keep her clawed fingers retracted. The fur was soft and warm. "It really is wonderful to have you all. We get visitors from all across Kalaraak, especially for the Falling Star Festival, but not usually from Altaea, unless I suppose they just don't say they're from Altaea? I know there's been some tension between our countries before, but I think it's silly. Reevan was telling me all about the land where you live. Are you really a Countess? That must be interesting! I bet it's a lot of work, though, to be in charge of so much land."

Callira said all of this very fast, like her mouth was struggling to keep up with the thoughts in her head. It took Lessie a moment to consolidate it. She blinked, processing.

Gods above. Did he tell her all of our business?

Lessie shot Reevan a look, which the kitskan avoided. She'd been enjoying not having to think about her nobility, and the reminder jolted unpleasantly in her gut. If she'd been able to, she'd offer the title to either of them right there. Ridiculous, archaic Altaean laws.

"It's a... recent change," she mumbled, unwilling to correct the title or discuss it further.

Callira only gave her a sweet smile. "You'll have to tell me the story, one day. I would love to hear it. I was telling Reevan about my own life, and I got a little carried away. I've been talking his ears off! I'm surprised he managed to get a word in enough to mention any of you. I've always wondered what Altaea was like," she said, violet eyes shining.

The kitskan woman spoke at length of wanting to travel, to see Altaea, and of wanting to build and own her own tavern one day. Lessie smiled and nodded along woodenly until Callira paused to take a breath, not trusting herself to know when a sentence had finished.

Reevan listened to every word, enraptured, and when Callira finally finished speaking, he turned to Lessie awkwardly and gestured to the signs behind the bar. They were covered in cheery, bold paint that depicted complicated-looking drinks with fancy embellishments.

"Callira invented all of these recipes from scratch," he said.

Lessie looked them over without reading them.

"Impressive," she remarked, trying and failing to appear interested, but it didn't matter. Callira had disappeared through a folding half-door behind the bar that must have led to the kitchens, returning a few moments later and placing another bowl of porridge in front of Lessie. A drizzle of honey and what might have been cinnamon were sprinkled on the top.

"Please, eat," Callira said brightly, sliding a spoon beside the bowl. "I've been told you're all guests of Bueno, and usually, that includes breakfast."

Lessie barely heard the conversation as she devoured the porridge, which had been unappealing until she took the first bite. The pleasant, surprisingly sweet flavour was enhanced by her hunger, and all of her attention became focused on finishing. Her spoon scraped the bottom of the bowl within minutes.

Callira continued talking about anything and everything, and Lessie let most of it wash over her without hearing it. Reevan nodded along enthusiastically, and jumped when Callira suddenly gasped and flew into the kitchens. Lessie and Reevan exchanged a vaguely quizzical look, but the kitskan woman soon returned to the bar, clutching a piece of paper that had been folded in half.

"Oh my gods, I forgot that Bueno asked that this be given to you upon waking. I'm so sorry! I got sidetracked."

Reevan took the paper. "It is an address I do not recognise," he said, inspecting the back. "Only that it is within Saluo itself."

Callira set down a steaming mug of tea in front of Lessie, who didn't have the heart to say she preferred coffee. She held it in her hands, letting the spices within the tea fill her nose. It was fragrant and invigorating.

"I suppose we should go sooner rather than later," Lessie said, unwilling to mention more in front of the unfamiliar kitskan. *Although Reevan's probably told her everything already.*

Callira glanced at the paper, her face brightening. "Oh, that's in the market district! Once you enter the gate, just keep going straight. You can't miss it. If you find yourself in the lake, you've gone a bit too far, but at least you'll be nice and refreshed after your walk in the heat!" She giggled a little at her own joke.

Reevan, who by his own admission had lived in Kalac for most of his life, visited Saluo often, and who Lessie was not entirely sure knew what a joke was, chuckled—*chuckled*—and gave Callira a grateful nod.

"Thank you, that is most helpful," he said. "Hopefully we shall not get too lost, or too wet."

Lessie could do nothing but blink and stare a hole into the side of Reevan's head, who was very determined not to look at her. He seemed to be running out of things to talk about with Callira. He looked around awkwardly.

"Do you enjoy working in a tavern, then?"

Lessie rolled her eyes and went back upstairs to gather the others.

The gates of Saluo were more intimidating than she'd ever admit.

Lessie readjusted her simple robe around her, grateful for the forethought she'd had to purchase one when she had grabbed Grundle's. Her practical travelling clothes were commonplace in northern Altaea, but Saluo fashion seemed vastly different. The last thing she wanted was to stick out. The soft, plain fabric covered her body completely, drifting in the slight breeze, and the oversized hood concealed her hair and gave her eyes some respite from the blinding suns. Although her skin was covered, she felt cooler than before. There was also something oddly freeing about knowing her belongings—and revolver—were concealed from passers-by.

Handing the odd little coin Bueno had given her to a stone-faced guard, Lessie felt a rush of panic, like he would denounce them as fakes and throw them out of the city. Would they detain them as criminals? Or simply deny them access? Would he ask to see what weapons she carried underneath her robe?

The guard returned her coin without speaking, gesturing for her to pass, and she remembered to breathe. She followed the others through the thick opening in the stone walls, her eyes struggling to adjust in the momentary darkness, feeling the soft crunch of the packed sand under her boots. Her thoughts came to her in Trixie's voice instead of her father's for once.

I have got to stop worrying about shit before it even happens.

Stepping out into the sunlight once more, Lessie blinked as she took in her first glimpse of the city itself. Reevan had said that things in Saluo would be different to the towns in Altaea, but she was not ready for the sight that greeted her.

It was beautiful.

Sandstone buildings, only one or two storeys high, lined the immaculate streets. Carts and horses bustled up and down the large pathways, no doubt busier due to the festival, but still with an air of normalcy as the owners called friendly greetings to each other. There were smaller paths paved with large sandstone bricks where people travelled on foot, separated from the larger middle by surprisingly lush shrubbery and trees lining them. The explosion of greenery against the sand was so bright it hurt her eyes. Many of the windows of the buildings were made with stained glass, causing patterns of coloured light to dance along the streets as the twin suns' rays shined through them. The entire city gave off an air of effortless beauty.

Lessie tried not to gawk as they made their way through the streets, the giant pyramid looming in the distance. She suppressed a shiver as she glanced towards it.

The man on the beach must be one of the Mahejerai. There was no better explanation for it, for the sinister way he had wielded the Arcane power he possessed. Lessie pulled her robe closer around her, suddenly feeling exposed, like she could feel his eyes on her.

Don't be an idiot. He's probably somewhere in Altaea, stealing some other god's power.

To distract herself from her own discomfort, she studied the others. Mae was looking around in wonder, smiling broadly, and Valandaras kept close to her, the scowl on his face apparent even through his cloth. The fabric looked a lot cleaner than normal. He must have washed it.

Reevan and Grundle led the way, but were both on edge, hoods low over their faces, the tension roiling over them like a pot about to boil over. Reevan had mentioned they were not from Saluo, but they were still clearly worried that they would be recognised.

Camden had an air of one who was trying not to be too impressed as he looked over the city, but Lessie caught his eyebrows raising as he took in the details that made it so impressive. The Lord of Nonchalance dropped his act before long, because it was too hard to maintain. Saluo was too enchanting.

The trees lining the streets had been decorated for the festival, with colourful banners linking between them. There were no pop-up vendors like the slums had offered, and the energy inside of the gates seemed more reserved than outside had been. The changes were subtle. People still smiled, but spoke quietly; children still played, but were quickly called back if they strayed an inch too far.

The city itself was just as diverse as the slums, with races Lessie had never seen before strolling the streets. One man towered above the others he walked with, horns like a ram's curling up from underneath the hair on his head. She tried not to stare, but it was hard to tear her eyes away from how interesting he looked. There were a great number of goblins, as well as many with orcish heritage—knowing they tended to hail from Kalac, it should have been less surprising, but it was beyond what she was used to seeing. Grundle had been the first goblin Lessie had ever spoken to.

The people around them moved with purpose, arms laden with food or other errands. It was the last day of the festival, so there would be many celebrations tonight, and it looked as though most of them were preparing. Some already wore masks upon their faces of varying designs, many quite plain, but others bursting with colour. Many on the street wore similar necklaces made of a dark cord, with jewels gleaming in the centre. A vague sense of déjà vu tugged at her, but she was too overwhelmed to give it much attention.

Lessie focused on trying to memorise everything she could about Saluo—the beautiful scenery, the sounds, the scents—so that she could tell Trixie about it later. Her sister had made no secret of her desire to see the other countries of their realm. It had seemed natural that she would end up travelling. In another life, she might have explored her Arcane gifts by studying at the temple within Saluo.

Of course, Trixie did travel far from home, but secluded inside an ancient Arcane school of knowledge somewhere in the Freemeres was something neither of them would have guessed at. Trixie had always insisted she'd never seen herself settling in any one place.

Lessie swallowed a lump in her throat that hadn't been there a moment ago.

I always saw myself staying home, helping Papa before taking over. But that's not an option anymore.

They walked for quite a long time; the city sprawling beneath them, taking in the different sights. Before long, the breeze brought with it a fresher scent, and Lessie glimpsed a small lake in the distance, sunlight glinting off of the still water. Callira had said that the markets bordered the lake, so they must be nearly there.

The 'markets' were a collection of businesses in single-story sandstone buildings, ringed around an open area occupied by a number of tents similar to those they had seen in the slums. Some of the tents were older and well weathered, suggesting they had commanded their spots for years. Others looked freshly erected and forced in between any available space, like they had opened for the festival and were trying to capitalise on the increased number of people within the city.

There were indeed a lot of people milling about, and the noise of their conversations overlapping was overwhelming, but Lessie gritted her teeth and marched ahead, following Reevan and Grundle as they wound their way through the stalls. Many of the stands offered trinkets, glittering jewels and stones, along with masks of all kinds. Others sold fresh meat and vegetables, or fragrant flowers that threw scent so strong it made her dizzy. One vendor even had exotic looking beasts in small cages, touting them as pets. A child giggled with delight as it tried to touch one of the brightly coloured parrots, shrieking at the bird's attempts to nibble their finger.

"We are almost at the address," said Reevan, gesturing ahead as they crossed through the middle of the markets. The newer stalls had formed a square around where the largest tent stood, which was a permanent fixture. It looked to be the original, with the others joining it over time as the city grew.

Lessie, distracted, did not immediately notice the wares of the largest tent until she was right next to it. What she saw made her stop dead in the street.

Are those... people?

The largest tent was full of slaves.

It had no sides, only a weathered canvas roof, so what dwelled within was visible from all angles. Cages with iron bars stood stacked against one another, filled with beings all dressed in the same brown robes. Many of the cages were stacked two or three high, with the people in the lower cages forced to sit or stand directly beneath those in the higher ones. There seemed to be no reasoning to it, but those in the higher cages looked healthier, less stressed than those below. There were many humans, as well as a few goblins and other races. One man looked as though he might even have been of true Elven descent, the tips of his ears long and pointed. They all looked miserable, some in the lower cages openly weeping as guards hissed at them to be silent.

Lessie blinked, eyes wide. She couldn't get her feet to move.

"What the fuck?" she whispered.

Reevan and Grundle had not stopped walking, had paid no mind to the horror that existed next to them. Mae took a shaky breath, her eyes shining with tears as she continued to walk, Valandaras putting himself between her and the tent as if to shield her from it.

Lessie stayed where she was.

"What the fuck?" she repeated, louder this time, and a couple of people glanced sideways at her. She felt a hand press firmly on the small of her back.

"Keep moving," Camden murmured in her ear, gently pushing her, and she reluctantly allowed herself to be led past the tent.

Lessie tore her eyes away from the tiniest goblin in a lower cage, bubbles of snot blowing from their nose as tears ran freely, and looked up at Camden in outrage. His face was a mask of indifference, but she could see the anger clouding in his eyes.

"Slavery is legal in Kalac," he said.

"Yeah, but—" Lessie struggled to form words, trying not to choke on her own rage. "They're just stuffed in cages until somebody comes along and *buys* them? That's disgusting. It's barbaric!"

"I know, Lessie," Camden replied grimly, refusing to look at her or back. "I know it is."

They reached the others, who had stopped outside one of the shabbier sandstone buildings that ringed the markets.

"We can't just leave them there, we have to help them. We can't just do nothing," Lessie spat.

Reevan whirled to face her. "Lessandra, unless you can afford to purchase every single one of them, you cannot help them," he said softly, tail twitching, one clawed finger scratching at the neck of his robe.

Lessie saw red. "What makes them any different from you?" she said, eyes darting between Reevan and Grundle. "The two of you managed to get out fine—"

"And you have no idea what it cost us to do so," Reevan hissed.

Something about the tone of his words had her retort die on her tongue. Her face burned.

Reevan sniffed. "Most of Kalac's slaves wear collars that track their movements by Arcane means," he said. "Breaking them out would only result in them being recaptured, as we have nowhere to harbour them all. They would suffer more for our attempt, and we would share their fate."

Mae stood next to Lessie, lacing their fingers together, and the comfort of the older woman's touch helped to ground her. Reevan regarded them all as if daring them to argue further with his reasoning. His bright green eyes came to rest on Mae.

"All places keep slaves. Some are merely more open about it," he said simply, before opening the door to the building and sweeping through it. Grundle followed immediately.

Valandaras and Camden both lingered in the doorway, before a nod from Mae had the Realmshifter head inside. Camden hesitated, like he wanted to stay, but Valandaras urged him forward, leaving the two girls alone in the alcove.

"I know what it's like to want to save them all," Mae murmured, staring back towards the markets with a faraway look. "To help them be free. I know. Sometimes, you just... can't."

Lessie caught a glimpse of immeasurable pain darken Mae's features, and it jolted her jumbled thoughts to focus. Who did Mae lose? Was it why she no longer served in a house of the Seven? Lessie had always been told that the Divines who volunteered to serve lived the best lives of all, but she'd never even met one before Mae. *Are Divines little more than slaves to the Seven?*

Mae blinked, and her eyes shuttered. She gave Lessie a shaky smile and squeezed her hand affectionately, though the Divine's skin felt clammy with sweat.

"Let's go," Mae said, tugging her towards the door.

Lessie took a deep breath. In for six, hold for three, out for six. She looked back at the slave tent one more time, fingers twitching.

You can't save them all, but someone should try.

25

LESSIE

A bell chimed merrily as they stepped into the shop, and Lessie tried to gather her composure. It was warmly lit by orbs of light that flickered on the ceiling, floating lazily and sometimes bumping into each other. Her lips tugged upwards at a memory of Trixie using those same orbs under her blankets to get away with reading late at night.

Whoever owns this place is Arcane, then.

The room looked like it had once been a warehouse. The walls were lined, floor to ceiling, with rolls and rolls of different fabrics. Every colour and texture she could imagine having existed, leaning haphazardly upon each other in spools thicker than rolled-up rugs. The plain stone floor was so old it had paths worn into it, and they weaved around pattern-measuring clothes mannequins, some humanoid, others shapes Lessie had no name for. A long desk with more fabric piled high upon it sat in the middle of the room, and behind it was a large divider blocking off any view of the back of the shop.

A small, bespectacled face peered around the divider and gave them a giant, toothless grin.

"Oh, new customers, hello there!"

The voice was so oddly pitched Lessie could not tell if the person was male or female or neither, but she supposed it didn't matter. The figure came out from around the divider and gave them all a deep bow. Lessie had no idea what race the shop's proprietor was—they seemed vaguely lizard-like, with shiny skin of a mottled orange-pink colour and no visible hair. The cadence of their voice was pleasant and melodic, with a lisp that became more prominent with each word they spoke. They were wearing the most impeccable navy blue day-suit Lessie had ever seen, complete with a soft white shirt and a vest with shiny brass buttons.

"Welcome to my shop, I am Satine, maker of Saluo's finest garments, the latest fashions designed perfectly for you," the lizard-person said, adjusting the circular golden rims perched on their nose. The spectacles magnified their eyes tenfold, giving them a bug-eyed look.

Reevan stepped forward, brandishing Bueno's note.

"We were given this address by an associate of ours," he said.

Satine gave them another gummy smile.

"Of course, Bueno's friends, I will be happy to help you, I only need to measure you," they replied.

A measuring tape around their neck unwound of its own accord and slithered along the floor. It snaked its way around Reevan, who bristled and seemed to be suppressing an urge to slash at it with his clawed fingers.

"Measure us?" Mae asked politely. "Measure us for what?"

Satine gave Mae an appraising once over before skittering towards them at a speed that had Valandaras reaching for his falchion and Lessie's own fingers twitch towards her revolver underneath her robe. The lizard-person did not seem to notice the defensive movements. They went straight past and reached for a few bolts of material, slicing samples with a delicate clawed finger and bringing them back to hold the colours against Mae's arm.

"Green for you, my dear, yes, I think it will do nicely," Satine said, marking down the measurements the tape had given for Reevan on a small notepad pulled from the pocket of the fine jacket. "Sometimes it can be clichéd, to place the red-haired ones in green, but when done right, it will be wonderful. Bueno says you are to attend the Night of Many Faces, you will need to look the part, nobody does a rush order quite like I can."

The measuring tape had moved to Valandaras, who stood deathly still. Probably to get it over with as quickly as possible. Lessie locked eyes with Mae. The Divine's face reflected the same question she was sure her own wore, although Mae seemed happier about the possibility. *Attend* the Night of Many Faces?

Camden perused the fabrics. "Is it too much to ask for a suit of pure gold? Or perhaps silver?" he asked, humour dancing in his eyes as he let his fingers brush over the soft material. "If we're going to a party, I want to look my best."

Gods, he is insufferable.

"I'll pay you extra if you make his itchy," Lessie muttered under her breath to the dressmaker as they placed swatches against her skin, mouth pursed in concentration.

"Miss, all of my garments are of the finest fabrics, they will be of utmost comfort, none of them will itch, you will never wish to wear anything else," Satine replied, missing the essence of what she was asking.

Lessie sighed. It was worth a shot.

"So it is a party, then?" Mae asked, a glimmer of excitement on her face. She giggled as the measuring tape wound its way around her playfully.

Satine looked up from comparing two fabric samples.

"It is the celebration of our first goddess, the Lady of Many Faces, held at the great Arcane temple where she returned," they said, hurrying over to mark the Divine's measurements in the notepad.

Lessie's eyes shot to Valandaras. What she could see of his face mirrored her own disbelief.

We can't go into the Mahejerai's temple. Does Bueno want us to die?

"The Arcane temple," Valandaras repeated. It was not really a question, but the dressmaker looked up at him from writing Grundle's measurements and nodded.

"Yes, the great pyramid of the Mahejerai, where those of Divinity return and those who study the Arcane ways belong, where the Weave is closest to the people," said Satine, as if it were the most normal thing in the world. "All those in Kalac with Arcane talents end up within the ranks of the Mahejerai before long. It is a great honour to be chosen."

A rush of suspicion came over Lessie.

"If all those with Arcane talent end up there, why aren't you there?" she asked Satine, eyes narrowing.

Satine paused from writing and slowly blinked at her. Their eyelids were vertical and blinked inwards, and Lessie tried not to show any outward discomfort by it, but her skin crawled.

"Miss, I only make dresses, I am not useful to the Mahejerai, they have no need for my parlour tricks," they replied slowly and pleasantly, like it should have been obvious. Lessie fell silent, and the lizard-person returned to measuring Camden's shoulders. Embarrassment washed over her.

What do I know of who the Mahejerai deem important? I've probably mortally offended them. Now my outfit will be the one that's itchy.

Reevan, however, cleared his throat, and when Lessie glanced his way, pointed surreptitiously towards the front of the shop. She followed his lead and assessed it with fresh eyes.

The shop had no displays in the windows facing into the street—it didn't really have windows at all, as the panes were darkened and used for storage of excess fabric bolts. There had been no sign. No advertisements. They had only known to go here because of Bueno's instructions; a man who prided himself on knowing all of Saluo's secrets. Even the tiny balls of arcane light could be momentarily mistaken for sconces.

All marks of someone who did not want to be found.

Maybe not all Arcanes end up with the Mahejerai, then.

Satine finished their measurements in silence, jotting them down on the notepad along with some rudimentary sketches of whatever came to mind. It was quite a fascinating process, but Lessie's mind was still reeling from the knowledge that they would be going inside the Mahejerai pyramid. She shivered. Kalac was a contradiction. A place of immeasurable beauty, with such horrible people lurking within. The horror of the slave market was proof of that. The only reason she hadn't run screaming for the Altaean border was the knowledge that the Mahejerai were probably closer to her home than here. Trapping more returning gods, syphoning more power.

Satine snapped the notebook shut and stuck the pencil behind the arm of their glasses. Lessie tried not to stare too long at the wire frames, but she was desperate to know how it stayed perched on the lizard's face, since Satine had no discernible ears. She found no answers. Arcane bullshit, then. It was oddly comforting to see it used the way Trixie did, as solutions to simple problems.

"I have everything I need, you will receive your garments before sunset, thank you for coming to visit me, be sure to tell Bueno how much you adore them," said Satine, already beginning to drift towards the back of the shop, humming to themselves as they started piling different bolts of fabric onto the desk. Most of the rolls should have been much too heavy for the tiny lizard-person to lift, but Lessie was beyond questioning at that point. She was the first to leave.

The damp breeze hit her again as she stepped outside of the shop, the bell tinkling to signal the crew's departure. Lessie stared into the horizon, where the hulking mass of the pyramid loomed over the city. She would bet it could be seen from any point in Saluo.

"Well, so much for avoiding the Mahejerai," she said. Reevan sniffed in agreement beside her.

As they began their trek back to Bueno's, Lessie's eyes fell again on the slave tent and hardened. A cold sense of purpose filled her. She knew they needed to speak to Lai'ireal for Mae, for answers on how to restore her Divinity. But what if, while the Mahejerai were off ransacking Altaea for returning gods, they could just waltz into the temple and take the power back? What if it was there somehow, stored within the pyramid? Or the secret to defeating those who had stolen it?

Lessie clenched her jaw. One way or another, she was going to find out. The Mahejerai had destroyed her home and ripped away the people she loved most. It was time she repaid the favour.

It's his turn to return home to see it go up in flames.

Head up, shoulders back. Breathe.

It was rare that Lessie heard her mother's voice in her thoughts, but it was instinctual to obey it. Though the movement sent pain shooting through her spine, Lessie pushed her shoulders down and tried to mask her discomfort. Each of her knuckles had already been cracked to oblivion, so she settled for stretching her neck. Something popped at the base of her skull, and she felt a little better, but couldn't shake the uncomfortable feeling of nervousness that had settled in her stomach.

Wafts of different smokes drifted from the open archway, bringing with them unique scents and the sudden urge for a cigarette. It had been years since she'd stolen from her father's tobacco pouch, but sometimes the craving would appear out of nowhere, lingering for a few minutes before disappearing just as quickly. She could have used the odd, calm feeling of the world's time pausing in the four minutes it took to smoke one. Lessie resisted the temptation to ask another patron for one of theirs—that would require her to talk, which she was not in the mood for.

Godsdamn it, what is taking everybody so long?

The ridiculous gown didn't help. Lavender and periwinkle fabric billowed around her, floating in the light breeze that danced past the front of Bueno's tavern, like the wind itself was taunting her. She shoved the skirts down, irritated. How could she be wearing so much fabric and still feel so exposed?

Probably because that godsdamned dressmaker forgot the other half of it.

The dress had been nothing like she expected. Gossamer sleeves fell off her shoulders to drape around her arms, beautiful and serving absolutely no purpose. The bodice was plain and fitted; the neckline plunging to her navel. The skirts were full and delicate; material floating with her movements like clouds, drifting dreamily around her ankles as she paced.

It was a dress fit for a princess. She felt both incredibly elegant and extremely out of place.

Lessie had tried in vain to wear her holster without interrupting the lines of the dress, but it was no use. The light-coloured fabric had made it too obvious, and she had sullenly left her beloved revolver locked in the chest in her room. Bueno had insisted that their belongings were safe there, that the tavern's upper levels were enchanted to keep away thieves, but it still felt wrong to be unarmed. A different kind of exposure, to not have her way to protect herself as she entered an unfamiliar city.

To attend a godsdamned party, of all things.

The Night of Many Faces.

The only real possibility of meeting Lai'ireal would be to attend the celebration of the god held on the last night of the festival. The grand ball was an exclusive event, but Bueno seemed to think they would have no trouble getting in once they had dressed in the clothing Satine provided. He had delighted in having the packages brought up to their rooms, saying they would not recognise themselves.

Lessie had been suspicious, and the feeling had only deepened as she had read the accompanied note, which mentioned 'adding to their tab' the cost of the garments. She had a feeling Bueno was such a successful businessman because he never forgot who owed him. Lessie didn't like owing anybody anything. But Bueno had a point—to get in, they had to look the part.

The gown was beautiful, she had to admit, as was the mask that had accompanied it. Decorated with delicate lace and sparkling stones, it covered the top half of her face, leaving only her mouth visible. The ribbons that held it in place had been woven into her hair, which she'd sat through without complaining, though the feeling of having someone else braid it and pin it to her scalp had made her skin crawl.

Mae had been beyond excited to help her, and Lessie had tried to enjoy it, but she didn't like casual touch at the best of times. It had been torture when Mae had darkened her eyes with a kohl-like paint, to 'make them stand out under the mask', and she could still feel the sensation of the wet liquid gliding along her eyelid, making her cringe.

Standing out was the opposite of what she wanted, and it went against how she'd been brought up. To be seen as too beautiful was to be seen as Elven, and there was still a deep mistrust of the Fae in Altaea. There had been a time when people had believed only those with Elven ancestry could possess Divine or Arcane abilities, which only sowed further discourse. Vry'iin had tricked them all, and the Elven people had upheld his lie. What else could they be hiding?

When Mae had tried to stain her lips with a terrifying shade of crimson, it had been Lessie's tipping point. She still remembered the look on her mother's face whenever Trixie had been accused of having Fae blood. Drawing attention to beauty was risking ostracisation. She had balked.

We're wasting time playing godsdamned dress-up. We just need to get this over with. Who cares if I wear lipstick?

Lessie sighed deeply. She'd stormed outside to wait for the others, but they were taking too long. She wanted to get a drink from the bar—or better yet, head back upstairs, apologise to Mae, and apply the lip paint. But going back inside meant admitting she had been wrong to leave in the first place. She hadn't. So she stayed outside and waited.

Her eyes drifted towards the city gates, torches beginning to glow as the last of the twin suns' light faded. Her stomach twisted. She had to find out if the Mahejerai were hiding anything within the temple. But so many things could go wrong. They could—

"Gods, look at you."

An amused voice cut through both the chatter of the crowd and her mind. Lessie glanced up just in time to see Camden give her an exaggerated once-over.

"You look like a woman befitting of your station. It's a miracle I recognised you," he added, eyes sparkling behind the silver mask he wore. He let out a low whistle of appreciation, a strange look on his face like he hadn't expected her to actually dress up. A stab of anger flared in her gut.

What did he think, that I don't know how to put on a dress? That I'd turn down the gown and wear my dusty trousers?

She would have preferred it, if it were an option, since then she'd have her revolver. But still.

"Thank you, Lord of Backhanded Compliments," Lessie responded in a deadpan. "And you'll look like every other useless idiot there, since Satine made you the most boring outfit in the history of the seven realms."

She was only half-right. The cut and colours of Camden's clothing were traditional, making the boring jab a safe one, but his outfit was just as well-made and fanciful as hers was—not to mention the lord's irritatingly perfect face and carefree demeanour had a habit of making anything he wore look like regalia. His suit wasn't pure gold or silver as requested, but there were touches; the buttons were shiny brass, the thread glittered subtly when it caught the light. He would have no trouble at all blending in with Kalac's affluent and idolised.

"You wound me," Camden said, sounding supremely unbothered. He pressed a hand to his heart as if injured. "We are aiming for anonymity, are we not? Perhaps you should change into something less remarkable, then, my *lady*."

He winked and brushed at the lapels of his fine jacket, smoothing imaginary wrinkles from the dark grey fabric.

Lessie crossed her arms and ignored him.

Pompous prick.

Camden sauntered closer, sipping from a glass he had probably swiped off a table on his way outside. She resisted the urge to snatch it from him.

"Dazzling the other guests with your dress aside, you should be careful tonight," he said, his tone suddenly serious. "We'll brush shoulders with Kalac's elite. Most of them consider Altaea to be a foreign enemy, and will speak poorly of it and its people. I know you won't be able to shoot them, since there's no way in the seven realms you've got a gun hidden under there," he gestured to her traitorous dress with a smirk, "but you'll still draw attention if you argue. Even if we discount the fact that you sound like you were born in the smallest backwater town Altaea has, you're not exactly skilled in hiding your emotions."

Lessie gave him a disgusted look. "And you are, I take it?"

Camden's smile only widened. "Remarkably accomplished. The amount of times I had to assure my dear father that I had been paying attention to whatever political drivel he had been spouting. That, or convince my poor mother I was sober, gods rest her soul in Requiem."

He tried to run a hand through his hair out of habit, but stopped before he ruined the styling. It had been slicked back to tame the curl in it; the length held away by the ribbons of his mask. It made him look older, more

put together. Lessie wasn't sure if she liked it. It didn't suit him. It was too...
neat.

"Nice to know you hate my accent, on top of everything else," she said,
trying to sound nonchalant, but the comment had stung more than she'd
admit. She liked how her voice sounded. It reminded her of home. Of her
family.

"I never said that. I actually find it quite charming," Camden replied.
"You sound like home. I only meant that you are unmistakeably Altaean,
and that in itself will raise eyebrows. I was taught to speak more... neutrally
in this kind of company."

Camden drained his glass and set it neatly on the ground in front of the
tavern.

"And don't expect me to bail you out of any awkward conversations you
do manage to get into," he added. "You'll need the practice for the Seven
when they begin to stick their noses into every facet of your life. You're a
noblewoman now."

Lessie ignored him, as she ignored the twinge in her stomach at the
mention of the Seven. At what waited for her back home. It was laughable
to think she could be a member of the nobility. She should never have
agreed to it.

*Lady Shilling. Gods help us. I need to find someone to give the stupid keep
to and leave as soon as we get back. Maybe I should just rip up the deed and
go back to Picking.*

Lessie and Camden stood in sullen silence until Reevan and Grundle
joined them. They were also in dark clothing, their masks undecorated and
covering their entire faces. Lessie supposed they didn't want to take any
chances on being recognised, and couldn't blame them for it, but the effect
was unsettling.

Valandaras strode outside, looking uncomfortable out of his armour.
He had been given a similar mask that covered the upper half of his face
completely, so that his cloth was not visible unless deliberately looked
for. He had worn his falchion at his side as usual, peace-bonded in the
ceremonial way most men of high station did. Camden had done the same,
the silver scabbard complementing the grey shirt he wore underneath his
jacket. Or was it purple? Lessie couldn't tell and didn't care enough to
clarify. She felt a stab of jealousy at the casual way both men could wear
their weapons. Neither of the swords would turn any heads.

Mae would.

Last to join them, the Divine bounded outside in a gown of deep forest green, figure-hugging and silky and perfect. The mask she wore resembled vines, swirling in intricate patterns across her eyes and the bridge of her nose, her painted lips all the more eye-catching with the rest of her face covered. Her fiery hair had been pinned up, with soft waves framing her face, the rich red in contrast to the sea of green that surrounded her. She could have been the Mother personified. Above all, though, it was the happiness shining from Mae's face that made her look so beautiful.

Lessie peered around Camden to see if she could catch Valandaras's reaction, and hid her smirk behind a hand. Indeed, the Realmshifter looked as if he had been struck by lightning.

"Miss Mae, you look wonderful," said Camden, giving Mae a small bow free of the mockery he had shown Lessie, but she was too wrapped up in her friend's happiness to be annoyed by it.

Mae beamed at them all. "Thank you. It has been a very long time since I felt quite this beautiful," she replied, twirling on the spot and lifting the skirts so that they could see the delicate silver heels she wore. They made Mae a few inches taller, putting her height comparable to Reevan and Camden. Lessie shook her head, lips pursing in amusement.

Back home, I was tall. Now the only one I tower over is Grundle, and he's a godsdamned goblin.

Valandaras still did not speak, but silently offered her his arm to escort her. Mae smiled again, pure joy radiating from her, and Lessie couldn't help but feel lifted as well, like the Divine's excitement was infectious. Seeing Mae smile how she had before this had all happened was wonderful, but it wasn't just the dress, or the ball, or even the anticipation of meeting an actual god. It was the hope that after tonight, they would finally start to get some answers.

Lessie had to watch her own feet as they took uneven steps on the sandstone walkway. The shoes that had been delivered fit perfectly, although she didn't remember Satine measuring her feet. She was grateful her dress kept them covered most of the time—it was less likely that people would see her trip. But she doubted she'd make it to the temple wearing them.

They made it barely halfway down the street before a carriage jerked to a stop next to them. The horses that pulled it whinnied as their reins were yanked abruptly, and the driver of the coach gave them a merry wave.

Lessie caught a glimpse of shaggy black hair and a flippant grin underneath the hood as the figure brought the horses to a standstill. It was enough to recognise her as the woman who was in Bueno's study when they had first arrived. She leapt from the driver's platform and landed nimbly in the street before them, throwing back her hood dramatically. The jagged scar running through her right eye did nothing to detract from their allure, with thick lashes and irises an astonishing ice blue. If anything, it only made her more attractive, since the rest of her face was just as striking.

She flashed them the kind of smile that promised she could charm them all into oblivion and leave them penniless in the streets if they gave her half a chance.

"Good evening, travellers," she said, voice clear and bright, with a hint of an accent Lessie couldn't place. "Halliday Greyholme, at your service. Bueno told me you might need an escort to the Night of Many Faces."

She unlatched the door to the carriage and gave them a theatrical, somewhat teasing bow as it swung open.

"Hop in."

26

REEVAN

The temple of the Mahejerai rose from the ground like it had pierced its way through the earth to touch the sky itself.

Even while atop a moving carriage, Reevan had to crane his neck, and the pyramid only became more imposing the closer they came towards it. The very building seemed to hum, to crackle with the energy of the many powerful beings it held within its weathered stone. A quiet, solid stronghold. A sanctuary of Arcane knowledge and Divine secrets. The colourful banners and twinkling lights in the surrounding trees were gaudy in comparison.

Reevan wrinkled his nose in distaste. His mask shifted a little, and he attempted to twitch it back into place before giving up and adjusting it with his claws. It was quite irritating to have his peripheral vision limited by the porcelain, not to mention heavy upon his ears, but he was grateful for the extra anonymity. He strengthened his grip upon the carriage's exterior handholds.

He glanced down at Grundle, whose dark floating robes and matching mask gave him the uncomfortable look of a small child's worst nightmare. The pair of them had elected to ride on the outside of the carriage rather than overcrowd the small seats within.

Reevan knew instinctively that a lot of things could go wrong tonight, and he breathed deep as the carriage rolled to a halt. He relished the chance to enjoy the fresh air—the fragrant spices and the calm the wind brought with it. He had always loved how crisp the air of the Kalac deserts could be when the twin suns sank beneath the horizon.

Reevan jumped from the rear of the carriage, padded feet landing softly upon the sandy cobblestones. Grundle appeared beside him, silent as ever, and the two Kalac natives enjoyed a moment of peaceful contemplation before the others joined them.

"So, what's the plan here?" Lessie asked as she climbed out of the carriage, gingerly holding the skirts of her dress aloft as she tried not to step on them. "We walk in, we wait in line to speak to Lai'ireal, and we walk out?"

She stood next to Reevan, eyes locked on the temple. They were even more striking with dusky makeup applied to them. Distrust and anger swirled within.

"I assume so, Lessandra," Reevan replied without looking at her. "This is my very first God Ball. I am unaware of the protocols in place for speaking to said gods."

He tested the limits of his peripheral vision in the mask by seeing if he could gauge her reaction. She might have rolled her eyes, but she did that for most things he said, so he could not be certain.

Halliday Greyholme gave them a farewell wave, gesturing to an area where carriages had already been stationed to wait for their guests. Reevan assumed this meant she would also be escorting them home. Hopefully, she would not have to wait for long.

Standing alone on the edge of the walkway, the six stood without speaking. The gentle thrum of surrounding activity did little to pierce the silence that fell between them. Reevan gazed up at the night sky through the slits in his porcelain mask, at the twinkling stars, tail twitching under his robes. He enjoyed the silence until Lessie broke it.

"What if we're not allowed to speak to Lai'ireal? What if they don't even let us in?" she asked, still staring up at the pyramid with dread and fidgeting with her dress. "Bueno didn't give us a coin for this."

Mae, who had been looking equally apprehensive, took Lessie's hand and clasped it within her own, squeezing softly. The simple motherly act forced a deep exhale from them both. It was like Mae's own fear retracted in the wake of comforting the younger girl.

"Worry about things as they come, not before," Mae said, giving Lessie's hand a gentle pat. "And as for being allowed in, I don't think we will have any problems. Bueno wants us to get inside the temple; he would not send us to our doom. Most of belonging is about believing that you belong, anyway. Follow my lead."

With that, Mae dazzled them all with a mischievous smile before squaring her shoulders and marching towards the entrance. Reevan followed without hesitation, the others trailing behind.

There were many guests in the first stages of arrival, and some congestion at the front of the pyramid. Reevan observed the crowd, looking for invitations, coins, anything to denote rightful entry, but could not spot anything concrete. Nobody was being turned away, however, which was a good sign.

A pair of guards stood at the temple's entrance, the weight of their full regalia already coating them in a light sheen of sweat despite the rapidly cooling evening air. Their plain masks covered their eyes, and their twin expressions of boredom told Reevan that they had been at this post for hours already.

Mae approached them, fearless, and the guard's faces flickered with interest. They bowed respectfully as she flashed them her teeth, but their eyes roamed over the silky green dress shimmering in the dim light. The look on Mae's face reminded Reevan of her mountain lion form, confident and predatory, and she captivated the guards completely. One of them even stepped forward to offer their hand as she ascended the three small steps into the pyramid itself.

A skittering of emerald sparks—subtle, but enough to mark her for what she was—cascaded down her bare arms as her fingertips lingered on the guard's hand. Mae bestowed a grateful smile upon the guard.

"Thank you," she murmured.

The guard went red.

"It is an honour," he replied, stammering, no longer able to make eye contact. Both guards waved them through, embarrassment and awe warring on their faces. Not a single member of the crew was questioned as they made their way inside.

Reevan's ear twitched in amusement. They worshipped Divines in Kalac, that was true, but perhaps there was also something to be said for wearing a shiny outfit.

Reevan followed the girls as they wound their way through the throng of people in the first antechamber, where some guests had paused to greet each other. Mae glanced back over her shoulder a few times, as if worried they would be separated.

Reevan was not concerned. It was fairly easy to keep track of where they all were, since all of their outfits matched. Camden's shirt was made of the same material as Lessie's floaty skirts, the light fabric rippling with an iridescent sheen. The stitching on Valandaras's jacket was dyed the same forest green as Mae's dress; the golden accents on his mask reminiscent of the vines that curled around her face. Reevan supposed that was a tradition for parties like this, for the guests to have complementary attire, since he saw many of the other guests dressed similarly. Perhaps he and Grundle were also matched because of it.

They stepped through a large stone archway and entered the ground floor of the temple. It was extremely large and open, with the walls stretching upwards twice as high as any room he had been in before, angling inwards as they followed the pyramid's shape. Thousands of tiny balls of Arcane light glittered as they drifted around the ceiling, giving the illusion that they were still under the stars. The floors were pure marble, polished so thoroughly they were like mirrors, reflecting the lights.

Music played from all around them, but Reevan could not find the source of it—another Arcane trick, perhaps. He kept one eye open for it as he watched the crowd.

Hundreds of people milled about, talking and laughing, sipping from refreshments. A few of the bolder guests already danced in the middle of the room, the dresses of the women swirling around them as they glided. The fashion choices ranged from the safe and boring to the outrageous and dramatic, and Reevan was glad to see that none of their own attire stood out. The guests all wore masks, some so elaborate and elongated that they were in danger of hitting other patrons as their wearers walked. One woman appeared to have the feathers of a peacock attached to hers.

"At least Satine made sure we fit the dress code," Camden remarked, casually lifting a glass of sparkling golden liquid from one of the nimble servers as they passed. He sniffed it delicately before downing the entire thing and smacking his lips together. "Now what?"

As he reached for a second flute, Valandaras placed a hand on the younger man's arm.

"Now we wait for Lai'ireal to appear, and do not attract attention," Valandaras said pointedly. Camden scowled, and Lessie snorted in amusement.

"If we weren't meant to attract attention, you should have warned Satine before they put Mae in that colour," said Lessie, eyes flicking to a few of the people around them, some of whom were staring openly at Mae. Reevan noted a few sneers, probably from jealousy, but most appeared to be in appreciation of the Divine's attire. Mae did not acknowledge them, but she did draw closer to Valandaras, her confidence faltering.

"At least it's a large room, right?" Mae said, giving them all a broad smile that did not reach her eyes under the mask. "Plenty of room to keep to ourselves."

They had stopped somewhat near the middle, where small alcoves had been created by placing high tables and narrow chairs in rings between the massive support pillars that lined either side of the room. Some guests had already claimed tables, and Lessie stalked towards the nearest vacant one, the legs of the chair scraping violently on the marble floor as she pulled it away from the table.

"So now we wait," said Lessie, fluffing the floaty skirts of her dress awkwardly as she perched on the narrow stool. "For Lai'ireal to appear, or for one of the thousand guards to realise we weren't invited and remove us. Fantastic." She glanced around, poorly concealed nerves plain even with her face covered.

Indeed, there were quite a few guards, all with the same glazed look of the two at the front entrance. Many were stationed at some of the various doorways that lead away from the main room, but their presence seemed to be ceremonial more than anything. Their blades were too clean. A couple of them gazed longingly at the sparkling drinks being offered to the guests. Reevan could see why; the drinks were multicoloured and bubbled merrily, glittering like they were infused with starlight.

Camden snagged a few more glasses off a nearby servant's tray and placed them on the table, before lifting a chair silently with his free hand and positioning it next to Lessie's.

"Relax, my *lady*," he said, shoving the last glass of iridescent wine towards her. "If you stop scowling, maybe someone will even ask to dance with you."

His comment only made her scowl more pronounced.

Grundle snickered.

"I don't want to dance," Lessie muttered, glaring at Camden.

"I wasn't asking," he replied. The young lord flashed an easy smile at a group of pretty women who passed their table, eyes glittering with mischief as they giggled.

Reevan watched the guests interact with mild interest. There were at least three other Divines in the ballroom, easily noticeable by the way the crowd gravitated towards them. They were all dressed in expensive clothing and dripping with jewels. A diamond the size of a marble glittered in one of the male's ears. The woman's brown skin seemed to shimmer with an iridescent glow, the contrast striking against her white gown. They did not look alike, but all three of them had an *otherness* which set them apart from the other revellers. It went beyond mere human attractiveness.

Reevan didn't know enough about the gods' Gifts to know which one each Divine served, but it was an interesting game to try to guess. The human man skittered golden light around his fingers, forming shapes of tiny sprites before sending them to dance around the Arcane light to the delight of those around him. The god of light and knowledge, Woki'Sune? Lai'ireal herself? A deity whose name was still lost to all but their most fervent followers?

Whoever granted their power, these Divines seemed much more comfortable showing their Gifts in public than Mae was. A by-product of her Altaean heritage. It was refreshing to see once more—Divines were given free rein in Kalac, even worshipped. Indeed, with every move the Divines made within the room, they were each followed by adoring admirers. Reevan had always found the Altaean nobility's treatment of those blessed with Divinity to be distasteful. They claimed to be protecting the Divines' power, but to Reevan, it smacked of indentured servitude.

There were a few figures in flowing purple robes that he understood to be members of the Mahejerai. The patterns were similar to those they had seen on the beach, although varied in design and intricacy. Some of the Mahejerai stood with drinks in hand, their hoods down, plain masks upon their faces as they spoke with guests. Others drifted between the partygoers, sending sparks of new light streaking from their fingertips into the cascade of artificial stars on the ceiling.

Reevan searched their faces out of habit, knowing all the while he would not recognise any of them from their altercation. None had left that beach alive. None except—

Lessie's glass tumbled from her grip.

It shattered on the marble floor, sending shards of crystal and glittery liquid cascading across it, and attracted the attention of most of the guests around them. Lessie didn't even seem to notice. Her eyes had gone wide with fear underneath her mask, locked on a point behind them. Reevan followed her horrified expression and found the source of her terror immediately.

At the end of the room, on a raised platform, cloaked in a familiar robe and mask, stood the hollow figure from the beach. The leader of the Mahejerai. The killer of Lessie's family and Mae's god.

Not transparent. Very much present.

And less than fifty feet away.

Reevan turned back to Lessie, intending to ask her to step outside, when Camden started laughing. The laugh was too loud, and it carried over the surrounding crowd. Lessie looked momentarily furious, face reddening from fear and embarrassment. Camden kept laughing, and the curious looks around them slid from Lessie and the glass to the lord as he shook his head in embarrassment. He pushed his seat backwards and rose, letting the legs of the stool scrape upon the marble obnoxiously, demanding even more attention.

"My lady, I am so sorry," Camden exclaimed, looking around as if for a napkin. "Forgive me for my clumsiness. Please, allow me to fetch you another!"

He waved his hand dramatically towards a server, who rushed towards them with another heavy tray. Camden snatched another glass of shimmering wine and pressed it into Lessie's shaking hands, all the while apologising profusely and proclaiming his mistake, speaking louder than necessary. He glanced at the strangers around them, flashing a sheepish smile as if disappointed in his own lack of coordination.

A few nearby guests murmured amongst themselves, commenting on the thoughtfulness of the gesture. Idle chatter around them resumed.

Reevan's ear twitched. Nicely done. The initial curiosity thrown their way had dissipated almost instantly. The lord was a natural at subterfuge.

Another server, a young, pale-skinned goblin, hurried to clear away the broken glass. Her robe shifted slightly as she hunched over, and Reevan felt a familiar twinge of horror as he eyed the collar around her neck. It was simple, black, with a glowing blue jewel in the centre. A slave.

The Mahejerai's leader cleared his throat loudly, and Reevan tore his eyes away from the slave collar as the guests all turned to face the dais. To face the one who had stolen the Godpower they had come to restore.

A hush fell upon the crowd. The hollow figure pushed back the hood of his intricately patterned Mahejerai robes and gracefully raised his arms to the guests in greeting. Once again, he wore a mask concealing his features, only tonight it was not out of place. The sea creature it resembled seemed otherworldly, casting shadows over the man's eyes. His voice boomed as he addressed the crowd, amplified by Arcane means.

"Welcome to the Night of Many Faces," he announced. "I am Oorata Boras."

As the crowd applauded, Reevan hesitantly clapped along with them. Beside him, Lessie loosed a shaky breath. Reevan found it useful that they finally had a name to put to the face. He exchanged an uneasy glance with Valandaras, grateful that the Realmshifter had elected not to bring that hideous black blade with him tonight. Surely its former master would be able to sense it.

Oorata Boras's words were solemn, as if in prayer.

"Long have the powers of the Divine and the Arcane been intertwined. Those chosen by the gods, and those favoured by the Weave itself, two sides of the same coin. For thousands of years, what was rightfully ours was denied from us by the Betrayer. Tonight, we celebrate the return of our most powerful beings—and with them, the magic itself."

Other members of the Mahejerai had fallen into step around him, and for a moment they formed a great ring. Reevan shifted uncomfortably and glanced around for cover in case any of them looked like they might explode.

Oorata raised his arms high. "On this night, one hundred and thirteen years ago, the first to Breach blessed Kalac and this temple with her glorious return. As the leader of the Mahejerai, I bid you all to join us in summoning Lai'ireal, the goddess of war, here tonight, so that we may honour her."

The robed figures around him began chanting in low voices, and a soft crackle of energy threaded between them, dancing through the crowd and reflecting off of the polished floor. Nothing like the raw power they had experienced on the beach, but controlled, muted.

Reevan blinked. It seemed like a show, a performance for the crowd, who indeed murmured with excitement as they felt the hum of power emanating from the Arcanes. It was effective—even Lessie swore under her breath, and Mae's knuckles had turned white as she gripped Valandaras's forearm. The two women were both more experienced than he at magical displays, and yet they seemed impressed, so he supposed he should be too.

The light became blinding, and Reevan squeezed his eyes shut against it. A shriek from one of the bejewelled guests had him opening them before the light had fully subsided, and he saw the last of the energy dissipate as it converged on a single spot in the middle of the room. A silence hung over them all, as if every person in the room were collectively holding their breath.

In the room's centre now stood a figure.

Female, clad in brilliant shining plate amour of silver and gold. She was tall, at least as tall as Reevan, and although her face was obscured by the helmet she wore, he could still feel her imposing stare as she looked over the crowd imperiously. She held a spear in one hand, the point razor-sharp and yet somehow delicate, and a heavy round shield graced her other forearm. A hazy glow surrounded her, blurring her edges. Waves of silky blonde hair streamed down her back, swaying slightly despite the lack of wind.

Lai'ireal slowly raised her spear above her head and the silence was broken.

The crowd roared. Guests clapped and cheered, all decorum forgotten for the moment. Divines sent shimmers of their gifts into the air, and the Arcane scattered among them shot coloured sparks up like fireworks. Mae applauded wildly, pushing up onto her toes to peer over the heads of the other guests.

The god was a mask of indifference. She kept her helmeted head high as the members of the Mahejerai bowed to her.

"Welcome Lai'ireal, Maiden of Battle, Lady of Many Faces, the god of war herself," Oorata Boras announced—more for the crowd, Reevan surmised, than the immortal being before him. Surely she knew her own titles. The Mahejerai's leader gestured to the dais behind him, where an elaborate golden chair had been placed.

"Your throne awaits. The Arcane and Divine among us will honour you with displays of their Gifts, so graciously bestowed by your Breach. Those who would speak with you will petition you individually, should you accept them."

Lai'ireal swept past the Mahejerai and ascended onto the dais without so much as a nod, balls of Arcane light reflecting in her shining armour. She dropped into the throne and did not remove her helmet. The god leaned back; her magnificent shield thudding onto the ground beside her, one gauntleted hand still gripping the deadly spear.

Reevan thought that she did not seem to want to speak to anyone at all.

The crowd paused, as if waiting for one individual to make the first move. A few nobles tittered nervously. Oorata gave them all a shark's smile.

"Let us show the Goddess how Kalac celebrates those of true power," he boomed, before sweeping into the crowd.

The music resumed, louder than before. The Mahejerai broke from their circle, beginning to mill about between the guests once more, and a few brave souls inched towards the dais, to ask for blessings or advice from the god now in their midst. Conversations resumed, the buzz of anticipation crackling around the room like a living thing.

Reevan could practically feel the excitement pouring off of Mae in waves. The Divine laced her arm through Valandaras's as if she intended to physically drag the Realmshifter towards the dais where Lai'ireal now lounged.

"She *has* to know," Mae whispered, face alight with hope under her delicate mask of leaves. "She will know how to help the Mother. If she truly was the first to Breach, she must know how to break free of it."

Valandaras was staring at the god with a hard expression—what little Reevan could see of his face, anyway.

"Lioness, we should give her a while. Wait until the excitement in the room has settled," he murmured, handing her a glass of sparkling wine. "Especially now we have somebody so dangerous to avoid."

He did not need to elaborate; they all knew who he meant.

Mae's brow furrowed, and she gave Valandaras a look that would have sent weaker men cowering.

"I can *wait* in line," she said tightly, placing her glass down onto the table and moving towards the dais. Valandaras only sighed and followed her.

Reevan had no desire to speak with the god himself, and neither did any of his other companions. Lessie had not taken her eyes off of Oorata Boras, and her jaw was clenched so tightly Reevan worried for her teeth.

Some guests resumed their dancing, though more timid than before, like they were worried the Lady of Many Faces might disapprove of their technique and strike them down where they stood. Reevan sniffed. He had heard of gods being petty or nonchalant, but none that would punish dancing of all things.

Camden stood tall, grey eyes narrowed as they swept over the crowd.

"At least the Mahejerai seem to be leaving Lai'ireal to her own devices," he said. "Oorata Boras is already halfway across the room, talking to a rather large gentleman." He gestured with his glass, a casual movement any bystander would mistake for a toast.

Reevan's eyes followed the gesture. And fell upon the one person he least wished to see.

Ashendi Braak.

The immense man's eyes glittered cruelly as he spoke with the Mahejerai's leader, and he wore no mask with his general's regalia. The sight of the crest of chains snapped Reevan's careful control over his own thoughts.

For a moment he pictured slinking through the crowd, his mask concealing his features, and sidling up behind his master before drawing his hidden dagger and burying it into Braak's spine. He smelled the blood that would gush, warm over his clawed hands, and heard the gasp of disbelief from the guests around him as Braak fell. He imagined what he would whisper into Braak's ear as he twisted the knife, so that the man would know exactly who had leaked his life's blood into the Silver Stream.

Reevan saw the guards closing in around him, too many to resist, Oorata Boras binding him through Arcane means. The shock upon the faces of his friends turning to horror. He saw no trial. He saw a black collar, a glowing gem, and a cage with iron bars...

Reevan moved before he knew what was happening.

He had already marked which guards had left their posts to gape at the god. He chose the nearest unguarded door and launched himself toward it, disappearing behind the flimsy decorative tapestry that had been hung to disguise them all.

He was vaguely aware of being followed, but for the moment, he could only focus on putting as much distance between himself and his master as he could. He did not trust himself to remain where he was; the temptation of seeing Braak bleed would eventually win out against his need to stay anonymous. If the Mahejerai removed him for trespassing, he would take it. He did not care if they killed him for it.

He would rather die than feel the pulse of a jewelled collar around his neck again.

27

REEVAN

He was not alone for long.

"Reevan, what in the seven realms are you doing?" Lessie hissed as she followed him down the dim hallway, heels clicking on the marble.

Reevan glanced up from where he had crouched in the shadows of another doorway. Lessie stood in front of him, glaring down. Grundle, in turn, glowered at her, while Camden looked mildly amused. Apparently, they had all thought it necessary to follow him into the forbidden corridor. He felt an odd pang of something, but he brushed aside the unfamiliar emotion.

Lessie gestured wildly, fingers splayed as if scolding a runaway child.

"We can't be here. The Mahejerai will notice for sure. The guards—"

"Lessandra, as much as I would love to see you converse with him," Reevan responded, cutting her off, "interacting with Ashendi Braak is not on my list of things to do tonight. It was in all of our best interests that I remove myself from his vicinity." He attempted to keep his tone as even as he could, though the image of Braak's blood on his dagger flashed in his mind once more, taunting him.

Lessie's mouth opened and then closed without speaking. She stared Reevan down like she wanted to argue, but thought better of it. Oddly, he knew she understood. After all, there were people in that room she'd gladly run from.

"Grundle wants to know why Braak and Boras know each other," said the goblin, black eyes glittering in the dim light. "He doesn't like magic."

A small spark of shame flared in the pit of Reevan's stomach. Grundle was most likely just as shaken by the sight of Ashendi Braak, but at least he hadn't run off to hide in the shadows.

Reevan sniffed, glancing around the hallway. "As do I, my small friend. It is most peculiar. Perhaps one of these rooms holds the answer."

Lessie snorted. "What are you suggesting? We sneak into Boras's bedroom and read his diary?"

Reevan peered down the hallway. There were a few corridors that led off from it, some with stairs that would lead to the higher levels of the pyramid. The place was a labyrinth; there was no telling where half of them might end up. The building was a hundred stories high, but it was hard to tell how much of it was functional.

Camden leaned against the wall. "Most of the party is preoccupied with trying to gain an audience with Lai'ireal," he said, crossing his arms over one another. "Maybe we should have a poke around."

"Look, I want to know what this asshole is up to more than anyone," said Lessie, "but I'm not about to go rifling through his stronghold while he's home. We're surrounded by guards, not to mention his personal team of Arcane assassins." She kept one eye on the door that they had come through, as if expecting an entire legion to burst into the corridor.

Grundle shrugged and started down one of the corridors.

"Grundle will look," he said. "Keeping to the shadows is what Grundle is best at."

Reevan nodded. "Grundle's right. We may not get this opportunity again," he said, rising from his crouch. He would have taken any excuse to put more distance between himself and Braak, but potentially helping Miss Mae seemed like a good one.

Lessie's jaw set. "Fine. Might as well die here. Where do we start?" She glanced around, as if there would be some sort of guidebook or map to the temple hanging on the wall. Her fingers reached for the nearest door and jiggled the handle, which was locked.

Footsteps echoed on the polished marble. Heading their way.

Already concealed, Grundle froze. Reevan melted into the darkness of the nearest corridor. His eyes met Camden's, who had pushed off of the wall and now stood between Lessie and the approaching footsteps.

Camden winked at Reevan, before grasping Lessie's wrist and spinning her into his arms. She gasped at the contact, the skirts of her dress swirling just as one of the temple's guards rounded the corner. Suspicious eyes followed the fabric's movement and found them immediately.

"What are you doing here?" the guard barked sharply, one hand resting on the hilt of their blade. "This area is off-limits to guests."

Reevan assessed the guard. He was on the wrong side of middle-aged, with too many sunspots and a rather glorious moustache. He seemed a little out of breath and disgruntled—like being pulled away from viewing Lai'ireal had annoyed him more than the actual trespass. If it came down to it, Reevan could silence him without much cause for concern. However, once they drew blood inside the temple, there was no going back.

Reevan's hand snaked around the hilt of his favourite dagger.

Camden gave the guard a courteous, vacant smile as he cradled Lessie to his chest. He did not look up as the guard spoke, nor gave any indication he agreed that he was guilty of any wrongdoing. Only vague annoyance at having his peace interrupted. Ever the pretentious noble, utterly convinced of his own importance.

"Of course, my good man," replied Camden casually, stroking Lessie's back as if in comfort. "My wife needed a moment of quiet. Crowds overwhelm her. We shall return to the main room when she is feeling better."

Keeping his eyes on Lessie, Camden dismissed the guard with a wave of his hand, the jewel in his signet ring flashing in the low light of the sconces. The meaning behind it was clear.

The guard bristled, annoyance rippling over his face. He was used to this treatment. Perhaps a lower-ranking member of the Mahejerai's guard, or outside protection hired just for the night. Either way, this man had experience with stuffy, pompous nobles who thought themselves the right to anywhere, and who listened to nobody. Reevan watched in fascination as the guard's stance visibly relaxed even as his anger climbed, dismissing the two young people as a threat.

Reevan was glad the guard could not see Lessie's face, for he may have reconsidered. Her mask did little to hide the outrage simmering beneath it. Her hands curled on Camden's chest, and the lord fought to contain the wince from her nails digging into his skin.

"I will escort you back to the main room *now*, sir," said the guard, voice still sharp but eyes less wary. Finally glancing up, Camden shot the guard an exasperated look over the top of Lessie's head, silently beseeching the guard to give them a moment. He took her hands in his, peeling them away from the grooves they had made in his fine shirt—and possibly the skin beneath it—and brushed his lips gently against them.

"Don't you worry, darling," said Camden, voice loud for the guard, but also somehow softer than Reevan had ever heard it. "You say the word, and I will send for the carriage. But let's try to enjoy ourselves a while longer. You did say you wanted to meet the Goddess."

Reevan could see a muscle in Lessie's jaw twitch wildly, but she only nodded, taking a deep breath in before exhaling and pulling herself together. She turned to face the guard, who offered her a small, stiff incline of his head and gestured to the corridor beyond. Lessie gave him a tight-lipped smile in return, not trusting herself to speak. Perhaps she worried her common-born Altaean accent would sound too suspicious when compared with Camden's, or perhaps she was simply too full of anger at his choice of deception. She sighed and began to walk.

Behind her, Camden's wolfish grin was not entirely theatrical.

"That's my girl."

Lessie's entire body stiffened after her first step. Reevan wondered which of Camden's limbs she was planning to maim first, and was grateful she was currently unarmed. A noblewoman drawing a firearm on her husband in a corridor in front of a guard was sure to attract unwanted attention.

Despite her obvious thoughts of violence, Lessie allowed herself to be steered back down the corridor with her eyes trained on the floor and her mouth shut. It was the most controlled anger Reevan had seen her display. He could practically feel the effort she was making, to not lash out, to hold back the string of expletives she was no doubt aching to sling at Camden. Her flushed cheeks and clenched fists, luckily, played into the role of the distressed wife rather than giving away their ruse.

Camden did not acknowledge the mollified guard other than to give him a slightly demeaning pat on the shoulder as they passed. The guard sighed, shaking his head as he watched them go. Pompous young nobles, it seemed to say. Thinking they were above the rules.

Reevan watched as the three disappeared back around the corner, the handsome lord's hand on the small of his 'wife's' back, guiding her gently in front of him. The guard followed closely behind, no longer on high alert, but determined to see them return to the celebration.

Leaving Reevan and Grundle alone in the corridor, completely to their own exploration.

Reevan sniffed, impressed. Lord DeFalcone was much more adept at deception than any of them could have guessed. Perhaps he was not so out of place on their journey as he had first appeared to be.

Two yellow eyes met Reevan's from across the hallway. Sparkling with the promise of discovering forbidden knowledge.

"Grundle sees something Reevan might find interesting," said the goblin, beckoning with a spindly finger.

Reevan grinned. One ear twitched back towards the ballroom, but he heard no other sounds of approach as the pair took their first steps down the dark passage. Strangely enough, it appeared to slope downwards. Grundle was right. He did find that interesting.

They would not have long. Even if no other guards detected their presence, there would be no telling how long the celebrations would last. If they spent too long here, they could find themselves trapped, with no way to alert the rest of the crew as to their predicament.

Of course, that was exactly the kind of challenge Reevan enjoyed most.

The further he and Grundle descended into the depths of the pyramid, the more Reevan tried not to think of how they would fight their way out if they were discovered. So far, the corridors and narrow stairwells they had found had been abandoned, with the Mahejerai attending the celebration above. The lack of opposition did nothing to assuage him. It would only take one pair of eyes to have them hanging from their ankles in the square. Or worse, to never leave the temple.

Grundle moved like a wraith, a diminutive shadow. He used the reflection in his favourite dagger to glance around corners, the only blade he kept free of the soot he used to blacken the others. It stopped them from glinting in light; an old trick they'd both learned as children.

Reevan wished he could remove his mask, but the anonymity it would bring should they be discovered was worth the uncomfortable feeling of it plastered against his fur.

They seemed to be going in circles, spiralling downwards. Reevan was intrigued by the pyramid's design. It was thirty stories high—why was such an expansive underground necessary? Was it common knowledge, or a secret the Arcane within these walls kept from the public?

Reevan and Grundle did not speak as they went, though they kept close to each other. Sometimes splitting to poke their heads into unlocked rooms, neither of them found little more than storage compartments or increasingly neglected study spaces. The hallways became less refined as they descended; the floor's polished marble gave way to simply packed earth that deadened the sound of their footsteps. It looked as though none of the Mahejerai bothered to visit this far underneath their sacred pyramid very often, if ever. The torches on the walls had been bewitched to be everlasting, but they saw no sign of regular use. Reevan's whiskers twitched inside the mask, itching. The whole thing was rather predictable, really. Perhaps this had been a waste of time.

The air changed.

Reevan smelled the water before he saw it. It was somehow... fresh, like the air rolling in off the ocean, like they were not underground at all. He ran a clawed finger along the wall to his left. It came away damp. He wiped it on his robes, frowning. That was different.

Grundle's eyes were pure black in the dim passageway, absorbing what little light there was. They met Reevan's as a sound came to them—the first in fifteen minutes.

A steady dripping.

Quiet. Irregular. Yet almost hypnotic.

It was coming from behind a door thirty feet down. Grundle inspected the door and pulled his dainty silver tools from their velvet wrap.

Reevan attempted to watch, but soon gave up and spent the next few minutes pacing, throwing furtive glances down the corridor. He chuckled as various whispered curses fell from the goblin's mouth. It had been a while since Grundle had found a locked door more than a mild inconvenience.

Finally, a sharp click. Grundle straightened and gave him a small nod. Reevan braced himself and pulled against the door, and it swung open silently towards them.

Revealing a wall of water.

Reevan shied back instinctively, jerking his body to the side to avoid the torrential pouring that his knowledge of basic physics told him would occur. No such event happened. The water stayed, immobile, as if an invisible force prevented it from falling into the corridor beyond. The scent of the ocean air swelled, overpowering Reevan's sensitive nose. It was dark, but not murky, and they could see through to what was presumably the other side. The water rippled, distorting their view of the dark chamber beyond it. It made no sound, eerie in its silence—the dripping seemed to be coming from further within the chamber itself. Towards the floor, green and brown kelp swayed gently in the water's current, like it was growing right out of the stone below it. A tiny fish swam past. Reevan had never seen anything like it.

Grundle and Reevan exchanged an uneasy glance. It could be a trap, an alarm of some kind. But if any room in the pyramid held answers, of course, it would be the one with the enchanted doorway.

Reevan reached a tentative claw towards the water, every hair on his body standing up in silent protest. His prickling fear gave way to fascination as he felt his hand go through the water. It was not thick—or *deep*, he supposed—and he sensed his fingers touching open air before he had submerged his arm beyond the elbow. Nobody attacked the disembodied hand that had presumably appeared on the other side, either, which was a good sign.

Reevan pulled his arm back and inspected it. His hand and robes had remained completely dry. It was as if the water had simply moved around him.

"This," said Reevan, twisting his outstretched hand, "is the strangest thing I've seen all night. And that is including a god. What do you think, old friend? Care for a swim?"

Grundle snorted. "Grundle is not going first."

Reevan shrugged, closed his eyes, and stepped through the wall of water. For a moment, all sound ceased, even the incessant dripping. He had the uncomfortable feeling of pressure upon his body, like he suddenly weighed much more than he were used to, and it was difficult to drag his limbs through the water. Before he could get used to the sensation, however, it vanished, and he found himself standing on the other side of the wall of water.

Ripping the porcelain mask away from his face, Reevan looked down at his robes, which were still dry. He grabbed them and shook them a little, just to be sure. They swished innocently. Even if there was absolutely nothing to be found inside this chamber, the experience of walking through that wall would be worth it.

Reevan waited just long enough to grow concerned when a small porcelain face appeared beside him. Seeing that Reevan had taken off his mask, Grundle removed his own and nodded, confirming what Reevan already knew. Nobody had come for them yet. But they would have to hurry if they were to remain undiscovered.

Trying to ignore the ominous rippling behind them, the kitskan and the goblin crept into the dark chamber. The entire room was made of stone, the same weathered slabs as the pyramid's outer structure, like it had been part of the original framework before the spire rose to the heavens without it. The chamber itself was dark and quite large, as if it mirrored the grand ballroom above, though the ceilings were not as high. It was devoid of any proper furniture, but some of the stone had been raised to create a dais in the centre of the room, along with some rudimentary structures that might have been benches. Oddly, there were interruptions in the stone floor, like tree roots had tried to grow up through them. Reevan took extra care not to trip over the uneven surface.

The smell of the ocean was stronger now that they were inside, the walls glistening with condensation, along with a strange metallic scent he couldn't place. Suddenly curious, Reevan skulked to the nearest wall and placed a claw into the water. Unlike the unconventional entrance, this water stuck, and his fingertip came away damp. He sniffed it before depositing the droplet onto his tongue. The taste of the salt water confirmed his theory. This was seawater. He watched, fascinated, as droplets of the water collected together to form tiny streams in the grooves of the stone walls, flowing downwards and then dancing along similar indentations in the floor.

Reevan's whiskers twitched as he followed the miniature rivers further into the chamber. The steady drip was louder now, able to be discerned from the trickling of the wall's water. Maddening in its slight irregularity.

Reevan and Grundle exchanged a wary glance. The unmistakable metallic scent grew stronger with each step, and they had both recognised it.

A flickering light had them both shrinking back into the safety of the darkness. Reevan watched the shadows dance along the far walls, the water shimmering with the reflections. He slowed his breathing and focused on the beats of his heart as he stilled. He did not move a muscle until he was certain that no living being besides themselves moved within the chamber. As deadly as he and Grundle were, they could not afford a fight that would cost their silence.

A minute crawled by. Reevan heard nothing but the incessant dripping.

Satisfied, he stepped forward. Closer inspection revealed a forgotten candle. The wick had curled over with the weight of the dying flame. Someone had set the candle at the base of a stone dais in the centre of the room, casting flickering shadows upon the statue above it. Reevan craned his neck upwards as he took in the sight.

The statue rose from the stone, towering above them, depicting a gruesome scene. The effigy was carved to resemble some sort of monstrous sea serpent, thirty feet tall, row upon row of stone teeth exposed as it held its maw wide, in the process of devouring a helpless soul depicted dangling upside down above it. All of the water in the room converged onto the statue, pooling around it, defying gravity as it raced upward and coated the monster's stone scales. The monster seemed to be crawling out of the dais itself, like the stone was nothing more than sand under waves. Again, Reevan had never seen anything like it.

Drip, drip, drip.

Reevan picked up the discarded candle from where it had been placed atop a small, thin box that sat at the edge of the dais. Lifting the meagre light source high, he heard Grundle's sharp intake of breath at the same instant his own eyes fully processed what he was seeing. He took a step back in quiet horror.

The humanoid figure being devoured by the creature was not part of the statue.

The figure was male, wearing a finely tailored suit, and the expensive jewellery he wore sparkled in the light as the candle passed over them. An elaborate mask was still affixed to the male's face. A rope had been placed around his ankles, suspending him from the ceiling to become a part of the grand display of stone.

But he was not made of stone.

He was flesh and blood.

And most of the latter had drained into the monster's waiting jaws. What little was left dripped, slowly, steadily, each drop spattering against the stone.

Reevan stared at the maw of the beast, watching the water converge with the blood, running between the monster's stone teeth and staining them a brilliant crimson. He had seen many disturbing scenes in his lifetime, but this was fast becoming one of the worst already.

"Well, this is a complication," Reevan murmured, feeling Grundle shift beside him. The goblin's eyes were wide, reflected in the candlelight, and he had already taken the small box that had lain at the foot of the statue. Reevan sniffed. Some things would never change.

"What god is this?" Grundle asked, robes shifting around the added weight. "Grundle has not seen it before."

Reevan stared up at the face of the stone monster. It did not look familiar. He could not even identify the species. If he squinted, it could have been a sculptor's strange interpretation of an underwater dragon, if it had been left there too long. The body was too long and sinewy for a true dragon, but he supposed most people had never seen one anyway, since dragons themselves were long extinct.

"It isn't," Reevan replied, circling around the statue. "I'll admit my knowledge of the gods is a little rusty, but off the top of my head I do not recall one who demands a sacrifice quite this literal."

He gestured to the unfortunate fellow, who had been relieved of all of his blood. Had he been a guest tonight? Would he be missed? Would there be people who would come to look for him, and find them?

Reevan felt a shiver travel up his spine, the fur along it rising. They needed to leave. Now. Not just the chamber, the entire temple. Preferably the city, too.

Grundle's lip curled as he stood before the leviathan, dwarfed beneath it. His head cocked to one side, like he were puzzled by it. Then the goblin spoke a single sentence that irrevocably changed Reevan's way of thinking.

"What if the god is not one of ours?"

Reevan had never once considered *that* before.

He started to expand on Grundle's theory, but the hairs on his neck stood up in alarm and he paused. Something was wrong. It took him a moment to place it.

The dripping had stopped.

The faint rhythmic sound replacing it was footsteps.

28

MAE

Finally, Mother. Soon I'll learn how to get you back.

The numbness in Mae's soul receded with every step, shrinking in the face of answers, of hope. It was all she could do to stop herself from sprinting across the ballroom, dragging Valandaras along with her. She wove her way through the crowd, letting the surge of guests carry her closer to the dais where Lai'ireal sat upon her makeshift throne.

There were many people waiting for an audience with the god; clamouring and jostling one another. They formed a line that curled around the dais and snaked along the edges of where couples danced. Mae refused to let it deter her. She tried not to count those ahead of her, nor the trickling of people who found their way behind her. To speak with Lai'ireal, she would wait all night if it were necessary.

Mae tried to contain her nerves by picking at the polish on her fingernails. Tiny red flakes fell onto the marble, reminding her enough of dried blood that she had to look away. One foot tapped in rhythm with the gentle music that played. Her eyes found the dancers, her body swaying in time with their steps. As much as she had hated her years living in Verestead, the extravagant balls had always been her favourite part. She barely registered when Valandaras moved away from her, probably to get another drink. Her thoughts tried to drift to decades past, but she yanked them back. She couldn't think of something as frivolous as dancing, not when the fate of her god hung in the balance.

I have to find a way to free the Mother. Lai'ireal must know something that can help.

A strong hand, gentle on her own, tugged her out of her head and the line. Valandaras had not gone to get another drink.

Mae pulled her arm back, brow furrowed in confusion. She made to join the line again, but stopped as his arm stayed extended. He wasn't leading her away.

Valandaras stood at the edge of the ballroom's dance floor, offering her his arm. He looked stiff, like he might drop his hand and return to the line at any second.

Like he was... embarrassed. Nervous, even.

"Lioness, when do you think we will ever get another chance to do this?" said Valandaras.

Mae's eyes went wide. *There's no way he wants to dance. He's doing this because he knows I do.* Her cheeks flushed with heat, and she was grateful for the mask that covered them.

"One dance, Val," she whispered, her tone a warning. "I can't miss her."

"You won't," he replied, taking her hand in his as he stepped out onto the dance floor.

Valandaras cradled her hand to his chest, before holding it in the appropriate manner for the type of dance they were about to attempt. Mae suppressed a shiver as his other hand rested on her waist, pulling her in closer to him. A sudden rush of nerves threatened to overtake her.

"I haven't done this dance in decades," Mae muttered. Her breath caught at the sound of his low chuckle in response. Even beneath the cloth and the mask, she swore she could see his eyes sparkle.

"When do you think I have ever performed this dance?" Valandaras whispered in her ear as the music swelled. She laughed aloud, drawing curious glances from the other dancers.

This is either going to be delightful or an absolute disaster.

And suddenly she was flying.

It was like remembering a dream, or a song not heard in an age. It had indeed been years since she had been in such a situation, a place that required a structured dance. But it felt familiar enough to come back to her. Mae let the notes of the music fill her soul, let the muscle memory of the steps take over as she twirled around the dance floor. The balls of arcane light twinkled around them, the crowd became little more than a blur.

Valandaras was not a brilliant dancer by any means, but he was steady and strong. He knew the basic steps. He held her tight when she pulled him towards her, and let her go when she needed only the slightest brush of their fingertips as she spun. When she forgot the next steps, he guided her into another spin, like he could tell from the pure joy on her face that they were her favourite part.

Emerald shimmered around her as she moved, the trickle of her Gift shining through like it, too, wanted to dance. For a moment, Mae sparkled like she were made of starlight. Terror at the unintentional flare of Divinity had her stumble a step, before remembering where she was. The people of Kalac revered the Divine. She was in no danger here for her Gift alone. Their entrance had already proven that.

Indeed, the others in the room that had shown their Gifts had made no secret of how they were favoured, whatever gods they served deeming their displays worthy. One of them was dancing close to them—a woman, her ebony skin glittering with iridescent light like she were bathed in the light from a stained-glass window. It was so stunning that Mae didn't immediately register who the Divine danced with until the crest of his house, displayed proudly upon his chest, came into view. Mae's heart faltered. She had seen that crest before.

This was the man Reevan had described as his former master, who controlled half of Kalac with his family's weaponry and subterfuge. The man who had stood on the edges of Crossroad and commanded an army of slaves to die for him.

This was Ashendi Braak.

Braak had not worn a mask, and Mae studied his features with a calculating eye. He reminded her of the enormous crocodiles that lazed along the rivers of the Freemeres. His eyes were beady and calculating, and his smiles had a sharp edge to them, like he could just as easily bite his companion as he could compliment her.

Valandaras settled them close, swaying with the music, in perfect earshot of the general. Mae felt a jolt of betrayal she knew she had no right to claim, but it coursed through her all the same.

Is this why he asked me to dance?

"Steady, lioness," Valandaras murmured, feeling her emotions shift, holding her closer than before. Mae narrowed her eyes and gazed past his mask, past his cloth, into his soul—and hoped eavesdropping on a dangerous enemy had not been the only reason Valandaras had taken her onto the dance floor.

If it had, though, it had been effective.

Ashendi Braak seemed to have been forced to dance with the Divine he now held due to some custom or protocol, but he did not want to engage with her attempts at conversation. A great hulking man, he towered over the delicate woman. The Divine appeared equally uncomfortable, and she wore her distaste openly, with a simple elegance. The conversation between the two was stilted, and yet Mae found herself listening intently.

"General, I have heard there have been more skirmishes at the border," the Divine said, her voice an air of polite indifference. "That the Altaeans continue to challenge you. Is that why you have remained in Saluo and not returned to Heartgate? Because of your failure at Crossroad?"

Braak bristled. "We have successfully halted the Altaean invasion," he replied stiffly, twirling the Divine around and then continuing to hold her at arm's length. The Divine smiled placidly.

"Ah, yes, of course, that's wonderful," she mused. "Kalac and its people are forever grateful for your continued protection, General."

Mae was grateful she had practice in keeping her expressions neutral. Only years of holding her face kept her brow from furrowing.

The Altaean invasion? Is that what the people of Kalac think?

Valandaras had stiffened in her arms, leaving them motionless. She stepped on his toe on purpose. He spun her again, a bit half-heartedly, but it kept them close.

"And what of your alliance with the Mahejerai?" the Divine asked. "Surely it has been useful having the Arcane join your ranks? Or do you count yourself amongst theirs now?"

The General regarded her with suspicion, eyes narrowing.

"The Mahejerai do not fight for me, nor do I for them. They are Arcane. They do not wear collars. They do not serve."

Mae chanced a glimpse at the couple. The Divine's face was impassive—as well as half-concealed by the stunning, jewel-encrusted mask she wore—but Mae thought she saw a flicker of something fiery in her eyes.

"No, General, of course not," she said. "All I meant was that you already command such a formidable and obedient army. Since the emperor's forces are preoccupied in the Freemeres, you are the southern cities' main defence. I would hope the addition of Arcane users would ensure that Kalac remains the powerhouse it always has been, with you to protect the border."

Mae and Valandaras shared a look. Whoever this woman was, she enjoyed the talk of war. Perhaps she was a Divine of Lai'ireal herself; it would explain the position of honour.

Braak's shoulders straightened and his chest puffed with pride. He enjoyed the praise.

"My force already rivals that of the emperor himself. I have much planned for this continent. The Mahejerai will merely play a small part in it."

"So Oorata Boras works for you, then?" the Divine asked.

Braak glanced towards where Oorata Boras stood, deep in conversation with an acolyte, and she twisted her head to follow his gaze.

"Boras and I have an... understanding," the general said with an oily smile. "He needs soldiers, and he pays handsomely for them. Altaea will suffer for their insolence. I dispatched their last High Marshal months ago—they are still scrambling to find order. We will continue to push into the borders they stole from us. They are weak. It's only a matter of time before they collapse."

Mae shivered. It was common knowledge that one of Braak's own men had assassinated the previous Altaean High Marshal. Hearing him openly brag about it, however, was enough to turn her stomach. Valandaras squeezed her hand.

The Divine's eyes narrowed. "And how much did that death truly cost you? I heard a rumour that you lost control of the Kiveri Czai shortly after," she remarked, letting the general spin her again, her delicate fingers alighting upon his shoulder once the turn completed. The tension between the two was becoming obvious, and other couples had moved further away, dancing circles to avoid crossing too near to them.

Mae was shocked at the Divine's brazen words. She knew from experience that those with Gifts often heard things not privy to the public, but there was an understanding that these things were to remain unspoken. Surely this was crossing a line, even for a Divine of Kalac.

Mae held her breath, straining to listen, suddenly frightened for the Divine. Valandaras had let her completely take over leading the dance, his own eyes boring into her without seeing as he concentrated on the conversation next to them.

The Divine had indeed said the wrong thing. Braak's nostrils flared and his lip curled, the lack of a mask giving his rage nowhere to hide on his face. For a moment, Mae thought he might simply shove her away and storm from the dance altogether.

"I did not *lose control*," he spat. "The Kiveri Czai's whereabouts are currently unknown because I wish them to be. Wars are not won solely by battles. Until you learn something of warfare, girl, hold your tongue."

"Of course, general."

The Divine continued to smile pleasantly, but did not attempt further conversation. Mae listened in vain, but they did not speak another word throughout the rest of the dance. The moment the music ended, Braak gave the Divine a stiff bow and stalked away, leaving her on the dance floor alone.

Mae could barely focus as Valandaras bowed to her, taking his hand in hers to pull her out of her polite returning curtsey. She sifted through the tiny pieces of information they had just learned, filing them away in case any of it could be helpful. Most of it appeared as though it would benefit Druitt and the military of Altaea, perhaps not much, but if they could get a message to them somehow—

Valandaras's lips brushed against her bare hand. Mae gasped softly, feeling a fluttering in her stomach. They were never this kind of close, never this... intimate.

"Thank you for the dance," he murmured, a hint of a smile tugging on his lips at her flustered expression.

Mae composed herself quickly. "I hope it was illuminating for you," she replied, raising an eyebrow, the effect ruined somewhat by her mask. Valandaras did not respond.

Mae kept her head high as she willed her shaking legs to carry her back towards the place where a few guests were still lining up to meet Lai'ireal. Thankfully, the ones she had stood next to before smiled warmly and beckoned her to resume her former place. Mae gave them a grateful smile as she did so. She could not afford any more time lost. There was certainly no more time for dancing. She needed to focus on what she had to ask the god, and hoped Valandaras would not mind if she did not speak as they waited.

But Valandaras did not join her in the line. Where had he gone?

Mae turned and watched from the sidelines, baffled, as Valandaras approached the Divine who had been dancing with Braak. The Divine assessed him with an exaggerated look up and down before accepting his hand and allowing him to lead her back onto the dance floor.

Mae told herself she felt nothing as she watched them dance. A muscle in her jaw twitched when the Divine let out an unexpected peal of laughter that rang like bells.

Mae shifted forward with the line of the devoted, ignoring the ringing in her ears, the burning sensation in her stomach. She tried not to watch, but her eyes never left Valandaras's back as he spun his newest dance partner around. The woman's dress glittered in the light like it were made of diamonds, and her body shimmered as her Gift rolled off her skin in waves, like there were no end to her power, like she were only letting a fraction of her true Gift show.

Mae swallowed the wave of jealousy that threatened to choke her.

A nasty voice whispered in her ear. *What if he means to recruit this Divine instead?*

Valandaras was her crewleader, and one who had kept her safe for half a decade. She had become useful to him using her Gift, and her ability to carry out jobs would be affected if she didn't free the Mother and restore her Divinity. She was afraid of losing that security, that was all.

You are replaceable, the voice whispered.

Except he had accepted her for who she was, Gift or no Gift, and had never once asked her to explain where she came from or who she had run from. He had taken her in before he had known what she could do. They had shared a table and a campfire for years. She knew what he was thinking half the time before he said it. She could read him like a book without even needing to see half of his face. Valandaras had seen her at some of the absolute lowest points of her too-long life, and still looked at her with something akin to reverence. Like she was a god.

A guard gestured to the people in front of Mae to step to the foot of the dais.

Perhaps that was what she was afraid of. Losing that casual intimacy, that peace of being able to simply exist with someone. The friendship, the camaraderie she shared with Valandaras didn't come easy. They had cultivated it through years of long night watches and abysmal weather conditions. Finding that level of trust again could well take another hundred years. A connection like that came once in twenty lifetimes.

The music swelled into a crescendo Mae knew well. It signalled the final part of the dance.

She'd been empty for so long. Valandaras had pulled her out of that trench, after sitting in it with her for much longer than any stranger should have felt obligated to do so. Perhaps she was afraid that if she lost him, lost the rest of the crew, that chasm would open up for her again.

No. I promised them I'd live. That I'd experience life, not just survive it.

If she regained her Gift or not, if she stayed with the others or not—that promise mattered above all else. The one she could never break.

The last guest to speak with Lai'ireal bowed deeply and melted back into the crowd.

Mae squeezed her eyes shut and took a shaky breath, willing her heartbeat to slow its frantic pace. How had her thoughts spiralled this badly? Valandaras had danced with someone else and suddenly she was reliving her life's worst traumas. She had thought little of how she was about to frame her questions to Lai'ireal, and now she was next.

She needed answers. *Mother, guide me.*

"Are you all right?" a soft voice murmured beside her. Mae's eyes flew open.

Valandaras stood beside her once more, like he had never left. He regarded her with a soft air of concern, like he could tell she had just lost her way inside her own mind and was struggling to claw her way back out of it. One of his arms reached out and grasped hers, squeezing gently.

"What do you need?" he asked. Even from beneath the cloth, she could feel his eyes searching her face.

Mae exhaled roughly. The guard standing closest to the dais beckoned her forward with an impatient wave. She took a single step forward, looking back over her shoulder at the Realmshifter beside her. All the animosity, the uncertainty fled from her mind in the warmth of his presence. He wouldn't replace her.

"Just stay with me," she whispered.

She didn't hear his response as she stepped forward and finally found herself standing before a god.

29

MAE

Mae bowed before Lai'ireal. The Lady of Many Faces, the Battle Maiden, the god of war herself.

Oh gods, which title would she prefer? Do any offend her?

Lai'ireal did not move other than a small incline of her head to indicate Mae could approach. Mae did so, fingers trembling, balling them into fists at her sides. Valandaras stood like a stone, beside her but also behind, letting her take the lead.

The dais wasn't tall, but it still made Lai'ireal's eyeline higher despite the god's seated position on her throne of honour. Mae stood at the edge and froze, panic gripping her as she realised she had absolutely no idea how to address a god.

The Mother only ever appeared in dreams, or like a feeling more than words. How strange that the first god I speak to in person should be not her, but another.

"Greetings, my lady," Mae said as she found her voice again, figuring standard noble politeness would suffice for the moment. Lai'ireal did not seem offended by her chosen formality, and Mae stifled her sigh of relief. She attempted to find the god's face behind the helmet, which had not been removed. Up close, the filigree engraved into the armour's surface was painstakingly detailed. A faint glow still came from within the gaps in the armour, like the Battle Maiden was containing her power for their benefit. It was unnerving, but Mae swallowed her discomfort and offered the god a welcoming smile.

"I hope this evening has been to your liking," she continued, hoping to forge a connection with the Battle Maiden before asking her to divulge her deepest secrets.

Another small incline of the head. Lai'ireal was not the talkative kind, then.

Mae cleared her throat, trying to calm the nerves coursing through her. She sent a skittering of her Gift rushing along her skin, letting the emerald spark just long enough for the god to see what she was. The only move Lai'ireal made was to drape one gauntleted hand over the edge of the throne. Her other still gripped her legendary spear, the point of which had been rumoured to pierce the walls of the Prison.

"I am afraid I have rather critical questions for you on this night," Mae said, keeping her voice light. She glanced behind her to where Valandaras scanned the room, one hand resting casually on the hilt of his falchion despite the peace-bind. Even without his armour, the Realmshifter still cut an intimidating figure, and those next in line to speak to the god were standing quite a way back, much more than they needed to.

Lai'ireal continued to stare down at Mae through the slits in her golden battle helmet. The metal armour clanged as she shifted on her throne, sitting slightly more upright. Mae took that to mean that she had the god's permission to continue.

"I follow the Mother," Mae said in hushed tones, terrified the wrong person would overhear. Her mouth still felt dry. "I do not know her true name, only that she is the god of all life, and she is in grave danger."

Lai'ireal did not respond.

"Her very essence has been syphoned and stolen, and I wish to find a way to restore it to her."

Silence.

"As you were the first to Breach, I thought you might know something about releasing that which has been captured. Anything that would help her reclaim it."

Silence.

"She is not the only god who has been targeted. Others will follow. Bor—whoever it is stealing their power intends to take it for themselves, perhaps even to ascend to a Mantle. They have to be stopped."

Silence.

Mae heard nothing but the pounding of her own blood in her ears.

She realised she was holding her breath and exhaled, letting the tension ease a little. She unwound her fingers from their fists, her nails having left little indentations in her palms.

Lai'ireal still regarded her without speaking, showing no indication she had heard, cared about, or even understood a single word. Did gods speak the common tongue?

Mae took another deep breath, willing the quaver in her voice to steady.

"Surely this concerns you, or at least troubles you a little?" she asked, a little less formally. She chanced another half-step forward, the toes of her silver shoes reaching the edge of the dais.

The god stiffened a little. Mae did not recede.

"Gods are being murdered," she whispered angrily. "Their very essence stolen, and with it the Gifts they bestow upon those who follow them. They are disappearing."

"What of *your* Gift, Divine?"

Lai'ireal had spoken at last. She leaned forward and fixed Mae with a pointed stare.

"Did the Mother's blessing fade slowly when she was drained like pus from a wound?" she said, her voice low and sharp. "Or was your connection severed like a blade through a limb?"

Mae flinched at the harsh descriptions.

"S-Severed," she answered, her voice suddenly hoarse. "What little I have left grows once more, but it is nothing compared to what I once held, and there are still Gifts I have lost, things I cannot do anymore."

Panic rose within her. How could she truly explain what had happened? How she had felt the Mother's essence tear from her very soul, how the absence even now ached within her like a death she could not mourn? Mae felt the numbness creeping back up over her, threatening to shut her down, and she pushed back on it desperately as she held the god's gaze.

Gods could be cryptic, petty, shallow beings, concerned only with their own fate. Maybe she had to make Lai'ireal see how it could happen to any god, even one of warfare.

"The Mother is not the only god to whom this fate has befallen," Mae said. "I fear more will follow, and losing them will do irreparable damage to their Divines. To our realm. Perhaps to our entire existence. Things may go back to how they were before the Breach."

Surely that has to be enough to worry her even a little?

Lai'ireal was silent once more, head tilted as she contemplated the information she had been presented with. Despite the urgency with which Mae had delivered her news, the god seemed supremely unconcerned. Metal clinked as her fingers tapped a rhythm onto the spear she held, vaguely in time with the music.

Mae felt her worry and fear warping, her agitation increasing by the second. She hated the note of desperation that had crept into her voice as she asked her questions, but now most of her willpower was being channelled into keeping from shaking with anger. She was running out of time. Perhaps a direct approach would be better.

"How can I stop these gods from being syphoned?"

Lai'ireal scoffed. "I am not an Oracle, child. I do not know."

But—

Mae's stomach twisted. They had come all this way, risked so much just for her chance to ask this question, and now there was no answer? It couldn't be.

"Then how do I help the Mother? How do I restore her?"

"Only death can restore life." Lai'ireal's eyes glowered from beneath the helmet.

Mae huffed. "What does that even mean?"

"It means that a god cannot be restored by a Divine's power alone."

Mother, this can't be happening...

Mae tried desperately to steer the conversation back to something useful. There had to be some scrap of information they could benefit from.

"But since you broke out of the Prison, you must have some idea—"

"I tire of your questions," Lai'ireal cut her off, waving a hand towards the crowd behind them. "It is time for you to return to the celebrations. Take care, Divine."

The god made a show of tilting her head past Mae to the next guests in line to speak, dismissing her entirely.

Like she was nothing.

Like her god meant nothing.

Mae felt the ripple of anger that had been building within her flare.

No.

In one swift movement, Mae stepped onto the dais.

The move drew gasps of shock from the patrons standing in line. The nearest guards started, stepping forward instinctively, before pausing as they realised rushing to the aid of the god of war could very well be seen as a grave insult. They satisfied themselves by creating a ring around the dais, but still gave it a wide berth. Mainly due to the Realmshifter standing at the base of it.

Mae felt the presence of Valandaras at her back, moving with her, standing between her and the honour guards. They faltered as they saw the light that pulsed beneath his skin, his uncovered hand faintly glittering as it hovered over the hilt of his peace-bound falchion. Perhaps they mistook him for Divine, above their laws and reproach; perhaps they had heard just how deadly a Realmshifter could be. Valandaras was calm, his face still covered by both mask and cloth, but his stance suggested he would fight the Battle Maiden himself if either she or the guards made a single move towards Mae.

Mae found herself looking down upon the seated god, and felt an unfamiliar flicker of true power, deep within. Heart racing, Mae pointed a shaking finger into Lai'ireal's face.

"If it were you," she hissed furiously, "syphoned, drained, ripped away from your Mantle. If it were your Divines who lost everything—were led to believe they could find answers with your brethren, only to be told there is nothing they can do to restore you—"

Lai'ireal had sat up straight, giving Mae her full attention at last. She lifted her chin, eyes still glowing under the helmet.

Righteous anger coursed through Mae as she stared at the god before her, so arrogant and nonchalant, so certain of her own indifference when it could have very well been her essence leeching into an ebony blade. Incapable of empathy, of putting herself in the place of another.

Mae would do it for her.

"You know what they'd do," Mae said. "What you would expect of them."

She felt her Gift rippling along her skin, like the Mother herself was listening and approving of her words. She straightened her shoulders, welcoming in the familiar feeling of it, and knew from the haze in her vision that her eyes had the faintest hint of an emerald glow to them, strangely similar to Lai'ireal's own spark.

The god inclined her head. A silent invitation for Mae to finish her thoughts. It was the most respectful move she had made all night.

"They would go to war for you," Mae said simply. "As I will for her."

And with that, she turned on her heel, stepped down from the dais and walked away. All the while feeling the violent, burning eyes of Lai'ireal boring into her back.

The adrenaline had worn off as Mae reached the table the crew had originally circled around, having stormed through the crowd as far away from the god as possible. Her heartbeat thundered in her ears, blood pounding.

Reevan and Grundle had disappeared. Lessie and Camden were still there, sullenly sipping their drinks and not speaking to one another, though the lord's hand rested possessively on the back of the ranger's chair as he stood beside it. Mae shook her head, too caught up in her own anger to comment on it. Those two were a wildfire waiting to happen.

"That bad, I take it?" Camden asked as she approached, bright smile faltering as he took in her expression.

Mae did not respond.

Valandaras, who had followed her through the crowd without a word after her altercation with Lai'ireal, sighed and rested his forearms upon the table. Lessie's eyes barrelled a thousand unspoken questions into him.

"We need to start thinking of other directions to explore," he said, keeping his voice low and level. "The Lady of Many Faces knew nothing of how to help us, or of how to free the Mother's essence."

"She cannot know *nothing*," Mae spat, slamming her fist upon the table. "She is a god."

A couple of nearby guests glanced her way quizzically, and Valandaras gave her a pointed stare that she felt even through the cloth and the mask. She didn't care.

"She refused to help. Lai'ireal dismissed my questions as if they were nothing," Mae hissed, feeling desolation try to settle upon her and violently shrugging it off. The rage was burning too hot for her to be numb. "Either she knows more than she let on, or she wants the Mother's essence to stay syphoned."

Lessie's eyes narrowed as she glanced between Mae and Valandaras.

"Could that be true?" she asked. "Could Lai'ireal have meant the Mother harm?"

Valandaras shook his head. "I do not think so, but there must be a reason she was not forthcoming with her answers. Perhaps she knew of Oorata Boras's plans already and wished not to talk in such a public setting."

Mae sighed loudly. "So we should do what? Waltz into a temple, pray, and hope Lai'ireal deems the area secure enough to deign to speak with me again? To give me another lot of nonsense riddles and rude dismissals? No. I need to question her again, here."

"This is not a moment to be brash, lioness," said Valandaras. "I believe we should—"

"Ah, you're all here. Excellent."

Reevan's polite voice cut through their conversation as the kitskan joined them at the table. He stood with his usual air of aloof casualness, but he was breathing hard under his porcelain mask, like he had recently run up several flights of stairs. He also smelled of salt, like he had spent the evening at the beach of all places.

"We need to leave," said Reevan firmly. "Immediately."

Grundle was already hovering by the door to the antechamber that would lead them outside. The goblin was doing his best to appear nonchalant, but he had the same disturbed posture, like he was ready to bolt from the room at the slightest provocation.

"Miss Mae, did you have the chance to speak with Lai'ireal tonight?" Reevan asked. Mae frowned, but slowly nodded, and Reevan's shoulders relaxed in mild relief. "Wonderful. Then we have tempted fate enough, and there is nothing keeping us from making a graceful and nondescript exit." He gathered his robes around him, already beginning to turn towards the doors.

Mae opened her mouth—whether to question or to argue, she hadn't decided yet—but stopped as Lessie and Camden both drained their glasses and slammed them down upon the table in perfect unison.

"Reevan's right," Lessie muttered, shoving the chair out from under her and rising to her feet, the periwinkle tulle floating around her like a cloud. "Besides, I don't want to be in the same room as that monster for any longer than I have to."

Mae didn't have to follow Lessie's glance to know that the girl had been fixated on Boras's location within the pyramid the entire time they had been here.

Reevan had caught his breath for the most part, and he began to edge away from the table. Valandaras fixed the kitskan with a hard stare.

"What have you done?"

"I did what we all came to do," Reevan replied. "I went looking for answers. But I do not think the Mahejerai would be very pleased with the answers that I found."

Mae glanced around. The celebration was still in full swing. People laughed and chatted, dancers whirled around the ballroom floor, members of the Mahejerai still stood talking with Kalac's elite. The Divines in the room still glittered with their Gift, basking in the praise of the common people. Lai'ireal still perched upon her golden throne, speaking to nobody, her form stiff as if she had turned to stone.

There did not seem to be any discord through the guards, no shouting or closing of rank, but if Mae looked closely, there appeared to be a few gaps in the line that had not been there before. It was entirely possible that they had moved elsewhere, but judging by Reevan's demeanour, they were most likely either dead or stuffed into a closet somewhere. Unless they were actively searching for him, in which case, he was right. They needed to leave now.

Mae hesitated. They couldn't leave now, could they? She hadn't gotten the answers she needed. She still had no idea how to free the Mother. A sharp pain jolted behind her left eye, and she pressed her thumb into it violently, feeling the mask shift. *Mother, forgive me.*

"I want a full explanation later," she muttered. Reevan gave her a small bow.

"Of course, Miss Mae," he replied, spinning on his heel and striding towards Grundle. Lessie and Camden had already left the table, hastening towards the temple's exit. Mae followed them, her silver heels making tiny clicking noises on the marbled floor, when the strangest sensation came upon her. Strange, and yet familiar. She paused, letting the feeling wash over her.

The faintest hint of a summer breeze, airy and warm, brushed past her face and slightly ruffled her hair. A single strand of red pulled across her vision and she reflexively brushed it behind her ear. It smelled like budding flowers, like the forest. Like home.

Confused, she looked back at Valandaras, who had stilled behind her. The Realmshifter, reading her face, rested a hand on her back, to comfort and guide her forward.

And over his shoulder, halfway across the vast, opulent room, through the mask of a demonic sea creature, Mae's eyes met those of Oorata Boras.

Narrowed, unforgiving eyes, which had started to fill with the first fragments of recognition.

30

VALANDARAS

The spark of fear on Mae's face was enough. Valandaras moved.

He did not look back to see what had caused her to tense. It was not time to ask questions. He strode forwards, grabbing Mae by the wrist and pulling her behind him, feeling her pulse beat wildly underneath his uncovered fingers. Valandaras did not run, but his back straightened, his pace quickened, and those in front moved like his demeanour alone commanded they part for him.

Together, they made their way towards the doors. Valandaras had already lost sight of the others in the crowd of guests, but they all knew the goal was to leave. He had to focus on getting Mae out first. The others were less conspicuous. She drew the most attention.

Valandaras did not slow. He kept Mae beside him, his arm across her shoulders like she was sick or injured, shielding her from the curious eyes that now lay upon them. His goal beat in his chest like a drum, like this alone was now his Path.

Protect them. Get them out.

That was all that mattered.

"He knows," Mae hissed, her voice on the edge of hysteria, nails digging into the flesh on his arm as she clutched it for support. Splotches of angry red started to appear across Mae's chest, creeping up her neck and into her hairline, the stress of the sheer panic marring her creamy skin. It clashed violently with the emerald of her gown. Valandaras did not have time to contemplate the strange feeling of his own golden light rushing to the spots underneath his skin, counteracting the pain, as it had begun to do in the last few months.

Protect them.

Valandaras caught a glimpse of Reevan, the kitskan moving swiftly through the large doors into the pyramid's antechamber. Lessie and

Camden followed through a moment later, the girl's dress swirling around her like spray from a waterfall. Grundle was probably already halfway back to Bueno's. Valandaras focused on making sure each one of them left the room before he did.

Get them out.

A flash of amethyst to his right had him reaching for his falchion on instinct, barely disguising the movement at the last moment, pushing away an attack that did not come. The peace-bond wrapped around the hilt snapped loudly. The Arcane in Mahejerai robes paused his display of lights as they brushed past, frowning in confusion, stumbling. Valandaras sensed the movement of the Arcane looking back towards Boras for instruction.

A murmur of dissent rippled through the crowd of guests.

Protect them. Get them out.

As they reached the massive doors, Mae's red-tipped fingernails curling around the handle and wrenching it open, Valandaras finally allowed himself a glance back into the ballroom. His eyes were immediately drawn to the leader of the Mahejerai.

Oorata Boras had made no move towards them, had not taken a single step from where he stood. But his face—what little of it that could be seen beneath the hideous mask of the sea demon—belied a thunderous rage that seemed to crackle along the very walls of the pyramid.

The balls of Arcane light flickered ominously.

Conversations around them fizzled and died.

In one fluid movement, every single member of the Mahejerai in the room turned to face them.

Valandaras felt the hairs on the back of his neck stand up as he slammed the antechamber door shut behind them.

They broke into a run.

They rushed through the smaller room, which was thankfully empty save for a few wide-eyed servers carrying overladen trays of food and drink back and forth from the main room. A few curious eyes met theirs and flickered away again, no doubt terrified to be seen not fully devoted to their assigned task.

Mae stumbled, and Valandaras paused long enough for her to gather the skirts of her dress in her hand, the other still tightly gripping his. She looked up into his face, eyes wide with fear, emerald skittering along her skin, and the thought clanged through him—that he could face no nobler death than to go down fighting if it meant that she got out.

Protect her.

A blast of cool night air hit his face as they burst through the pyramid's entrance. The guards who stood at the main doors of the temple shouted in alarm, but he did not stop to see if they were followed, rushing down the stone steps towards the street below. Their faster gait drew attention, Mae's silver heels clicking sharply on the pavement, a few patrons outside going so far as to point and exclaim.

Valandaras spotted Lessie and Camden also running, all decorum forgotten, focused only on putting as much distance between themselves and the pyramid as possible. Over his shoulder, Valandaras caught a glimpse of movement near the pyramid's entrance, though he could not discern much else. Every instinct he had was roaring at him to turn and fight, to eliminate the threat rather than run from it. But he knew that if he did so, he was putting countless innocent bystanders at risk. Even without the Mournblade, Oorata Boras was an enigma. Determined to become a god. They had no idea what he was capable of doing to get what he wanted.

And he wanted the last spark of the Mother that still flickered inside of Mae.

Get her out.

Mae gave a choked sob of relief, and Valandaras looked to where their carriage still stood, horses hitched to a post and idly awaiting their return. Halliday Greyholme lounged upon the roof of the carriage, booted feet dangling over the side, a thin plume of smoke rising from the cigarette in her hand as she stared up at the starry sky.

She bolted upright with a bloodcurdling shriek as Reevan came barrelling out of the shadows, took a flying leap, and landed next to her, jostling the carriage. He must have informed her of their current situation, for she let out an extremely vulgar curse word that even Lessie might have cringed at and leaped into action, unhooking the reins of the horses from the post they had been hitched to.

Reevan yanked the door of the carriage open from above it, and Grundle's masked face poked out, long fingers beckoning to them. Valandaras and Mae reached the carriage at the same time as Lessie and Camden. The two men shared a solemn look as the women clambered inside, Mae shoving Lessie in before her, a piece of the girl's dress tearing as it caught on one of the steps. Lessie ripped it free, snarling in frustration. As Camden hurriedly entered the carriage, Valandaras turned back towards the pyramid.

Oorata Boras stood alone at the entrance to the temple.

His eyes were glowing purple.

"You'd better get in!" shouted Halliday, who had finished readying the horses and vaulted nimbly back into the driver's seat. Somehow her cigarette had stayed lit and perfectly balanced between her lips. She took a violent drag that burned up half the remaining paper and gestured wildly to the open door.

Valandaras slammed the carriage door shut, hooked his boots into the outer step, and slapped the roof. Halliday shrugged and gathered the reins between her fingers, the sharp crack they made echoing through the relatively peaceful night. The carriage lurched, the horses nickering, stressed from the scent of fear in the air, steps unsteady as Halliday urged them to go as fast as possible. Transports like these were not designed for speed, and the wood groaned as the powerful bodies of the horses dragged it forward much faster than they were used to.

Valandaras did not take his attention from the leader of the Mahejerai.

So he saw when Boras raised a pointed finger towards them. He saw the malicious smile on the man's face illuminated by the Arcane glow of his eyes. Valandaras saw the purple light grow brighter. And he saw the crackling ball of energy as it hurtled towards them.

There was no possible way to outrun it.

There was nothing he could do to stop it.

Or was there?

Protect her.

Valandaras tore off his mask, sending it clattering onto the street. He yanked at the cloth beneath it, pulling it down and exposing his entire face for the first time in decades. He opened his eyes and stared straight into the sphere of rippling energy. Golden realmlight streamed from him, a beacon meeting the sphere. For an agonising second, it was as if the Arcane energy had been made even stronger.

Valandaras raised his hand, closed his fingers around the open air, and *pulled.*

It was like he had ripped a hole in the very fabric of the world.

A tear appeared in the air itself. Blinding light poured from within it like blood from a wound. The carriage did not stop, and the jagged tear began to close the further they moved away, like the ripple of a boat in the water. Valandaras cried out as he forced his hand downwards, widening the split as best he could, still gripping the side of the carriage to stop himself from being torn from it. His eyes burned, and he fought the urge to squeeze them shut.

The ball of Arcane energy passed through into the tear of light he had created, the air around it sizzling with heat as it disappeared in front of him. A sickening sensation coursed through him where the sphere should have annihilated them all.

His hands shook. His fingers burned. One horse whinnied in terror, and Valandaras could hear screaming, though he didn't know where it was coming from.

He couldn't hold it any longer. He let go.

The tear immediately began to seal up, folding the light within like it was eager to become whole again, trapping the Mahejerai's sphere inside. In seconds, it was as if it had never happened.

Valandaras's vision swam with dark spots, and he squeezed his eyes shut, fumbling with the cloth that had pooled around his chin, desperate to have it covering him again. He blinked furiously under the cloth, willing his vision to return to normal. He strained his eyes towards the temple, searching for signs of another incoming attack. None came.

They were too far away, now, for him to make out any details beyond silhouettes. The figure standing alone at the base of the pyramid did not move. No energy sparked or crackled.

But as the carriage turned a corner and disappeared into the night, Valandaras swore he could feel a sense of deep, unfathomable fury radiating, not only from the man who stood upon its steps, but from the temple itself.

They rode in silence.

Nobody spoke as they jostled from the rocking of the carriage as it took corners too fast, as it twisted through side streets and changed directions abruptly. Valandaras knew that the Greyholme girl was laying down a foundation of confusion, to disguise which way they had gone, but with the most powerful Arcanes in the city hunting them, it would only last so long.

None of them had bore witness to what he had done, having all been inside the carriage, and he was not going to explain it unless he had to. After they had turned the corner, he had wrenched open the door and swung inside while the carriage remained in motion, and the only sound since had been their heavy breathing as they tried to calm their racing hearts.

It was cramped inside the carriage with all six of them. Lessie hissed expletives under her breath as her elbow cracked against the window, having twisted in her seat to avoid physical contact with Camden, who had tried to give Valandaras some room on their side. A light sheen of sweat covered them both. Mae stared at the floor, wisps of auburn dragging free of the hairpins as she swayed with the carriage's movement, elbows on her knees, utterly dejected. Grundle sat next to her with his favourite dagger unsheathed and angled towards the carriage door.

Reevan, to his credit, appeared completely at ease. The kitskan tapped out a rhythm on the carriage's wooden window frame with one clawed fingernail, gazing out of the shuttered window like he was on a daytime sightseeing trip. Valandaras soon became aware of the sound of Lessie cracking her knuckles, one by one, as if she were desperate to relieve even the smallest amount of pressure within her. Once she had finished, she clasped her hands together and broke the silence.

"Reevan," said Lessie through clenched teeth, "what... the *fuck*... just happened?"

Reevan seemed momentarily perplexed at Lessie's question.

"I think that went quite well, all things considered," he replied. "We have information we did not before, and we did not become captured or die horrible deaths at the hands of the Mahejerai."

"What information?" Mae said despondently, still staring at the carriage floor. "Lai'ireal gave me nothing."

"Well, for one, we now know that Boras's choice of headwear is not merely for aesthetic," said Reevan, and he gave the others a brief description of what he and Grundle had discovered lurking miles beneath the pyramid. Their faces twisted from apprehensive to downright disturbed as they listened. When he got to the statue of the sea creature, Lessie interrupted him.

"And it had a dead person hanging on it?" she asked in horror. Her face had gone pale underneath her freckles.

"Yes, Lessandra," Reevan confirmed. "An extremely well-dressed one. I could have retired on the rings alone, but I thought it best not to disturb them. Beautiful suit, made of velvet, if I'm not mistaken."

"Oh, Mother," Mae whispered, voice full of dread. "They were Divine. I saw them when we first arrived, but I thought he must have left."

Valandaras searched his memories of the night, but did not recall seeing a Divine in a velvet suit. Perhaps Mae had a sense for those things, or had seen a Gift be used in a way more subtle than the other Divines. Regardless, it was a horrible way to die, and proof that the Mahejerai were not above killing to get the Divinity they were seeking. But even as revulsion for the senseless death filled him, a small part of Valandaras sagged in relief.

It's not about her, he thought. *At least, not only her.*

Reevan described the statue in detail, as well as their journey leaving the chamber, avoiding the acolytes sent to check on the Divine's body, and returning to the ballroom. Towards the end of Reevan's tale, it was Camden who interrupted.

"If you were so sure nobody saw you, why did we need to leave immediately?" he asked, his brow knitting together in confusion. "And why did every Mahejerai in the building seem to know who we were?"

"Grundle took something."

The goblin had melted in between Reevan and Mae so completely it had been easy to forget he was there. He now leaned forward and produced a long, thin box from within his robes.

It resembled the kind of storage vessel Valandaras had seen belonging to travelling performers, to keep their instruments safely packed away between cities. He had once met a kitskan woman who carried a contraption within a similar box that, when attached together, formed a powerful device that allowed one to see the stars as if they were up close. There could be any manner of things inside it.

Mae reached for the box, running her delicate fingers along the side, where delicate runes had been carved along its surface, though some were faded and hard to see.

"It's beautiful. What's inside?" she asked Grundle, the flicker of curiosity in her eyes momentarily outshining the dark shadows underneath them.

"Don't know. Won't open."

"Oh, godsdamn it," Lessie swore, throwing her hands up. "We've made enemies with the strongest Arcane faction in all of Kalaraak because y'all stole a box, and you don't even know what's inside of it?"

"In Grundle's defence, they were already our enemies, Lessandra," replied Reevan. "I will say, seeing Braak schmooze with the Mahejerai was worrying. He has little reason to still be in Saluo."

"He's supplying Oorata Boras with soldiers," said Mae, picking at what was left of the polish on her nails. "Whether to serve as a distraction while the Mahejerai cross into Altaea to harvest gods, or simply to give them the protection of a larger force, I don't know. They have an 'understanding', whatever that means. What little we overheard was muddy."

She sighed deeply. "He told the Divine it was to 'halt the Altaean invasion'. He even bragged about using the Kiveri Czai."

Lessie and Camden's faces wore twin flames of outrage.

"Us invade them?" the young lord spluttered incredulously. "That's preposterous."

"Absolutely ridiculous," said Lessie. Camden smirked and she threw a look of disgust his way, annoyed they had been like-minded.

"What did he say about the Kiveri Czai?" Reevan asked. "It's been a while since I've heard that name."

Mae told the others what they had overheard during their dance. Valandaras said nothing, but his mind continued racing, trying to put the dots together. He kept coming back to Braak's bragging of the Altaean attack. Did Braak bring a legion of soldiers down upon Crossroad just so that the Arcane with the Mournblade could come for Mae? Was that the 'understanding' between Braak and Boras?

The carriage lurched to a stop, and Valandaras kept one hand on the hilt of his falchion, the peace-bond long snapped. Others did the same, reaching for weapons, even Camden's hand hovering nervously over his sword.

Halliday's hooded face appeared in the door.

"We're covering our asses," she explained, yanking the door open and gesturing to exit the carriage.

Valandaras glanced around, but could not pinpoint where in Saluo they were. The alley was empty except for another carriage, smaller than theirs with heavily curtained windows. The driver of the other vehicle, still and hunched over the reins, was so enveloped in their dark clothing that Valandaras could not discern their gender or race. The only light came from a small lantern, the raised edges of Halliday's scar standing out more against her pale skin in the flickering light as she held it aloft. She spoke in hushed tones as she guided them into the second carriage.

"That one," Halliday said, jerking her thumb backwards towards their first carriage, "will make its way back into the upper half of Saluo. I'll take you out of the northern gate and circle around back to Bueno's."

The crew silently shuffled out of their seats and into the smaller carriage, disappearing one by one into the dark cabin. Valandaras lingered between the carriages, seeing the others safely inside. Halliday gave him a crooked smile.

"If I were you, I'd grab your shit and get ready to disappear," she said. "Luckily you have the best damn smuggler this side of the Freemeres with you." She adjusted her cloak until her face was barely visible before approaching the other driver.

Valandaras noted the somewhat brazen exchange of coin between Halliday and the figure who had taken her place upon the original carriage. Even from a distance, by the size alone, it was more coin than Druitt had paid them for Camden's liberation. The stranger's pouch was a lot heavier than it had been mere minutes before, but the risk to their life had also increased substantially with the Mahejerai on the hunt.

When does it no longer become a worthy trade, gold for life?

Halliday caught his eye and grinned, tipping an imaginary brim of a hat she did not wear.

"Relax, Realmshifter," she said, hoisting herself into the driver's seat of the new carriage and adjusting the length of the reins in her gloved fingers. "Your secret is safe with me, and Bueno is a man of his word. No harm will come to you and yours while you're dealing with us. We'll get you out."

"Why would he be so invested in our survival?" Valandaras asked. He had found promises like that to mean little.

Halliday's smile only widened. "Because you intrigue him. Bueno has been around for a very, very long time, Realmshifter, and he has seen it all. You presented him with a story he didn't immediately know the ending to."

She patted the seat next to her, and Valandaras gave it a hard stare before slamming the door to the carriage closed and climbing up beside her. For a smuggler, she certainly was cheerful.

Halliday's demeanour only improved as they made their way through the northern gate. The guards stationed there were bleary-eyed and receptive to both the charming smile she flashed and the coin she presented. They did not comment on the carriage or ask to look inside.

Valandaras's hand did not leave the hilt of his falchion until long after the gate had disappeared from view.

Halliday commented on the night's weather more than once, like she wanted to start up a conversation, but Valandaras remained silent. He knew she had witnessed what he had done, how he had stopped the Arcane attack, and the shame and guilt of that alone threatened to undo him. A melting pot of emotions radiated from inside the carriage, fear and anger the strongest, and he grappled with the uncomfortable feeling of not knowing what to do next. He always had a plan, a strategy, and for once, he was at a complete loss. His Path was unclear.

There have to be others we could speak to. Other Divines, perhaps, in Verestead, or one of the major cities. We should focus on preventing Boras's plans to take a Mantle, or to find a way to release the syphoned power, and then that will bring about the Mother's freedom. But nothing feels right. These are not clear Paths.

Valandaras breathed a small sigh of relief as the shape of Bueno's tavern finally loomed in the darkness. Halliday halted the carriage directly in front and gave him a surprisingly serious look.

"I'll give you ten minutes," she said, "and then I'll get you back into Altaea alive. Don't keep me waiting."

Valandaras nodded. Unfinished business or not, their time here in Kalac was done. He opened the carriage's door and ushered the rest of the crew inside. The explosion of sound that greeted them within Bueno's was even more potent than before, and they did their best to avoid the crowd, the party in full swing celebrating the Night of Many Faces for those who had not received an invitation to the ball at the pyramid. Reevan gazed longingly towards the bar, eyes searching for the dark-furred kitskan, but was urged forward. They ascended the staircase to the inn's sleeping quarters. Valandaras paused long enough to see them run towards their respective rooms, gathering the belongings their formal attire had forced them to leave behind, before he strode into his own room.

The first thing he grabbed was the Mournblade, and had barely finished sliding it into his belt when a high-pitched scream of surprise made his blood run cold.

It was Mae's scream.

He hurtled from his room, narrowly avoiding smashing the flimsy wooden door from its hinges as he charged straight across the hall. Mae and Lessie had both frozen in the doorway, Mae's hands covering her mouth like she could force the scream back in.

There was someone already in their room.

Lessie's eyes darted wildly between the stranger and the trunk at the foot of her bed where her revolver resided. Mae had looked towards him, her face clouded with confusion. Falchion half-unsheathed, Valandaras stared at the uninvited guest.

It was the Divine from the temple. The one he had danced with.

Still in her sparkling gown and elaborate mask, the Divine's ebony skin glowed softly from within. She perched on the edge of Mae's bed as if it were a throne, like she had been waiting there for hours. At the temple, her glow had been so bright that it blurred her edges, but now it had dimmed, as if muted in their presence. She rose gracefully in one fluid movement and gave them all a curt nod.

"It took you longer to return than I had hoped. We do not have long to speak," she said. Her voice was low and sharp, with a strange overtone to it, like she were speaking from two pitches at once. It had not sounded that way within the pyramid. True, she had not said much during their short dance, and in his rather pathetic bid to appeal to her for information, Valandaras had only asked her a single question—one she had laughed at.

Mae stepped warily into the room.

"Why would you come all this way to speak with us?" she asked, eyes narrow with suspicion. There was a note of open hostility in her voice that Valandaras had not heard before.

The Divine did not answer Mae's question. She reached both hands behind her head and unravelled her mask. Valandaras noticed a few things all at once.

How the muscles in her arms rippled with the quiet strength of a seasoned fighter. She had seemed quite diminutive for a human woman while dancing with her—but standing before him now, she was at least as tall as he was. Her eyeline matched his easily.

Now that her skin wasn't shimmering so brightly with the iridescent light, it became apparent that she was covered in scars. Some were pale white and tiny, others dark, some angry and raised and red. Criss-crossed and intersected between each other, a thousand cuts, old underneath new. Many he recognised as the tell-tale marks of a sword or an arrowhead.

Battle scars. The scars of a warrior.

And lastly, Valandaras took in the set of her jaw, the grounded stance of her feet, the confidence in her posture. He remembered that this woman had stared into the eyes of Ashendi Braak—Kalac's most infamous war general—and shown not one ounce of fear.

Only fire. Only challenge.

The Divine pulled the mask from her face. Mae gasped.

Her face was otherworldly, ethereal; she was so beautiful it was almost painful to behold. Her features seemed to shift in the dim light, like her very skin was struggling to contain it all in one place. Now free of the mask restricting it, her long, curly hair framed her like a dark halo, tumbling around her, snagging behind delicately pointed ears.

She regarded them all with glowing, golden eyes. It was like looking into sunlight.

"Because I am Lai'ireal, the god of war," she said. "And I have heard a lot about you, Mae of the Valefork."

31

VALANDARAS

Realisation coursed through Valandaras like lightning.

The Lady of Many Faces.

The god's own nickname should have told them. The god of war had indeed been at the Mahejerai's temple, but she was not the apathetic warrior who had lounged on a throne before them; she had not answered the questions Mae asked. Lai'ireal, the true Lai'ireal, now stood before them, resplendent in her gown, preternaturally still and looking impatient as she regarded them all with glowing violet eyes.

Mae had gone pale as death.

"How do you know of the Valefork?" she asked warily, stepping further into the bedroom. Valandaras repressed the urge to yank her backwards, hand drifting not towards his falchion, which he had sheathed, but to the Mournblade shoved hastily into his belt. He wished he had been able to don his armour before this confrontation, though he knew even with it he would be little match for the god of war herself. She could obliterate them all without a second thought.

"Long have there been Divines who... stand out," said Lai'ireal. The god's perfect face was a veil of vague indifference. "Their gods take special interest in them. The Mother always spoke fondly of you, having followed her for a century and made such creative uses of your Gift."

Mae blushed, a strange mix of pride and grief filling her face. She perched on the end of the rickety bed and stared at the floor, the fabric of her beautiful dress wrinkling and bunching. Lessie hovered in the door beside Valandaras. She caught his eye and mouthed silently, 'a century?', her own eyes wide.

Wisely, he did not respond. Some Divines were rumoured to be ageless.

"Your Gift only strengthened when you found your way back to the Mother after your tragic loss," Lai'ireal continued. Mae's head shot up, eyes full of warning, but the goddess did not seem to notice. "We had thought perhaps that was the catalyst, but we were mistaken. No matter."

"What catalyst?" said Lessie from the doorway, who regarded the god with her usual suspicion. "And who is 'we', exactly?"

Lai'ireal turned glowing eyes towards Lessie, as if noticing another in the room for the first time. She seemed irritated that Lessie had dared speak to her first.

"The Pantheon of Gods, young one," she replied, ignoring Lessie's frown at her wording. "After spending an eternity in a cage, we keep a close eye on the plots against our power. We have had a mere hundred years to rebuild what was stolen from us, and still there are Mantles that sit empty, some who may never return."

Lai'ireal paced, her shimmering gown melting away to reveal a set of regal plate armour identical to what her decoy had worn while in the Mahejerai's temple, though without her distinctive helmet. The engraved detailing on the shield at her back drew Valandaras's eye as it glinted in the dim candlelight. It depicted a scene from an ancient battle, where Lai'ireal and Haropheth had together slain an army of ten thousand led by a rival god. He had heard the legend from his Pod leader, who spoke at length of Haropheth's harsh judgment of the traitors.

Lai'ireal turned back towards them, even more imposing in her armour. The top of her head was close to brushing the ceiling, making her easily eight feet tall. When had she become so tall?

"The Betrayal has made more than a few of us paranoid and more inclined to meddle, though it is forbidden. Even so, I cannot interfere much, other than to offer some guidance."

Lessie edged into the room and sat upon her own bed, pulling at the ribbons that kept her mask attached to her face. Strands of her long chestnut hair came with it as she ripped it free, and she swore under her breath before opening her trunk and shoving the mask inside. Valandaras did not miss how the movement brought her closer to her revolver, pulling it from the trunk and into her lap in a fairly stealthy move. Beneath his initial disapproval, he admired her gall.

The girl would draw a gun on a god, he thought, closing the door and leaning against it.

Mae followed Lessie's lead, delicate fingers weaving through waves as she slowly unwound the vines of her mask and removed the pins from her hair. It swirled around her as the style came apart, wreathing her in a temporary halo of flame. She kept her face passive and her voice even, but Valandaras could practically see her heart pounding as she spoke.

"Why come to me here, now?" Mae asked. "Why not speak at the temple?"

"The celebration for my return has long since devolved into shameless carnival tricks, a mockery of what it once was," Lai'ireal replied, the strange double-tone of her voice less prominent as they became used to it. "People of no faith, come to gawk at a god. I usually do not bother with it. I have been sending my most faithful Divines to serve in my place for decades. The mewling crowds have never noticed the difference."

Lai'ireal scowled, eyes darkening in anger.

"But there have been whispers of treachery I could no longer ignore. The Mahejerai have long tried to connect the Weave of the Arcane and the Gifts of the Divine together, to increase their power and their influence in this world, which is their prerogative. But this new leader has gone too far. When I felt the stirrings of a new war begin, I had to know more of his plan."

Lai'ireal turned and crossed the room again, like she was a wild animal unused to being confined in such a small space. The ancient spear strapped to her back behind her shield was so tall it would have scraped the ceiling had she let it; the main tip so sharp it had supposedly pierced the Godprison itself. Solarium, it was called. The point of the sun. A Sliver—and a powerful one, since it was wielded by the god it belonged to, rather than gifted to a Divine or lost to the ages.

Valandaras felt Mae's eyes on him for a split second, but when he returned the glance, her eyes were on the goddess. Perhaps he was mistaken.

"We saw you dance with Ashendi Braak," Mae said, questioning in her tone, along with wisps of that unfamiliar hostility.

Lai'ireal continued her pacing. "There were parts of this plan that I could see clearly, but others are clouded. Braak's involvement is one. I even resorted to *talking* with the man, but he was... reluctant to discuss his newest alliance. He seems to think he is the one to fear, the mastermind behind it all. He is a fool. Oorata Boras holds the key to this entire realm's undoing. A powerful Arcane, who has stolen enough Divine essence to become a god himself."

"Has he, though?" asked Lessie, not looking up, focusing on removing her dainty shoes. She threw one into her trunk like it had offended her.

"Because I've personally stopped him from syphoning gods at least twice now."

Despite the situation, Valandaras felt the corners of his mouth twitch.

Lai'ireal ignored Lessie and continued to address Mae.

"Oorata Boras is extremely dangerous. In his quest for power, he has entangled his fate with something not of this realm. Only a god can freely bestow an unclaimed Mantle, so he searched the seven realms for one that will grant him what he wishes. He has been gathering Divinity ever since, possibly as a way to break that god through into this realm."

At this, Mae's eyes met Valandaras from across the room. He knew what she was thinking. The statue of the sea creature. It *was* a god.

"Yes," Lai'ireal said, like she had read their thoughts. "Not all gods are created equal, just as not all realms are as vast as this one. Some gods rule alone. Unchecked and isolated, unable to leave the realm they command. Most of them prefer it that way. Boras has found one that craves more. We know him as Daigon, the god of darkened depths. He is the sole god of Keanos."

Valandaras felt his heartbeat quicken. He had been to Keanos—the realm of water—only once in his life. It was a simple realm, tiny compared to others, home to a few peaceful semi-aquatic races and more deep, open ocean than he had seen before or since. His Pod had searched the entirety of it for signs of Vry'iin in less than a decade. He had not met the god of darkened depths himself, but they had left the realm a member short.

Lai'ireal, for the first time, looked troubled.

"You *must* prevent Boras from doing this, from bringing a god into this realm that was not meant for it. Daigon craves destruction. No doubt Boras has promised him all the havoc he desires should he grant a Mantle. But Daigon has spent a hundred millennia in his tiny realm with only his own murderous thoughts for company. He is insane. I have seen the war that he will wage upon this realm. There will be no survivors."

The goddess looked down upon Mae, watching the Divine wring her hands nervously. Her expression softened slightly.

"My Divine gave you the performance the Mahejerai needed to see, but also the answers that you seek. Only death can restore life. Only killing Boras will release the power he took. Slay him, and you will return the Mother to her former glory."

At last, a clear goal. A solution. Valandaras held back a sigh of relief.

Mae took the news poorly, anger clouding her features.

"But you, I mean, *she* also said that a Divine's power cannot stand against a god's. If he's stolen enough power to become one, how are we supposed to slay him?"

Lai'ireal smiled, though to Valandaras it seemed little more than a courtesy, as it did not reach her eyes.

"That is why I have come to you, Mae of the Valefork, faithful disciple of the Mother—for only a Divine of great loyalty and understanding of the true sanctity of life could be trusted with this secret. A tome, written tens of thousands of years ago, forged in the fires of Ignatia, where it remains to this day. It contains the residual Divinity of a long-forgotten god. Retrieve it. It will give you what you need to defeat Oorata Boras and the mad god he summons."

"Ignatia?" Mae squeaked. "The realm of fire?"

Valandaras squeezed his eyes shut under the cloth as the unpleasant memories surfaced. He had been to Ignatia a few times in his youth. The realm of fire was, as its name suggested, unbearably hot and largely inhospitable, and Pods never stayed long. His own had spent less than a day there, but it had felt like weeks.

"This is a godsdamned joke, right?" said Lessie, shaking her head. Her patience with the evening had run dry, and her fire was beginning to consume her. Valandaras cleared his throat in warning. Lai'ireal still did not acknowledge the girl, but the goddess's back stiffened as if she were offended, irritation flickering over her too-perfect face.

Lessie either did not notice or did not care.

"It's not exactly an easy place for us mere mortals to get to," she said, sarcasm dripping from every word. "We can't just hire a carriage to take us there. What are we supposed to do, ask Boras to transport us on his way to pick up Daigon? And for that matter, I'm sure the tome is just sitting out in the open, on some ceremonial plinth for us to pick up, with absolutely no mortal peril to suffer through—"

Lai'ireal finally snapped. "It is an artefact capable of destroying gods. It is not supposed to be easily accessible, child." The goddess glared at the girl, who glared right back.

"Lessie has a point, though, my lady," Mae mused. "How are we supposed to get this tome, to reach Ignatia? I thought the realms were all disconnected by Vry'iin."

"Alas, they were," Lai'ireal answered, "and yet, for a select few, they are connected just the same. Even the gods cannot traverse the realms freely anymore, but there are still ways to access them." She raised a gauntleted hand and pointed to Valandaras. "Because of ones like him."

All three women turned to Valandaras. Three sets of eyes bored into him. It was extremely uncomfortable.

She cannot mean for me to take them.

Lai'ireal stared into Valandaras's eyes so intently he had to fight not to look away. She had not acknowledged him until this moment. He kept very still, reading the predator in her expression, her posture. Everything about this woman, this god, screamed dominance. The urge to defer to her power was overwhelming, but he did not bend.

"Realmshifting is a dangerous practice, especially alone," said Valandaras carefully, speaking for the first time in the goddess's presence. "Without another Realmshifter or a Sliver to anchor me, I could just as easily tear a hole straight to Requiem. I will not risk their lives for this."

Not even the Mother was worth Mae's life.

Lai'ireal crossed the room until they were nearly nose-to-nose. Valandaras did not flinch despite the urge to cringe away. His cloth helped with the burn from her glowing eyes as much as it did his own.

"Surely you know what it is you carry with you, Realmshifter?" Lai'ireal asked. Her voice was dangerously quiet, like a snake about to strike.

He did not respond.

"That," said Lai'ireal, gesturing to the Mournblade, "is the blade of the god of death. And you are all extremely fortunate that Nim'iean is not alive to claim it."

Valandaras blinked. He had been right all along.

The Mournblade was a Sliver, forged with the essence of the god of death. He possessed an extremely powerful and dangerous artefact; a weapon capable of hurting gods themselves. More importantly, having a Sliver attuned to his light would stabilise his realmshifting abilities, as he could channel that holy power through the blade. He would be able to realmshift alone, without needing another member of his Pod to anchor him. After more than a decade of searching, his Path to finding a Sliver in this realm was complete. His commander would demand he return to the Pod immediately should she hear of it. Valandaras looked down at the obsidian sword shoved into his belt, still wrapped in a cloak. As always, the energy from it seemed to emit a dark hum.

And yet I still feel that it is not mine to wield.

"You have relieved Oorata Boras of the Sliver he means to control Daigon with," said Lai'ireal. "That is why he hunts you. The Mournblade would make receiving godpower more... straightforward. But losing it will not stop him from enacting his plan. He will find other ways."

Lessie and Mae had both frozen, and the two women shared a look before the younger spoke.

"The god of death is... dead?" Lessie asked hesitantly.

Lai'ireal sighed, the most human reaction she had shown during their entire conversation.

"I do not know for certain, child. He was not in the Prison. Perhaps he was syphoned or slain, perhaps he exiled himself into a mortal avatar to avoid it. Vry'iin himself may have destroyed him. No one has heard from him for an age. But I knew him for an age before that, and believe me, he would reclaim what is his were he able. Be thankful that for whatever reason, he is not."

Mae had stopped trembling, though her knuckles were white within her clasped hands, and the colour had started to return to her face, but she still looked pale and withdrawn.

"Where do we even start?" she said, voice forlorn. "I have but scraps of my Gift. I won't have the power to find the tome, let alone use it."

Lai'ireal ceased her pacing, her head cocked, reading the pain in Mae's expression. Then the goddess did something unexpected. She crouched down in front of Mae, so their faces were level.

Like an equal.

Valandaras held his breath as Lai'ireal forced Mae to look at her.

"In the centre of Ignatia's hottest fires, there stands a temple to a god who vanished long before the Prison. There you will find the tome. It is the only way to grant you the power of a god without sacrificing one of my brethren. It is not to be used lightly. And I must tell you that in payment for its power, it may claim your life."

Valandaras went deathly still. He could barely hear over the dull roaring that had begun in his ears. The goddess placed both of her scarred, glittering hands on Mae's own.

"Use the blade, embrace the power of the tome, and remember. Only death can restore life."

Mae gave a shaky nod. Lai'ireal straightened and looked to Valandaras with the air of a general about to give orders.

"The protection I have placed around this building will not last long. Oorata Boras will make his move soon. Be sure she is ready, Realmshifter."

Valandaras flexed his fingers, which had balled into fists. His hands felt like ice. *It may claim her life.*

"This is not the way realmshifting is used," he protested. "It is forbidden to take others with us between realms. This is not my Path." *And I cannot watch her die*, a voice inside him shouted.

The goddess smiled, light glinting from the white of her teeth. It looked more like a snarl.

"Then I hope you find your true Path, Realmshifter," Lai'ireal said simply, "before Daigon devours it, along with this entire realm and everyone upon it."

The iridescent shimmer of her glow brightened again, and soon it was hard to look upon her. Lai'ireal spoke once more, though it sounded far away. The double-tone of her voice made the statement all the more imposing, the message all the more foreboding.

"Do what has to be done. All of you."

The light became blinding, and Valandaras had to cover his face with his arm. Even beneath the cloth, his eyes still stung, and he closed them against it. When it subsided, he opened them again to find Lai'ireal no longer in the room. The god of war had delivered her message and left them. The air suddenly felt colder, calmer. He felt a dull ache begin throbbing in his temples.

Insanity, he thought. *To realmshift alone, and be expected to take them with me...*

Mae and Lessie still sat on their respective beds, wearing twin expressions of worry. Mae's crescent fingernails were bare; none of the crimson paint had made it through the night. Lessie had her head in her hands and was pressing her thumbs into her eyelids aggressively, as if trying to erase the interaction from her mind. A low groan of frustration escaped her as she inspected her hands, which had come away blackened from the makeup she had no doubt forgotten had been applied hours earlier.

Valandaras felt his pulse racing, and took a deep breath as he fought the tempest of thoughts that threatened to undo him, his hastily repaired semblance of control.

A tome that will claim her life to use, in exchange for the life of her god. To prevent a man obsessed with becoming a god himself. This cannot be my Path. I cannot have been led here only to watch her die.

A polite knock at the door had them all jump.

Valandaras wrenched the door open to find Reevan standing in the corridor, knuckles still held up to the wooden frame. He wore his travelling robes and had his pack secured to his back.

"Forgive me, I was under the assumption that we were leaving," said Reevan, mild confusion crossing his features at seeing them all still dressed in their finery. "Do you need assistance with gathering your belongings? Has there been a change of plans? You all look like you've seen a ghost."

A terse silence hung, before Mae laughed bitterly. She stood and walked to the window, the silky emerald fabric of her gown in perfect contrast to the unruly auburn hair now spilling down her back. Her silhouette framed by the soft glow of the dying lanterns, she could have been a statue; a painting of a deity. An homage to a forgotten god.

Valandaras's stomach jolted.

The power may claim her life.

She had been his only constant for so many years now. His reason to keep going, to continue his Path. More than she knew. More than he would admit, even to himself. No god was worth losing her.

I will not let her die.

Mae did not look back as she spoke.

"Not a ghost. A god."

32

LESSIE

Bueno's study was silent.

A small miracle, Lessie figured, given the number of people now gathered inside it. On the floor, she drew her knees up tighter against her chest, wrapping her arms around them. Her fingers twitched, desperate to rub at her eyes again, but the black staining on her knuckles helped her to resist.

This has been the second longest night of my life.

After Lai'ireal disappeared, Halliday Greyholme had barged into their sleeping quarters, swearing about time-wasting and the dangers of letting the Mahejerai catch up. When she learned of their impromptu upstairs visitor, however, she had immediately herded them all back down the hallway into the small study and gone to wake up the tavern's proprietor.

Bueno himself now sat behind his desk, bleary-eyed, wearing silken sleeping clothes and a luxurious, fluffy dressing robe that a king might have thought excessive. He said nothing to anyone as he shuffled past, and his only act had been to throw open the large window, letting the chill of the witching hour's winds drift gently into the room.

The frigid air kept them awake, but it also sent goosebumps prickling over her exposed skin. Lessie wrapped the sides of her father's plaid shirt tighter around herself and wished she'd picked up her jacket. For a godsdamned desert, it was freezing at night.

Maybe the ice settling in her bones wasn't only from the brisk air. Every time she closed her eyes, she saw him. Oorata Boras. Gesturing grandly before an adoring crowd like he was anything other than a callous murderer and a hypocrite. Praising the power of the Arcane, when he had used his to try to rip her sister's magic from her body. Celebrating the Divine, while he wielded gifts stolen from the gods they followed.

Lessie also hadn't shaken the feeling of his gaze boring into her back as she ran from him. Again.

I'm tired of running.

Sitting on one of the oversized cushions, she was thankful for the brief pause they had been given to get out of their formal clothing. Some, like Reevan, had changed the second they had made it into their rooms. Others, like Mae and Valandaras, were too focused on the impending task at hand to worry about attire. The material of Mae's green dress swished audibly as she paced back and forth over the rug. The rest of the crew listened to Mae's breathless explanation as she recounted her bizarre conversation with the god of war. Camden's eyes glazed over halfway through it, and Reevan looked like he was constantly on the verge of interrupting, but they had managed to keep silent and pay attention for the most part.

Lessie kept hers on Valandaras, who stood preternaturally still by the large window, half-listening to the retelling, looking out at the city. No doubt already planning their next move. Which apparently involved slicing their way to another realm with the god of death's blade.

Lessie shivered again, this time not from the cold.

Halliday had perched on a barstool and frowned through the entire story, a look that plainly said she didn't understand and wasn't sure if she wanted to. At one point they locked eyes, and Lessie found herself matching the grimace.

Hell, I don't understand most of it, and I had a front-row seat.

Bueno now stifled a yawn poorly between his fingers. A ring with a ruby the size of a coin glittered in the dim candlelight.

"I'm afraid you will have to explain it again, my dear," he said. "I was only halfway into wakefulness."

Mae paused in her pacing to shoot a look of incredulity at Bueno. She gave a frustrated sigh before condensing the story even further.

"Lai'ireal appeared to us and told us of Oorata Boras's plan to bring Daigon, the god of Keanos, here to Kalaraak," she said, wringing her hands. "To stop him, we need to find an artefact—a tome that lies in an abandoned temple. In Ignatia."

Lessie shook her head. A prickle of amusement washed over her.

When you put it like that, it sounds easy.

"Yes, yes, of course," said Bueno, rubbing at his eyes, "and what part of this warranted my being torn from my bed after a night of well-deserved celebrating?"

"Honestly, boss, it was more of a courtesy thing," said Halliday, jumping from her stool and disappearing behind the bar. "I figured you'd want to know if gods were materialising into your guest rooms. It puts a dent in your security protocols." She poured herself a generous glass of whiskey and drained it in a single swallow, smacking her lips together obnoxiously. "There's also the fact that I had to pull a carriage switch just to get them out of the city proper. That Mahejerai maniac nearly blew the first one halfway to Requiem."

That got Bueno's attention. "Oh dear," he said, tutting. "I sent you with my favourite one. Is it damaged?"

Lessie scoffed.

"Obviously all of you are all right, my dear, because you are all here and whole in front of me," Bueno remarked, giving her a sleepy smirk. "And so I worry about my best carriage. Greyholme, tell me, how bad is it?"

Halliday levelled her icy blue stare at Valandaras's back.

"Not a scratch."

Bueno looked genuinely relieved, pressing a hand to his chest and sighing dramatically, but Lessie's curiosity peaked at the strange look that had passed over Halliday's striking face. Something had happened. She had seen Valandaras do something.

Lessie didn't know if anyone else had noticed. Camden was half asleep, and Reevan and Grundle kept their eyes on the door for the most part. Mae had continued to pace in the middle of the room before drifting towards a bookshelf, aimlessly running her fingers along the spines of the books. Like she wasn't sure where to go from here.

None of us do. Who knows what to do next?

Valandaras seemed to sense the eyes on his back.

"Realmlight is unstable," he murmured. "I could not have held it longer than those few seconds. But with the Mournblade..."

Valandaras turned to them at last, pulling the sword from his belt and unwrapping the cloak that surrounded it. Lessie had not seen it uncovered since it had come into their possession. She suppressed a shudder as the obsidian blade glinted in the light, feeling as always that the blade was humming, whispering to her in a language she couldn't understand.

Valandaras lifted the Mournblade, turning it over in his hand.

"Lai'ireal confirmed this to be the blade of Nim'iean, the lost god of death," he proclaimed. "It is a Sliver. I can use it to anchor myself when I realmshift, so I can do so alone." He shoved the weapon back into his belt without covering it again.

Lessie didn't know what a Sliver was, and after tonight she wasn't sure if she wanted to. Camden shifted on the pillow next to her, their knees knocking together slightly. The movement sent a waft of cinnamon, wood-smoke and something vaguely citrusy over her, which she'd come to recognise as whatever scent he wore. Eyes on the Mournblade, he missed the scowl she gave him. She couldn't explain why, but it was irritating how good he smelled. Normal people didn't bother with such frivolous things as cologne, especially while travelling. It was distracting.

I probably smell like whiskey and gunpowder.

Nobody seemed to know what to say after Valandaras's declaration. There was a long, pensive silence, which Lessie had always hated. There were two types of quiet, and she greatly preferred the kind that came with wind and rain; a crackling fire and wildlife. Unloaded quiet. Silence like this meant that something was wrong. Whether it was the absence of birdsong before a gunshot, her father's unvoiced disapproval hanging in the air, or the odd emptiness of her bedroom without Trixie's constant stream of chatter bouncing off the walls—true silence felt unnatural to her. She was usually the first to break it, and this time would be no exception.

"Well, hell," Lessie muttered, echoing her father's favourite sentiment. "I guess we're going to the realm of fire, then."

"*I* am going," Valandaras corrected. "There is no need for any of you to accompany me."

Lessie blinked in confusion. "What?"

The rest of the room showed similar expressions, but none so thunderous as Mae's, who came out of her thousand-yard stare to regard him incredulously.

"Absolutely, there is a need," Mae said, snapping shut the book she held and slamming it back down, ignoring Bueno's pained sound of protest as the shelf rattled. "Lai'ireal said that only a Divine could retrieve the tome."

All eyes went from Mae to Valandaras and back. Valandaras straightened his spine, looking oddly as though he were preparing for battle.

"It is forbidden to take others with us when we realmshift," he said carefully. "I must go alone."

Mae's face contorted as she stared at Valandaras in disbelief, fury glittering behind her eyes. She advanced on him, showing uncanny similarities to the mountain lion even in her human form.

Lessie covered her mouth with her hand to hide her amusement. She had seen them disagree on things before, of course, and they had been civil most of the time, but of this magnitude? With this much at stake?

Here we go. My money's on Mae.

"If you think I'm letting you go without me, Val, then you don't know me at all."

"A Realmshifter does not interfere with the course of other's lives. My Path—"

"Half a decade, and you believe I would sit here on my ass and let you do it for me?"

"I have been to Ignatia—"

"Good, then we'll know what to expect."

"The entire realm is volcanic. Rivers of lava, toxic fumes, unstable ground—"

"I'm not planning on living there—"

"Even Realmshifters can only spend days at a time there. It is extremely dangerous."

"All the more reason to have somebody there to watch your back."

"It is not a place for those who cannot defend themselves."

"You think I can't defend myself? Just because I can't Change? I can still handle—"

"Realmshifting is *sacred*. I cannot take—"

"Civilians? Is that what I am?" Mae's voice had risen beyond what was proper during the arguing, but now it dropped drastically.

Valandaras froze.

Mae's eyes sparked, like she knew she'd hit a sore spot. A skittering of green raced along the Divine's skin as if her Gift was a living thing inside of her, desperate to prove it was still there. They had moved closer to each other while speaking, and now Mae stepped into Valandaras's space.

"Am I a *liability*, Val?" Mae hissed.

Valandaras flinched.

Lessie raised an eyebrow. Next to her, Camden snickered. *Point one, Mae.*

Mae's voice was a snarl. "Lai'ireal came to *me*. She told you to take me there. I'm going."

Valandaras did not respond, but his mouth was set in a hard line. Mae's eyes had flooded with the emerald light, rivalling the Realmshifter's own glow. The two had come nose to nose during their argument, but now Valandaras returned to the window, putting some distance between them.

When he spoke again, his tone was clipped, like he was forcing himself to remain calm.

"The longer I hold open the way alone, the more people I take, the higher the chance of failure. I will not risk killing you all. Not even for this."

Halliday snorted from the corner. "Gods almighty, you're both so dramatic. Just let him go."

Lessie gave Halliday a withering look. She was right, but she didn't need to be so loud about it. *Besides, Valandaras can't seriously think we would stay behind?*

Lessie wanted to argue her point, too, but getting in between Mae and Valandaras seemed like the stupidest possible thing to do at the moment. She'd have more luck talking Bueno into giving her the deed to his tavern. She dropped her gaze into her lap, chewing on the inside of her lip to keep from speaking, mind spinning with a dozen counterpoints.

We don't all have to go. Just enough of us to guarantee we get the tome and get out. But Valandaras is insane if he thinks he's going alone.

Next to her, Camden was ashen under his tan, deep in thought as he ran a hand along the reddish-brown stubble that shadowed his jawline. He rose from his cushioned floor seat with surprising grace and opened his mouth to speak, ignoring her hiss of disapproval.

"Perhaps there is another way Mae could join Valandaras in the realm of fire?" he asked, eyes darting between them, palms up like he wanted to calm the fire of the fight before it burned out of control. "It's, uh, legally ambiguous, shall we say? And ridiculously expensive. But you can get anything you need in Verestead if you're willing to pay for it."

At the mention of Altaea's capital, Mae stiffened. She glared at Camden, who held himself relatively well against it, stumbling over his words only slightly as he continued pitching his idea.

"Besides, not all of us need to accompany you to Ignatia itself—there has to be something we can do here. We could go to the king, implore him to march his armies against the Mahejerai—"

The emerald glow of Mae's Gift drained from her face, and her eyes went hollow. The change was drastic. It was as if she had aged a century. *Another century.*

"I will tear my way through the realms to Ignatia myself before I take a single breath inside the walls of Verestead," said Mae, voice full of ice.

Camden wilted under the weight of Mae's stare and quickly fell silent, but the ghost in her eyes did not recede. Even Valandaras had paused in his brooding to assess her. Lessie searched memories of their conversations, looking for a reason, but she couldn't recall a single moment that would explain the pain that now lingered on her friend's face. Mae had never once mentioned Verestead before.

Lessie got to her feet, intending to either comfort Mae or kick Camden; she hadn't decided yet. Maybe both.

Reevan, however, took the opportunity to contribute to the conversation, clearing his throat loudly.

"Lord DeFalcone brings an excellent point to the table," he said, lounging on one of the larger cushions in the corner. "There should be a number of us who remain behind, if only to gather further information on Boras's intentions. I am assuming nobody knows exactly when he is planning on unleashing his monster of a god into our realm? Or whereabouts on Kalaraak he means to do so?"

The others met him with blank stares. Lessie grit her teeth.

Oh, godsdamn it.

Reevan sniffed. "I thought so. This is extremely important information that we're going to need, so we must split up. Some of us can return to Altaea, or poke around here some more to prepare for whatever it is that the Mahejerai are planning. Would that relieve some strain on your realmshifting, Valandaras?"

Mae's eyes flashed in triumph, but Valandaras did not acknowledge Reevan's words or move from his place at the window. Reevan seemed unbothered as he scratched behind one ear with a razor-sharp claw.

"Personally, I believe some of us will be much more useful committing domestic espionage and gathering allies than dodging volcanic eruptions and tomb raiding," he said.

Camden looked visibly relieved, running a hand through his hair. It was essentially the same idea he had suggested, without the emotional damage mentioning Verestead had seemed to cause.

Lessie felt the exhaustion of the night catching up, and she rubbed at her eyes again, swearing as more black came away on the back of her knuckles. Of course, Reevan was right.

We have no idea how long we have to try to pull this off. A year? A week? Hours?

Bueno stood from behind his desk and stretched, yawning loudly.

"All of this sounds wonderful, yes, an excellent plan," he said, voice thick, edging around the desk and heading for the study's exit. "Please let me know which of my services you require in approximately eight hours. Greyholme will know where to find me."

Reevan's tail twitched. "Is there a time limit on your assistance?"

Bueno laughed as he wrenched open the heavy door, breaking whatever enchantment it held and allowing sounds from the last of the revelry below to drift into the room.

"No, no, my dear kitskan friend, I just need a long rest. Goodnight again, my delightful, interesting foreign guests. Next time, allow the suns to rise before involving me. I will be much more helpful."

Bueno swept through the door, luxurious robe trailing behind him, before poking his face back around, so that his head appeared to float against the door frame.

"Also, if you would be so kind as to not touch any more of my belongings—many of them are priceless and irreplaceable. Greyholme, that whiskey will be added to your ledger," he added casually, and Halliday froze with another glass halfway to her lips. "Rest well, when you eventually make your way to your own beds."

With that, Bueno disappeared, shutting the door firmly behind him, and they were bathed in the artificial silence of the room's enchantment once more. Halliday rolled her eyes dramatically and made an obscene gesture at the door, but the effect was ruined somewhat by the yawn she fought to keep off her face.

Lessie stifled a yawn of her own, glancing at an ornate clock perched high on one of Bueno's shelves. Despite the tiredness sinking into her bones, the true lateness of the hour surprised her; the night would give way to dawn in just a few hours. It seemed as though they'd left for the temple only a short time ago.

Bueno's got a point. How are we supposed to think clearly after a night this... messy?

"Grundle will stay in Kalaraak," said Grundle from the corner of the room, moving for the first time in half an hour and spooking Halliday so badly she dropped her drink. The empty whiskey glass clattered onto the bar before she snatched it back up. "Grundle has no need to go to other realms," the goblin added.

"A wise choice, my small friend. As will I," said Reevan. He rose from his seat on the floor and looked towards Lessie and Camden. "I suppose the two of you will be more inclined to seize the opportunity to explore Ignatia?"

Camden shook his head, absently twisting the silver ring he wore around his finger.

"I'm afraid I must decline," he said. "My father would flay me alive if I went gallivanting off to another realm of existence—and then Druitt would find a Divine to heal me, and then *he* would kill me." Despite his clear relief at having the option to stay, Camden looked vaguely disappointed. He sighed heavily. "Of course, they're probably already going to, after all this."

Lessie's brow furrowed. Camden hadn't said a word about his family's opinion of his impromptu vacation to Kalac. Suddenly, he cared what they thought? Why would he willingly turn this big of an adventure down?

"What happened to 'broadening your horizons?'" she asked, her opinion evident in her tone.

Camden laughed. "I meant stepping out of my own province, honey, not an entirely different realm. Besides, I don't particularly care for the heat. I've always preferred the colder months."

Lessie side-eyed him. "So you're a coward," she said, wrinkling her nose. "Good to know."

His eyes narrowed. "I would have thought you, of all people, would understand what having to put your family's needs first is like, my *lady*."

"You don't know shit about what I've done for my family—"

"Ahem," said Reevan, clearing his throat and holding up a large paw-like hand. "Can we keep the fighting to one conversation at a time, please?"

Temper flared, Lessie choked down the barrage of insults that had sprung to mind. How dare he insinuate she didn't put her family first? Even as her face burned, she kept her eyes on Camden, determined to not be the one to look away.

The Lord of Cowardice, for his part, clenched his jaw and flashed her an insincere grin before turning away, dismissing her entirely. It made her feel like screaming, but she shut her mouth, crossed her arms, and pretended he was no longer in the room. If she breathed in shallowly enough, she could even block the scent of him.

Godsdamn him. Even Ignatia wouldn't be far enough away.

"I'm going with you," Lessie announced loudly, causing both Mae and Valandaras to break their stares and look her way, reminding her painfully of her parents. She ignored the jolt of emotion, just as she ignored how

Camden's head had whipped around again to stare at her. "The tome's temple is probably a death trap. I've spent my whole life dodging my sister's weird Arcane backfires. Magic leaves traces. I'll know what to look for."

It was a flimsy justification, but she needed to go. There had to be something that would convince them. She squared her shoulders.

"Plus, someone has to keep y'all from killing each other," she added.

Valandaras's voice was firm. "No."

"Boras is as much my problem as he is yours, and he knows my face," Lessie said. "I can't spy on him, but I deserve the chance to be involved in taking him down." She tried to appear unemotional about it. The strain in her tone was obvious even to her, though, and Valandaras remained unmoved, his mouth set in a hard line.

Gods above, you're a stubborn ass.

Lessie tried a new angle. "Look, Mae deserves the chance to get to the tome. I want to help her. Sure, using it might kill her, but Daigon and Boras definitely will, along with the rest of us."

Valandaras sighed, rubbing his hand along his forehead, his new cloth already stained from the fallout of the night.

"The rules of walking the Path are clear," he said. "We are never to interfere with the natural way of things. We cannot upset the balance of the realms. I cannot move a living person from one realm to another without facing serious repercussions." He sounded weary. Maybe he'd seen the repercussions for himself.

Mae's face was still shadowed in anger, but her eyes were rimmed with tears.

"I *have* to do this," she said, an edge of pleading to her voice that had not been there before. "For the Mother. For all the Divines who've lost their gods. For—for me."

An angry tear escaped, and Mae hurriedly brushed it from her cheek. Valandaras jerked an arm out towards her, but stopped as if catching himself. Lessie and Reevan exchanged a pointed glance.

"I am sorry, my lioness, but I cannot do this."

Valandaras's words were so soft, so gentle, that Lessie had the uncomfortable feeling of intruding on a private moment between the two. Mae's crestfallen face, Valandaras's clenched fists, the tension between them taking on a melancholic quality that hurt worse than the shouting. Lessie shifted awkwardly and looked away.

Mae's voice broke.

"Val, please."

33

LESSIE

Wait, you're serious, then?

In about ten hours.

Lessie, I don't understand. What do you mean, you're going to Ignatia?

I mean we're going to Ignatia. How much clearer can I be?

Ignatia.

Yes.

The realm of fire.

Yes.

The eternally burning, full of fire demons and volcanoes and gods know what else, extremely dangerous Ignatia?

Trixie, how many Ignatias are there?

All right, I was just checking, because the last time I saw you, you weren't insane. How are you even going to get there? It's not like you can hire a carriage. Is that why you're writing to me now? I think maybe one of the more ancient teachers at the Quillkeep might know how to realm-shift, but I don't know if I've been here long enough to beg them to teach me... I'm pretty sure it's banned, anyway. I don't think regular people can just pop to other realms for a holiday.

Trix, you don't have to. Valandaras is taking us.

Oh, right, no shit. I'd forgotten that he's a Realmshifter. That's convenient. I've heard their rules are really strict, though. I remember Papa talking about one who came to Picking when he was a kid. Isn't being a Realmshifter a big secret and they can't show anyone how it works?

Yeah, he's pretty pissed off that he's doing it.

Is he still in love with Mae?

Definitely.

Of course. It was never even a question of if he'd do it, then, was it? Gods, that's so romantic! And kind of sad, though. Imagine spending all your time ignoring the feelings you have for someone when you could just be with them instead. That must be so frustrating for them, pretending like they don't like each other that way. It's like they want to be unhappy. What's so bad about letting yourself be loved?

Less?

Lessandra P Shilling, you better not be ignoring me.

HELLO?

Yeah, I'm still here, calm down.

I thought you'd fallen asleep or dropped your journal or something. Don't blame me for freaking out. It's been ages since we've had time to sit and write at the same time. I miss you.

I miss you too, Trix.

I miss Mama and Papa so much. I just know they'd be interested in what I'm studying. It's all complicated as hell, I love it. Did you know that there's different classifications of Arcane energy, and some Arcanes can only access parts of it? I thought it all just kind of came from the same place. The Weave has always felt like a big well to me. There's a girl here who can control the elements. She literally makes fire burst from her fingertips, it's so hot. I asked her to lunch the other—hey, how's that annoying nobleman going? What's his actual name again... Carden? Caspian?

Camden.

Yes, him. Is he still drinking like a fish and complaining about everything?

Yes.

Good, someone's gotta step up when you're busy.

I didn't agree to use this journal to be insulted.

No, you agreed to use it to help me study the effects of long-term enchantments on inanimate objects with a varying degree of distance separation, in the hopes of successful stable replication in the future. And also because I'm your favourite sister, and you love me.

You're my only sister.

Even better reason to make sure I succeed, isn't it? We can't all become war heroes and be bequeathed titles and castles to live in, I

have to figure out a way to support myself. Oh, you'll have to make sure you write while you're in Ignatia. I want to see if there's any complications on the enchantment from being on a different realm.

It's not a godsdamned castle. And I've already told you, I'm not keeping the title. I just have to find someone else to take it.

It's got a tower. It's a castle, your ladyship. But sure, whatever you say. Try not to push Camden into a volcano.

Gods, Trix, I'm not a murderer. Besides, he's not coming.

Why, what did you say to him?

Trixanna.

What?

Why do you think it was something I said to him?

Because the last time you wrote in here, you referred to him only as 'the Lord of Insufferability'; derisively recounted an extremely long anecdote he told about drunkenly hijacking a bard's performance in a tavern; and questioned if either of his parents paid any attention to him as a child. I just kind of assumed you're also saying this stuff out loud.

If he didn't want to be called the Lord of Insufferability, he could try to be less insufferable. But no, he's going back to Altaea to speak with his brother, and anyway, it's dangerous for too many of us to go. It's only Mae, Valandaras and me. We leave for Ignatia in the morning.

To find a dusty old book that once belonged to a god?

A tome, yes.

And this tome is going to help Mae get her Divinity back? So she can fight the Arcane? Oorata Boras?

That's the plan.

Good. I still can't believe you found the bastard. I wish I could be there with you.

The Quillkeep is the safest place you can be right now, Trix.

I know, I know, and getting to study Arcane gifts instead of hiding them is incredible... but I would have liked to help. I don't know how healthy this pursuit of vengeance is, but I get it. It's not fair that it all got put on you, ~~especially since you're Mund~~ Papa would be really proud of you, you know. Stressed out about how far away from home we both are, but definitely proud. Gods, I miss him. I miss Mama, too. It's been over a year... It still doesn't feel real.

I have to sleep.

Look, I know you don't want to talk about it yet. You're going to have to one day, you know that, right? You can't keep pushing it all down, you're going to explode. Make sure you write when you're in Ignatia, when you're not busy dodging lava explosions and robbing an ancient library. Love you.

Love you too, Trix.

Lessie...

Yeah?

You're gonna make him pay for what he did, right?

Yeah. I am.

Valandaras's face still had a shadow of resigned frustration Lessie easily recognised, for she had often seen it on her own father—simmering below the surface, carefully hidden beneath the need to support the ones he loved. Instead of the smoking remains of a failed Arcane experiment, however, Valandaras stared at an empty spot on the wall of his room. He remained motionless, kneeling on the floor in full plate armour and two heavy travelling packs. The Mournblade lay unsheathed and glittering before him.

He did not speak.

He did not acknowledge Lessie, nor Mae, who stood patiently beside her.

He had not given any indication that either of them was to do anything.

And so they waited like sentinels at his back while he meditated upon the black blade. For the first few minutes, the tense silence had been intriguing, and Lessie imagined stairs of flame or a kaleidoscope of colour springing to life within the room, perhaps spiralling out of the sword, or even Valandaras himself. Who knew how the Realmshifter's most secretive powers would manifest? Despite the severity of the situation at hand, she felt a certain anticipation—excitement, even—for what was about to happen. Something new.

As time trickled by, nothing had happened at all. Valandaras had simply frozen, like he had entered a trance. Lessie huffed an errant strand of hair away from her face.

Who knew realmshifting would be so godsdamned boring.

She adjusted the pack at her back, resisting the urge to check for yet another time that all of her belongings were secure inside. She transferred her weight from side to side, feeling the supple leather of her worn boots as they shifted with her movement. She studied the wall as she tried and failed to keep from chewing on the inside of her cheek. When she could stand the silence no longer, Lessie leaned closer to Mae.

"Is he going to explain what he's doing, or do we just have to wait an hour for anything to happen?" she asked, speaking out of the side of her mouth without moving her lips. It was barely more than a whisper, but she knew Valandaras would still hear it.

"I'm sure he knows what needs to be done," Mae replied, pursing her lips to keep from smiling.

Lessie sighed. "Couldn't he have done it earlier, then?"

"Shh," Mae whispered, patting her arm gently. "He'll tell us when he's ready."

Lessie crossed her arms over her chest, trying not to pout.

He could have been ready before we got here.

Finally, Valandaras rose to his feet, obscured eyes still fixed on a point they could not see.

"You are about to witness something that is sacred. A practice that is not meant for outsider eyes," he said, gauntleted hand gripping the unsheathed Mournblade. He did not turn towards them, but Lessie still felt the urge to stand up straighter as he spoke. "Realmshifting was our greatest gift granted by Haropheth, and it is to be used only to help us further down our Path. To serve him in fulfilling his oath of vengeance. To find Vry'iin."

He shook his head as if in disappointment as he faced them. Resplendent in his armour, shield strapped to his back, tattered red cloak shifting with his movement, he looked every inch the confident warrior. But the lines on his face were set with worry.

"Even with a Sliver, realmshifting alone is dangerous, and to take you with me is incredibly reckless. If my Pod, my leader, or Haropheth himself were to learn of this, I will be punished beyond measure. If we were to survive it."

Despite the already rapidly warming day, Lessie shivered.

"I know what this means for you, Val," said Mae solemnly. "And if there were any other way, I'd take it. I only hope I can make it up to you one day." Her voice was stiff, like she had not forgiven him for the way they had quarrelled the night before, but her eyes were shining with gratitude.

Valandaras held Mae's gaze. Not for the first time, Lessie had the uncomfortable feeling like she was intruding on an intimate moment between the two. She looked away, shuffling her feet awkwardly, like she could give them privacy by pretending she wasn't there. Valandaras did not respond to Mae's words as he turned back towards the bare wall, and Lessie resisted the urge to stick out her tongue at the back of his head.

Then Valandaras did something Lessie had never seen him do.

He reached for the cloth that covered his face, tugged gently at the knot that held it, and pulled it down—exposing his eyes.

Mae inhaled sharply.

The light pooling beneath Valandaras's uncovered eyes was warm and had a wild energy to it, like it was searching for a way to spill around the final barrier of his eyelids. Even though he kept them closed, the room brightened as if the twin suns had crested over the horizon.

A warning twinged in her gut, like her subconscious knew that Valandaras had just become much more dangerous.

"You both should shield your own eyes," he said. "My light could damage your vision beyond repair should you face it."

Mae buried her face in her hands. Lessie did the same, but immediately gave into the urge to peek through her fingers.

Like hell am I missing this.

Valandaras focused on the same spot he had spent the last half hour meditating upon and opened his uncovered eyes. The room flooded with light so strong that it stung.

Lessie flinched, squinting, trying to adjust her sight as she watched every inch of Valandaras's bare skin glow brighter, his usual faint luminescence amplified a hundred times over. The light from his eyes spilled out onto the empty wall, illuminating everything before him. Only the Mournblade seemed to resist it, absorbing the light with its own stubborn blackness. Valandaras lifted the Mournblade. The obsidian sword glittered in the brightness, and as he continued to look directly at it, the blade emitted an audible hum—one Lessie knew for certain she wasn't imagining. Golden sparks skittered across the surface, sinking into the metal, until the whole weapon became as blinding as Valandaras himself.

When so much of the light had absorbed into the sword that none of the Mournblade's original ebony steel could be seen, the Realmshifter raised it high and slowly dragged it downwards through the air.

The air *split*.

The light that poured out of the slice in the air was so blinding it caused a sharp pain to shoot through Lessie's eyes into her brain, and she couldn't contain the hiss of pain that escaped her. She shrank backwards, blinking furiously, momentarily blinded as she tried to clear the sun spots that had formed in her vision. For a few seconds she could see only the pale pink of her eyelids overlaid by a pattern of shifting, burning circles. It felt as if she had been struck by lightning, or been forced to stare directly at the sun.

Valandaras repeated the movement a few more times, the process slow and methodical, like he was carving the air itself. He seemed to use his eyes to find the path to the realm as well as to guide the Mournblade. Sometimes the obsidian sword would appear to partially disappear inside the tear, with only the hilt visible, like he was pushing it through the light. Through the realms? She couldn't tell. Understanding it would take much more than what observation could give her.

Lessie tried to watch as much of it as she could out of sheer curiosity, but the combination of the Mournblade's sinister hum and Valandaras's raw radiance threatened to make her sick. Mae shifted beside her, eyes still covered.

"Almost," muttered Valandaras, sweat beading on his brow, frowning in concentration. "—that's it."

He thrust the Mournblade into the light, wedging it into nothing—but somehow it stayed suspended in the air, crackling with energy. He let go hesitantly, as if half-expecting the blade to clatter to the ground, but it held.

Valandaras ran his fingers around the edges of the tear he had created, the Mournblade acting as a tether to keep the connection open, and pulled carefully at the light around the sword.

A piece of the room they stood in ripped away entirely. Where once had been air and ground, now a shining portal of pure light remained.

The balance of the world tilted, and Lessie's stomach tilted with it. Squeezing her eyes shut against the onslaught of brightness, she felt the gentle touch of Mae's fingertips on her shoulder, in comfort and in solidarity. The Divine was trembling from holding herself back; whether she wanted to help Valandaras or launch herself into Ignatia, Lessie wasn't sure.

Valandaras kept his hands locked around the piece of the realm he had torn apart, like it would snap back the second he let go of it. It appeared to be pushing against his grip. Somewhere, a high-pitched keening noise cut through the silence of the room.

"Go. Enter. Now, before it is too late," he said, voice straining slightly. He twisted away awkwardly so they would not walk into his eyeline. "But whatever you do, do not start walking without me."

Mae stepped forward immediately, the skirts of her dress swirling around her. She hesitated for a fraction of a second, before squaring her shoulders and stepping into the light. Just before she disappeared from view, she turned, and it was as if she were backlit by the seven realms themselves. A halo outlining her form and blurring her features, fiery hair shining, emerald glittering over her body as if greeting the golden glow.

Mae reached a slender hand back towards them, fractals reflecting through it like rays of the sun, veins glowing. Despite the danger of what they were attempting, a fierce smile of pure joy radiated from her face. If there was a god of light, in that moment, Mae would have outshined them.

Suddenly Lessie felt very, very small.

"Lessie?" Mae's hand was outstretched, beckoning to her. Valandaras grimaced as he struggled to keep his grip while still angling his gaze away from them. The keening noise grew louder. The Mournblade began to shudder.

She couldn't move. Her limbs were filled with lead.

I can't do this.

"Lessie, come on!" shouted Mae. A phantom wind whipped her hair around her like flames licking at her skin, devouring her voice and making her sound a thousand miles away instead of right in front of them.

One of Valandaras's hands slipped. The passageway faltered.

Lessie managed a step closer, every instinct she had screaming to run in the opposite direction. Panicked thoughts beat in her mind like a drum.

What in the seven realms am I thinking? I'm not Divine, I don't have Arcane powers, I'm as Mundane as people get. How will I survive Ignatia? I can't die in another realm, Trixie will kill me...

Valandaras swore and let go of the light.

The edges immediately began to knit together as it started to seal. He returned one hand to the hilt of the Mournblade and reached for her wildly, not daring to turn his exposed eyes in her direction lest he risk damaging her vision permanently.

But if I don't go, Boras wins, and they died for nothing.

Lessie felt her control over her body return just as Valandaras's fingers closed around the front of her shirt and yanked her into the light. She collided with Mae and scrambled to keep upright in the blindingly bright space, eyes forced shut, disturbed with what little she had managed to take in.

What had looked like a door now felt like more of a corridor; an extended hallway of luminescence. Valandaras's realmlight, imbibed into the Mournblade, had created a passage. A small bridge of light, a single thread of gold. Beyond the light of the carved space, all around them, was nothing but an inky black void. Utter darkness.

Lessie knew instinctively that to go into the darkness would be to die.

The ground tilted again and the heat at her back vanished. Lessie had a vague understanding of the portal closing on the outside before Valandaras pushed in front of them. She squinted against the brightness, desperately trying to make sense of her surroundings. Now that the tear had resealed, only the light from Valandaras's eyes and the Mournblade were keeping the black void from devouring them.

The Realmshifter surged forward, like unleashing the light gave him speed beyond his normal capabilities, and she felt his urgency as he dragged them both onwards behind him, encouraging them with murmurs and gestures. He never looked back; the light still poured from his open eyes, shining into the black and creating a path—the Path?—for them to stay upon.

Mae wrapped her slender hand around Lessie's, and only the feel of the Divine's skin upon her own let her know she wasn't disintegrating.

"Hurry!" shouted Valandaras.

Lessie squeezed Mae's hand until she thought her bones might break and ran for her life.

Her footsteps felt weightless as she ran, trying to keep herself from tripping over nothing. Only Valandaras's light kept the darkness at bay, and the sensation of the passageway closing in behind them filled her with terror. As they sprinted through what felt like all time and space, she had a brief, maddening thought of launching herself sideways into the void, and she clung to Mae's hand to keep from going insane.

They came to the end of the passageway's light suddenly and lost their footing, the sharp drop downwards unexpected.

Lessie threw her arms out to steady herself, losing her grip on Mae's hand and cursing as she stumbled and hit the ground. She skidded, hard rock cutting through the skin on her palms. She heard Mae's exclamation of pain as the Divine fell close by.

Everything was quiet. The light no longer assaulted the outside of her eyelids. Either they'd made it, or she was dead.

Lessie pushed herself up into sitting, wincing as she inspected the grazes on her hands. Annoying, but not life-threatening. An involuntary hiss escaped her as she tried to brush the debris from them, pain shooting through her like shrapnel.

She was almost definitely alive, and she knew they had reached their destination. It wasn't the barren, rocky land that stretched in every direction, or the towering mountains that surrounded them.

It was the wind.

Dry. Hot. The kind of wind that left skin burned before long; that tore her hair from the braid and whipped it across her face with little mercy. Wind that brought with it the scent of charred wood and sizzling rocks, the faint trace of sulphur and something more sinister.

That wind felt more foreign than Kalac ever had.

Lessie dragged herself back to her feet and looked around, ignoring the sting in her palms. A trickle of blood ran down her fingers and dripped onto the craggy ground.

A faint rumbling behind her made her spin, and she watched in awe as one of the furthermost mountains exploded skyward with a cascade of molten rock, so hot it glowed a violent orange even from a distance. For a moment, her eyes refused to believe what they were seeing.

"Holy shit," Lessie whispered, speaking aloud without meaning to.

Valandaras had done it. They had realmshifted. And she now stood upon truly foreign soil, on a completely different realm of existence.

The realm of fire.

Ignatia.

34

REEVAN

Reevan was beginning to grow tired of the décor in Bueno's study.

Not because it was uncomfortable or garish, quite the opposite; the man had impeccable taste and an impressive assortment of rare and intricate objects. No, Reevan had simply taken in everything interesting about the room after spending the better of two weeks inside it, and it was driving him mad. Camden and Grundle were showing similar signs of cabin fever.

Valandaras, before he had left, had assured Reevan and the others that he intended to realmshift back to Kalaraak through the same Path he made leaving, and that it was safest to sit tight and await their return. If they made good time, they would be gone for little less than a week.

That was thirteen days ago.

Valandaras, Mae and Lessie had been gone for thirteen days. It had been an oversight by all of them that those left behind had no idea of knowing if the Realmshifter had been successful. Reevan and the others did not know how long it would take for the tome to be retrieved—of knowing at all if their allies had failed. If they were even still alive.

Reevan did not usually worry, but it was unnerving.

Bueno thought it prudent for them to lay as low as possible while the enraged Oorata Boras ordered the Mahejerai to lock down the city and find them. The fury radiating out from the temple had dampened the spirits of the entire city. The Festival of the Falling Star had officially come to a close, so people were attempting to leave Saluo in droves, but instead found themselves subjected to bottlenecked lines and invasive searches. Passage through the gates had slowed to a trickle, with the process taking days instead of hours. There was no simple way out for anyone.

The only reason the Mahejerai had not involved the Perqeit and used the city guard forces to tear Saluo apart, Bueno had commented drily, was because that would require admitting they had been outsmarted—something Oorata Boras would not allow. Reevan supposed they were bound to catch a break somehow.

Instead, the Mahejerai were conducting a quiet, methodical search, sweeping through the buildings of the city one after another while they kept the city's foreign guests in a chokehold. The rumours of the Mahejerai's ability to use Arcane means to track their enemies had made all of Saluo uneasy, and the underground market for cloaking and concealment had exploded in popularity. Regular people who usually revered the Arcane were becoming suspicious, turning to the Divines among them for help.

Bueno had insisted his study was the safest room in Saluo, with all manner of unnamed enchantments woven within the very walls. He waved off talk of Lai'ireal's temporary blessings fading, saying the tavern itself was protected too, but not to such a scale as his own personal quarters. Since their greatest chance of survival depended on staying out of the Mahejerai's way, sequestering themselves inside the study—for a time, at least—seemed like the best course of action. Reevan had suggested using their considerable contacts and leaving Saluo altogether, but Halliday had made a fair point that the roads out of the city would be the first place the Mahejerai would send scouts. Oorata Boras knew places they were likely to retreat to, especially if he had recognised Lessie. Reevan did not know how much she had told the others of her family's fate, probably next to nothing, but he would not further jeopardise her home town.

No, they had to wait until the Mahejerai stopped searching for them. Until they gave up on whatever lay inside of the box Grundle had taken. It was either very dangerous or very powerful—perhaps both. Grundle had not figured out how to open it, though he tried constantly. The goblin brought the thin box with him to the study every day, running fingers around its edges, testing each of his shiny tools against the box's hinges—the only reason they had cause to believe it opened in the first place—and searching every inch for a weakness.

He had found none. Perhaps it did not open at all.

Reevan had looked at the box for a grand total of thirty-four minutes before giving up. He wondered if they should just return the box, leave it on the ground in front of the pyramid, since it had proven quite useless. It had obviously been sealed via Arcane means, therefore nothing he knew would override that. Arcane abilities were far beyond Reevan's understanding. They weren't Grundle's forte, either, but the stubborn goblin would sooner die than admit the box had bested him. He grew more frustrated as the days passed, but all of his time within the study remained focused on it.

Camden had given the box a nonchalant once-over and said that the runes looked somewhat familiar, but could not place them. Reevan had been sure that while locked in a room with a bar, the lord would drink himself into a stupor before long, but Camden had surprised him—remaining subdued and quiet, nursing a single whiskey for the majority of the day as he curled up on a floor pillow and worked his way through Bueno's bookshelves. Reevan was not entirely convinced that the lord was actually reading the books, due to the speed that the pile dwindled, but at least Camden kept himself occupied.

Reevan's favourite thing to do was to study the map.

It was a thing of beauty, Bueno's map. Most map-makers had a strong bias towards their own lands, and finding a detailed depiction of the entire Kalaraak realm was rare. Bueno's map not only showed the major cities of all the countries, but also most of their landmarks and places of interest, as if he had taken a native map from each land and somehow combined them. Some of the smaller towns seemed to have been added in by a different hand, possibly Bueno himself. Bueno must be an extremely well-travelled man for his age, Reevan had mused, tracing a path with a claw from the northern island of the Ruby Isles all the way to Saluo. Or perhaps Bueno simply employed a well-paid cartographer.

On their eleventh day in hiding, a low-ranking member of the Mahejerai arrived and demanded to search the tavern. After initially rebuffing and refusing him—which was to be expected of any slums proprietor—Bueno had generously conceded and allowed him inside. Bueno had then accompanied the Arcane acolyte, taking him on an unnecessarily thorough tour of the lower floor, all the while keeping up a string of inane complaints so glorious that the irritated man barely glanced around before making a hasty exit, leaving the upper floors unchecked.

Reevan himself had not seen it, since he was in the study at the time, but Callira, the enchanting kitskan bartender, had described it in great detail as she brought them refreshments in the afternoon.

"And then, the Mahejerai man sighed so loudly I'm positively surprised you didn't hear it, even all the way up here, and he tossed his robes about himself, spun on his heel and practically ran out of the bar," said Callira, placing an ale mug in front of Reevan, who took it and drank deeply. She had made a game of finding the perfect blend of spices to add to his milk, and even something so simple was transformed when made by her deft hand.

"Once again, this is delicious," said Reevan, trying to avoid the milk staining the fur around his mouth. "You have a talent. When you do procure the means to build your own tavern, you should open it in the village near Falcon's Watch. I would visit all the time to try all the newest varieties of your spiced milks."

"Do you really think so?" Callira asked in wonder, bright eyes shining at the praise. Reevan nodded, draining the mug and setting it down. Why would he give a compliment if he did not think it to be true? Women could be quite strange.

"I do," he confirmed. "I believe you would be an absolutely wonderful addition to our community. I would build the tavern myself it if meant I could drink this every day."

If there was one thing Callira was passionate about, it was the dream of her own tavern. She gushed, first enthusiastically giving Reevan an in-depth analysis of the spices she had used in his milk and how they differed from the day before, before talking at length of the architectural choices she would make if she were to design the building from the ground up. Even the novelties had been thought of. Callira had described in detail her vision of a giant cauldron in the centre, where patrons could purchase various powders that would produce coloured smoke or fireworks that would rise in the air above the tavern, further advertising it to others..

Reevan listened as well as he could, offering little in reply, content to let the charming kitskan woman dominate the conversation. He sometimes had trouble understanding Callira, but not for the same reasons he did for other people. It was partly because she spoke too quickly, like the words were racing one another as they left her brain toward her mouth; and partly because he often found himself so distracted by her charming mannerisms. She gestured a lot, long fingers flailing gracefully in the air in front of her and razor-sharp claws glinting; and her face was extremely expressive, which was a blessing for one who often failed to pick up on the underlying emotion of a conversation.

Despite Callira's visual clues, however, Reevan had to stop and reprocess a lot of the things she said to make sure he had heard them correctly. It did not make the experience any less enjoyable. Reevan often noticed people only asked questions in conversations to be polite—they did not care about his answer, merely waiting for their chance to speak again. Callira had no such fake methodical way of her speaking. She only paused in her stories when she genuinely wanted his opinion. He liked it. As his involuntary seclusion dragged on, their daily conversations were the only thing keeping him from breaking down the soundless door of the study and taking his chances with the Mahejerai.

Callira had been talking for close to twenty minutes when the door to the study swung open again and Bueno strode inside. The man looked a little weary, but also pleased with himself. The carriage driver, Halliday Greyholme, sauntered in after him.

Grundle immediately covered the box with his robes. He had not told Bueno about it, as he had an odd suspicion that Bueno would try to take it from him. Reevan thought that was ridiculous, since Bueno's shelves were already fit to burst with trinkets, but Grundle could be strangely possessive. If it made him feel a little better, then so be it.

Bueno raised an eyebrow at Callira and the beautiful kitskan flushed scarlet under her fur, and she hurriedly gathered her tray to return downstairs to the bar. Reevan watched the tip of her tail snake around the door with a slight pang of sadness.

"Well, friends," said Bueno, dropping into the chair behind his desk. "It appears that we have successfully evaded the Mahejerai's first attempt to find you. You are, of course, most welcome."

"Thank you, Bueno," said Camden, eyes still on his latest novel.

"It was nothing," Bueno scoffed, waving his hand dismissively. "I have long wished to test my defences upon a foe of this level. I'll add this favour to your tab, but I must warn you, it's getting quite lengthy."

Camden looked up, mild irritation flickering over his face at being forced to interrupt the page he was on.

"I've been meaning to ask you about that," he said. "I assume you will be expecting payment shortly. Whatever it is, I can cover it, but I can't access anything from the DeFalcone vaults until I'm back home."

Bueno accepted the drink Halliday placed in front of him, propping his slippered feet onto the same haphazard stack of books as he always did. Reevan suspected that the books were on the desk for that particular purpose.

"That is no trouble, dear boy," Bueno replied. "You will be able to give more before you depart. But if the debt remains unsettled, since Greyholme will be escorting you all across the border when the time comes, you can send anything left that you owe back with her."

"With Halliday?" Camden asked. "Why her?"

Halliday's smile was crooked. "I'm a smuggler. I smuggle things. It's what I do," she said, hopping up onto a barstool and selecting a toothpick from the jar on the counter. "In this case, people. In most cases, really, come to think about it."

Halliday chewed on the toothpick and flashed Camden a grin, but the lord's frown only deepened as he gave the woman a doubtful look.

"What is 'left' of our debt?" asked Reevan. "Have we already contributed?"

"Of a sort, my kitskan friend," replied Bueno. "Not all debts are paid in gold. To be the Eyes and Ears of Saluo, I have to know everything that goes on in Saluo, yes?" He raised his half-empty glass in a toast to them. "You have already upheld your end of our original agreement. I have learned much more about what goes on within that awful building, now I know where to look. The confirmation of the underground levels' existence was a nice touch. I have you two—" he inclined his head to both Reevan and Grundle, "to thank for that."

Grundle looked less than pleased at the praise, one small hand still lingering on the fabric concealing the thin box. He was acting a little obsessive about it, but it was probably the result of their confinement. If there was one thing Grundle hated, it was an unpicked lock.

"Do you think it will help our current problem?" asked Reevan.

Bueno shrugged. "Perhaps. I have only just begun to dig, and accessing the bowels of the pyramid is proving, shall we say, challenging for my spies. I have not discovered any information about where our Boras plans to enact his insanity, but I may have an inkling of when."

Bueno sipped at his drink, musing, before sighing and setting it down.

"My friends, in case I was not clear, I cannot do this for free. As much as I would love to bestow my services from the goodness of my heart, the fact remains that the Mahejerai will come after you all. There is a decent chance they will discover I have assisted you. I place my life, and the lives of those around me, in mortal peril for this. I must assure that I am properly compensated."

"So what do you want, then?" asked Camden. The lord shoved a stray paper into the book in his hands, holding his place, and rose from his cushioned reading nest. "Gold? Or information about us? About Altaea?

I can't speak for these two, but I don't know shit. About Altaea's military movements, about my father's plans for the conflict with Kalac once he reascends. None of it. Any secrets I tell you would be useless to you."

Bueno seemed mildly disappointed, but the smile he gave was warm.

"Ah, knowledge is never useless, my boy, but you misunderstand me. I do not expect you to commit crimes against your country. I deal in secrets, yes, but I also dabble in favours. Like the one your dear brother now owes me for taking you under my wing."

Reevan's tail twitched. "You wish for us to owe you a favour?"

"Oh, you already do, many times over at this point," said Bueno, laughing. "But I suppose this would be a more official one. A heavier one. More gravitas, as they say." He looked around at each of them expectantly.

Camden sighed and gave a small nod of assent.

"I'm sure I'll regret this," he muttered under his breath.

"Wonderful," Bueno announced, clearly delighted. "Since we are in agreement, I will help you uncover what those awful Arcanes are planning, and then we can get you on your way. You'll be back in Altaea in no time." He clapped his hands together as if that settled the matter completely, before reaching once more for his drink.

"I wish I'd been able to get closer to any of them at the temple," said Camden. "But I didn't want Lessie to have to go anywhere near Oorata Boras. What little we overheard from guests was prattling, or the occasional comment about the Arcane prowess of the Mahejerai. And we still don't know why they need Ashendi Braak, either."

"Grundle knows why," the goblin murmured from the corner.

Bueno jumped. "My small friend, you were quiet so long I thought someone had turned you to stone."

Grundle did not seem to read the jest in Bueno's comment.

"Grundle would not turn to stone. That is impossible."

Bueno opened his mouth, frowned, and closed it again.

"The Arcane ones do not number many," Grundle said. "Braak gave them slaves to fight. They are afraid to lose blood of the Weave."

"That only makes things worse," said Camden. "Not only do we not know when or where Boras plans to bring Daigon through to Kalaraak, but we also have no idea what kind of force we'll be up against." He nodded to Reevan. "You just barely managed to stop him last time, and it left Miss Mae out of action for a week. That was a disastrous fight."

Reevan sniffed. "We prevented the full siphoning of the god. I would not call that disastrous."

Camden's eyebrows practically disappeared into his hairline.

"You wouldn't? Let's review it, then," he said, counting off on his fingers. "Mae almost died. The spikes nearly electrocuted you, not to mention the Mournblade. Valandaras was almost crushed by a possessed behemoth of a shipwreck. Lessie lost her godsdamned mind trying to keep you all covered, and I had to stop her from flinging herself over the cliff after you. Boras took ninety-eight percent of the Mother's power. *And he wasn't even really there.* I'd say that is fairly disastrous."

Perhaps the young lord had a point.

"Gentlemen, please," Bueno said, shaking his head dramatically, eyes glittering with amusement as he glanced exaggeratedly between Reevan and Camden. He placed his hands out as if to block physical blows. Reevan thought that odd, since they were nowhere near close enough to each other to do so. "Do not quarrel. We will—"

The sharp sound of a gentle knock interrupted Bueno. Reevan's ears perked up, having already memorised the pattern and cadence of the knock. Mildly annoyed at the interruption of what was sure to be a pun of some kind, Bueno cracked the door before pulling it open. It revealed Callira, who stood awkwardly in the corridor, unwilling to speak for the first time Reevan had ever noticed.

Bueno noticed it too. "Girl, you are uncharacteristically quiet," he mused, raising an eyebrow. "Has the day finally come where you tell me you are leaving to build that whimsical, moonstruck tavern of yours?"

Callira's skin flushed scarlet under her fur.

"N-no, Mr Bueno, sir," she answered, though she seemed to not want to meet any of their eyes. "Orembar sent me up here, he—"

"Orembar knows better than to pull my best bartender away from her duties during the early dinner rush," Bueno said, cutting her off. "I suppose he has grown tired of guarding the stairway to my private quarters and has decided to expand into the management of my staff."

Callira stumbled over her words. "Y-yes, sir, but he said you would want to be informed. Something odd is happening outside. The Mahejerai—"

She suddenly had the attention of all five occupants in the room. Halliday and Camden rose from their seats. Grundle stepped away from the box for the first time that day, reaching for his dagger. Reevan, whose attention had been on Callira since her first knock, hoped that he did not make her uncomfortable with his prolonged focus.

Bueno's voice dropped low. "Are they here?" he asked evenly, hand casually returning to the handle of the door. Reevan had a sudden urge to pull Callira through the doorway before her employer slammed it in her face, leaving her outside of the room's added protections.

Callira shook her head, throat bobbing, and a few sighs of relief exhaled simultaneously. Bueno's shoulders relaxed. Reevan was not so easily assuaged.

"What is it, then?" Reevan asked, hoping Bueno would not mind his hijacking of the questioning. "What have the Mahejerai done?"

Callira's violet eyes were wide and fearful as they flickered between Bueno and himself. It seemed as though she had never had to deliver bad news before. She was quite good at it. The suspense had built up nicely. He would be so relieved to have an answer that it wouldn't matter how horrible it was.

Callira found her voice.

"The Mahejerai are no longer in Saluo," she whispered, voice trembling. "They left."

35

REEVAN

The Mahejerai had left Saluo.

Left Kalac altogether, if Bueno's informants were to be believed. Halliday had swept from the room muttering about getting stories straight, and it had taken less than an hour for her to reappear.

"It's true," said Halliday, pushing the door open so forcefully that it bounced off the wall and caused both a chip in the wood panelling and a pained noise to escape from Bueno's mouth. "They've completely cleared out. Heading north-east."

Reevan's first thought was at least now they could leave the study.

"Do you know *why* the Mahejerai left?" he asked.

Halliday shook her head. "Only that they left in a hurry. A few low-level acolytes remained at the temple, keeping up appearances, but the vast majority of the Mahejerai's order exited the city through the north gate." Her icy blue eyes were alight with the thrill of a new challenge. "Also, boss, you said to tell you if Braak was with them. He's not, but he's left too. Out the eastern gate, heading for Heartgate."

"Interesting," mused Bueno.

"I can guarantee that Braak's army will have also mobilised in aid of the Mahejerai," said Reevan. "He will deploy them from Heartgate, but they work for the Mahejerai now, too. Braak will move them to wherever Boras is planning to summon the god of Keanos."

"He expects resistance, then," said Camden. "Why bother taking an entire army with them if he didn't?"

Bueno returned to the seat behind his desk. For once, he did not lounge, but stayed rather alert.

"I must say, this is perplexing," he said, shuffling through a few discarded papers. "I had it on good authority that the Mahejerai were dependent on the solstices for a ritual of this magnitude. I thought we'd have more time—at least a few weeks. Months, if my informant was correct."

"Good authority?" questioned Camden. "How good can it be, if they did not predict this?"

Bueno fixed him with cold eyes. "Good enough that the informant died for it."

Camden fell silent.

"We must get back to Altaea and stop this," Reevan said. "Or at least be ready to meet him in battle. Oorata Boras cannot be allowed to take the power of a god, and Braak will only use this as an excuse to wage war upon the other countries of Kalaraak. With the power of a god behind him, he will become unstoppable."

"What are you suggesting *we* do, my kitskan friend?" asked Bueno. Reevan didn't have time to wonder why Bueno had inflected certain words, he needed to speak his thoughts aloud before the plans ran away from him.

"First, we find out what we're up against," Reevan said. "We need all the information you have on the Mahejerai—the temple, the ritual, the connection with Daigon. Anything that could give us an edge. We find out where they're heading, what they're planning. Then, we utilise Miss Halliday's services, and we get out of your hair. Gather allies."

"We could go to Druitt," Camden suggested. "He might not be able to sway the acting High Marshal into using Altaea's armies, but those who fought at Crossroad will want to fight, at least."

"Indeed," said Reevan. "We take the fight to Braak. We oppose the army, interrupt the ritual. And in doing so, we buy Miss Mae time to return with the tome and stop Boras from summoning Daigon."

The unspoken *if* hung in the air.

Bueno had not taken his eyes from Reevan. "That is a very generous amount of information you are asking me to give," he said. A small smirk passed over his face. "As well as the use of my best smuggler. You ask a lot, for which I fear I would not be receiving much in return. This would be the moment to barter any secrets you're offering."

Halliday snorted, and Reevan caught the last of an eye roll as he glanced towards her. The self-proclaimed smuggler had been lounging upon one of the bar stools—impressive, since Reevan had found them to be quite uncomfortable—and she winked at him as she leaned back, propping her elbows on the bar.

"I'm good, boss," she quipped. "I've learned my lesson about sharing secrets with you. Now I'm stuck dragging this lot back to Altaea. Never planned on setting foot in that mess of a kingdom again."

"You want a secret? I'll share a secret," said Camden. "I hadn't planned on it, either."

This confused Reevan. Camden had made it plain that he had not particularly enjoyed his time here in Saluo. He had complained about almost everything, from the weather to the way the food disagreed with his stomach. Why would he wish to stay?

Camden must have noticed Reevan's quizzical expression, for he sighed. Eyes on his whiskey glass, he spoke with the tone of a man trying very, very hard to be indifferent.

"When we return to Altaea, I won't be going back to the West Keep to continue my life of beloved debauchery," Camden said. "I must join my father in Verestead, so he can instruct me on what my duties as *heir of the house* are when he reascends. Even though that won't be until after the next winter's solstice. He said it would take more time than usual to *train* me." A muscle in his jaw clenched.

Bueno sat up straight for the first time, brow creasing, true alarm on his face.

"Your brother, is he not—"

Camden started. "No, no, he's fine. Never better, actually," he said, throwing his hands up in apology as he realised what he had insinuated. "Living the life he always dreamed of. Better late than never, I suppose."

Camden took in their confused expressions and laughed, but the bitterness in the sound was surprising. Although Camden enjoyed the drama of drawing out the story and keeping them in suspense, Reevan could tell that the lord had also, perhaps, not intended to tell this one at all.

"Druitt abdicated," Camden explained. "Gave it all up. The name, the gold, the birthright to one day be king. He wants to be the next High Marshal instead. As far as Altaean law is concerned, he's no longer a DeFalcone."

Reevan looked around the room. Of the five occupants, only Camden himself was Altaean-born, as far as he knew, but they all seemed to grasp the gravity of such a decision. Halliday looked mildly impressed, Bueno delighted. Grundle did not react.

"Druitt wrote our father a letter," Camden said, "saying the battle at Crossroad was the catalyst for him and that Altaea needed him as a protector on the front lines more than it ever would bootlicking the Seven as a king. Father was absolutely furious; even travelled all the way from Verestead to talk him out of it. Druitt threw his signet ring in the mud at Father's feet."

Camden ran a hand through his hair, the silver ring on his own finger glinting. Reevan recognised it now—it was larger, more ornate than the one Camden had worn in the past, and a jewel glittered within it. Reevan had not recognised the significance of the change. He wondered how hard it had been to clean, or if Camden's father had ordered a new one made.

"Father always hated how much Druitt loved being part of a team," Camden said. "Hated how serious he was about the military, how he worked his way up without leaning on our name. Kept pressuring him to give it up for the *family business*. At least with this stunt, Druitt finally got Father to take him seriously."

Underneath the nonchalance, a fierce pride for his brother shined. Camden was obviously proud that Druitt had managed to avoid the pressures of future kingship, but also annoyed he hadn't thought of it first.

"But now, alas, the spare suffers. There I was, at the best tavern Roost Keep has to offer, minding my own business, celebrating our success at Crossroad and having quite a lovely conversation with my favourite barmaid, Claudette, when Father barges in and starts giving me a lecture on how the DeFalcone *heir* should behave in public."

Camden flourished in mockery of his father's entrance, before his shoulders slumped as if an invisible weight of responsibility now settled upon them. He looked older than he had appeared just moments ago.

"That's why I declined to travel to Ignatia. As much as I'd love to explore realms far and wide, it now matters a great deal more that I stay alive. There's nobody after me. The DeFalcone line would cease to be part of the Seven. Though, honestly, maybe it should. We all know I'll make an awful king."

Camden smiled, but it was more of a grimace. "Perhaps Father can name Lessie heir, instead, now that she's a minor noble of our house. I don't know which of them would be more disgusted, but I'd love to see it. Falcon's Watch was meant to be my job, so palming it off to someone was the last piece of Druitt's escape plan. Made it airtight, too, since Father tried to contest it." He fidgeted with his ring. "Lessie probably wouldn't be afraid to stand up to him, either," he muttered.

"Forgive me, my lord," asked Reevan, confused, "but if it matters more for you to stay alive, accompanying us to Saluo may not have been the best of decisions."

Camden grinned sheepishly. "Ah. Yes. I'm afraid I took the news of my promotion about as well as my father took Druitt's resignation. He is currently unaware of the extent of my recent travels. I may have insinuated that I was merely delivering the news that Bueno was ready to host you, and that I would be taking care of Falcon's Watch while you did so."

He sighed and plopped himself back down among his towers of books. "My original plan was to drop you all off in Saluo, and then keep going until I found a town I liked enough to stay. Preferably somewhere not a single person could put the name DeFalcone to my face. Running seemed like the best option I had."

Reevan wondered what had changed Camden's mind, to back out on his plan of disappearing. In all honesty, it sounded delightful.

"With a bit of luck, my father will remain blissfully ignorant of my current location." Camden shrugged. "Although I've since rethought my decision to permanently relocate, I deserved one last act of defiance. If Father discovers my treachery, well—I suppose he can always disown me."

Bueno roared with laughter. Halliday's eyes flickered to the door of the study, like she was picturing the Archduke DeFalcone battering down the door and dragging his son back to his newfound duties. Reevan watched their expressions with mild interest. It all seemed a bit dramatic, really.

"My boy," said Bueno, wiping a tear of mirth from his face, "you are more like your brother than you may ever realise. That was a wonderful secret, yes, thank you."

Camden grinned as he watched the older man laughing, looking lighter for having shared his troubles. Reevan cocked his head. Maybe there was something to be said for divulging what bothered you. He wouldn't, of course. But it could be helpful.

"And what about you, Reevan?" asked Bueno, dark eyes sparkling like he already knew. "Your friend's story has paid for your safe return. But what will you tell me, in exchange for the knowledge you seek?"

Reevan stared hard, but Bueno only smiled pleasantly. The man was goading him to reveal his hand, and he would have loved to play the game. But they were out of time. Reevan looked at Grundle, wordlessly seeking his permission. Fear filled the goblin's face, but it hardened into resolve as his long fingers flexed around the thin box, still concealed behind him. Grundle had never owned anything; it was always stolen.

Reevan sighed. "I will tell you my secret, *alone*, and along with it I will offer you a favour to collect when you see fit. But for that, I do have an additional request."

"You've got my attention," admitted Bueno, smiling. "I've never had a caveat attached to a trade like this before. What does your deepest desire happen to be?"

Reevan nodded to Grundle, who hooked one long finger into the neck of his robes and yanked downwards. In doing so, he exposed the slave's collar fastened around his neck. It was smaller than most others, the dark cord only half an inch wide and delicate, and the glittering gem set in the middle of it seemed dull and lifeless.

There was a sharp intake of breath from the other occupants of the room.

"That one day," said Reevan evenly, "when I eventually return to this city, you will help me to remove every last one of these wretched devices from around the necks of those who wear them."

Bueno had gone still. "How did you do it?" he asked, eyes alight with interest.

"Can't remove them," muttered Grundle. "Can only turn them off."

"Grundle has many talents," said Reevan. "but the ability to tinker with things he shouldn't be able to has always been his most useful. He has perfected the art of deactivation. Most slave collars are designed to inject the wearer with some sort of inhibitor should they stray too far from their allocated area. But Grundle found a way around it."

Halliday whistled. "That's actually very impressive, little guy."

Grundle glowered at her. He had probably never been referred to so informally. She winked at him.

"But still, there are mechanisms in place that prevent total removal," Reevan said, turning his emerald eyes on Bueno. "I want it gone, and I want them freed. Do that, and I will gift you with all the knowledge I have ever acquired as a member of Braak's inner circle. This is my price."

Bueno nodded to himself, the wheels in his brain turning.

"All of my knowledge on the Mahejerai's plans, in exchange for how to deactivate the most barbaric form of slave control I, for one, have seen in any realm," he mused. "I believe I am getting the better end of it. You have a deal, my friend."

Bueno extended a hand, and Reevan shook it. The room fell silent for long enough that if Lessie were there, she would have broken it twice over.

Eventually, a different young woman did.

"So what now?" Halliday asked.

"We plan," said Reevan. "We gather resources. We track Braak's movements, and uncover Boras's motives for leaving Kalac. Lord Camden and his brother will find us soldiers to oppose Braak's armies."

"We have to do this quietly," Camden added. His face was hard. "We'll have the godsdamned fight of our lives trying to keep this from becoming a war. My father will take any excuse to declare it upon Kalac once he reascends. And if he learns of my travels, he'll lock me in a tower himself this time."

"No problem," said Halliday. "Stealth is my middle name. I'll get you back into Altaea so quietly even your daddy won't know what city you're in until you're right behind him."

Bueno scoffed. "Don't think this frees you from your debt, Greyholme. You've still got a while to go."

He started shuffling through the papers at his desk. Halliday stuck her tongue out at Bueno's back.

Reevan sniffed. At least they had the beginnings of a plan. Something to do while they waited for the others to come back, besides sit on their hands and agonise over the future.

Over the next few days, they would discuss many tiny details; such as working out what would happen when Valandaras, Mae and Lessie returned to Saluo—or never returned at all. Bueno was delighted to learn the first titbits of Reevan's promised information, practically salivating beneath his calm exterior. They would spend an unimaginable amount of time deciding what to do and what not to.

There was one thing, however, that Reevan had known from the beginning that he would have to do. It would be vital to his plan's success. And he was not looking forward to it.

"As for us," Reevan said, tail twitching as he indicated himself and Grundle, "it is time we paid our former master a visit."

36

MAE

Unforgiving.

If Mae had to describe Ignatia with a single word, it would be unforgiving.

The desolate, sweeping plains of the realm of fire offered little respite against the heat and even less protection against the wind, which raged endlessly. Hot and dry, whipping their hair about and searing their faces. The only relief they found was the darkened sky, but that in itself was uncomfortable. Perpetual dusk distorted their perception of time.

Their deadliest enemy became dehydration. They had been travelling for less than a day, and already Mae felt the dull throb of a persistent headache hanging above her brow; the now familiar burn creeping into her eyes and muddling her thoughts. Her mouth had a constant dryness to it that she knew would only worsen with the small sips of water she allowed herself, resisting the urge to dump the entire thing over her head.

Valandaras's extra pack had contained nothing but waterskins, carrying gallons and gallons of life-preserving water. He had divided the precious commodity between the three of them when they had first landed on the realm, once they had recovered enough to move. They planned to ration the water as best they could, but it quickly became obvious they wouldn't make it to the temple if they did. They just had to hope another water source would be located before it ran out.

Mae exhaled heavily. Even the breath leaving her lungs was hot. It was an odd sensation, feeling overheated without direct sunlight beaming down on her as the obvious culprit. The skies were thick with ash and smoke from the volcanic mountains. If there was a sun, she had yet to spot it behind the billowing clouds. It did not matter. The heat in Ignatia radiated upwards from the core of the realm. Mae could feel it in the soles of her boots as they walked. It was unsettling to think there were mere miles between her feet and the rest of the molten rock that sometimes burst from the tops of mountains, flowing down the sides in great scarlet rivers.

The urge to stop, to sit down, to give up was stronger than she'd ever admit. Her feet were sore and kept threatening to blister, and only the trickle of her Gift kept her upright. It was constantly drained to nothing, and she felt the hollow ache tug at her soul.

The somewhat decent amount of healing power Mae had managed to store had been depleted the second they had reached Ignatia. Falling from Valandaras's portal of light, she had landed awkwardly, felt something snap in her ankle, and the spark had rushed through her body without a conscious decision on her part. Knitting the bone back together had drained her reserves. It was necessary—without healing the injury, she would have been unable to walk—but it hurt in more ways than one. Mae had seen Lessie's bleeding hands, felt her Gift sputter, and had not been able to do a single thing to help.

Mother, this is my nightmare. Powerless, unable to use your Gift for its true intention, to help people, to restore life.

Luckily, Valandaras appeared to have been keeping a few of his own gifts quiet.

Mae watched in disbelief as the Realmshifter approached Lessie. The cloth was carefully placed over his eyes once more, and he wrapped the Mournblade back within the cloak. Underneath his gauntlets, however, he had not wrapped his hands as he usually did, and the faint golden glow of his skin hummed with a pulse that felt slightly familiar.

Valandaras crouched before Lessie and took the girl's hands in his own. How *she* would have. Mae was surprised at the flash of envy that threatened to envelop her.

Lessie flinched away from the contact, ripping her injured palms away from him and into her lap. Valandaras kept his own hands outstretched, waiting patiently, until she sighed and placed her hands back within his grasp.

Mae limped towards them both and folded herself down next to Lessie, doing her best to ignore the tiny barks of pain from her ankle as the last of her Gift's trickle settled into the injury.

Lessie did not meet either of their eyes. Mae suspected the girl was embarrassed about her moment of inaction, and made a note to reassure her of it later. Lessie had frozen, it was true, but it was nothing to be embarrassed about. Mae had seen her shake it off before Valandaras had pulled her into the abyss. It was normal, natural to fear the darkness.

Mae couldn't explain why the void had not terrified her. Why, instead, it had felt like finally coming home.

"Since when were *you* the healer?" Lessie mumbled, and Valandaras chuckled.

"To tell you the truth, I am not exactly sure," he replied, taking one of Lessie's injured hands in between his own. The golden light flared inside them like he held a miniature sun within his fingertips. "I have not always had this ability. It has manifested itself in the last year or so. Perhaps the longer I serve Haropheth, the more power he bestows upon me."

Mae frowned. That didn't make sense. "Can any other Realmshifters heal injuries and wounds?" she asked.

Valandaras stiffened at her voice. He did not immediately respond, attention focused on Lessie's other hand as the light glowed brighter again.

"Themselves, yes," he answered, avoiding Mae's gaze, but thankfully not her question. "Most Realmshifters can heal minor cuts and wounds on their own bodies, albeit at a slower rate than I have found I can. Usually while they are asleep. But not others, no, not that I am aware of. It is not part of the Path, to consider others. The Path is only to locate the Betrayer. Our ability to heal ourselves is to keep us healthy on our Path."

Curiosity bloomed within Mae, and she forgot that she and Valandaras were not really speaking after their fight in Bueno's study. The questions spilled out of her mouth before she could stop herself.

"So all Realmshifters can heal themselves, but your healing is faster? How much faster? And now you've discovered you can heal others? Or has nobody thought to try to heal someone else before? How long have you been able to do this?"

Valandaras finally raised his head in her direction. His eyes met hers, as always, as if the cloth did not exist, and Mae searched them for any signs of the truth. But for once he was unreadable to her, his face held in a carefully constructed neutrality.

"Since Holdfast."

Mae's heart sank.

Their disastrous bounty in Holdfast, months ago now, had been the first time she had been unable to keep every member of the crew safe. The first time her Gift had not been enough to help them all. When she had been the one who needed saving. She was still unsure how they'd all escaped with their lives. She should have died. Had *Valandaras* healed her?

Despite the oppressive heat, Mae shivered. Holdfast had scarred her. She had long vowed to live a life of optimism, a glass-half-full existence, but the last year had landed more blows than she could count. Holdfast had been the hardest—it had triggered a regression within her. She had been withdrawing, worrying more about the consequences of a job failing than she had before, voicing those concerns out loud to others instead of being the one to soothe fears away. Things had finally started to feel better when the Mother had been attacked and she had lost everything.

And now I sit here, useless, as Val does the job I'm supposed to.

When Valandaras released Lessie's hands, she held up her palms, angling them as if inspecting his handiwork. The flesh had been healed, but the blood and dirt remained, so it was hard to see any improvement. She flexed her fingers, apparently satisfied.

"Not even a scar," Lessie remarked, sounding disappointed. "Thanks. I was a little worried I'd have a glowing golden line to have to explain for the rest of my life. Or that you'd realmshift my fingers to Requiem without me." She cracked each knuckle in turn, oblivious to Mae's flinch at each tiny snap.

Valandaras kept his head down, using his waterskin to rinse the worst of the blood away. But even as he responded to Lessie, Mae felt his attention slide to her.

"That is not something you need to worry about," Valandaras said. "This healing light, whatever it is, does not come from the same place as my eyes. I can feel them. They are separate. This light is... gentle. Calm. It comes from a place inside of me I was not aware existed until the first time I needed it."

Beneath her shock, Mae felt a small smile bloom. She knew that feeling all too well.

Valandaras turned his dimly glittering palms over, shifting uncomfortably. "I cannot figure out why I have it, only that I can use it to heal."

Mae held back a scoff. *He doesn't understand the power, so it scares him. How typical. No wonder I've never seen him use it before.*

Valandaras began sorting through his pack, keeping his eyes averted, but he spoke clearly enough that they knew he still addressed them as he re-wrapped his hands.

"The light of a Realmshifter, on the other hand, is designed to... carve. To see beyond the realm I physically stand upon and find a path through the void to the others. That light cannot heal, as its purpose is to destroy the natural barriers the realms should have between them. To cleave the very fabric of the world. That light reflects Haropheth's desperation at the moment he created us—it is unforgiving, and unstable, and chaotic in its cruelty. But that light is also necessary. It is what kept us alive today as we travelled within the void."

Lessie went pale under her freckles. "So if you didn't wear that cloth over your eyes, you'd just be walking around ripping open portals to other realms?" she asked.

Valandaras nodded gruffly in response, pulling out another waterskin from his pack. It was clear he now considered the conversation over.

Mae stared at him, stunned, finally having a solid answer for why his skin glittered with the golden light, for why he kept his eyes obscured from the world. The knowledge felt like it had done nothing but raise more questions. And the healing light coming from a different place? That felt strangely familiar. It sounded like *her* light.

Gods, it's like he is Divine, in a way.

The questions only mounted as they continued their trek across the barren wasteland of a realm. Valandaras had assured them that he knew the direction they should be going. The 'pull of the Path', he called it. The invisible string that guided him to the place he most needed to be. Mae couldn't help but wonder if that thread had tied him to her, or if she'd yanked him off his Path the day they had met.

Ignatia was infinitely strange. It had first seemed a desolate wasteland, but upon closer inspection it was teeming with life. Fat lizards lay content under flattened rocks, warming their bellies on the ground. Now and then, the silhouettes of strange birds would pass over them as they dipped below all but the lightest of the ash clouds. Craggy rocks and pointy brown plants dotted the landscape. Every so often they would come across a flowering plant, the explosion of colour a stubborn defiance of its own surroundings. Mae found herself smiling.

Mother, once you get used to how hot it is, this place is beautiful.

Valandaras spoke little as they travelled, but he occasionally pointed out small settlements and villages whenever they could be seen. Mae was embarrassed that the realisation had shocked her—of course there were, of course sentient humanoids existed on other realms, but she had never stopped to think about them. What their lives would be like, what they wore, what languages they spoke. Did Ignatia have a single language? Or did they, too, have a common tongue? A mismatched patchwork born from millennia of trade between multiple races, like how those on Kalaraak all used Dwarven terms for masonry and metalwork no matter their race. There probably had been an Elven word for the techniques, once, and a human one too, but nobody used them anymore. Language was beautiful like that.

Mae felt the spark of her Gift flicker happily as her mind swirled with the curiosities. She swore her step felt lighter, her feet more cushioned against the underground heat.

The dwellings Valandaras pointed out were hard to see, built into the sides of the tallest mountains. Mae guessed it was cooler further away from the surface, so the homes had been built as high as possible. How did the Ignatian natives know which mountains would not erupt into molten death, becoming boiling rivers to carry them straight to the Silver Stream itself? Perhaps they had fortified their homes somehow.

I know Val said we should avoid speaking to anyone, going anywhere near them, but wouldn't it be so incredible to? What if we—

Valandaras stopped abruptly, and Mae barely caught herself as she kept walking and collided with his back. She avoided his concerned look.

Maybe the heat was getting to her. She felt a little *too* lost in her thoughts.

The trio rested often, but with the ever-present ash clouds obscuring clear indication of time passing, it was hard to judge when to pack down for the night. They settled on whenever they found decent shelter, an open-mouthed cave or a grouping of bone-dry rocks large enough to give the illusion of safety.

Sleep was elusive. The ground was too warm. Every time Mae felt herself starting to drift, a trickle of sweat would roll down her neck, or a minute position shift would send a sharp rock digging into her skin. She volunteered for the longest watch of the night.

Mae sat, lost in thought again, as the night's quiet stillness blanketed them. Only Valandaras's soft snores and the occasional nonsense sentence of Lessie's sleep-talk interrupted the silence. Even at night, the heat simmered under the surface. Mae was itching to get away from it. If there had been trees nearby, she might have climbed one, if only to be further away from the ground.

For the first time since the Mother's essence had been stolen, Mae found herself weighing up the consequences of a Change attempt. Perhaps into one of the birds they had seen, leaving the ground far below. She could fly above the ash clouds, see what nobody else in Ignatia ever had. She had always loved flying. It was indescribable. The feeling of being above it all—inconsequential to politics and power plays, unbound by invisible borderlines. Where she could see things for what they were. In a strange way, it felt like a death of her human self. Disconnection, unable to reach those below, but also untouchable freedom.

Mae knew attempting to Change would fail; that part of her Gift's well had remained bleakly empty. But the longing to fly, to be free, stayed with her.

The ash clouds rolled slowly across the dark sky.

She did not try. But she came close.

They moved slower the next day, beginning to feel the effects of limited water. What little signs of other life disappeared behind them as they wound their way around rocky outcrops and steep valleys, trying to avoid climbing too high or fall too low. The surrounding mountains were smaller and angrier, spewing trickles of molten rock that slid down to converge into lava rivers. They avoided the largest of these rivers; the heat radiating from them unbearable, but Mae noticed a few of the smaller streams broke off and created a path alongside them that Valandaras seemed to follow them more often than not.

Lessie didn't speak the entire time, other than a few mumbled curses under her breath as she scribbled furiously into her journal. Mae knew the girl felt out of her depth. In a different time, a lighter adventure, Mae would have tried to lift Lessie's spirits, but holding up her own in this heat was debilitating enough.

Valandaras knows where he is going. He has to.

"You know what?" Lessie muttered. "I'm starting to think Lai'ireal just wanted to kill us. 'In the centre of Ignatia's hottest fires', sure," she scoffed, poorly imitating the goddess's strange overtone. "What kind of direction is that? What are the odds that we're going to have to climb into a volcano?"

Valandaras shook his head. "We will not."

Lessie kicked a dusty rock as she walked by it, the dirt exploding into a miniature cloud of dust.

"How can you be so sure? Your Path? The *invisible string*?"

Valandaras turned, the heavy pack at his back slipping, and he set it down upon the earth, resting for the moment.

"Yes," he replied. "I have explained this to you before."

"You haven't explained anything," Lessie snapped. "You make vague allusions to higher powers and then expect us all to blindly follow you. I don't know if we're going in the right direction, and I hate it. Can't you at least give us a couple of landmarks to aim for?"

Valandaras sighed heavily, which only served to make Lessie angrier.

Mae kept walking. She absent-mindedly followed the path of a tiny lava stream, wandering alongside it. The way the liquid rock flowed, slow and methodical, was oddly calming.

Valandaras's voice drifted towards her. "I have also explained that it is not the way of the Path to discuss its innermost workings. I am a Realmshifter. Guarding the secrets of the Realmshifters is part of what it means to be one. I have told you that my Path pulls me in the direction I am supposed to go, to achieve the goal I have set out to accomplish. It is a feeling. It is not a mind map. I do not have Bueno's tapestry draped over my eyes."

The voices of her companions seemed much quieter than they should be, since Mae had not walked that far ahead of them. Had the wind changed direction? And how was it possible that it was blowing even hotter than before?

"All right, whatever," said Lessie, mollified but still annoyed. She gestured at the risen earth that surrounded them, the volcanic peaks in the distance. "But what if we're meant to be going up one of these godsdamned mountains?"

Mae reached another small cliff. The little lava stream flowed off the edge into the valley below. Her eyes followed it down.

Oh, Mother.

"We're not," she called over her shoulder.

Her voice must have sounded strange, for it pulled both sets of eyes upon her back. The conversation stopped. The sound of a pack being pulled from the ground. Footsteps rushing to her side.

Valandaras's arm brushed her shoulder as he came to stand beside her, his golden glow more noticeable in Ignatia's muted landscape. The movement sent a skitter of her Gift down her side, the emerald spark still playful like it was greeting a friend. He tensed as he looked down into the valley below.

The land itself was completely desolate. No trees, plants, not even a stray boulder marred its surface. The ground within the valley was flat—unnaturally so. The only interruption to the surface were the lines of fire left by the molten rock that flowed through it. At the valley's end, the smaller streams of lava converged into the great molten river, which disappeared once more into the horizon.

But not before they intersected, again and again, making patterns in the otherwise solid ground. The effect was hypnotising, as if someone long ago had dug tiny trenches to encourage the lava to flow in the places that would form a design only viewable from above.

It looked like... wings.

Glorious feathers of fire. Arcing over the ground, like a bird about to take flight. Stretching for the entire length of the valley itself. Impossibly intricate. There was no chance this had formed naturally, not if given a hundred millennia to form. Tears pricked at her eyes at the sheer beauty of it.

And in the middle, where wings that size would join onto the body of the creature, the beast or bird they belonged to—instead there was a deep impression in the hard ground. Circular and shrouded in shadow. Some of the lava streamed along the edges of it, disappearing below.

If Mae squinted, reflected in the glow of the lava streams, she thought she could see the beginning of stairs embedded in the rock. Descending.

An entrance.

"We're not going up," Mae said calmly, ignoring Lessie's sharp intake of breath beside her. "We're going down. Ignatia's hottest fires are within. The temple is underground."

37

MAE

Being underground still felt like a relief, despite the lack of a sun to escape from.

Mae descended the circular steps of stone slowly, giving her eyes time to adjust to the darkness. The only light came from the silent lava trickles along the walls, and the stairs were narrow and covered with millennia of dust. Valandaras followed; hand perpetually glued to the hilt of his falchion.

Lessie trailed behind them, reluctant. "I don't know why I expected a nice, calm, above-ground temple," she muttered under her breath. "Of course, if we're going to die in another realm, it might as well be underneath the rivers of boiling hot lava, where nobody will ever find our bodies."

Mae winced, but her lips tugged upwards at the dramatics. Lessie had a tendency to overuse sarcasm to cover up her true emotions—in this case, fear.

Mother, grant her strength. She is terrified of being underground.

Though it was hotter the further they descended, since they were drawing closer to Ignatia's molten core, the temperature of the underground temple was a less violent heat than above. Their main source of discomfort was no longer the unforgiving wind's whip to their faces. It had been replaced by a heavy, oppressive heat that weighed on them, like a living thing pressing upon their bodies from every angle. Even the air felt thicker; an ever so slight resistance through it as they walked. Each inhale felt like a battle.

The circular stairwell ended in a small antechamber, scarcely big enough for the three of them. The walls were made of the same ashy, uneven stone as the steps, suggesting the entire cavern had been formed by giant rivers of lava long ago. Although the colours within the stone were somewhat chaotic, there was an elegance to it—the surface of the walls and floor were refined, the kaleidoscope of sand and stone smooth. Minute grooves in the walls allowed the lava to flow where it was needed, giving them light without impeding their movements. If Mae looked too long at any one stream, she could see the air warping beside it; the lava was so hot that it drove away what little moisture remained.

They paused at the bottom of the stairwell, and Mae took a moment of quiet reverence. Whoever the followers of this forgotten god were, they had spent years building this temple. Smoothing the walls, carving the paths for the lava. The steps alone could have taken decades.

The antechamber was empty, and twin archways of stone stood on each side of it; the curve of the hallways beyond suggested they were following the wings of fire above. Perhaps the entire temple mimicked the shape of the beast. Her respect for the long-dead Divines of this temple increased. Mae smiled, feeling the quiet hum only a holy place could manage. Somehow, she knew, they were safe here.

For now, anyway.

"Stay here and stay quiet," Valandaras said, his tone a warning. "We may not be alone."

He strode to the right archway, weapon half-unsheathed, and disappeared through it without a second thought. Mae listened as the slight echo of his footsteps faded, following the curve. She felt a bead of sweat roll from the nape of her neck and disappear into the back of her dress. She refused to shiver as it trickled down her spine. Her resistance to rolling her eyes at Valandaras's abrupt exit was substantially weaker.

For a minute, the two women stood in silence. Lessie's fingers gripped the handle of her gun so tightly Mae could have counted the lines on the girl's knuckles. She forced herself to take a deep, calming breath. It didn't work. Her mind raced. It was one thing to stand back and let Valandaras handle something completely outside of her skill set—like realmshifting, for example—but assessing a hallway? They could have all gone together. It was ridiculous to leave her behind.

Why does he always do this?

"Mae, don't," Lessie warned, but Mae had already set off after Valandaras.

She walked through the arch with deliberately overconfident steps, straining her eyes and ears for anything amiss. The only signs of life she found were a single trail of familiar bootprints in the dust. Lava glistened through the cracks, illuminating the passageway and casting odd shadows upon the walls. The shimmer of Mae's Gift down her arms helped to keep her unease at bay, as if the Mother were there with her. You are not alone, it seemed to whisper, and you are on the right path. Her Gift glittered brighter on her left, meeting the glow of the wall, lighting it up.

Mae's attention followed the glow and paused.

The stone walls had carvings etched upon them. Intricate, detailed drawings. Those at the start of the corridor had been so simple she had dismissed them as decorative, but now she turned and glanced back with fresh eyes.

"Lessie, come and look at this," Mae called.

The only response was a muttered curse from the antechamber. Mae shook her head in amusement. Lessie would have happily waited above for them and avoided the underground temple altogether if the girl's own stubbornness had let her.

Lessie's grumbling became clearer as she caught up, but stopped abruptly as she noticed the walls.

"Holy shit."

"I know," Mae replied. She pointed at the first panel, which she had now recognised words carved into its surface. "It's in Elven, but it's ancient. The language is almost indecipherable. This must be thousands of years old."

Lessie whistled. "Can... can you read it?" she asked.

They both ignored the underlying question all Altaeans feared most.

Mae stepped closer to the walls, where the tiny trickles had illuminated them enough to read by.

"I was taught Elven as a child," Mae admitted. "It's in an obsolete dialect, but I understand parts. It says it 'foretells what comes after, and records what comes before.' It's a story. A prophecy and a history."

Lessie frowned. "Of the tome? Of this god?"

Mae nodded. "It appears so. I can't imagine who else it would be about."

Spurred by their discovery, the two women followed the carvings as they continued down the passageway, Mae doing her best to translate as they went. Where parts of the story had worn away with time or were too complicated to decipher, they relied on the intricate illustrations for context. It was fortunate they had pictures, since some of the language was vague and hard to decipher. The sheer age of the texts was baffling, even to someone as long-lived as she was.

I have never felt quite so insignificant in time before.

"From what I can understand, the people who followed this god believed that it took the form of a giant being made entirely of fire—a bird," Mae said, tracing the depictions in the air with her fingertips, feeling the heat from the lava trickle radiating beneath them. "Unbound by the realms, it flew freely between them. Then the story of a cycle begins."

Mae's eyes shifted eagerly to the next panel, following the passageway on a gentle slope downwards.

"Are we sure it's the god?" asked Lessie. "Maybe it was a Divine. Could you Change into something like this?"

Mae pretended she didn't notice the disappointment on Lessie's face when she shook her head. "Wings are complicated, even without adding fire to the mix. This has to be the god."

Mae pointed at an illustration that showed the firebird, wings folded, surrounded by an odd geometric pattern.

"It became encased in... something... and was eventually freed by those who 'knew the truth'."

"'Knew the truth'? Could that mean its followers? Or Lai'ireal?" Lessie asked, keeping her eyes ahead. The girl had only glanced at the carvings, trusting Mae's interpretation of them while she guarded them both and looked out for Valandaras. "Lai'ireal knew about this place, after all. Is it talking about being freed from the Godprison?"

"Possibly," Mae replied. "It's not clear. This next one shows a rebirth, an unplanned return. So the encasing might very well reference the Godprison."

Lessie's eyes narrowed. "Though didn't Lai'ireal say this god never came back?" she asked, turning to squint suspiciously at the wall. "That they vanished *before* the Godprison? But that would make this temple..." Shock flitted across her face.

Mae nodded. "Hundreds of thousands of years old, most likely. I know. It's incredible. We could be the first people to set foot within these walls in millennia."

The numbers were staggering. No living being on Kalaraak knew for certain, but it was widely accepted that Vry'iin's betrayal had happened upwards of fifty thousand years ago.

"But isn't that a god tree?" Lessie asked, pointing back at a carving they had just passed. "Did this god manifest on Ignatia how the Mother would have on Kalaraak? I thought gods didn't do that unless they had been syphoned into the Prison by Vry'iin. Otherwise, where is it coming back from?"

Mae sighed. She had heard how the younger girl's voice had caught when mentioning the Mother. It hurt, but she also appreciated Lessie trying to be mindful of her feelings.

"I don't know, Lessie," Mae replied, placing a hand on the girl's elbow to show she was all right. She knew Lessie didn't believe her. "It's very complicated and confusing, but I suppose most gods and prophecies are. Like here, see—this one says that the returned god... was granted power? Granted power. To someone else?" Mae shook her head. "It's unclear. The Elven word here could mean 'power' in the general sense, but I've seen it used as 'alliance' before. And here, this one..."

Mae lost herself in the story. It was complicated, but still felt familiar. Like re-reading a favourite book after decades, only recognising the barest of details. Lessie drew closer to her, eyes wide, the aloof mask of indifference falling away to stare at the walls with a curiosity bordering on reverence. Together, they made their way down the sloping hallway.

"The firebird raised an army of... something... I don't know that one, I'm afraid," Mae continued, struggling to decipher the ancient tongue. "Befriended an enemy, then fought another, more powerful one. A being of unfathomable evil, whom they refer to only as 'the Outsider'."

Lessie shook her head. "If this bird did all that, no wonder it disappeared. My head hurts just keeping track of what it did."

Mae stopped at what seemed to be the last panel, as the walls after it remained smooth. The design was the most intricate one yet. The firebird, wings outstretched in mid-flight, mouth open in a silent scream. A swirling, faceless void that represented the Outsider twisted around it. Those who had carved the walls had seemed reluctant to depict the evil, leaving it deliberately ambiguous, but even the lack of lava to illuminate it gave the entity a dark, ominous energy. The two beings were frozen in eternal combat, laying waste to each other in the sky as a sprawling battle below them raged. Thousands of bodies, depicted sparingly so as not to pull focus, fought upon the ground below, with what looked like both steel and Divine or Arcane means.

Mae came so close to the last panel that her nose might've burned from the lava, but she couldn't make out any faces or clothing upon the army. Had they been the firebird's followers? Was that why they were all gone?

Mother, imagine nobody being left alive to know you. What a tragedy that would be.

It could be a trick of the light, but the lava that ran down the walls also glowed brighter behind the firebird's wings than it did in any other etching. In this final panel, however, they appeared to be melting off; the firebird's expression twisted in pain.

"And this is where the firebird god 'became death'," Mae whispered, a cold sense of foreboding washing over her and making the hairs on her arms rise. "To defeat the Outsider, bring back order, and restore the god's... rebirth."

Mae sighed, reaching a finger out towards the firebird's face as if she could comfort it. "I wish I knew what that means."

"Your translation of ancient Elven is quite good, lioness," came a low voice from behind them, stepping out of the shadows.

Mae jumped, spinning on her heels, hands flying to her face even as she recognised Valandaras's voice. Lessie ripped her revolver around and had half pulled the trigger before his sentence finished, swearing and yanking it back as he came into view. He did not flinch at the weapon pointed at his face, his attention focused solely on the carved stonework.

"But it does not say 'rebirth'," Valandaras continued. "In this instance, I would interpret it as 'balance'. The firebird 'became death' to defeat the Outsider, and restored the balance of the gods."

"Holy gods in Prison," Lessie swore loudly. "I nearly took your godsdamned head off."

Mae giggled, despite the wave of exhaustion that washed over her. It was like her body knew that Valandaras could take over protecting them, so it took the opportunity to let go.

Valandaras did not respond to Lessie's outburst, only beckoning them further down the passageway.

"I have found where we are meant to go," he said tightly, ghosts of the tension they'd had ever since their fight still lingering in his voice.

Mae knew, even underneath her own grievance, that it would pass. One fight could never undo all that they shared. She was still annoyed with him, but he had brought her here despite how he felt about it.

"So are we alone down here?" Mae asked, allowing a hint of teasing back into her tone. "Or did you find somebody else lurking in the shadows?"

Valandaras's face was unreadable, but she swore she saw a flicker of amusement twitch across his mouth as he replied.

"Of a sort."

Valandaras took them to the end of the hallway, where the rest of the walls had stayed blank until they reached a set of heavy stone doors. The doors themselves were carved to resemble the firebird, with wings stretching across each side so that the bird would take flight if they were to be opened.

Valandaras also showed them how if they were to continue on down the corridor, it would eventually slope back towards the antechamber and the stairs to return above ground. It explained how he had doubled back around and come up behind them. Mae noted with fascination that the prophetic carvings of the hallway were mirrored—the first carved panel beside the heavy doors bearing the same words that had been on the first she had read. If they were to complete a full circle of the hallways, both starting and finishing in the antechamber, then the story told on the panels would repeat itself twice.

There were minor changes in the left-hand hallway, but Mae dismissed them as differences of opinion or even carving skills. Divines have long squabbled about the 'correct' interpretation of their god's will. The gods themselves did not come down to tell their own legends—except perhaps Lai'ireal, she supposed.

Valandaras pushed open the winged stone doors, leading them through to another passageway. This one was straight and narrow, stretching on for what seemed like a mile. The walls here were undecorated, with no sprawling stories etched into them, but the edges of the passageway were not empty.

Along the corridor stood stone statues of warriors. Rows and rows of them, standing floor-to-ceiling at ten feet tall and frozen at attention like they were guarding the way forward. Each was depicted wearing beautifully detailed armour, the plates fashioned to resemble the feathers of the firebird, pauldrons stretching outwards to mimic wings. They were so lifelike that when Lessie waved her hand in front of the nearest one, Mae let out a small sigh of relief when it did not respond.

"Symbolic guardians, I suppose," Mae murmured, more to herself than the others.

"Thank the gods," Lessie muttered, eyeing the nearest statue's longsword, clasped by stone fingers twice as thick as her own. "So what are we supposed to do once we have the tome? Are we going to realmshift back home straight away?"

"That is the plan," said Valandaras. "Wherever we find it, I will then attempt to find a Path to return us to Kalaraak. It will be difficult within the temple, so we will have to return to the surface before I do so. I cannot see any clear path down here."

"Is that normal?" Mae asked, curiosity outweighing decorum. Valandaras had always been tight-lipped about realmshifting, but that was before he had realmshifted with them. He stiffened automatically at the question, then relaxed.

"Honestly, I have never seen anything like it," he replied. "There is no path. It is as if we are not within a realm at all. It might just be from the walls, molten and moving as they are. I will reassess once we find the tome."

"And then what?" Lessie said, eyes shifting between Valandaras and Mae. It was clear her faith in the mission was fading.

I don't know, Mae thought hopelessly. *I have no idea where to go from here.*

"I will study the tome," Mae answered, hoping the false bravado in her voice would be enough to spur them on a little longer. "Figure out how to use it, I suppose. After all, we need it to stop Oorata Boras and return the Mother."

"We do not need it for that," said Valandaras stiffly. "We will leave it as a last resort. I will use the Mournblade to kill Boras before he can summon Daigon to Kalaraak. Then you will not need to risk yourself. Need I remind you that Lai'ireal said it will—"

"I know it might claim my life," Mae snapped. She felt the beginnings of heat rising in her cheeks. Valandaras had always supported her before. Why was this any different? "That is my choice to make. I am prepared to make that sacrifice."

Valandaras stopped walking. "I cannot understand why you would risk dying, especially to such an unnatural death."

Mae saw red, although she didn't know if it was with rage or exhaustion. All she could think as she spun on her heel to face him was how tired she was of not saying what she thought. She was done hiding. No more obscuring the truth. Not from him.

"I am a hundred and twenty-one years old, Val," Mae said. "I am not sure if I *can* die a natural death. In fact, it would be welcome at this point. I have long wished for it."

The hardness in Valandaras's face took on a strange quality she had not seen before. He stepped towards her, and for a moment she thought he would start shouting. Instead, he put his hands onto her shoulders and bent until they were nose to nose.

"Never, ever say that again," said Valandaras. This close, she could feel the burn of his eyes even with the cloth between them. It was like he looked into her soul. She fought the urge to squirm under the intense contact and did not respond.

"Promise me, Mae."

Her eyes met his defiantly. It stung this close, but she refused to flinch.

"Why should I? Death is not so bad. It's the living after it has touched you that tears at your soul."

What does he know of living long after you have stopped caring to? What does he know of being able to go anywhere but the home that's no longer there?

"Because I cannot lose you," said Valandaras. "Not after all of this."

Whatever retort Mae had begun to voice died on her lips. She felt a sharp sting of sudden tears threaten to spill from her eyes, but she clung to them stubbornly. Valandaras tightened his grip on her shoulders, and she felt the comforting warmth of his strange glow seep into her skin.

It might have been an eternity before Lessie's pointed cough broke the tension between them. As if remembering they had an audience, Valandaras dropped his hands from Mae's shoulders and let them hang awkwardly by his side. Mae gave Valandaras a small nod, refusing to acknowledge what the moment had meant.

They walked the rest of the corridor in complete silence and did not speak when they reached a second set of stone firebird doors. Valandaras pushed them inwards without waiting, and the three filed in.

This chamber had been designed for worship. The ceilings were much higher than the corridor they had just passed through, giving the room a less oppressive feel than the rest of the temple. Generous rows of stone pews curved around in both directions, on either side of an aisle that led to the back of the room. More carvings highlighted by the lava seeping within them covered the stonework, as complex as the prophetic stories on the corridors before them. The back wall's depiction was made up entirely of one image—a massive god tree. It glowed fiercely from the streams of lava that made up its willowy branches, which stretched over the edges of the walls, continued around the corners, and swept to the floor. The heat rolling off the carved walls made the room the hottest yet, and Mae nervously reached for one of the last waterskins.

The god tree dominated the space with the way it was sculpted out of the stone, making it feel like a once-real tree that had been petrified. Even the flow of the lava seemed to pulse, like it was a living thing. Mae couldn't help but smile at it. It didn't feel that different from the god tree she had once felt the Mother radiating from. Perhaps some things were the same no matter what realm they stood in.

The worship chamber was otherwise empty except for a large statue of a bird at the foot of the tree. It was so lifelike that she'd frozen when she first noticed it. Mae had never seen the type before, but it bore a close enough resemblance to the wall carvings that she knew it was the firebird for which this temple stood. It reminded her of the great cranes they had seen flying overhead outside, so its kind was most likely native to Ignatia. It towered over them, ten feet tall, perched on a glittering obsidian plinth with wings outstretched as if about to take flight.

"Beautiful," Mae murmured, approaching the statue for a closer look, ignoring the disapproving noise from Valandaras as she did so. He would, of course, want to sweep the room for hidden horrors before they moved a finger.

Mae was done waiting. She had already spotted something. Nestled at the bird's feet, facing the room, stood a lectern.

And on that lectern lay a book.

Mae felt her pulse quicken as she stepped up around the plinth, scarcely daring to breathe as she took in the sight of the aged leather tome, exactly where Lai'ireal had said it would be. It lay closed upon the lectern, preserved by the ancient magic that had created it, since a mundane book would have long since crumbled to dust. It was smaller than she had expected. The embossed edges glowed with a faint reddish tinge, and it bore no title, only an outline of the firebird that mimicked the design they had seen in the valley above. The pages were thick and held closed by metal clasps. Each corner of the tome was edged with gold plates that resembled feathers, tarnished but still grand.

The rush of relief was so strong it nearly brought Mae to her knees.

Oh, Mother, it's here. All is not lost.

Mae brushed a finger delicately down the edge of the book. The bound pages within looked impossibly fragile, but somehow still untouched through the millennia of laying idle in this room. How many thousands of years had it sat here, waiting? For her?

Mae looked over the top of the lectern at Valandaras and Lessie, who wore twin expressions of apprehension. She smiled and picked up the tome to show them they had been successful.

And as her fingers curled around the bound leather, lifting the surprisingly heavy book into the air, an earth-shuddering sound shook the foundations of the room. A sudden heat warmed her back as the lava that made the branches of the carved willow flared, brightening the room and illuminating the fear on her companion's faces. But it was not the sight of her friends that made Mae's stomach drop.

As one, all of the stone statues in the corridor turned their heads towards her.

38

VALANDARAS

One by one, the stone guardians shuddered to life.

Valandaras felt the beginnings of battle adrenaline rise within him as the keening of two dozen obsidian stone longswords wrenched from their sheaths. A sinister glow built as molten lava flowed through the statues like blood through veins, illuminating them as well as awakening whatever form of sentience they had been bewitched with.

Mae wrapped her arms around the book she held protectively, like she could shield it from their view. It would do little good. These were constructs—the tome's removal had triggered them. It was possible they could not see at all. There was nothing but blank stone behind the carved slit in their helmets. They were not alive, and they could not be reasoned with. Gods designed these sorts of defences for a singular purpose.

"They will kill us before they let us leave the temple with the tome," Valandaras said, keeping his voice calm as he unsheathed his falchion. He stepped forward and settled into a defensive stance.

Beside him, the clicks of a chamber being spun echoed on the high ceiling.

"Then what do we do?" asked Lessie, her revolver already in hand and aimed at the nearest stone effigy, though a bullet would do little more than bounce off and hurt one of them instead. "I don't know about y'all, but I'm pretty set on leaving the temple."

The nearest stone soldiers stepped free of their plinths and began a slow, methodical march up the corridor. As if a wave had activated them, further ones followed suit, until a neat, miniature army moved towards them, one by one.

Valandaras could do nothing to halt their advance. There was nowhere to retreat. His only option was to fight.

The first guardian reached the entryway into the room, brandishing a sword that glowed so hot from the fire within that Valandaras could see the air warping around it. He swung his falchion, testing the statue's reflexes, and it brought its weapon up to meet the strike. His blade hit the stone and bounced off hard, making his hands ache.

Valandaras retreated a few steps, cursing under his breath. Lessie fired low into the statue's legs, but it did not slow its pace. It did not even seem to notice. A small chip in the stone surface was the only evidence that the girl had found her mark. All the shot had done was reverberate in their ears.

"Of course, they're godsdamned invincible," Lessie muttered. "Only a god could get through stone."

Only a god, Valandaras thought. *Or perhaps a Sliver.*

As other guardians began to force their way inside the chamber, Valandaras acted on instinct before he could doubt his decision. He shoved his falchion into Lessie's hands, ripped the Mournblade free from within the cloak that contained it, and struck at the first stone guardian that stepped into the room.

The black blade sank into stone flesh and stayed there.

The statue faltered. Valandaras had managed a decent strike to the neck, but now the Mournblade had wedged into the groove it had made, and Valandaras was forced to let go of the sword as a hand the size of his head pushed him backwards. He hit the floor hard, pain jolting up his spine, seeing stars as the back of his head cracked against the floor.

Mae's scream echoed in his ears.

The guardian bore no visible face, but as it moved towards him—the Mournblade still embedded in its neck—Valandaras felt the mild tone of surprise, regardless. Perhaps these beings had never been challenged before, or perhaps any would-be thieves they had deterred had long since turned to dust. Either way, it was clear the statues did not expect resistance.

The first guardian brought a longsword of stone slashing down towards him and Valandaras only just managed to roll out of its reach. The weapon was six feet long and too heavy to cut like a true blade, and having missed him, it slammed into the floor and cracked it. Fissures spread from the impact point like spiderwebs.

The stone guardian's next strike swung upwards, missing Lessie by inches and colliding with the ceiling. Debris and dust rained down upon them all. The statue pulled its blade back, unaware of the damage it had caused to the temple, and readied another attack.

Valandaras planted his boot onto the statue, yanked the Mournblade out, and swung again. This time, he cleaved its head from its shoulders. The stone crashed to the floor, splitting, trickles of lava pouring like blood from the fissures.

Valandaras did not stop until he had severed both arms, the stone sword shattering on impact as it hit the floor next to the guardian's unseeing head. The statue stilled, collapsing to the floor, the molten heartbeat slowing before dimming completely. Dust rose from the pieces.

The other statues continued their march down the passageway.

"Get back," Valandaras shouted to Lessie, praying to all the gods the girl would listen. She still gripped his falchion, but it was no Sliver; she would be pulverised.

Valandaras fought back the taste of bile as he adjusted his grip on the Mournblade's hilt. Yes, the Sliver's power was designed to cut through the magic weaved by gods, but a single one of these guardians had almost knocked him out. There were over a dozen.

The sound of stone feet slamming against the floor started to echo his own heartbeat.

Mae backed up against the far wall, dragging Lessie with her. The girl seemed torn between wanting to protect Mae and helping Valandaras, but there wasn't much she could do for either. The glow from the carved god tree's branches had become so bright it was white, making them hard to see.

"Val, you have to realmshift us back home!" Mae yelled, an edge of hysteria creeping into her voice. Her knuckles were white around the tome.

"I need time for that," he said through gritted teeth. *And a Path*.

Valandaras kept swinging, hoping to slow the statues with the fallen bodies of their comrades. A second guardian went down. It knocked one of the hinged doors as it fell before cracking against the floor and remaining still.

Valandaras breathed heavily as he ducked part of the firebird's wing, which had broken off the door. He heard vague sounds of a scuffle behind him, like Mae and Lessie were disagreeing on whether they could help, but he knew that Mae would keep the girl out of harm's way. The sweat building from the heat in the room soaked him, stung his eyes under his cloth, made his armour feel like lead.

This was not a fight he could outlast.

Another shot rang out. Lessie reappeared by his side, down to her tunic, her shirt singed and smoking. She had aimed not for the stone guardians, but for the cracks in the corridor's ceiling above the fallen door.

"If we block the door, maybe it will keep them out," she shouted above the crashing stone. "We can fight them one at a time."

It was the best idea they'd had.

Valandaras threw all of his strength into closing the remaining unbroken door. It protested as his full weight slammed against it, catching on the broken slabs of the floor and causing a high-pitched keening so unpleasant it made his teeth hurt.

He managed to close the door just as another guardian reached it and swung blindly for him. A chunk of rock chipped off of the door and flew past him, grazing his cheek and nearly ripping the cloth from his face. He briefly considered using his realmlight against the guardians as a last resort, but it was too unpredictable in such a small space. He could drag them all straight into the void.

The statues bottlenecked around what was left of the opening, stumbling against the remains of the first two that had fallen. They did not seem to be truly sentient, but there was a sense of mounting frenzy as they crashed into one another while trying to enter the chamber. Debris choked the heated air as one guardian knocked a second, who hit the wall and cracked from the force of it.

Valandaras breathed in and felt hot dust burn his lungs. They would suffocate before the guardians stopped coming.

We can't fight them all.

Valandaras leapt onto the pile of stone that had been the first guardian and entered the corridor.

The Mournblade's sinister hum buzzing in his ears, he lunged for the guardian in front, prompting a defensive strike of the statue's sword. As he predicted, it swung upward again, smashing once more into the ceiling—which had already been weakened by Lessie's bullets and the cracks around it. The surrounding statues followed suit, bringing their weapons high to protect themselves, unknowingly contributing to their own undoing. A thick, dark powder rained down upon them all.

A sudden low rumbling had them all pause. Then all Valandaras could hear was Mae.

"Val!" she screamed from inside the chamber. "Get out of there!"

The entire corridor began to collapse.

Valandaras turned and tried to climb back inside the chamber, the guardians he had felled and the rubble around them hindering his way in. The walls had begun to shake. Pieces of rock bigger than his head fell from the ceiling, smashing into the statues behind him. The heat was unbearable—like the collapse of the ceiling brought with it the burn of the lava above them. Trickles of molten rock dripped from the ceiling like blood, sizzling as it hit the stone below.

Valandaras did not have time to stop and see how many of the stone guardians had been buried under the rubble. He dragged himself over the top of the makeshift blockade, even as searing pain shot through him. Something had hit him or fallen onto him, but he didn't know what. He didn't care.

He just had to get to her.

Valandaras landed heavily on the other side of the stone blockage, one of his legs crumpling underneath him, just as the rest of the corridor's ceiling collapsed behind him.

A brief blanket of auburn crossed his swaying vision before everything went black.

Valandaras awoke all at once, the cracks in the partially crumbling ceiling slowly coming back into focus. The quiet of the room did little to ease the ringing in his ears.

"Hey, you," came a voice from the side, and he turned to see amber eyes. They softened as they met his.

"Nice of you to rejoin us," Mae said, teasing, though the skin on her face looked raw and her eyes were rimmed with red. "You seemed like you needed a nap."

Valandaras winced as he drew himself up into sitting, recognising immediately that he had damaged something vital in his leg. Pain shot through him. He groaned, doing his best to contain the shout that longed to wrench from him. He inspected the wound as clinically as possible. At least two bones were shattered, possibly more. One of the women had tied a makeshift bandage around it, which he recognised—the bright blue fabric contrasted strangely with the dull silver of his armour. It criss-crossed around his leg, forming a brace.

"We didn't remove your greaves," Mae said, gesturing to their rudimentary first aid. "I figured the metal would do better to support it than it would to take it off."

"Right," Valandaras said, though he was focusing on retaining consciousness. His entire lower leg pulsed with pain, and he bit the inside of his cheek to keep from screaming.

His knee was practically useless; along with the swelling around his shin and ankle making it impossible to bend or move it. The strange healing power he possessed had been keeping him alive while he slept, working feverishly to knit his bones back together, but he could tell it would take time before he could walk unassisted again.

Mae and Lessie had moved him away from the door, closer to the shelter of the firebird statue and the god tree behind it. Not too close, as the heat radiating from the lava streams of the willow's carved branches had reached dizzying levels with the room sealed. But he was no longer underneath the unstable ceiling. At least the lava of the god tree had returned to how it was previously, the pulsing of the molten rock gentle and rhythmic as it flowed down the walls.

Mae sat beside him with her hand rested gently on his thigh, skin touching through a tear in the fabric. Emerald sputtered between her fingertips, and Valandaras knew she was draining every last drop of her Gift into healing his injury. A rush of affection flowed through him. She had her own cuts and scrapes, probably from falling debris and stray rocks, but still she gave everything to him.

He didn't deserve her.

Clattering sounded from behind him, and Valandaras strained to get up, to reach for his falchion, to protect Mae. She placed a gentle hand on his chest, pushing him back into sitting, a seemingly involuntary *tsk* of disapproval rushing from her lips. He stifled the feeling that bloomed from her touch and searched for the source of the noise.

Lessie had positioned herself at the edge of the chamber, guarding the remains of the caved-in entrance. Her pack had been upended, probably at first to find medical supplies to help him, but now her belongings stayed littered around her. She sat cross-legged on a cracked statue's torso, furiously scribbling into her journal.

"Gods in Prison, I am going to die in Ignatia, and Trixie's going to be so pissed off at me," she muttered darkly, punctuating every syllable with a stab of her quill. "It's no use. I'm not getting through. Guess it doesn't work cross-realm."

The quill snapped, and Lessie let out a strangled growl of annoyance as she tossed the broken pieces to the ground. Lessie's neck and collarbones were blotchy and red, the flush from the heated room adding to the oppressive feel even more now that the entrance had been blocked.

"She's not handling the cave-in," Mae whispered. "She was completely calm until we finished patching you up, but she's been getting worse since. She tried to remove some of the rocks from the door, but it hasn't worked."

Lessie began pacing around the remains of the chamber door like a wild animal trapped in a cage. Errant strands of hair had been ripped free of her braid during the scuffle, and she pushed it out of her face, agitated. Dust from the collapsed ceiling had settled into her clothing, and parts of it were singed from the close calls with the molten walls. Her plaid shirt had been wrapped around her waist, parts of the material blackened.

Valandaras knew he looked just as bad, if not worse. He wiped a trickle of blood from his nose, the crimson soaking into the wrappings on his hands. He slowly unwound them, piling the fabric beside him. The glow of the realmlight beneath his skin seemed muted, dulled in comparison to the healing that glittered from his palms. He gripped his knee and winced at the sharp stab of pain that resonated from it.

Lessie had not abandoned her search for an exit, but was becoming more erratic with her suggestions.

"What about that?" she asked, pointing to the tome that lay beside Mae. "It's supposed to hold the power of a god, right? Can we use it to get out? I know you were reading it before."

Mae's fingers curled around the tome, moving it closer to her. Valandaras was annoyed she had gone through it alone, in case it had hurt her, but he supposed he couldn't blame her. They were all reaching desperate levels.

Mae shook her head. "Most of it is in ancient Elvish, but from what little I understand, I... It requires the user to Change," she said. Her face flushed, and she hung her head, refusing to meet their eyes.

Lessie stared at her blankly. "So? You've done that hundreds of times."

"Not since the Mother's essence was syphoned. I... I do not have enough of my Gift to even attempt it."

The pain in Mae's voice was evident. The tome was unusable.

Lessie's jaw clenched. She seemed to be fighting the urge to scream, or perhaps to grab the book and throw it across the room. On that, at least, Valandaras would have let her. They had all nearly died, he had broken so many tenants of his Path... for a power Mae could not access. If Lai'ireal appeared at this very moment, Valandaras would throw it first.

Still, part of him was relieved. If Mae could not use the tome, then it could not claim her life.

"It's all right, it's fine," Lessie said. "Valandaras, you're awake now, so you can realmshift us out from here. We're not trapped. We're perfectly fine." Her eyes held a hint of mania, like she was close to snapping the careful control she had kept herself under since the moment they had arrived in Ignatia.

Valandaras felt a seed of fear take root in his stomach. He sat up straighter, feeling Mae's hand hovering behind his back.

"I cannot see a path down here," he said. "There is too much interference from the god that once dwelled. Or perhaps it is this tree, or simply the amount of molten rock upon these walls."

Lessie ceased her pacing. "I don't understand," she said, biting tone on every syllable. "It's a realm, isn't it? You're a Realmshifter. If you can't shift realms, then we can't get out." She wrung her hands, knuckles cracking like tiny gunshots, and stormed up the aisle between the pews towards them. Her eyes were beginning to glaze over with panic.

Valandaras struggled to stand, hating how much he needed Mae's help to pull himself up to his full height. He looked around anxiously, as if a Path would reveal itself to him, but the room was as eerily empty as ever. He could try to meditate upon it, but he needed a starting point, and this chamber held none.

Had he doomed them all?

"We brought the door down to give us time," Valandaras said, grimacing as he tested his weight on his leg and found it could bear almost none. He leaned heavily on a stone pew. "I could not have foreseen the entire corridor collapsing. Even if I could see a way, right now, I cannot walk. The way of the Path—"

"*Fuck* your Path," Lessie exploded. "We're going to *die* down here!"

"Lessie..." said Mae, stepping between them, and the soothing softness in the Divine's voice had the opposite effect.

"Don't," Lessie spat, eyes flashing. "I don't want to hear you take his side again. You're both hypocrites, keeping all this bullshit to yourselves and expecting everyone else to trust you with the details, when you can't even look each other in the eye and say what you mean. You—" she jabbed an accusatory finger at Valandaras, "who's always leaving us out of the planning, who's always claiming to be 'following the Path', when really you're just doing whatever the fuck you feel like, never giving a damn what anybody else thinks—"

"I—" Valandaras spluttered, but Lessie had already rounded on Mae.

"And *you*, who I trusted, who I volunteered to follow into this godsforsaken lava pit because I believed in you—You can't even use the power we almost died for? You, who are apparently over a century old? How is that even possible? What else are you lying about? What else am I not being told? What else am I being *left out of*?"

Lessie's face had gone red, and Valandaras believed she would attempt to claw her way to the surface with her bare hands.

"I'm going to suffocate to death in this underground tomb and never see my sister again because you couldn't take two seconds to investigate a book before you picked it up—"

"Lessie, calm down," warned Mae.

"DON'T TELL ME TO CALM DOWN!" Lessie shouted. "You're not my godsdamned mother! Who would still be ALIVE if it wasn't for your gods and their *bullshit*!"

Mae moved, and for a second Valandaras thought she was going to strike Lessie. Then Mae's arms encircled the younger woman and pulled her into an embrace that undid the last shred of restraint Lessie had been clinging to. The howl that escaped her was miserable, primal—the pain of a loss she had not let herself feel for too long.

Lessie collapsed into Mae's arms and broke down completely.

Mae brought Lessie with her to the floor and held her while she cried. Lessie's words were indecipherable, shuddering breaths and choked sobs interrupting them, half buried in Mae's chest. The only thing Valandaras could properly make out was a single sentence.

"It's my fault." Over and over again.

Valandaras locked eyes with Mae as she stroked Lessie's hair, feeling a kind of uselessness he had not experienced before. This was a heartbreak nothing could mend—not time, nor Divine healing. Tears tracked down both women's faces, Mae's gentle, Lessie's a torrential flood.

"What am I meant to do with it?" Lessie heaved in between choked sobs. "All my questions. I still have so much I need to ask them. And they're just *gone.*"

"I know, sweetheart," whispered Mae softly. "I know."

"I can't die here and leave Trixie alone," Lessie wailed. "I can't—I promised them I'd p-protect her, and I haven't, and now we're stuck and I can't—I can't do anything about it—"

"I know, honey."

They stayed that way for a while. Mae's gentle shushing and Lessie's cries echoed in the cavernous space.

Valandaras tried to give the women as much privacy as he could. He lowered himself onto the stone pew and concentrated on the strange light he possessed as it poured into his injuries. The golden healing wasn't subtle like how Mae's felt, possibly because he hadn't had years of learning how to control it like she did. It pulsed like a heartbeat, not much, but enough to know that with some assistance he could at least walk again in a matter of hours.

After a while, Lessie's sobs quietened, and the last waterskin was shared between them. Valandaras tried not to think about what that would mean for them later if they couldn't find a way out of the chamber.

"I just wish I could tell her," Lessie said, her voice small and melancholic. "Everything we've done. Mama was a bit... she kind of hated what Papa and I did with all the monster hunting and the Maw. I couldn't talk to her about it. She was worried all the time. About me, about Trix... But I could have shown her Falcon's Watch. All the plans we have for it. I think she would have loved it."

Most of Lessie's tears had dried up, leaving streaks in the ash that had settled on her face. Occasionally her whole body would shudder, breath pulling in rapidly, like her nervous system was desperately trying to regulate itself.

For the first time, to Valandaras, the age difference between them all became stark. She had always carried herself with an air of hostile maturity, but here, Lessie seemed like a child. Too young to have endured the losses she already carried with her, and exhausted from pretending they didn't matter.

"Papa and I were always so close, I think I made her feel like I didn't need her," Lessie said. "But I did—I do. I just wanted her to be proud of me. I could never tell."

Mae held Lessie's face in her hands, wiping away the worst of the tears.

"Your mother would be so very proud of everything you've accomplished," Mae said, "and she would want you to not be so hard on yourself all the time."

Lessie laughed. "You don't know that. You never met my mother."

"Not *your* mother, perhaps," Mae replied. "But I am still a mother, and we all feel it. All she ever wanted was for her girls to be safe, and you've done that for your sister. Yourself, not so much, but we're doing our best."

"I—what?" Lessie asked, breathless, momentarily overtaken by confusion. "You're a mother?"

The moment the words had left Mae's lips, it made perfect sense to Valandaras. Her tone, her selflessness, the words she chose, the careful attention of everyone's emotions around her. But he had never heard her so much as mention it before. A mother?

Mae seemed to regret the words. Her fingers drifted to her bare nails, where she found no polish to pick, and the cuticles suffered for it. Her golden eyes held emotions Valandaras had no name for.

"If you promise to stay calm and rest before we figure out a way out of this mess, then I will tell you," Mae said. There was a note of hesitancy to her voice, and Valandaras knew immediately that she could never say another word and he would accept it.

Lessie had gone red again, not from anger this time, but embarrassment.

"No, it's your private—you don't have to..."

Mae smiled softly, and the lines near the corners of her eyes creased.

"It's fine," she said. "It is painful to tell it, yes, and I will warn you now, it does not have a happy ending. But I have gone too many years not speaking of my life."

Mae glanced at Valandaras and patted the cold stone floor as if it were the most luxurious cushion in Bueno's study. *I need you next to me for this*, the simple gesture seemed to say.

Valandaras barely noticed the pain in his leg as he joined her on the floor and readjusted to give her his full attention.

"It's time," Mae said. "I'll tell you my story."

39

VALANDARAS

"From the moment I was born, I have felt the Mother's presence."

Mae sat beneath the petrified god tree, yellow dress tucked underneath her legs, and led the sermon of her life Valandaras had never thought he would be privileged enough to hear. Her hands were shaking, but her voice was clear and warm.

"It did not matter that the Mother was imprisoned, for she is the god of life itself, and life is all around. It is impossible not to believe in the wonder of it. I marvelled at the simplest things—people, animals, plants, and how they all connect. It was fascinating to me.

"I was still a small child when the Breach occurred; when the powers of the gods could reach us once more. I remember it vividly. I was playing outside my home and found a mouse that had been hurt. It was quivering all over and breathing so fast, and I could feel its tiny heartbeat hammering as I picked it up. I knew it would probably die, and all I wanted to do was help."

Mae cupped her hands in her lap as if she could still see the tiny rodent nestled in them.

"I hoped and wished that something could help, and for the first time, I heard the Mother whisper back—that I could. I stroked that tiny furry head of his, and the smallest emerald spark came from my finger and buried itself into the mouse. Naturally, I was terrified. I think I dropped the poor thing." Mae shook her head in embarrassment. "But the mouse landed on his feet, washed his little whiskers and scampered away. He was completely fine. I had helped him."

Mae smiled broadly, and Valandaras saw the woman he knew best shining through. It had been a long time since he had seen it, with the loss of the Mother dampening Mae's spirits. Her simple joy at helping another soul. It was like feeling the warmth of sun rays again after a long winter.

"From that moment, I thought of only the Mother," Mae continued. "My own mother had died giving birth to me, and while my father tried his best to take care of me, he was old and tired from working the lands. I don't know for certain if either of them had Elven blood; my father never spoke of it, despite teaching me the language. He knew nothing of the gods other than Vry'iin, like most of the common people. I had to figure it out alone.

"I soon found comfort in speaking to the Mother, in learning the Gifts she had blessed me with. As an adult, I tried my best to ease my father's aches and pains, but he was adamant that I should hide my Gift. He didn't like me to use it, even in the house, and certainly never in view of the others in our village. After the Breach, the Seven had quickly called for Divines to join their houses; he feared the nobility taking me away. I thought him old and foolish. After all, it is not compulsory for Divines to serve. They have to be *willing*."

Mae's humourless laugh was the bleakest sound Valandaras had ever heard her make. She shook herself before she kept talking.

"I ached to see more of the Mother's world, more of life. I told my father I would travel for a year. He argued against it, but ultimately wished me luck and safety. I think he knew he would not live to see me return. I left the Valefork for the first time in my life when I was twenty-eight years old. I think I had plans to go as far as Moengraan, or perhaps even the Ruby Isles. I wanted to see how other countries treated their Divines. If I could make a life for myself somewhere I would not have to hide what I was. But it was in Grenglade, the very first city I visited across the border, where I met the person who would change my life's trajectory forever."

"Who were they?" asked Lessie, captivated by the story.

Mae's skin flushed scarlet.

Valandaras felt the strange absence of her attention, like she was pretending only Lessie was present, but it was unnecessary. Of course, she must have had lovers, especially for the amount of years she had been alive within this realm. It would be insanity to think she had not. Besides, it bore no effect on him. *They* were not lovers. They did not owe each other anything.

"Time has lost his name to me, I'm afraid," Mae said. Valandaras wasn't sure if he believed her. "But he had eyes of the most peculiar shade of blue. Not like the sky, or even the water. They were like the ocean—murky, sparkling, endless. Looking into them was to sink and drown and die happily. I'd never seen that colour blue before. And how the lines by them would crinkle when he smiled... it's always the eyes that tell you so much about who a person is on the inside. They were mesmerising."

Mae sighed.

The nostalgia contained within the small sound ripped open a pit of jealousy Valandaras had not been aware existed within him. He wrestled with it silently, disguising his uncomfortable shift by adjusting his injured leg. He forced himself to look straight at Mae, face a mask of polite interest. It did not matter that she hadn't seen his eyes, because nobody had. That was a simple fact of being who he was.

Lessie glanced between them awkwardly.

"So what happened to him?" she asked.

"He left, of course," said Mae with a sad smile. "I knew he would. That man didn't know how to let me love him the way he deserved to. I hope he found someone who did, in the end. It would never have worked. Divines are long-lived and most mortal men are... not. But what little time we had I would not change, because it gave me the greatest gift I had never even dared to dream of. I did not think it was possible for one like me."

Mae's hand drifted, and for a moment, rested low on her stomach. The smile she gave Valandaras belonged to a ghost of a woman he had never met.

"I returned to the Valefork with life stirring in my belly," Mae said, patting her abdomen. "And although I was frightened beyond belief, I was never alone. The Mother was there, in the cracks of light, in my dreams, offering words of comfort that were real enough to get me through it. I gave birth to my girls, twins, alone in the home where my own mother had died birthing me. It is only through the Mother's Gift that I survived it.

"People are not meant to be alone to bring life into this world. We are supposed to care for one another, to help when things become overwhelming and the everyday mundane becomes impossible. The support a mother does or doesn't receive stays with her forever. I had nobody. Our home was far from most towns, and I could not risk the village's persecution. I had no choice but to learn how to take care of my girls and myself alone.

"It was daunting and frustrating and humbling. I don't think I slept more than a few hours straight for two years," Mae said, though the words were uttered fondly. Like the torture was worth it.

Lessie gave Mae a rare, broad smile that transformed the girl's face from harsh to beautiful.

"What did you call them?" she asked.

"Aurora and Luna," Mae replied, pride shining. The glow of the molten willow branches behind her made her eyes appear even more golden than they usually were. "My sun and moon. It was fitting—they were night and day, opposite souls. Though they were so identical, it was uncanny. They looked so much like me. I would call them my tiny duplicates. All besides those eyes of purest ocean blue. They were full of life. Wild, silly, thoughtful, and smart—so, so clever. They bickered constantly, about the most ridiculous things, like what colour to paint their nails, or who had not finished their chores. But their love for each other was rivalled only by mine for them. The Mother blessed them with her Gifts as she had me, and we made a life together. Just the three of us.

"Whispers of who I was must have reached the people of the village, and sometimes desperate souls would arrive on our doorstep, seeking help for ailments. I helped them as best I could. How could I not? I had to show my girls what a Gift truly was."

Mae shook her head, lost in the memories like a fog.

"Years flew by, and I saw my precious girls grow from babies to children to teenagers, on the cusp of becoming young women. Watching them grow, helping them learn, teaching them the ways of the world and all of the Mother's life in it. It was the most wonderful time in my entire existence. There was no greater privilege and no simpler joy. I could not have been prouder of them."

The smile fell from Mae's face, and the change in her demeanour was obvious. Valandaras fought the urge to take her hand, not wanting to interrupt her train of thought, but the sadness that poured from her affected the whole room. Even the glowing from the willow's molten branches seemed to dim.

"I don't know how they found us," Mae said. "I still can't... sometimes at night I go over it in my head, even now. There had to have been *something* that I could have done differently, to keep us safer, to—"

Mae cut herself off, tears pricking in her eyes.

This time, Valandaras did not stop himself from reaching for her hand. It was delicate and warm, and he cringed internally as his calloused fingers brushed against her soft skin, but he needed to comfort her. He didn't know *how* to send his strange healing light to her, or if it only worked on physical pain. But he tried anyway.

Mae's fingers crushed his for a moment before loosening their grip, but she did not let go. She took a few deep breaths.

"But no matter the how," she said, voice barely above a whisper. "Rumours reached the capital of a Divine whose Gift could heal, but who was not in service to the crown. The ascended king sought to rectify that."

"But... service is voluntary," said Lessie, voice trailing off as she questioned her own knowledge.

Mae smiled sadly. "That's what every Altaean thinks, don't they? I believed it too. Once."

Valandaras's bare fingers felt another squeeze.

"The king at that time was practically a teenager, but he suffered from a disease that would end his life prematurely, as it had his predecessor. It was the very reason he had the burden of the crown that young, and he was determined to evade his fate. He dispatched a group of his personal guard to... *persuade* me to enter his service. Of course, believing it was the choice of the Divine to serve, I politely declined. The next time I opened our door, the king himself stood on my doorstep."

Lessie's hands folded over her mouth, muffling her gasp.

"I bargained with the young king," said Mae. "I pleaded, I threatened, I refused. He said he could not 'force' me to serve, but he could command my girls to come with him. Back then, any mundane, low-born person could be compelled to join the king's staff. An archaic law. The king did not know that my girls also had the Mother's Gift, and I could not correct him, because then he would never have let them be."

Mae's jaw clenched, like she was back in that grove, on that doorstep, fighting for her life. For her children.

"In the end, I offered fifty years of my life to the king's own court, his ancestral house, in exchange for my daughters to go free," she said, eyes flashing with anger. "They were furious with me. I can still hear them screaming as he escorted me into the carriage. 'You can't leave. I'd rather die than lose you. Mother, come back.'"

Mae's voice broke. "My mind distorted it so badly I was convinced I could hear their infant's wails all the way to Verestead. I was sobbing with my head in my hands for the entire journey. The king did not say a word."

A dull roaring had begun in Valandaras's ears. If this king still lived, he would not for long.

"He was a cruel man and an awful king. It was lucky his reign was soon to end. He stayed in Verestead when he descended and spent the next five decades scheming, trying to secure advantageous marriages for his horrible children and political sway for his house. I served them faithfully for half a century. I healed his sickness. I kept him pain-free and comfortable as he advanced in age, cheating death itself. I healed his sons when they complained of wounds from the training arena that were little more than scrapes, I smoothed his daughter's skin so that she would appeal to lords of higher station. I helped deliver his first grandchild and stayed up nights rocking them, tears streaming down my face as I pretended it was one of my own girls. I watched him reascend the throne when he should not have been fit to rule even once.

"But all those years, I never lost hope that one day, my time would be up and I would go home. I would see my girls again. If they had moved on, I would find them. I would spend a lifetime finding them. We were all Divine, after all. Some Divines are rumoured to be almost ageless. I could still have had centuries with them."

Mae stared at the wall. Molten lava reflected in her hollow eyes.

"To the day, on the fiftieth year, I entered the king's chambers and informed him that our bargain was completed and I was going home to my girls. He laughed in my face."

Mae laughed bitterly, echoing what she must have heard that day.

"He told me my girls were criminals. That they had conspired to get me out of the palace, to defy the king's right to 'request' the service of any Divine. And they had almost gotten me out. My smart, brave, reckless girls had tried to rescue me."

Valandaras realised Mae had been speaking of her children in the past tense. Foreboding dread washed over him. Mae's eyes were as empty as the void between realms.

"The king discovered their deception and ordered them both executed for treason to the crown. Their souls entered the Silver Stream to Requiem before he had even descended the throne, before I had even served a year of my self-imposed exile. My Aurora, my Luna. My sun and moon. They were both gone."

A tear slid down Lessie's face. She swiped at it angrily, not daring to take her eyes away from Mae. Valandaras could see why. Mae was less of a person at that moment and more of a force. Within the void, a spark of rage had ignited. Not how her Gift did, but darker.

A reckoning.

"For fifty years, I had served this horrible man and his despicable family, only for the promise that I would one day see my own again. When my children had both been dead the entire time. He had known—he had looked into my eyes every single day and said *nothing*. He only cared about using my Gift to save his own skin. He would have sold me any lie to keep it.

"I..." Mae hesitated. A muscle in her jaw twitched. She opened her mouth once more to speak before slamming it shut again. Her eyes closed, and she took a few deep breaths.

"It is a bit of a blur after that," she said finally, rubbing at her eyes like a wave of fatigue had rolled over her. "I left the chamber and started running. Not caring where, just needing to get out. I remember thinking wildly that I wished I could become a bird and just fly away. That was the first time I Changed."

Valandaras knew her well enough to know that there was a part of the story she was omitting, but now was not the time to press it. If there were some things she wanted to keep to herself, then that was her choice.

"I became a sparrow. It was strange, but I was too encompassed by pain to be frightened of it. I flew as far as my tiny wings could take me until I ended up in a forest outside of Verestead. I Changed back mid-air and almost broke my legs falling. I did not heal a single cut or bruise. I wanted to suffer.

"I was angry at the Mother. She was the god of life. How could she have let my precious girls cross the Silver Stream so young? When they believed in her, devoted their lives to her just as I had? I was furious. My mind shut down. I cut off the Mother. My body rejected my Gift. I did not feel a connection to her for months, as I made my way back to my empty home, only to find the Valefork grove had reclaimed it. There was nothing but a gutted skeleton of a building, collapsed by ivy. No proof my girls, my life, had ever existed. I wanted to burn the entire forest down."

Valandaras would, without hesitation. Even now, if she still wished it, that was where they would go. He would carry the torch the entire way.

Mae rubbed at her temples and sighed deeply. "I look back now and understand I was never truly angry with the Mother," she said. "I was angry with myself. For not being there, for not protecting them, for not realising they would do exactly what I would have done if they had been taken. But nothing could change the fact that my sun and moon had been stolen from my sky, and it plunged me into darkness. Grief consumed me.

"And still, the Mother lingered, whispering to me, keeping me afloat, but letting me feel the pain of crushed hope and longing that threatened to destroy me. If I ignored it, it would only kill me faster. It is a strange state to live in. I wanted to die, but I was also terrified to."

Mae stared at the floor. Her voice was heartbreakingly small as she made the confession.

"Although I say I would welcome death, in truth, even now, I am afraid of it. Afraid of walking into Requiem and finding Luna and Aurora had not made it there. Afraid of not making it to Requiem myself, of being sent to Antithiia instead. Afraid of facing my girls. How full of pain and anger their eyes would be, knowing I could not protect them from their fate."

"They would not. They would understand," said Valandaras, interrupting Mae for the first time. "And they would have made it to Requiem. No souls that strong would lose their way."

He could not be sure, of course. He had not been to Requiem. It was the one realm that Realmshifters did not return from. But the relief that bloomed upon Mae's face was worth saying it. Her hand gave his another grateful squeeze before she spoke again.

"I eventually found my way back to the Mother, and she helped me through the darkest time in all my years. I spent months on end in a Changed form, only returning to my own body to sleep. Not thinking, letting the animal's instinct take over—winding my way through the forests and plains, never staying in any one place for long. I don't remember how many years I did this. I did a lot of soul-searching. My girls would be furious with me for wasting my hard-earned freedom, but it hurt to feel emotions other than pain. I knew I still wanted to see as much of this realm as I could, but I could never return to Verestead, nor make my home a city where the Archdukes ruled—I had served in the house of one of the Seven and then disappeared. But the borders were fiercely guarded, and I was a fugitive. I just wandered for years.

"And then I met... you, Val."

Valandaras started. He had forgotten that he had a part to play in this narrative.

"I remember," he said gently. "You scared me half to death. I thought you were a corpse."

Mae laughed through a sob. Seeing Lessie's confused expression, she smiled fondly.

"I had fallen asleep while Changed," Mae explained. "It was not a subconscious thing. Back then I had to choose to keep myself in a form, so I cannot hold it if I'm not awake. I've since learned to hang onto it a little longer, but usually I would just Change back to be safe. It had been an awful night, and I wasn't thinking straight. I curled up to sleep as a fox and woke up a woman with a giant glowing warrior peering over me. I thought I had finally been found by the Kingsguard. I accepted my fate. Do you remember, Val?"

Valandaras remembered.

He had been on Kalaraak for less than five years, trying to follow his Path to a Sliver as best he could, but with nothing to show for it so far. He had seen red hair peeking out from below a bush off the edge of the thoroughfare, and something had tugged at him to investigate it. He'd thought her dead until he'd gotten close enough to see her breathing. When she had stirred, the relief that shocked through his body like lightning.

Her first words to him had been *'please, just make it quick'*.

Valandaras had never seen melancholy like that before. He had stared into those haunted eyes, such a peculiar colour and filled with desolation, and decided then and there that there was nothing he wouldn't do to see them full of life once more.

Present Mae giggled, a tiny wisp of her true laugh, but the sound still rang like silver bells.

"Luckily, you had no idea what I was talking about. There was probably quite a large bounty on my head. You could have retired a very rich man."

He wouldn't have considered it, not even for a second. Once she turned those eyes on him, he was hers.

"I believe I asked you if you had misplaced your bedroll, and if you needed to borrow another," Valandaras said instead.

Lessie snorted.

"Val knows the rest from here, but I'll summarise for you, Lessie," Mae said. "I quickly realised that Valandaras, being a Realmshifter, was perhaps the only person I'd ever met who operated outside Altaean law—and could therefore keep me safe if the Kingsguard came knocking. So I decided to make myself indispensable to him."

Valandaras shook his head. Indispensable, indeed.

"He needed someone to talk for him. Regular people don't feel particularly comfortable conversing with an intimidating, surly Realmshifter. And when they won't speak to the Divine, they don't think to hold their tongue around the songbird on the windowsill. You never told me what you were looking for, but you also never asked who was looking for me, so I just went with it. Before I knew it, we were picking up mercenary jobs." Mae's mischievous smile grew wider. "Turns out we work quite well together."

Valandaras returned her smile. Those early days had been... strange. She had been somehow both closed off and an open book. She joked with him, smiled at him, tried to get him to open up. It hadn't really worked—he hadn't told Mae a single thing about himself, but she had just... accepted him anyway. He knew she had stayed with him for safety, and he had decided very early on that he would have done anything to keep her safe.

"So, your daughters..." said Lessie hesitantly.

"...are most likely buried in an unmarked grave for prisoners," finished Mae. "All I can hope for is that someone spoke the words, that their souls made it safely to Requiem. I may never know."

Lessie's face was drained of colour, tear-streaked and ashy, with red-rimmed eyes and dark circles. The younger woman hugged her knees.

"I feel even worse that I shouted at y'all now," she mumbled. "Sorry."

Mae's eyes flickered to Valandaras. "I didn't tell you all of this to make you feel bad," she said. "Or for you to pity me. Quite the opposite. I tell you this so that you know I have felt both sides of a mother's love, and I can say that even to her very last breath, your mother was thinking of you."

Mae reached for Lessie's hand, taking it between her own. "And she was grateful that you did not share her fate. There is nothing a mother wouldn't do for her children. Your mother would have fought tooth and nail to get out for you, but she would have also walked straight in if it would have kept you safe. That kind of love cannot be severed by death."

Lessie sighed shakily and did not respond. She gave Mae's hand a small squeeze of her own, before wrapping her arms around her knees. Content to let the silence sit, for once.

Mae laid her own hands upon Valandaras's leg once more and let her emerald spark dance among his golden one. Together, they poured all they could into knitting the injury back together. The sooner he could walk, the sooner they could solve the problem of getting them out of the temple. Valandaras stared at the mingling colours of the energy, the divine motes of light, and lost himself in thoughts.

Mae watched their sparks as they intertwined. "I can't explain it, but that's how I feel when the Mother speaks to me," she whispered softly. Her voice was hoarse from talking. "Like there's two sources of the Divinity. Hers, and mine. It's how I know we will find a way home. I feel her, even here."

Mae gave the firebird's tome a curious look. "It is similar, in a way, to how the followers of this god must have felt to lose her over and over. I have felt the Mother's presence through so much. The Godprison, the syphon, even the pull to Requiem itself. Each time I thought I had lost her, the connection was instead reborn, stronger than before." Her eyes were shining with tears once more. "Grief is just love, after all. Perhaps you cannot truly know one without the other. I would rather have lost her than never known her at all."

Mae's emerald glow, despite being constantly drained by her healing of his leg, flared brighter than it had in months. For a moment, she sparkled.

Valandaras tried to understand, but his mind was exhausted. He began to feel... hot.

Behind them, the glow of the carved god tree had brightened, as if in answer to Mae's flare of Divinity. Different than before, when the guardians had awoken. This glow was a golden, white light, and before long it became impossible to look at. It had to be a trick, but it looked like the very branches of the willow tree were moving—swaying across the stone wall like a phantom breeze had ruffled them.

Lessie scooted backwards towards the entrance, cursing madly. Valandaras pulled himself to his feet again, trying to ignore the bark of pain that still shot through him despite his and Mae's combined healing efforts.

The heat from the carved god tree reached unbearable levels. Valandaras threw his arm up to block his face, and the heat from the wall warmed the metal of his vambraces even at a distance.

Mae got to her feet, captivated. No fear, only curiosity. She cocked her head, eyes wide.

"Do you suppose..." she said, absent-mindedly tracing the gentle sway of the branches with her fingers.

"Don't—" Valandaras said, but as usual, Mae didn't listen.

This woman will be the death of me.

Mae reached out a hand, fingertips sparkling with emerald, and tried to touch one of the glowing molten leaves. And instead of melting her skin off, two of the largest willow branches brushed lazily aside, revealing part of the trunk that had been covered.

And embedded in the petrified wood was a door.

40

LESSIE

Lessie stared in disbelief at the door that had appeared before them.

The branches of the giant carved willow swayed, molten lava flowing gently from them in a perpetual waterfall of motion. Pulsing with a soft, golden light. Reacting to Mae's Divine spark, like it had finally recognised the nature of who dwelled within the chamber. The trunk of the willow was wider than she was tall; so it was fathomable that the lowest branches had been concealing the opening. It looked rather ordinary—arched, following the natural curve of the petrified statue's grains, with no discernible knocker or handle. Only a faint outline and a promise of escape.

"Never thought I'd be happy to see a lava statue come alive," Lessie muttered, shaking her head. *Especially since a bunch of them just tried to kill us.*

Normally, Lessie would have been suspicious that such a convenient solution to their problem had presented itself. But that wild panic reared its head once more and threatened to choke her, still clawing at her mind from where she'd shoved it down. Adrenaline pumped through her, and her palms felt slick with sweat. She immediately started shoving her belongings back into her pack, scrambling to grab them from where she'd strewn them earlier in search of her journal. The mysterious god tree door meant she didn't have to die here, which made her much more willing to accept it.

Mae and Valandaras both sized up the door. Mae in abject wonder, Valandaras in blatant mistrust. Lessie knew who would make the first move.

"After you," said Lessie, gesturing to Mae.

Valandaras made a pained noise as Mae reached for the door. She pushed on it gently, avoiding the minute trickles of lava that ran down beside it and framed the edges. The door pressed inwards, revealing a dark passageway.

It was impossible to see where it went, or even how long it was. Even with the glow of the lava, the tunnel soon swallowed the light beyond what the human eye could see.

"So we're going through the tree, right?" Lessie asked hurriedly. "It's probably a back door the Divines of the firebird built in so they didn't have to climb all those stairs after they'd finished in here."

Valandaras was sceptical. "This is highly irregular," he said, frowning. "It could be a trap, like the guardians. It could be full of them."

Lessie readjusted her pack. It could be full of snakes and scorpions and Mahejerai for all she cared. If it came down to a choice between the mysterious tree tunnel and staying in the caved-in temple miles underground a lava lake, she was taking her chances with the tree tunnel.

"Val, this could be our one chance," Mae said. "I've got a good feeling." She offered her shoulder to Valandaras to steady him. The Realmshifter had healed remarkably for how shattered his leg was, but it would be days until he could walk unassisted.

Lessie knew that Mae would not leave him if he pushed it. She also knew that Valandaras would do anything that Mae asked of him, and was tired of disagreeing with her, especially with the harrowing story of her former life still fresh in their minds. Mae gave Valandaras an imploring look, and Lessie could see his resolve crumble. Good.

I will not die underground.

"Right," said Lessie, striding forward. "If Mae's got a good feeling about it, then it's settled. We at least see where it goes."

As predicted, Valandaras did not have the energy to argue with them. He only sighed and put his arm around Mae, gingerly testing the weight of his bad leg.

Lessie took point. Holding her breath, she edged past the door into the passage beyond.

The change was immediate. It reminded her of when the door to Bueno's study closed, but for all her senses—like the passageway had cut them off from everything behind them. There was no longer any smell of disturbed rock, no blistering, oppressive heat radiating from the walls. Only a gentle silence, but one she had never heard quite so loud.

The passageway was pitch black except for the faint glow of Valandaras's skin and Mae's palms. Lessie blinked, struggling to adjust. Waving a hand in front of her face, she could barely make out her own fingertips.

"It would be nice if I could see a godsdamned thing," Lessie muttered under her breath.

Like she'd spoken a command word, tiny balls of firelight dotted the ceiling of the passage. Lessie stopped dead, causing Mae and Valandaras to nearly walk into her.

"It just..." she sputtered in disbelief. The lights twinkled, hovering among the grooves of the uneven ceiling. Sparkling like laughter. Like they were... alive.

Mae's smile was brighter than the phantom lights.

"It can understand us," she said, delighted.

"It?" Lessie asked, confused.

"The god tree," said Mae, gesturing to the tunnel. Like it was the natural conclusion to make.

Lessie looked closer at the walls of the passage now that she had light to see. It was not, as she had first assumed, uneven, scratchy stonework, but thousands of branches and vines, knotted and twisted together, arching softly around them. It was like they were inside the trunk of the god tree, but it had extended outwards, creating space for them to walk through. Soft moss, leaves and twigs formed the path's floor, blanketing the passage and dampening their footsteps. The lights twinkled high above Valandaras's head; the height of the tunnel stretching to accommodate him. It was small, but not too cramped.

Lessie still felt the familiar tang of claustrophobia creeping up along the back of her neck. She shuddered and pressed on.

I probably shouldn't say 'godsdamned' inside a god tree. Shit.

"It cannot be..." Valandaras murmured, before a hiss of pain escaped him as he stepped awkwardly around a raised vine. Mae's arm tightened around him.

"What?" said Lessie, eyes forward. She half expected another stone guardian to appear in front of them. Valandaras only shook his head and kept walking.

Lessie led the way, anger and fear a jumbled mess inside her. Every time she thought of her outburst, her cheeks burned. She had shouted at her two closest friends, called them names, ridiculed them for not being able to get them out safely, when she herself was completely dependent on their magic to do so. That was the crux of the matter.

Lessie felt useless, ordinary. *Mundane.*

It was an unofficial term for people with no magical prowess or Divinity, and it wasn't a neutral one. Trixie had mentioned it once, and it had devolved into one of their worst fights; the slur casually thrown around within the Quillkeep by Arcanes who had spent too long being ostracized for abilities they were born with. Being persecuted by people who didn't have a drop of natural magic in their veins.

It was true, but it stung regardless. Lessie had never been a natural at anything. Every single skill she possessed was a result of years of trying, of careful practice, of honing a craft.

And precisely zero of those skills helped me get out of that godsdamned temple. Or to save my parents.

More tears pricked behind her eyes, though she didn't know how her body managed to find the moisture to make them after spending the past week in Ignatia. The god tree's passage provided a reprieve from the oppressive heat, at least. Lessie couldn't remember crying this much in her life.

Of all the emotions roiling inside her, shame hurt the most. She had ranted and blamed Mae's god for her mother's death, when really the Mother was no more to blame than Mae was herself, and still she'd felt obligated to explain. Lessie's meltdown had made Mae relive the worst days of her weirdly long life. Mae had already lost her children, and then lost the Mother to Boras. It wasn't Mae's fault. If anything, she deserved revenge just as much as Lessie did. Against the Mahejerai for her god, and whichever noble house had stolen half her life. In their own way, the nobility of Altaea were just as evil, if not worse.

As Lessie walked, plans began to form.

It all comes down to stopping Oorata Boras, but I wouldn't mind taking a swing at the Seven, either. Maybe the Lord of Debauchery can help with that one.

They kept going until Valandaras's leg gave out and he could go no further.

Lessie threw her pack down onto the soft moss and rushed to Mae to help lower Valandaras to the floor. He was battling frustration at his impairment, and as soon as he was comfortably sitting he resumed pouring his strange healing light into his leg. He feared being useless as much as she did. *A liability.*

"We can rest here," Lessie said.

Mae settled next to Valandaras, resting a gentle hand upon his knee. The glittering emerald mixing with the gold reminded Lessie of sunlight upon grass, and an unexpected rush of homesickness flooded through her. She dug through her pack for her journal before remembering she'd snapped her last quill. The lack of connection to Trixie made her uneasy.

Lessie shivered. The sweat that she had become used to during their time in the temple had now dried on her skin, and a faint breeze from nowhere sent goosebumps skittering over her body. She shrugged herself back into her jacket, cringing at the ash that fell from her shirt as she disturbed it, and stared at what little she could see of the path ahead. It sloped gently, enough to feel her calves protest the angle, but she couldn't tell if it was enough to take them to the surface.

"Do you think we're going to hit the surface anytime soon?" she asked. "This passage could go on for days. We don't have enough supplies to outlast that. Besides, it's godsdamned cold down here."

If they were heading to Ignatia's surface, they should've still been warm. Instead, the unbearable heat had been replaced by a gentle, tepid temperature, coupled with the phantom breezes that occasionally cooled their faces. It would have been absolutely wonderful if it weren't so unnerving.

Mae had noticed it, too. "It doesn't feel like we're even in Ignatia anymore," she said. She held a waterskin delicately. Lessie knew it was almost empty. "I'm starting to think that's not where this leads. But why would the god tree reveal the passage to us if it wasn't trying to help?"

Help. Like it was a sentient being, instead of blind luck. Why would the gods even try to help at all? It seemed to Lessie as if every time they interfered, they just made things worse. The burning of the nameless army on the firebird's temple carving was proof of that, as well as Lai'ireal sending them to get a tome Mae couldn't unlock the power of.

Well, if they weren't in Ignatia anymore, one thing was for certain. *Trixie's going to kill me for not testing if the journal works in... wherever this is.*

Lessie sighed deeply. "If it's not Ignatia, then where is it?" she asked half-heartedly, not expecting an answer.

"I have a theory, but it is an outlandish one," replied Valandaras.

Of course he does.

"Oh, please tell us," Mae asked. She probably never wanted to tell a story of her own again. Lessie's stomach flipped again as she thought of

Mae's story, of her daughters. What a loss she carried with her. One more reason to hate the Seven and all the pompous bullshit they hid behind. How they denounced places like Kalac for keeping slaves, when the Divines who 'volunteered' within their houses were prisoners themselves.

Mama was right. The nobility are monsters. And now I'm one of them.

Valandaras looked as though he were struggling to find the right words. "I once met someone. In Adrai'ica," he said eventually. "He believed that all the god trees in the realms were connected long before Vry'iin created the Godprison. That the gods once needed to traverse between the realms unseen, and used the connection between the god trees to do it."

"Incredible," said Mae, face alight with curiosity. "Who was this person? Were they Fae?"

A prickle of dread ran down Lessie's spine. She'd seen all manner of strange monsters, horrors any regular person would blanch at, but the only people her mother had taught her to fear were the Fae.

Valandaras nodded. "One of my brothers was tasked with attempting to learn the whereabouts of a potential Sliver from him," he said. "He spoke of the Oaken Eternal, as he called it, and said things like how it 'connected us all'. I knew god trees themselves were real, as I had seen them, but I believed the connection to be more of a metaphorical one. Saelin thought the Fae was trying to trick us into trying to walk into a tree."

Lessie had never heard Valandaras speak of another Realmshifter by name before. She wondered if they had all been raised together, fighting over space and stealing each other's cloth the way Trixie had raided her meagre wardrobe and broken her things with accidental Arcane flares. The thought of a teenage Valandaras was immeasurably amusing to her. Had they played pranks on each other, or bickered over their Path? Did they all return for Solstices?

Valandaras had a faraway look. "Saelin did manage to locate the Sliver," he said, lips pursed in amusement. "But not before this particular Fae confused him so much that he almost gave up and left Adrai'ica altogether. I suppose it is good that he didn't, for then I would have been the one to claim Aasimon's Fang, and would have had no reason to search Kalaraak at all."

Mae smiled. "How lucky we all are for that Fae, then."

"Was he cursed?" Lessie asked, trying to sound nonchalant. Her mother had spoken in hushed tones of the curses the Fae would bestow, upon each other or anyone unlucky enough to cross them. "Your brother?"

"No. The Fae meant him no harm. But he was quite mad, even by Fae standards," Valandaras replied. "Spoke to thin air, jumped at small noises, wandered off mid-sentence. I confess I had forgotten his words before now because I simply did not believe them. He was infamous for not making much sense."

"I'll say," said Lessie. "Why call it the Oaken Eternal if half the trees are willows?"

The Fae spoke in lies and deceit, just like their False God. Even the name was a trick. They weren't Fae at all, but exiled Elven, driven mad by the realm they'd been banished to. Picking a new name for themselves didn't erase what they were.

"Maybe it is a translation issue," Mae mused. "The Elven people have many more words for plant-life than the common tongue. I cannot even pronounce some of them. It could be that each of these passageways connects to a different type of god tree, that grows native to the realm it originated from."

Valandaras coughed suddenly and violently, like the fresh air of the passage had managed to move the ash of the chambers from his lungs. Lessie felt similarly. She could sense the slight rattle within her chest when she inhaled.

"I just hope we find the tree that leads to Kalaraak," said Lessie darkly. "I don't know how many more of those thorns I can take."

Before they had stopped to rest, they had discovered one or two other passageways which branched off from the one they were on. The openings were heavily obscured by bramble, and even the gentle lights overhead shied away, leaving them in darkness. Lessie had tried pulling some of it aside, and was rewarded for her efforts with thorns piercing through her glove into her skin. Wherever those paths led, the Oaken Eternal did not want them following.

Mae handed them both tiny cups of lukewarm water. Lessie tried not to think about how long it had taken her to wring it from the waterskins.

"Whatever it is, we will figure it out as soon as we can," said Mae. "Rest. I'll take first watch."

Lessie wanted to argue, but her eyes burned from the ash and the crying. So she crawled into her bedroll, closed her eyes, and let thoughts about what they would do if the god tree couldn't get them to the surface lull her into an uneasy sleep.

Lessie dreamed of home.

The plains of Picking in early summer, her favourite time of year. The wide open spaces, the grass rustling gently in the breeze, the faint smell of the wild daisies and fields of poppies her mother loved so much, that dotted the countryside with bursts of white and pink and yellow and red. Her sister's laughter, shattering a peaceful silence, but so genuine that she could not help but join in. Trixie squealed in amusement, looking years younger than she really was, juggling a ball of lavender Arcane light like a carnival trick. Her mother and father, faces blurry but beaming, standing on the front porch of the home she had been born in.

This was the reprieve. That small window of time that only came a few times a year, where the mouth of the Maw was silent and the world was safe without them having to fight for it. Lessie breathed in happily, closing her eyes, the smell of the summer air grounding her. The seeds of a dandelion flower drifted past her in the wind. She could hear Trixie, talking so fast the words blurred together, about nothing and everything all at once.

Her next inhale had her unexpectedly choking. Smoke filled her nostrils and stung her eyes. Lessie looked up and saw only the skeleton of her home, charred beyond recognition. Flames licked at the burning frame, crackling ominously. The sky darkened. Her sister's talking turned to screams.

Everything started to dissolve.

Lessie wheeled around, and her vision blurred around the edges. She looked back for her parents, but they were gone, and as she ran inside her home she instead saw the blackened front gate of Falcon's Watch, blown apart by their rescue attempt. Instead of fire, water poured from the cracks in the stonework, filling the courtyard until the bodies that littered it were floating.

Every single one of them held a face that she knew.

Reevan, fur singed and smoking, robes billowing around him in the murky water. Grundle, face down, even tinier in death, scarlet blood seeping around him. Mae and Valandaras, arms outstretched as if they'd died trying to reach one another. Every other body bore the faces of her parents, frozen in pain, over and over and over again.

Lessie choked back bile as she waded through the waist-high water, past the twisted corpses of her friends and family. A misstep saw her stumble and nearly go under, the salt in the water stinging her eyes as she struggled to right herself. She just had to get home. She had to find Trixie. Her sister could reverse it, could fix what had been broken. That was what Arcane magic was for.

Camden was there, his silver suit covered in blood and ichor as he shouted to her, beckoning from the doorway to the keep. A rush of relief coursed through her as he pulled her from the water, her boots sloshing, the fabric clinging to her. His hand on her back, guiding her inside, felt like tiny bolts of lightning to her skin, and the feeling was confusing, conflicting, it didn't make sense.

Except it didn't go away. The lingering of the physical touch began to burn. Lessie clawed at her shirt, ripping at her skin, but the sensation only got worse. Camden either didn't notice or didn't care as she struggled, shouting, and he dragged her along through the keep, up the winding stairs that went on for hours, urging her on, deaf to her protests. All the while the feeling underneath her skin spread like wildfire.

Lessie forgot everything as they reached the open doorway of what had become her bedroom. Trixie sat behind her desk, scribbling in her journal. Lessie breathed a sigh of relief. She tried to speak, but her throat wouldn't let the words out.

Her sister rose from her chair and Lessie's blood ran cold. Trixie's eyes were glowing with an amethyst fury. Smoke wafted from them like it was burning her from the inside.

"Do you really think anything you did will make a difference?" Trixie said. Her voice was not her own. It sounded like how the void between realms had felt. Utter desolation. "Idiot girl."

"You're not my sister," Lessie said defiantly, regaining control of her voice. The thing that wasn't her sister cackled. Lessie tried to back out of the room, but Camden's hand wouldn't move from behind her.

"It's probably better off this way, my lady," he said, sneering her title like a slur. "You can face this on your own."

Lessie reached for her revolver, but it wasn't there. Her holster was empty. She scrabbled at her body for a weapon, but found nothing. Not-Trixie's head tilted at an inhuman angle.

"Worthless," she laughed. "No Divinity. No Arcane power. Completely and utterly ordinary. Mundane. Why do you even try? They're all dead, anyway. You can't save them."

Lessie blinked and Not-Trixie was beside her. She could do nothing but watch as delicate fingers reached upwards and dragged a nail slowly down Camden's face. She had too many joints in her fingers, they were too long.

Lessie was still staring in horror as Not-Trixie's grip tightened around Camden's throat like a lover, and a strange, possessive burst of anger jolted through her.

Then there was a sickening crunch and Camden's neck snapped. He crumpled to the floor beside her wordlessly and the scream stuck in her throat.

"They'll all die," Not-Trixie said in her ear. "Even me."

The glint of her revolver's barrel caught in the candlelight. Her sister's tiny hands with the too-long fingers wrapped around the hilt with her own initials engraved upon it. Not-Trixie grinned as she shoved the revolver she had made under her own chin. Her teeth were black.

"No," Lessie protested, attempting to wrestle the gun away. "No, Trix, I can't—no, no, NO—"

Lessie jolted awake.

The echo of a phantom gunshot rang in her ears. Her heart pounded. For a moment she stayed frozen, panting, staring up at the tiny lights as they drifted lazily around the ceiling. She couldn't remember where she was. Sweat drenched her whole body. She didn't know if she'd shouted aloud, and she sat up, terrified that she would see the floating bodies of her friends instead of their concerned faces. She looked around wildly, squinting in the dim light.

Mae and Valandaras were both asleep.

It was supposed to be Mae's watch, or perhaps the torch had already passed, because Valandaras sat upright with his torso pressed against the bramble of the walls like he had been staring at the passageway beyond them. His head drifted to the side, snoring softly, the usual glow of his eyes dimmed beneath his cloth.

Mae had curled up beside him, her head rested in Valandaras's lap, her fingertips still lingering on his injured leg. The firebird's tome lay open in front of her, like she'd been reading it as he slept.

Lessie was so grateful to see them both alive that she didn't mind they had abandoned their watch in favour of sleep. She watched the rhythmic pattern of their subconscious sparks until her heartbeat returned to normal.

Every so often, a tiny glimmer of emerald would come from underneath Mae's fingers, sending sparks through Valandaras's skin and healing him. In turn, Valandaras's unwrapped hand had curled over Mae's back protectively, and the brighter glow from his bare palm would flare and warm her shoulder.

Despite her dread, Lessie smiled. *Even when they're asleep, they care about each other. It's instinctual.*

Mae shivered. Lessie got up and draped her bedroll over the sleeping woman's legs. They could rest as long as they needed to. It was her turn to keep watch. She wasn't going back to sleep tonight, anyway.

When they awoke, neither Mae nor Valandaras acknowledged their intimate sleeping positions beyond a few awkward stretches. Mae apologised for not keeping to the watch schedule, but Lessie waved her off. She didn't care.

At least they weren't awake to hear me screaming my head off.

They continued on much as they had the day before. Valandaras's leg had improved somewhat, but he could still not walk on his own, and therefore their pace was slow.

Lessie focused on searching for something, anything, that showed they were going the right way, but it all looked disturbingly similar as they walked. Only the absence of their own footprints in the floor ahead convinced her it wasn't a single giant circle.

"What do you think we're looking for?" Lessie said as they rounded yet another gently curved corner. "We could follow this tunnel forever."

Valandaras was also concerned. "There has been little change in the terrain," he said, gesturing to the expanse of tangled bramble that formed the arch. "I cannot see a single line with which to realmshift, either. This might as well be the void. I don't know how we could possibly know which realm we're even heading towards."

Mae looked thoughtful. "Why don't we ask it?"

Lessie's instinct was to laugh, but she hadn't thought of anything better.

"I suppose it worked for the lights," she replied, shaking her head.

After all the things I've seen, speaking to a bunch of ancient trees shouldn't seem so weird.

"Uh, hi, Oaken Eternal," she said aloud, feeling incredibly stupid for doing so. Mae's mouth quivered like she was suppressing a giggle, and Lessie threw her a withering look. "We need to reach Kalaraak, please. I want to go home."

Nothing happened. The lights wound within the bramble didn't go out, but they didn't brighten either. No path presented itself. Lessie didn't know what she'd expected, but she'd hoped for something, at least.

"Maybe it only speaks Elven," Mae said.

The glimmer of amusement in Mae's eyes reminded Lessie of her sister, and her stomach lurched as the dream-image of Trixie casually breaking Camden's neck flashed into her mind.

Mae saw her expression and patted her shoulder. "I'm sorry. I was only trying to lighten the mood."

At least Mae was feeling more like her usual self.

Lessie sighed. "Whatever. Let's keep going."

They pushed onwards, walking in tense silence. They came across another divergence from the main path, but it was immediately clear that it was not the way home. Parts of the walls around the arch had blackened in places, the vines glistening as if wet.

Lessie reached for one, but shied back as she took in the scent of the vines. A damp, mouldy sweetness wafted from them, cloying and sinister. Black ichor dripped from a few, pooling beneath the moss at their feet, which squelched unpleasantly even as they gave it a wide berth. Further out, hundreds of clear crystals grew along the branches and twigs, like salt water had dried upon them.

"They look poisoned," said Mae darkly. "This is a perversion. The Mother would hate this."

"I'm just glad that's not the passage we have to go down," said Lessie.

Indeed, the vines and bramble had grown over this particular pathway so thickly it was almost completely hidden from view, like the Oaken Eternal itself were trying to block the way. The growth bowed towards them. As if something very large had been pushing on the other side, trying to get out.

Lessie shuddered.

The lights above them flickered. The ones behind, where they had walked from, extinguished altogether. Ahead, around the next curve, a brighter light pulsed.

"It's a sign," Mae said. She adjusted her grip on Valandaras's waist, the Realmshifter having gained back more movement in his shattered leg. "Lessie, follow it."

Lessie bolted, running towards the light. She rounded the corner and her breath caught.

It was another pathway. Another divergence. But this one was open.

The lights pulsed like a heartbeat as they surrounded the new passageway's arched entrance. Lessie peered down the passage, but the tiny light could only penetrate the blackness so far before it was swallowed completely. It did not seem long, but the darkness could be deceiving.

"There's another passage!" Lessie shouted.

"This has to be it," Mae said as they caught up. "Look at the lights, the way the branches fold inwards. The Oaken Eternal is telling us to go down here."

Lessie eyed it warily. There were a hundred ways this could go wrong. Maybe the lights were work of the Fae, leading them to their untimely demise. Perhaps the passage was a trap. Maybe it would take them straight back into the firebird's temple.

Anything is better than slowly suffocating in an Ignatian tomb.

Still, there was a sense of... rightness about it. The phantom breeze rushed towards her, smelling of lavender and citrus. She couldn't explain it, but it felt like home. She glanced towards the ceiling.

"Thanks," Lessie whispered, feeling foolish.

The lights twinkled merrily.

Mae held out her hand. "We all go in together, this time," she said. "Nobody gets left behind."

Lessie knew there was a good chance this would be the last thing she ever did. She took a deep breath in, held it, and exhaled just as deeply. Every time she did, it was like her father's phantom hand on her shoulder. She'd struggled to trust anyone other than him with anything, even now. Accepting that he was really gone, that she was on her own, had been harder than she'd ever admit.

But she liked to think she was getting better at trusting those around her.

For the second time in a week, Lessie wrapped her hand around Mae's and stepped into a passageway between realms—that could lead to exactly where she needed to go, or to certain death.

PART THREE
THE GOD OF DEATH

41

LESSIE

Everything went white.

Lessie heard Mae whisper beside her, "Oh, thank the Mother," and figured it was safe to open her eyes. She blinked furiously at the flash of light that stung them. That was the unmistakable glare of the twin Kalaraak suns blinding her. She inhaled. Her lungs rejoiced at the cool air that filled them. No sulphur, no heat. Not even the sandy winds of Kalac. Only the scent of crisp autumn flooded her senses. Stone, grasses, a hint of citrus. Altaean sky above her, and Altaean soil beneath her feet.

Home.

They were in Altaea, but that was where her certainty ended. They were in some sort of garden. The ancient willow tree they had stepped out of was a twin to the petrified behemoth deep within the firebird's temple. Its branches stretched outwards and down majestically, stark shade and bright sunlight dappling her companions as the wind shifted. Long, feathered leaves swished around them, brushing the earth and keeping them concealed within.

Looking through the willow's branches, Lessie could see other trees, along with patches of colourful flowers in the gentle light. Clover blanketed the ground around them, dots of white and pink the only interruption to the soft green. Further away, a stone wall ringed the greenery, suggesting it was a protected area.

It was serene and beautiful, and Lessie recognised nothing. She took a few deep breaths to stop herself from sinking to her knees. In for six, hold for three, out for six.

Thank the gods. Or the god trees, I guess.

"Where are we?" she wondered aloud.

"For a moment, I thought we had found Adrai'ica," Mae replied softly, voice full of reverence.

Lessie's blood pressure spiked. No. It couldn't be. Adrai'ica was home to the worst of those who had worshipped Vry'iin. The grotesque, chaotic and fanciful. The Fae. Adrai'ica twisted and deformed those who dwelled within it.

Lessie had been taught to fear anything to do with the Fae, including Adrai'ica itself. Though she was starting to question a lot more of the things her Altaean education had taught her.

Lessie took a deep breath. They were not in Adrai'ica. Her instincts would not betray her like this. Everything here was too... normal.

"This is Altaea. I know it," Lessie said firmly. *Gods help us if it isn't.*

Valandaras looked around, mouth set in a hard line as he took in the towering buildings outside the walls. He winced as he put weight on his injured leg.

"Lessie's right," he said, pointing outside the garden's walls. "I have been here before. We're in Roost Keep."

Lessie scanned the walls and landed on a particularly large building with stone eagles perched atop the roof like gargoyles. She had never been to Roost Keep before, but the name sparked recognition. It wasn't Altaea's capital, but it was important. People visited the sprawling city for all kinds of trade in the northern parts of Altaea, and it was home to one of the Seven. Possibly DeFalcone territory, but she couldn't remember for certain. The thought of the DeFalcones, of Camden, made her stomach churn.

"How are we going to tell the others where we are?" Lessie asked, panic building again. "They're still in Saluo. We're on the other side of the godsdamned continent again."

Mae looked to Valandaras, who remained stoic. "We will find someone to send a message to them. It is all we can do," he replied.

A smile blossomed on Mae's face despite the heavy fatigue evident in the dark circles under her eyes.

"If we're in Roost Keep, then this must be the Evergreen Gardens," she said. "I've heard stories of it. It stays like this, no matter the season. Nobody knows if it's Divine or Arcane work, only that it's been this way since before the Breach."

Lessie had no time to appreciate botanical wonders.

"So what do we do?" she asked. The scent of the burning embers within Ignatia still clung to her clothing, mixing with the wildflowers, confusing her senses and setting her nerves on edge.

"Druitt DeFalcone," said Valandaras, still leaning heavily on Mae. "He is stationed here with the Roost Keep guard. He was working with the acting High Marshal when we last spoke. He can assist us in getting a message to the others."

A sharp cry of pain escaped Valandaras as he tried to put his full weight on his damaged leg. Mae helped to lower him to the ground, the Realmshifter's unwrapped knuckles going white as he gripped her arms for support.

"I have to rest it, just for a short while," he said, irritation warring with pain on his face. Mae hovered over him uncertainly, and Lessie knew at once that she would not leave him. It was a mark of just how badly he had injured it that their healing combined had taken this long.

"Stay here," Lessie said, gesturing to the god tree. "I'll go. I'll find Druitt. We can work out what to do from there."

Mae nodded. "I'll keep him here. We'll get it healed up soon enough."

With that, Lessie squared her shoulders, pushed aside the nearest flowing willow branch, and marched into the garden. It was incredibly beautiful, and in another life she would have loved to have spent years here. A life where she had time to care about the types of greenery that were bursting from every corner of the place.

Unfortunately, I have to focus on saving the realm from insane gods.

Lessie located the entrance to the gardens, a simple, unmanned archway, and stepped into the streets of Roost Keep. Valandaras had given her a rough idea of what to look for, and after she got her bearings, she hastily set off towards the heart of the city. The wind was biting for this time of year. It was much too cold. Lessie grimaced and pulled her jacket tighter around her, grateful for the chance to wear it again.

It probably only feels cold because I've just spent a week in a volcano.

At least her jacket was semi-clean, offering a small respite from the judgemental looks of Roost Keep's citizens. As she followed the cobbled path towards the centre of the city, Lessie became acutely aware of how filthy she was. Ignatia's ash and soot had stained her clothing, and their tussle with the guardians had left parts of it torn and singed. Her hands were coated in a layer of grime that made her cringe to think of how her face looked. Still, she met the eyes of passers-by as defiantly as she could.

She needed to get to the guardhouse and find Druitt DeFalcone. Then they could figure out what to do next.

Lessie trudged forward, carving a path towards the city's centre, where Valandaras had said the High Marshal's guardhouse would be. The streets were quiet, but what few pedestrians there gave her a wide berth as they hurried past, punctuated by curious whispers and quiet disgust. She knew they had reason to—she looked like she'd narrowly escaped a wildfire. The look on her face alone was enough to scare them out of eye contact.

It's no different to being home. To protect people, only to see them scorn you.

Still, it stung a little, especially after what she had just been through. Lessie gave up trying to stare them all down and looked past them instead.

There was one man walking towards her that hadn't felt the need to cross to the other side of the street. Maybe he was too focused on his own task to notice how bedraggled she looked; his arms were overloaded with a large amount of parchment, haphazard documents and loose papers, hastily tied together with a ribbon. Lessie found herself fixating on him, wondering when he would look up, if he would notice her at all, or if he blindly expected her to move. Why should she? Temper flaring, she immediately resolved not to. The man shifted his weight, pulling the largest stack from the top, struggling to carry it all. He finally glanced upwards just before they collided.

Their eyes met.

Through the haze of stress, of exhaustion that threatened to collapse her, Lessie had the strangest thought.

He reminds me of—

The papers hit the ground with a thud. Parchment scattered to the wind.

The cold disappeared as the man dropped everything he held and pulled her towards him. Warm arms wrapped around her in a tight embrace, and the cinnamon wood-smoke scent hit her before she had a chance to panic.

"My lady," said Camden DeFalcone thickly, "it appears you have *quite* a story to tell me."

Lessie clamped down on the inexplicable urge to cry and let him hold her for a moment. Before long, her fingernails dug into his back, but he didn't flinch, and she gripped him so hard she thought she might collapse if she let go first.

After a while, Camden pulled away and held her at arm's length, inspecting her clothing and searching for injury, or perhaps to confirm she were indeed truly present. She felt colder now he'd pulled away, and suddenly self-conscious of her clothing's present state as she noticed the marks her ash-stained tunic had left on his tan coat. Camden's hands seemed hesitant to let go of her shoulders, like he was afraid she would disappear if he did.

"How in the seven realms did you manage to make it home?" he asked, suddenly panicked. "What of Mae? Valandaras? Did they make it?"

"They're fine," Lessie assured him, and he sagged in relief. "Valandaras is hurt, but they're fine. They're here."

As the shock of seeing him wore off, suspicion crept up within her. The others were supposed to be in Saluo. They had said they would stay hidden, with Bueno. Why was Camden, of all people, on the streets of Roost Keep?

Why didn't they wait for us to come back?

"What are you doing here?" she asked. She struggled to keep the accusation from her voice.

Camden smiled, bemused. "I should ask you the same thing, my lady. Do you realise how long you've been gone?"

"A week? Ten days, maybe?" What did that matter?

Camden laughed, and then his eyes widened in disbelief as they flickered between hers, searching for a joke she hadn't made.

Lessie frowned. "What?"

"You've been gone for months," Camden said. "Almost a season. The winter solstice is practically upon us."

It was Lessie's turn to laugh. "Bullshit. You can't be serious."

"As the grave. How else would we have arrived in Roost Keep before you? Unless Reevan somehow learned to teleport us all, of course, but even he's not quite that fast."

Teleport? Camden was making less and less sense. She tilted her head as he stammered, his confidence sliding from his face. He ran his hands through hair that was definitely longer than it had been when she last saw him. What was going on?

"What?" Lessie repeated.

"Look, it's an inside joke, I—oh, godsdamn it, the plans..."

Camden remembered the papers he had dropped and knelt to gather them again. Lessie automatically bent to help, and as she reached for the parchment, her fingertips felt moisture. She pressed her hand to the ground in confusion. It was the kind of damp that suggested there had been recent snowfall. She flinched at the biting cold of the cobblestones, prickling her skin like shards of ice.

Camden gingerly rescued a couple of mud-splattered scrolls from an errant puddle. "Druitt's going to kill me," he muttered, shaking the parchment.

Lessie realised now why she hadn't immediately recognised Camden—he looked different with a beard grown in, neatly trimmed and reddish-brown. Older. More refined. Even more annoyingly handsome. The dark jewel in his silver signet ring glinted as his fingers brushed stray droplets from the paper.

Lessie glanced around in disbelief. Branches of trees stood bare. Passers-by pulled cloaks tighter around them against the wind, their breath visible as they puffed towards their destinations. In a nearby building, a glowing fire crackled merrily behind the glass of a window, distorted from frost on the panes.

Disbelief gave way to dread. The stiff wind picked up again and a stray leaf blew past her, shrivelled and browned. A shiver ran through her that had nothing to do with the weather.

"Months?" Lessie whispered in horror.

Camden's grey eyes shot to hers. They were unreadable.

"We thought you were all dead," he said quietly. "We came here to help my brother organise a defence against the Mahejerai. It's going about as well as you'd expect it to be."

He finished gathering the fallen papers and straightened. Lessie didn't remember him being quite that tall. He undid the silver clasp on his heavy winter cloak and draped it around her shoulders before she could protest. The woollen material felt strangely comforting.

"Let's get you inside," said Camden, still looking at her like she was a ghost. "We'll send for the others. You've got a lot to catch up on." A flash of mischief saw the Camden she knew shining through the familiar stranger before her. "Besides, you are in desperate need of a bath. You smell... burnt."

Druitt's office was small, but mercifully warm, with the fireplace in the corner heating the room without much effort. For a person who usually preferred the cold, it would have been stifling. Normally she would have hated it. But Lessie was used to warmer temperatures lately.

Druitt himself hovered behind his desk, which was as full of jumbled papers as he had made the table in the West Keep a lifetime ago. Lessie struggled to stay focused as he and Camden bounced between topics, trying to fill them in on what had happened during the time they had lost. The stress of the journey had drained her, and now that her adrenaline had dried up, she wanted nothing more than to curl up and sleep for a century.

She was also acutely aware that the soft linen shirt she'd been given to wear after her scalding hot bath had once been Camden's, because cinnamon wood-smoke kept assaulting her nostrils despite him being seated on the other side of the room. Even without the familiar scent, she would have guessed, because the Lord of Self-Satisfied Smugness kept glancing at it and smirking.

He probably thinks I'm sullying his noble garment with my peasant blood.

Valandaras hadn't spoken at all. He was furious that Ignatia had stolen so much time from them in Kalaraak. Apparently he had only been there for a day or two at most, and as such had not noticed the missing pieces of time from his life. Or maybe there were other realms where time slowed, and it had evened out for him.

Lessie didn't want to think about it. She stared out the window, watching tiny flakes of snow gather on the iron grates that patterned the panes. She stared at the floor, where a thick rug had been pulled awkwardly underneath the desk, probably to cover a stain of some kind on the carpet. She tried her best to keep up with the conversation, but she was secretly relieved when someone else asked the first question.

"I'm sorry, where did you say Reevan is?" asked Mae.

She paced behind Valandaras protectively as a grizzled Divine worked to heal the rest of Valandaras's injury. The man had been called in by Druitt, and served not the Seven but the city itself. If Mae was a hundred years old and looked thirty, then this Divine must have been about a thousand, if the silver hair and deep lines upon his face were any indication of age. He had come from the Roost Keep's infirmary, where he apparently specialised in bone breaks. Lessie didn't know what god he served to be granted such a specific Gift—and if he gave it freely—but he seemed solely focused on his task.

"Reevan is on Aelmor Island," replied Druitt. "It is where the Mahejerai have set up their defences. When they left Saluo in a hurry, we spent weeks tracking both the Mahejerai themselves and the army they ally with. Reevan volunteered to do some scouting before we sent our forces in, and Grundle went to join him about a week ago."

Druitt jabbed his finger onto the large map in the centre of the table. Lessie could see someone had hurriedly added to it. The Kalac regions were filled in more than when she had last seen it. The tiny island had been added by hand, nestled within a ring of land masses at the top of the Kalac and Altaean coasts.

"It's fortunate that you returned when you did," said Druitt, pinching the bridge of his nose. "I've been waiting on the High Marshal's approval to take a regiment up to defend Aelmor, since it's disputed land. So far, she has only allowed me to take men who volunteer themselves, and I pulled a lot of strings to get even that. We had to be covert about my troops' involvement. Strictly volunteer only, that sort of thing. None of it is official Altaean business."

"Why? Doesn't the king care?" Lessie asked. "Surely this concerns all of us."

Camden and Druitt shared a dark look.

"With the Kingswitch only weeks away, nobody wants to be seen making any hard choices," Druitt said carefully. "Although, just between us, we're lucky Father hasn't taken the throne. He would love the excuse to declare outright war on Kalac. But either way, I understand the High Marshal's hesitation—she has only my word that this is even happening. Braak and Boras have covered their tracks too well."

"So it's up to us to handle this," finished Camden cheerfully. "Saving the entire realm? No problem. Child's play, even. At least Claudette let us use the big office. Druitt's regular one moonlights as a broom closet."

"I still can't believe Boras didn't already destroy the entire realm while we were gone," muttered Lessie. "What is he waiting for?"

"Timing," answered Druitt. "It's one of the two things he needed. He found the place, now he needs the right time. We think it's to do with the winter solstice. So far, nobody's been able to figure out what's so special about the island itself, but hopefully Reevan has."

"It will be a weak point," said Valandaras. He shifted awkwardly in his seat, his damaged leg propped up for the old Divine to work on. Pulling the map towards him, he drew a finger down it. "There are points across any realm where the divide between them is less substantial. It is where I find it easiest to realmshift. If this island is on one of these fault lines, so to speak, Boras's ritual will be more successful there."

Lessie looked at the map, now with added Ignatian grime from Valandaras's uncovered fingers. The curved lines that crossed over the realm made a pattern that tugged at her.

Valandaras scowled at the map. "Combine that with the rotation of the realm around our suns, and you get a few days a year that are most favourable for Arcane rituals of this magnitude. In other words, we need to get there as soon as we can." He winced as a sapphire spark of the old Divine's healing travelled up his skin and sunk into an errant cut on his neck, erasing it. Mae gave the old Divine a grateful look.

"It will be extremely hard to get you in," said Druitt. "From what Reevan has managed to tell us, Braak's army is doing the brunt of the defensive work. They've made it impossible to advance further inward. Our plan is to attempt a siege, but they could last weeks."

"Weeks we don't have," Mae said. "If Val's right about the weak point, then Boras will attempt to bring Daigon through on the day of the winter solstice."

"Ah, my favourite holiday," remarked Camden. "I'll be sure to toast a marshmallow for all of you in celebration, since you'll be missing it. I'll try not to peek at your presents, but no promises."

"You're not coming with us?" asked Lessie, judgement clear in her tone.

"Absolutely not," he said. "Wouldn't catch me dead on that leaky boat Druitt calls a ship."

Lessie scoffed. "What are you so afraid of?"

"Death, mostly," replied Camden conversationally. "And spiders. Not too fond of heights, either, as I discovered when Reevan tossed me out a window."

Lessie glared at him, feeling some of her fire return through her exhaustion. *Is he physically incapable of answering a serious question with a serious answer?*

"Camden is not coming," Druitt said firmly, "because one of us needs to stay alive, and it recently became infinitely more important that it be him. This was the deal, Cam. I made this happen for you because I owed you."

Behind the frown, the look between the brothers was surprisingly tender, with an unspoken apology written all over Druitt's expression.

"I know, I know." Camden threw up his hands in surrender, then caught Lessie's eye and winked. "It's a long story, my lady. Maybe one day I'll tell it to you, if you can stand to be in my presence for that long."

Lessie rolled her eyes. That was unlikely.

"We will have an Arcane get a message to Reevan that you have returned," said Druitt. "It's not much, but he will know to expect us. I wish we could wait for you to recover more, but we're running out of time. We depart at first light. If you're able to, we'll need all the help we can get."

The gruff old Divine motioned for Valandaras to stand, and he did so gingerly, testing the weight on his injured leg. He didn't collapse, so it must have felt better.

"Two weeks. Rest. Stay off," the Divine said in a clipped voice.

Valandaras only nodded. Mae grasped both of the Divine's hands in her own and thanked him profusely before he shuffled from the room.

Valandaras did not sit back down.

"We'll go with you," he declared. "Tomorrow. We'll plan on the way. We will finish this."

Lessie shook her head. So much for staying off his damaged leg for two weeks. She stared down at the sprawling map before her and stifled a yawn.

Already, they had somewhere else to be. Time was moving too fast, like it was trying to make up for the months they'd lost to Ignatia. Lessie felt drained. Her mind was spinning, and her body, still stiff and sore despite the bath, screamed for sleep. She supposed true rest would have to wait until they were on the ship.

Oh, gods.

Somehow, being stuck on a ship sounded worse than realmshifting.

42

MAE

It was later than she planned when Mae finally knocked on the door to Valandaras's cabin.

The war galley Druitt had procured was not designed for privacy, but there were a few rooms once designated for officers, with small cramped bunks and single cots inside. Mae was sharing with Lessie, but the ranger spent the majority of her time on deck, fascinated by the ship and its workings. Left to her own devices, Mae had been slowly losing her mind in the small room. She had read the firebird's tome cover to cover around a dozen times by now, and something about the story was bugging her. She needed a second opinion.

That was the reason she told herself, anyway.

Valandaras wrenched open the wooden door as the ship swayed, and Mae burst into the room without waiting for an invitation.

"I think there's something we're missing about the tome," she said, spinning on her heel to face him. "We—Val, you're..." she trailed off, blushing scarlet.

"Undressed?" he supplied. Mae could see the raised eyebrow beneath the cloth. It was white again; he had donned a fresh one from the supply she'd found for him in Saluo. He wore only a pair of loose linen pants, no shirt, and his arms were unwrapped. The glow of his skin was brighter with so much of it visible.

"It is the middle of the night," Valandaras added, feigning ignorance. "Contrary to the rumours, I don't always sleep in my armour."

Mae stared at the floor, willing her pulse to settle. It wasn't like she hadn't seen him unclothed before; she'd patched him up so many times she'd lost count. But something about the tiny room and the faint glimmer of his casually exposed skin jumbled her thoughts.

"It's barely eleven," she stuttered, "and I was going to say, you're up and walking, not—I'm sorry, I just—can you put a shirt on? I'm having trouble remembering what I came here to talk about."

Her cheeks only heated further as Valandaras smiled, a little smugly, but he obliged her.

"Very well. What was the revelation?" he asked.

Mae held up the tome. "This doesn't just have the entire written history of the firebird's reign in Ignatia. It also tells of how it left behind the power to be reborn again. It has explicit instructions on how to 'take in' that power, from the book. Any Divine with an ability to Change, which most of the firebird's followers appeared to inherit, could take on the 'form of the phoenix', as they called it. It's incredible. Those stories upon the walls of the temple, all of those battles—some of them were not explicitly the god itself, but the Divines who followed it, harnessing the power that it offered freely to them. It's a give and take. They can use it for a limited time, as long as they have access to the Sliver it was stored in. This Sliver."

Valandaras's forehead creased. "And is that something you could do?"

Mae nodded. "In theory. I understand it. I've read the words a hundred times already. Some of them lost their bodies to the form, but I don't know if it's because they misused it, stayed too long... it's unclear."

She flicked through the pages, searching for the passages that explained it further, before growing frustrated and snapping the tome shut once more.

"The problem is I don't have access to the Mother's true power, so I cannot Change. But I've been thinking. Why would Lai'ireal send us after this if she already knew I could not use it? Was it just so we would kill Boras? I think there is a way. What if it's not just the tome that can store godpower? What if I could pull the Mother's power back through the Mournblade?"

Valandaras's eyes flickered to the corner of the room, where the obsidian blade lay wrapped once more. If she concentrated enough, Mae could hear the sinister humming, and deliberately repressed the shiver it tried to give her.

"I suppose it would depend on whether the power remained within the Mournblade," Valandaras said slowly, considering her words, "or if Boras syphoned it through into himself. And I have never heard of taking back a Gift."

"It was not a true Gift. It was stolen. Perhaps I can force it to return to where it belongs."

This has to work, or it was all for nothing.

Valandaras was unconvinced. "What makes you think a thing like that would even be possible?"

Mae's stomach lurched. She knew if she avoided it, he would not press her. That he would trust her without the truth. But this was the moment.

"To explain that, I need to tell you something."

"Anything, lioness."

The nickname stung, and Mae almost abandoned her words altogether. She picked at her fingernails, delaying the seconds until he would look at her differently.

"I left out a part of the story about my... departure from serving Altaean high society," she said carefully. "And it is important to me that you know the whole truth. In case something happens."

Valandaras frowned underneath the cloth. "I am not sure I follow, but I'm listening."

Breathe.

"I killed the king."

There. She had said it. Mae flinched inwardly, cringing in anticipation, waiting for the change in his demeanour. The judgement, the disappointment, the shock and fear that would eventually twist into hatred. Valandaras was such a paragon of justice, of right and wrong. Surely, this would affect how he felt about her.

For the moment, Valandaras just looked puzzled.

"How?" he asked.

Oh, gods. Mae knew she would have to elaborate, but part of her had thought he would turn her away before she would have a chance to. She took a deep breath.

"My Gift," she whispered. "I took it all back."

"What do you mean?"

"I can't explain it," Mae said, the words tumbling out. "When the king told me my girls were gone, I imploded. I was so consumed by the shock, the rage I felt at having my family ripped from me. I don't know how I did it. But I stood before this man and I felt every tiny spark of the Mother's Gift I had ever wasted on his miserable existence, and I reached out, and I pulled, and I took it all back. He crumbled."

"I see," said Valandaras, unreadable. "And that killed him?"

Mae nodded. "He was old, and his body should have succumbed to his disease years before he met me. He was dead before he hit the floor."

Her face burned. To fight an armed enemy was one thing, but this? It was nothing short of murder. *I preach of life and the Mother, who am I to decide when someone should die?*

"So there you have it," she said. "I killed the king of Altaea. It was unintentional, but I cannot say I regret it. He did not deserve the Mother's Gift."

Valandaras's glow from beneath his cloth grew dim, closing his eyes in contemplation. He did not move from the bed beside her, but Mae felt the tension surround them, radiating out of her body the way his glow did. She wanted to run, like she had from the castle. To leave the room and never say the other things she had been waiting years to. But even if she could move, she knew it would do no good. Everything else aside, they were on a ship—there wasn't really anywhere for her to run.

And so the Divine and the Realmshifter sat in the most uncomfortable silence they had ever experienced with each other. Mae's confession hung in the air between them.

Valandaras did not speak for a long while, long enough that Mae wondered if he would ever speak to her again. They both stared out of the porthole window, the only sound the waves knocking into the sides of the ship outside.

Finally, Valandaras sighed deeply.

"From what you said, he was an awful human being, and an even worse king," he said. "Unintentional or not, you did the realm a favour."

Mae laughed aloud at the sheer rush of relief that flooded through her bones, even as a tear rolled down her cheek.

He didn't hate her. He didn't think her a murderer. She exhaled deeply and found the strength to look at him again. His brow had creased with worry, and he had curled his arms by his side in that way he always did, like he were keeping himself from reaching for her.

"You think so?" Mae asked, trying to keep the grin off her face, but she felt giddy. "It's a truly terrible thing to have done. Are you sure you don't want to turn me in? You could probably still collect on the bounty."

She had been harbouring guilt for the act for a decade, and now the absolution of the one person whose opinion mattered most threatened to unhinge her completely. Valandaras kept staring at her, and she kept laughing through her tears, and eventually, he joined her. He wrapped an arm around her in comfort, squeezing her gently, and the physical touch made her Gift sing in response.

"You are the most complicated person I have ever met, Mae of the Valefork," Valandaras said, shaking his head as if in awe. "But I must admit, I have enjoyed learning each complication."

Valandaras stood, and before she could protest, he had retrieved and unwrapped the Mournblade.

"Go ahead, then. See if you can pull it back."

Mae eyed the blade warily, before focusing on it as hard as she could. The sword's humming grew louder without being covered, and she resisted the urge to block her ears. She reached out with the trickle of her Gift, emerald sparks glistening across her arms, and called to the Mournblade to release what it had stolen from her.

Nothing happened.

The stab of disappointment hurt so much it rendered her speechless. Mae blinked back tears of frustration.

Godsdamn it, Mother, what will it take to get you back?

Golden fingers gripped her shoulder gently.

"It was a good idea, lioness," Valandaras said softly. "All this means is that the Mournblade did not store the power within itself. It flowed directly into Oorata Boras once he held it. Perhaps only the phoenix god knew how to keep their power within a Sliver."

Mae pouted and sank back onto the bed. She pretended not to notice when Valandaras joined her once more, the Mournblade having been returned to its wrapped exile in the corner. She was too disappointed to think about it.

They fell into their usual comfortable silence, which gave Mae enough time to gather her thoughts and work out what she wanted to say next. But Valandaras's next words shocked her.

"If you could pull enough of your Gift back from me, would you be able to Change?"

"Absolutely not," she said immediately.

"I do not think that is true," he replied. "You have poured so much of yourself into my injuries over the last few years. Surely that is enough to Change. As much as I don't want you to use the tome, if it is what you wish, then I will help."

"I am only going to say this once, Val," Mae said firmly. "I would rather face Daigon, Oorata Boras and Ashendi Braak alone, armed with only a rusty bread knife, than take back a single drop of the Mother's Gift from you. Besides, I don't think I can pull a true Gift. You deserved it every single time."

Valandaras's face clouded in confusion. "Why tell me this, then?" he asked. "I thought it was so I would know it was possible to take back a god's Gift from one you had healed. What other reason could there be?"

Mae shook her head. It was now or never.

Mother, give me strength.

"I could not face this fight without you knowing all of me," she whispered. "I worry you only see the best in me. I needed to know that you truly knew the worst. Because your opinion of me matters more than anyone else's."

"Why?"

Mae's heart was pounding. If she dared to look down, she would not have been surprised to see it beating visibly in her chest. Her hands felt clammy and if she picked at her nails any more, they'd start bleeding.

Of the two confessions, strangely, this was the one she'd been more frightened to make. Even the thought of using the firebird's tome, of losing her body to the phoenix form, scared her less than the fear of rejection that she invited by speaking her thoughts aloud. If she never said it, she could pretend she didn't know his answer. Even though she *knew*, she could keep it safe and not risk ruining it.

But she had stood at the edge long enough. It was time to take the leap. If she fell and her bones crushed, so be it.

"Because from the moment I was born, I have been taking care of everyone around me," Mae said. "My father. My village. My girls. The king's court, the Archdukes of the Seven. I have been planning and worrying and constantly carrying the stress of others for a century. For some, I did it willingly, gladly. But you? You were the first person I've ever met who wanted to take care of me. Who cared if I was looked after. Who saw me not for what I could do for them, but simply for who I am. You didn't know what I could do when you asked me to stay with you. You just wanted to make sure I was safe."

Valandaras had frozen.

Mae didn't stop to think. She let the truth spill out, because to keep it inside any longer was a worse kind of death than the one that faced them with the coming sunrises.

"I have seen many kinds of love," she said, voice shaking, "and I have felt its maddening touch. It takes more forms than I can. But true, peaceful love is not black and white, or even shades of grey. It's golden, like the sun's rays—like you. Love is the daylight streaming onto the leaves of the trees. Love is hot tea pushed into cold hands. Love is noticing. Love is silence. Love is looking at somebody and just knowing that they want you to be there with them. And I look at you and I just... know."

She placed a hand gently on Valandaras's chest. He inhaled sharply.

"So that is why I had to tell you everything. Because I do not wish to be anywhere other than at your side, facing whatever comes towards us. And if Lai'ireal was right, if I figure out how to use the tome, perhaps I will finally die, so... I could not go to Requiem without saying this aloud. I love you, Val. I know you know. I've been in love with you for years. But I needed you to hear it."

Forget facing Daigon. This was the bravest thing Mae had ever done.

Valandaras looked as if he had been temporarily rendered paralysed, and for a moment, her heart faltered. Had she made a mistake? Then a faintly glowing golden hand curled over her own, pressing them both into Valandaras's heart. The warmth of his strange healing jolted through her skin.

"I could search the seven realms for a thousand years and never find someone I wished to be beside," Valandaras said quietly. "And I would rather die on this Path with you than live a thousand lifetimes having never walked it."

It wasn't exactly what she had expected him to say, but it said enough. And when Valandaras reached for her, Mae found herself hearing the words he hadn't said as his fingertips grazed her skin.

"Stay with me."

Mae did not return to her own quarters that night, or any of the nights that followed. She figured Lessie needed the uninterrupted rest.

After a week of smooth sailing, the tension on the ship mounted as they came upon their destination. The ring of islands surrounding Aelmor were difficult to navigate, and the war galley was older than was perhaps ideal for harbouring this many people. The twin transport ships that trailed behind them carried the bulk of the soldiers that made up Druitt's volunteer companies, but those ships had been sourced last minute and had little function other than basic defences. If they were to be attacked, now was the worst possible time.

The day of the winter solstice came, and they arrived just in time. Slowly, they picked their way through the shallow waters, praying their hulls remained intact and not ripped to shreds by the jewel-bright coral reefs that glittered below them. Reevan had responded to the Arcane's messages, telling them where to bring their ships, and it was Reevan who greeted them within the tiny cove they docked in.

Reevan waved to them, beckoning, and he looked vaguely surprised when Lessie hugged him. It was brief, and the kitskan's arms hovered awkwardly over her back, but it was as warm a greeting between the two as Mae had ever seen.

Reevan led them through the areas he and Druitt had coordinated for the soldiers. He looked exhausted. There were deep circles under his eyes, visible even through the sandy fur on his face, and he had lost an alarming amount of weight in such a short time. His gaunt face made his eyes appear even larger. Reevan offered no explanation for his appearance, or how he had obtained the information he now shared with them.

He explained how Braak had stationed pockets of his army along the rocky beaches, supplemented with the lower-ranked Arcanes of the Mahejerai. Braak had instructed them to kill anyone who tried to enter the cave systems that separated the beaches from the middle of the island. The caves were housed within cliffs so high it would be insanity to even attempt to scale them, with dense forest growing at their peaks, the snow-capped trees hundreds of feet tall. Nobody had seen what lay at the centre of the island; only that Boras and his inner circle spent much time there.

"What are they doing in there?" asked Lessie. She had peppered Reevan with questions as they disembarked, but the kitskan did not have answers for most of them.

"I have not been privy to the island's central location, Lessandra," Reevan replied, using her full name as he always did, ignoring her flicker of annoyance. "But I have it on good authority that it is where the ritual will occur."

Reevan had been sending information back and forth to Druitt for months, and they discussed their newest plans as the meagre army they had managed to assemble readied themselves upon the shore. As far as plans went, it was a shaky one; Valandaras was to lead a team of Druitt's best men to the cave entrance that led to Boras's last known location. Valandaras would then attempt to bring down the Mahejerai's leader with the Mournblade, which would release the power it had taken from syphoned gods. At first, Reevan had offered to go with Valandaras, citing his superior knowledge of the twisting cave tunnels as the main advantage.

"Perhaps I should wield the Mournblade," Reevan suggested. "I have been observing Boras, and for all intents and purposes, he appears to be mortal, but using that blade might yield more favourable results. I have the better chance of getting closest to him—"

"No," replied Valandaras. His gauntleted hand wrapped possessively around the hilt of the Mournblade even as he gave it a fleeting look of disgust. "A mortal should not wield a Sliver. It would sooner kill you than serve you. I alone have been trained to wield such weapons so that their unpredictable nature cannot affect me."

Reevan shrugged, nonplussed. "It was merely a suggestion."

Reevan's second suggestion was more well-received—that he would accompany Lessie and Mae through the caves to further map Boras's movements while the armies clashed. It was a thinly veiled attempt at keeping the two women away from the bloodshed, and Mae bristled as Valandaras immediately agreed to it. Lessie had been mortally offended at the suggestion, despite the kitskan's praise of her reconnaissance skills. She wanted to fight. Mae felt the same.

This is my battle, too. Perhaps more than anyone.

Eventually, it was settled. Mae would go with Lessie and Reevan, not to avoid battle, but to get closer to the island's centre, in case Daigon came through before Valandaras could slay the Mahejerai leader. Once Valandaras killed Boras, she would have the Mother's power once more, and they could stop the ritual before Daigon set foot upon Kalaraak. If—and only if—Daigon became a threat that couldn't be solved by Valandaras and the Mournblade, then Mae would attempt to harness the power of the phoenix tome. As a last resort.

Mae knew Valandaras would rather die than have her use it. It didn't change the fact that they *had* to keep it in mind. She hadn't told anyone, but she also had a feeling that the Change attempt might kill her before the tome got a chance.

Mae had wanted to kiss Valandaras goodbye, but it had seemed too final. Too dramatic. Like it tempted fate to make something tragic of their story. They had all the time in the world after this. Realmshifters lived incredibly long lives—perhaps even longer than Divines did. For the first time in a very long time, Mae felt unabashedly optimistic about the future. Like she could finally begin to find her old self again, after this was all over. The person she'd promised to be.

Watching Valandaras disappear into the ranks of the soldiers had still planted a tiny seed of fear within her stomach.

Mae and Lessie followed Reevan down the narrow passageway. He chose his path easily, like he had travelled them a hundred times before. The tunnels were a labyrinth. They changed direction multiple times, until Mae could not tell which way they had originally been heading.

"Is Grundle down here?" asked Lessie. "Or did you lose him?"

She squinted in the dim caves, the only light from the small lantern Reevan clutched in his clawed fingers.

"Grundle is where he needs to be," replied Reevan. "And soon we will be, too."

They rounded a corner and came upon a larger cave. It was uneven, split in half by a chasm more than thirty feet deep. It would take them a long time to climb down it and up the other side. Time they didn't have. Lessie eyed the gap doubtfully. Mae felt a pang of longing for her mountain lion form, who could have cleared the jump with feet to spare.

"Reevan," Lessie said through clenched teeth. "I don't know if you know this, but not everybody can jump like you."

"I know, Lessandra," replied Reevan. "I am counting on it."

Mae smiled at their banter. A rock shifting across the cavern caught her attention, and she looked up. The smile on her face froze.

Standing directly across the gap was Ashendi Braak.

The enormous man stood in his general's uniform, eyes glittering cruelly as he regarded them. Behind the massive man stood Grundle, a tiny shadow already forgotten.

"The prodigal son returns," Braak said, sneering down at Reevan. "I'm disappointed it took so long. I was beginning to suspect the Kiveri Czai had lost his touch."

Lessie drew her revolver hesitantly, but faltered as she brought it up.

"What is he talking about?" she asked. "Reevan?"

Reevan did not reply.

Mae was stunned. She had heard the name, of course, they all had. The Kiveri Czai of Kalac— the assassin who murdered Altaea's last High Marshal, the ghost who had terrorised Braak's enemies for near on a decade... Reevan? There had to be some mistake. Even if he were, even if he had, Reevan was their friend. Her friend.

"I don't have time to listen to this prattle," said Braak, waving a meaty hand dismissively. "These caves will all be underwater before long. Bring the Divine and be done with it. Kill the girl if you have to." With that, the Kalac general turned away, dismissing them all without a second thought, like he saw no threat from any of them. Grundle followed along behind him, disappearing into the shadows.

Oh, Mother.

"Tell us it's not true," Mae whispered.

Lessie's eyes were slits; her stare boring into the side of Reevan's head.

"Reevan?" she repeated. Mae could hear the doubt creep into her voice.

Reevan's only reply was to knock Lessie's gun out of her hands with his staff. The revolver clattered to the floor before tipping over the edge into the chasm below. The scream of rage that tore from Lessie's throat echoed in the hollow cavern's walls as she threw herself after it, clutching for it with panicked fingers, cursing as the weapon evaded her and fell to the bottom of the crevasse.

"You... you..." hissed Lessie, speechless with fury. She clenched her fists, dirt scraping, and Mae was suddenly sure that in that moment Lessie would have torn Reevan apart with her bare hands.

Reevan twisted his staff, and the end retracted, revealing a deadly blade. Three feet long and serrated, the wicked point of the glaive he held kept Lessie at arm's length, separating them. She eyed the glaive hatefully, but Mae could see a hint of triumph underneath the rage clouding her features. Lessie had been waiting for it. Waiting for a betrayal, for one of them to let her down, for her unwillingness to trust them to be justified. The vindication in knowing she'd been right warred with the devastation of knowing she'd been right.

"I knew it," Lessie whispered angrily. "Why else would you leave?"

Reevan's tail twitched. His giant emerald eyes were pools of black in the dark passageway. Perhaps it was what Mae wanted to see, but they seemed sad.

"I am sorry for this," he said. Then he grabbed Mae around the waist and leapt twenty feet across the cavern.

Mae's shriek of surprise ripped from her without warning. She didn't have time to panic, even looking down into the abyss below. They cleared the chasm with inches to spare, Mae's hair streaming behind her, rocks and debris clattering down into the drop.

"Reevan!" yelled Lessie from the other side of the chasm. "Godsdamn you."

"Please don't follow us, Lessandra," Reevan called, like a father warning a child against climbing a particularly tall tree. "These caverns are quite confusing. You'd be better off following the trail back and joining Valandaras. Trust me, only someone incredibly skilled at tracking could keep up."

Mae's stomach lurched. Valandaras could be on the other side of the island by now, fighting. How would Lessie make it to him alone? What if she couldn't make it out before it flooded?

A voice in her head whispered that she should probably worry about her own fate, too, but it was easier to fear for Lessie. Mae knew Lessie wouldn't leave the cavern without retrieving her weapon first, and the climb down would cost her precious minutes.

Ashendi Braak shouted from the passage he had already disappeared down. Reevan's ears twitched towards the sound. He was being summoned.

Lessie pointed a finger forcefully over the gap; her hand shaking. The fire in her eyes burned too hot for tears.

"You can't just leave me here in the dark," she said. A note of pleading had edged into her voice, hidden mostly by the dizzying anger. The mother in Mae heard it, and it cut through her chest like a knife.

Mother, you can't leave.

Reevan leaned down, and as he did so, his robes shifted—and for the first time, Mae saw the black cord fastened around his neck. Delicate, interwoven, with a glowing sapphire that pulsed in the centre of his throat. She inhaled sharply.

Reevan did not react to her as he gently placed the lantern on the ground. The shadows that it cast around the cavern threw their faces into stark contrast. It was the kindest thing he could have done, given the situation.

Mae didn't know how to feel about that.

"Farewell, Lessandra," said Reevan. There was no empathy in the goodbye, no soul reflected in the black of his eyes. The emerald had long disappeared in the darkness.

Lessie shrieked in pure frustration.

Mae felt the last spark of hope within her blink out. The numbness rose up like a wave; a comforting blanket wrapping around her and smothering the sorrow and rage that thrashed underneath it. Her fingers curled tighter around the tome of the phoenix, a dead weight in her arms, hugging it to her chest to keep from shattering. They had been through so much, too much, all for it to end up here.

Mae barely struggled when Reevan's soft claws wrapped around her arm and pulled her further into the darkness.

43

VALANDARAS

As the Altaean troops marched along the beaches of Aelmor Island, trudging through sand and bracing themselves against the cold, Valandaras tried to enter the place in his mind he reserved for battle. But where he would usually find peace, he instead found roiling discontent.

Valandaras had fought across many of the realms, and had more horrific memories than he could count. He had seen first-hand the devastation of Antithiia, the shattered realm of the damned, and the eternal war that raged upon it. He had held gasping soldiers as they bled out; had slain grotesque creatures, had killed and almost died in pursuit of his Path many times over. He had seen death in too many forms. Over the course of his long life, he had witnessed things he couldn't bring himself to speak about. By now, he considered himself numb to it.

Seeing an enemy force come into view still made his stomach drop, knowing the unnecessary loss of life that would soon occur. It could be his as much as anyone's. Death did not play favourites. He had to focus.

And yet my head is full of her. At least she is sheltered from this misery.

The island itself, they had quickly discovered, was a place best left uncharted during the winter. Everything about it was unwelcoming. The wind's bitter howling as it dragged salt water across their faces. The patchy rain that fell, churning the ground beneath their feet and soaking through the gaps in their armour into the clothing beneath until a chill settled deep within their bones. The wet sand that lulled them into a false security by giving them more purchase, before it trapped their feet should they linger too long and sink down into it. At one point, the freezing rain fell as snow upon the beaches. Valandaras had never seen such weather upon Kalaraak, but he had not ventured this far north during the winter.

Hopefully our enemy will have little idea of how to handle such conditions, either, he thought grimly. *Being from Kalac cannot possibly be an advantage here.*

The Kalac army that had amassed below the edges of the cliffs milled about nervously. With a practised eye, Valandaras counted around ten companies' worth. A thousand soldiers, give or take. Some of them would be unwilling participants, unable to disobey the orders given by the one who had fastened the collars around their necks. Most of them looked agitated, like they were itching for the fight to begin, to finally have something to do to warm their bones upon the freezing sands.

As he watched the tense soldiers, one thing became clear—there was a distinct lack of Arcane. There were no purple Mahejerai robes, no sparks of the Weave that Boras had promised to Braak's army. Not even the tell-tale sign of a Divine's healing glittered. As far as Valandaras could tell, there was no magic among this group of Kalac soldiers at all.

That alone should have warned Valandaras that something was amiss.

Druitt's men had marched around almost half of the island, and Valandaras knew that they were tired and stiff from days at sea. Valiantly, they wore it as well as they could, but at least some of them were regretting volunteering for this assignment. Valandaras was a source of cautious inspiration for them, since some of these soldiers had fought with him at Crossroad, so he made a show of standing tall and unafraid. He settled into a casual offensive stance, readying his body for the attack. The posturing worked, and many of the men imitated him, shaking off their own nerves. Outwardly, Valandaras was ready for the battle.

His mind, however, was not on the fight in front of him.

He could not recall a time where he had been more distracted. Even the pull of his Path tugged back the way he had come, but he buried it in the back of his thoughts. Mae would be safe with Lessie and Reevan. They were already sequestered away within a cavern, to emerge only once the fighting had stopped and the ritual halted.

Valandaras had not expected Mae to agree to it, but he was glad. He had to focus on taking Oorata Boras down. Mae would know when he had succeeded, because the Mother's essence would be freed from the Mahejerai. She would be able to join the fight when she had control of her Gifts. It was risky, but it was better to keep her away from the ritual in case she tried to stop it herself.

The last time I told her to stay out of a fight, we all nearly died. I know better than to try and forbid her from helping altogether.

The last few days had been like living inside a dream—one where he did not have a lifetime of searching stretched out ahead, or only a vengeful god to answer to. Valandaras knew reality would soon come crashing down around them, and he was determined to defeat it. Rest on the ship for him had been practically non-existent. He had fashioned a thousand escapes for his predicament in the haunting hours between midnight and dawn; with Mae curled beside him on the tiny cot and sleep eluding him in favour of watching her back gently rise and fall with her steady breaths.

He could not abandon his Path for her. That was simple. Realmshifters had to serve a god. It was written into their very being, when they were chosen. Valandaras was bound by his duties to Haropheth to follow the Path, to find the Betrayer. Logically, he knew he must have been pulled to Mae in order to find the Mournblade, to complete his search.

But the pull of the Path had lingered even after discovering the Sliver. It had to be something else, something to do with Mae herself, or the Gift she possessed.

Valandaras had changed his mind with every sway of the waves. Every imagined solution seemed more ludicrous than the last. He could take the Mournblade to his Pod, gift it to another Realmshifter, and have them return him to Kalaraak. He could explain the pull of his Path. Request council of Elastrad, his Pod's leader, confide in her his suspicions. He could denounce his god altogether and refuse to serve any longer. Beg they strip his abilities from him. Become as mortal as any other man.

It was a precarious line of thinking. He didn't know if being a Realmshifter was something that could be taken away. Nobody had ever done it. His Pod could attack him for even suggesting it, or worse, execute him for treason or blasphemy. Haropheth himself could strike him down.

But if they didn't, then Valandaras could be free. A taste of a truly normal life, so foreign in concept and even harder to picture in practice, could now be within his reach. He and Mae had not talked much of what they would do after—when the battle was over and the Mother's essence had been restored—but Mae had made it clear that she intended to go where he went. Valandaras couldn't begin to think of what he'd do if he lost her now.

The biting wind brought clarity. Valandaras shook himself. He had to kill Oorata Boras, first. One problem at a time.

Druitt DeFalcone stood beside him, in well-worn leathers and a heavy breastplate. He no longer wielded the blade with the unique wing-tipped cross guard, but a standard issue sword. Despite its simplicity, it was well cared for, and shined even in the dull light obscured by the thickly clouded skies. The message behind it was clear. Druitt had officially rejected his heritage, and stood beside his men as an equal. Only his military rank mattered.

Valandaras drew his falchion, letting the familiar curve of the seasoned blade and the feel of the hilt between his fingers calm him. His heavy shield, the lion's mouth frozen in an eternal roar, hung over his arm. His weapons were simple, too. He would not use the Mournblade unless he had to, but he had unwrapped the Sliver from the heavy cloak that deadened its hum and strapped it to his back. Ready for the Mahejerai's leader, but no other. It would be unjust to wield such a weapon against an ordinary soldier.

"This is not going to be pretty," Druitt muttered, grey eyes narrowing against the glare of the suns on the white sand. It occasionally cut through the dreary clouds, adding yet another obstacle to their fight.

Valandaras stared through the enemy lines to the cave entrance behind them. Reevan had said that Oorata was working within, putting the finishing touches on a ritual that would bring about the destruction of their realm. He had also advised that there would be little opposition around the island until they reached this point. So far, his intel had been correct; the troops had spotted only scouts and the occasional clifftop archer who tracked but did not loose.

"Give me as much time as you can," Valandaras replied, and Druitt nodded grimly.

The plan was simple. Druitt's men were to keep the enemy occupied, while Valandaras barrelled straight through them to confront Boras inside. Hopefully, they could hold their own until the Mahejerai's death turned the tides in their favour.

The captain made the call to advance, and the first of their soldiers edged forward with caution. Braak's army did not respond. Perhaps they couldn't without their master present. There was no sign of Ashendi Braak among them, and it showed. There were no discernible officers, no order to the men—they mingled archer and infantrymen like they cared little for the formations they would have been taught. Despite what Valandaras had learned of Braak's prowess as a general, his army barely resembled an army at all.

That should have seemed strange, too.

Druitt gave the order to charge, and the first wave of the Altaean soldiers surged forward. Valandaras felt the wrongness of the moment pass through him like a shiver. Their enemy readied their weapons, holding their positions. The hair on the back of his neck stood up.

The air above the sand rippled.

A warning died in Valandaras's throat as the front line of Altaean soldiers stepped past an invisible line in the sand and evaporated into red mist.

No noise.

They didn't even fall.

They died running, obliterated into matter within seconds. A hundred men's souls sent straight to the Silver Stream at once.

Chaos erupted.

Druitt's soldiers halted, shouts of dismay and fear flooding through them. The enemy force of slave soldiers flickered like a disturbed reflection, then disappeared altogether.

Instead of a thousand men, ten cloaked figures now stood between them and the cave. The closest ones wore intricately patterned robes, and their faces were passive, devoid of any emotion. One had collapsed; his energy spent by keeping the illusion intact for so long. Another seemed to have misted along with the Altaean soldiers, a light splatter of crimson the only evidence they had existed.

"Fall back," Druitt screamed, trying to restore order.

The Altaeans were panicked. The front lines were blinking blood out of their eyes; drenched in what was left of their fallen comrades. They broke ranks, scattering, shoving one another in desperate attempts to flee the Arcane ones before them. Immediate retreat seemed their only option.

The nearest Mahejerai smiled wickedly and raised his arms skyward. A second shimmer caught Valandaras's eye.

"Stop!" he shouted to Druitt. "It's a trap!"

Genuine fear gripped the captain's face, and he shouted for the men to halt. Valandaras shoved to the front, expecting another misting, but he instead found their soldiers paused in their retreat, skittish and snapping at each other like cornered animals. A second Arcane collapsed altogether, and the air around the beach shifted, bending the light around them oddly and making Valandaras's stomach lurch.

Braak's army *was* there.

The Altaeans had marched straight past them.

The soldiers bearing the crest of chains had been cloaked beneath an Arcane illusion. Jewels of obedience glittered at their throats. They stood in perfect, uniformed tactical formations. They rose from the icy waves of the water. They pulled away from the shadows underneath the unscalable cliffs. Swords were unsheathed, arrows were nocked. Twice as many as had been reported.

The Altaean army, already terrified of the Arcanes behind them, had nowhere to go.

It was not a battle. It was a slaughter.

They fought for what felt like hours. Braak's army had freshness and fervour; they were well-rested and faced fates worse than death should they not deliver. The Altaeans were outmatched and outnumbered, though the majority still faced their deaths bravely. Swords and polearms clashed, arrows loosed, and all around men died screaming. The Mahejerai spread out and manipulated the Weave from the edges of the battle. Balls of Arcane fire fell upon soldiers, Altaean and Kalac alike, and violet flame seared through steel armour to flesh below. Terrified screams pierced the air as burning men discovered seawater did nothing to quench the fire's thirst.

Bodies began to pile along the shoreline.

Valandaras swung blindly through the masses as he made his way back towards the caves. He couldn't stop to help others. He had to disable the Arcane ones, or they were all dead. He lost Druitt almost immediately. The captain was trying desperately to keep his men motivated, in between fending off the enemies trying to swarm him. Only Druitt's lifetime of military training kept him alive, but the odds of any of them surviving were dropping drastically as each second ticked by. Valandaras wanted to stay, to fight beside him, but he pressed on.

Valandaras killed his way towards the caves. The Mahejerai standing at the entrance watched him coming, unconcerned. Smirking like predators; wildcats waiting for an exhausted mouse to move within their reach. The closest Arcane smiled and sent a ball of energy crackling towards him from forty feet away.

Valandaras threw up his shield. The steel heated as it absorbed the impact, searing the flesh on his forearm. He cursed and dropped the shield, ripping feverishly at buckles on the metal vambrace below.

His strange healing light, still devoted to repairing the very last of his injury from Ignatia, rushed to his aid and replaced the angry red on his arm with the bright pink of new skin. A jolt of pain shot through his leg and his step faltered. Flame licked across his shield, the metal misshapen and dented, and the engraved lion's roar upon it now resembled a defiant scream of pain. His discarded armour piece had burned so hot it had melted into the sand.

He had to keep going. She needed him to. Valandaras wrapped both gauntleted hands around the hilt of his falchion and left his shield embedded in the blood-soaked sand.

He approached the Arcanes warily, goosebumps rising on his exposed arm. Instincts roaring, drowning out the army at his back. This was the bigger threat.

"Weren't we supposed to leave that one alone?" one of the Mahejerai commented mildly.

The human woman who had sent the ball of energy only grinned wider, lightning crackling between her fingertips. Valandaras dodged her next attack, throwing himself to the side at the last second, sand sticking to the freezing rain soaked through his cloth.

"It's just a man," she hissed. "Look at his mundane steel. Watch how it crumbles."

She began to chant in an unfamiliar tongue, and two others picked up her words, amplifying the sound. This time, Valandaras couldn't dodge the lightning that reached for him, but it stopped just short and snapped to the blade of his falchion like moths to a flame.

Veins spread across the metal. A sizzling sound popped in his ears.

Another of the Mahejerai lunged for him. A sword of violet light formed in the Arcane's hands, and Valandaras acted instinctively as the phantom blade swung towards his head. He blocked with his falchion and felt the blade crack. As the Arcane pushed down, the steel of Valandaras's sword began to splinter. Pieces of the falchion chipped off and broke away. It was as if the cracks of light had shattered it from the inside. One tiny piece of the steel embedded itself in his cheek, and a trickle of blood join the freezing rain already streaming down his face.

Valandaras pushed, straining, and managed to throw the Mahejerai off-balance. The Arcane was not a swordsman, and he went sprawling into the sand. The Mahejerai woman snickered. They held no care for their brethren.

"The kitskan scum did warn us against it," said the male Mahejerai, spitting sand from his mouth and dusting off his robes. "He said that we would fall against the Realmshifter. I think he was trying to save all of the glory for himself."

Valandaras steadied himself.

One look at his falchion told him the blade was useless. Another hit and it would shatter completely. He slowly backed away, sheathing it, feeling the fragile metal bend and creak as it slid into its scabbard. He should find Druitt, fight their way back to the others. At least it sounded as if Reevan had tried to get the Arcanes to avoid him.

But if Reevan warned the Mahejerai not to engage me, then why would he not tell us they would be here with this army?

"This one will die as all mundane men do," the Arcane woman said, somehow still audible over the din of battle, spitting her words like slurs. "Will you bleed light, Realmshifter? Like the other one did?"

They had killed a Realmshifter. Within Valandaras, the anger of his god roiled. Haropheth was furious that one of his chosen had fallen. Valandaras struggled to stay in the moment, to keep the foreign rage contained.

The Mahejerai woman advanced on him, grinning, more violet energy beginning to spark between her fingertips. There was a casual cruelty to her words that most soldiers lacked, absent even from the Mahejerai around her. She wanted him to suffer.

"Will your pretty Divine bleed green?" she asked him, malice glittering in her eyes.

The Arcane man laughed.

Valandaras stilled.

There was only one reason they would know to taunt him about Mae. They were still after her. They knew she was important to him. The fight around him, the needless death and destruction—it had been a ploy to separate them. To keep them apart. So he wouldn't be there to protect her.

And he had readily agreed to it, like a fool.

Valandaras swayed, the realisation threatening to bring him to his knees.

Have I sent them to their deaths?

A pulse from the centre of the island rang out like a shockwave, and the Arcanes were knocked to the ground. Valandaras barely caught himself. The battle behind him reached a crescendo of chaos. Even more men screamed. Arcanes threw power with abandon, frying the slave army fighters as much as the Altaeans.

"The ritual is complete," one of the Mahejerai called, seemingly to his companions, but it was Valandaras he stared at for a reaction. The pulse had thrown him closer, and he laughed manically as he dragged himself back to his feet. "The Master will soon ascend."

For a moment, Valandaras felt despair wash over him. They were too late. Was Mae gone? Had he lost her?

A flicker of his golden healing pulsed in his palms as if in answer. Mae was not dead. He would know if she was.

And so he would go to her.

A cold, calm sense of purpose settled within his bones. It was not Haropheth's anger that ignited inside him, foreign, to be struggled against and pushed down. The fury was purely his own. He let it sink in, course through his veins. He accepted it, welcomed it. It was how he was *supposed* to feel. This rage was all encompassing, righteous, and he would not ignore it. He would embrace it.

The Arcanes around him smiled like sharks, descending upon him, crackling energy bouncing between them as they eagerly muttered incantations.

Valandaras reached a steadily glowing hand behind him and slowly unsheathed the Mournblade. The black blade's hum became audible, even among the frightened shouts of soldiers and the distant rumbling of the ritual.

The Mahejerai woman scoffed and hurled her spiderweb lightning towards him again. Lazily. Like she expected the blade to crumble as his falchion had. It was a fair assumption.

Valandaras did not try to block the attack. Instead, he raised the Mournblade, and the jagged obsidian blade flickered ominously as he poured his realmlight into it.

The Arcane lightning hit the Mournblade and fizzled out. The blade absorbed the energy into itself and took on a curious, dark glow.

Valandaras had felt it when using the Mournblade to realmshift. Perhaps the moment he had first held it in his hands. It was a Sliver, made by the gods. It was designed to absorb Divinity, to act as a conduit for a god's power.

Arcane energy—and realmlight—were no different. He could imbibe it himself.

The nearest Arcane conjured his phantom sword again and swung at him, still sneering. Valandaras twisted upwards and met the strike. The sword hit the Mournblade and disintegrated mid-air, turning to nothing but violet mist in the Mahejerai's hands. He sputtered in disbelief, arms flailing, losing balance.

The killing calm settled over Valandaras.

Today, he was Death's deliverer.

The Arcane looked at Valandaras with hatred burning in his eyes, and more violet energy started to crackle within his fingertips. The beginnings of a new sword began to form, and he lunged.

Valandaras cut downwards and sheared the Arcane in half.

Pieces of the fallen Mahejerai's body slumped silently onto the sand, smoking faintly. The Mournblade took on an eerie violet edge to its dark radiance, illuminating Valandaras's face and pulsing in time with the rage that coursed through him. His mind was clear.

The other Mahejerai paused. The Arcane woman took an uneasy step back. The confident look on her face faltered.

Valandaras unleashed himself upon the Mahejerai.

44

REEVAN

Reevan knew the path to the centre of the island with his eyes closed by now, so he led the way.

Ashendi Braak had taken custody of Mae the second they cleared the last cave. With little difficulty, he twisted Mae's arms and bound them behind her back, though at first she had put up an admirable fight. Braak's shin must have been sporting a decent-sized bruise by now. She had only fallen silent once he threatened to deliver her to Boras in pieces. The small book she carried tumbled into the dirt during the scuffle, and Reevan picked it up gingerly at his master's behest.

Reevan knew Braak wanted to be the one to present Mae to Boras, though his master was terrified of anyone who wielded Divine or Arcane gifts. Reevan didn't roll his eyes, but he did exchange a quick glance with Grundle, whose face had not shown a single emotion for days. The goblin had not left Braak's left side since he had joined Reevan on Aelmor, and was showing signs he had regressed quite badly. Grundle barely spoke and obeyed every order without question. Reevan had found himself almost missing the goblin's odd attempts at conversation. Reevan couldn't blame Grundle for the regression, though. They had both been under Braak's ownership for their whole lives. It had been easy to fall into old patterns. Being on their own had been strange.

Reevan wondered if he had made the path complicated enough that Lessie could not follow; that the girl would see chasing them into the labyrinth as pointless. There was no doubt in his mind that she would attempt to climb into the crevasse and retrieve her weapon. She would then do one of two things—either retreat to Druitt and Valandaras for assistance, or track them down to try to rescue Mae and seek revenge upon him. Reevan was mildly interested to see which choice she would make.

The final cave passage opened onto a bluff that overlooked the central lake of Aelmor. In the midst of deep winter, it had frozen over, and the frigid winds coming off the ice seemed to blow right through Reevan's fur into his bones. It was a flat, empty space, devoid of the beautiful plant life that ringed the inner lake or the pebbly beaches that covered the outer shores. It served only as a stage for the horror they were about to witness.

Standing on the edge of the bluff, gazing into the horizon, stood Oorata Boras.

"Ah, you've arrived," he said, raising his arms as if in warm greeting, despite the coldness in his eyes. The wide sleeves of his ceremonial Mahejerai robes billowed in the biting wind. "I was beginning to think you were having trouble delivering, Ashendi."

Reevan's master bristled, and he shoved Mae forwards roughly. Reevan and Grundle remained where they were, to await further instruction. Obedient. Silent.

"I brought you your army, and now I send my finest to fetch for you like a dog," Braak snarled. "I'm done doing your bidding, Arcane."

Boras smiled, a shark's smile that matched his hideous mask.

"And yet, you still failed to retrieve my blade," he said coolly.

Braak fell silent, seething, and Boras turned his attention to Mae.

"I've been dying to properly meet you, Divine," he said, eyes glittering with malice. "I've heard so much about you. Ones like you have always been of... *special interest* to me. Your god's power has been most helpful in achieving my goals."

Boras raised an arm that sparked with a familiar emerald glow. It was harder somehow, less natural, but it was recognisable enough. Silent tears began to stream down Mae's face.

"And yet I sense this power is... incomplete," he said, irritation clouding his features. "And it is because of your belief. Faith that strong becomes a living thing—it might as well be a part of the god themselves. There is a piece of them that you hold inside of you."

Boras regarded Mae curiously. "Of course, I have successfully drained that from others before, but you managed to evade me. That has made it... challenging to wield the gifts. You have irritated me to no end, Divine."

Mae said nothing, but behind the terror, pride burned in her heated cheeks and set jaw. Reevan thought it was the clearest compliment the Mahejerai could hope to give her. Oorata Boras was obviously annoyed by

Mae's clear connection to the Mother, but also oddly impressed. Perhaps even jealous.

It also explained the corpse of the Divine beneath the Mahejerai's temple. Reevan hoped that not all drainings were quite that literal.

"Braak's lapcat tells me that you shifted realms to try to get your power back," Boras mused. Reevan bristled before he could catch it. From the mouth of the Mahejerai, calling him a cat was a grave insult. "An admirable feat. I suppose when your own is not enough, using the power of those around you is the next best thing. We are more alike than you would think. I used a Realmshifter once, too, to first invite my guest to this realm. I found they lacked the... control I needed. Their power is not easily taken, either. It was disappointing."

Boras's tone did not leave much hope for the fate of that Realmshifter. Reevan wondered how hard it had been for Boras to kill them, since Valandaras was sure to come looking for Mae before long, and he was sure to be violent beyond belief once he learned of the Mahejerai's plans for her.

"But no matter," said Boras, gesturing out to the lake. "Like the Realmshifters would say, I have found another... Path."

Reevan watched Mae's eyes follow Boras's outstretched hand and come to the same uneasy conclusion he had when he had first beheld the sight. She even stopped struggling for a moment and stared, wide eyed in wonder.

The Mahejerai had found another god tree. But this one was different.

The god tree at the centre of Aelmor's frozen lake made the one that had housed the Mother's essence look like a sapling. The gargantuan trunk must have been fifty feet wide; branches thicker than bodies stretching across the sky, casting shadows upon the icy water. The island that it stood upon was tiny in comparison, the land completely swallowed by the oak's roots, giving the impression that the god tree rose directly from the ice itself. The water that still flowed underneath the frozen surface was so calm and clear that the bottom of the lake was visible despite its depth, and the roots of the god tree spread out like tentacles before disappearing into the soil below.

A ring of Mahejerai hovered in the air around the god tree, each grasping a silver spike and holding it aloft. Midnight blue strands of Arcane energy glittered both around them and within the god tree itself, like they were channelling all of their power into it. The beam of light grew steadily brighter as it jumped from one Arcane to the next, searching for the spike they held like anchors for the energy. Each Arcane looked exhausted, faces contorting in pain at the continual strain of holding themselves aloft while the energy coursed through their bodies.

There were no grounded spikes to unearth this time, no reachable element to interrupt. The Mahejerai were not taking any chances.

"The Oaken Eternal..." Mae whispered in awe.

Reevan knew it had something to do with how she and Valandaras had returned to Kalaraak, but surely they would have noticed if the path had led to here. It would have saved them quite a lot of time.

"I will deal with you after," said Boras to Mae, turning his back to them. "First, I have a ritual to complete."

Boras raised his arms skyward and sent his own deep blue energy spiralling towards the circle. It reminded Reevan of the glow behind Valandaras's eyes, though different in hue, and he wondered if the power the Mahejerai now threw towards the god tree once belonged to the Realmshifter who had met a violent end at Boras's hands. The Arcanes began to chant, eerily in unison, in a language Reevan didn't know.

When the energy had finished arcing through each Arcane's spike, it filled the entire god tree with a murky blue radiance. Still they continued, voices mingling and rising louder, chaotic in their delivery. Instead of continuing upwards, disappearing into the clouds, the light from the Arcanes seeped down into the water. A great creaking joined the humming of the energy.

The chanting grew more fervent, the power brighter.

"It is high time," Boras intoned, "that my guest be allowed passage into this realm, so that he can grant me what is mine."

There was a deafening crack, and the great god tree split in half like it had been struck by lightning.

The ice around it shattered, arcing outwards like spiderwebs, tiny cracks splintering the surface. A column of sapphire light shot into the sky, connecting the god tree to the clouds above, sizzling audibly even from a distance. Inky blue energy trickled into the ground upon the god tree's platform and disappeared into the frozen water beneath it.

Like the god tree itself was the portal. Like it had been the path all along.

The ground beneath them shook, sending small rocks careening into the icy water below the cliff's face. Mae whimpered. Braak increased his grip on her arms, wrenching them tighter behind her back. Reevan frowned. There was no need for that. Mae was unarmed, her hands were bound, and she had merely a trickle of her true power. But Arcane power and

Divinity had always made his master uneasy. Ashendi Braak was afraid of the Weave. Reevan was still surprised that Braak had aligned himself with the Mahejerai in the first place. It was one reason Reevan and Grundle had been favoured, but also why they had remained deliberately uneducated in Arcane dealings.

"Finally," said Boras. The rumbling stopped. For a moment, there was only peace. It was almost beautiful.

Then, one by one, the Arcanes exploded.

Flesh dissolved into red mist as their essence, their very selves, gave over to the power of the ritual. Reevan could still picture the terrified face of the Arcane who had given his life to syphon the Mother. If only one Arcane life had been needed then, this ritual would surely destroy the entire tree and any god that it currently housed. The energy the Arcane's bodies had held coalesced upon the behemoth oak's broken trunk, and the light spilling forth from the hole was interrupted by a shadow.

The head of a hideous, gargantuan sea creature emerged from the hole in the god tree's split trunk.

It looked eerily close to the statue Reevan had come across in the bowels of the Mahejerai temple, except magnified a hundred times over. The maw of this beast alone could have swallowed them all whole. He had a sharp, elongated face, and tendrils of dark blue energy floated around him, as if one of the fabled dragons of old had rotted and bloated at the bottom of the deepest ocean.

Daigon, god of darkened depths and the terror of Keanos, took his first breath upon the realm of Kalaraak.

He smiled wickedly, revealing yellow teeth longer than the blade of Reevan's glaive. A giant clawed foot hooked around the remains of the god tree, and Daigon wrenched more of his elongated body through the portal. His overlapping scales shone like sapphire armour, catching in the cracks of light from the suns as he moved. Some seemed to have their own luminescence, like they were his light source in his usual dwelling. Many of them were marred, with massive scars rippling over parts of the god's body, long-healed and ancient but brutal in their size and depth. Reevan wondered what could possibly exist in the waters of Keanos to have caused that kind of damage to its only god, but he supposed that whatever it was, Daigon had defeated them.

Daigon's eyes were yellow and pupilless, but Reevan still felt their direction change as the god lifted his massive head and regarded them all upon the bluff. He towered over them, even without his full bulk through the portal.

"I have been waiting too long for this," Daigon purred. The strange overlapping tone that all god's voices seemed to have made his baritone even more sinister, like it came from two places at once. "You have angered me, young one, by taking this long."

Reevan sniffed in amusement as Oorata Boras's whole body stiffened in irritation. Clearly, the Mahejerai did not consider himself young. But to an immortal, perhaps they all were.

"Welcome, great one, Daigon, ruler of darkened depths," said Boras, voice projected across the frozen waters by his Arcane prowess. Strands of emerald, midnight blue, and amethyst raced along his body as he spoke, stolen Divinity mingling with his own Arcane gifts. "You will have your chaos. First, grant me what you promised. The Mantle of the Weave itself, that lies unclaimed across our seven realms. I have proven myself a master of its arts. Share your godly essence to give me this, and I will grant you the souls you seek."

Daigon barely glanced their way. The leviathan uncoiled his long body, propelling him high enough to see over even the highest cliffs. He seemed to have noticed the army of slaves, currently locked in combat with Druitt's army. Daigon's deep inhale was clear. He had scented blood.

"After I... feed," he said, laughing cruelly, deep voice rumbling across the land and rippling chunks of ice in the water around him. He turned away and ignored them completely.

Boras's eyes hardened under the mask.

"Braak," he said evenly, keeping his eyes on Daigon. "It is time. Have the Divine killed."

Braak pulled Mae towards the edge of the cliff, cursing under his breath as she struggled against him.

"No," said Mae. "No, you can't—"

Braak shoved her, hard, and she went sprawling into the dirt at Boras's feet. Reevan gripped the handle of his glaive so tightly he could see the skin beneath his fur.

"It is a shame," Boras said. "You would have made an interesting member of my order."

Braak pulled the silver shortsword from his scabbard, beady eyes alight with the promise of violence. Reevan felt Grundle's long fingers grasp his wrist beneath his robes.

"No, Ashendi," said Boras, without looking at them. He sounded irritated, like he was sick of having to give all the orders. "Have the Kiveri Czai do it. Prove his loyalty. He has been out of action for so long, after all."

Reevan, thankfully, held his eye roll. The Kiveri Czai. He had always hated the moniker. Braak had started the talk, believing the fear of an assassin to have as much to do with reputation as it did the deaths he delivered. He had been spreading rumours of Reevan's deadliness for years before he even stained his first blade red. Translated to the common tongue, it meant something along the lines of 'Bringer of Fanged Death', which made no sense. Braak had butchered Reevan's native language, just as he had obliterated Reevan's own knowledge of his kitskan heritage.

It had been effective, though. People were terrified of the Kiveri Czai.

Braak bristled. "We agreed that we would not give each other orders, *Oorata*," he hissed, before clicking his fingers towards Reevan. "Finish it."

"Do you have any preferences as to the method, master?" Reevan drawled, with the air of one supremely bored with his latest assignment. He resisted the urge to scratch at his collar.

"Just kill her, slave," ordered Boras dismissively. "With the last spark of the Divine released, I will have the Divinity required to bend Daigon to my will."

He turned back to the insane god he had summoned, who was finished ripping the last of his enormous body through the portal of the god tree and now advanced upon the warring armies on the other side of the cliffs. Once again, Oorata spoke before his master could answer, and the rage that simmered in Braak's eyes reached dangerous levels. He gestured to Reevan angrily, impatiently. *Get it done*, the unspoken order said.

Reevan stalked towards them and raised his glaive high. He spun the pole a few times with a flourish, just for show. His master had always preferred dramatic assassinations, and this would be no different.

Mae struggled to get up, her bound hands impeding her ability to move, but still she fought with fire. It was commendable, but she needed to be careful, or her thrashing would send her and Boras both off the edge of the cliff. Reevan's emerald eyes met hers, and he saw the fear within them, and he knew that she was unnerved by the lack of emotion upon his own face as he raised his glaive above her. It was the way it had to be. He couldn't say it now, of course, but he had quite liked Miss Mae.

Death didn't comment. It just did what had to be done.

"It is time for the power to return where it belongs," Boras intoned, raising his arms to the sky as if in prayer, ready to receive the final spark of the Mother's stolen Divinity and take his place among the gods.

Mae exhaled deeply and squeezed her eyes shut.

"I completely agree," said the Kiveri Czai.

In one swift arc, Reevan brought the silver blade upwards. Then there was nothing but the sickening sound of the glaive's serrated edge tearing through clothing and flesh.

Blood spattered onto the hard rock.

Grundle inhaled sharply, the first sound he'd made in days.

Mae's eyes flew open.

Oorata Boras crumpled to the ground behind her.

Reevan had moved too quickly for the Mahejerai to react, and there had been no defensive manoeuvrer, no bracing, no flinch. The perfect slash of the impossibly sharp blade had ripped straight through Boras's robes and into the flesh on his back, exposing his spine, soaking through the purple with the burgundy of his blood. He sank to his knees, breath coming in quick gasps, mouth opening and closing like a fish, eyes wide in disbelief.

It was the Kiveri Czai's most dramatic assassination yet.

Time seemed to slow. Reevan watched with mild fascination as strands of glittering emerald and midnight blue poured from Boras's body. Sparks of stolen Divinity, returning to the gods to whom they belonged, perhaps. The blue dissipated quickly, shimmering like starlight before fading from view, but most of the emerald remained, hovering over Mae.

Reevan sighed in relief as the emerald sparks sank into Mae's body, where they were supposed to be. He didn't really understand how these things worked, but he had hoped. He would never have gotten close enough to Boras without delivering Mae. It would have been better if he'd managed to kill the Mahejerai before the ritual completed, but it was better than nothing. He'd been delicately balancing the act since he'd arrived. It was a complicated dance, and he had missed a few steps.

Mae struggled to sit up, trying to pull her body away from the person rapidly bleeding out before her. Reevan angled the blade of his glaive with surprising precision and severed the bonds that held Mae's hands behind her back. The small act cost Reevan his freedom. Ashendi Braak's giant arms closed around his chest.

Mae rubbed her wrists. "Why?" she asked.

Reevan could barely hear her over the enraged shouts of his master, but he saw it. Mae let out a gasp of pure shock as the Mother's Gift returned to her. The emerald glittered brighter than ever, healing her cuts and scrapes like they were nothing.

Struggling against Braak's grip, Reevan pulled the phoenix tome from beneath his robes. It fell at her feet.

"I believe you said you needed the Mother's power back in order to Change, Miss Mae," said Reevan.

Mae's eyes began to glow.

45

LESSIE

Lessie knew she'd go after Reevan before the tip of his traitorous tail had finished disappearing into the darkness.

She hauled herself up over the side of the crevasse just in time to catch the lantern before it burned out. Cursing, she wiped her brow, which was slick with sweat despite the chill in the caverns. The climb up had been less hazardous than the descent, but the effort to yank herself over the edge forced her to wait while she caught her breath. She pulled out her revolver and inspected it, righteous anger coursing through her.

'Trust him'. *How dare he*.

Lessie stared into the dying fire of the lantern, weighing up her choices. The smart thing to do would be to go back. To go for help, now that she'd retrieved her revolver, which thankfully had not been damaged when it fell into the crevasse. To find Valandaras, or Druitt, and figure out a course of action that involved showing up to rescue Mae with an army at her back. To strategize, to plan.

But Lessie was done planning. There was no time. And she now had a visceral need for revenge against not one, but two souls on the island.

The caverns were mostly rock, which was unhelpful for tracking, and likely why Reevan had assumed she would be unable to follow them. Squinting in the dim light, Lessie found signs of a scuffle, where Mae had obviously tried to evade capture. From there, tiny signs lit up like candles, showing her the way. A drag in the dirt here, a patch of flattened moss there. A regular person would have missed them, but to Lessie, they might as well have been pointed arrowheads leading her out.

Lessie wasn't a regular person. She'd grown up tracking demons through the Maw. Reevan had sorely underestimated her.

Precious minutes ticked past, and Lessie picked her way through the labyrinth of tunnels within the unscalable cliffs, using the smallest traces of the trail to guide her. Before long, the echoing shouts and screaming led her to the bluff.

Lessie exited the caves and found chaos.

Oorata Boras, broken and bleeding and leaking some sort of Divine energy, was crawling back from the cliff side. A trail of blood marked the small distance he had managed to drag himself. The man had minutes to live, if not seconds. He glanced up at her briefly, hatred plain on his bloodless face, before he collapsed. Lessie stared at him, transfixed, disappointment and satisfaction warring within her.

Looks like somebody already got to him, at least.

There was a bright flash of light from behind the dying Mahejerai. Mae, unbound and alive, stood at the cliff's edge, her body flooded with the Mother's essence. Somehow, she had done it—the power of her god had been released. Head thrown back in ecstasy, green sparks washing over her skin, fingertips still clutched around the firebird's tome.

Eyes glowing with raw energy, Mae exhaled deeply and smiled. Then she dropped the book and Changed. Her human body shifted and bubbled, losing form. The Change, usually emerald and familiar, sparked a gold so bright it was almost white, and Lessie threw a hand over her face to keep her eyes from being branded.

Mae became a being of pure light.

She lifted her arms and feathers emerged, sparking with fire as they became wings. Her body grew, shifting and twisting, and she launched herself off the bluff. For an agonising second Mae disappeared over the edge, and Lessie screamed, but the sound of beating wings became deafening and an answering shriek pierced the air.

Mae arose. She had Changed.

Shimmering fire radiated off her. Tiny ember sparks and tendrils of grey smoke poured from her feathers. There was no record of this creature in living memory, but Lessie recognised it instantly. The firebird from the temple. The form of the phoenix. Mae had harnessed its power.

Mae's phoenix form flew skyward, a plume of fire following her ascent, before nose-diving towards Daigon.

Lessie stared after the firebird in awe, before the scuffle in front of her drew her attention back to the ground.

Ashendi Braak had pinned Reevan down. Both his hands were wrapped around the kitskan's throat, the muscles in his powerful arms rippling. The enormous man was furious, rage overflowing as he pressed downward, cutting off Reevan's air. Reevan struggled, trying to get his legs underneath to kick Braak off, but the general's armour and positioning made it impossible to find purchase. Reevan's glaive lay uselessly in the dirt behind them.

Lessie's knuckles tightened around the handle of her gun. Reevan had failed to keep Mae contained, and now his master was punishing him for it. That was it. He had double-crossed them, and was now paying for it. It was what should happen.

Her hands still shook as she levelled the revolver at him.

Traitor or not, Reevan doesn't deserve to die like this.

"After all I've done for you," Braak roared. "Took you in, raised you like a son, taught you skills the mewling masses could never dream of, made you the infamous Kiveri Czai of Kalac—this is how you repay me. That band of misfits won't even mourn your pitiful death."

Braak clutched at the collar around Reevan's neck and pulled, and there was a horrible keening noise as the rope snapped. Reevan screamed in pain as the collar came away, ripping inner barbs from his flesh—the entire cord had been embedded in his skin. Braak tossed it aside and laughed. The jewel shattered on the rocks.

"I don't know how you did it, but if the collar didn't kill you, I will," Braak sneered. "Were your pathetic little friends worth it?"

Lessie stilled.

Reevan had been working against them. He had sold Mae out and given her to Boras. He had been doing it on Braak's orders. He had left her in a cave to die.

Reevan had betrayed her.

Hadn't he?

Her heart lurched. *What if he didn't? What if I don't have to hate him?*

Slowly, carefully, Lessie brought her revolver up. Braak didn't even notice her. He was too focused on seeing the light leave Reevan's eyes. She had half-pressed down on the trigger when she caught a glimpse of movement behind them.

"You... forget..." Reevan wheezed as Braak's hands pressed down upon his windpipe.

"What, slave? What did I forget?" snarled Braak, rage clouding his senses, yanking Reevan's face toward him until their noses touched. "How much of a snivelling traitor you are?"

Reevan tried to speak again, but couldn't get the words out. Sensing a trap, Braak eased his pressure only slightly—not enough for Reevan to wiggle free, but enough for him to speak. He slammed Reevan's body further into the packed earth.

"*What* did I forget?" Braak growled, repeating his question viciously.

"The same thing everyone forgets," Reevan rasped, still scrabbling at Braak's hands with his free claw, trying to pry himself free. "That of all the slaves you made into killers, the Kiveri Czai was not the deadliest."

Ashendi Braak's confused expression froze upon his face as a tiny, blackened dagger lodged to the hilt in the side of his neck.

Grundle looked terrified as he ripped the blade free, the wound immediately spurting hot blood onto his face and clothing. Braak's hands left Reevan's neck and clutched his own, beady eyes going wide as he desperately tried to stop the blood flowing. He turned, searching for his assailant, and Grundle flinched as one of Braak's fists swung for his tiny face and missed, hitting him in the chest instead and sending him flying backwards. The movement cost Braak precious seconds of what little was left of his life, the adrenaline and rage coursing through his body only causing further blood loss.

With his master's attention gone, Reevan shoved himself out of reach, his robe tearing, clutching his throat gingerly as he put himself in between Braak and Lessie. Braak lurched towards them, but the man was rapidly becoming less of a threat, his face pale and bloodless, his thick fingers grasping at nothing.

All Lessie could do was peer around Reevan and watch in horror as Ashendi Braak's lifeblood leaked out of his body into the Silver Stream.

Gasping, Braak collapsed, and Reevan must have decided that it was finally safe to approach. He skirted around, staying well out of reach, and retrieved his glaive. Using it like a polearm, Reevan shoved Braak onto his back from where he'd fallen. The dying man's mouth was moving, but none of them could hear if he had any final grand words to say. Wildly, Lessie felt a rush of guilt that she still didn't know the funeral rites. She didn't know what words were needed to make sure Braak's soul made it to Requiem.

But perhaps some souls didn't deserve an easy journey.

"I had hoped it would be me who killed you one day, master," Reevan said casually, but his voice rasped and his emerald eyes were hard. "At least it was someone who deserved it. But you did teach me that it's better to be sure."

Reevan brought his glaive down into Braak's chest. Lessie had never heard such an unpleasant sound. It squelched as the kitskan twisted the staff, rotating the blade. Braak exhaled slowly and did not inhale again.

"Sorry you had to see that, Lessandra," said Reevan. His voice was strained, dipping in and out from the strangulation. "I'd rather hoped to have this all taken care of by the time the rest of you caught up."

"Reevan, you..."

"I told you to trust me," he wheezed. "I knew you'd make it up here in time. Actually, you were even quicker than I thought. I had to take a gamble that you'd know what I meant."

Lessie didn't know what to say to that.

"Right," she replied, dazed.

Reevan had protected Mae. He hadn't betrayed her. All the hatred bubbling up inside her had nowhere to go. Boras was dying and Reevan was her friend.

A strange gurgling came from behind them. A realmlight tear hung in the air, much in the way Valandaras had opened a rift between the realms, but it was *wrong*. The split was jagged and dark, sinister—no blinding light poured from it like how Valandaras's portal had. Only ominous shadows.

Lessie had whirled just in time to watch the end of Boras's blood-spattered robes disappear within the tear. A shower of amethyst sparks shed from the portal's edges like starlight.

"What in the..." said Lessie, before all sound ceased around them. She felt the pull from the portal at the same time, like it were calling to her, beckoning to her blood like a Fae curse her mother had always warned about.

Reevan took a single step towards the dark portal before Lessie grabbed him and yanked him backwards. They hit the ground with a dull thud, pain shooting up her back at the sharp rocks underneath her. Reevan groaned beside her, shaking his head, ears twitching.

"Thank you, Lessandra," Reevan said. "I hear it, too. I wouldn't go near that if I were you, it could lead—Grundle, NO!"

Reevan's sharp cry was so loud Lessie flinched, but it had no effect. Grundle either couldn't hear him or elected to ignore him. The goblin's face was oddly blank, his large golden eyes absorbed by the lack of light blanketing their surroundings. They were too far away, and could do nothing to stop him.

Grundle stepped into the dark portal and vanished.

"Godsdamn it, Grundle!" Lessie shouted, but the goblin had already disappeared from view. The tear in the realm's fabric began to heal, and in seconds it had sealed itself. There was no way to go after Grundle, even if they could brave wherever the tear had led to.

A crash shook the earth. Lessie and Reevan ran from the cliff's edge, the ground uneven and crumbling under their feet. A screech had them both cover their ears.

Lessie looked out over the lake and saw Daigon, the water god of Keanos, and she realised immediately that nothing she had ever fought within the Maw would have prepared her for this. Her own father would have turned and ran for his life.

The leviathan had draped his body along the cliffs, knocking trees aside to get to the warring armies beyond them. Squinting, Lessie could just make out the shape of bodies in his claws as he raked them along the beach below, but could not tell if they were Altaean or Kalac. Daigon did not seem to care.

The frozen lake had shattered into chunks of ice with his heavy steps, like he had been unaware of his path in his quest for blood. The water god had been solely focused on the death and destruction of the army below, but now his coiled body unwound like a rattlesnake to strike at the golden firebird in the sky above him.

Mae, who had taken the form of the phoenix, commanded the firebird god's power as if she was born to it. She drew Daigon's attention desperately, trying to keep him from devouring the soldiers in his wake. Though she must have been over thirty feet long, the phoenix still looked woefully small as it flew around the leviathan's head, a trail of fire streaking the sky behind her.

Her distraction worked, with Daigon turning from what was left of the dying army to snap at her. Mae and Daigon clashed again and again, and it was clear that the phoenix was at a disadvantage, but her intensity had caught Daigon off guard. The god of Keanos had not expected adversity, and the old scars of his previous battles now had some new contenders.

"What do we do now?" Lessie yelled over the screeches of the phoenix and Daigon's roars. "Boras was supposed to control that thing, but he's gone."

Oorata Boras had to be dead. She had seen the void during realmshifting; nobody could survive it. She felt a strange sense of emptiness at the thought. It was over. The man who had killed her parents and threatened her sister, who had ripped her life from her, was dead. Wasn't she meant to feel better? All she felt was hollow.

Reevan gazed up at the warring gods, looking more frightened than he had when he faced death at the hands of his master. He snatched up the phoenix tome, which was still smoking slightly, and stowed it safely within his robes.

"We stay out of their way," he replied, "and we hope that whatever power Mae borrowed from the tome is enough to finish Daigon off. And then we get off this island."

Lessie looked out at the lake. The portal to the Oaken Eternal's path that Daigon had ripped through still lay open, sapphire light pouring into the frozen water around it, filling what little branches of the destroyed tree that were left with an ominous glow below the surface. Inky blue strands of Divinity snaked through the icy water like veins underneath skin, staining the sand as they searched for the one they belonged to. Daigon's power was leaking from his own realm into theirs as he drew more and more of it through the portal.

Daigon roared in anger, crashing onto the ice, giant jaws snapping at Mae as she flew near. The behemoth rose up, his strange serpent's body balanced upon powerful hind legs.

Mae's fire raged like a third burning sun in the sky, heating the crisp winter air around them and turning it to steam, melting the ice below and weakening it. She already looked tired, like the power was burning through just as hard as she was, but she dove again and again for Daigon, slashing at him with golden claws and burning him with her fire.

"We need to leave," Reevan yelled, "before they tear this island apart."

Lessie knew staying atop the bluff was suicide, but she couldn't look away. Lai'ireal's voice clanged in her head, strange double-tone reminding her that using the firebird's power might claim Mae's life.

Mae became little more than an outline against the grey sky, the phoenix burning brighter than realmlight. Lava spewed forth from her wings, raining down upon the waters, peppering Daigon with molten rock. The sound of the god's agonised roars shook the island's foundations.

Lessie felt Reevan's clawed fingers wrap around her own and was strangely grateful for the comfort.

How long has she got?

The fight between the two took to the skies. It should have been impossible, but the firebird's powerful claws had sunken into the scales on Daigon's back and lifted him skywards. The leviathan bellowed as he became airborne, spewing forth black fire from his mouth, thrashing against her grip. They grappled in mid-air, twisting, each trying to find purchase.

Lessie screamed as Daigon's teeth sank into Mae's flesh.

Mae tried to drop him, screeching, but Daigon did not let go. Teeth the length of trees pierced through her body, and together the phoenix and the god of Keanos plummeted to the earth. They rolled through the air, barrelling towards the cliffs.

Lessie and Reevan ran for their lives as two gods collided with the earth.

46

GRUNDLE

Grundle saw the void.

The inky black sky and roiling violet vortex that might have been clouds or galaxies, the swirling expanse of nothingness between realms. Grundle had never realmshifted, so he had nothing to compare this to, and he assumed that he was dead. Grundle was currently wrong—he was still very much alive. He could still breathe; he could still see. If he had the time or wish to explore it, he would have found himself on a tiny pocket of ground, perhaps a fracture of a realm that had broken off in some ancient war or meteor swarm.

Grundle did not have the time or the wish to explore. Grundle had climbed through the strange portal he had seen Oorata Boras conjure for reasons he could no longer remember, and now wanted only to confirm his suspicions and return to his friends. But now he was struggling to stay focused. The weight of his crimes were threatening to undo him.

The only source of light came from the crumpled figure of Boras, which was pulsing a faint purple. His body floated before Grundle, suspended in the air above. Grundle paid it little mind. Most of Grundle's thoughts were consumed by the feeling of his master's lifeblood spilling from his body onto Grundle's gloved hands. He wiped at the material frantically, but the soft leather remained soaked. He removed them, throwing them to the ground, but the blood had seeped into the fabric and stained his skin. Grundle held up his hands, staring in horror at the wet blood that glistened on his dark skin even in the lack of light. His master's soul had been released into the Silver Stream because of Grundle.

What had he done? How could he have done this? Braak was the only father Grundle had ever known.

Grundle was a traitor. Grundle had killed his master. That was a very bad thing. But Grundle had protected his friends, had saved Reevan. So that was a good thing? Maybe Grundle did not need to die in penance. He had saved more lives than he had taken on this day.

Traitor traitor traitor beat in his head like a heartbeat.

"Have you come to finish me off, assassin? To kill me like you did your own master?"

The eerie voice rattled straight through Grundle's bones. Boras's mouth had not moved. He had not spoken aloud. The sound had sprung to life inside Grundle's own mind.

Images of Grundle's life flooded through him, like someone was sifting through his memories. Blurry shapes that might have been his own true family. Events he had blocked out. His first kill. Scrabbling underneath a chained fence. A hand, raised not in genuine anger, but in annoyance, and the sting of a blow. Assassinations. Weapons designed to hide, poisons designed to kill slowly. Other images were clearer. Valandaras, shaking his hand like an equal as he hired them. Lessie swearing as he beat her hand at cards. Reevan's eyes, wide with gratitude as the jewel in his collar dimmed. Miss Mae humming to herself as she slowly knitted Grundle's wounds from the Mournblade. Gentle.

Emotions Grundle didn't have names for threatened to overwhelm him as he struggled to bring himself back to the present conversation.

"Boras will soon die without Grundle's help," said Grundle aloud, though he didn't know if it was necessary. "Grundle came to make sure."

"Quite the contrary, small one," Boras replied. "I think you will find that Oorata Boras has been dead for some time now. In fact, I do not believe you ever met him."

Grundle didn't know what that meant, but the eerie voice had started to feel disjointed, like it was losing its tether to the one it belonged to. The airborne body of the Mahejerai's leader had been slowly rotating, and now it turned to face Grundle.

Boras's head was at the wrong angle. Grundle had orchestrated enough falls to know that no humanoid could survive their neck being bent so far in one direction. And yet the Mahejerai leader's body continued to pulse with the same violet glow—like he was trapped within his own power. Where Boras's eyes had been, only two black holes remained. Swirling with the violet clouds of the void around them.

Grundle watched helplessly as the black holes widened.

"Oorata Boras fought hard, I will admit. He lasted months. It was commendable enough, if not irritating. And it gave me time to learn all I needed to."

The voice in Grundle's head started to laugh. Quietly at first, but soon the noise reached a level where it reverberated inside Grundle's skull so loud that it made Grundle scream, squeezing his eyes shut against the pain. Grundle fell to the ground, cradling his head in his hands. He pressed his fingers into his temples, the mounting pressure bringing him a slight sense of clarity.

"Oorata Boras was a smart man. He knew much of the Arcane and Divine of this realm. It was interesting to absorb his knowledge. It gave me... ideas."

The laughter inside Grundle's head had split into two distinct voices—one of them Boras's, the other unknown. The other voice was cold as death. As devoid of emotion as the void itself.

"But unfortunately, thanks to the meddlesome nature of your friends, Oorata Boras has now reached his limit of usefulness," the strange voice intoned.

Grundle opened his eyes.

The blackened void within Boras's face burst over, splitting skin and muscle. Grundle heard the sickening crunch of bone before part of the man's skull cracked and shot towards him. Grundle dodged the projectile on instinct, but more followed, and he could do nothing but curl into a tiny ball on the ground and hope that the sounds of shattering bone would not become his own.

"It is fortunate that I have been wanting a reason to leave this body for some time now," the hollow voice intoned.

Grundle watched in horror through spindly fingers as Boras's body collapsed in on itself and crumpled to the ground below. For a moment, it was still, wisps of violet smoke rising from the corpse.

Grundle had the nerve to hope that it was now over. That whatever had possessed the Mahejerai had lost the fight within itself; that it was unable to continue without a body to support it.

Grundle was wrong.

The creature that emerged from within Boras's mangled remains was so unspeakably horrific that for a moment Grundle forgot everything. His tortured mind went completely blank.

Which is exactly what it wanted.

"Thank you for bringing me a new one, Grundle."

47

MAE

Mae knew the form of the phoenix would not last long.

The borrowed Gift flooded her senses and coursed like fire through her veins. Her skin bubbled as the feathers shifted, shimmering, forming the shape the firebird's tome had shown her. Her body sang with joy at the Mother's essence, the emerald warmth keeping her from being torn apart by the intensity of the phoenix. The Mother's voice had once more become a chorus, a symphony after months of whispers, and the gentle reassurance helped Mae to keep her head.

The firebird's Change was not gentle. It was not the Change of a sparrow or mountain lion; she had borrowed the power of a god. It was less of a form and more of a force. Every muscle movement, every heartbeat, every thought felt amplified a thousand times over. This phoenix had lived a hundred lives, been reborn through countless Divines, and while Mae wore her skin, she held their wisdom and rage like it were her own. She was both stranger and expert of the Gifts the phoenix had bestowed upon her.

But it was tough to master, and Mae didn't have the time to learn. She had lost control as she'd dragged Daigon skywards, and his teeth had pierced into her side, tearing at her flesh and ripping flaming feathers from her body. She'd narrowly avoided a catastrophic crash as they'd ploughed through the mountainside. Even as she lay beneath the mound of displaced dirt, a chorus of a thousand abilities and memories shrieked courses of action within her mind. Past lives of the phoenix, disjointed and warring for her attention.

It was too much. Overload.

But she just needed enough to defeat Daigon. Even to get him down, to incapacitate him enough so that Valandaras could realmshift the god back to the realm he belonged in. That could be enough.

I'll drag Daigon through the Oaken Eternal all the way back to Keanos myself if I have to.

Groaning internally, Mae commanded the phoenix to rise. The wings burned so hot that the forest was ablaze from where she'd levelled it. Mae felt a pang of guilt for the felled trees and rock scattered over the land. They had ripped part of the cliff away altogether. Drawing upon strength buried deep in the reserves of her borrowed Gift, Mae tore herself from the rubble of the cliffside and dove again for the leviathan. His yellow eyes narrowed in anticipation of her attack. One of them had swollen half-shut, a trickle of molten fire from a blast dragged across the pupilless expanse. His head bobbed, jerking, trying to guess her next move, and he screamed and shot waves of raw energy at her as she clipped his shoulder, tearing sapphire scales from his flesh.

Daigon was a force of pure fury. He wanted only to feed, to gorge himself on the blood of the soldiers left scrambling upon the beaches. He had already ripped scores of them from the ground, devouring them whole before Mae had managed to capture his attention. The waves seemed to respond to Daigon's growls, the tide ebbing further out than it should be, leaving bodies exposed on the blood-soaked sand. Crimson seafoam bubbled at the shoreline. The icy water of the lake had turned midnight black from the energy leaking out of the Oaken Eternal's portal.

Somewhere, distant in the back of her consciousness, Mae felt a warning. The firebird's Gift was not infinite. She was almost out of time. If she burned the phoenix for too long, it would consume her.

But I have to keep him away. My friends are on that beach. Val's down there.

Desperately, she dove again. She had to keep him occupied until... she didn't know. Valandaras could realmshift him back to Keanos. Valandaras could use the Mournblade. The Oaken Eternal, perhaps. Her thoughts were becoming muddled, her brain heating along with her body. She had to think of something. *Anything.*

"You dare to challenge me, child?" Daigon screamed, furious at her evasion. "I have fought your kind before. I am older than time itself. I saw the end before it began. I watched the pitiful rulers of these realms fall for the False God's lies. I watched as they faded into nothing. He dared not touch Keanos. Vry'iin himself would not challenge me!"

Mae swerved in mid-air, but she misjudged the angle badly. One of Daigon's massive hooked claws slammed into her, forcing the wind from her lungs and almost knocking her out of the sky. A jolt of panic coursed through her as Daigon's massive form loomed over her.

Daigon sneered. "He could not contain me, and neither will you."

The giant claws closed around her foreign body. Mae twisted, but his grasp stayed firm. Daigon drew himself up to his full height, towering hundreds of feet over the ruined island. He held her up to the sea. The waves had grown erratic and dark, smashing against the shore with an anger unlike any natural tide. The black water of the icy lake trickled towards the ocean like the tiny rivers of lava in Ignatia.

A new type of fear choked her.

"Perhaps I will make my new home here," Daigon said, his low voice cruel in its amusement. "I will bend these waters to my will."

Mae struggled to break his grip. She could hear the distant screams and moans of the dead. Souls would be flooding the Silver Stream. Daigon's hot breath upon her face made her stomach turn as he pulled her close, blood-stained teeth stinking of flesh and carrion.

She flared the fire, but he held strong, even as the scales on his clawed hands burned. He seemed to be enjoying the pain. He held her high above the last of the dying soldiers and regarded her, eyes glittering with malice.

"What do you think becomes of a firebird if it is drowned, little one?" Daigon asked. "Can a phoenix rise from the ashes if they are scattered to the sea?"

Mae reached inside herself, desperately searching for a way out, and found her own Gift mingling with the phoenix fire. Together, the emerald and red-hot flame melded and pulsed white. A hundred voices screeched at her not to; that it was too dangerous. But buried among them, one voice whispered that she would be all right.

She trusted that voice more than anything. It might have been the Mother, but it might have been her own.

Mae's fire turned inward.

The firebird's form pulsed. Feathers whitened and her body glowed, the fire building within, her core heating beyond even her imagination. The phoenix warnings inside her mind became shrieks. She was burning too hot, too much, all at once.

She was going to die.

But if it claimed her life, then she would take Daigon with her.

Daigon faltered, trying to let her go, but what Mae had at first been desperate to escape she now clung to like a funeral pyre. He tried to tear her from his grip, but only succeeded in fusing his other claw to her burning body. The leviathan roared, first in anger, then in agony as his flesh began to burn away. He flailed wildly, Mae's phoenix form melting through his scales. All the while the firebird's Gift rose inside her, building until the heat was so intense she thought she might explode from it.

Mae rocketed upwards, dragging the serpent god with her, until they were so high they might have touched the suns themselves. Mae could feel the phoenix Gift reaching its limits. She was much too high. She needed to go back down. But she couldn't lose the chance to wound Daigon enough that the others would be able to contain him.

The spark flared.

Daigon bellowed in horror as the last of the flesh melted away from his claws. He plummeted back down towards the island, long serpent's body spiralling.

The phoenix shone, alone in the sky, like the brightest star about to implode. Mae sighed. It felt like the souls of a hundred phoenix Divines embraced her.

And with that, it was gone.

Mae felt the last of the phoenix's power drain and knew she would not survive its loss.

A terrible shriek tore from her throat as the tome's Gift ripped the wings away, as the most powerful Change she had ever attempted thrust her back towards her human body. Flaming crimson feathers scattered into the sky, turning to ash and raining down upon the beach below. Her body hurt little compared to her mind, which was forced to sever the connections it had just made to those who had used the Gift before her. The Mother's gentle whispering barely kept her conscious.

As the phoenix relinquished the last of itself and returned her to her own body, for a single moment, Mae was weightless. For a single moment, the sky was perfectly clear, and above it all, she could see everything for what it was.

She saw the broken bodies of allies and enemies, patches of scarlet staining the sand beneath them. Indistinguishable from one another in death.

She saw the Oaken Eternal, massive trunk splintered and branches spread like they were reaching for help, midnight energy leaking from the cracked wood's polluted roots into the lake around it.

She saw the hulking form of Ashendi Braak, intimidating even in death, the last of his life's blood merging with the gentle waves that lapped upon the shore of the lake his body floated in. The bluff they had stood upon had been obliterated; blasted to rubble by her and Daigon's rapid descent into the cliffside.

She saw Daigon. Skin blackened and melted, slithering back up out of the water, a feral grin curling around his vile mouth. Her stomach dropped. The evil god was wounded, but the phoenix had failed to destroy him.

She saw her friends, bloodied and exhausted, trying to reach one another. Trying to hold on. To survive against the impossible. Alive, for now.

Mae observed death as a neutral outsider for what seemed like an eternity.

Then all at once, she was falling.

Mae hit the ground as herself and heard, rather than felt, her bones crunch. Only the grace of the Mother's Gift kept her from losing consciousness. Sound exploded from all around her, but it seemed miles away. Her ears were ringing, and the metallic tang of blood flooded her mouth. She swallowed it, panicking, and the sickness in her stomach lurched unpleasantly. One of her arms was bent at an odd angle. She couldn't move her legs. She couldn't even feel them. She had shattered her spine.

Her Gift raced through her, trying to knit all the injuries closed, but she knew even with the Mother's essence released from the clutches of Boras, the damage to her body was overwhelming. If this were someone else, she would have shaken her head and offered her deepest regrets at not being able to help.

She was not a miracle worker. There was no stopping a soul who had already begun to cross the Silver Stream. The Mother's presence was like a soft blanket thrown over her, a comforting hand that could ultimately offer little else.

Mae was vaguely aware that she was dying.

Trying to catch her breath and unable to move, Mae lay on her back and stared up at a beautiful, cloudless patch of sky, where the phoenix fire had burned so bright it had chased away the clouds. In the diffused winter light of the twin suns, she could also see the faint outline of the moon already beginning its journey across.

Her sun and moon would have been proud.

At least I'll finally see my girls again.

A weight pressed in upon Mae's chest, her Gift desperately trying to re-inflate her crushed lungs, the catastrophic extent of her injuries threatening to overcome her.

Mae drifted in and out of consciousness.

I'm not afraid to die. How strange.

Shouting came, and she tried to turn her head to the sound, but her neck felt like it would snap from the effort. Her vision wavered so badly she couldn't see who it was, but soon the golden light warmed her face and she knew.

"Oh, Mae," said Valandaras, more to himself than to her. "No, no, no."

Mae sighed as he came into view above her. More covered in ichor and blood than she had ever seen him. His armour was dented, scratched and blackened, and he was wielding the Mournblade, whose sinister hum she could pick up even amongst the din of the fighting. Still, she felt peaceful. At least she would not die alone.

Valandaras knelt beside her. He threw the hideous black blade to the ground, ripping his gauntlets away and tearing at the wrappings on his hands. She realised what he was trying to do just as he reached for her.

"Val," Mae said, voice hoarse. "Don't waste it. It's too late."

Valandaras did not respond. He placed his golden, glowing hands onto her face, cupping her cheeks. The light that spread from them met the glittering emerald of her own Gift, still trying desperately to keep her conscious. Their Gifts coming together in one final dance. Mae inhaled sharply as the strange healing he possessed jolted through her. It was not subtle like hers was. It was raw, untrained, born of a visceral need to keep her alive.

He could not. There was too much damage to heal this. But Mae felt herself come back from the edge, just a little. She managed a small smile.

"Take it from me," Valandaras pleaded. "The healing. Anything. Take it all back, if you need it. I don't care. It all means nothing without you."

Mae shook her head, or at least tried to. She couldn't. To take back a Gift, to pull power from within someone—she had to mean that. And even if she could, she wouldn't. Every single drop of the Mother's Gift that she had given to Valandaras belonged with him.

"I can't," she whispered. "It's yours."

Valandaras choked on a sob and pulled her into his arms. Mae felt a distant keening protest from her bones at the movement. The part of her mind that healed tried to take stock of her injuries again, feeling all the ways her body was broken beyond repair, but once she reached a certain point, she stopped listening to it.

She was still dying.

Valandaras stayed kneeling in the sand before her, cradling her like he could shield her from the entire seven realms. Perhaps, in another life, where they were both regular people unattached to gods, he could have. What little she could see of his face held only devastation, and the other emotion they had both refused to acknowledge for far too godsdamned long. No sense in avoiding it now.

Mae tried to pull air into her exhausted lungs, the shallow inhale sending a sharp, stabbing pain through her chest, and stared up into the face of the man she loved. She was glad he would be the last thing she saw.

The cloth that covered Valandaras's eyes was as filthy as the day they had met. Mae reached for it, and Valandaras flinched as her fingers brushed the cloth.

"Don't—" he protested, but Mae had already begun to pull at it.

He tried to stop her from tearing the cloth down, but he couldn't deflect her fingers without jostling her, and she knew he would refuse to relinquish hold of her. Not now. Not when they had so little time left. Mae pulled at the cloth until it pooled around Valandaras's neck, leaving his face exposed. The light glowed more brightly from his uncovered eyes, but Valandaras wouldn't look at her. He squeezed them shut, shaking his head.

"Val," Mae whispered. "Look at me."

"Lioness, I will hurt you. You are in enough pain."

"You can't hurt me. Look at me."

"I can't."

"Val, I—" Mae coughed, and felt a vague sense of horror as flecks of crimson blood spattered onto Valandaras's face. His grip on her skin tightened. "Please."

His eyes met hers.

It was like staring into the sun.

Mae refused to blink. In the back of her mind, her instincts roared at her to look away, to avert her eyes, but it sounded dull and far away. She stared, transfixed, perhaps the first person to look directly into the eyes of a Realmshifter. She looked into his eyes like they were the only tether keeping her from joining the Silver Stream, because they were.

And the light didn't sizzle into her like a weapon. Valandaras's eyes did not cut through her in search of another realm of existence. Instead, the golden glow bathed over her like daylight and warmed her skin down to her bones. It didn't burn, although she felt an odd sensation—familiar, not painful like it should have been, but calming, like perhaps the light itself knew not to harm her. It felt like his healing hands, amplified a hundred times. Perhaps it was. She couldn't tell. She couldn't think. Mae could do nothing but gaze into Valandaras's eyes for the first time since they had met, a lifetime ago.

Behind the dazzling white, they might have been green. Warm, inviting. The colour of the forest in its most resplendent days of summer. The colour of her Gift, healing and comforting. The colour of home.

Mae smiled.

"I see you," she said, reaching a hand to his face and letting her fingers graze his skin. They left behind a streak of blood and dirt that neither of them noticed. Valandaras shivered. A tear rolled down his cheek, leaving a tiny stream of clean skin amidst the grime of the battle.

"Stay with me," Mae whispered.

Valandaras kissed her. It was somehow both gentle and desperate. A tear fell from his face onto hers.

"I would stay by your side for a thousand lifetimes," Valandaras replied thickly. "I would follow you through any world, any realm you asked of me. Nothing could keep me away. I would carve through the realms with my bare hands before I let you go."

Valandaras wrapped his arms around her, enveloping her in the warmth of his embrace, and Mae smiled against his skin. In her long life, the arms of the Realmshifter had been the only place she'd ever truly felt safe. She could let go.

"You were my Path," Valandaras whispered. "I knew that from the moment I met you. But I still chose to love you. Every day. It was always you."

She knew.

His eyes had not hurt her, but they had not healed her, either. Her own Gift slowed to a crawl and her breathing laboured. Her lungs felt deflated, like she couldn't take in enough air. Her Gift had nothing left.

Valandaras placed a gentle kiss on her forehead. Mae closed her eyes.

"I believed in nothing before you, Mae," said Valandaras. He sent the golden shimmer from his hands cascading over her again, desperate to keep her breathing. "You are why I can heal. I fell in love with you so completely, you Changed me. You are the only goddess I ever saw fit to worship."

Valandaras's Gift sputtered and drained completely. Mae sighed. It was getting harder to inhale. Her hands were numb from the freezing wind, but she felt warm and sleepy.

Perhaps—

"There you are," snarled a voice.

The ground shook next to them. Mae's eyes snapped open.

Daigon, the great god of darkened depths, the terror of Keanos, dragged his bleeding and blackened body in the sand. He looked badly wounded, but his eyes still glittered with a cruel insanity. His front legs were completely missing, melted away by the phoenix fire. The cauterised stumps made trenches in the sand as he slithered towards them. Dark blood poured from a dozen wounds on his body. Mae noticed with satisfaction that she had burned a lot of his skin. He had not liked that. Her mind felt fuzzy. She was too numb to be afraid.

"This ends now," Daigon growled, and flung himself towards them.

Valandaras threw himself between them instinctually, but was knocked violently aside as Daigon's massive head snapped for him. The force of the god's strike sent him sprawling. He rolled, golden light from his uncovered eyes spilling over the sand. Much too far away. Valandaras screamed for Mae to run.

She couldn't run. She couldn't even stand.

Mae gazed up at the behemoth, so close now she could see the tiny droplets of water still clinging to his yellowed teeth as he grinned.

"Pretty, broken thing," Daigon snarled. "Thought you could cheat death by pretending to be a god." He opened his mouth wide, intending to swallow her whole.

Mae tried in vain to push herself backwards, her unresponsive legs dragging in the sand. She felt the very last of her Gift run dry. Her healing ceased completely and pain flared all over her body—which gave her a moment of odd lucidity.

She looked about wildly, moments before having accepted that death had come for her, now determined to fight it tooth and nail for reasons she could not name. Her hands sank into the sand behind her, scrabbling for purchase, and brushed against something discarded, half buried.

Mae's fingers closed around the hilt of the Mournblade.

She looked up into the gaping maw of Daigon, at the endless cavern beginning to envelop her. The serpent laughed maniacally as he bore down upon her, the low sound booming.

She saw her death, and she accepted it. Welcomed it, even. But she would not accept the death of her realm on account of this creature.

Mae's eyes danced with the final wisp of the Mother's Gift before the emerald blackened and pooled into glittering obsidian. It flowed down her body like enveloping shadows. A calming, welcoming embrace.

The Mournblade had stopped humming.

Mae got to her feet.

Mae gripped the hilt of Mournblade with both hands, and the sinister thrum it had always emitted flared again. Became a symphony.

Daigon had not slowed in his descent towards her.

The last thing Mae saw was Valandaras, still running back for her, ready to fight a god with no weapon for her. She saw him slow, his face warped in confusion and terror, but behind it she saw the love for her that had always been there. No matter how obscured. Plain as day.

Mae smiled.

"Death comes for us all," Mae said. "Even gods."

Daigon's jaws closed around her body.

Mae drove the Mournblade through the roof of his mouth, directly into his brain.

48

VALANDARAS

Daigon closed his jaws around Mae, and the world stopped.

Valandaras felt the air still. The din of battle quieten. There was absolutely no way he would reach them in time to stop the leviathan from devouring her. He had been knocked too far away.

Valandaras didn't care. Nothing else mattered in that moment. He didn't even stop to cover his eyes. He would get Mae back if he had to use realmlight to slice his way through Daigon's belly to reach her.

Valandaras unsheathed his falchion, the weak points of the blade still barely intact from the earlier Arcane attack upon it. It would soon shatter, but he had no alternative. He had lost the Mournblade. He was cursing its wretched existence when he caught the faintest glimpse of the black blade in Mae's hands.

Before Daigon's jaws closed, Valandaras swore he saw Mae smile.

Had she still been able to stand before?

A thunderclap rocked over the sands. It was loud enough that Valandaras was forced to his knees, desperately pressing his hands over his ears. He looked up, uncovered eyes squinting in the fading light of the sunsets.

Daigon had frozen in place, his massive serpent's form looming over the beach. Splinters of light crackled through Daigon's scales like lightning. At first Valandaras thought it looked emerald in colour, before shifting darker, like black veins with an opalescent shimmer. They spread over the water god's body, crossing over each other and intersecting until they covered him completely. The black glow that surrounded him sunk into the rivers they had created and spread, pressing down like a blanket of pure night. Soon all Valandaras could see was the giant god's eye, pupilless and frozen open in fear.

There was a strange noise, like the wind being sucked from the air all around. Then Daigon's body began to disintegrate.

Valandaras watched in awe as Daigon's scales collapsed in on themselves like they had turned to ash. The leviathan's long body uncoiled, twisting in agony, and the particles of blackened dust swirled around themselves, creating a whirlwind. More and more pieces broke away and joined the storm.

A horrible wailing, low and guttural, rumbled through the air, as if Daigon could do nothing but scream as his own body was ripped away from him. All around was chaos. Valandaras could hear shouting, but he could not tell if it were friend or foe, they were too far away.

The wind picked up more fervently, and Valandaras shielded his eyes as the sapphire scales of Daigon, sharp as razors, flew through the air and surrounded the collapsing god. Daigon seemed to be shrinking, like his very flesh and bones were being drained from him. A hundred feet long became fifty, then ten, then nothing.

Daigon's hoarse cries were pitiful, before abruptly cutting off as the creature's mouth crumbled into the blackness. The glow from within became brighter somehow, despite the dark, like the iridescent shimmer kept it from becoming all-encompassing.

The last of Daigon's body shattered outwards without warning. Valandaras threw himself to the ground.

Spitting sand from his mouth, the Realmshifter scrabbled to find purchase. A tornado of obsidian dust barrelled upwards into the sky, with what was left of Daigon having joined it.

And in the centre of it all stood Mae.

In the eye of the storm, her hair faintly rustled by the obsidian tempest that swirled around her, with both hands clasped around the hilt of the Mournblade as she held it skyward. Glowing in the black.

Valandaras's heart lurched. Mae looked much taller than he knew her to be, and even as he stared, she grew in size. Ten, fifteen, twenty feet, until her colossal figure towered over the beach. Mae's face was blank, devoid of all emotion, her eyes pooled with black darker than the void between realms. The humming of the Mournblade became unbearable, like the enlarged blade also amplified it, and the vibrations of the hum shook the debris and burnt trees around them.

"Mae!" Valandaras shouted against the howling of the wind around her. Sand buffeted against him, debris and dark tendrils swirling.

Mae paused. Slowly, she looked around, but it was like she was disoriented. At that height, she could probably see everything all at once. Finally, her eyes found him.

Valandaras searched within the endless black pools for the woman he loved, and he swore he saw a flicker of amber.

Mae shook her head and lowered the Mournblade.

"Oh, no," she said, in a strange, double-toned voice, and the sound boomed across the island, shaking trees and making ripples in the water. Valandaras clapped his hands over his ears, wincing. He craned his neck upwards, amusement flashing through him at the chagrined look on giant Mae's face. The emotion, so out of place with everything else he was feeling, threatened to undo the last thread of composure he clung to.

Mae reached out a hand to the tempest still howling around her, and at her touch, the wind quietened. The black dust started to dissipate, and Valandaras watched in fascination as it funnelled into the Mournblade itself. Mae sighed in relief, gesturing gently, and her form began to shrink. The fifty foot tall goddess that had dwarfed the island slowly returned to a more familiar height. Before long, Valandaras found himself eye-to-eye with her once more. He held his breath as she approached.

Mae had changed.

The face that Valandaras knew so well had been enhanced beyond all comprehension. Mae was magnificent; so devastatingly beautiful that he now knew why people said the gods themselves had once been Fae. It was indescribable—she looked how she always had, but now an otherworldly, ethereal beauty blanketed her already stunning features. Painters could spend centuries trying to capture its essence, poets could spend their whole lives trying to put it into words. Wars would be fought over her face should she ask. Even Lai'ireal herself couldn't compare.

Mae revealed the tips of delicately pointed ears as she brushed her hair absently behind them, the auburn locks moving gently despite the lack of wind. Her eyes were still black, swirling with a faintly pulsing light, but if he looked hard enough, he could glimpse the more familiar amber behind it.

Mae's dirtied dress had transformed into a gossamer robe, black as night and rippling in a phantom wind as it draped over her frame. A dark veil blanketed her, like the tendrils of the storm that still swirled around them, and shadows skittered over her skin not unlike the Mother's emerald once had.

Mae raised the Mournblade as if she had only just remembered she was still holding it. The obsidian Sliver had stopped its sinister humming, the last of Daigon's black energy having coalesced upon it. Mae turned it over in her hand and frowned.

"Oh, this won't do," she said lightly, the strange double-tone of her voice less painful and yet more distinctive now she had returned to her regular height. She let go of the blade, and it hung suspended in the air before them. Mae stood deep in thought, staring at it for a while, then waved a hand.

Before Valandaras's eyes, the Mournblade shimmered.

The obsidian steel melted, swirling like liquid, while the hilt elongated and stretched in the air before him. Pieces of felled trees around them flew through the air, joining the Mournblade and solidifying its new shape, wood and vine knotting together seamlessly. It became a staff, taller than he was. The blade itself transformed into a delicate glowing hunk of blackened metal that formed an orb at its peak like a fallen star. It was as beautiful as any Sliver Valandaras had ever seen.

Mae adjusted her grip on the obsidian staff and hummed thoughtfully. Her eyes finally became fully amber once more.

"I suppose I shall have to think of a new name for it," she said. "It's not exactly a blade anymore, is it?"

Valandaras let out a choked sob of amusement.

Mae wasn't the same. But she was still in there.

Mae surveyed the island and the destruction her phoenix form and Daigon had rained down upon it. The cliffside forest they had crashed through had collapsed the caverns within it, leaving a clear path right into the icy lake. Rubble and half-cleaved rocks littered the landscape, felled trees buried under sand, chunks of ice melting into the shoreline. In the centre of the lake, a weak pulsing came from the remains of the god tree.

Mae's ghostly form gestured towards it curiously, and suddenly they both stood before the ruins of the ancient tree. Valandaras threw out his arms to steady himself, stomach lurching. It was as if they had blinked out of existence to appear where she wished them to.

Mae gave a small gasp of surprise.

"Oh," she exclaimed. "I only wished to see it closer."

She inspected her fingers, wisps of smoke curling around the black-tipped nails, as if an explanation for her new power lay with them. "I suppose that will take some getting used to."

Mae crouched and placed her hands upon the roots of the giant oak, split apart by Daigon's arrival. Her brow furrowed before softening. A halo of black energy still lingered around her head like a crown.

"It still lives," she breathed. "But it has endured too much. It deserves to rest."

Valandaras felt the tug before he saw it.

Mae raised her arms, and the staff that had once been the Mournblade resumed humming, a light pulsing faintly from the orb at its peak. The hum was no longer sinister, but somehow comforting and peaceful. She gripped it in both hands and tapped it lightly upon the earth.

The fallen sides of the trunk rose. Branches knit together, reaching towards the sky once more. The gargantuan oak groaned as it reformed, the wood creaking and pulsing with its light once more, but it was muted and sputtering. Mae's smoky wisps hit the icy water, where they turned into inky swirls. They curled around the roots of the god tree, twisting, blanketing the struggling glow. Soon the tree was almost as it had once been.

But there were still splinters, cracked pieces where Daigon had ripped his way through a portal that had not been meant for him, and a few of his sapphire scales remained embedded within the wood.

Valandaras had the strangest urge to reach out with his own light, and he followed the instinct. Slowly, gingerly, he put his hands onto the trunk of the great willow. The gentle, golden glow he knew had come from Mae herself flowed through him, surrounding the errant scales of the water god and dissolving them. Soon, the entire tree was whole once more.

There was a sound like the tree heaving a great sigh, before it turned black and stilled.

Mae echoed the sigh. "It is at peace now," she said. "It cannot serve as a portal anymore, but the Oaken Eternal will not suffer for it."

Valandaras couldn't think of anything to say to that, so he simply nodded. Mae accepted it, and together they stood before the petrified god tree in the silence that only came when two people understood each other on a level beyond comprehension.

"I believe you are no longer a Divine, lioness," said Valandaras. His voice wobbled a little, but they both ignored it.

"I think you're right, Val," said Mae. "The Mother has been freed, but the power I feel within me is not a Gift. I cannot be sure, but I think that capturing Daigon's essence awoke the Mournblade to its true purpose—serving the god of death. And since the Mantle was empty..."

Valandaras almost fell to his knees as the comprehension struck him.

Mae smiled sadly. "It appears as though I now have more of a permanent job to do." She turned her hand over in front of her, watching the smoky tendrils waft around her fingertips. "I can feel the pull to Requiem already. It is in desperate need of someone to watch over it."

Valandaras felt the despair threaten to overwhelm him. They had fought so hard, given so much. A thousand possible remedies for their situation raced through him, each one more outlandish than the next. How could he fix this?

"I have to go," Mae said softly. Her eyes darkened as they fixed on a faraway point. Valandaras's heart pounded in his ears.

I cannot lose her. Not after all this.

But who was he to ask a god to stay?

Valandaras said nothing, but wordlessly reached for Mae. Just as he had a lifetime ago, when he had offered her a hand out of a darkened place on the side of a road. Her fingers curled around his own, and her smile told him she was thinking of it too. She embraced him carefully, wary of her new, unpredictable power, before sighing and sinking into his arms. A lump formed in his throat as her fingers gripped his back tighter than they needed to.

"I'm sorry," Mae whispered.

Valandaras rested his chin atop her head and blinked back tears. He had forgotten to retie his cloth, and he felt exposed. He closed his uncovered eyes, grounding himself, feeling his different Gifts coexisting uneasily within his body like oil and water. Haropheth's power of realmshifting roiled inside him, avoiding the golden light he now knew came from Mae herself. It was foreign as the day he had discovered it, and somehow yet more natural, like a lover from a past life. It had woven itself around all the parts of his soul he kept secret, safe even from his own doubts, mistakes and self-loathing. Golden. Pure. Haropheth himself could not have touched it, could not have ripped it from him.

Valandaras could still feel it—the pull of his Path, towards her. It had not changed. From the moment they had met, it was like his Path had veered off and became fluid, dependent on her.

What if she was never part of my Path at all? What if she was my destination?

The words were out of his mouth before he knew it.

"Make me your Divine."

"What?" Mae asked, taken aback. She looked at him like he had lost his mind. Maybe he had. But if it meant he got to keep her in his life, he'd gladly go insane. It would be a small price to pay.

"Let me serve you," said Valandaras. "Be to you what you were to the Mother."

Mae seemed wary. "Val, I—"

"All gods have Divines. Chosen. Allow me to become your first. Perhaps I already am. We both know this comes from you." He held up a gently glowing palm, the strange healing glittering within his skin.

Fear flickered over Mae's face. "I do not even know what is expected of me. How can I expect it from you? What if I accidentally doom you to eternal servitude?"

He was already doomed to eternal servitude. This would be something he had never had before. A choice.

"I do not care, lioness," he said firmly. "I have been yours for years now. This would merely be making it official."

At that, Mae smiled, the true beaming smile of pure joy that he'd missed all these months, and the glow threatened to blind him.

"Divine," she murmured in agreement. "Yes."

She placed a hand upon his cheek, and for a moment, Valandaras could truly feel the gravitas of what he was doing. The world spun a little. Like it was giving him a push. He dropped to his knees in the blood-soaked sand, closed his eyes, and inhaled deeply.

For the second time in his life, Valandaras knelt before a god.

There was a pause.

"I'm not really sure what to say," Mae admitted.

Valandaras smiled. "Whatever you wish to. Whatever feels right."

"Very well, then, but you asked for it," she said, eyes glittering with amusement. She gestured grandly, the former Mournblade's orb glimmering faintly.

"Valandaras, protector of the seven realms. Realmshifter of Haropheth. Valiant warrior; stubborn, overprotective leader of mercenary crews. Incredible lover, wonderful friend, average dancer. Love of my life—and now possibly immortal existence."

Mae giggled at her own grandeur. Valandaras only looked up at her and smiled, shaking his head. Trust her to make light of their most serious moment. It was so... *her*. She was everything to him. Fearless, complicated, an enigma he could spend twenty lifetimes trying to solve. He hoped it took twice that long.

Mae took his hand in her own. It was freezing cold, but it fit perfectly, so he didn't mind.

"Do you choose to serve me faithfully as my Divine? To go where I need you to go, do what must be done? To forsake all other gods and follow me?"

"I do."

"Do you truly wish to become a Divine of the god of death?" Mae asked, uncertainty creeping into her voice. "To use your Gifts when people need them, to do what is right even when some may demand differently? To protect your Divinity from those who would seek to misuse it?"

Valandaras knew what she feared. He would never willingly serve another. Not the Seven, not Altaea or Kalac, not even his Pod or Haropheth himself. If they tried, he would spend an eternity fighting it if he had to. He belonged with her and her alone. He was hers.

"Yes."

"Will you stay with me? If not in body, then in spirit?"

Tiny drops of freezing rain soaked Valandaras's uncovered face, washing away the gore of battle. He felt clean, for the first time in years. Mae did not shy away from his gaze. His realmlight couldn't hurt her now. Even as he stared up at her, he felt the light that spilled from his open eyes cooling. Calming. Darkening.

"Of course," he said. He had never been more sure of anything.

Mae's amber eyes were full of tears. "Do you swear it?"

Valandaras finally understood.

As soon as he had been old enough to speak the oaths, he had been sworn to Haropheth. To the Path. To hunting Vry'iin, and enacting a revenge he had no part in. For nearly a century, he had felt like his destiny was not his own. That he was shifting through realms, searching, not for the False God—but for a purpose. Now he knew.

Every single thread of gold had led him to this moment. To Mae.

So he could choose her.

It was the easiest choice he would ever make.

"I swear."

49

LESSIE

Lessie didn't remember how she made it back to the ship.

It was a blur—screaming, shouting, blood. Ash and freezing rain pouring from the sky. Stumbling over fallen soldiers. Waves crashing upon the shore, dragging lifeless bodies out to sea. The ground of the island keening as it broke apart. Reevan's clawed hand laced around her fingers, her knuckles white and aching, but too terrified to let go. Running until her chest burned. Blindly trusting Reevan to get her out, because she couldn't see through her tears.

Making it back to the cove where they'd first landed. Barely enough crew left alive for the last ship to be functional. Druitt shouting orders to inexperienced sailors, his arm in a makeshift sling. Turning too late, scraping against the coral, feeling the ship shudder. Wondering dully if the bottom remained intact, or if they would take on water until they slowly sank to a watery grave. Watching what was left of the other two ships break apart, as the shockwaves from the middle of the island had sent them careening into the sharp rocks in the shallows.

Screaming. Bodies. Death.

Mae was not there.

Valandaras's uncovered eyes, glowing. No realms tearing open.

Pulling what little survivors they could find from the water. Altaeans, Kalac slaves, it made no difference. A shout from the crow's nest. A tiny body, floating face down. Hauling a goblin on board. Grundle vomiting sea water and black bile across the deck. Braak's blood still stained his hands.

Slowly, against all odds, the ship made it out of the ring of islands. Somehow, they stayed afloat. What was left of Aelmor Island faded into the distance.

Mae was not there.

Lessie didn't want to think about why it hurt so much. The hole inside her soul tore open a little wider.

Nestled in the captain's cabin. Debriefing, comparing experiences. The cold seeped into her bones so deeply her teeth chattered. Her hair was soaked. She ripped the braid free, letting it hang limp around her face. A threadbare blanket clutched around her shoulders. Arguing. Barely listening to the conversation. The phoenix tome, blackened and dull, open upon the table. She couldn't read elven.

Valandaras had said Mae was gone. A god. What?

Grundle rocked back and forth, eyes empty.

Reevan stood at the door like a sentinel, tiny spots of blood soaked into the sandy fur around his neck where a barbed slave's collar had once pierced his flesh. Lessie tried to count them, but her eyes wouldn't stay focused.

A cook's assistant brought them all drinks. Lessie mumbled her thanks as he knelt in front of her and pushed a chipped mug of something warm into her hands. Cupping his around hers. A silver signet ring glinted in the dull glow of the lantern. Grey eyes.

"It's absolutely abysmal coffee, I'm afraid," Camden whispered. "Would you prefer whiskey, my lady? I can probably rustle some up."

Lessie didn't have the energy left to be surprised. Of course, Camden was there. The pompous idiot was always there when she actually needed him. Lord of Perfect Timing. She managed a small smile, tears stinging at the attempt, and the creases by his eyes deepened as he gently squeezed her knee. His expression was so soft that it inexplicably made her feel even more like crying.

Druitt's face went slack. "Camden," he said, teeth clenched, "what in the seven realms are you doing here?"

"I decided I couldn't bear to see you have all the fun without me," Camden replied, winking at Lessie. His hair was carefully dishevelled, his clothes worn and stained; probably stolen from another member of the ship's mess. "Besides, somebody needed to keep an eye on the ship."

"*You are not supposed to be here!*" Druitt yelled. "You were meant to stay in Roost Keep until the reascension. Father is going to kill us both. You promised—"

"—to stay alive, and away from the fighting," Camden countered. "I did both. Considering none of you noticed me, I believe I was completely safe the entire time. Besides, if I hadn't told this lot to ready the sails when I did, you'd be shouting at me from driftwood floating in the water. You're godsdamned welcome."

Druitt went red, pinching the bridge of his nose, muttering under his breath as if reminding himself that he couldn't throttle his brother with a broken arm and witnesses present. Lessie knew that feeling all too well. The rush of homesickness threatened to choke her.

I need my sister.

Maybe she could travel to the Freemeres. See Trixie in person, finally know for certain that her sister was all right, that the Quillkeep had been the right choice for her. She had the money to. Maybe, with Boras gone, Trixie could come home, now that Lessie could protect her again. They needed each other.

I want to go home.

"So," Camden said, pulling up a spare stool and rubbing his hands together. "Now that I've finished fetching all your drinks like an overworked barmaid, tell me everything that happened."

Lessie's throat felt like she'd never speak again, but she managed. They sat around the cramped wooden table, and together, Reevan and Lessie spoke of how Boras and Braak had been taken care of by Reevan and Grundle, respectively. Reevan handled most of the talking, especially when it came to Mae and Lessie choked up, unable to speak. He explained Mae's transformation in a fair amount of detail, considering he was being attacked at the time.

Druitt filled them in on the army's disastrous offence upon the beach. How ninety percent of the people who had sailed here with them now sailed to a different realm altogether.

Valandaras told them all of how Mae had slain Daigon with the Mournblade and became a god herself. It sounded ridiculous. Like Mae herself had wanted the most overdramatic reason for not being there. Lessie didn't want to believe it.

But Mae wouldn't leave them unless she had to. Lessie felt the hole in her chest pull a little wider, the wound no Divine could heal rip a little more.

I can't keep losing people.

"Godsdamn," Camden whistled. "So Boras was right. A mortal can become a god, with enough power. Luckily it was Mae and not him. Are you sure he's dead?"

Everybody turned to Grundle. He had not spoken. Someone had draped a blanket around him, and he perched upon his seat with his arms wrapped around his knees. His eyes were overly wide and unfocused, staring into nothing as he gently swayed with the ship's movement. The goblin had clearly seen horrors beyond comprehension within the dark realmlight tear.

"Is Oorata Boras dead, Grundle?" asked Valandaras. "Did you see him die? Can you confirm it?"

Slowly, Grundle nodded. There was a collective sigh of relief. Lessie expected a rush of satisfaction, but it didn't come. All she felt was cold.

At least Trixie is safe from him now. Mama and Papa's souls can rest.

It was over. Her enemy was dead. She could go home. Back to Picking, where she could rebuild her parent's farm and resume defence of the Maw. No more mercenary work. No more nobility, either. It was laughable that she had kept it this long. She should refuse her title, or pass it to another. Falcon's Watch needed a proper noble to run it. She wasn't a DeFalcone, after all. She didn't owe anyone anything. She could go back to her old life—an outsider, but one free of having people to lose.

"All of the Mahejerai on that island are dead," said Valandaras. "Those upon the beaches, as well as those who gave their lives for the ritual."

His voice suggested that he was largely responsible. Nobody asked him to elaborate.

"As fantastic as that is, it doesn't bode well for our neighbourly relations," Druitt said darkly. "There are a lot of dead soldiers on that island, not to mention the loss of Arcane life, which they hold sacred. Kalac's emperor will want Altaea to answer for this."

"There is also the matter of the slaves on board our ship," said Valandaras. His uncovered face appeared to be as foreign to him as it was to Lessie; he kept reaching to adjust cloth that wasn't there. "Their master may be slain, but they still hold allegiance to Kalac. We will have to return them to their homeland if they do not seek asylum within Altaea. They may not be welcomed back warmly."

"I do not believe that will be a problem," rasped Reevan. His voice was still strained from the attempted strangulation. "Grundle can disable their collars if they still find themselves influenced. We can send word to Bueno, have him help find them refuge within Saluo. They will return free."

"And I'm sure Bueno will appreciate the chance for us to owe him yet another favour," said Camden wryly.

"Besides," Reevan added, "we need Kalac natives to spread the news. Today saw not only Oorata Boras and Ashendi Braak fall, but the Kiveri

Czai himself. The collar of Kalac's most feared assassin lies broken at the bottom of the island's rubble. His defeat signifies the fall of Braak's influence over Kalac."

Reevan stood tall, despite the horrified looks from everyone in the room, but the end of his tail twitched uncontrollably beneath his tattered robes. "I believe even the Emperor will hesitate to retaliate, knowing he has lost the majority of what made his southern cities so formidable."

Druitt's face was a mask of stone. "Should I even ask?"

Reevan's emerald eyes held sorrow, but also peace.

"The Kiveri Czai is dead, and he will have no mourners. Only sighs of relief."

The others waited for an explanation, but Reevan did not supply one. Lessie didn't think he needed to, but eventually the silence became too much for her, even in her nerve wracked state.

"Won't Altaea want to retaliate, too?" she asked. "Druitt... you said once that your father would be itching to start a war when he reascended. Is that war going to start now?"

Did we start it?

"Kalac has been severely weakened by this turn of events," added Reevan. "The southern cities will likely turn to the emperor for aid, since Braak's army kept their borders. If Altaea wished to expand its own, it would be a perfect time for the Seven to push their luck."

Lessie felt sick even thinking of it. The families of the Seven had their own agendas, mostly consumed with furthering their own political gain. Didn't they have enough? How many of them kept Divines like Mae, who did not wish to serve? Who had been coerced, forced, threatened into using their Gifts to further the interests of the Altaean nobility? Anger washed over her like a flood and settled in her bones. Mae had lost half her life to serving, not to mention the lives of her daughters. Who knew how many others there were in the same situation? It didn't matter. The Seven were untouchable.

Somebody needs to stop them. Put an end to it. Just like the slaves in Saluo.

Camden and Druitt shared a look that Lessie recognised. It was the face Trixie gave her when one of them was about to take the fall for something big.

"I can take the news to Father," said Camden, with an air of resignation. "I can tell him the abridged version of what happened here, leaving out the parts about how decimated Kalac's southern army is. Father won't risk war with Kalac just because our borders are no longer threatened; he still has the emperor to worry about. It might not prevent a war altogether, but it'll stave off an immediate response, at least."

Druitt looked shocked. "Father will believe it coming from you, but he'll be furious you knew about it before he did," he said. "And the fact that you left Altaea? You'll be lucky if he doesn't forbid you to leave his sight for years. I'm surprised you aren't trying to bargain your way to more time here first."

"I've put off going to Verestead long enough," Camden replied wearily, before giving Druitt an exaggerated false smile. "Unless we have any other pressing end-of-the-world matters to attend to? I rather enjoyed this one."

Druitt glowered. He was still annoyed that Camden had managed to sneak on board the ship without his knowledge.

"I say this not as a former DeFalcone, but as your brother, because I love you," he said. "*Promise me* that this is your last act of defiance against being heir. No more adventures."

Camden laughed. "Oh gods, I'd be lying if I said I didn't want another ten. But yes, I suppose it was. I can't go around putting myself in mortal danger every week. It's very unbecoming of a prince." His eyes rolled so hard he was in danger of losing them inside his skull.

Former DeFalcone? Prince? What were they talking about? Lessie's mind was swimming again. She pressed her fingers in her temples, silently begging the pounding to subside.

"Heir?" she mumbled.

Camden gave her knee a gentle pat. His eyes were twinkling, but also sad. "I told you it was a long story, honey," he said.

Druitt laughed. "Now that, my dear brother, is the understatement of the century."

The sound of laughter felt unnatural to Lessie's ears. The others began to discuss the logistics of the Kalac refugees, or indeed if their ship would make it back to the Altaean port before they needed to stop for repairs.

Lessie's attention slid in and out of conversations, half-listening, drifting with the gentle rock of the ocean's waves. Occasionally, her ears pricked up as the others discussed Falcon's Watch. She had once had plans for it, of course, but she was going to have to trust that the other people in this room could handle it.

Her thoughts kept coming back to Mae. Throughout the talking, Lessie still kept looking around the table for her. It had become a habit to meet the Divine's eyes across the room while others spoke. Mae had always been smiling at her, encouraging her to participate, trying to get her to open up. Like the older sister she had always wanted. Like the older sister *she* might have been, had she not spent her life resentful and frightened, hiding and fighting.

Mae was gone. Was a god. The god of death. For a woman who had been remarkably full of life, it was strangely fitting.

Lessie had seen too much death, lately.

She knew partly why she couldn't make sense of her thoughts. She was grateful that her friends had escaped Oorata Boras, but in a way, Reevan had stolen her thunder. The vengeance she'd poured her heart and soul into for over a year had come to a head with no real resolution. She hadn't been able to confront Boras.

Lessie didn't know what she would have said when it came down to it, despite a thousand imagined conversations. Ones where she shouted and cursed; ones where she stood silent as he begged for absolution with her revolver pressed against his temple. Where she screamed her parents' names into his broken face, over and over.

It didn't matter, because she hadn't been able to do any of them. Now it was over—despite the niggling feeling in the back of her mind that insisted it remained unfinished.

It's over. Oorata Boras is dead.

Lessie found herself watching Reevan. The kitskan's attention stayed politely upon whoever was talking, but now and then his emerald eyes would flicker upwards to meet her own. She knew he was as exhausted as she was, but the looks he gave her were warm and comforting. Reevan had trusted her, had believed that she would know he had not betrayed them. But she hadn't. She had been determined to destroy him before Braak had got to him first. Shame burned her cheeks as she pictured it. She was going to let him die.

A small voice inside her objected, reminding her how she could have killed Reevan before Braak had the chance to. She'd had the perfect shot. She hadn't taken it.

I didn't want to believe he'd betrayed me, even when it all pointed that way. Blind faith like that usually gets you nothing but burned.

But she had needed Reevan's friendship to be real, because it was the first time in a long time that she hadn't felt alone.

Her parents had needed her, but the truth was Trixie didn't. Lessie needed her sister—needed to feel needed—but Trixie was finally happy and safe, and Lessie couldn't be a part of it. So she had thrown herself into pursuing Oorata Boras to fill the void. Working alone, needing nobody, focusing single-mindedly on revenge had been the only way to avoid more pain.

But there had been moments where she could have chased that vengeance, except it would have resulted in losing her friends. The altercation on the beach. The Mahejerai's temple. Even the pull of Boras's realm tear. She could have gone rogue, exacted her revenge without considering what would happen to the rest of the party.

Lessie had picked her friends, every time. And they had proven over and over that they needed her as much as she needed them.

Mae had believed in her, encouraged her. Valandaras had trusted her judgement. Reevan had trusted her to keep him alive, even when he knew she could have killed him instead. Even Camden, who got on her every last nerve, but who stood up for her when it really mattered.

Her mother would have told her to be wary of what they wanted from her. Her father would have told her to trust her gut. And her gut was telling her that they cared.

Trust and faith were more alike than she had first thought. Once, Lessie had thought little of either. Now what she had to trust was her own faith in the people around her. That they needed her not because of what she could do for them, but because of who she was.

And to trust herself that she was making the right decision.

"Will you be returning to Falcon's Watch now, Lessandra?" Reevan asked, interrupting someone else's sentence that she hadn't heard the start of.

Lessie waited for the flicker of irritation at his address, but it didn't come. Instead, a rush of affection coursed through her. Reevan used her full name because he liked it. Liked her.

Reevan stared at her politely, awaiting an answer to his simple question. Lessie felt Camden's eyes on her like a hawk. Breathing felt like shards of metal piercing her heart. Who was she, now vengeance had failed to fill the wound that death had left in her soul?

In for six, hold for three, out for six.

Despite her exhaustion, the corners of her mouth tugged slightly upwards.

"Yeah. I can't wait to go home."

50

REEVAN

THREE MONTHS LATER

Reevan awoke slowly.

The sunlight streaming through his window was pleasant at first, but soon heated his bedroom beyond even his taste. He rose reluctantly, descending the smaller staircase into the back of the keep with a vague idea of breaking his fast in the kitchens rather than the main dining hall. There had been many guests of late, and he did not feel the need for idle chatter.

Avoiding the kind eyes of the main cook, who had quickly learned his tight-lipped smiles and swift exits to be marks of respect rather than rudeness, Reevan stole just enough food to be comfortable and ambled out of the kitchen's back entrance into the courtyard.

The western entrance to Falcon's Watch had finally been fortified. A proud wooden gate stood in the space where Reevan had once strolled in, a collar around his neck and Grundle at his side, to rescue a pompous noble for a fee. It had been more than a year, but sometimes it felt like it had happened mere days ago. Still, Reevan thought, if those Kalac runaways were to walk through now, it would be difficult to recognise them. The events of the past had changed them too much.

Grundle had changed perhaps most of all. He had begun to recover from his accident, although it was hard to get him to open up about what had happened to him within the vortex he had fallen into. He had refused to speak of it—or at all, really—for weeks after, and seemed to struggle to remember even basic parts of his former life. Killing Braak had seemed to place a block within his mind—like he couldn't think of anything that had happened before it.

Reevan had felt partially responsible for Grundle's condition and had taken to trying to work through Grundle's issues with him. They had started at the beginning, Reevan talking through their childhoods, of how Braak had treated them, before moving on to how their lives had improved once they were no longer under his control. Recently, they had made some progress. Grundle had mentioned, unprompted, a conversation they had while disrupting the god tree's ritual on the beach. He'd gotten some of the details wrong, like he was remembering it from a different perspective, but progress was progress. Reevan felt confident that with time, Grundle would make a full recovery.

Until then, the goblin was content to remain in his dungeon-turned-workshop, poring over old designs and attempting to bring them to life. The obsession with opening the thin box had returned, too. That part of his mind, at least, had not been lost.

One of Grundle's first brilliant designs had, for once, not been a weapon. It was a trench system designed to support plant life more easily, using less manpower to draw from the wells. Lessie, along with Cutty and a small group of guards and workers around Falcon's Watch, had spent weeks mapping it out before putting it into action. They had planted an array of vegetables, fruiting trees and wildflowers that had at first seemed like a chaotic mishmash.

But as the sunny days and watered soil continued, the seeded land produced an astonishing amount of greenery. Bursts of colour surrounded them, buds of every hue opened and reached towards the twin suns. Fruit swelled and ripened in days, and nearby villagers wept in joy as the vegetables they harvested yielded better results than they could ever have dared to hope for. The grounds of Falcon's Watch and the surrounding fields had come to life as if the Mother herself had blessed the soil.

Valandaras had helped too, though his blessing was complicated.

Reevan did not pretend to understand how Valandaras's new power worked. His allegiance had changed, and with that change came others. He was still considered a Realmshifter, though he had not attempted to do so, and he still kept his eyes covered, although Reevan suspected this was more out of habit than anything. The light that glowed from underneath his cloth was gentler now. Cooler, and yet somehow more welcoming.

Valandaras was also now Divine in his own right; his Gifts bestowed upon him by the woman—the god—he loved. They were a little strange; he still had his healing hands, and he could breathe life into things that were an inch from death. But that did not always mean he should. After all, death came for them all.

There had been many casualties that day on Aelmor Island. Of what was left of Druitt's crew, most had retired, and a few of them had taken up employment within Lessie's guards. They had seen enough death for a lifetime. They seemed less scared of it now, though. There were quite a few new followers of the one they had started calling Mae'ruhn.

Reevan supposed believing in the god of death was easy when they had bore witness to her ascension, though he didn't understand why they had to change her name. He had even researched it looking for an answer, digging up ancient Elven traditions and citing religious texts that claimed those gods without a postfix would struggle to hold their mantles. Superstitions were tough to shake, he supposed. For a culture terrified of repeating the Fae's mistakes, the Altaeans sure liked to follow their rules. 'Ruhn' being the Elven word for 'death' had made it simple enough, but it still seemed unnecessary. She would always be Miss Mae to him.

It was still odd without her. Quieter. Less laughter.

Reevan made his way around the keep, chewing on the flatbread he had pilfered from the serving plate until he found who he was looking for.

Lessie crouched over a patch of wildflowers, her father's plaid shirt wrapped around her waist, the tops of her shoulders already freckling in the early spring suns. Reevan could hear her cursing as he approached.

"Gods... damn... it," she muttered under her breath as she pulled at a weed with her bare hands. It was putting up a decent fight. "Shit!"

"Lessandra, I believe there are protective gloves for this sort of task," Reevan drawled as a way of greeting. "Those plants have thorns for a reason. They do not want you to de-home them."

"I didn't bother getting my gloves because there was only one weed," Lessie replied, glowering at the offending plant before she gestured behind her. A trail of uprooted weeds marked the path she had taken. "And then I noticed one more, and one more, and so on." She sighed. "You slept in."

"I did," said Reevan. "I suppose there is a first time for everything."

Lessie gave him a half smile, wiping her brow and smearing it with soil. She either didn't notice or didn't care.

Reevan stood in silence for the next minute while Lessie wrestled with the weed. She hissed in triumph as it finally relinquished hold on the ground, tearing from the earth with a spray of loose dirt.

It was easy to see why Lessie had fixated on the weeds encroaching on this particular earth. A small part of the eastern grounds had become Lessie's pet project, where she had resolved to create the garden Mae had once described. Lessie had poured her grief into the garden, filling it with the brightest flowers and the lushest greenery Reevan had ever seen.

It was a perfect homage. Lessie had even commissioned a Divine of the Maker, a stone shaper, to fashion a small memorial statue of Mae. It stood proudly in the centre of the grove, a tiny plaque at its feet. The plaque bore no words, just a simple engraving of a sun and a crescent moon. Reevan had asked why there was only a single sun, since traditionally sun designs were carved after the fashion of the twins in their sky, but Lessie's eyes had welled with tears and he decided he should not have pointed out the mistake.

Lessie looked up at the statue now, fingers still curled around the weed. Mae's frozen face smiled benevolently down on the pair of them. It was an uncanny likeness, born of Divine methods, although Reevan doubted the Maker himself could have captured Mae's spirit within stone.

"She's not coming back, is she," said Lessie quietly. It wasn't a question.

The loss of the older woman had hit Lessie harder than she would ever admit. Another strike on the tally of people she had cared about and lost. Mae'ruhn may exist as the god of death, the keeper of Requiem and guardian of the Silver Stream, but they had still lost the Mae they knew and loved.

"I do not believe so, no," Reevan replied. "But I suppose we shall all see her again at some point, unless you have plans to become immortal. She is the god of death, after all."

Lessie raised her eyebrows as she contemplated his words.

"I never thought about it like that," she said, standing and stretching, the weed sprinkling dirt onto the ground around her.

Reevan gestured to the statue. "Most people try not to make a habit of thinking about death. But at least this way, we know we won't greet a stranger at the end of our lives. We will cross the gates of Requiem with a friend instead."

Lessie looked marginally less morose, which Reevan was proud of. He had simply been stating a fact, but for once it appeared to have brought some comfort. They stood in a comfortable silence for a minute or so before Lessie cracked and broke it.

"I've been meaning to ask you something, Reevan," said Lessie, giving him a sideways glance that he artfully avoided.

"Of course."

"When Braak—at the Night of Many Faces, your master said that he wanted people to think you were outside of his control."

"Yes, Lessandra."

"And then you really were outside of his control..."

Reevan looked at her expectantly. He had been waiting for this question, and was honestly surprised it had not come up sooner. A clawed finger longed to scratch at the ring of tiny scars around his neck.

Lessie's voice was deceptively casual.

"Exactly when did you stop following his orders? Was it before or after we started working together?"

Reevan raised his eyebrows. "Does it matter?"

He would tell her, of course, if she pressed. But he knew there was a good chance that she would not like the answer.

Lessie gave him a long, hard look. He thought he saw a flash of doubt in her eyes, but it disappeared quicker than he had seen for others. A much rarer emotion filled them instead.

Trust.

"I guess not," Lessie said. "Thanks for not killing us all."

"There's still time, Lessandra."

"Did you just make a joke, Reevan? I think that brings your grand total up to two."

Reevan chuckled. "I am capable of humour, you know. I believe the problem lies in that most of what I find humorous flies over people's heads. Callira happens to think I am quite funny."

"Of course *she* does, she's—"

"Hello," came a voice from beside them.

Lessie swung the corpse of the weed in surprise and smacked Grundle in the face with it.

"Godsdamn it, Grundle!" she exclaimed. "How do you *do* that?"

"Sorry," said the goblin, voice even quieter than it had been before. "Letter came for you, but Cutty could not find your whereabouts. I said I could help."

He held up a thick roll of sealed parchment with his long, spindly fingers. Lessie's eyes darkened with concern as they flickered to Reevan. She had noticed, too. It was quite jarring. Reevan gave her a look that he hoped said to ignore it, for now. Although there might soon come a time when it could no longer be ignored.

"Thanks, Grundle," said Lessie, taking the parchment from him. Grundle did not say anything else before he walked away, presumably to return to his workshop. He was still a little unsure of his surroundings, of his steps, and his face still dropped into vacancy more often than not.

Lessie watched him go, forehead creasing with worry.

"Tell me you heard that," she said quietly to Reevan. She shivered despite the warmth of the day. "It's so... unsettling."

"Trust me, Lessandra, I know," Reevan replied. "I have known Grundle almost my entire life. To hear him suddenly change his speech patterns... I do not know what to make of it." He shrugged. "Perhaps it is a good thing, for it may mean he now feels a sense of self outside of being owned, now that Braak swims the Silver Stream."

Lessie kept her eyes on Grundle's retreating form as she broke the seal on the parchment she held. Reevan wondered if it would be rude to remain while the lady of the estate read her private correspondence, but Lessie quickly unfurled the scroll, read the top line and groaned loudly.

"It's from the Lord of Vexation himself," she said, making a face at the parchment before reading the letter aloud for Reevan's benefit.

"'For the bewitching eyes of the Most Esteemed Lady Lessandra Shilling, Beloved Viscountess of Falcon's Watch and Protector of its Surrounding Lands'—gods, he is insufferable—'my lady, I hope this letter reaches you well and thriving in your little patch of Altaea. You will be delighted to hear I shall visit you shortly, as my confinement to Verestead has been paused to attend your official inauguration into nobility. You are almost a year overdue for this, after all! Since my father will no doubt be busy with his recent re-kingship, it falls to me as heir to represent house DeFalcone—besides yourself, of course.'"

Lessie made a choked, disgusted noise before continuing.

"'It may seem frivolous and pointless, and that's because it is, and that's what the Seven are best at. Remember, you will need to extend invitations to all dignitaries of the Altaean nobility, no matter how much you wish to keep it a *private affair* between us. Write to me if you require any advice on which meals to serve or how to properly decorate the main hall for such an event—I don't know if I can trust your taste alone. And please reach out to Bueno. He can commission Satine to make you another remarkable gown to wear.

"'I will arrive a few days beforehand, so I can make sure all the dressings have been made to the standard of a DeFalcone event—and so I can sample the wares of that wonderful new tavern I hear has opened in Falcon's Watch. The Smoking Cauldron, if I am not mistaken?'"

At that, Lessie looked up and gave Reevan a rare, genuine smile, although a slightly exasperated one. Reevan could only shrug in return.

Callira's tavern had been constructed in record time and was proving popular so far. The townsfolk adored her, and they had gone too many years without a proper place to relax or celebrate. Reevan's favourite evening activity was to join the night guard on the parapets of the keep, so he could gaze down at the distant village and watch colourful sparks and clouds of lavender haze drift from the Smoking Cauldron's oversized chimney. Callira's dream had been easy to fulfil.

It had been quite a shock to see her on their doorstep, bright-eyed and bushy-tailed, ready to start building. But Reevan supposed that technically, he had offered. He was just lucky that Lessie had been in favour of it.

"How is this drivel still going?" Lessie muttered, shaking the parchment as it drooped. "'Druitt has said that our dear father the King has commended our actions on Aelmor Island, minus a certain cook's assistant, so I'm unfortunately not disowned yet. Your inaugural ball can double as a celebration of how we saved the entire realm, perhaps. I look forward to seeing how Falcon's Watch has flourished under your care. At least, I hope it has, because I have to be the one to tell Father how it's going. Please don't make me disappoint the king, my lady, as I can assure you he is most unpleasant... when disappointed, I mean. Hopefully, your standing with him shall be more pristine than mine can ever hope to be. Either way, I eagerly await your invitation, and will count the minutes until I can once again dodge silvery projectiles from your deft hand. Perhaps I'll even ask you to dance.

"'Yours forever and always, most sincerely, Crown Prince Camden of House DeFalcone, Current Heir to the Throne of Altaea and Hoping the Next Seven Years Pass Quickly and Without Incident,'" Lessie concluded.

She shook her head, dark eyes skimming over the indigo ink as she re-read the words over. Reevan peered over her shoulder curiously, impressed with Camden's surprisingly striking penmanship.

"Gods above, he's even more of a pompous prick in written form," Lessie muttered. Her cheeks had reddened.

"If I recall correctly, Lessandra, last time he was here, you did tell him to write a letter in future if he needed to reach you," said Reevan, though he did not blame her for forgetting. It felt like a century ago that the young lord, now a prince, graced their doorstep unexpectedly. It was incredible just how much had changed in such a short time.

"Right," Lessie said, shaking her head. "Well, I'll burn this when I go inside, then."

Reevan sniffed in amusement at her nonchalance. Then he watched out of the corner of his eye as Lessie carefully folded Camden's letter three times and placed it into her pocket. Together they stood, side by side, looking out onto the sprawling grounds of the keep.

"I have to hold a ball," said Lessie quietly. Reevan nodded.

"And I have to invite members of the Seven," she added, sighing.

"It appears that way."

Lessie's face was pensive, looking out onto the fields around them. Reevan knew she despised the Altaean nobility, and had spoken of half-formed plans to liberate the Divines currently under their control. They were about as likely as Reevan's own plans to eliminate slavery in Kalac, which he still dreamed of. One day, he would go back and call in Bueno's favour, but after the disaster on Aelmor, Reevan had stayed with Lessie. She had not said it, but she needed him.

They were all slaves to something, even if it was their own responsibilities. And friendship was a surprisingly easy master to serve.

"Although..." Lessie mused, "his royal Princeship didn't say anything about *only* inviting the Seven."

Reevan cocked his head in confusion, which only made her smile grow.

"What do you think, Reevan? Maybe we should invite some of our own friends, too."

Friends?

Reevan turned to Lessie to see mischief sparkle in her eyes, taking years off her face. Her smile was as broad as he had ever seen it.

"How do you think the pompous pricks of the Seven's nobility will handle meeting the Eyes and Ears of Saluo himself?" she asked, holding back the beginnings of laughter. "Better than they'd handle Halliday Greyholme?"

Reevan stared at Lessie for a moment, then began to laugh with her.

It was a nice feeling, to have a friend.

51

VALANDARAS

Valandaras could feel Death, and she called to him.

He spent every dawn in the memorial garden Lessie had made for Mae. Not only was it tranquil and peaceful, but the presence of the statue made him feel less foolish when he addressed her aloud. She did not reply in words, but he felt her anyway. He would kneel before the stone figure and meditate until the warmth of the suns rose behind her and warmed his face.

The statue wasn't enough to represent the hole Mae had left in the realm, in him. It should have been a thousand foot monolith; a petrified ancient oak, or a cascading waterfall that bubbled how her laugh had. The cool stone couldn't show how warmly she had lived; in screaming colour, bursting with life.

The memorial wasn't for him, and he was glad of it. Nothing could be made that would properly symbolise his loss of her.

Outwardly, little had changed, but inside, Valandaras barely recognised himself. He still wore his armour, though he had retired his tattered red cloak. The lion etched into his old, misshapen shield meant something different now. Valandaras still wore his cloth, but no longer for the safety of those around him. No longer for the fear of tearing through the realms. Now he wore the cloth to keep the people close to him at ease.

For if they stared too long into the cool light behind his eyes, they might catch a glimpse of their own destined place in the Silver Stream. Instead of realmlight flooding when he opened his eyes, carving a Path between realms, now Valandaras saw the light within the living.

Only faintly, and only if he concentrated. But if he searched for it, Valandaras could see a spark within each person. Their soul. It had been jarring at first, to see the glimmer within his own friends. To have an idea of how long their lives would be, how much time their journey towards the Silver Stream could take. It was tough to interpret, especially since Valandaras knew almost nothing of his strange new Gifts.

But he was starting to pick up on the differences between the soulsparks. Lessie's light was strong, though it blinked out once or twice, steadily shining within her. Reevan's, on the other hand, crackled like lightning, jumping all over the place, extinguishing for an instant before sparking brightly again. And there were some he couldn't find at all, like Grundle's.

Valandaras didn't know what the sparks meant for those who carried them. Perhaps one day he would.

As a Divine of death, Valandaras could feel when someone was about to begin their last journey to Requiem—and if they could be pulled back a little. If the gentle glow that pulsed warm underneath his fingertips could still reach them. He could give a little more time, or a little less, if he chose to. Valandaras also understood that although it would be his choice to make; ultimately, death would come for them all. There was an odd beauty in the inevitability of it.

Distracted, Valandaras watched a smoky tendril roll through his fingertips playfully, like a living thing. The almost imperceptible glisten of his skin had become cooler, softer, and occasionally he found shadows skittering along them, reminding him painfully of the way Mae's skin had once sparkled with emerald. Everything reminded him of her, in the simplest ways.

He had not seen her since that day.

Some mornings, as he gazed into the stone eyes of a woman he could no longer stand beside, Valandaras felt torn. They were one and the same, and yet, his heart belonged with two completely different entities.

Mae'ruhn was his god. The god of death, who had bestowed his Gifts upon him. Who had freed his soul from the eternal contract he had been born into and offered him a choice to serve her instead. The impassive, neutral god who had filled his heart with true purpose.

Mae was the kind, fierce woman he would love long after it had stopped beating.

"I spoke the words for you again, yesterday," Valandaras said softly to the statue. "I did not expect there to be so many, so soon. This land has seen more than its fair share of death."

Lessie had asked Valandaras to stay in Falcon's Watch for the time being, and he had already been cautiously approached by some of the townsfolk in the village nearby—to heal a grievous injury, or stay with an elder as they passed. Surprisingly, the people had also requested that he speak formally over their dead. To say the prayers they believed would help the souls find their way to Requiem. It had been a tremendous leap of faith for them. Valandaras knew they were nervous about interacting with him, and rightfully so. There had never been a Divine of the god of death in their living memory. He was the first.

Valandaras knew the prayers were a formality—he could find a lost soul regardless—but he had still learned the words in every tongue. It made the living less anxious about their dead, and it made his task a little easier. He had a duty, now, to guide souls to the gates of Requiem when it became their time. It was all Mae'ruhn had asked of him.

He wished she would ask more. Then perhaps she would have more reason to materialise upon Kalaraak, and he could see her. What he wouldn't give to see those amber eyes upon him once more. Sometimes, he felt weary, like he had already lived enough for ten lives. He would not look for his own time to cross into the Silver Stream, but he hoped it would not be another century before he saw the gates.

What a curse a Divine's long life turned out to be, he thought, *since it only keeps me from her.*

"I miss you, lioness," he whispered to the statue.

There was no reply, but he felt the presence deep within his bones. It was a twin to his own longing, a resigned ache that mirrored his own. Logically, he knew it was the way things were meant to happen. The realms had needed the mantle fulfilled.

It still stung to lose her.

Valandaras felt the pull to Mae'ruhn as easily as breathing. It was a connection not unlike how she must have felt to the Mother. He thought it ironic that now he finally understood how she must have struggled when that connection had been severed. He had only to ask, to think it, and the Gifts she bestowed would flow from him.

Occasionally, Valandaras would feel another, very specific pull, out into the deserts of Kalac. It was becoming harder and harder to ignore. He would meditate upon it, listening to the eerie call within himself, trying to discern its meaning. So far, he had been unsuccessful. He would have to investigate it soon before it drove him mad. Perhaps it was the remains of his Realmshifter's Path, calling desperately for him to find a Sliver he no longer needed. It could be Haropheth himself, seeking restitution for the warrior he had lost. The vengeful god had not yet appeared before him, or indeed sent any of his former Pod members to accuse him of treachery and attempt to deliver what they believed to be justice.

They would, in time. And he would greet them without shame.

If Valandaras was a traitor to his kind, he would accept it. He had forsaken the god he had been sworn to, and with that choice had come consequences. He was no longer a Realmshifter—even if he had a Sliver, he could feel deep within that he would not be able to shift through the realms as he once had. He couldn't see the lines anymore. He only saw the realm he stood upon, where he was supposed to be, whole and bursting with colour around him. Like how Mae must have seen it her whole life.

Valandaras thought he would have mourned it more. The death of who he was. But it was peaceful.

He felt her strongest here, alone, surrounded by gardens inspired by her, nurtured by the Mother's essence. A few of the tiny patches of flowers had blackened, only to bud brighter and stronger than before. Only death could restore life.

Valandaras rose from his prayers and watched as the suns slowly rose, ringing the stone Mae's head in a temporary halo of light. From this angle, for a moment, it was almost as if her eyes sparkled.

Another day began in earnest, and sunlight warmed his skin and momentarily chased away the shadows. Light didn't hurt his eyes. He could stare directly into the suns. He couldn't remember a time when he had simply looked at a horizon and seen it for exactly what it was.

Valandaras could not see Mae. But he felt Death beside him. And death whispered gently that he was loved, and protected, and would join her when it was truly his time to. He was not afraid of what the future held for him. It had all been worth it.

Valandaras would gladly serve the god of death for an eternity than live a single day without the woman he loved.

52

EPILOGUE

MAE'RUHN

Mae'ruhn, the new god of death, stood at the gates to Requiem.

There was no nail polish to pick off, no Changed form to hide inside. No forced laughter or fake smile to wear like a shield against the nobility. Worst of all, there was nobody beside her, no friends to urge her forward or caution her steps.

She was on her own.

Mae stared up at the gates in wonder. They were impossibly high, thousands of feet, so tall that the tips disappeared into the cloud that blanketed the sky around them. Resembling wrought iron, dark as night and twisted into intricate patterns, the metal spires were imposing but also strangely welcoming. Across the iron, delicately coiling around the latticework of the gates themselves, were two magnificent snakes. One with scales of shining ebony, one pale as the moon itself, but otherwise equal in size and stature, the fifty-foot-long delicate serpents had stayed perfectly still as Mae approached.

They did not move, but she couldn't shake the feeling that they were real. Their glittering eyes were too intelligent to be carved from anything other than flesh and blood.

Above her, a river of cascading starlight flowed in the air, passing through the gates and beyond into the darkness of Requiem itself. Sparkling with every colour in the rainbow and beyond, some she had no name for, shimmering together until they melded into one opalescent light. Twisting gently, current ever-moving, as graceful as an earthly river. Carrying the souls of those who had passed into the place where they would rest for all eternity, if they so wished.

The Silver Stream.

Mae had always hoped, but to actually see it, to confirm its existence, felt like finally being able to breathe after a lifetime of struggling for air.

To know that it was true, that souls were delivered to Requiem gently, and safe, and free of the pain and suffering many of them must have felt when dying—it made the knot in her chest that had dwelled there for a decade loosen, ever so slightly.

Mae had paused at the entrance to her new domain, sifting through the overwhelming expanse of knowledge she now possessed. Some things she knew instinctively. Her purpose, her duty, her strange new abilities. Other knowledge only caused further questions—like what being the god of death, the guardian of an entire realm, had to mean for her. How she had changed. How she had once felt cautiously long-lived, and now stared down the barrel of true immortality.

Other things, still, that she could not think about. How she could never truly be with the ones she loved again. Her friends. Valandaras.

"It will get easier, you know," came a soft voice. One that had guided Mae for her entire life.

The comforting presence of the Mother stood beside her. Not quite corporeal, but the gentle emerald glow that surrounded her shaped into a feminine figure easily enough to recognise as similar to her own.

"Mother," Mae said, frowning. The strange cadence of her own voice was still foreign to her. "I—should I even call you that?"

I am a god. Should I not know the answers to simple questions?

The Mother's presence smiled fondly.

"You may call me whatever you wish, my child," she responded, and the double-tone of her voice was natural and soothing, healing, barely noticeable to Mae. "I can give you my true name, but you have spent a long time with this one. It can be hard to change."

"Believe me, I know," Mae said, sighing. "Whatever you decide, I'll respect. You are the god of life, after all."

"Ah, but we are equals, you and I," said the Mother. "Two sides of the same coin, for life cannot exist without death. You, Mae'ruhn, are of utmost importance, now that the Mantle of Death lies upon your brow. Nim'iean's continued absence has caused the Silver Stream to suffer, and there are many souls that will need guiding into their proper places within Requiem. He will have to answer for that, when he eventually shows himself."

"Nim'iean lives?" Mae asked, shocked. The former god of death had never once shown his face upon any realm, Kalaraak or otherwise.

"I do not believe what he has done could ever be called living. But yes, Nim'iean will awaken once more, now that his Sliver—" the Mother gestured to the Mournstaff, which hummed happily in Mae's hands "has returned to its former glory. He will challenge you for it, and his Mantle back, when he decides he wants it again. But that could be millennia from now. It is a heavy burden to be a god."

Mae gazed wistfully at the swirling stream of souls.

"I never wished to become a god. I only wanted to save you."

"You saved much more than I, my child," said the Mother. "You saved your realm from a terrible fate. And there were others, trapped, who are now free to connect with their realms. To shape their Divines and make their worlds better places."

"I must say, I didn't expect... this."

The Mother placed a hand upon Mae's shoulder. The ebbing flow of dark shadows brushed themselves softly aside in the wake of the Mother's touch. Her emerald fingers glittered strangely upon the dark clothing, and Mae felt a pang of longing for her bright dresses. That part of her, at least, still felt as human as the day she was born.

"Would you still have done it? Knowing what you would have to give up?"

Mae thought for a minute. "I believe so." *I would have done anything to save them.*

"Then all is as it should be," the Mother said gently.

Mae gripped the Mournstaff. It no longer hummed with a sinister undertone. The almost imperceptible noise it now emitted was peaceful, calming. The orb at the top, nestled between the intricate, branch-like steel claws, glowed with a faint golden light that gave her a strange jolt of homesickness.

Mae gazed up into the unmoving eyes of the twin serpents guarding the gates into her new domain and did nothing.

"Why do you hesitate?" asked the Mother.

Mae stared into the swirling galaxies within the Silver Stream. If she concentrated, she could see every individual pinprick of light and the soul it represented. She could sense their entire life, follow it forwards, pinpoint when and where they would cross through the gates. If she wished, she could even manipulate it, giving a soul a tiny nudge one way or another. The stream carried them here, to the gate, but Mae'ruhn held the keys. She decided when they would enter.

The knowledge of the power she held whispered caution at that one. Meddling in the lives of the mortals had a price, and she had already paid too much.

"I am afraid that I will not come back out," Mae admitted. "I have seen too much of death, and I do not wish to return to watch it claim those who I love. Now I am the death that greets them, that tears them away from life. Who am I to decide when somebody's time is finished? Who am I to hold death in my hands, to bestow it upon them without bias? How can I watch as they march closer to their own time in Requiem, and do nothing?"

"Only death can restore life," said the Mother knowingly, "because it is only through death that we learn how precious the life we had truly was. It is natural to want to spare those you loved from this pain, but it is the impermanence of life that makes it precious."

"I feel foolish," Mae said, staring once more into the glittering souls of the Silver Stream. She could see one in particular, glimmering a little more golden than those around it. "I wasted so much of the time I had, especially towards the end, by keeping my feelings to myself. I know his heart is mine, Mother, but it's not the same. I cannot see him, I cannot touch him. He serves. I did not want to bind him to me, to give him no choice."

"If there is one thing I know, it is that all there is in life is choice, even when you do not believe it," replied the Mother. Her round face held immeasurable kindness. "And that man has chosen to follow you for every single day since the moment you two met. Why do you think I placed you in his Path?"

"Mother?" Mae asked, aghast.

"You have held a Changed form while sleeping before, my dear," replied the Mother, and for the first time, Mae heard a hint of mischief within the immortal being's tone. "But the two of you deserved to meet."

"I—" Mae stopped, incredulous. "You orchestrated it?"

"Just a tiny push. We are not supposed to meddle in much," said the Mother. The crinkles around her eyes made them almost disappear when she smiled. "But you were alone for so long, and I could do nothing but watch as you suffered. You knew too much sorrow. You deserved to be taken care of, if only for a little while."

A lump formed in the back of Mae's throat and tears stung her eyes. She fell silent. For a god, her emotions certainly still felt human. Maybe that was the great deception of it all—that the gods had just as much humanity within as the rest of the living.

The two gods stood without speaking for a while. Perhaps it was a minute, or decade, or an age. Time worked strangely within Requiem.

"You are strong," the Mother said softly. "You are brave, and you are kind. You will learn, with time, how best to handle your new Divine purpose. And you will see them again."

Mae knew. She could feel it now. All of it. Those who were close, and those who would not meet her for centuries. She would come for them all, eventually. And she would greet them as carefully and delicately as she could.

Mae exhaled loudly, squared her shoulders, and approached the gate. The serpent's eyes glittered like diamonds, but they held no malice. Slowly, the bodies of the snakes unwound until they had left the middle of the gate. They each inclined their heads in respectful greeting.

Mae glanced behind her one more time. The Mother was nowhere to be seen, but Mae could still feel her. That kind of connection didn't need constant reassurance.

Mae struck the ground three times with the Mournstaff, and the gates of Requiem swung outward towards her. She took a deep breath, gathered her thoughts, and stepped inside the realm of the dead.

The first thing that she registered had her immortal heartbeat skip.

Two souls, waiting just inside the gate. Pacing. Like they had been there for some time, and were becoming increasingly impatient. Both wearing brightly coloured dresses, one yellow, the other blue. Clouds of auburn hair drifting in the gentle breeze from the Silver Stream above.

Four blue eyes met two of glowing amber.

"...Mother?"

THE KALARAAK CHRONICLES
will continue

GLOSSARY

ADRAI'ICA — the realm of Cursed Fae. Where Haropheth banished the Elven people of Kalaraak in punishment for following Vry'iin so fervently. Adrai'ica is said to be the strangest of the realms, with warped time and little adherence to laws of physics or morality.

ALTAEA — a country in the realm of Kalaraak. Once seven independently governed duchies, the houses combined their lands to create a single, united kingdom, with kingship shared among the heads of each noble house. They are outwardly mistrustful of Arcane users, and most Divines who live there end up serving in the king's courts or with the wealthiest houses of the nobility.

ANTITHIIA — the realm of the damned. Home to Vry'iin's fortress, as well as an army of demons and creatures made of nightmares. Souls who are unworthy to enter Requiem usually find their way to Antithiia.

ARCANE — an individual who can manipulate the magic of the Weave itself, usually without any sort of god's blessing. As the weave is difficult and unpredictable, many Arcanes are subject to scrutiny, and are prone to experiencing injury or death attempting to learn their craft. Altaean citizens tend to mistrust them. There are places across the realm where the weave is practiced openly and Arcanes are taught to hone their skills, but the locations are heavily guarded.

ARCHDUKE — the leader and governing member of a House of the Seven. They are responsible for the family lands and those who dwell upon them, as well as managing those with smaller titles. They will become

King of Altaea for seven years when it is their turn in the rotation of the Kingswitch.

THE BETRAYAL — the act of when Vry'iin tricked his fellow gods into the Godprison. Vry'iin trapped them, took all of their power unto himself, and ruled as the only god of the Seven Realms for millennia.

BETRAYER — see Vry'iin. Also known as the False God or Hollow God.

THE BREACH — the act of the Godprison finally breaking open, 113 years before the events of *The Kalaraak Chronicles* begin. Most of the gods had been trapped within the Godprison for upwards of fifty thousand years. There is discourse as to which god first managed to cause the Breach; most scholars accept a combination of Lai'ireal and Haropheth.

DIVINE — an individual who has received supernatural gifts from the god they follow. Gifts range from carnival tricks and glamours to healings, blessings, and living weapons. Most Divines were cut off from their Divinity until the Breach. A god did not have to be returned from the prison to manifest Divines, although those with returned gods are considered to be stronger due to their connection.

ELVEN/FAE — a race of people now mostly lost to Kalaraak. Legend tells that they were Vry'iin's most fervent supporters, and he favoured them by blessing them with great beauty as well as Divinity at a much higher rate than other races. When Vry'iin's betrayal was revealed, the Elven people were collectively banished from Kalaraak altogether by other vengeful gods. Some surviving Elven made Adrai'ica their home, where the realm's twisted time and atmosphere transformed them into what we now call the Fae. Some humans on Kalaraak can still trace Elven in their bloodlines, but it is unwise to make this public knowledge.

THE FREEMERES — a country in the realm of Kalaraak. Full of lush forests, craggy mountains and deep marshes, they tend to stay neutral during any conflicts between their neighbours.

GOBLIN — a race of people mainly native to Kalac, but can be found all over the realms. Short in stature, they have similar lifespans to humans, with their main differences being their elongated fingers and sharper teeth.

GODPRISON — where the gods were held after being tricked by Vry'iin. While some escaped by releasing their immortality, hiding, or outright refusing to listen to the Betrayer, it is said that most gods were held within it for several thousand years.

HAROPHETH — once the god of judgement, Haropheth made a deal with another inside the Godprison and bound their power to his own. Once he made the Breach, he could not return to his former Mantle, and instead became consumed by vengeance against Vry'iin. He cursed the Elven Divines, along with their entire people, for following Vry'iin. He created the Realmshifters when traversing between realms proved unstable for his volatile physical form.

IGNATIA — the realm of Fire. The realm is hottest at its core, and radiates heat from within.

KALAC — one of the countries in the realm of Kalaraak. The oldest living empire in memory, Kalac is a sprawling land with thousand-mile deserts separating its major cities. It is said that the southern cities, closest to Altaea, are largely ignored by the Emperor, despite their efforts to expand Kalac's borders. Kalac regard those of Divine or Arcane power to be above regular station and treat them akin to worship.

KALARAAK — the realm of Earth. Considered one of the largest realms with the highest population, Kalaraak is home to many distinct races and land masses. Kalaraak has remained cut off from other realms despite the Breach.

KEANOS — the realm of Water. It is entirely oceanic besides a few small islands, with many underwater cities and mostly aquatic races. It is tiny in comparison with the other realms.

KINGSWITCH — the process of governing who the ruling house is to be within Altaea. Every seven years, one house of the Seven's Archduke steps down and another is crowned as king, to rule for equal amounts of time.

KITSKAN — a race of people who resemble cats, although they would be offended at the comparison. They are of similar heights and lifespans as humans, with their main differences being fur, whiskers, and claws. Kitskans are also famous for being extremely fast.

LAI'IREAL — the god of war and battle. She has many names, including the Battle Maiden, the Lady of Many Faces, and the Falling Star. It is said that her beauty is too great to capture in any one face, so it is customary to not try to depict it in artwork. She is widely considered to be the first god to Breach the Godprison.

THE MAKER — one of the oldest gods known to the Seven Realms. He is the god of creation, and his followers worship by crafting. His practises and rituals were not lost as the others were, as the Dwarven people in particular remembered his ways. He was not tricked into the Godprison and instead shattered a piece of Antithiia into a haven for himself, which he named 'Kharodrum' (Dwarvish for 'solitude'). It is widely believed that this splinter in the realms eventually led to the Breach being possible.

MANTLE — the title of a god. There are many Mantles, such as the God of Battle or the God of Magic, and they designate a god's purpose upon the seven realms. Not all gods retain possession of their Mantle indefinitely. A Mantle can be lost, given up, or left empty due to the god's disappearance or unwillingness to perform the duties associated with it. An empty Mantle can even be bestowed upon a mortal if they possess enough godpower. Taking control of a Mantle requires a Sliver to syphon the godpower through, otherwise holding godpower would be too much for a mortal body.

THE MOTHER — the god of life and nature. She is one of the oldest gods, and one of the strongest, as her influence was only dampened by the Godprison rather than being cut off completely. Her true name is lost to time.

NIM'IEAN — the lost god of death. He was not caught in the Godprison, and many assume he gave up his Mantle and bound himself to an immortal body to avoid it. He has not been seen since before the Betrayal.

OAKEN ETERNAL — a series of ancient trees which form passageways between the realms. They are older than time itself, and although they may be crafted by the Mother, it is possible they predate even her existence. They were once the only connection between any of the realms.

QUILLKEEP — a secretive place of Arcane study. A sanctuary for the persecuted in the Freemeres, its precise location is fiercely guarded.

REALMS — self-contained worlds which were once connected, until the Betrayer disconnected them all using the power stolen from the gods. The only way to traverse between them now is by way of Realmshifting, besides a few secret methods unknown to most.

REALMSHIFTER — a holy warrior of the god Haropheth, who gave up his Mantle to seek revenge upon Vry'iin. Realmshifters were given the power to travel through the void between the realms using the holy light from their eyes, but it is volatile and difficult to control without multiple realmshifters (or a Sliver) to ground them.

REQUIEM — the realm of the Dead. Souls travel the Silver Stream to Requiem once they have passed on from their respective realms. Requiem is an eternal resting place, but not much is known of it, especially since the god of Death has been missing for millennia.

RUBY ISLES — a cluster of three islands in the northern Alsuran ocean, ringed by reefs of a peculiar crimson coral. Known for pirating and general debauchery, they were once home to peaceful colonies before being exploited by traffickers. The southern island in particular is fiercely guarded by its residents, allowing few outsiders within its borders.

SLIVER — a weapon of a god, forged in times before the Godprison. They were said to be so strong they could kill or hurt gods themselves, as they retained tiny pieces of the ones who first imbibed them. Slivers are conduits of godpower and can be used to syphon or store it. Haropheth instructed his Realmshifters to obtain as many Slivers as possible; both so they can realmshift unassisted and so they would be able to wound Vry'iin if they were able to track him down.

SEVEN, HOUSE OF — one of the noble houses who originally ran an independent duchy before Altaea formed. Now shares responsibility for the entire kingdom when their turn in the Kingswitch occurs.

SILVER STREAM — the river of starlight that weaves through all realms and ferries passed souls to Requiem.

THE TRIMOUNT — the mountain range central to Kalaraak's biggest landmass. It divides the three main countries of Altaea, Kalac and the Freemeres. It has many settlements around its edges, but the range itself is extremely dangerous and remains mostly unexplored.

THE WEAVE — the term for the true source of all non-divine magic. Arcane users draw their power from the Weave. It has been unstable since the Betrayal, and most Arcanes struggle with mastery of their power.

VRY'IIN — the god of lies and deceit. He has many names, including the False God, the Hollow One, and the Betrayer. Vry'iin tricked most other gods and imprisoned them, taking their powers unto himself. For millennia, Vry'iin was the one and only god of Kalaraak, until the Godprison was finally breached and his betrayal came to light. After the Breach, Vry'iin disappeared, and has never been seen or heard of in the 113 years following.

Acknowledgements

When I first sat down to write this book, I don't think I had an inkling of what life had in store for me. Two years, three job changes, and an official adult ADHD diagnosis later, there are many people to whom I owe my thanks.

To my incredible husband, Matt—this was your world first, so thank you for trusting me to use it as the blueprint for bringing this novel to life. Thank you for putting up with my incessant questions, my late nights and endless complaints of fatigue. You are the smartest person I've ever met, and I am continually in awe of the crazy shit you come up with. You are my soulmate, and the best Dungeon Master a player could ever hope for.

To the original Kalaraak campaign players—I have taken many, many creative liberties, and this is not the story we told at the table, but without you breathing life into these characters I wouldn't have known where to start. Thank you for trusting me with the parts of your soul (and unresolved trauma) D&D characters always come from. Our times at the table have been the happiest and most ridiculous hours of my life, and I'm forever grateful to have the most incredible tablemates by my side—I've never met a bigger bunch of dumbasses and I wouldn't have it any other way. I still think this was a safer option than streaming. Thank you, all of you.

To my best friend, Stephanie Wickham—who took the time to read any little scrap I sent her, hyped me up, but still told me when something I'd written made absolutely no sense. Thank you for your endless support, and your incredibly helpful drawings. My first ever fanart of Reevan jumping out the window is priceless, and I promise I'll get around to framing it sometime in the next twelve years.

To Lucas Lex DeJong—the official first person to read this novel in full, long-time best friend and First Published Author in the framily, our conversations of 'Things we have Googled for writing that have definitely put us on a List' never fail to make me laugh. Thank you for your honest feedback and for always finding time to inspire me. And for pushing me to finish this book out of pure spite, because if you can write six, why the hell can't I finish one? (DELUGE, out now at all good book retailers)

To Mike, my incredible cover artist—your art now lives not only on my body in the form of multiple beautiful tattoos, but now also as the first piece of my soul to exist outside of it. Thank you for dealing with my endless revisions, unhinged pinterest board dumps, and ADHD concentration levels. I know you worked your ass off to deliver and stressed yourself out way beyond what you should have. You created the cover of my dreams, and one I'm sure will cause many people to judge the book within favourably. I hope you're ready to make the next one!

To my beta & advanced copy readers—whether long time friends or kind Twitter strangers, your interest in reading this book is what kept me going. I will never forget the feeling of waking up to see people had responded to my ARC application form. When trying to market yourself, it's easy to feel like you're annoying people as you shout PLEASE LIKE MY THING into the void. Bob, Esmay, Kylee, Kris, Jamedi, all of the twitter Spark fanclub. Thank you for devoting your time and resources to reading, reviewing, and sharing my book. Every one of you is appreciated beyond words.

To my parents—thank you for instilling a fierce love of reading and buying your daughter any number of books she begged for. Sorry I used all the memory on our giant cream windows 95 PC writing terrible fan fiction in word documents. And to my grandmother, who stayed up with me way past my bedtime because I begged to read a thirteenth book before sleeping. Who saved literally hundreds of books in storage so that I could read them to my own children. I miss you every day. If I didn't know better, I'd think you were reading to me now.

To my children—Jensen, my beloved bonus child, every time I see you up late reading I pretend I don't, because I love knowing you're lost in a fantasy world. You're brilliant, don't soon forget. And to Kira, my starlight, you are more magical than any Arcane or Divine. I wrote this story to show you that you can do anything if you have an idea—and you put in the work to see it become a reality. You are my world.

Of course, to you—if you've made it this far. There are a lot of cool books out there, so thank you for choosing this one. I hope you fell in love with this place and these characters as much as I did. I hope this story captures your imagination, and maybe even pushes you to take the leap to join a D&D group or write that novel in your own head. I promise you, any fan art I come across will be printed and framed on my walls.

And if you noticed the many, many Taylor Swift references peppered throughout this novel, what if I told you none of it was accidental?

ABOUT THE AUTHOR

*Louise Holland has dreamed of
writing a novel since the age of 8.
This is her first time finishing one.*

Milton Keynes UK
Ingram Content Group UK Ltd.
UKHW041012041223
433750UK00004B/50

9 780645 889611